All an Illusion

The Douglas Files: Book Three

Nathan Birr

Beacon Books LLC

Published by BEACON BOOKS, LLC

Cover Image Copyright ©
welcomia/iStock/Thinkstock

THE HOLY BIBLE, NEW INTERNATIONAL VERSION®, NIV®
Copyright © 1973, 1978, 1984, 2011 by Biblica, Inc.®
Used by permission. All rights reserved worldwide.

Library of Congress Control Number: 2015914990

ISBN: 978-0-9967691-0-5 (hc)
ISBN: 978-0-9967691-1-2 (sc)
ISBN: 978-0-9967691-2-9 (e)

www.nathanbirr.com

Also by Nathan Birr

Overnight Delivery
The Douglas Files: Book One

Black Male
A Douglas Files Short

Three's a Crowd
The Douglas Files: Book Two

Coming Spring, 2016:
God, Girls, Golf & the Gridiron
(Not Always in That Order)
. . . A Love Story

To Tiffani—
I picture us going back to Vegas one day and
having a George and Brad "remember when"
conversation in front of the Bellagio.
Until then, we have our memories . . .

Chapter One

"HI, JACKSON, IT'S Hillary McKenzie."

He nearly dropped the phone.

Hillary.

He was dumbfounded, unable to imagine why she had called him. Their last goodbye, a year ago, had been little more than an acknowledgment of departure. No fond farewell. No best wishes. No inclination that their paths would ever cross again. Or that she wanted them to. And yet, it was her unmistakable voice in his ear.

"I need to talk to you," the voicemail message continued. "Please return my call at this number. Otherwise, I'll try you again later this evening."

He stood in stunned silence for several minutes, staring out sliding glass doors at the distant ocean without seeing it. He'd heard the phone ring, but since it hadn't sounded a familiar ringtone, it hadn't warranted putting down his Xbox controller. Now, heart thudding in his chest, hands shaking, he replayed the message to see if Hillary had left any clues as to what she wanted. But a flood of mental images drowned out any potential insight he might have gained. Images of long, golden hair fluttering in the Southern California breeze. Of blue eyes that could look right through him. Of an explosion. Fire and smoke. Caskets.

Robotically, Jackson returned to his Xbox. The memories and images continued to plague him as he lethargically played the second half of a Rams-49ers game. They weren't grainy and blurry like so many memories tended to be. These thoughts were vivid and razor sharp as they sliced through his brain, more than once distracting him from the game. When it mercifully ended, he put away his controller and debated returning her call.

Since they had parted ways the previous August, he had no more desire to see Hillary than she had to see him. Thoughts of her came now and then, but he quickly slammed the door on them. They were links to a previous life, one he was

1

trying hard to forget. Now, thanks to the voicemail, he couldn't dislodge the images planted in his mind. Of her. Of them. Of it.

He hoped some exercise and a change of scenery would clear his head, and it had been a while since he'd last cut his neighbor Connie's grass. At least he thought so. The days and weeks had started to run together of late. He had taken only two cases since the suicide of his pseudo-client Ryan a month and a half ago. Neither had paid much, and Jackson's finances were starting to run on fumes. Fortunately, whiling away the days playing *Madden* and *Call of Duty* didn't run up too hefty of a bill.

Video games were a distraction, the same way remodeling his house had been in the wake of the accident that had taken the lives of his parents and brother sixteen months ago. Killing virtual terrorists and rebuilding the once proud (Los Angeles) Rams franchise made the pain, regrets, and general disenfranchisement fade into the background. Until a memory intruded on his consciousness and made him acutely cognizant of it all again.

Jackson pushed the mower at a feverish pace, sweat blinding his vision. He couldn't stop wondering what Hillary wanted from him. There had been urgency in her voice, and yet complete and total calmness. He'd observed it before. Most people, when in want or need, lacked composure. Not Hillary. There was no uncertainty in her mind. She would get what she wanted, allowing urgency and composure to coexist in a state of absolute control.

Finished in record time, Jackson left the mower out to cool and hurried home before Connie came out to chat. He drained a glass of iced tea and went upstairs to take a cold shower, fighting thoughts that clawed their way into his brain. He stayed under the frigid water as long as he could, and emerged cooler and a little cleaner. He stared at his reflection in the mirror—the dirty blond hair that hung over his eyebrows and almost to his shoulders, the hollow blue eyes that looked more like a painting than the real thing, and the face that had almost forgotten how to smile.

He broke off his gaze and sighed. He had paid enough attention in his sessions with Dr. Zachary to know that he needed to face his problems. And he knew Hillary well enough to know she wasn't going away. Not if she wanted something. So he dressed and went downstairs, grabbing his phone and dialing her number before he talked himself out of it.

"This is Hillary."

The voice was pure and velvety.

He cleared his throat. "Hey, Hill, it's Jackson."

There was a slight pause before she spoke. "I'm surprised you called me back."

"I'm a little surprised myself. What's up?"

"I need to ask you for a favor," she said with authority. It was not a request.

"What's that?"

"You're still a private investigator, correct." Again, not a question.

Jackson paced into the dining room, raking his free hand through his damp hair. It was in stark contrast to his mouth, which was suddenly dry.

"Jackson?"

"Yeah," he said. "Yeah, I'm still a P.I."

"Good. I have a case for you."

"A referral?"

"Not exactly."

Jackson turned back toward the living room. "What's going on?"

"I have a meeting in Santa Monica tomorrow afternoon. Are you free if I stop by around five?"

"Uh, yeah, I guess." Jackson sat down on the edge of his coffee table. Right on his TV remote. "Agh!"

"Everything all right?"

"Yeah, fine."

"You do live at the same place?"

"Yeah."

"I'll see you tomorrow at five."

"Okay."

Before the word was out of his mouth, she ended the call.

*   *   *

Three and a half years ago . . .
Monday, May 25
12:21 p.m.

ONE OF the unwritten rules in the Douglas household was that father and sons always played a game of catch on Memorial Day. Every now and again, they'd toss a football back and forth, but usually, like today, it was a baseball. Taking advantage of a typically beautiful San Diego afternoon, Jackson and his dad played long toss across the expanse of the backyard until Hannah Douglas emerged from the house carrying a tray of raw hamburger patties.

"All set, dear?" David Douglas asked.

"Ready when you are."

David fired one more fastball into Jackson's mitt and headed toward the deck. Jackson filled a glass of iced tea and sat down next to his grandpa Leroy on the glider swing.

"Grant just called," Hannah said as she began setting the table. "They're a few minutes out."

David checked his watch. "Right on time. Traffic must have been good."

"Knowing Grant they left at dawn to be safe," Jackson said.

"How long has he been seeing this girl?" Leroy asked.

"About a month," David answered, looking at Hannah for confirmation. She nodded.

"What about you?" Leroy asked, digging his elbow into Jackson's ribs. "You got a girlfriend yet?"

"Nope."

"Got any prospects?"

"As there are fish in the ocean . . ."

Leroy chuckled, scratched his head, and took a drink. Jackson followed suit, then turned his eyes toward the grill. Tongues of flame suddenly shot up, and David repositioned a few patties.

"Son, I like my burgers rare," Leroy hollered.

David's reply was interrupted by the shrill ring of a cordless phone.

"Good grief," Leroy said as Hannah answered the call. "That could wake your grandmother."

"Probably Grant letting us know he's in the driveway," Jackson said.

"Yeah, well, he gets his thoroughness honest."

Hannah lowered the phone, muffling it against her shoulder. "David, it's for you. Admiral Sullivan."

All three Douglas men frowned.

"Jack, tend the burgers, will you?" David said as he came to take the phone from Hannah. He disappeared inside.

"I like mine—"

"Rare," Jackson said as he stood. "I know, Grandpa."

Careful to cook the burgers evenly—and to leave a couple rare—Jackson pondered reasons for David's former boss at ONI to be calling. He was interrupted when he heard car doors closing, followed by muffled voices as Grant and his new lady friend made their way around the side of the house.

Jackson was anxious to meet her, especially after Grant's sterling portrayal. Then again, he'd heard similar rave reviews from his brother before. If she bore any resemblance to Grant's previous girlfriends, she would be smart, stoic, unfunny, and mediocre at best in the looks department. Preferring substance over style was one thing. Sacrificing style for it was another. The worst part was always the "So what do you think of her?" conversation, similar to the "Wow, I've always wanted one of these" exchanges after a crummy Christmas gift.

Jackson closed the grill lid and looked up as Grant and his girlfriend appeared around the corner. Then he fumbled and nearly dropped the spatula.

Standing beside Grant was the most strikingly gorgeous female Jackson had ever seen. "Smoking hot" would have been an understatement, and far too crass to describe such beauty. She was tall—close to six feet—with a delightfully proportioned figure and creamy, flawless skin. General decency and Christian propriety notwithstanding, Jackson wouldn't have been able to help staring at her body if not for the magnificence of her oval face.

Golden hair was drawn back into a loose ponytail that glistened in the sunlight. Icy blue eyes sparkled like sapphires, and firm, ruby lips guarded perfect teeth. Her nose was small and chiseled, her cheeks high and smooth. Subtle makeup accentuated her faultless features, as did a playful silver necklace and hoop earrings. She wore a white chiffon cap-sleeved blouse and a dark denim skirt cut just above the knee, along with platform sandals that increased her height by a few inches.

"Hey, Jack," Grant said, climbing onto the deck.

"Grant," Jackson said, forcing his eyes to his brother. They shook hands as they always did.

Grant smiled. "Jack, this is Hillary."

Jackson reached out and shook a soft, smooth hand. Fighting the cotton that had suddenly taken over his mouth, he offered a quiet, "Hi."

"It's nice to meet you," Hillary said, forming a crooked little smile that sped up Jackson's heartrate. Wow. The "So what do you think of her?" conversation was quickly going to morph into a "Does she have a sister?" talk. "Or a single mom, for that matter? Distant cousin?"

"Hey, Grandpa," Grant called over Jackson's shoulder. Hillary waved at Jackson with her fingers as she and Grant moved on to greet Leroy, leaving

Jackson with a dumb look on his face and a greasy spatula in his hand. After standing there like an idiot for a moment, he scraped the burgers off the grill.

When David and Hannah emerged, introductions were made all around, and the group sat down around the picnic table in the lawn. Hannah's side dishes included potato salad, baked beans, and an array of fresh fruit and vegetables. As usual, everything looked delicious.

"So where'd you go to school, Hillary?" David asked after he had blessed the food, the nation, its troops, and the leaders of half the free world.

"UC-Santa Barbara, and then Pepperdine Law School," Hillary replied.

"*Summa cum laude,*" Grant said.

"Wow, that's very impressive," Hannah said.

"At Pepperdine or UCSB?" Jackson asked.

Hillary smiled demurely before answering softly. "Both."

"Wow," Hannah said again.

"And you're sure you're dating the right guy?" Jackson asked. "I mean, Grant's no dummy, but he wasn't even top of his class at UCLA."

"At least he got in. My sister's boyfriend had to go to USC."

She said it very innocently, but flicked her eyes at Jackson for just a fraction of a second. The rivalry between the two L.A. rivals was a source of contention between the Douglas brothers, and, while it was possible Hillary was unaware of Jackson's two years at Southern Cal, the fleeting glance suggested otherwise. Either way, the mention of a sister had most of Jackson's attention.

"You play any sports in school?" David asked.

Hannah groaned.

"Honest question in this family."

Hillary smiled as she sipped her ice water. "No, I get that a lot because of my height." She shook her head. "I played intramural basketball at UCSB, but that's it."

There was a brief lull in conversation while everyone sampled and complimented Hannah on the food. Grant added a, "Good burgers . . . Dad," with a sideways wink at his brother.

"A little overdone," Leroy commented, not so subtly nudging Jackson with his elbow.

"I can't help but notice you're choking it down just fine," Jackson replied.

Leroy nodded as he stuffed the last bite into his mouth. He chewed, then stifled something between a cough and a belch into his napkin, and asked, "How'd my grandson get you to agree to go out with him anyhow?" He followed up his question with what could only be described as a dry heave. Typical old guy eating sounds.

Hillary flashed a quick smile. "He just asked."

"So what," Jackson said, "'I hope they nail your client to the wall, and by the way would you like to have dinner?'"

"Not exactly."

"We were both working the same case," Grant said. Then he shrugged. "Sort of. We picked up a guy for a B&E and petty theft, who turned out to be the key witness in getting her firm's client off on a string of burglary charges."

"Key witness how?"

"He was actually the culprit."

"How very *Perry Mason*."

"I was the arresting officer, she was working for CD&R, and over the course of a week or so, we got to know each other beyond the basic cop-lawyer formalities. One thing led to another . . ."

"Nothing like a couple of cat burglars to bring two people together."

Hannah elbowed Jackson in the ribs from the other side, and he returned to his hamburger.

David continued to ask profiling questions, albeit gentle ones, and Hannah apologized for him and made short work of befriending Hillary. For her part, Hillary made pleasant conversation and seemed to enjoy the would-be in-laws.

"What'd Sully want anyhow?" Jackson asked when burger number two was safely down and conversation had again lagged.

"Admiral Sullivan, you mean?" David said.

"Aye, sir."

"He wanted to know if I could come by in the morning."

"For what?" Grant asked.

"He didn't say, just that he had something important he wanted to talk about."

Grant frowned. "You've been retired for a decade."

"Probably pulling your pension," Jackson mumbled.

"Just so long as he doesn't want you to re-up," Hannah said.

"I'm too old for that, dear. They want brave, young, strapping men."

Grant grinned. "That's why you washed out, Jack."

"Ah, go kiss the cannonmaster's mother."

Leroy chuckled and nearly choked.

"Son, do you by any chance mean the gunner's daughter?" David asked.

"Whomever."

Hannah stood up. "Dear, will you help me with dessert?"

"You'd better believe it," he said with a goofy dad smile.

They adjourned to the house and Leroy got up to refill his tea.

"You were in the Navy?" Hillary asked.

"Army, and only technically."

"What happened?"

"He opted out after two months," Grant said. "Entry Level Separation."

"How come?"

Jackson reached for a wedge of pineapple. "It just wasn't what I was expecting."

Grant began humming.

"Really, dude? *Story of My Life?*"

Grant shrugged. "It's a pattern. USC, San Diego, every job you've ever had."

"Well, we can't all be blessed with a lifelong focus."

"You two squabbling again?" Leroy asked.

"He started it," Jackson said in a purposefully childish voice.

"Yeah, and you no doubt finished it."

Hannah and David returned carrying generous slices of lemon meringue pie. They were slowly savored while the Douglas family got better acquainted with Hillary. When everyone was as full as could be, Hannah began to clear the table, refusing any help. Leroy ignored her and pitched in as always. Grant and David worked off their lunch with a game of catch. Jackson, feeling the effects of a pound of beef and all the sides, not to mention an extra-wide slice of pie, reclined to the glider. Hillary offered her assistance in the kitchen and, being a guest, had it refused by Hannah. So after looking around for a moment, she strode over to Jackson.

"Mind if I join you?"

He swallowed, stopped his rocking, and scooted over. "Sure."

Hillary sat down and the aroma of her perfume swirled into Jackson's nose. Best looking and best smelling girl he'd ever seen. For the first time, he admitted to himself that he was jealous of his brother.

Slipping off her sandals, Hillary crossed her legs at the ankle and sat back. Citing the ways in which admiring his brother's girlfriend's legs was immoral, Jackson tried to focus on David and Grant's game of catch. But peripheral vision made it hard to watch two amateurs lob a baseball back and forth. So he tried another diversion.

"This thing between you and Grant serious?"

Hillary turned her head and possibly lifted her chin a fraction. She studied Jackson for a second and shook her head. "Not yet."

"He brought you to meet the family. And you haven't run away."

"Not yet," she said with a thin smile.

"Well, Grant's playing show-off, so he must like you quite a bit."

"And you're playing smart aleck, so what does that mean?"

"Not so much playing as reverting to form."

Hillary smirked. "Grant was right."

"What?"

"That you were a wise guy."

"You sure he didn't say 'wise man'?"

"Oh, I'm pretty sure."

Jackson shrugged. "It's not the greatest reputation, maybe, but one I can easy live up to."

"Are you always this cavalier?"

"Are you always this subtle?"

"I'm used to dealing with hostile witnesses. I'm a lawyer."

"Does that mean you're billing some poor schlep to talk to me?"

Hillary just turned a placid smile toward him. "No, I'm the only one paying for this."

Jackson looked up as Grant walked over, wiping a thin bead of sweat off his forehead. "You two friends yet?"

With just a flit of the eyes toward Jackson, Hillary smiled again and answered nonchalantly. "Not yet."

Chapter Two

AS JACKSON SWUNG open his front door, the words "You're late" formed in his brain. They never made it to his lips.

Hillary stood on his front step, looking as breathtaking as ever. She wore a charcoal blazer open over a light blue V-neck blouse. Her knee-length skirt matched the blazer. So did the two-inch heels. Her wavy blond hair was in a ponytail, tight enough to look professional, loose enough to be stylish. Gold earrings, necklace, and bangles on her right wrist were immediately noticeable without being overwhelming. Her left hand, which carried a manila file folder, was adorned with a gold watch, probably a Rolex. She lifted her right hand to tuck a strand of hair behind her ear, no doubt blown loose during the ride in her Lexus convertible, now parked at the curb.

They eyed each other for just a second, Hillary's frosty blue eyes cutting into Jackson like lasers. Then her unsmiling mouth parted to ask, "Are you going to let me in?"

Her soft voice was another anchor dragging him back to the past, creating a churning sensation in his gut. There was no sensation in his mouth, which had suddenly gone drier than the dirt in his yard. Without a word, he stepped out of the way, and she strode into his modest living room. Hillary hadn't seen the remodeled place, and quickly glanced around. "You finally finished."

The previous owners had been drug dealers, and between raids by the LAPD, the place had fallen into disrepair and ultimately foreclosure. That's when Jackson had entered the picture, and after all his renovations, he was quite pleased with how it had turned out. Especially considering he was just an amateur when it came to home remodeling.

Jackson cleared his throat. "Working was therapy."

"It's quaint," she said. It didn't sound like a compliment.

"You want something to drink?" he asked.

"I'm fine."

He nodded. "Uh, have a seat."

Hillary sent a distrusting look at Jackson's couch and recliner. She selected the former, sat, and crossed her legs at the knee. Jackson eased back into his recliner.

"You look good," he said, immediately regretting his choice of words. It was the type of thing a guy was supposed to tell a female acquaintance after not seeing her for a while, especially when she looked as good as Hillary did. But she was not an acquaintance, and it had come out a little blunt.

"I mean, it looks like you're doing well."

"And you look like you've let yourself go."

Jackson shook the hair off his eyebrows. "It's been a rough couple of months."

Hillary smiled—more accurately, grimaced—politely.

He took a deep breath. "What can I do for you?"

"I need you to find a woman named Arielle Coal."

"*You* do?"

"Yes."

"*You're* the client?"

"Yes." She had the look of a teacher waiting for a remedial student to finally figure out the obvious.

He shook his head. "Who's Arielle Coal?"

"As far as I can tell, she's a rather high-end Las Vegas call girl."

Jackson sat back. "What's your interest in a Vegas call girl?"

"Does it matter?"

"If you want me to find her, it does."

"Have you forgotten that you owe me?"

"I wouldn't have opened the door if I had."

Hillary exhaled.

"Who is she?" Jackson asked again.

"I believe she has information about a client of mine—information that could impact my appeal."

"You lost?"

"It's complicated."

"Un-complicate it."

"I'm sure even you've heard of attorney-client confidentiality."

"Just like you've heard of investigator-client confidentiality."

"Yes, one of the more sacred oaths."

Jackson took a deep breath. Hillary didn't blink.

"Can you change the names to protect the—ahem—innocent?"

Hillary left the folder unopened on her lap. "Several months ago, I was approached by a friend who asked me to defend a friend of his. He was accused of burglary and had only procured a public defender. My friend asked me to take the case *pro bono*, and since my workload was light and the case intrigued me, I agreed."

Jackson found himself staring, mesmerized by Hillary's voice. It was a problem he'd often had, getting completely lost when she talked. There was just something about her voice, a texture that he couldn't quite define. Her diction was perfect, her words coated with honey. He forced himself to concentrate.

"The evidence was stacked against my client, but it was mostly circumstantial, and there was more than enough room for a good attorney to create reasonable doubt."

"Create?"

She shot him a quick glare. "However, there was DNA evidence that implicated my client, and juries love DNA."

"Crazy juries. It's not like it's irrefutable science or anything."

"DNA evidence is highly accurate but it's not infallible, especially when it comes to its application to a particular case." She paused for a breath. "Aside from the DNA evidence, one of the weak points of my defense was my client's lack of an alibi for the night the alleged crime was committed. He said he was home alone, with no witnesses."

"Don't they always?"

"However, that night he both received and made a call from a number that we identified as belonging to a woman named Arielle Coal. He had also made a call earlier that day to the same number. When I asked him about it, he claimed it was a mix-up—a series of wrong numbers and misdials. He claimed he didn't know anyone named Arielle Coal, had only exchanged the three mistaken phone calls with her, and most definitely wasn't with her on the night in question."

"He married?" Jackson asked.

"No."

"Got a girlfriend?"

"Not that I'm aware of."

"So why would he lie about it, if she could have been an alibi?"

"Why do any men cover up meeting with a prostitute?"

"You're looking at me like I should know."

Hillary gracefully moved on. "I don't know his specific reasons. I've asked him at length and he won't tell me anything further. That's why I want to talk to her."

"You think he's covering for her somehow?"

"I don't know. I just know I don't believe for a second that they accidentally exchanged multiple phone calls, not on the same day he allegedly committed a crime that has him serving three years in prison."

Jackson shook his head. "How come you didn't pursue this during the trial?"

"The public defender originally assigned to the case took my client's word that he was home alone and had no one to confirm his alibi, and thus he didn't bother to search for any evidence that might prove contrary. When I took over, I subpoenaed his phone records, but I didn't get the results until the day before the trial started. I asked the judge for a continuance, but was denied. Since my client wouldn't divulge any further details, I had to go forward with what I had. Unfortunately, it wasn't enough."

"So why now? He clearly doesn't care. Why's this stuck in your craw?"

Hillary shrugged indifferently. "Arielle Coal is a loose end, and I want it tied."

"That it?"

She took a deep breath. "I took an oath, Jackson. It is my sworn duty to provide the best possible legal defense for my client, even if he's not totally compliant. Besides, I want the truth."

"What's truth got to do with being a defense attorney?"

Hillary's eyes blazed, but she didn't take the bait. "I don't like losing, especially cases I should win. If I can talk to Arielle Coal and find something that will help me win the appeal, I can get this blotch off my record."

"How altruistic of you."

"I really don't think you're the person to lecture me on ethics and morality, do you?"

They stared each other down for several intense seconds.

Jackson blinked first. "Why don't you subpoena her?"

"Because to subpoena her, we'd have to find her to serve the subpoena."

"And you don't have some minion at CD&R who can do that?" He met her eyes. "Or am I the minion?"

"We have people for that," she answered, "but I don't want to send them to Las Vegas on what could be a wild goose chase, especially on a *pro bono* case."

"You'd rather send me instead?"

"You do owe me."

Jackson hung his head. "Yeah, and I knew you'd call it in someday."

"I believe that was your deal, '*quid pro quo*.'"

Jackson rubbed his forehead.

"Unless you plan to back out," Hillary said.

He sighed. "No, a deal's a deal."

"Good. Then you'll find her?"

"What am I supposed to do, drive to Vegas and bring her back here, Dog Chapman-style?"

"No, I'll be going with you."

"Great."

Hillary stood. "Are you free this weekend?"

Jackson also stood, and hesitated. He wanted very much to tell her that, actually, his weekend was busy. He had to play the Colts and the Cardinals in an attempt to lock up the NFC's number one seed in the playoffs. Plus there was a mission to stop nuclear missiles from destroying the Eastern Seaboard. But with one look at Hillary's expression he realized it hadn't really been a question.

"Yeah, I'm free."

"Good. I have a quick interview Friday morning, but I've cleared the rest of my schedule. I'll pick you up around ten."

"Whatever you say."

Hillary gave a perfunctory smile and extended the folder to him. "Here's what I was able to compile, mostly from public records."

Jackson took the folder and opened it to see a single sheet of paper with a driver's license photo and a few lines of basic demographic information.

"I'm surprised you don't have this on a tablet or your phone or something."

"I do," she answered. "I thought this would better suit your technological aptitude."

He looked down at the info, following her as she strode for the door. It was hard to tell from a black and white photocopied driver's license, but Arielle looked rather attractive. Medium height, brown hair, green eyes, just twenty-four years old. It wasn't much to go on.

"This all?" he asked.

"You're the investigator," Hillary said. "Investigate."

Before he could utter a reply, she was out the door, her heels clicking on the driveway. Jackson watched her almost to her car, then eased the door shut. He resolved never to check his voicemail again.

Chapter Three

JACKSON'S PHONE STARTLED him awake. He glanced at the clock, the red numbers temporarily blurred. Then he sighed. He'd set the alarm for nine, giving him an hour to shower, pack, and grab some breakfast. He sighed again. Twelve extra minutes of consciousness wouldn't kill him.

Jackson sat up in bed, and shook his head to clear the remaining cobwebs as he picked his phone off the nightstand. "Yeah?"

"Good morning to you, too," Hillary said.

"I don't suppose you're calling because you decided to issue a subpoena instead."

"I'm calling because some clumsy moron just backed into my car."

Jackson nodded, waiting for the correlation. Maybe he was just slow this morning.

"It's not exactly totaled, but we'll need alternate transportation today."

"Oh, and you accidentally called my number instead of Hertz's."

Hillary failed to mask a sigh. "I don't have time to banter. Can you drive?"

If she didn't have time to banter, then he didn't have time to tell her that he still drove a 1976 Ford Granada. A gift of sorts from his grandpa, the car was still in pristine shape. Well, maybe not pristine, but after three and a half decades, it still ran without complaint. Well, much of a complaint. In addition to being a sentimental reminder of his childhood with his grandparents, Jackson considered the old car a classic. There were others who saw it only as a piece of junk.

"Yeah, I can drive," he answered.

"Good."

"You need me to pick you up at . . . wherever you are?"

"I'll take a cab home."

"Same place as always?"

"Yes."

"When will you be back?"

"Pick me up at ten."

Hillary disconnected the call before he could reply.

Twenty-six minutes later, Jackson had showered, shaved, dressed, and packed a weekend's worth of clothes and personal items into a duffel bag. Feeling a little bit like a death row inmate whose call from the governor hadn't come, Jackson hit the road. It was another sunny day in Los Angeles, this one accented with the stereotypical smog that turned the sky a sick blue-gray.

Hillary lived in a condominium in Thousand Oaks, on the other side of the Santa Monica Mountains. Jackson had been there a few times and had no trouble finding the place. Seven minutes before ten, he parked in the morning shade of a large oak tree. On the other side of the tree, a fountain placidly spilled into a large duck pond around which the complex's four buildings were situated. The air was clearer here, the view of the mountains unobstructed by smog. Lawyering paid very well.

Jackson got out and trudged to Hillary's door. All day Thursday, he'd mulled potential ways of backing out. Short of just reneging on his word, he couldn't think of one. And even if he could summon the courage to let Hillary know he was welshing, it wasn't an option. He honored his word. A word he never should have put himself in position to give.

With a sigh, he rang the bell. He'd become rather adept over the past sixteen months at walling off certain emotions, and he'd spent the rest of his Thursday constructing another mental barricade. Jackson wasn't really sure why Hillary evoked such strong feelings in him. There were plenty of other triggers in his everyday life that had far deeper and more relevant ties to his parents and brother. But his mind closely associated Hillary with their deaths, and thoughts of her—fleeting as they had been—were like smelling salts that made him acutely aware of the pain again. His therapist said he needed to let the pain out bit by bit, but he wasn't prepared to be vulnerable in front of Hillary. Why give a sniper a clear shot?

He was about to reach for the bell again when he heard a click and the door swung open. Hillary wore a jade short-sleeved blouse and black dress pants. No shoes. Even so, she looked Jackson in the eye.

"You're actually on time."

He cleared his throat. "You of all people should know I'm never late."

"I just got back a few minutes ago. Come on in."

She turned with a flick of her hair—loose and luxurious—and Jackson followed her into the condo, the familiarity coming back to him like a bad odor. It was ironic, since her condo smelled like the perfume department at Macy's. The décor was sleek and modern, very urban loft. It seemed cold to Jackson, but that was appropriate. Then again, maybe it was just the air conditioning.

While Hillary changed, Jackson wandered into the living room. The eight by ten of Grant that always sat on the end table by Hillary's couch was gone. It had been replaced by a smaller framed photo of Hillary's parents. A collage on the wall showed her and her sisters, college friends, and a few candid shots of the family. There were no photos of Grant.

Jackson turned and examined a small computer stand in the corner. An empty laptop dock sat beside a laser printer. Like everything else in the house, the small desk was free of dust and clutter. There was, however, one item out of place. An unframed photo was tacked to the back of the desk, behind the printer. It was a guy, young, dark-haired, tanned. He was grinning, wearing a polo shirt and an earthy necklace. One arm apparently held the camera. The other loosely and casually held Hillary.

Jackson stepped into the dining room. He, Grant, and Hillary had shared a home-cooked dinner around her dining room table one night, a bonding exercise that had turned ugly. Not an unfamiliar story.

Hillary met him in the kitchen, a duffel bag twice the size of Jackson's over one shoulder, a smaller travel bag and a purse over the other. She had changed into a navy polo, white Bermuda shorts, and canvas shoes. No socks. Her hair was drawn back into what was technically a ponytail, but too loose to really be compared to its namesake. It was held not with a band or tie, but by a wide clip.

Jackson turned his eyes down to Hillary's luggage. "Just how long are we going to be gone?"

"Depends on how efficiently you work. I figured I'd better be prepared."

She flicked off the lights and followed Jackson out the door. He waited while she locked up, then led the way down the curved sidewalk to the parking lot. He heard Hillary stop behind him.

"You still drive that rolling junkyard?"

"Whose car is running right now?" he asked.

"I told you, someone backed into me."

"And you could have sprung for a rental. Which brings up the question of how our little *quid pro quo* covers expenses."

"I'll pay," Hillary said with a huff.

"Good, because I'm tapped."

"How surprising." She shook her head as she placed her travel bag in the wheel well of the trunk. "Maybe I should have hired a real private investigator."

"'Hire' is an interesting choice of words."

She dropped her duffel bag into the trunk next to his and turned on her heel. He slammed the lid. This was going to be fun.

*　　　　　*　　　　　*

10:21 a.m.

"IS THERE a reason you haven't turned on the air?" Hillary asked. Wind whipped through the open windows of the Granada, taking her hair with it, and making conversation difficult.

"It doesn't work," Jackson replied.

"You're kidding."

"The vent isn't much better."

"Well it's a good thing it's only a hundred degrees then."

"We're going to Vegas," Jackson said. "It should be hot."

"Speaking of that, do you think we could go a little faster?"

"Downhill, yeah."

"What?"

"It's a thirty-five-year-old car, Hill."

"Hillary."

"It has its limitations."

"Sixty miles per hour?" she asked, leaning over to see the speedometer. "Really?"

Jackson craned his neck to see the gauge better over the wheel. "Wow, sixty, that's actually pretty good."

Hillary pinched the bridge of her nose and sighed. But she didn't say anything else.

Jackson opted for the back roads, skirting the San Gabriel Mountains via the Mojave Desert, rather than L.A. sprawl. Hillary watched the scenery out her window, ignoring Jackson completely. He was just fine with that.

They joined up with Interstate 15 in Victorville, where the only thing green was the golf course. I-15 would take them northeast through the desert to Nevada and put them in Las Vegas three hours later.

Hillary didn't say a word until Barstow, where Jackson asked if she was hungry. "Sure," was all she said, and he pulled into a Taco Bell just off the interstate. The lunch rush was past, and they had no trouble finding a solitary booth.

"What intrigued you?" Jackson asked after a bite of his Cheesy Gordita Crunch.

"Excuse me?"

"You said something about this case intrigued you. What was it?"

She shook her head. "Why does that matter?"

"Because I'm trying to find a potential witness. I think context is relevant."

"I don't," she said, tossing her salad with a spork.

"Is this how it's going to work?" Jackson asked. "You're going to give me the old 'need to know' line whenever I ask a question."

She sighed. "My client allegedly broke into a Beverly Hills residence but was chased off by the homeowner. My client has no record and no known ties to the homeowners, and the prosecution was unable to establish a motive for the burglary."

"So how'd the jury ever convict?"

"His DNA was found both in the house and in the bushes outside the window through which he allegedly entered."

"So how do you explain that?" he asked as he took another bite.

"That was the sticking point. That and his lack of alibi. If I can provide the latter, it might go a long way in creating reasonable doubt as to the former."

"And you think his alibi is that he drove five hours to Las Vegas to meet up with a hooker?"

"I don't know. I just know that he called her that afternoon, then forty-five minutes before the alleged break-in."

"So now even the break-in is alleged?"

"You know what I mean." She swallowed. "Arielle returned his call fifteen minutes later, thirty minutes before he supposedly broke in. I don't know why they exchanged the calls, where they were, what they did or didn't do. That is why I want to talk to Arielle. Something about this doesn't sit right. Yes, his DNA was found on the premises. But that in and of itself should not warrant a conviction. My client got a bad verdict, and I don't want that on my record."

Jackson nodded. They ate for a minute. Then he sat back, taking a big slurp of his soda. "Do you think he did it?"

Hillary looked up. "What kind of question is that?"

"You said he got a bad deal. Does that mean he's innocent?"

"It means he should have been found not guilty."

"Yeah, but did he do it?"

Hillary paused a beat, then shook her head and returned to her salad. "That's not my concern."

"What if it's murder, then do you care?"

She looked back up. "My job is to provide my client with a fair defense."

"Even if he's guilty?"

"Justice isn't just for the alleged victims."

"Spoken like a true lawyer."

"Thank you."

"It wasn't a compliment."

Hillary set down her spork. "I should think you of all people would appreciate a lack of bias on the part of defense attorneys."

Jackson decided to study the landscaping out the window. It was sparse. Barstow was in the middle of the desert, and even the river was dry. So was his soda, and he got up to refill it.

He observed Hillary as the Baja Blast filled his cup. Her beauty was paralyzing, her personality enervating. Her eyes seemed to bore directly into his soul, and her words cut him like a scalpel. He generally shrugged off insults, but hers always found their mark. Maybe because she had intellectually proven herself his equal time and time again. No, not his equal. His superior.

He decided the banter and hostility weren't working. Maybe some diplomacy was in order.

The soda started to run over, and Jackson yanked his cup away, sloshing the sticky liquid onto his hand and his pants. Licking off his fingers, he returned to the table.

"Maybe next time you should ask a grownup for help," Hillary said.

He winced and sat down. So much for diplomacy.

They finished eating in silence, and before Jackson could be a gentleman and take her tray, Hillary was on her feet. "We should get going. It's going to take a while at sixty miles per hour."

Jackson dumped his trash in the bin and followed her out into the baking afternoon sun. The leather seats were painful through his T-shirt and blue jeans, and had to be searing against Hillary's partially exposed legs. She didn't even flinch.

20

After blistering his hand on the metal seatbelt fastener, Jackson put the car in gear and gave tact another try. "So how have you been?"

Hillary frowned, as if he'd asked her for details on her last physical.

"Fine," she answered at length.

"I mean, since the accident. I've only talked to you—"

"According to you, I don't have anything to be sad about, remember?"

"I never said that."

"I believe your exact words were, 'It's just a fiancé.'"

"I didn—"

"You also used the phrase 'dime a dozen,' if I recall."

"It was a bad choice of words."

"How out of character."

Jackson thought about apologizing, taking whatever tongue-lashing she wanted to dish out, all in the name of steering away from the proverbial cliff. But her condescension was starting to get to him, and he was out of straws.

"You know what, you're right—I don't equate losing a boyfriend with losing an entire family. I didn't think you were experiencing the same kind of pain and loss I was, and I still don't. So sue me."

Hillary's eyes were on fire. "Don't you dare tell me what I lost, Jackson."

They were on the interstate by now, the Granada maxed out at sixty-two. Windows down, wind whipping in, but their voices were plenty loud.

"Yeah, well, I'll tell you what I lost," Jackson continued. "A mother—irreplaceable. A father—irreplaceable. A brother—irreplaceable."

"And Grant was the love of my life," she said, her words like shards of ice. "He was irreplaceable."

Jackson had her, and he resisted a smirk as he licked his lips. "The photo I saw on your desk suggests otherwise."

Her head whipped to the side. "How dare you!"

"What, observe your living room décor?"

"No, act like you know anything about love. You treat women like Bond girls, and have the gall to tell me how I should have felt when I lost my soulmate. Or how I should feel now."

"I'm just saying, sixteen months seems pretty quick to get over the 'love of your life.' Your exact words."

She shook her head. "I thought maybe you had changed. Matured. But you're the same smart-aleck brat who doesn't know half as much as you think and pretend, your mouth writing checks your brain can't cash, hiding all of your insecurities behind a stupid smirk. Well I see past it all, Jackson, and I see a pathetic loser who will never have what Grant and I had—fleeting as it may have been."

"Apparently you're already having seconds."

"And you're still sitting at the kiddie table playing with your food. Don't tell me what it's like to have my heart broken when yours has never been whole. And don't tell me how to live my life when you clearly don't have a clue how to live yours!"

They fumed in silence for several miles while Jackson sharpened his dagger. He knew he should keep it sheathed, but he didn't. "What did Grant ever see in you?"

"Funny, I was about to ask you the same thing." She parried his thrust, and buried his own knife into his chest. "The only thing is, he chose me. You, he was just stuck with."

Chapter Four

3:21 p.m.

THE HEAT INSIDE the Granada rivaled that outside. Neither Jackson nor Hillary spoke again, an invisible line splitting the car in two, until they were in Nevada. For her part, Hillary didn't even look Jackson's way, and he appreciated the irony of her blistering words and frigid attitude.

The first sign that they were nearing Las Vegas was billboards spaced evenly along the side of the road. They advertised hotel rates, casino deals, show tickets, sex, real estate—everything Sin City was known for. There was nothing to suggest the advertised entities were real, just miles of sand and rock in every direction.

"Do we have reservations?" Jackson asked, his voice dry. It sounded foreign.

"I booked rooms last night," Hillary said without looking his way.

"Where?"

"A Holiday Inn Express on Flamingo."

"Wow, you're quite the travel agent there, Hill. Come to Vegas and you stay in a Holiday Inn."

"This isn't Jackson's bro trip. We're here on business."

"Yes, ma'am."

They crested a small rise, and the Las Vegas skyline took shape like a smoky mirage. In a few minutes, distinct buildings began to emerge from the haze as golf communities and outlet malls sprung up along the interstate. Friday traffic from L.A. had been moderately heavy, but it intensified as they approached America's Playground.

Jackson exited the interstate just south of the airport and turned north onto Las Vegas Boulevard—"The Strip." As they passed the famous "Welcome to Fabulous Las Vegas Nevada" sign and the procession of massive resort hotel-and-casinos began, he found himself in awe.

"Your first time?" Hillary asked, a little less hostility in her voice. Was she making an attempt at civility?

23

"No," Jackson answered, checking out the replicas of the Sphinx and Egyptian obelisk in front of Luxor Las Vegas. "No, Grant and I came out here once."

"Grant? How'd you manage that?"

"I sold him on the adventure of it. He'd just read *Wild at Heart.*"

They stopped for the light at Tropicana, and Jackson used the opportunity to take in the sights. Behind him were the castle-themed Excalibur, the pyramid of Luxor, and the resplendent gold surface of Mandalay Bay. Ahead on his left, a reproduction of the New York City skyline towered over replicas of the Statue of Liberty and the Brooklyn Bridge at New York-New York. To the right, the famed golden lion stood guard in front of the uniquely green MGM Grand. By comparison, the massive Tropicana out Hillary's window looked ho-hum.

"Green light," Hillary announced.

"Thanks."

They cruised past half a dozen more mega resorts before reaching Flamingo Road. Hillary simply said, "Right," as they approached the intersection. Jackson made the turn and, a moment later, spotted their hotel on the south side of the street.

It looked like a shoebox compared to the edifices lining the strip. In reality, it was a brand new, four-story building surrounded by immaculate green lawns and an assortment of palm trees and bushes. Jackson parked as close to the front door as he could, and Hillary had her door open before the engine died. Jackson got out, the full brunt of the heat assaulting him like a blowtorch. Hillary was a statue at his back bumper, and he hurried to open the trunk. He reached in and handed her smaller bag to her, and would have slung her duffel over his shoulder had she not taken it from him first. With a shrug, he grabbed his bag and followed her inside. Sophistication and relaxation welcomed him, along with chilled central air. Suddenly he felt the weariness of heat and travel and wanted nothing more than to collapse onto a plush hotel bed.

Hillary had other things in mind. They checked in, took the stairs to their second-story rooms, and spent a few minutes freshening up. She knocked on his door as he was washing his hands, and knocked again before he could get to the door.

"Wow, impatient much?" he asked, jerking it open.

"You ready?" she asked.

"As I'll ever be." He pocketed his key card. "You have any idea how to find this Arielle Coal?"

"I'm supposed to do your work?"

"Look, I take it she's not in the phonebook, or you could have found her that way. And I'm guessing you've already tried the cell number that you traced to her."

"Not in service anymore."

"What about the photo? You get an address off her driver's license?"

"It's old. An apartment building that was torn down two years ago."

Jackson shrugged. "You check Facebook or Twitter, see if her name came up on the internet anywhere? She work for an agency, maybe?"

"Amuse Escorts."

Jackson sighed and shook his head. "Why wasn't that on the file you gave me? And what exactly do you need me for again? You just trying to ruin my weekend?"

Hillary pushed her way into the room and closed the door behind her. "I don't need you just to find out where she is. I need you to find her."

Jackson felt like the slow kid in the room. "What are you talking about?"

She took a step closer. "I need you to bring her to me, under the auspices of soliciting her services."

The light went on. "You want me to hire a hooker?"

Hillary nodded.

"Are you out of your mind?"

"I didn't say 'sleep with.' Just hire."

"You're serious? This isn't your version of *Candid Camera* or something?"

"I'm serious, Jackson. Why do you think I came to you, of all the P.I.s in the world?"

"What's that supposed to mean?"

"I figured this would be your cup of tea."

Jackson wasn't sure to what extent she meant the insult, and he didn't care. "Forget about it."

"You owe me."

"A favor. Not this."

"I don't recall splitting hairs when you came to me."

"I didn't ask you to break the law. Prostitution's illegal, even in Vegas."

"It's a misdemeanor," Hillary admitted, "but you're not going to engage in prostitution."

"Right. 'Your Honor, I just wanted to talk with her, honest.'" He shook his head again. "Do you think I'm stupid?"

"Judging by your track record?"

Jackson pretended to fume while considering how bad her proposal really was. This was certainly not what he'd envisioned when the idea of becoming a private investigator first appealed to him. He would take real cases, help real people. Not proposition and pump hookers for court testimony to get a guilty guy off.

"'I'll do anything,'" Hillary said. "Weren't those your words on the phone?"

"It's a figure of speech, Hill. 'I'd give my right arm for fill-in-the-blank' or 'I would die for dot, dot, dot.' It's not supposed to be literal."

"Fine." She put up her hands. "You know what, forget I asked. I should have known better anyhow. Your word never did mean anything."

"That's not true."

"Yeah? Prove it."

Jackson stared at her for several seconds. She stared right back.

"Just arrange to meet with her," Hillary said. "Use an alias, whatever. If you get into any legal trouble, I'll get you out of it."

"Super. I'm sure that will look great on my rap sheet too."

"Please. In your line of work it will probably be a badge of honor."

"Says the defense attorney."

Hillary glared at him. Glare was really too light of a word to describe just how her eyes raked him. He ultimately looked away, scowling and pacing across the room, just to make sure his displeasure was clearly noted. Then, the fight drained out of his body, he collapsed into a chair, resting his head into his hand.

"Okay, how do I go about soliciting a hooker?"

"You mean you don't know?"

"Do not push it," Jackson said, jumping out of the chair. "I owe you, and a deal's a deal." He sighed. "I call her, I set up the meet, and you get your answers. And then I never want to see your face again."

"Good," Hillary said. "This will work out even better than I thought."

*　　　　*　　　　*

4:14 p.m.

THE RECEPTIONIST at Amuse Escorts had never heard of anyone named Arielle Coal, and the agency didn't allow clients to request escorts by name. Even if the escort came highly recommended, as Jackson claimed. So he described

26

Arielle from the dossier Hillary had provided him, insinuating that he was looking for someone of her ilk. He was told there were several possible matches. When he asked to see photographs, he was directed to their website.

Feeling as if the degradation of his character had taken another leap, Jackson opened Amuse Escorts' website on Hillary's computer. The receptionist had guided him to the personnel directory, and he perused the photos of several women, all posed as seductively as possible in slinky evening gowns. There were no names, and it was hard to tell given the disparity between Arielle's driver's license photo and the "Glamour Shots" on the website, but he didn't think any of them were her. He thanked the receptionist anyhow and hung up.

Jackson had insisted Hillary return to her room and give him some privacy for the call. After closing down the Amuse website, he knocked on her door.

"How'd you know she worked for Amuse?" he asked.

"Her W-2 form," she answered, her eyes on her phone, not him.

He closed the door behind him. "Did it have an address?"

"Yeah, an apartment on Santa Paula Drive. I called the landlord. She moved out in January."

"Great. Well, they've never heard of her at Amuse either."

"And you believe them?"

"Does it matter?" He explained that he had been able to see photos of escorts "matching" Arielle's description and that none of them fit the bill.

Hillary waited for a second, as if expecting more. "Okay, so try something else. Imagine that you actually wanted to find her."

Jackson let out a gigantic sigh. "Fine." He handed the computer to Hillary. "You stay here and see if you can find anything."

"Do you always make your clients do your job?"

"The sooner we find her, the sooner we both get to go home."

Hillary took the laptop. "What exactly am I supposed to find?"

"The dossier you gave me is pretty flimsy. Go online and see if you can learn anything else about her. Like I said, is she on social media, is she a model or an actress on the side with her own website, anything? Check out other agencies' websites and see if you find anyone who looks like her. And I'm assuming CD&R has some sort of database you can tap into. You know, how you determine jurors' pressure points and stuff like that?"

"Where do you think this dossier came from? I've already done everything you said."

He shrugged. "Do it again."

"And what are you going to be doing?"

"Associating with the unwashed masses," Jackson answered. "Call me if you get anything."

For once, Hillary didn't slap a scathing little comment onto the end of their conversation, and Jackson left before she had a second chance. After sitting all day, he had energy to expel and decided to walk instead of drive. Besides, the Granada's leather seats had been exposed to the sun for at least half an hour, and thus would be unbearable.

Jackson thought about praying for wisdom as he walked the sidewalk along Flamingo, but praying and trolling for hookers didn't seem to go together. So he contemplated how to find Arielle as quickly as possible and get back to L.A.

His previous trip to Las Vegas had taught him a few things. One, the house did always win. The resort hotels that lined the Strip were monuments to that. Two, gambling wasn't the only reason Vegas was called Sin City. Sex was for sale everywhere—marquees, bus stops, taxi placards, and handouts available on every sidewalk. Poor slobs with absolutely no self-respect hawked flyers for everything from Grand Canyon or Hoover Dam tours to burlesque shows and hookers. They practically forced them on you as you walked down the street, and if you weren't confronted by a peddler, the next corner was sure to have several bins full of the things.

He was sweating by the time he reached Las Vegas Boulevard, and he stopped to take in the scene. Directly ahead of him, across about ten lanes of traffic, was the majestic Italian-inspired Bellagio with its famous fountains. Adjacent to it across Flamingo, the iconic Caesars Palace loomed against a bright blue sky. Left, down his side of the Strip, he saw Bally's and the half-sized Eiffel Tower at Paris. To the right, a conglomeration of hotels and casinos not quite as famous or nearly as sprawling as Bellagio or Caesars Palace were crowded together. They looked a little shady, so he backtracked to the pedestrian bridge that crossed Flamingo and headed north.

Already, the Strip was active, its sidewalks crowded with tourists. The sound of traffic was constant, and music emanated from unseen sources. In the right moment, the hustle and bustle and edgy vibe would have appealed to Jackson. But not now. All he wanted was to be home, on his deck, looking out at the Pacific.

The first hawker Jackson encountered boasted that he had the best deals on Grand Canyon helicopter tours on the Strip. The next two were moving too fast down the street, shoving leaflets as they went, and Jackson couldn't even get his question out of his mouth before they were gone. The fourth guy turned out to be a woman, old and rugged, as if she'd spent years in the sun. Jackson met her in front of Casino Royale, across the street from the Volcano at The Mirage. It was currently dormant.

The woman had long brown hair, braided, and wore an orange vest that nearly covered her sleeveless T-shirt and shorts. Three pouches in the front of the vest held various flyers, and at least a dozen buttons adorned the top half of the vest. One of them had the letters A and E shaped into the form of a woman, with Amuse Escorts scrawled in cursive below the logo.

"Excuse me," Jackson said, and the woman turned from a couple of female tourists to him. "You work for Amuse Escorts?" he asked.

She squinted through cheap sunglasses. "You want their brochure?" she asked, reaching into her pouch.

Brochures were for timeshares and power wheelchairs, not hookers for hire, but Jackson wasn't going to quibble. "I'm actually looking for someone particular. Arielle Coal?"

The woman pulled out a flyer. "Don't know the names, buddy. Here you go."

Before he could reply, she was off, honing in on a trio of guys who had just jaywalked over from The Mirage. Jackson scanned the flyer—nobody who looked like Arielle—and stuffed it in his pocket. He followed Las Vegas Boulevard as it curved to the northeast, past The Venetian and The Palazzo, before he crossed over to Treasure Island.

He turned back south, along the "gangway" in front of a faux pirate village, scanning the sidewalk for more peddlers. He finally found one in front of the Caesars Palace Forum Shops. He too had a braid, but it was gray and matched by a long, flowing beard. His flyers were not for the Grand Canyon or Hoover Dam, a fact Jackson learned as he stuck one in his chest. Jackson took it and pocketed it without looking at it.

"I'm trying to find a woman named Arielle Coal," he said. "Works for—"

"I don't know names," the guy said, starting to walk away.

"Worked for Amuse Escorts," Jackson called, a little louder than he would have liked. They weren't exactly alone on the sidewalk.

The man turned and took a step back. "Try the Rio."

"She work—"

"Ask for Johnny."

"Johnny at the Rio?"

"Usually hangs out poolside."

Jackson mulled the information for a moment as his tipster moved on to the next mark. The Rio was west of the Strip and west of I-15. Jackson decided he was sick of walking, especially given the heat of the day, which wasn't diminishing with the onset of evening. So he headed back for their hotel, calling Hillary as he crossed another pedestrian bridge to the east side of Las Vegas Boulevard.

"You find her?" she asked.

"No. A lead maybe." He explained briefly and said that he was coming back to get the car before heading to the Rio.

"You're already halfway there."

"Now I'm already halfway back," he said.

"Fine. I'm going with you."

"I'm five minutes out. Meet me at the car."

She was waiting for him at the passenger door, and he acknowledged her with a mere raise of his eyebrows. The leather seats were indeed murder, so to take his mind off them, he asked Hillary if she had found any new information online. Her reply was a terse, "No." He shelved his next question, if she had even tried.

Although not on the Strip, the Rio was still a Vegas landmark. Its fifty-one-story curved tower glowed purplish-blue and red, as did the three prongs of the hotel. Abundant palms surrounded the property, their leaves fluttering languidly in the late-afternoon breeze. A hot breeze, for what it was worth.

Jackson parked on the west side of the building, and he and Hillary walked through the interior to the pool. There were actually four pools, of various shape and size. One looked like a cornucopia (with a sand bottom); another some kind of exotic fish. Chaise lounges littered the deck, with plenty of sunbathers drinking in the last of the afternoon's sunlight. Hundreds of palm trees provided seclusion for Jacuzzis and private cabanas. The music was festive, salsa maybe, but there was too much ambient noise for Jackson to make out much of it.

"Did your pal say how we were supposed to find this Johnny character?" Hillary asked.

"I'm guessing with some help from Mr. Lincoln."

"Five bucks? Serious?"

"Okay, you're handling expenses. Cough up Mr. Jackson."

Hillary dug into her purse and provided Jackson with a twenty-dollar bill. He took it to one of two full-service bars and plopped it on the counter. The bartender eyed it, then him. "What can I get you?"

"We're looking for a guy named Johnny. I was told I could find him here."

The bartender simultaneously pocketed the twenty and pointed across the deck to a row of chaise lounges by the far pool. "Front row. Third from the left."

Jackson shaded his eyes, and nearly lost his lunch. He counted four stomachs, all rolling around on top of each other. In fairness, two of them might have been man boobs. Johnny wore red, white, and blue trunks, and a white robe that hung off his shoulders and flowed onto the ground like the train on a wedding dress.

"Thanks," Jackson mumbled, and turned to Hillary. "Maybe you should hang here. I'll talk to Butterbean."

"Suit yourself," she said, taking a seat at the bar.

Jackson made his way through the sunbathers and around the pool. He counted the occupants of the front row again, just to make sure, before approaching Johnny. He had a buffer of several chairs around him, and Jackson sat down on a vacant chaise lounge. The odor from Johnny's sunscreen nearly toppled him backwards.

"You Johnny?" Jackson asked.

The man made no movement, keeping his eyes trained at the pools from behind visor-like sunglasses. "Who wants to know?" he finally asked, his voice a sort of high-pitched gravel.

"I'm looking for a girl," Jackson said.

"You're looking the wrong way," Johnny answered with a lecherous smile. He then made some sort of oohing sound as a young woman stepped out of the pool.

"Her name's Arielle Coal," Jackson said. "She worked for Amuse Escorts."

"She left Amuse early this year," Johnny said. He reached for a drink on the opposite side of his chair. It was yellowish green, with an umbrella in it. A real man's drink.

"Any idea where I can find her?"

For the first time, Johnny turned his head to look at Jackson. He slid the sunglasses down to his neck. Then grinned as a girl—perhaps of legal age—in a two-piece walked by. His eyes followed her to the far end of the pool.

"Last I knew she was dancing at Coyote Ugly at New York-New York," he said, his big round eyes now back on Jackson. "But that was several months ago."

"Thanks," Jackson said, having no interest in how Johnny knew what he did.

Jackson headed back to Hillary while Johnny returned the shields to his eyes and resumed lusting.

"Well?" Hillary asked.

"Good news," Jackson said. "She's no longer a hooker. Now she dances on tables."

Chapter Five

6:16 p.m.

"LET ME GET this straight," Hillary said. "You're afraid to go into the bar, so you're sending me in?"

She and Jackson were on the floor of the New York-New York casino, not far from the Statue of Liberty with a blustery skirt, à la Marilyn Monroe. It had taken them longer than it should have to exit The Rio, drive a few blocks to New York-New York, find a parking spot, and walk to their present location. As a result, Hillary had already been cranky before Jackson told her he wasn't entering Coyote Ugly.

"I'm not afraid," he answered. "I'd just prefer not to."

"Are you kidding? They're not strippers, Jackson."

"Nope."

"So what's the deal?"

"I don't feel like it's the type of place I should go into."

"You went to the pool."

"Yeah."

"There were girls there. Some of them even in swimsuits."

"Swimming and dancing on a bar are different."

Hillary blew out an angry breath. Then composed herself. "So let me get this straight. You refuse to go in there because it's some den of iniquity, but you have no problems letting me go in?"

"It's girls dancing, Hill. A little different for you than it is for me."

"And what about the degenerates watching with wide eyes?"

"So you get cat-called a few times. I'm sure you're used to it. Besides, if any of them try anything, one look would turn them into an ice cube."

She nearly proved it with him.

"Take it or leave it, Hill. Makes me no difference either way."

Giving him a final look of utter contempt, she turned and headed for the mezzanine level of the casino. Jackson leaned against the side of a slot machine

33

and pondered the hill on which he'd taken his stand. He'd just spent an hour trying to hire a prostitute, but he wouldn't go into the Coyote Ugly Saloon.

He blamed it on the movie. When *Coyote Ugly* first came out, Jackson had assumed—like any decent young Christian—that it was pure filth. He'd heard from one source that it was just harmless fun, a lot of loud dancing, singing, and fancy bartending tricks. Others told him it was practically pornographic. He'd never watched it to find out. Nor did he have any clue what specifically went on inside the real bar. And he didn't have any interest finding out, just like he didn't care how good the wings were at Hooters. He had lines. This was one of them.

That was only part of it. He also wanted to take control back from Hillary. If she thought he was going to be her little lackey, going wherever and doing whatever she told him, she had another think coming. It was important to push back now and again, just to set boundaries.

While he waited, Jackson watched the hubbub in the casino. The jingling, clanking, repeating tunes from the slot machines; the neon and flashing lights; the shouts of winners and would-be winners—it was at the same time enthralling and annoying.

Hillary was gone maybe fifteen minutes. Instead of walking up to Jackson, she strode right past him.

"Anything?" he asked after a few quick steps to catch up with her.

"You're really something, you know that?"

"You know who else wouldn't be seen dead in place like that? Grant."

Hillary stopped. "For your information, Grant would much rather have gone in there himself than have me do it."

Jackson sighed. "I take it you didn't get a chance to talk to her."

"She doesn't work there anymore."

"Girl can really hold down a job."

"I got the name of another agency," she said.

"Great. We can start this whole business over."

Hillary resumed walking, headed for the front exit. Jackson followed.

"You gonna share it with me?" he asked.

"Good Night Escorts."

"Is that a double entendre?"

"Do you even know what that means?"

"I thought so," he said with a frown. "Maybe not."

Hillary sighed and shook her head again. Jackson kept a few paces behind, fatefully humming the Black Eyed Peas' "I Gotta Feeling."

The sun had dipped behind the mountains while Jackson and Hillary were inside the casino, and as night fell, Las Vegas was transformed. The mammoth resorts and casinos were just inanimate buildings during the day. At night, they came alive, megaliths with personality. Jackson stood on the sidewalk for a minute and took in the panorama.

Lights flashed everywhere. The new properties that had sprung up along the Strip had largely abandoned the neon of old Vegas, but had replaced it with every color of the rainbow, from the bright white spotlight atop Luxor's pyramid to the vibrant blues and reds adorning the towers of the fairy tale castle at Excalibur to the familiar green façade of MGM Grand. All the casino exteriors, if not colored themselves, were bathed in soft blues and yellows and whites, all of them ringed with light. The names were brightly emblazoned on the buildings, from the red Caesars Palace to the shining gold of Mandalay Bay. Their marquees boasted giant, live screens with advertisements for headline shows and coming attractions. And individual clubs, bars, and restaurants all had their own signage, all bright and beckoning.

The streets and sidewalks, busy during the day, were now flooded with people coming and going from restaurants, casinos, shows, attractions, bars, and clubs. Some were just out and about for the sake of it. Whatever their reason for being on the streets and sidewalks, their screams and shouts combined with music from the casinos and the constant traffic on Las Vegas Boulevard to form an energetic buzz. It pulsated, like Times Square on New Year's Eve or Staples Center just before tip-off of a playoff game.

Jackson couldn't help but drink it all in. Until Hillary pulled his arm.

"Come on. You've got another call to make."

"What about some dinner?"

"After you make contact."

He sighed and followed her around the front pond with spitting tugboats and Lady Liberty, then across the footbridge spanning Tropicana Boulevard, to a small front parking lot at Excalibur. Jackson had been gawking at the mock New York City skyline earlier and had missed the turn onto Tropicana, forcing him to park elsewhere. He didn't mind; it gave him a chance to take in more of the Strip's ambiance. Hillary, on the other hand, might as well have been in a factory hallway.

They drove back to their hotel in silence. Hillary found the number for Good Night Escorts on her phone, and Jackson retreated to his room to make the call in private.

"Good Night Escorts," a slinky female voice declared. "How can I help make your night unforgettable?" She accented every syllable in unforgettable.

Jackson rolled his eyes and swallowed the bile in his throat. "You could let me spend it with Arielle."

The voice on the other end paused, and he thought maybe she was about to hang up. "Is this your first time with us?" she finally asked.

"Yes. I was recommended by a friend."

Another pause. "Well, we have two young ladies by that name working for us. Did your friend happen to describe her to you?"

Jackson fought off a smile. His foot was in the door. Now not to lose his shoe. Or his soul.

He looked down at the dossier Hillary had provided. "She's a brunette, beautiful auburn hair, and 'maddening' green eyes." He choked internally.

"Arielle with an E," the operator said. "Hang on one second, Tiger, and I'll get her number for you."

"Great," Jackson said. He took the opportunity to wonder where on the sleazy scale hiring recommended call girls fell. After all, there was sleazy and then there was *sleazy*.

The minx returned and gave Jackson a phone number, Las Vegas area code. Then she went over pricing and terms, her words making it very clear that Good Night Escorts only provided companions. Her tone was another matter entirely.

Jackson ended the conversation just as someone knocked on his door. He saw through the peephole that it was Hillary.

"Well?" she asked when he admitted her.

"Just a second, I think I have to wash my ear out with soap."

"Quit being melodramatic."

"I got her number."

"Call her."

"There's a little procedure to it," Jackson said. He relayed the operator's directions. Good Night's escorts required a twenty-five-percent retainer up front. Consider it a reservation fee, the receptionist had said. The rest would be placed in an escrow account, managed by the service. Afterwards, assuming there were no complaints on either side, the money would pass to the escort. The original twenty-five percent was theirs no matter what. And of course, Good Night took a cut, although the lady never said anything about that. From the way she talked, she wanted Jackson to believe that Good Night merely played a matchmaking role, out of the goodness of their hearts.

"Did you give them your credit card?"

"Uh, that would be a no. I believe the client was going to cover expenses for this little junket."

"And how is it going to work when you give them my name on the credit card?" she asked.

"You expect me to put it on my card?"

"I'll pay you back."

"They keep track of credit card transactions, Hill. There's certain things I'd kind of like kept off my record."

"Maybe you should have thought of that a year ago."

He swallowed a growl and consented to using his credit card.

"Good. Now call her."

"Not with you standing here."

"Come on."

"I never make a date with one woman in front of another."

"You know, you're not half as cute as you think you are."

The first response that popped into Jackson's head was that Hillary was twice as cute as she had ever been told. Even in a shirt that was rumpled from a day in the car and a plain pair of shorts. But there was no way he was telling her that. So instead, he resorted to a Captain Jack Sparrow rip-off that felt cheesy as soon as it left his tongue.

"Ah, but you have agreed that I'm cute."

Hillary gave him a "whatever" shake of the head and turned on her heel. She let the door close with plenty of force, and Jackson took a deep breath before dialing.

As he punched in Arielle's number, he couldn't remember the last time he had even asked a girl out on a date. Sure, he and Sam—and at one time, Maggie—hung out a lot, but there were none of the butterflies-in-the-stomach phone calls to see if they'd have dinner. Even past girlfriends had just sort of fallen into place. Now, here he was, wondering how to ask a call girl out to dinner.

And dinner was part of the deal. The smooth-voiced receptionist stressed that Good Night Escorts charged an initial flat rate, and billed hourly after six hours. In other words, their girls liked to be wined and dined.

Jackson listened through three rings, then heard voicemail pick up. "This is Arielle. I can't take your call right now, so please leave a message. Thanks." The voice was soft, innocent sounding. He had expected a chain-smoking gurgle like Ursula from *The Little Mermaid*. Arielle sounded more like, well, Ariel.

He disconnected the call before the beep. He was not about to ask out a hooker via voicemail.

Next he phoned Hillary's room, told her he got voicemail, and again suggested they get something to eat. She sighed but agreed, and he met her in the hallway. Jackson proposed the Hard Rock Café, and Hillary, apparently tired of arguing, agreed again.

Easily detectible by the giant eighty-four-foot neon guitar by its front entrance, the Hard Rock Café sat on the corner of Harmon and Paradise a few blocks east of the Strip. It was close enough to their hotel that Hillary persuaded Jackson to walk. Even though the sun had set, the air was still warm and a trace muggy. It was a perfect night for dinner with a beautiful girl in a glamorous city. Just not this beautiful girl, and not this city, given their reason for being there.

On a Friday night, the Hard Rock was packed, and Jackson and Hillary had to wait twenty minutes to be seated. They perused the gift shop and checked out the rock and roll memorabilia on the walls, anything to avoid conversation. Not that it would have been easy, with everyone from The Who to Aerosmith to Maroon 5 pumping through the restaurant's sound system.

When they were finally shown to a booth, Jackson and Hillary looked over their menus and ordered without so much as a word to each other. After the waitress left them, Hillary leaned over the small two-person table to ask a question. Elvis was singing "Jailhouse Rock," the quietest song of the night. Still, the din of the crowd forced Jackson to lean forward as well and ask Hillary to repeat herself.

"What's your next step if you can't get a hold of her?"

Jackson paused a beat. "Dessert."

She rolled her eyes.

"Call her again," he said.

"You should have left a message."

"It's Friday," Jackson said. "She's probably out leaning on the arm of some tractor salesman from Des Moines while he gambles away the family nest egg."

Hillary sat back and crossed her arms, saying nothing more until their food arrived. She'd ordered a salad; Jackson a mushroom and Swiss burger. After a few bites, he asked how her salad was, another attempt at being cordial.

"Fine," she said without looking up, and their dinner conversation was over.

There was a lull between U2 and Kings of Leon or Jackson never would have heard his phone. He quickly checked the display, and announced to Hillary, "It's her." She stopped mid-bite as Jackson answered. "Hello?"

"Hi there," said a soft, demure voice. "It's Arielle."

"Hi," Jackson said back. "Just a second."

He stood and made his way through the restaurant, out into the desert night, where he could hear. Sort of. His ears were still ringing.

"Sorry about that," he said. "You know Vegas."

She giggled, straight out of a can. "You called me earlier?"

"I just got to town, and I was looking for somebody to show me a good time."

"What did you have in mind?" Soft, demure, and yet a little playful.

Jackson leaned against a palm tree and waited until a car whooshed by on Paradise. "Well, how about a late dinner and then we'll see."

Another giggle. "I assume you spoke with my agency."

"I did."

"So you know our billing procedure."

"I do."

"Any idea how long 'we'll see' might take?"

"I've got all night," Jackson said, feeling as if God was holding the Book of Life and signaling to the archangel Michael for an eraser.

"That makes two of us," she said.

"Great," Jackson said. "Tell me, Arielle, where do you like to eat in this town?"

"That depends what you're in the mood for."

He thought for a moment. He'd already eaten half his burger, but Hillary was footing the bill.

"I'd love a good steak."

"SW Steakhouse is top of the line, if you can afford it."

Jackson grinned. "Money is no problem."

She giggled yet again.

He rolled his eyes.

They bantered for another minute, set the time, and covered finances. Jackson then called Good Night Escorts back and made a deposit via credit card. As he closed his phone and headed back inside, he almost felt guilty for the trap he was setting for Arielle.

Almost.

Chapter Six

HILLARY PRACTICALLY LASSOED the waitress for the check when Jackson returned with the news that he had booked a "date" with Arielle.

"What's the rush?" Jackson asked as she signed the credit card slip. "I'm not meeting her till nine-thirty."

"Do you have reservations?"

"I have to call," he said, pretending he'd already thought of it.

"And you might want to shower first," Hillary said, "considering you've been in a car and running around the Strip all day."

"You realize this is just a sting, right?" Jackson said. "I'm not actually spending the night with her."

"You have to get her back to the hotel," she replied.

"Ha. The pope could get her back to the hotel."

They paid and headed north along Paradise. Carrying the remaining half of his burger, Jackson had to speed walk to keep up with Hillary. Fortunately, she had her head in her phone and wasn't moving at max speed. "SW Steakhouse?" she asked suddenly, not breaking stride.

"Yeah, what's wrong?"

"Did you happen to look at the menu?"

"Why?"

"There's not a dinner on here for less than forty dollars."

"What can I say, I'm a high-roller, baby."

"Maybe the high-roller would like to cover his own expenses."

"What'd you want me to do, give her a choice between McDonald's and BK?'"

"Do you think, given the fact that you've already eaten, that you could at least not order the most expensive cut on the menu?"

He shrugged. "Why not? I'll get a filet mignon. That sounds small and probably cheap, right?"

Hillary ignored him and kept walking. When they returned to their hotel, instead of going into her room, she stood behind Jackson as he retrieved his key from his wallet.

"Would you like to come over?" he asked over his shoulder.

"What do you have for clothes?" Hillary asked as he opened the door. She followed him in.

"More of the same."

"That's it?"

"You didn't say to pack for a night on the town."

She rolled her eyes. "Did it ever occur to you to bring along at least a semi-formal outfit?"

"I don't own a semi-formal outfit," he said.

"You really just have jeans and T-shirts?"

Jackson unzipped his bag and set it on the bed. "Look for yourself."

"Not a chance."

He heaved it back to the floor.

"I assume you remembered a toothbrush."

Jackson snapped his fingers and gave a mock sigh.

Hillary rolled her eyes again. "You can't go to SW Steakhouse in blue jeans and a USC T-shirt."

"Then can I have the plastic? I'll hit Armani."

"We don't have time for you to go. What size shirt do you wear?"

"Medium."

"I mean dress shirt."

"I don't know. Whatever fits."

Hillary bit off a scream. "Pants?"

Jackson bent down and peeked into his bag to check his blue jeans. "Thirty-four."

"Length?"

"Thirty-four too. I'm very easy."

"Give me your key."

"What?"

"So I can get in when I get back."

"Door opens from the inside too, Hill."

"You need to shower, shave, get a man's haircut. Seriously, when was the last time you looked in a mirror?"

"I forget, was I this big of pain when I asked you for a favor?"

41

"Oh yeah. You probably just don't remember, seeing as how you . . . You know what, we don't have time for this. I need the car keys too."

"Walk."

"Jackson."

He hesitantly reached for his pocket, then tossed her the keys, underhanded but without a lot of arc.

"What, like I could do any damage to it."

If it hadn't been for the fact that she had his car, Jackson would have been halfway back to Los Angeles by the time she returned. Instead, he was showered, shaved, and dressed—same jeans, different shirt—when she knocked and admitted herself to his room. It was ten after nine, twenty minutes before he was supposed to meet Arielle.

"We don't have much time," Hillary said as she set bags from two stores Jackson had never heard of on the dresser. He peeked into the first and pulled out a blue button-down shirt. UCLA blue. There was no way that was a coincidence. The second bag contained a pair of dark, semi-formal dress pants and a belt.

"I didn't have time to buy shoes, so come up with an explanation for why you're wearing sneakers."

"How much did you spend?"

"Why do you care?"

"I feel a little bad about not having steakhouse-appropriate clothes along."

"Feeling bad doesn't do us any good now. Get dressed."

He retreated to the bathroom and quickly changed. Tennis shoes and white socks didn't go too well with black pants, but the pants were long enough that if he kept from crossing his legs, no one would know. And they were sort of comfortable too.

He emerged from the bathroom and Hillary lifted an eyebrow. "It'll do, I guess. Only this isn't *Miami Vice*. Button your shirt."

Jackson had left the top two buttons open, figuring it made him look casual and cool. He didn't bother arguing with her, but buttoned the lower of the two. "Anything else?"

"Yeah. Don't mess this up."

"Not sure I could if I wanted to."

"You should get going," she said, tossing his keys back to him. "I'm keeping the room key. I'll be in here waiting when you get back. Send me a text when you're on the way."

"I don't have texting on my phone."

"Every phone has texting."

He shrugged.

She blew out an angry breath. "Fine." She cut her eyes to the door.

"Um, aren't we forgetting something?" he asked.

"What?"

"Cash. I'm buying, but you're paying."

"Use your card again."

"I'm not wild about racking up all these charges."

"I don't care what you're wild about. I'll pay you back. And I didn't have time to get to an ATM. Now go."

"One more thing," he said.

"What?"

"When I get her back here, and she finds you lying in wait like a court stenographer, how do we keep her here?"

"Stand by the door."

"Great," Jackson said. "Forceful detainment against her will. Well, I don't see how this can go wrong."

*　　　　　*　　　　　*

9:27 p.m.

JACKSON WAS short on time, so he utilized the valet parking at the main entrance of Wynn Las Vegas. Named for business mogul Steve Wynn, the forty-five story hotel had opened in 2005, followed by its twin, Encore, in 2008. Wynn was a far cry from the glitz and glitter of old Las Vegas, featuring glass inlaid marble floors, exquisite décor, and shopping to the tastes of Dior, Cartier, and Louis Vuitton. Most of the shops were in the Wynn Esplanade, an interior walkway that curved around the Lake of Dreams and The Mountain, a conglomeration of rock, pines, and waterfalls that was the defining feature visible from the Strip. That and the building's curved contour.

SW Steakhouse was just off the casino—which was refined and upscale as well—with outdoor terrace seating that overlooked the Lake of Dreams. A three-acre body of water, the lake was backed by a forty-foot waterfall set against The Mountain. Every half hour after sunset, the lake came alive with over 4,400 LED lights and a variety of holographic images.

A maître d' showed Jackson to a table on the terrace. Arielle had not yet arrived, and Jackson was seated as one of the lake shows began, this one involving two glowing balls that seemed to hover over the surface of the water as they "danced" with one another. With the entire lake water lit, accompanied by a stirring musical score, the show was quite impressive.

A waiter who was better dressed than Jackson brought him a wine list and a menu, and Jackson perused the latter while keeping an eye out for Arielle and taking in the ambiance of the restaurant. It had all the typical trimmings—fine linens, flowers and candles on each table, more glasses and silverware than Jackson knew what to do with—augmented by the tranquil beauty of the lake, the privacy provided by the surrounding foliage, and the charm of an evening breeze.

If only he wasn't there to meet a lady of the evening.

Jackson didn't wear a watch, and he felt like checking his phone would be a touch gauche in such a place. So he passed time by devouring warm, delicious rolls brought to him by the waiter. He'd only eaten half of his burger, after all, and they practically melted in his mouth.

After the third roll, he couldn't resist. He withdrew his phone and checked the time. Ten till ten. Arielle was twenty minutes late. He was temporarily buoyed by the thought that maybe she wasn't coming and he wouldn't have to go through with this. But there was no way Hillary was letting him off that easy, and for that reason, he hoped Arielle would show soon.

She didn't. At ten, he decided to call her. He stood and made his way out of the steakhouse before dialing. Arielle didn't answer, and he disconnected and tried again. Ten rings total, no answer.

With a sigh, Jackson returned to his seat and had another roll. He waited until quarter after when he was told very politely by the waiter that the kitchen was closing and if he was going to order, it had to be now. Jackson said that his "date" must have had something come up and apologized for the inconvenience. He was not charged for the water or the bread, but left a ten-dollar tip anyhow. Hillary would reimburse him.

Just to be sure, Jackson loitered outside the entrance to the restaurant until ten-thirty. When Arielle still didn't show, he called again, not surprised that there was no answer. He left a message, his tone more concerned than wanting a refund. Maybe something had come up?

Clapping his phone shut, Jackson scanned the casino floor one more time. The crowd was thinning somewhat, and still no Arielle. Jackson picked up his car, tipped the valet, and called Hillary as he started back to the hotel.

"Jackson?" she answered.

"She didn't show."

"What?"

"Probably took one look at my sneakers from across the room and realized I wasn't her type."

"This is not the time for jokes."

He finally was able to turn left onto Sands Avenue. "Maybe she's onto us."

"How could she be? Did you try calling her?"

"Twice. Left a message a little while ago."

"Where are you now?"

"I figured I'd hit the craps tables."

Her lack of comment was scathing in its own way.

"I'm on my way back," Jackson said. "I'll be there in a f—" He heard her disconnect before he could finish.

Jackson took his time getting up to his room, scanning the breakfast area for a microwave with which to heat up the rest of his burger. Those rolls had been good, but not filling. The door to his room was propped open on the slide latch, and he found Hillary sitting at the table, staring intently at her laptop screen. She had changed into blue jeans—probably designer—and a white, long-sleeved blouse. She wore heels that came to a point, and her hair was clipped behind her head. She was the casual lawyer, ready for interrogation.

"What happened?" she asked before Jackson could close the door.

"Well, these two balls started floating on the water, a red one and a blue—"

"Jackson, so help me I will smack you if you don't cut this flippant attitude."

"What part of 'she didn't show' confused you earlier?"

"You didn't see anything off? Nobody watching you, anything like that?"

"Nope."

"What'd you say in your message?"

"'It's Jack, I'm at the restaurant, where are you, give me a call.' I kept it light and playful, in character."

Hillary checked her watch. "You should have waited longer."

"She was forty-five minutes late, Hill."

"Hillary."

"The kitchen was closing, what was I to do? She was a no-show."

Hillary stood and paced. Jackson crashed on the bed and reached for the remote. The Dodgers were seven games behind the Giants in the N.L. West, but had a chance to spoil San Diego's wildcard hopes. It was worth monitoring.

45

"Call the agency," Hillary said.

Jackson dropped the remote on the bed. "I doubt they know where she is."

"Find out."

"Yes, ma'am." He went out into the hallway to call Good Night Escorts. He was greeted by a voice similar to but different from the first one. He pictured a blonde instead of a brunette. "I was supposed to have dinner with one of your clients, and she didn't show," he explained after she issued the same greeting as the first.

"I'm so very sorry about that," the woman said. "Can I please have your name?"

"Jackson Douglas," he said with a sigh. He'd only given Arielle his first name, but when he'd called the agency to make payment, he had been forced to give them his full name as it appeared on his credit card.

"One second." The woman tapped on her keyboard. "You were scheduled with Arielle, is that correct?"

"That's right."

"That's strange. She hasn't contacted us, which is protocol if a complication arises. Have you spoken to her?"

"Not since we made the date."

"And what time was that?"

"Eight, ballpark."

"I see." More tapping. "Well, Mr. Douglas, I am very sorry for your inconvenience this evening. I will certainly refund the remainder of your payment back to your credit card. Before I do, could I possibly interest you in another of our escorts. I know it's late, but I'm sure we could find someone available."

"Actually, any chance you can tell me where I could find Arielle. I was really looking forward to meeting her."

"I'm afraid I can't do that."

"Not an address, home phone, anything?"

"No, sir, I'm afraid not."

Jackson didn't push, and in two minutes, he was off the phone with a confirmation number for the reimbursement. He returned to his room and broke the news to Hillary.

She sat back and sighed. "Now what?"

"I don't know, but this has an odd taste. There's something not right about this girl. Keeps switching jobs, moving, changing cell numbers."

"All the more reason to see what she knows."

"So you're not going to let me watch *SportsCenter*, get a good night's sleep, and go home tomorrow?"

She shook her head.

He sighed and opened his phone.

"Who are you calling now?"

He held the phone to his ear and ignored her. On the fourth ring, his friend Mouse answered. "Hey, dude." Wide awake, probably killing aliens online. It was how he spent the majority of his time, in addition to some harmless hacking for the sake of it. If there was information to be found on the World Wide Web, "Mouse" was the guy to find it.

"Hey, I need a favor," Jackson said. "Can you track down a phone number and get me the address?"

"You don't need me for that, dude. Try Google."

"It's a cell."

Mouse sighed. "Give me the number."

Jackson read him Arielle's cell number, and Mouse said he'd call back shortly. Jackson dropped back onto the bed and waited. Mouse returned the call in two minutes.

"Baltimore Gardens Apartments," he said, adding the apartment number. "Just west of the Stratosphere in Las Vegas. Whose place is this?"

"Friend of a friend," Jackson said.

"Arielle Coal? Sounds like a stripper."

"Thanks, man."

"Sure thing."

Jackson closed his phone and asked to borrow Hillary's laptop. It only took him a few minutes to map the location while he relayed Mouse's information to her.

"Let's go," she said.

"And what if she's there?" Jackson asked. "We just knock on the door and ask to depose her? I go, in character."

"And what, claim you're stalking her?"

"Better me than us," Jackson said.

Hillary sighed. "What's your plan? Kidnap her? Interrogate her yourself?"

"I'll improvise."

"Oh, fabulous."

"You know what, Hill, I've had about enough of your disdain. The fact is, I am actually pretty good at what I do. I've gone along with everything you've asked, no matter how degrading, so I'm calling the shot on this one. I'm going to my car. I have over a hundred bucks in cash. Either I go to her place, alone, or I'm getting a room with a view, ordering room service, and heading back to L.A. in the morning. Your choice."

Hillary stared at him for a moment, just long enough to be unsettling. Her face revealed nothing. "Call me and let me know the second you have something," she finally said.

He grabbed his keys without a word and headed for the door.

*   *   *

11:19 p.m.

JACKSON HAD no idea what he would do if Arielle opened the door. As he approached her apartment, he began to doubt it would get that far. He would probably be shivved in the back for his shoes long before he rang her buzzer.

To get to Baltimore Avenue, Jackson had gone north on the Strip. It had still been rocking. Just a few blocks north and west, the venue was completely different. Matching stucco apartment buildings lined both sides of the street. More were visible at the end of the block. It looked like military housing. The obligatory palm trees swayed in the darkness they helped cause by blocking out a pair of streetlights. He guessed Arielle went to most clients and not the other way around.

Jackson pulled to the curb and got out. Looking behind him, he could see the giant spire of the Stratosphere towering over the palms. The opulence of Las Vegas tourism one block, cookie cutter tenements the next.

Entering the building, Jackson navigated to Arielle's apartment on the second floor. He rapped on the door and waited. There was no answer, and he leaned toward the door to listen. Loud music was vibrating through the hallway, but it wasn't coming from her place. He knocked again.

Nothing. Jackson tried the knob. He couldn't help it. As a private investigator, he was vocationally bound to try the door. It opened, and with a look up and down the hallway, Jackson slipped into her apartment. The lights were on, a lamp in the living area and ceiling fixture down a hallway on the right.

"Arielle?" Jackson called. "Anyone here?"

No answer.

Somewhere in the distance, a police siren sounded. The loud music switched beats but kept playing. All that was missing was a crying baby from the next apartment.

Arielle's place was a paradox. It was old, small, not located in the best part of town. But she had amenities, such as a flat screen TV and a laptop computer on the couch (a plush couch, for that matter). Artwork on the walls conveyed a tropical theme: a blown-up photograph of a small sailboat alone on a tranquil sea, a conch shell collage, a painting of a palapa on the beach at sunset.

Jackson peered into the kitchenette. A sleek, single-brew coffeemaker was next to a bright blue and green margarita machine. He also saw a blender and a smoothie maker. And more Caribbean knickknacks. The oldest profession apparently paid pretty well.

Before trespassing too far, Jackson called Arielle's name again. She was clearly gone, and he talked himself into a thorough look around. It was their only lead to her, and if he didn't check the place out, Hillary would just send him right back.

There were a couple of bills on the table, nothing unusual. Two issues of *People* sat on the living room coffee table. Wary of leaving fingerprints, Jackson opted against opening the laptop on the couch. Instead he quickly scoured the kitchen before moving to the bedroom.

He stopped in his tracks.

A cell phone lay on the floor, a picture of a man on the screen. Jackson bent to look at the picture and the name above it, and that's when he saw the arm.

Slowly he stood and advanced toward the open closet door. The arm gave way to a shoulder and a head, and then the rest of a body clad in a silk robe that, like the body, was spattered in blood. Several bullet holes were clearly visible through the fabric and in the flesh above the collar. The face, drained of blood, showed panic and pain. The eyes were rolled back into the head. Wet, tangled hair was splayed in every direction—across the face, onto the floor, and over some of the wounds. Even so, Jackson had no difficulty recognizing the corpse.

It was Arielle Coal.

Jackson realized he was standing in dead hooker blood. He stepped back and wiped his shoe on the carpet. He didn't see a gun anywhere, or shell casings, but didn't dare get closer to look in the closet.

He studied the blood on the floor for a moment, and the phone. Had she been calling when she was shot, or had she tried to call afterwards? Not a forensic expert, he guessed the former.

He didn't have long to think about it. He heard the door to the apartment opening and realized the siren had grown much louder. Red and blue lights flashed outside the window.

Jackson turned toward the door to announce his presence. Before he could, a police officer appeared in the doorway, gun drawn. "Police! Don't move!"

Chapter Seven

Thirteen months ago . . .
Saturday, August 20
6:24 a.m.

SERGEANT CASPER SET a Styrofoam cup of coffee on the table in front of Jackson. He gave a friendly-ish nod, then backtracked and left him alone in the interrogation room. Casper was the only other white guy at the station, and for this reason, he and Jackson seemed to have bonded.

With cuffed hands, Jackson reached for the steaming cup. Funny, it looked just like the stuff in the grill grease traps at McDonald's. McDonald's . . . he could kiss that job goodbye. He wouldn't much miss the minimal wage, at least until his savings were totally depleted. Nor would he miss the awkward teenagers and college dropouts who had manned the grills and assembly lines with him. But the activity—the menial physical labor, the having something at all to do that just maybe would keep his mind from the searing, constant pain—that he would miss.

Jackson sipped the coffee. Tasted about like the stuff in the grease traps too, and it immediately made him nauseous. Or rather, just revived an existing sensation. Without swallowing a drop, he dribbled back into the cup. Right over his split lip, and for a moment, it stung worse than the pounding in his head. Setting his jaw, Jackson licked the cut and set the cup of grease out of reach.

The door opened and Hillary strode into the interrogation room. She stopped and stood with her back arched, her mouth just a line, eyes bullets. As always, she was dressed to the nines, even on short notice. A tan skirt suit over a brown blouse, hugging her body perfectly, was accentuated by a sophisticated bead necklace. Her hair was up but still stylish, and she carried an expensive attaché case in her left hand. Expensive, Jackson knew, because he had been with Grant when he picked it out.

Jackson's mouth was dry and his stomach flip-flopping, now for two reasons. Because it would matter, he sat up slightly. "Thanks . . ." He cleared his throat. "Thanks for coming."

Hillary finally moved from the door, which Casper closed behind her. "You look terrible," she said, setting her attaché case on the table. She unbuttoned her blazer and sat down. Bangles on her wrist clanked against each other. Vanilla-scented perfume wafted across the table. Finally, a smell other than sweat and urine.

"I feel terrible," Jackson said.

"What happened?"

"You see that Vin Diesel-looking guy on the way in? We 'exchanged.'"

"Why?"

"Because he was the baddest dude in the holding cell."

"So what, you felt provoked to attack him?"

"That's how it works in here."

"You're an idiot."

Jackson shrugged. "I landed a few."

Hillary retrieved a notepad and pen from her case. "Start at the beginning. Tell me everything you can remember."

Jackson took a breath. "A guy at work, Orlando, he mentioned that he and his cousin Paco occasionally hang out at Griffith Park."

"And by hang out, you mean 'get high.'"

Jackson nodded. "He invited me along a couple of times. Last night I said yeah."

"How stupid . . ." Hillary mumbled under her breath. She didn't look up from the pad. "Go on."

"Orlando and I met Paco and his pal Eddie. Paco passed out joints, and we walked down into the ravine and smoked them."

"How many?"

"One."

"One?"

"Yeah."

"You sure about that?"

"Pretty. But it might have been more of a blunt than a joint. I'm still learning the vernacular."

Hillary rolled her eyes. "Then what?"

"We were waiting for some guy named Miggy to show up."

"Who's Miggy?"

"Beats me. Some guy. He never came. The cops did."

"And they hauled you all in here for smoking a blunt?"

52

"I think O and Paco had a few more."

"How many more?"

"I wasn't counting."

"Estimate."

"A few."

"What about Eddie?"

"No idea."

Hillary wiggled the pen between her fingers. "Is that it?"

Jackson looked down. "Uh . . . Paco and Eddie were delivering a few dozen joints to Orlando. It was supposed to be four dozen, so Eddie had Orlando's extra cash. Cops found it all."

"So Eddie was the supplier?"

"I don't know."

"Because you just said Paco passed out the joints."

"He was the one who physically handed me the joint. Or blunt. Or whatever. Eddie was the one who had Orlando's cash."

"So they were partners?"

"They drove together is about all I know. I wasn't exactly taking minutes."

Hillary leaned forward. "They're holding you on possession with intent to sell. That's two to four, Jackson. You may want to start applying yourself here."

"I wasn't selling, or intending to sell. I was just there."

"To get high. Yeah, you're an innocent bystander. It's guilt by association."

"That going to be our defense?"

"I'm not sure I'm representing you," she said, capping her pen. She closed her notepad. "By the way, bail's twenty grand."

"The bail or the bond?"

"What did I just say?"

"So two grand."

"Do you have it?"

"Not on me."

"No kidding."

"I can get two grand, but it's kind of going to wipe me out."

"Don't do the crime if you can't do the time."

"Is that what they teach at Pepperdine Law?"

"No, they teach us not to commit crimes and not to 'hang out' with people who do."

"I'm sorry, but don't you make a living defending people who commit crimes?"

"We defend people who are accused of crimes."

"Sure, and none of them are ever guilty." Jackson turned in his seat. "You must really be loving this, playing all high-and-mighty. Go ahead and gloat, Hill. You're better than me. You would never dream of doing anything so stupid."

Hillary gritted her teeth, but quickly regained her composure. "No, I wouldn't. And you know why, because I have something you'll never have—character." She leaned halfway across the table, eyes blazing. "You think I'm not hurting? You think this is easy on me? I lost my fiancé, Jackson!"

"So get another boyfriend! I lost my family, Hillary!"

Hillary stood up, and Jackson thought she was going to leave. She stopped at the door and faced him. "I'm going to pretend you didn't just say that, because if you had ever been in love you would know how imprudent and insensitive it was."

Jackson looked away.

"Do you have any idea what day it is today?" she asked.

"Saturday?"

"The date."

"August . . . twentieth?"

"That date ring a bell?"

He frowned. "Should it?"

Hillary's grin was actually a grimace. "No, it probably shouldn't to you." She pulled her chair back out and sat down. She sighed. "I'm going out on a limb here, but let me guess, you don't have the money to pay for a lawyer either?"

Jackson wanted to crawl under the table. "I was hoping you could do it on the house, a family discount."

"'We aren't family. We never will be.' Isn't that what you said?"

Jackson was beat and he knew it. He hoped a hangdog expression would count for something. He put as much pout into his lower lip as he could without looking ridiculous. "Look, Hill."

"Hillary!"

Jackson tried not to sigh. "Hillary. You're right, I'm an idiot, a moron, a meatball. What I did was stupid and senseless, okay? I don't deserve your help, and yes, I'm only asking you because I'm in trouble. I'm exploiting what little of a relationship we have."

She tilted her head and licked her lips. Jackson had seen similar looks from prey animals on *National Geographic.*

He continued. "Grant raved about you, which means behind the smugness and piety and disdain you have for me, there must be some Christian decency inside you. So I'm appealing to that. I'm begging, Hillary. Please help me. I didn't have anything to do with selling drugs. I smoked a joint. I'll take my slap on the wrist, but you gotta get me off the hook for selling. Do that, and I promise I'll never ask you for anything or bother you again as long as we live. As far as you're concerned, I'll be dead too."

Hillary sat back and crossed her legs. She stared at Jackson for several minutes, he was sure just to make him squirm.

"And I'll owe you," he added. "Help me, Hillary. And I'll help you."

"How are you ever going to help me?"

He shook his head. "Any way I can. Any time. You name it. Call it *quid pro quo.*"

She rolled her eyes and stared for another minute for good measure. Finally, she spoke. "Tell me what you know about Orlando, Paco, and Eddie."

"You'll do it?"

She opened her pad again, and uncapped the pen. "Tell me what you know."

Jackson scooted his chair closer to the table. "Orlando and I work together. He's just a recreational user, a little bit of a knucklehead."

"Paco and Eddie?"

"I don't know. Orlando mentioned Paco a few times. I'd never heard of Eddie until tonight."

"And this person, Miggy?"

"No clue. A guy who was supposed to meet us."

"To buy? Sell?"

Jackson shook his head.

"What will the three of them say about you?"

"Orlando, I don't know. Paco and Eddie are mad. They think I turned on them." He pointed to his lip and a somewhat blackened eye. "They were on Vin Diesel's side."

Hillary was unimpressed. She wiggled the pen some more. "You are a first time offender, and if you testify first, we may be able to work a deal. Are you willing to testify against them?"

"I'll tell the truth: Orlando bought pot, Paco and Eddie sold it. I watched and blew one."

"Maybe leave that out."

From her attaché case, Hillary pulled out a cell phone. "Let me make a call. If I talk to the A.D.A. now, we may be able to get your charges reduced, which means getting your bail reduced."

"Thanks, Hill. Ary."

She began to dial and Jackson leaned back. He'd been tormented by an image ever since the cops had put him in the back of the squad car. It was of his parents, sitting on a heavenly cloud, floating just off the surface of the earth. They were watching him burn hash, and they were frowning sternly.

He tried to concentrate on other things. He watched Hillary pace and talk. She was speaking legalese, fast and quiet, and he couldn't make much from one side of the conversation. After ten minutes, she clapped her phone shut.

"I got his assistant. He's going to make a few calls and get back to me. But it sounds favorable."

"What's favorable?"

"With your testimony, you'll probably avoid jail time."

"What about my record?"

"At worst a misdemeanor. You can still buy guns and vote."

Jackson smiled. "Thanks, Hillary."

"Tell me something, Jackson. Why? Even from you, I didn't expect this."

He sat back and took a deep breath. "I was desperate. I thought it might . . . might numb the pain for just a little while. I know it's stupid, but nothing else has helped, and I couldn't stand it anymore."

"So did it?" she asked. "Did it numb the pain?"

Jackson looked at the floor under the table. "No." When he lifted his head, Hillary was standing.

"It could be a few hours," she said. "I'm going to see about getting you different accommodations."

He nodded. "Hey, Hillary."

She paused at the door.

"What's today? August twentieth?"

She smiled sadly. "It was supposed to be our wedding."

Chapter Eight

DETECTIVES BAXTER AND Cruz were playing a modified game of good cop-bad cop. More of a Mr. Feeny-Jonathan Turner. Baxter laid down the law; Cruz looked for ways Jackson could get around it. They'd been at it for close to an hour, after letting Jackson hang out in the Las Vegas Metropolitan Police Department holding cell for most of the night. Or so he assumed. He had no way to tell time.

"Murder One could get you the death penalty in Nevada," Baxter said. He wore a tie, pressed shirt, and pleated pants, and he talked with the voice of an appliance salesman.

"Come on, tell us why you did it," Cruz said with a wink. He was short, with spiked hair and tats on the inside of his arm, jawing gum like a cold-turkey quitter. He was already sitting on the edge of the table, while Baxter leaned back in his chair, legs crossed as if he was doing the Sunday Times crossword.

"Unless you got Grissom in the back room cooking something up, you're forgetting one little detail," Jackson said. "Evidence."

"You were caught at the crime scene," Baxter said with complete disinterest. "Your DNA will be all over the place."

"Juries love DNA," Cruz said, popping his gum.

"So I've heard. Say, would you two mind sitting a little closer together? I'm getting dizzy from the back and forth."

Baxter scanned his tablet. "Says here you were arrested last August for possession of marijuana?"

"Is that so?"

"You struck a deal, got by with community service and therapy." He looked up. "I guess it didn't work."

Cruz winked again. "You confess now, strike a deal, maybe you get a reduced sentence."

"Or since I'm innocent, I walk."

Baxter shook his head. "There is no way you're walking." He looked at Cruz. The cue.

Cruz appropriately shook his head. "Afraid not."

"Well, then I guess I don't have a choice," Jackson said. He leaned forward slightly. "I'll have to wait for my lawyer."

Baxter pursed his lips. Cruz showed the first signs of annoyance and assaulted his gum.

"She's a real bulldog," Jackson said. "Not much of a looker like all the lady lawyers on TV, but she's a terror in the courtroom."

"And she just happens to be in Las Vegas?" Baxter asked.

Jackson held out his palms.

"Once she gets here, the deal's off the table."

"What deal was that again?" He looked to Cruz. "And is that even legal? Isn't there something in the Constitution about not punishing the accused for wanting to talk to his lawyer?"

Before either of them could speak, the door opened and Hillary marched in.

"Jackson, don't say anything."

Baxter and Cruz both turned. Cruz's gum nearly fell out. Baxter sat about three inches taller.

Hillary stood all of her six feet, plus three inches from her stiletto heels. She wore a charcoal gray, form-fitting skirt to the knees and a powder blue sleeveless blouse with a shirred collar cut low enough to offer a suggestion. No jacket. Her hair was down, very wavy, Erin Andrews quality. It would explain why she had been late, although Jackson was pretty sure she rolled out of bed ready to shoot a TRESemmé commercial.

"I'm Hillary McKenzie, Mr. Douglas's lawyer," she said, handing Baxter a business card.

"McKenzie?"

"That's right. These charges are ridiculous."

"He was found in the victim's apartment, with the victim's very dead body on the floor."

"You are?"

"Detective Marshall Baxter."

"Detective Marshall," Jackson said. "Is that like a lieutenant colonel or a sergeant major?"

They both ignored him. "Has he been read his rights?" Hillary asked.

"Yes, ma'am," Cruz said. "First thing."

He winked at her too. She did not wink back. "Your name?"

"Detective Anibal Cruz."

"Detective Cruz, I suggest you remove whatever is lodged in your eye, because I would hate to get the wrong impression and have to sue you for sexual harassment. Now, may I have a moment with my client?"

"A moment," Baxter said. He motioned at Cruz, who unblinkingly followed him from the room.

Hillary sat down. "What have you told them?"

"Name, rank, and serial number."

"That it?"

"A few funnies."

"Jackson, be serious."

"I haven't told them anything."

"What happened?"

He explained every detail, from entering Arielle's room to finding her body to accidentally stepping in the blood to the cops showing up. Hillary asked a handful of questions. Did you see any evidence of the killer? Did you admit to anything to Baxter and Cruz? Did you touch anything?

No, no, no.

"Well, except for stepping in the blood," Jackson said.

"You're an idiot."

Jackson picked at something on his jeans.

"Let me do the talking," she said.

"Sure thing."

Hillary stood and opened the door. "Mr. Douglas is willing to make a full statement, in exchange for having all of the charges against him dropped."

Cruz smiled. Baxter snorted. "We have your client at the scene of the crime."

"So you have no evidence that he committed the crime. How was the victim killed?"

"Multiple gunshot wounds to the chest," Cruz answered. "Looks like a .45."

"And did you find the murder weapon when you searched Mr. Douglas?"

"No," Baxter admitted.

"Did you find it anywhere on the premises?"

"Not as of yet."

"So your theory is Mr. Douglas shot the victim, left to dispose of the gun, and then returned to the scene of the crime?"

"We're not sure what he did with the gun."

"Did you test him for gunpowder residue?" Hillary asked.

"He could have worn gloves," Cruz offered.

She turned a very sharp look his way. "Did you find any gloves on the premises?"

"No." Head bowed, gum still smacking.

"So you assume Mr. Douglas deposited them with the murder weapon. Did he by any chance take out the victim's trash and recycling too?"

Go, girl.

"A lot of people have been convicted without a murder weapon," Baxter said.

"None of them were my clients," Hillary replied.

"His DNA is at the site. We found a partial print on the apartment doorknob."

"My client doesn't dispute being in the building. Is that a crime?"

"Breaking and entering, at the very least."

"Do you have any evidence that he broke in to her apartment?"

Cruz shook his head.

"Do you?" Hillary asked again, looking this time at Baxter.

He muttered a very soft, "No."

"So for all you know, the door could have been open," Hillary said. "Not only do you not have one shred of evidence to suggest that my client killed this young woman, but nothing to suggest that he was in her apartment illegally. What exactly do you have?"

Baxter stood and rested his knuckles on the table. "We have your client at the scene of a murder, shortly after the murder, standing in the victim's blood."

"I'll grant you he's clumsy. Is that a crime in Nevada?"

"No, that's not it. We have repeated phone conversations between your client and the victim, five calls between them last evening. We have a credit card transaction—your client's credit card—processed by Good Night Escorts, the victim's employer. We've spoken with them, and they gave us your client's name and his cell phone number from when he called to make payment for a date with the victim. We have more than enough to hold him and, I think the D.A. will agree, to try him."

"Tell me, Detective Baxter, is it against the law to hire a companion from Good Night Escorts? I assume the answer is no, or with your evidence-gathering skills, you no doubt would have shut them down by now."

Baxter didn't answer.

"So at the very most you have my client attempting to hire a woman to spend time with him last evening. If you have credit card statements—for which I would very much like to see a warrant—then you also should have record of a return transaction for seventy-five percent of that money, and can no doubt verify from the staff at Good Night Escorts that the alleged intended meeting never took place. You can also confirm with the staff at SW Steakhouse that Miss Coal never showed up."

"Maybe your client got stood up," Cruz suggested. "It hurt his male ego, and he decided to take a little revenge."

"Let me ask you something," Hillary said, looking to Baxter as means of ignoring Cruz's theory. "Did your investigation also uncover that my client is a private investigator?"

"With a record," Baxter replied.

"And it never occurred to you that a private investigator might have reasons other than murder for being in the apartment of a Las Vegas prostitute?"

"Oh, it occurred to me," he said. "But so far your client hasn't said a word about what that reason might be."

Hillary looked at Jackson. He shrugged.

"He's working for me," she said.

Cruz actually stopped chewing his gum, for a moment. Baxter sat back in his chair. "This should be good."

"I hired him to find a potential witness."

"Arielle Coal?"

"That's right. I knew that she worked as a call girl in Las Vegas, but didn't know where specifically to look. Mr. Douglas is a private investigator, and thus more suited than I am for tracking down a person with no known contact information. Furthermore, as a man, I thought he would better be able to make contact with Miss Coal and get her to agree to an interview."

Baxter looked at her. She resumed.

"I had Mr. Douglas contact Miss Coal through Good Night Escorts and arrange to meet her for dinner. The plan was for him to bring her back to our hotel room, with her consent, and question her there, with her consent."

Jackson didn't know so much about the "with her consent" business, but Baxter at least seemed to be buying it.

"Miss Coal didn't show to dinner," Hillary continued. "The time of Mr. Douglas's phone calls, plus the nature of voicemails left on her phone, should corroborate that, as will the staff at SW Steakhouse, as already mentioned. Unable to reach Miss Coal this way, we divined her home address and Mr. Douglas went to speak with her there. When he arrived, he found Miss Coal unresponsive. The officers arrived before he could notify the police."

When it was apparent she was done, Baxter nodded. "How'd your client 'divine' Miss Coal's home address? We spoke to Good Night Escorts and they were quite clear they don't and didn't give out that information."

"He's a private investigator. Please give him some credit."

"Ms. McKenzie, I've never heard of Conway, Davenport & Rankin. Is it a local firm?"

"We're in Los Angeles."

"Los Angeles. Well, I assume you often hire investigators to research potential witnesses in cases like this, correct?"

"Yes."

"Do you often accompany them across state lines?"

"No," Hillary said, and Baxter smiled. "Only when I want to speak to the person I've hired them to locate."

"What," Cruz asked with a cocky grin, "the two of you have a little action on the side?"

"That is not only highly inappropriate and unprofessional, but also baseless and inaccurate. Not to mention thoroughly repulsive. And if you persist in making these types of comments, I'm going to have to initiate legal action against you personally and this department for sexual harassment and slander."

"Calm down, Ms. McKenzie," Baxter said. "Detective Cruz didn't mean anything by it."

"I apologize," he said.

Hillary continued on the offensive. "May I ask what time the murder was committed?"

"Sometime between eight and eleven."

It was Hillary's turn to smile. "My client was in his hotel room, with me, until quarter after nine. He was at SW Steakhouse with any number of witnesses from nine-thirty until ten-thirty, and was back with me again by quarter to eleven. When in that time do you allege that he committed the murder? Or would you mean to implicate me as an accomplice?"

Baxter kept his mouth shut. Cruz jawed away at his gum.

Jackson didn't mention that Hillary had been clothes shopping until about nine, leaving him alone in their hotel. It wasn't his lie.

"You have nothing to tie my client to the murder," Hillary continued. "Your timeline is sketchy at best. He was not present at the scene of the crime until well after the time you stipulated the murder took place. You have nothing to suggest that he entered Miss Coal's room illegally. And you now have my testimony, which carries with it the weight of Conway, Davenport & Rankin, Attorneys at Law."

Neither detective moved.

"Like I said, my client will give you a full statement, in exchange for dropping the murder charges. There's not a grand jury in the world that would even indict on what you have, much less twelve Americans who would convict him. Don't waste my time, his time, your time, the D.A.'s time, a jury's time, and the taxpayers' money with this. And don't let your investigation grow cold following a red herring."

Baxter looked to Cruz. "Give us a minute," he said.

They left the room.

Hillary turned to Jackson, finally taking the time for several deep breaths.

"You're a real pit bull, you know that," he said.

She sat and crossed her legs. "There's nothing you're not telling me, is there?"

"I can't think of anything. I do sort of wonder who called the cops."

"A neighbor likely heard the shots."

"And the cops just happened to ID the right apartment? It was a ghost town when I got there."

She shrugged.

"So what do I tell them, in this statement of mine, if they agree?"

"What I just told them," Hillary said. "But use your own words."

"Sounds ethical."

She leveled her eyes at him.

"Did you mean that bit about being a competent private investigator?" he asked.

Hillary hid a faint smirk. "I'm pretty sure those weren't my exact words."

"Ask you something else?"

She nodded.

"After I called this morning, how much time did you spend on your hair?"

She rolled her eyes and said nothing.

"And why did you have a pair of stiletto heels on this trip?"

Baxter's minute turned into five. He returned with a notepad and pen. He tossed them onto the table. "Tell us what happened."

"Do we have a deal?" Hillary asked.

"Murder charges dropped, but that doesn't mean he's clear. Depends on his statement, depends on the rest of the investigation."

Hillary nodded at Jackson.

So he regurgitated Hillary's story, which was a regurgitation of the truth. He went to Arielle's apartment, found her dead, accidentally stepped in the blood, would have called the cops but they beat him to it, the end.

Baxter and Cruz re-questioned him on several points, checking details, comparing his answers to Hillary's. Then Baxter nodded at the legal pad. "Write it down."

So he did, with a complaint midway about writer's cramp. Then Baxter outlined the rules of Jackson's release. Notify us before you leave town. Be prepared to answer any further questions. We'll be contacting you if any new evidence arises. He agreed to everything.

"Is that it?" Hillary asked.

"Just a few more questions."

"Shoot," Jackson said. "Uh . . . sorry."

Baxter glared for a moment. He nodded at Cruz, who pulled out his phone. He set it on the table, and displayed a picture of the phone Jackson had found on Arielle's bedroom floor.

"You know this guy?" Cruz asked.

Jackson studied the photo. Dark hair, dark complexion, medium looking. The display said his name was Tony.

"No, never seen him."

"This was on the display when you found the phone?" Baxter asked.

"That's right."

"You touch it?"

"I already told you, I didn't touch anything."

"Except the blood."

Hillary sighed, loudly.

"One more," Baxter said. "You happen to know a Warren McKenzie?"

Jackson slowly turned to Hillary, expecting to see the color drained from her face, the aura of confidence gone. Perhaps for a flash, but with a smooth, quick lick of her lips, she re-gathered her poise.

"Why do you ask?" she said.

"We found his business card at Miss Coal's apartment. Do you know him?"

"Warren McKenzie is my father."

Chapter Nine

CRUZ STOPPED, HIS gum hanging in his open mouth. He slowly started chewing again.

"Your father is Warren H. McKenzie?" Baxter asked.

"Yes."

"Lives in Santa Barbara?"

"When he's in the States. He travels a lot."

"Is he traveling right now?"

"He's been gone for several weeks," Hillary said.

"Where?"

"Asia."

"What's the nature of his travel?"

"Business."

"What kind of business?"

"I'm sorry, you said you found a business card?"

Baxter nodded at Cruz again, and once again he called up a photo on his phone. He slid it to Hillary, and Jackson leaned over to take a look. The card was ivory, ridged surface, with just the name, a phone number, and an e-mail address in black block print. One look at Hillary's face indicated it was her father's contact information.

"You said this was found in Miss Coal's apartment?" she asked, returning the phone to Cruz.

"That's correct," Baxter answered. "It was on her nightstand, tucked inside a book."

Hillary shook her head, confused. It was a new expression for her.

"Do you have any idea why a Las Vegas call girl would have your father's business card?" Baxter asked. Jackson noted he had ceased referring to Arielle as Miss Coal.

"No," Hillary said. "I'm sure you won't believe this, but he is not the kind of man who would hire a call girl."

"Maybe he was investigating her," Cruz said.

Hillary's eyes drove him back into his chair.

"What do we know about Coal, other than her chosen profession and the fact that she had my father's business card?" Hillary asked, her entire body turned toward Baxter—and away from Cruz. "Which by the way, she could have gotten from anywhere."

Baxter flipped open a small notebook. "She's twenty-four, been with Good Night Escorts for a few months, an assortment of places before that. She is what she is. We're more concerned with her killer."

"I assume you've thoroughly searched the apartment."

"We have."

"Any clues pointing to any other suspects?"

"Why don't you let us do our job?" Cruz said.

"Because all you've done is bungle it so far."

"That's not fair," Baxter said. "We found Mr. Douglas at the crime scene. What were we to assume?"

"I didn't think you were to assume anything. You're supposed to find the truth."

"We will." He paused to gather himself. "In the meantime, if we have any further questions, we'll contact you."

Hillary smiled—it wasn't sincere—and she and Jackson stood to leave. She waited until they were on the steps outside the station to speak. "Who would want to kill Arielle?" she asked.

"Beats me," Jackson said. "Somebody who knew she was about to talk to you."

"Nobody knew that."

"I mean, somebody who knew why we were here."

"Nobody knew that either."

"So somebody who knew what mysterious ties Arielle has to your client and who knew that if someone was looking for her, it might be for that reason."

"So who tipped this somebody off, Johnny at the Rio?"

Jackson shrugged. "You take a cab?"

"I had to. The Granada's still at her apartment."

Jackson sagged his shoulders. "I can kiss my hubcaps goodbye."

"A real loss."

"Say, it was really nice in there, wasn't it, the two of us not trying to kill each other?"

Hillary responded by signaling for a cab. She gave the driver the address for the Baltimore Gardens, and he gave her the once-over. Twice, maybe. But then he headed south, toward the Strip.

"I assume this means we're headed home," Jackson said.

"Wrong. Arielle's death could still be connected to my case."

"Or she could be another dead hooker. Face it, Hill, it's over."

"It's not over, not until I get some answers about why she exchanged calls with my client and what, if anything, she knew that could have exonerated him."

"Where do you expect to get those answers?"

"We'll start by checking her apartment."

"Pretty sure the police alread—"

"They always miss something."

"You sound like a bad detective show."

"You would know."

"Hill, if we get caught in there, they'll run both of us into jail. Is this one case really worth that much?"

She answered with a quick glare across the backseat of the cab.

"Wow, you take losses hard."

"I want the truth."

Jackson shook his head.

"And I want to know how she's connected to my father."

"Why don't you call him and ask him?"

"Because last I heard, he and Mom were headed into the back country of Bangladesh for several weeks. They aren't reachable."

He looked out the window as they turned onto Baltimore Avenue, thinking about suggesting she wait several weeks. Instead, he said, "This is a bad idea."

"You have a better one?"

"How about breakfast?"

"When we're done."

The driver, who had been listening to Latino music and acting for all the world as if he didn't care what Jackson and Hillary were talking about, dropped them off behind Jackson's unharmed Granada. "Should we at least work up a cover story?" Jackson asked as the cab pulled away.

"We won't need one. Come on."

Jackson followed Hillary inside and then led her up to Arielle's apartment. The door was closed, blocked with police tape. "Now what, Miss Ethical Standards?"

"Now you aspire to the highest ideals of your craft and pick the lock."

"You want me to break the law?"

"I want you to pick that lock."

"'If anyone causes one of these little ones to sin . . .'"

"Just do it."

"Sorry, the cops confiscated my lock picks."

Hillary slid her purse around her shoulder to the front of her body and delicately opened it. A moment later, she pulled out a pair of bobby pins. "Will these work?"

"Really, a bobby pin? Your Aunt Netty won't mind?"

"Will you just shut up and pick the lock?"

He took the pins. "Believe it or not, I am not an expert lock pick."

"You not being an expert at something is supposed to be hard to believe?"

"I wonder if it's too late to sign a confession for Baxter and Cruz."

"Pick the lock."

Scanning the hallway to make sure it was clear, Jackson knelt down and began working the bobby pins into the lock. Magnum could always pick a lock, even with a couple of Dobermans bearing down on him. Maybe that's what Jackson needed—some urgency.

He got it in the form of a voice in the stairwell, and suddenly the tumbler clicked. "We're in," he whispered, ducking under the police tape. Hillary followed right behind him, closing the door quickly but quietly.

"Welcome to the dark side," Jackson said.

"Take the bedroom."

"What exactly are we looking for?" he asked.

"Why is it that I have to keep telling you how to do your job?"

Jackson shook his head and headed for Arielle's bedroom. In broad daylight, even with the blinds drawn, the room looked drastically different. And sterile, except for bloodstains still on the carpet.

Several interesting items caught Jackson's attention. The bed was made. There were no clothes on the floor or in the bathroom. There was a small hamper in the corner, and Jackson lifted the lid to find several days' worth of clothes and a bath towel. He reconstructed the scene. Arielle's hair had been wet when he found her, meaning she had just showered. There were no clothes left behind anywhere, and the towel was on top of dirty clothes in the hamper. Arielle had showered, put on her robe, and gone to the closet to dress. Had she just been putting on pajamas for the night, she wouldn't have bothered with the robe. No, she had intended to keep the date with him, and had been in the act of selecting her outfit when the shooter had gunned her down.

So how had he gotten in? Had she let him in? Jackson doubted she showered and dressed for a date with a client while a man was over, but then again, he wasn't real up to speed on the behavior of prostitutes. The other option was that he had broken in. Either way, it didn't give Jackson a clue as to why Arielle had been murdered.

There were no medications in the bathroom or nightstand, other than standard pain relievers, some antacid tablets, birth control pills, and cold medicine. There was a lot of makeup, which didn't come as a huge surprise, and several hair highlight kits. Apparently Arielle went from auburn tints to jet black and back.

Jackson returned to the bedroom. On the nightstand by the bed was a single book. The cover showed sunbeams peeking through the clouds, and the title and subtitle suggested it contained some sort of self-improvement mumbo-jumbo. He didn't touch it. Assorted odds and ends in the drawer of the nightstand all seemed to belong. There wasn't a journal or diary with a "So-and-so is out to get me" entry, but it was never that easy.

He dropped to his hands and knees and looked under the bed. No shell casings, and as he crawled around the bloodstains on the carpet, he saw none on the floor of the closet either. He did see about a million pair of shoes and an assortment of dresses and evening gowns. On a shelf above the hanging clothes were some folded sweaters and blue jeans. He moved to a dresser by the wall and found a drawer of T-shirts and tank tops, another of shorts, and two more of socks, underwear, and assorted intimates. He didn't linger.

None of the clothes told him anything about Arielle. Nor did a survey of her purse, which was hung on the doorknob of the closet. He stood and examined the room again. Clearly the police had gone over the apartment with a fine-toothed comb, finding anything to be found.

He was about to return to the living room when he took notice of a photo frame on the dresser. It held three photos, and Jackson picked it up to take a closer look. One photo showed Arielle sitting on a couch beside a shriveled up woman with a blue turban cap on her head. It wasn't Arielle's couch. Another showed Arielle and a young woman, both dressed for a night on the town, posing in front of some club. The third was of Arielle and a guy at a party. They weren't posed like a couple, and yet their body language suggested they were more than just friends.

He committed the three other faces to memory and placed the frame back on the dresser as he turned to leave the room. He was a little too haphazard and the frame fell, clunking on the floor and bouncing toward the closet.

"What was that?" Hillary asked.

"Just destroying some evidence," Jackson replied as he bent to pick up the frame. The glass had not broken, but it had come loose from the frame and backing, spilling two photographs onto the carpet. As Jackson picked the first up, he saw a small key beneath it on the carpet.

He set down the photograph and the pieces of the frame to inspect the key. It was smaller than a car or house key, its head circular and inscribed with a number. C13. An apartment? A locker? He slipped it into his pocket and pieced the frame back together. When he exited the bedroom, Hillary was sorting through the mail on the kitchen table.

"Be sure to get your fingerprints all over those," he said.

"The police already dusted. How do you think they got your print off the doorknob?"

"You find anything?" he asked.

"Nothing of interest. You?"

Before Jackson could answer, he heard the sound of a key in the lock and saw Arielle's doorknob begin to turn.

Chapter Ten

JACKSON SHOT A quick glance at Hillary as the front door swung open and a woman pushed her way past the police tape.

She stopped suddenly when she spotted Jackson and Hillary. "Who are you?"

Jackson eyed the woman while formulating an answer. She was short and a little plump, but not fat and not unattractive. Her blond hair was straight, uneven, and a little bleached, naturally or otherwise. She wore a red UNLV T-shirt and denim shorts. Her eyes and nose, like the shirt, were red.

"Jim Taggart," Jackson said just before Hillary opened her mouth. "I'm a private investigator. This is my associate, Evelyn Martin." He glanced at Hillary before turning his eyes to the woman.

"Shelly Patrick. You're a private eye?"

"That's right. You got a business card on you, Angel?"

Hillary, to her credit, played along. "Sorry, Jimmy."

"Angel?" Shelly asked.

"A nickname I gave her. Can you blame me?"

"And you're Jim?"

"That's right."

Shelly grinned. "I've seen *The Rockford Files*. Wanna try again?"

Jackson studied her eyes. Aside from being a little red, they were brown and focused. Shelly did not appear to be gullible, so he would have to tell her the truth. Or something more believable.

He turned again to Hillary. "Do you have a business card, for real?"

She looked at him for a moment before nodding. She reached into her purse and withdrew a card, which she handed to Shelly. Once again, Jackson spoke just before Hillary did.

"I'm Ray McKenzie, Miss Coal's attorney. This is my associate, Jackie."

Shelly looked from the card to him, her brown and red eyes dubious. "This says Hillary McKenzie."

Jackson sighed. "Technically, my name his Hillary. I go by Ray."

"Your name is Hillary?"

"Been in the family for years. French, I think. And it sounds and looks very regal on company letterhead, but please, call me Ray."

After a few moments' pause, Shelly nodded. "I didn't know Arielle had a lawyer."

"How do . . . did you know Miss Coal?"

"We were friends," Shelly said, rushing her words to get them out before a sniff. She held the back of her hand in front of her nose. "I can't believe . . ."

"I'm very sorry for your loss," Jackson said. "You were close?"

"I liked to think so."

"Did Miss Coal confide anything in you recently?"

"Confide? Like what?"

Jackson shook his head. "Anything. What I'm asking is, did she have any secrets? Was she suspicious of someone out to get her? Anything like that?"

Shelly shook her head. "No. Well . . . It's nothing suspicious . . ."

"Anything could be important."

"About a week ago, Arielle asked if I could have my boyfriend pull up some footage of Senator Moore's speech at UNLV last month. Cory—my boyfriend—is an assistant production manager at KLAS. She wanted to know who one of the guys standing behind the senator was. She didn't say why."

"Did your boyfriend identify him?"

"No. He was a nobody."

"And she didn't say anything about why she wanted to know?"

Shelly shook her head. She frowned. "Why do you want to know all this?"

"Miss Coal recently took out a wrongful death policy and made some amendments to her will. Naturally, given the circumstances of her death, we're looking into things."

"Isn't that a job for the police?"

"Of course, but we like to conduct our own investigation as well."

Shelly bit her lip. "Arielle did seem . . . I don't know, a little different lately."

"How so?"

"She was always so laidback and fun, very carefree. But for the last month or so, she seemed withdrawn and uptight. Almost as if something was gnawing at her. I asked her about it once, but she said it was nothing, just the stress of her job. I know she hated the life." Shelly bit her lip again. "Anyhow, I just came by to . . . to feed her fish," she said, pointing at an aquarium in the corner that, until now, had not attracted Jackson's attention. "I know that seems silly in the light of things, but . . ."

"It's not silly at all," Hillary said with more sympathy than Jackson considered her capable of.

"Have you spoken to Darla yet?" Shelly asked.

"Darla?"

"Arielle's aunt, Darla Fazekas."

"No, not yet."

Shelly's eyes welled up. "I wonder if anyone's even told her. She's the closest thing to family Arielle has. Had," she corrected, then began crying. Hillary actually approached her and embraced her. Jackson again marveled at a side of Hillary he had seldom seen.

He didn't think it prudent to continue questioning Shelly, and they now had a few leads to follow. So once Hillary had consoled her, Jackson thanked Shelly for her help, offered his condolences again, and guided his "associate" from the apartment.

"That was quick thinking," Hillary said as they stepped out into the sunlight.

Jackson stopped walking. "Whoa, was that a compliment?"

"I didn't say it was good thinking. Claiming to be a private eye when you're a private eye? What's up with that?"

"I thought if there was something suspicious going on with Arielle, a P.I. snooping around her apartment would be plausible."

"So why fake names?"

"Anonymity," Jackson said as he unlocked his car door. He got in and reached over to unlock Hillary's door.

"And you pick *The Rockford Files* for your aliases?"

"Jim Taggart was Rockford's fallback. I figured nobody in my general age demo has any idea who or what Rockford was."

Hillary nodded. "Is Evelyn Martin really his associate?"

"Uh, more like a friend."

"What about 'Angel'? Was that you trying to be clever, or did Rockford really call her that?"

"Everybody called Evelyn Angel," he said, making a U-turn. "Besides, you think I'd compliment you if I didn't have to?"

They headed back toward the Strip.

"And what was with claiming to be Hillary?"

"Ingenious, huh?"

"More like insane."

"I figure people will only buy a lie if it sounds really good or really ridiculous, as in too ridiculous to make up. So, I made up something that ridiculous."

"Why not just let me handle things?"

"Hmm, I wonder."

Hillary shook her head. "You find anything?"

"As a matter of fact, yes." He reached into his pocket and pulled out the key. He handed it to her.

"Looks like a safe deposit box key," she said. "Maybe an airport locker."

"Or a train station, or bus station, or roller skating rink, hotel safe, private gun closet. Could be for anything."

"Where'd you find it?"

"Behind some pictures in a photo frame."

"You didn't see a safe in her bedroom?"

Jackson smacked his head. "Shoot, there was a safe under the bed. I never thought to try the key in it."

Hillary jabbed her tongue into her jaw.

"I saw nothing else of even the remotest interest. You?"

"Unfortunately, no."

Jackson turned onto Flamingo.

"I thought you wanted breakfast," Hillary said a moment later when he entered their hotel parking lot.

"In clean clothes, preferably."

"And after a shower, maybe?"

"Yeah, sure."

Twenty minutes later, Jackson met Hillary in front of her room. She was in denim shorts and a creamsickle-orange baby doll top. Her hair was down. Jackson wore faded jeans and a Dodgers tee, equally casual, but he felt underdressed.

He had heard good things about Excalibur's Roundtable Buffet, so he and Hillary joined the mid-morning crowd at the medieval-themed hotel, many of whom looked as if they had been in jail overnight too. Hillary was appropriately restrained; Jackson packed it in like the Gallic warriors the place honored. It was a trait he inherited from his grandpa—if they offer you all-you-can-eat, take them up.

Hillary finished and sat back with a look of bemusement as Jackson started on his third plate, piled high with eggs, bacon, biscuits and sausage gravy, waffles, and a made-to-order omelet. Her plate, which was promptly cleared away, had a few fruit rinds and stems remaining. Some people didn't understand how a buffet worked.

"So I've been thinking," Jackson said.

Hillary, to his shock, didn't comment.

"The cops said Arielle was killed between eight and eleven. From what I could make of the scene, she intended to keep the date."

"What did you make of the scene?"

He ingested a third of a waffle before explaining how he'd found her clothes under a towel in the bathroom hamper, with no clothes out on the bed or on a hanger in the bathroom. She had been found by the closet in her bathrobe, which Jackson deduced meant she had showered and was preparing to get dressed.

"But you have no idea what she was going to wear."

"No."

"So how does that prove anything?"

"Not a lot of people shower at night, then put on a bathrobe, then change into their jammies. If she had taken a bubble bath before bed, why the robe? She was getting dressed to go somewhere, and it only stands to reason it was to meet me," he said with a shrug. "Not sure what that tells us, other than it seemed things were business as usual until she was killed."

"And it means the time of death was closer to eight than eleven, assuming she was going to be on time. Probably before nine if she wasn't even dressed yet."

"Unfortunately," Jackson said as he piled scrambled eggs onto his fork, "it doesn't tell us why anyone would want to kill her."

"No, but maybe this guy she wanted identified has something to do with it."

"Yeah, that was strange. Why would she want to ID a guy from the background of a politician's speech? I thought they just propped up any Tom, Dick, and Harry they could find who wouldn't make rabbit ears behind the guy."

"Sometimes. But a lot of times they have family and staff or VIPs related to whatever's being spoken about."

"So you think it's someone who worked for or with Senator What's-his-name?"

"Moore, and I don't know. But I intend to find out."

"If Arielle was—ahem, ahem—involved with a senator or one of his staff members, it could open the door to a lot of possible motives." He chased a bite of omelet with a bite of Danish. "It would—" He swallowed "—also explain all her nice stuff, say if she was blackmailing somebody."

"She did seem to be living pretty well."

"Considering her trade."

"No. A lot of high-end call girls make a very good living. Trust me, in my profession, you meet all sorts of people. What I meant is that she wasn't living in a real nice part of town or a classy building. But she had a big TV, a nice computer, plenty of kitchen gadgets, not to mention some pretty upscale artwork."

"Wardrobe wasn't bad either."

Hillary nodded. "It's just odd, if he was making good enough money to afford the lifestyle, why not move into a little better environs?"

Jackson shrugged. He resumed eating while Hillary watched with a morbid sort of fascination. When his plate was clear, he felt as if he'd swallowed a bowling ball. He sat back and groaned.

"Lovely," Hillary said. "If you're going to vomit, could you at least try to make it to the men's room first?"

"I'll keep that in mind." He downed the remaining third of a glass of orange juice. "Any of this—Moore, some guy at his speech, paranoia from a hooker who can afford a different machine for every type of beverage—have any connection to your mysterious client?"

"No. Not that I can see."

"Or to your dad?"

She shook her head.

"So we still have nothing."

"We have Arielle's aunt, Darla. And we have a key."

"Great. You go grill her bereft family and I'll start trying locks at every bank in town. I should be done by Christmas."

Chapter Eleven

DARLA FAZEKAS HAD stringy red-blond hair, weather-beaten skin, and teeth that had seen more cigarettes than the Marlboro man. Her hair had mostly fallen out of a ponytail, and bags under her eyes suggested she felt as ragged as she looked. Darla wore a rayon maid's dress over fleshy tights, sneakers, and a black cardigan even though it was ninety degrees outside. A large purple purse was slung over her shoulder as she half sat, half leaned on the stool in front of a slot machine. A slot machine she was steadily feeding quarters. While smoking. Darla was a shrewd manager of her finances.

Setting up a meeting with her hadn't been easy. After their buffet brunch, Jackson and Hillary had driven back to their hotel and quickly found Darla's address and phone number online. They had placed several calls to her home, sandwiched around some very brief research on Senator Moore. When the second call had been unanswered, they had driven to her house in a neighborhood north of downtown that made Arielle's living conditions seem palatial by comparison. There a neighbor had informed them that Darla worked at the Vegas Club Hotel & Casino.

It took some doing on Hillary's part, but she had finally been able to speak with Darla in the middle of her shift, and she had agreed to meet with them when it was finished around two. Jackson and Hillary had staked out the casino floor at quarter to and waited nearly forty-five minutes before assuming Darla had blown them off. To be sure, they had wandered through the dimly lit, smoky casino, thinking perhaps she had meant a different set of slot machines than she had told them on the phone. After not spotting her there either, they had returned to their original location, on the east corner of the building, to find her plugging away.

"Darla?" Hillary asked as she took an empty stool next to her, at the end of the row. Jackson leaned on the vacant slot machine.

"That's right," Darla said, pulling on the lever. It resulted in a combination of numbers and fruit that that didn't pay.

Hillary introduced herself and Jackson, offering their condolences.

Darla sniffed and nodded. "Thank you." She slid on her stool to face them. "I'm sorry I'm late. I just finished talking to the police."

"Do you mind if we ask you some more questions?" Hillary said.

"No, I guess not. How did you say you know Arielle?"

"I'm a lawyer working on a case that might involve her. I was hoping to talk to her, and now I'm hoping you might be able to provide some information for me."

"I don't know what I would know," Darla said, "but I'll try."

Hillary nodded.

"Do you mind if we walk and talk?" Darla asked. "I'm freezing in here."

It was not freezing outside. The temperature had, if anything, gone up, with no breeze to speak of. Even so, Darla kept her sweater on and walked with her arms crossed as they strolled along Freemont Street.

In the old days, downtown had been the essence of Vegas. As the mega resorts had sprung up along the Strip, downtown had needed to find a new way to remain viable. Thus, the Freemont Street Experience had been born. Covered by a four-block-long, ninety-foot-high barrel vault canopy, Freemont Street had been turned into an outdoor strip mall amidst the downtown hotels. Souvenir shops sold everything from four-for-ten-dollar T-shirts to personalized shot glasses to little Elvis suits for kids. Kiosks in the middle of the street hawked cheap gadgets, caricatures of famous celebrities, and Vegas cityscape calendars. After dusk, the canopy became a movie screen for dazzling light and audio shows that would literally stop vehicle and pedestrian traffic. Between shows and during the day, the old Vegas landmarks like the Golden Nugget and Binion's Horseshoe dominated the scene. Everything was ablaze with neon, from building exteriors to hotel signs to the famous giant cowboy smoking a cigarette.

He was not alone. Darla nursed a cancer stick too as she walked between Jackson and Hillary and answered all their questions. Arielle Coal had been born Amanda Coleman. Her mother, Yvonne Coleman, had been Darla's sister. Had been, because she had died of skin cancer in 2010. Jackson wondered if Yvonne was the woman in the photo frame on Arielle's dresser.

Like her daughter, Yvonne had worked every bar top, pole, and street corner in Las Vegas, Reno, and a truck stop on I-15. She had never wanted that sort of lifestyle for her daughter, but according to Darla, hadn't done a lot to prevent it.

Darla didn't know Arielle's father, didn't think Arielle knew him, and wasn't sure if Yvonne even had. But he clearly hadn't played a role in Arielle's life.

Neither had Darla, for that matter, until near the end of Yvonne's life. She and Arielle had leaned on each other through a difficult time, but had subsequently drifted apart again, despite living just miles from each other.

"Did Arielle have any other living relatives?" Hillary asked as they waited for vehicle traffic at Casino Center Boulevard, the only street to cross the Fremont Street Experience.

Darla took a drag on her cigarette. "Not really. Yvonne had another daughter, back in . . . '84? She gave her up for adoption right after the birth. She was in no condition to be a mother."

Jackson could see the lawyer in Hillary wanted to follow up on that last statement, but she let it pass as they crossed the street. "Do you know her name, know where she lives? Do you know her father's name?"

Darla shook her head. "He was in the Army, I think, stationed somewhere around here."

"Still?" Jackson asked.

"No, he became some big venture capitalist or something fancy sounding, I don't remember. Yvonne just mentioned once how successful he was . . . compared to her."

"But he wasn't a part of Arielle's life in any way?" Hillary asked.

"Not that I know of," Darla said, drawing on her cigarette and blowing a puff of smoke out her nose. "As for the daughter, I don't know anything about her. I don't think Yvonne really did either. It's sad."

"Was Arielle seeing anyone?" Hillary asked after a few steps.

Darla huffed. "Considering her profession . . ."

"I meant outside of work."

"I don't think she had a boyfriend. There was one guy, Matt, that she mentioned once or twice. I don't know what their relationship was."

"Do you know his last name?"

"Sorry."

"What about friends?"

"We didn't talk all that much, you know," Darla said. "In fact . . . I hadn't spoken to her in at least a week."

Jackson went months without talking to his aunts and uncles. Then again, they didn't live across town.

Darla sniffed and lifted the cigarette back to her lips with a trembling hand. A long drag steadied her. "There was one girl, Alex, that she hung out with a lot.

Brought her by once. Pretty girl, short black hair, looked a little bit like Arielle. I'm sorry, but I don't remember her last name."

They were almost to Neonopolis, a two hundred fifty thousand-square foot shopping mall at the end of the Freemont Street Experience. "Darla, can you think of any reason why anyone would want to harm Arielle?" Hillary asked.

Darla licked her lip and looked down. "No. Arielle was a sweet girl. I know that probably sounds funny to you, her being a hooker and all, but she was the nicest person . . . She wouldn't hurt nobody. And . . ."

"Darla?"

"It's nothing," she said, digging through her purse for another cigarette.

"Anything could be helpful," Hillary said.

Not until she found her cigarette—which took some time—lit it, and had a long draw on it, did Darla answer. "I told the police this too, and they just sort of shrugged it off."

"Hispanic guy?" Jackson asked. "Chawing gum?"

"Yeah, and a cranky tall guy."

"Cruz and Baxter."

"What'd you tell them?" Hillary asked.

Darla blew out another puff of smoke. "Arielle came in to some money recently."

"How much money?"

"I don't know. I just . . . She kind of went on a spending spree all the sudden, telling me about the stuff she'd got. A new TV, a Blu-ray player, a bunch 'a new clothes. I told her to get outta that crummy apartment."

"How long ago?" Hillary asked.

"Three, four months maybe."

"And the police didn't take any interest in that?"

"Said they'd look into it. You know how it goes. Thing is, I don't know where she got the money. Poor thing couldn't keep a job."

"Is there anything else you can think of?" Hillary asked.

"No, I don't think so. It just doesn't make sense."

Hillary extracted a business card from her purse. "My cell's on the bottom," she said. "If you think of anything else, will you please give me a call?"

Darla nodded as she took the card. "You one of them prosecuting attorneys or the other kind?"

"Most definitely the other kind," Jackson said, despite the glare from Hillary.

Darla nodded again and stuffed the card into her purse, where it was likely lost amongst loose cigarettes and slot machine tokens. Jackson and Hillary thanked her for her time and expressed their condolences again, and Darla turned to leave.

"One more thing?" Jackson asked.

She stopped and looked back at him, cigarette between her lips.

"Do you happen to know a guy named Tony, average looking, dark hair?"

Darla nodded. "Sounds like Antonio the Magnificent."

"Who's—"

"A two-bit magician, another friend of Arielle's."

"Just a friend?" Hillary asked.

"I don't know," Darla said. "About six months ago, out of the blue, Arielle called me up and wanted to meet. Suggested we go see this friend of hers perform. It wasn't much to see. I think she mentioned his name once or twice after that, but nothing that sticks in my memory."

Hillary thanked her again and they watched her start the slow, plodding journey back toward the Vegas Club.

"A call girl strikes it rich, somehow," Jackson said as they started walking back to the Granada. "She keeps living in the slums, keeps selling her body for cash, may have been hiding a deep dark secret that could keep your client from wrongfully going to jail, and . . ." He looked at Hillary. "How come you didn't ask her about him?"

Hillary shrugged. "She said it herself, they didn't interact much. Darla was fuzzy on names and details, so even if Arielle mentioned some obscure phone calls, I doubt Darla would remember anything relevant."

He thought about it for a moment and concluded that was fair. "Anyhow, and now she's dead. Oh yeah, and she may have known your dad."

"That about sums it up."

He took a deep breath. "Well, you like magic?"

Chapter Twelve

3:13 p.m.

BACK AT THEIR hotel, Hillary gave Jackson her laptop to research Senator Moore while she took her tablet and phone to her room. She tasked him with expanding on their basic bio. He had argued that technically his work was done, having found Arielle Coal. She told him to adhere to the spirit of the law, not the letter of it. He made a crack about her profession and methods, and she retorted about his needing those methods the previous August. He silently took her laptop back to his room and turned on the TV. It was a lackluster day of college football, but any was better than none.

Before meeting Darla, they had discovered that Moore had been a major in the United States Air Force prior to turning to a career in politics. After three stints as a Nevada state senator, he was currently in his second term as a U.S. senator. A right-wing Republican, he was pretty well liked by his constituents, especially those in rural areas, and was likely not to face a serious challenge when his term ended in a couple of years. That had been about all they'd learned before heading for downtown.

With a Georgia-Arkansas game on in the background, Jackson got to work. He searched Moore's website and a couple of political blogs, and had just logged onto a website showing all senate voting records when Hillary banged on his door. He admitted her and she immediately turned her eyes to the TV.

"Turn that off," she said.

He muted the announcers.

"I said turn it off."

"Yikes."

She sat on the edge of the bed. "What did you find?"

He reported back.

"That's it?"

"I just got started."

And was momentarily distracted by the final two minutes of the first half of the game.

Hillary exhaled and began speaking. "Carson Andrew Morelli was born to Italian immigrants in 1953 and changed his name shortly after leaving the Air Force?"

"You find out why?"

"No, but his military record is spotless." She glanced quickly down at her tablet. "He got his start in local politics in Reno before moving to the Nevada and U.S. senate. I'll take a closer look at his voting record, but he's been clear on what he stands for since day one."

"Which is?"

"Guns, big military, small government, people's and states' rights. He's pro-life, anti-same-sex marriage, middle of the road on the environment, although he is a member of the Sierra Club. He's a Roman Catholic from a long line of Roman Catholics, and attends mass faithfully every Sunday. He's been married since '86, no sign of scandal—personally or professionally. No kids, no siblings, his parents are deceased."

"You learned all that?"

"I actually worked."

"How?"

"How did I work?"

"How did you learn all that? His website is bare bones and the political blogs are all slanted."

She sighed. "Mostly from a friend in the California lieutenant governor's office with some connections. I also ran his name through the CD&R database. And I wasn't distracted by football."

"Well, you find any ties to Arielle?"

"No."

"So we have an Air Force major who is now a beloved U.S. senator with absolutely no ties to our case."

"Except that Arielle was looking into him."

"Not him. Some lackey on the podium at a speech."

"To that end, I called Shelly and she told me the specific speech Arielle had asked about. Senator Moore spoke on immigration reform and the need to stem the flow of illegal aliens across the border. I've been combing the dignitaries and who's who in attendance, but so far, no names have popped. Without a name to check for, there isn't much to go on."

"An immigration speech at UNLV had dignitaries?"

She sighed again.

"Well, there has to be a connection of some sort," Jackson said. "She must have seen this guy somewhere else, then spotted him at the speech and realized it would give her a potential way to identify him."

"Or she thought she knew who he was and wanted confirmation that he was indeed tied to Moore."

Jackson shrugged.

"I also found another connection to my father," Hillary said.

"What?"

"He and Moore were both stationed at the same Air Force base for almost two and a half years, from January of 1982 to June, 1984."

"Which base?"

"Blane Air Force Base, about sixty or seventy miles north of here in the middle of the desert."

"Could be coincidence. Had to be a lot of guys stationed there."

"I also found that Dad made several contributions to Moore's re-election campaign four years ago."

"How much?"

"Why does that matter?"

He shrugged. "I might give a hundred bucks to a guy if I like a speech of his."

"I doubt it."

"It's another thing to give several grand. It implies more than a spur of the moment, he's-an-old-friend-so-I'll-break-off-a-Benjamin contribution. It implies you believe in their cause."

"Twenty-five hundred dollars," Hillary said quietly.

"I assume that even for your dad that's significant."

"Yes."

"So what does that mean?"

"I don't know. But it's the second time Dad's turned up in our investigation, and I find it pretty coincidental." She sighed. "At any rate, we have to go. Bring the laptop. I want to check Moore's voting record while you drive."

"Drive where?"

"We're meeting an old friend of Dad's."

Jackson had several questions, but Hillary was already moving. He unplugged the laptop, grabbed his wallet and keys, and followed her down to the parking lot. If anything, it had gotten hotter, and the seats of the Granada threatened to sear the denim of his blue jeans right into his flesh.

"You want to tell me where we're going?" he asked as he started the car.

"Red Rock Canyon, west of the city."

"Any id—"

"Take Flamingo west to the Beltway, then north to West Charleston."

He nodded and exited the parking lot. He waited until he had crossed the Strip and I-15. It didn't take long for America's Playground to turn into typical commercial and residential sprawl.

"So who is this friend of your dad's and why are we driving into the desert to meet him?"

"He and Dad worked together at Blane. They were good friends, and Dad kept in touch with him afterwards. He was one of the few."

"And he just happens to live here in Las Vegas?"

Hillary nodded. "Since we've found several connections to Dad, I thought maybe he might have a clue how he's tied up in all this. I gave him a call and he agreed to meet with us."

"Okay, so why in the middle of the desert instead of a Cold Stone on the Strip?"

"He's former military, and when I gave him a few of the details, he seemed hesitant. I said it was important and when he agreed and suggested the location, I wasn't about to argue."

The houses along West Flamingo were different but all the same, tan or beige with a roof that was some shade of red. They were packed close together, with small yards, a decent amount of trees, and swimming pools. The wind whipping through the Granada's windows was stifling, and Jackson dreaded listening to a Hillary interrogation in the desert.

When they reached the Bruce Woodbury Beltway, they followed it west and then north, where it intersected with West Charleston Road. The Strip on the eastern horizon was obscured by haze and another resort complex, making the Vegas suburbs resemble those of any other southwestern city. Jackson turned west, away from an outdoor mall, and they drove past several cookie cutter communities. Then, just that quickly, they were in the desert.

A few miles later, Jackson turned onto a one-way drive leading into the Red Rock Canyon National Conservation Area. In addition to the obvious red rocks, the park contained sandstone cliffs up to three thousand feet tall, making it an ideal destination for hikers and climbers. Wild burros and desert tortoises were some of the animals to frequent the two hundred thousand-acre park, which offered over thirty miles of hiking trails and a thirteen-mile scenic driving loop. After Jackson paid his admission fee at the front gate, Hillary told him to pass on the visitor's center and take the scenic drive.

"Do I have to wait until dark and flick my headlights a few times?" he asked.

She glared at him while working to pull her hair into a ponytail. For some girls, a ponytail was a way to get hair out of the face and little else. It was practicality over style. Not so with Hillary. Maybe it was a natural wave, maybe it was the few strands left loose and tucked behind her ear, or maybe it was just her. Somehow, a quick ponytail was as stylish as a prom-night updo.

"You want to watch the road?" she asked as Jackson nearly veered off the single-lane surface.

He said nothing but drove on, meandering over and around hills and arroyos, the barren terrain dotted with scrub. Off to the right, a large wedge of red rock and sandstone jutted up from the earth, piercing the hazy blue sky. Ahead, the mountains were more traditional for a desert scene, their pine-speckled ridges and gorges contrasts of sun-splashed brightness and dark shadow. It was beautiful in a desolate, forsaken, wilderness sort of way.

They passed a parking area on the right, and Hillary instructed Jackson to take the next turnout. It was half a mile along, and the only car parked in the small lot was a beat-up old pickup truck with two bicycles strapped in the bed. Jackson parked a few stalls away and cut the engine.

"How are we supposed to ID this friend of your dad's?"

"I told him to look for a decrepit old car."

"Funny," Jackson said, throwing open his door. He got out and stretched, his skin instantly baked by the sun. They were on top of a ridge, with a dry streambed behind them and the craggy red rocks just in front of them. Jackson leaned back against the rear bumper. Hillary joined him, her posture remaining ramrod straight.

"When he gets here, let me do the talking."

"Remind me again why I'm not sitting on my couch watching football?"

She didn't have time to answer. A charcoal gray mid-'80s model Camaro turned into their parking area. Jackson recognized it, having seen it parked at the previous turnout. The driver, hidden behind tinted windows, parked one space over from them, his door open almost before the car had come to a stop.

He was short and stout, with arms like pythons. His brown hair was buzzed short, almost as short as the stubble on his jaw. He wore work khakis and a plain

T-shirt that matched the Camaro in color. Despite having just slits for eyes, he quickly surveyed the scene before walking to the back of the Granada, where Jackson and Hillary met him.

"Hillary McKenzie," he said with an upturn of the mouth that could be categorized as a smile. His voice was like flint.

"Captain Donovan, thank you so much for meeting us," she said, extending a hand.

He waved at her formality, then shook. "Please, those days are long past. Roy's fine."

"Roy, this is Jackson Douglas."

"Boyfriend?"

"No."

"Too bad," Donovan said with a wink as he shook Jackson's hand.

"Air Force?" Jackson asked.

"Eight years."

"Thank you for your service."

For just a moment, the eyes showed life. "You're welcome," he said, gripping Jackson's hand a little more firmly before letting go. He turned to Hillary and stuck both hands in his pockets. "You said you had questions about your father and his time at Blane?"

Hillary nodded and launched into a brief explanation of why she and Jackson were in Las Vegas and the ways Warren's name had come up in their investigation of Arielle's death and research on Senator Moore.

When she was finished, Donovan squinted into the late-afternoon sun. "I'd been stationed at Blane about six months when your father arrived. It was a small base, so it didn't take long for two captains to get to know one another. He was one of the few, to steal a term from the Marines."

"The few?" Hillary asked.

"The best of the best. Resources were stretched pretty thin at the base. In addition to his regular duties, Warren was pressed into service as a doctor."

"A doctor?" Jackson asked.

"Dad went to med school for a couple of years before enlisting," Hillary said.

"He never complained," Donovan said. "Worked his tail off, harder than anybody on the base, and he always had time to help the next guy."

"That sounds like him," Hillary said.

"He's a man of integrity through and through. An honor to serve with him. I have to say, I don't think your father is involved in anything sordid." He nodded at Hillary. "I could see the concern in your eyes."

"I don't think he's involved in anything sordid, either," she said. "But he is tied to Arielle and Senator Moore."

"Did you know him?" Jackson asked, not caring that Hillary was supposed to run the conversation.

"Then-Major Morelli? Yeah, I knew of him. We didn't strike up quite the friendship Warren and I did."

"Any particular reason?" Hillary asked.

"Nothing more than a couple of personalities that didn't jive. It wasn't hostile. We just weren't pals."

"What about him and my father?"

"I couldn't say. Although," he said, looking around again to make sure they were still alone, "I'm pretty sure they were both a part of Silver Dawn."

"Silver Dawn?"

"Classified research project conducted at the base. I don't know any of the details because it was need-to-know and I didn't have the need."

"But Moore and Dad were involved?"

"It was classified, but that didn't stop most of the base from knowing it existed, even knowing some of the players. Your father, being by-the-book, didn't talk and I didn't ask. But I always suspected he was part of it."

"Why?" Hillary asked.

"A lot of little things. We held the same rank, but he had access to restricted areas on the base that I didn't, meetings at all hours that I wasn't privy to, private phone calls and whispered conversations that ended abruptly when I arrived, off-base visitors that weren't on his official schedule, different stuff like that. Some of that can be explained by our having different jobs and responsibilities. But there was so much secrecy, and . . . I can't explain it, really, but you get a sense about these things." He looked away, then back. "There were actually rumors about a second component to Silver Dawn, a 'Phase Two.' I couldn't help but wonder if your father was part of that as well."

"Why's that?"

He lowered his voice. "Hangar 5."

"What's Hangar 5?" Hillary asked.

"A hangar at the base, off limits to almost everybody."

"But not my father?"

Donovan shook his head.

"What's the deal with Hangar 5?" Jackson asked.

"Late one night, like midnight late, a buddy and I are coming back from a raid on the mess, and we see this white bus—like a painted school bus, blacked out windows, no markings. It pulled right into Hangar 5. A couple other guys reported seeing the same thing at other times, a plain white bus coming or going, always late at night. We had no idea what was going on, but you can imagine, the rumors started flying. We assumed it was people, but we didn't know who they were, why they were there, how many of them there were, what their living arrangements were like. They could have been stretched out on cots like a refugee camp or lived in sophisticated dorms built inside the hangar. I guess, for all we know, the buses could have been empty or carrying anything. People just made the most sense."

Jackson and Hillary exchanged a look, trying to comprehend what they were hearing.

"I saw your father coming out of the building once, and I mean nobody had access. I never asked him about it, and he obviously never said anything." Donovan shrugged. "Could have been nothing more than an emergency medical visit, but like I said, I couldn't help but wonder."

"Do you know that Hangar 5 was tied to Silver Dawn?"

"No, but a base that size, there are only so many projects that could be taking place at once. And I doubt anybody would be involved in two of them."

Hillary took a moment to digest. "And Morelli was part of Silver Dawn as well?"

"That was the scuttlebutt. I have no proof."

"Do you have any idea what the project was?" Jackson asked. "Silver Dawn or Phase Two?"

Donovan shrugged again. "There are a lot of rumors, none of which are worth repeating. It was the early '80s, still in the Cold War, and we were always looking for another weapon or a leg up. Could have been anything."

"Why Blane?" Jackson asked.

"Blane's about as isolated as they come. I guess they figured it was a good place to hide."

"Hide what?" Hillary asked before Jackson could.

"Their experiments."

The temperature in the desert dropped about ten degrees. Despite the sun, Jackson felt a shiver creeping up his spine.

Again, Hillary beat him to the punch. "What kind of experiments?"

"I shouldn't have said that. It's one of the rumors." He sighed. "But I was a supply officer and processed orders for obscene amounts of lab and medical equipment. Way more than would be needed normally. Factor in the buses, tight security on Hangar 5, your dad being recruited for his medical skills . . . Truth is, I don't know what they were doing, and, frankly, never wanted to, other than for curiosity's sake."

Hillary took the news in stride with a simple head nod.

Donovan warily eyed a passing sedan.

"Who was behind the project?" Hillary asked. "The Air Force?"

"Who knows that either? We had Army guys coming and going, civilians, probably the CIA. Anybody's guess."

Hillary moved in another direction. "Have you kept in touch with my father lately?"

"We exchange phone calls now and again. I haven't spoken to him in a couple of years. Haven't seen him since . . . '92, was it, in Portland, with the whole family? You'd have been, what, seven or eight?"

She nodded.

"We talked more back then, but you know how it goes."

"Did he ever mention Arielle Coal to you, mention anything about being in Las Vegas?"

"No. The closest he came was that he mentioned he had a layover in Las Vegas a couple of years ago, thought we could get together for a drink. I was out of town."

"Do you remember when that was?"

"February, maybe early March, of '09."

Hillary nodded.

"What happened to Silver Dawn?" Jackson asked.

"Project was scrapped in 1988. Few years later, the base was decommissioned too. Budgetary reasons."

"The base or Silver Dawn?"

"The base. No idea on Silver Dawn. A buddy mentioned it had been terminated. For all I know, that was cover or he was misinformed. I was out of the Air Force by then, so I didn't pay too much attention to it."

"Anything else you can think of?" Hillary asked. "Anything that might explain the apparent triangle between Dad, Senator Moore, and Arielle?"

Donovan shook his head. "No, afraid not."

She nodded.

"But it's like I told you earlier, whatever your father was involved in while in the Air Force and whatever tie there is to this Coal girl, your father was a man of integrity. Always was, and I'm sure he is now."

"Thank you."

"And if I may, a word of advice?"

"Of course."

"Be careful asking too many questions about Silver Dawn. The military doesn't take too kindly to civilian investigations into military business, especially when it comes to classified projects. I don't know what Silver Dawn was. Maybe it's perfectly innocuous. But tread lightly."

She nodded again. "We will."

Donovan extended a hand. "Give your father my best the next time you see him."

"I'll do that."

"Jackson."

They shook hands again, then Donovan retreated to his Camaro. As quickly as he had come, he was gone, burning rubber down the one-lane scenic drive. Jackson watched the Camaro around the corner, then turned to Hillary. "So what do you make of all that?"

Her stare was past him and out at the desert floor. "I have no idea."

Chapter Thirteen

6:07 p.m.

FROM THE PATIO at P.F. Chang's at Planet Hollywood, Jackson and Hillary had a view of the Fountains of Bellagio, which had just finished another magnificent choreographed performance, this time to Celine Dion's "My Heart Will Go On." They were seated in the shade as the sun had dropped behind The Cosmopolitan. Even so, it was hot.

After the meeting with Roy Donovan, they had finished the one-way drive through Red Rock Canyon National Recreation Area and headed back to the city. In addition to viewing Senator Moore's voting record (there were no surprises), Hillary had used the drive time to look up Antonio the Magnificent, a.k.a. Tony Ribaldi. He performed nightly at eight, at a club on Paradise Road known as AiR. Hillary had called the club and spoken to Tony. He had heard about Arielle and was distressed, but the show must go on. He'd actually said it. Tony had already spoken to the police, but had agreed to meet with Jackson and Hillary after the show. He had been emphatic that it be after. He'd had enough bad vibes already.

Since they hadn't eaten lunch, Jackson and Hillary had both been hungry and he'd let her pick the place. She'd been quiet most of the drive back, and he couldn't blame her. His parents were dead. The next worst thing would be finding out one of them had a secret that involved a U.S. senator, a classified military project, and a dead prostitute.

The silence continued as they avoided conversation for most of the meal. For them, it constituted getting along. Vegas was a hard place to talk anyhow. Something somewhere was always making noise, most recently the show at Bellagio.

Hillary pushed around the last of her Mandarin chicken with her chopsticks. "What does your gut tell you?"

"My gut?" Jackson asked. He took a drink of iced tea.

"Don't all private investigators operate on gut instincts and hunches?"

"I don't know about all, but I go where the evidence leads me."

"Now who sounds like a bad detective show?"

Jackson stabbed a shrimp. "What does my gut tell me about what?"

"Who killed Arielle."

"Oh, are we working that case again?"

"What's that supposed to mean?"

"Seems we've sort of shifted from her to your father."

"Same investigation."

Jackson ingested the impaled shrimp. "How should I know who killed her? She's investigating the pal of a U.S. senator, holding contact info for a rich philanthropist, hanging out with magicians, and oh yeah, she's a hooker. Pick your poison."

"Forget I asked."

Jackson cleaned up his moo goo gai pan and watched Hillary pout. It wasn't a typical until-I-get-my-way pout, but more of a setting of the jaw, a how-dare-you-cross-me? sort of a thing. It had the same effect.

"Truth is, Hill, I think it was a pro."

"A pro?"

"Yeah, or somebody who watches crime shows."

"Why's that?"

"They policed their brass. No shell casings anywhere."

"In case you forgot, the police had the scene before us."

"Yes, but I saw none when I was there the first time either. Could have missed them, or they could have all rolled under the bed. But you asked for my gut, and that's what it says."

Hillary sat back and smiled politely at the waiter who took their plates and promised to return with the check. "Okay, so why were pros after Arielle?"

Jackson shrugged. "Best bet is it has to do with the money her aunt mentioned."

"So where did it come from?"

"Big tip?"

Hillary didn't smile.

"Hush money. Slept with the wrong guy and overheard something?"

"Or just the wrong guy, period," she said. "He was married, influential."

"You think . . ."

"More like the guy she tried to ID at his speech."

"You said you had a list of people in attendance. We should ask Shelly if her boyfriend can get us a photo of the guy."

"Already did. She's going to e-mail it to me."

The waiter returned with the check and two fortune cookies. Jackson reached for a cookie and the check as well. "This one's on me."

Hillary frowned.

"I'd have to eat anyhow this weekend."

She was too stunned, it appeared, to say anything, and Jackson whipped out his Visa. Then he cracked his fortune cookie. He grunted.

"What?"

"'*The path you are on will lead to success.*' I'm guessing this wasn't Arielle's fortune," he said as he crunched into the cookie.

The waiter took the check and Jackson drained his tea. "What's yours say?"

Hillary broke open her cookie.

"If it happens to be the numbers from *Lost*, I want it," Jackson added.

"'*There is someone rather unpleasant in your life you need to listen to.*'" Hillary dropped the paper onto the table. "Okay, speak."

He faked a laugh. "We got plenty of time before the show," he said. "Explore a little?"

She shrugged, and Jackson stood to leave.

"Don't you want your credit card back first?"

He winced and returned to his chair until the waiter returned again. He signed for dinner and pocketed his Visa. Then he and Hillary crossed the street and took the covered walkway leading to Bellagio's entrance. On the sidewalk, another crowd was beginning to form in anticipation of the next fountain show. But Jackson and Hillary headed inside, where the opulence was on full display.

Everything about Bellagio screamed class. Or rather, softly whispered it. The marble floors. The flowing chandeliers. The exquisite décor, including the incredible *Fiori di Como* glass sculpture, a chandelier comprised of two-thousand hand blown blossoms of every color that hung in the lobby. Even the casino floor was refined and understated, not the typical cheap, clangy, smoky environment.

Jackson and Hillary took their time strolling through the Conservatory & Botanical Gardens, around the luxurious pool courtyard, through the casino itself, and down Via Bellagio. An upscale shopping center, Via Bellagio dropped such names as Armani, Chanel, and Tiffany. Just window browsing made Jackson feel extravagant.

They emerged on the north side of Bellagio, across the street from sprawling Caesars Palace. It was one of the patriarchs of the Strip, the forefather of mega resort hotel and casinos. Through the years, it had grown and added on and undergone renovations, and it was still the king.

"Which way?" Hillary asked, turning her head south then north then toward Jackson, blond hair flopping across her bare shoulders. She fit in with the Vegas crowd—gorgeous, hip, at ease. And she seemed relaxed, almost fun. This was the sister-in-law Jackson had hoped for, the kind of girl you would like to hang out with, in Vegas or anywhere else.

"Let's go see the volcano," Jackson said, deciding to strike while the iron was hot. They crossed Flamingo Road and continued past Caesars Palace to The Mirage. Like Bellagio, it had a lagoon in front. Unlike Bellagio, it erupted with fire instead of water. Situated in the middle of what would have been a crescent shaped pond was a fifty-foot-high mound of faux rock, backed by a palm forest. It was innocent enough now, with nothing but water cascading over the side of the mountain.

Jackson leaned against the railing, soaking in the atmosphere. It was that moment sometime between dusk and darkness where a hint of day remained but the energy of the night was starting to take over. Such moments were far more prolific in Vegas than anywhere else, what with the warm desert air, the grandeur of the architecture, and the excitement of all the gamblers and partiers that was palpable.

And of course, with the knockout standing next to him. There were plenty of good looking girls in Vegas, but Hillary broke the meter. A few years ago, Jackson had entertained thoughts of Mosaic Law, of one brother filling in if another died. That was back when their relationship was only strained; and before the potential opportunity had become a devastating reality. Still, Jackson had to admit she sure improved the scenery.

"You're staring," Hillary said, catching Jackson as he watched the breeze lift the ends of her hair off her arms.

"Thinking," he quickly covered.

"About what?"

He noted the suspicion and made sure they moved on. "Arielle and your dad and possible connections."

"Before you say it and get a punch in the teeth, he didn't hire her."

"I wasn't thinking that."

Hillary tossed her hair onto her back with a subtle flick of the head. "I don't even know where to start."

Jackson had several questions, but before he could ask them, Hillary's phone rang. She checked the display, then gave Jackson an "excuse me" look and headed down the sidewalk. A blissful, "Hi," was all he heard before she was out of range.

He turned and leaned his back on the railing, watching the sights and sounds. Across the street was the Venetian, a perfect recreation of the famed Italian city, right down to the gondolas in front of a replica of St. Mark's Campanile. If he wasn't mistaken, the Venetian was home to Madame Tussauds Wax Museum. Creepy and intriguing. He had no idea how long they'd be in Vegas and wondered if he could talk Hillary into a little excursion. All work and no play . . .

Hillary returned after a couple of minutes, phone back in her purse. She didn't offer an explanation, and Jackson didn't ask. Before they could resume their previous conversation, the volcano erupted.

From the top of the fifty-foot-high mountain, flames shot up an additional forty feet. Rivulets of "lava" flowed down the side of the mountain and into the lagoon, out of which dozens and dozens of fireballs exploded. It was all set to an aggressive and perfectly complementary percussion rhythm that made the volcano come to life. So did the fire cannons, close enough to the sidewalks that Jackson could feel their heat. The naysayers had degenerate gamblers and prostitutes to complain about, but proponents of Vegas certainly had their ammunition as well.

When the show was over, Jackson and Hillary started back the way they had come. They arrived back at Bellagio between shows, and agreed to wait for the next one. Jackson rested his forearms on one of the concrete supports, right where the Ocean gang had said farewell.

"You were talking about connections to Arielle and Dad," Hillary said. "Come up with anything?"

"Nothing concrete. What's your father up to these days?"

Jackson knew that Hillary's dad was literally a millionaire, probably several times over. He had been involved in aerospace somehow, and made a fortune on the design of an airplane wing or a rocket engine or something. Jackson had always tuned out Hillary when she started in on the family fortune.

But that had been years ago. Warren had retired, and he and Danae McKenzie had started their own non-profit. They now spent their time jet-setting around the globe, doing whatever their little philanthropic hearts desired. If

Hillary had ever mentioned specifics, Jackson hadn't been paying attention. He just knew that Warren and Danae's humanitarian efforts were legendary.

"He and Mom have been in Dhaka for the last few weeks, waiting out monsoon season," Hillary explained.

"Dhaka?"

"Bangladesh."

"For what purpose?"

"Building schools, libraries, water treatment facilities, emergency response stations."

"Hands on."

"Some people write a check. Mom and Dad write the check, deliver it, and start putting the money to work."

"What about before Bangladesh?"

"They were home the last half of the summer. Before that, in Haiti and Guinea."

"You talk with them much?"

"Is that relevant?"

"To a caring human being," Jackson said.

She looked at him. "Is that relevant?"

Jackson stared at the water, contemplating how good it would feel to toss Hillary over the wall. He pictured her fighting to the surface, coughing and spluttering.

"No," she said. "A phone call after they got to Dhaka, a few e-mails. They keep pretty busy."

"Their work always the same?"

"Variations on a theme. Whatever the people need."

"They ever work in the U.S.?"

"Work, no. Donate, occasionally."

"Any chance they might have donated money to somebody in Las Vegas?"

"You mean like Arielle?"

"I didn't mean anything."

"I doubt it," she said after a moment.

"Your dad have any business associates in Vegas?"

"None I know of, but that doesn't mean no."

Jackson shrugged. "Maybe he gave a crony a business card, he lost it, and—"

"And Arielle picked it up. That's your theory?"

"It's one of them."

"It stinks."

"Thanks."

The crowd began to press in, and Hillary came around to Jackson's other side to avoid a trio of glittery teenage girls. Jackson used the lull in conversation to study the Bellagio, its yellow exterior bathed in a pale purple hue, towering over the tranquil pond in front of it. Fifty stories above the strip, the signature cupola was an epicenter, drawing the eye from the surrounding buildings with both elegance and insolence. It also tied the massive hotel to the quaint shops and restaurants clustered on the shore of the pond, a scene seemingly transported from the Lake Como coastline. Within the heart of Las Vegas, in the middle of the desert, Bellagio was a slice of Italian serenity. And that was just the exterior.

He dropped his eyes back to Hillary, who stared indifferently across the lake. "How long has he been retired?" Jackson asked.

"Four years this June," she said without looking at him.

"How much was he worth?"

Now she turned. "How can that possibly matter?"

"Goes to motive, Your Honor."

"Motive for what? You're just making stuff up."

Jackson shrugged.

"He did quite well."

"Boeing was it?"

"He had his own company, McKenzie Enterprises. They worked with Boeing, Lockheed Martin, some of the major companies."

"And how did he get to McKenzie Enterprises from medical school?"

"He intended to be a surgeon, but—"

"Washed out?"

"No, enlisted after his uncle was shot down in Vietnam."

"Oh."

"Once he left the Air Force, he got a job with Northrup for a few years before founding McKenzie Enterprises."

"What about your mom?"

"What about her?"

"She work?"

"Am I being deposed?"

"Wouldn't that be a kick?"

"She worked part-time, mostly charitable work."

Jackson nodded. He paused. "I have to ask, Hillary."

"No."

"Was there ever any sort—"

"No," she repeated, her eyes matching the fire of The Mirage Volcano.

"I'm not asking if your dad cheated. I'm just asking, how was the marriage?"

"None of your business."

"If we're looking for—"

"Looking for a connection to Arielle? The only connection down that road is one I'm telling you doesn't exist. Period."

Jackson put up his hands. "Okay."

"I'm not trying to clear my father's name because I think he might be involved in something sleazy. I'm confident he's not and I'm trying to clear away what to some would be suspicion." Her eyes connoted that she considered Jackson in the "some" category.

They stood side-by-side for several minutes.

"How are your sisters?"

"What?"

"How are your sisters?"

Hillary looked at him as if he'd just stepped off a spaceship. "Heather got engaged last month," she said finally, "and Holly is working in San Francisco as a barista at a coffee shop and still trying to get her singing career off the ground."

"Singing career?"

Hillary nodded.

"Like professionally?"

"That's the goal."

"Has she tried *Idol?*"

"Once."

"Hmm," Jackson said.

"Hmm, what?"

"Heather got engaged."

"So, what's that have to do with Dad and Arielle? What does any of this have to do with them?"

"Nothing," Jackson said. "But it might explain why you've been so uptight."

"Excuse me?"

"You're sublimating your anger, frustration, and the feeling of rejection now that she's getting married and you lost your fiancé."

"Sublimating. You get that from your court-ordered therapist?"

"I got that from having keen insight. In fact . . ."

"What?"

"How long have you been seeing What's-his-name?"

"Maybe you should try your 'keen insight' on our case instead of playing twenty questions with my personal life."

"So you don't deny it?"

"I have nothing to deny."

"That's a very lawyerly answer."

"You know what, I've had enough of this," she said. "I thought you were actually working, actually trying to help. You're just trying to pry. Sublimating *your* anger, frustration, and the feeling of rejection from losing your family."

Jackson knew his face revealed that her comment had struck a nerve, but he looked her in the eye anyway.

"I was trying to be nice," he said, "seeing as how questions about how your dad and a dead hooker are linked could be kind of unpleasant."

His reasons hadn't been entirely that altruistic, but he was mad. She had crossed the line, and he wanted a fight.

But Hillary deftly sidestepped. "I'll walk back to the hotel."

He lowered his head in disgust. "Fine."

"Antonio's show is at eight," she reminded. And with that, she was gone, and the nice moment they had shared that evening disappeared like a desert mirage.

The fountains started, with Elvis as the backdrop, singing "A Little Less Conversation." How fitting, Jackson thought, as he turned—just like the Ocean gang—and walked away.

Chapter Fourteen

10:07 p.m.

LOCATED AT THE south end of the Strip, across from the airport, Mandalay Bay, with its gold exterior, was a beacon to approaching gamblers and a landmark in its own right, despite being little more than a decade old. Jackson had parked in a lot south of the main tower, and he and Hillary had hiked through the best-smelling casino—if not place altogether—in the world to THEhotel, a forty-three-story addition to Mandalay Bay. On the ground floor of the tower was THElounge, a swank, cozy place to relax, watch some TV, or play a game of billiard. Jackson and Hillary had settled in plush leather chairs to wait for Antonio.

They had gone to AiR and watched Antonio's show. It had been subpar, except for the trick where he had made a tall, blond volunteer from the audience disappear. He had sent word through his "lovely" assistant—who had escorted Hillary back to the club's dining room—that he would meet with them, but not at AiR as originally planned. Dolores, the assistant, wouldn't say why, but told Hillary to meet Antonio at THElounge at ten.

Hillary, despite multiple pleas, had not revealed any further details about how Antonio had made her disappear.

While they waited, Jackson sipped a coffee—his purchase—and caught late football scores on the TV over the bar. Nothing exciting had happened during the day, so at least he hadn't missed much running Hillary's fool's errands.

Antonio the Magnificent arrived ten minutes late. He wore a lavender polo shirt and blue jeans over cowboy boots. His hair was lazily spiked, as was the trend, as it had been in the picture on Arielle's phone. He nodded at Hillary and Jackson and sat down. "Hello again."

"Thanks for seeing us, Antonio," Hillary said.

He nodded. "Call me Tony. Antonio's just a stage name."

"Okay, Tony."

He smiled. "I hope I didn't embarrass you too much on stage."

Hillary returned the smile. "Not too much."

Was she flirting?

"And I'm sorry for the switch of venues, but I saw a face in the crowd tonight."

"A face?"

"Yeah. The same guy was there several days ago. I'm pretty good with faces."

Jackson sat forward. "What happened several days ago?"

Tony bit his lip. "I don't know how much I should say. The cops asked a lot of questions earlier. I think I'm on the short list of suspects."

"I know the feeling."

Hillary explained, as she had on the phone earlier, that Arielle was possibly a very important witness in a case she was appealing. Or rather, might have been an important witness. Finding out what had happened to Arielle could still play a vital role in the case. She appealed on behalf of justice. As always, she won.

"What do you want to know?" Tony asked.

"You mentioned a familiar face in the audience," Hillary said. "Why'd that scare you off?"

"About a week ago, Arielle called me." He accepted a mixed drink from a waitress, tasted it, then continued. "She wouldn't tell me what was bothering her, but something clearly was. She was afraid, and whatever it was, it was getting worse."

"Why do you say that?"

"I've known Arielle for a year, and she's gradually gotten a little more . . . skittish."

"Skittish?"

"Yeah. She seemed on edge, paranoid. Last week, she said she thought someone was following her."

"Why would someone follow her?"

"I don't know," Tony answered. "And neither did she. At least, not that she would tell me." He took another drink. "I told her to come by the show, we'd talk."

"Did she?"

"Yeah. That was the night that guy was there, and now he shows up again when you want to talk about Arielle. I thought it was too much to be a coincidence."

"What night was that?"

Tony studied the ceiling. "Must have been . . . Monday, maybe Tuesday. The days run together."

"You perform every night?" Jackson asked.

"Except Sundays."

"Did this man see you talking with Arielle?" Hillary asked.

"No, we grabbed a pizza at Metro. We drove separate." He shrugged. "He might have seen us chatting for a minute, making plans, but I chat with a lot of people after the show."

"What'd he look like?" Hillary asked.

"Shorter than you," he said with a glance at Jackson, "thinning black hair, kind of a gruff face, a pronounced chin dimple, and really dark eyes. I know that's a cliché, but they were dark. And he had a look, like he knew he was trouble and was afraid other people would recognize him or something. It's hard to define, but he definitely stuck out."

"What did Arielle tell you when you met?" Jackson asked.

"Not much. Just reiterated that she thought someone was following her. She was really on edge, like she had something she needed to do but couldn't figure out what it was or how to do it. But she wouldn't tell me the details. I said I couldn't help if I didn't know what was going on, but she said just being there helped."

"What exactly was the nature of your relationship?" Hillary asked.

"Just friends," Tony said dismissively.

"*Just* friends?"

He swallowed. "We hooked up a couple of times, in the beginning. We both agreed it wasn't right for us. Since then, it's been platonic."

"On both ends?"

"Yeah."

"Did she say anything else—anything at all?" Hillary asked.

Tony thought for a minute, took another drink. "She didn't *say* anything. But, she was more paranoid than ever. Looking over her shoulder, fidgeting. I mean, it doesn't take a genius to see something was wrong."

Hillary nodded.

"And she had a bus ticket."

"A bus ticket?"

"It was sort of sticking out of her bag. I checked it when she went to the restroom, then asked her about it. She said something about visiting a friend."

"Where was the ticket to?" Hillary asked.

"And when?" Jackson asked.

"To L.A., but that's the thing—it was open-ended."

"A getaway," Jackson said.

"Had she said anything about running away?" Hillary asked.

"No, but it was in her body language. She had the look of a rabbit in the bush, ready to dart."

"When did her paranoia start?" Jackson asked.

"A couple of months ago, maybe. We don't talk all that often, every week or two. But she got a wad of money a while back, and that's when it seemed to start."

Jackson and Hillary exchanged a quick glance.

"How much money?" Hillary asked.

"I don't know, but she was suddenly flush. She didn't talk about it or anything, but you could tell. She dressed different, started eating at some swanky places, and her apartment is fitted."

"You've been to her apartment recently?"

"We hung out a few times. Honestly, that's all it was. A way to relax."

Hillary nodded.

"She give any clue where the money was from?" Jackson asked.

"No, but I got the feeling it was something shady. She really didn't want to talk about it." He shrugged. "And it wouldn't be the first time somebody in her line of work got involved in something paralegal."

Hillary winced at his choice of words. "Were you aware that Arielle had switched jobs several times?"

"Yeah, she wasn't happy with her previous agency."

"Amuse?"

"Yeah. She said their clients were . . . unsophisticated. Her words."

"What about Coyote Ugly?"

Tony shrugged. "It wasn't her thing. Don't get me wrong, it wasn't like being a call girl was either. But she said it was more . . . personal."

"That it would be," Jackson muttered.

"At the bar, strangers watch you dance. As a call girl, at least you sort of get to know the person a little. And you know, come to think of it, the money seemed to start flowing shortly after she switched to, what's the name, Good Night Escorts. I don't know, maybe they just paid really well or had exclusive clients."

"Do you have any idea why she might have been trying to call you last night?" Hillary asked.

"No. The cops asked the same thing. Arielle and I hadn't talked since Monday, Tuesday, whatever it was."

"Did she have any enemies that you knew of?" Hillary asked. "Anyone from her past who might want to harm her?"

"No, of course not. Everybody loved Arielle. She was easy to get along with. Nobody'd want to hurt her."

"Anything else?" Jackson asked. "Anything the police asked you we didn't?"

"Where I was last night. On stage, with a couple dozen witnesses, then at the club till almost eleven. Pretty standard most nights. But, they didn't seem convinced by a magician's alibi," he added with a smile.

"What about your assistant?" Hillary asked.

"Dolores?"

"How long has she been working with you?"

"Two years now. She's a prelaw student at UNLV."

"Is there any history between you two?" Hillary asked.

"No. Anything you see is just part of the show. Dol's a sweet kid."

Hillary nodded.

"How long have you been a magician?" Jackson asked.

"Professionally, six years. I've been messing around all my life. Kept making things around the house disappear, and of course I couldn't tell my parents where they were. Magician's code and all that."

"So I suppose there's no way you'll tell me how you made Hillary disappear?"

"Afraid not," Tony said.

"I was hoping to try it myself later."

Tony's eyes went between them. "You two aren't together?"

"No," Hillary stated flatly.

"Hmm. You have chemistry. This tag-team questioning. You're better than the cops."

"That I don't doubt," Jackson said.

"One last question," Hillary said. "Do you know a friend of Arielle's named Alex?"

"Sure, Alex Chapman. Why?"

"Arielle's aunt mentioned her. If they were close, Arielle might have confided in her."

"Yeah, Alex sings at a club downtown named Seven-7." He checked his watch. "Probably there now. I think the club caters to the late crowd."

"Thank you," Hillary said. She extended a business card to Tony. "If you think of anything else, please give me a call."

"I'll do that. And like I told the cops, if you find out what happened to her, please let me know."

"We will."

The trio stood and shook hands. Tony departed, and Jackson and Hillary remained for a moment.

"Chemistry," he said.

She just huffed. "Come on."

"Don't tell me, you want to take in a late-night show at Seven-7."

"The sooner we talk to Alex, the sooner we get some answers."

"Yeah, because that's working so well. All we have is more questions."

"Clearly we're on to something. She switched agencies, suddenly struck it rich, and at the same time got paranoid and thought someone was following her."

"Another sordid tale in a city full of them."

"How do you ever solve a case with this sort of attitude?"

"Easy. I observe things."

"Like what?"

"Like the fact that Arielle was planning a Greyhound getaway."

"So?"

"So," he said, "if she was planning to make a run from whoever she felt was after her, maybe she also had the goods on them, either to blackmail or give to the authorities or whatever. And maybe, just maybe, she—"

"Stashed it in a locker at the bus station. The key."

"And thank you, Lassiter, for stealing my thunder."

"Who?"

"Lassiter, from *Psych*."

She shook her head.

"It's set in Santa Barbara, how do you . . ." Now he shook his head.

"Can we just go get the key?"

Jackson reached into his pocket. "One step ahead of you."

"Must be nice for a change. Come on."

As they walked to the car, Hillary used her phone to locate the Greyhound bus station. She also called Seven-7 to ask if she could speak to Alex Chapman. After several minutes, she was informed that Alex was unavailable, but that she performed at eleven p.m. and two a.m. She told Jackson as much as they got into his car. It was ten-thirty at night and still hot and unpleasant.

The Las Vegas Greyhound station was located west of downtown, just south of the Plaza Hotel and Casino on Main Street. Taking I-15 instead of Las Vegas Boulevard, Jackson made it in just over ten minutes. He parked in a surface lot and they made the short walk to the entrance, passing several homeless people on the street. Hillary, as beautiful as ever despite the long day—and wearing an eye-catching orange top, no less—stood out and made an easy target. Jackson doubted she would suffer anything worse than a catcall or two, but he kept a watchful eye out nonetheless.

Inside, things weren't much better. An old man sat in one corner, one foot bare, mumbling to himself and repeatedly digging through his pockets. As Jackson watched him for a moment, he realized he wasn't looking for something, but repeating the same series of motions over and over, almost in rhythm. A woman who—from Jackson's limited but recent experience—was likely a hooker, nearly sucked her cigarette flat through lips caked with bright red lipstick. It was a drastic contrast to her green dress, accentuated by black fishnet stockings. She eyed Jackson for a moment before breaking away. A Hispanic guy bounced to his own music as he leaned against the wall, wearing a bulky black jacket despite the heat. Likely hiding drugs. Just down the way from him, sitting against the wall instead of standing, was a gruff-looking woman holding a cardboard sign asking for money.

A handful of other, less conspicuous people sat in the waiting area or stood in line to purchase tickets. None of them seemed overly pleased to be at the bus station at quarter to eleven on a Saturday night. And none of them, save for a black guy in a Mets cap who was seeking spare change, cast more than a passing glance at Jackson or Hillary. That included a security guard who looked as bored as the passengers.

"Dregs of humanity," Jackson muttered to Hillary.

"Your kind of people?"

"Let's just get in and get out."

The lockers were around the corner, next to another seating area. It was almost empty, the only inhabitants a young blond woman biting her fingernails and a heavyset woman eating a Jimmy John's sandwich. And, Jackson saw as they drew closer, a man of indeterminate age lying on the floor in the corner. He had a dirty gray beard, worn clothes, and a distinct stench that was stronger and more pronounced than that which permeated the rest of the station.

"You have the key?" Hillary asked.

Jackson handed it to her. She found the corresponding locker, C13, and inserted the key. It opened and she withdrew a canvas backpack as the intercom squawked with an announcement for an impending departure. Across the room, the blonde collected her purse and stood. Hillary took a quick peek to make sure the backpack was the sole content of the locker before closing the door and pocketing the key. She then unzipped the main pocket of the backpack.

"Change of clothes, a small box of priceless treasures, and a romance paperback?" Jackson asked.

"Not exactly," she said, handing him the bag. "See for yourself."

Jackson grabbed it and peered inside. Reflexively, he lifted his head and scanned the room. He turned his eyes briefly to Hillary before lowering them again to the backpack.

It was filled with cash.

Chapter Fifteen

10:51 p.m.

JACKSON QUICKLY ZIPPED the backpack. "We need to put this back."

"Why?"

"Um, because this is evidence."

Hillary shook her head. "We don't know that."

"You're right, a backpack full of cash in a bus locker probably has nothing to do with a hooker's murder."

"Keep your voice down."

"My voice is down. Besides, Bootlegger Club is too busy inhaling her sandwich and Pigpen's only half conscious. Hill, we cannot take this bag. We have to call Baxter and Cruz."

"We'll discuss this later, somewhere else."

"After we've contaminated the evidence?"

"You're holding it in your hand right now. It's already contaminated. Now come on."

He sighed and hoisted the backpack onto his shoulders. "Do me a favor and don't make eye contact with any security cameras," he said.

Hillary ignored him, walking confidently and purposefully toward the exit. Jackson tried to mimic her, but felt as if every eye in the station was on him and on the backpack. In actuality, most of them were turned toward a commotion near the ticket counter, and Jackson and Hillary, despite passing a couple of sketchy characters on the sidewalk, reached the Granada safely. Jackson chucked the backpack onto the floor at Hillary's feet and locked his door as soon as it closed.

"How is this not evidence tampering or interfering with an investigation or something?" he asked.

"Because we don't know that it's evidence," Hillary said as she buckled her seatbelt.

"Isn't that for the cops to determine?"

"If they had been the ones to find it, yes. It's not our fault they didn't find the key at her apartment."

He shook his head.

"I also saw a notebook in with the money," Hillary said. "We'll take it back to the hotel, see how much money is there, see what's in the notebook, see if anything else is in the backpack. Then we'll decide what to do."

"It must be nice being a lawyer," he said, "making up the law as you go along."

"Please, like if this were any other case you'd be running to the police instead of trying to solve it yourself."

"If this were any other case, I'd have given up a long time ago."

"If this were anything else at all, you'd have given up. Now drive."

"Where to?"

"Seven-7."

"You really want to go clubbing with a backpack full of cash in the car?"

"Yes, because no one in their right mind would break into this car to steal something."

"After our last stop, it's not people in their right mind I'm worried about."

"Drive."

Jackson did. Seven-7 was just a few blocks away, in the shadow of the Freemont Street Experience. Jackson had to circle the block a few times to find a parking lot. Then, stowing the backpack in the trunk, they set out on foot.

With so much neon and so many flashing lights, Seven-7's relatively small marquee (a large red numeral 7 with the word "Seven" etched in white script across the top of the 7) was easy to miss. It hung above a doorway that appeared to be little more than a crevice between two buildings. In actuality, it opened to a poorly lit entry hall, off which were restrooms, a coat nook with a payphone, a door marked "Employees Only," and another labeled "Kitchen."

On their right, across from a life-size photograph of Elvis in a white jumper open almost to the navel, his face contorted as he squinted at his microphone, was an opening leading to the club itself. As Jackson and Hillary turned the corner, they were greeted by a sultry, somewhat husky female voice. She was singing a song Jackson had heard before but couldn't place. He also couldn't see. Seven-7 was only marginally better illuminated than the hallway. Smoke hung like blue haze under a recessed ceiling, partially obscuring a disco ball in the center of the room. Beneath it were maybe a dozen circular tables. Another ten or twelve booths lined the right and left walls, creating several alcoves separated by potted ferns. A V-shaped bar jutted out from the near wall, providing seating for another ten or twelve people on barstools. Stained glass chandeliers hung over the bar and above the booths. Along with candles on all the tables, they provided the room's only light, save for a trio of spotlights pointed at the stage along the far wall. Stage was being generous, given that it was simply a carpeted platform a step or two above the rest of the dining room.

"I assume Gene Rayburn and Charles Nelson Reilly are sharing a drink somewhere in here," Jackson said, noting maybe half of the tables had occupants. It was too dark to identify much about them, but they appeared to be the same crowd that flocked to $3.99 buffets and one-dollar cocktails at the off-Strip casinos and played nickel slots at eleven a.m.

Hillary didn't answer, instead leading the way past an unmanned hostess desk. The floor beneath them was carpeted the same bright red as the stage. The walls were covered by dark wood paneling to match the tables, chairs, and booths. The room smelled of cheap booze and meat gravy, the latter of which made Jackson's mouth water.

Hillary picked a booth on the right, near the stage. Jackson slid in the opposite side of the semicircular booth and turned his eyes to the stage. A black curtain was drawn to the sides, revealing a red curtain as a backdrop. A baby grand piano sat in the right corner, its ivories tickled softly by a lanky black man with gray stubble for hair. He was joined onstage by a woman in a floor-length black dress, slit high, with a plunging neckline, and long, flared sleeves. She wore a gaudy jade necklace that hung to her torso and earrings that dangled to her shoulders and reflected the flickering candlelight as she leaned forward and swayed while singing into a cordless microphone. Large curls added texture to dark brown hair that flowed behind her as she moved gracefully across the stage.

The only thing out of place was the face. It was young. Dressed as she was, wearing what she was, and singing where she was, the woman should have been old enough to be Jackson's mom. Instead, she was incredibly young, low to mid-twenties, and cute despite the '70s hairstyle and outfit. Even without a photo or description, there was little doubt this was Alex Chapman.

She finished her number and bowed to moderate applause. Including Jackson's. Hillary shot him a look but he ignored her. A waitress (with a face that belonged on stage) brought them cocktail napkins and glasses of water, along with menus. Hillary declined, but Jackson immediately opened his and began scanning it.

"You can't be serious," Hillary said. "You already had dinner and nachos at the club."

"Relax, I'll buy."

She shook her head.

"You can't tell me you don't ever get cravings for a five-dollar midnight cheeseburger."

She shook it again. Onstage, Alex had wandered over and now leaned against the piano as she began singing "How Sweet It Is (To Be Loved By You)." Her voice was rich and strong, and she had an aura about her that was captivating. Or maybe she was just cute. Either way, Jackson determined that watching and listening to her for an hour wouldn't be so bad. Especially if he could eat and annoy Hillary at the same time.

Jackson ordered a cheeseburger and fries, then clapped a little louder when Alex finished her second song. She then slid behind the piano, playing a duet with the lanky guy for a few minutes. Hillary drank her water sullenly.

"Ask you a question?" Jackson said when the duet was finished and light applause again filled the dining room.

"Mm, what's that?"

"Have you ever had a good time?"

"Excuse me?"

"You're always so straight-laced and proper and professional. Do you ever just cut loose and have fun?"

She took another drink before answering. "I have plenty of fun, Jackson. I just don't like to mix—"

"Business and pleasure. Very original."

"You know, I could ask you the same question in reverse."

"Forget I said anything."

"That's right, duck even the appearance of responsibility."

He was saved from further comment by the arrival of his burger and a plate of steak fries, and by the onset of another song. Alex had taken up the microphone again, and as she sang a slow, sensual ballad, she stepped down from the stage and slowly circulated around the tables.

"Oh, please," Hillary muttered as Alex "sat" on the lap of a middle-aged man at a front-row table. She sang a few lyrics to him, smiled seductively, then moved on. She made the rounds as she sang, not visiting Jackson's lap but offering him a wink. He returned it as he reached for a fry, drawing an audible huff from Hillary.

"Are you jealous?" he asked after more applause.

The confusion—maybe even shock—on her face seemed to be genuine. "Of what?"

"I show the mildest interest in Alex's singing ability and suddenly you're cranky—er—and snarking under your breath."

"I'm not snarking. But you are once again flirting with the first pretty girl to come along."

"I'm trying to be memorable. I thought it might help us get a word with her after the performance."

"Whatever you say."

Jackson ignored Hillary for the rest of the show, enjoying a pretty decent cheeseburger and a pretty decent (and just pretty) singer. Alex's last number, a powerful rendition of "Ain't No Mountain High Enough," elicited genuine applause, not the half-hearted courtesy clap to be expected. Alex bowed again, blew a kiss, and gestured toward the lanky guy at the piano, who had done a fair job of his own, before she disappeared behind the curtain.

"So how do we get an audience with her?" Jackson asked.

"Like this," Hillary said. Lanky had ambled down off the stage and was headed past them, toward the bar. Hillary stood and stepped deftly into his path. "Excuse me," she said.

The man stopped. "Yes, ma'am?"

"I'm wondering if it would be possible for us to speak with Miss Chapman."

"Are you friends of hers?"

"We knew a friend," Hillary said. They'd been stretching the truth for two days, so why not a little further?

"Well let me go speak to her a moment. Can I give her your names?"

"I don't think she'll know our names, but it's about Arielle," Hillary said.

"Arielle. The young woman who was killed last night?"

Hillary nodded somberly. "That's right."

"I'll let her know you're here. Please wait here."

"Thank you," Hillary said.

He nodded and turned back toward the stage.

"Seeing dead now counts as knowing?" Jackson asked.

"Did you have a better idea?"

He shrugged. Around them, the lounge was turning over. Half of the audience was on their way out. The other half was settling in for the night. A stagehand was wheeling the piano behind the curtain in preparation for the next performer. A minute later, Lanky returned. "Come with me," he said.

Jackson tossed a ten on the table next to his plate and he and Hillary followed the man onto the stage, behind the black curtain, and into a narrow hallway that ran beside the dining room. It was at least well-lit. Lanky rapped on the second door on their right, a door marked only with a "B" in the center. He pushed it open and stuck his head inside. "Alex, a couple of people to see you."

He then backed out and nodded at Jackson and Hillary. They entered a standard, spacious dressing room. Posters on the wall showed Charo, Phyllis Diller, Cher, Rita Rudner, and Celine Dion. Alex sat on a backless chair in front of a vanity, turned so that she faced them. She held a tapered blush brush in her hand, not that she needed any more makeup. Her hair was now wavy, shorter, and a few shades lighter, and Jackson saw that her stage tresses were actually a wig hung over a mannequin head beside her.

"Miss Chapman, thank you for seeing us," Hillary said.

"Please, Alex. You knew Arielle?"

"In a manner of speaking," Hillary said. She introduced herself and Jackson and explained why they were there. Once again, she softened the pitch by mentioning her pursuit of justice.

Alex's dark blue eyes studied Hillary intently, then settled on Jackson. "You don't look like a P.I."

"You don't look like a 1970s diva."

"Yeah, well, it's a gig." She turned around and finished applying a touchup of blush to her cheeks. Then she set down the brush and swiveled to face them. "Okay, what do you want to know?"

"We spoke to Arielle's aunt Darla and Antonio the Magnificent," Hillary said. "They both told us that she had seemed paranoid of late. Did you notice anything unusual or suspicious?"

"I don't know that she was paranoid, but something was off."

"How so?"

"You can just tell. I got the feeling she was in some kind of trouble, but she wouldn't talk about it."

"What gave you that feeling?"

"Different things. Her temperament was always fun and feisty, but she'd been muted the last month or two. She'd get these faraway stares on her face and just blend into the wall. That was never her. And there was the money."

"The money?" Hillary asked.

"I don't know where she got it, and she wouldn't tell me. A couple of times, I got the feeling she wanted to but couldn't bring herself to say anything. It's the way she was in general lately, like she wanted to get something off her chest but didn't dare."

"Do you have any idea where it came from?" Hillary asked.

"Or how much it was?" Jackson asked, thinking about the backpack in his Granada, parked on the street, unguarded.

Alex shook her head. "No, but it was substantial. As for where she got it, I have a theory, but like I said, she wouldn't say anything about it."

Hillary waited.

Alex continued. "Arielle mentioned to me once, a few months ago, that she was moonlighting. She'd just started with Good Night Escorts, and they paid better and serviced better clientele than her previous agency, but I know they didn't pay as well as she was living. Anyhow, shortly after she started there, she said something about working on the side too. She wouldn't tell me for who or how often, but it could be that's where the extra income came from."

"Do you know if it was another agency or just another person?" Jackson asked.

"No, I don't. Don't even know what it was she was doing. I tried to bring it up again a while back, and she just got that stare."

"Had she said anything in particular about someone being out to get her or being after her?"

Alex bit down on her lip. "I'm trying to remember, but I don't think so. The last few weeks, we didn't talk about much of anything. She seemed so out of it that I just tried to lighten the mood. We basically talked about nothing."

Hillary allowed an appropriate pause to transition to her next question. "Can you think of anyone who would want to harm Arielle?"

"No," Alex answered with a frown. "I never knew anybody who didn't like her."

"Was she seeing anyone?" Jackson asked.

"You mean besides every night?"

"I mean did she have a boyfriend?"

"No. Well, there was Matt, but I don't know what they called whatever they had."

"Do you know Matt's last name?" Hillary asked.

"No."

"Any idea where he and Arielle met or where we might find him?"

"Not really. I gathered from some comments she made that he ran in pretty high circles, but I don't know anything specific."

"Had she said anything to you about leaving town?" Jackson asked.

"No, why?"

He explained about the bus ticket Tony had spotted. Alex shook her head, saying it was news to her.

"Can you think of anything else that might shed a light on Arielle's murder?" Hillary asked.

"I can't. The cops asked me the same question, and I've been thinking all day, but I've got nothing. Sorry."

Hillary, as had become custom, handed Alex a business card. "If you do think of something—anything—please give me a call."

"I will," Alex said.

"Thank you for your time," Hillary said, turning to leave.

"I enjoyed the show," Jackson said with a wink.

"Thanks."

Hillary again rolled her eyes as Jackson closed the dressing room door behind him.

"What?" he asked.

"I suppose you were flirting now to spur her to call us if she remembers something?"

"No," he said with a grin. "I was flirting this time because she was cute and I liked her singing."

Chapter Sixteen

"TWENTY-FIVE BIG ONES," Jackson announced, setting the last stack of bundled cash on the end of Hillary's bed.

"Exactly?"

"Unless one of these stacks is short."

There were twenty-five bundles of cash, each the same height. Jackson had counted three of them, finding fifty twenty-dollar bills in each. He'd done the math three times before announcing the total to Hillary. There were no markings on the paper straps binding the bills, but they were crisp and new.

Hillary, meanwhile, had begun thumbing through a college-ruled notebook that had been bound with a heavy-duty rubber band and wedged in with the money. Aside from a small pouch with basic toiletries and first-aid supplies, they had been the only contents of the backpack.

It now sat on the floor beside the bed. Like a scene from Poe's *The Tell-Tale Heart*, it ate at Jackson. Not so much because it and the money and the notebook could lead the police to Arielle's killer, but because he was sure Baxter and Cruz would find out that he and Hillary had taken it and not called them. It was one thing to have a hotshot—and plain hot—lawyer get you off once. It was another thing to have her do it twice, especially if she was in the next cell.

"You find anything in there?" he asked Hillary.

"Plenty."

"Mind sharing?"

"In a minute."

He got up and paced. It was all starting to make sense. Arielle had been moonlighting, had made a wad of cash, had suspected—accurately or otherwise—that someone was after her, had prepped for her getaway, and hadn't made it in time. But what exactly had she done to cause someone to want to kill her? Slept with the wrong person? Seen or heard something she shouldn't have?

Extorted in addition to moonlighting? What did Senator Moore have to do with anything, and the guy at his speech, and the "face" Antonio the Magnificent had seen in the crowd?

"Okay, read the first couple of pages," Hillary said. She handed the notebook to Jackson, who fell into a chair.

Arielle's writing was fast and messy, lacking any feminine flirt or chic swirl. As Jackson read, his questions began to have some answers.

She wrote that she had begun working for Good Night Escorts back in June, where she had met a man named Matt Brenner. He worked for the agency, as "talent management." He and Arielle developed a friendship that became something more than friendship. Like Darla and Alex, Arielle wasn't able to classify what that something was.

In early July, Matt approached Arielle and asked if she would be interested in making some extra money. She was sick of her current life and thought money would be the way out, so she said yes. Matt introduced her to a man named "X" who explained the gig to her. He and "his people" would provide her clients, aside from those who came through Good Night Escorts. Arielle's job was to seduce them, show them a good time, and invite them back to her hotel suite, where she was to slip them a knockout drug and leave. Each case was different. Sometimes all she had to do was meet a client; other times she actually needed to lure a would-be client to the hotel, the means of doing so left up to her.

Still other times, she was told to come to a certain room where an unconscious man was waiting. Her job was to wait until he awoke and pretend as if they had painted the town red then spent the night or weekend together. She would be given a basic script and told what to say and do to convince the person that what had happened should indeed stay in Vegas. Empty liquor bottles, drug paraphernalia, and staged photographs were just some of the props at her disposal.

Arielle asked both X and Matt what was happening to the men she drugged, and they both told her it was above her pay grade. She didn't like the idea, but the money was really good. She also convinced herself these men had it coming, although she knew that wasn't necessarily the case.

Jackson looked up. "Why did she keep her diary in a bus locker?"

"I think it's more of a tell-all," Hillary answered, looking up from her laptop. "Keep reading."

The man known as X paid her after each "date." When a second inquiry into what was happening was met with a harsh warning to never mind and enjoy the money, Arielle again questioned Matt. He told her it was best she didn't know. But her conscience got the best of her, and one night after drugging another client, she hung around to see what would happen. Five minutes after she left the room, she saw two men enter. They emerged a few minutes later carrying a huge duffel bag between them, which they loaded into a black van.

About a week later, she watched as two men again removed a duffel that she presumed held the body of the man she had drugged. That time, she had her car ready and followed the van. It entered a parking garage downtown, and she watched as the duffel was transported from one unmarked van to another, this one with government plates. A few weeks later, she saw part of Senator Moore's UNLV immigration speech on TV and spotted a familiar face in the crowd behind him. She was almost positive it belonged to a man she had seen at what she dubbed "the body exchange." She talked to Shelly, whose boyfriend provided Arielle with footage of the speech. She was even more positive the faces matched, but was unable to identify the man or learn his name.

Jackson turned the page to find a flow chart containing half a dozen different names, some of which he recognized from Arielle's previous entries and some of which were new to him. The next page contained a list of completely new names, along with dates, various hotels, and some scribbled notes. It appeared to be a log of Arielle's clients, perhaps ones provided by X?

Jackson looked up. "Did you get to any part where we find out who killed her?"

Hillary swung her legs off the bed and stood. "Did you really expect it to be that easy?"

"No, but I'm not in the mood for trying to find the link between a bunch of Johns Arielle seduced and drugged." He held up the page showing the names.

"That isn't the end."

"Sum it up for me."

"I haven't read it all. I stopped there," she said, nodding at the notebook.

He tossed it on the bed. "Well I'm bushed. You can stay up all night reading the sordid details if you want. Better yet, call Baxter and Cruz and let them read it."

"Not yet. Not until we know that what we have is evidence in her murder. And not until I know if it provides any clues about my father."

"Suit yourself," Jackson said. He walked toward the door, then stopped and looked at the stack of cash still on the bed. "You might wanna deadbolt this behind me."

*   *   *

7:30 a.m.

JACKSON DREAMT he was a magician who kept making Hillary disappear, but every time he did, she reappeared, like Hugh Jackman in *The Prestige*. At least she didn't keep getting cloned. One Hillary was plenty.

He was roused from his nightmare by a piercing ring. He flailed at his alarm clock, assaulting the poor thing in attempt to make the noise stop. After several rings, he realized the shrillness was emanating from the phone. He reached a clumsy hand for it and knocked the receiver onto the floor. With a groan as he saw the time on the assailed clock, he reeled in the receiver by its cord.

"Hello?"

"Did I wake you?"

"No, I was just doing my morning calisthenics."

"Good," she said, ignoring the sarcasm. "I'll be over in a little while and we can get to work."

"Stellar."

He hung up and buried his face in the pillow. From one nightmare to another.

Slowly, he dragged himself out of bed, pulled the comforter up to the headboard, and rummaged for clean clothes. He was to the last of his socks and underwear, so either this was their final day in Vegas or he needed to hit a Wal-Mart.

Jackson took longer than normal in the shower, attempting to let the warm water wake him. It didn't work, and threatened to put him back to sleep. Finally he forced himself to get out. His mind was like oatmeal, unable to remember half of what he and Hillary had learned yesterday, much less put the pieces together. Then again, maybe it was because none of the pieces had defined edges.

He was coherent enough to say a prayer for wisdom just before someone pounded on the door. Jackson spat out his toothpaste, quickly rinsed his mouth, and reached for his plain red shirt. He pulled it on and, shutting the bathroom door behind him, put his eye to the peephole.

It was Hillary, hair in a pony, wearing the hideous powder blue of UCLA. As if she knew he was at the door, she rapped on it again. He took a deep breath and undid the deadbolt. "Hey," he mumbled.

"Morning," she said, thrusting a Styrofoam cup of coffee at him as she entered.

"Arsenic?"

"Black," she replied. She set a small plate on the dresser. It contained a large muffin, a few pieces of strudel, and a cake donut. "Also brought you breakfast."

"Maybe I'm still dreaming."

"Pardon?"

"Uh, nothing. Thanks."

"Consider it a peace offering," she said. "I've been a little brusque, and that crack about hiring a hooker being your cup of tea was out of line."

Just that one crack was out of line? He decided to let it go. If she was making the effort . . .

"Thanks," he said again. The muffin looked particularly gooey, so he peeled the wrapper and began eating. "Where'd you get these?"

"Continental breakfast downstairs."

"Hmm. Good."

"So, you want to come over? We'll get to work."

"Uh, yeah. I'm still a little foggy this morning. We did spend the night at a magic show and a '70s lounge sandwiched around finding twenty-five grand at the city dump, right?"

"More or less."

Remembering the stack of cash he'd left on Hillary's bed woke Jackson up more than the coffee, and he followed her back to her room. The bed was perfectly made, all her clothes were packed away in her suitcase or the dresser beneath the TV, and the room smelled like vanilla instead of morning breath. The cash was now stacked on a chair beside the dresser/entertainment stand, twenty-five bundles of Andrew Jacksons.

Jackson took his muffin and wandered to the window. It was a gray, hazy morning. Wet spots in the parking lot indicated it had rained overnight, but they were quickly drying. He was sure more heat was on the way.

"So what's the plan for today?" he asked between bites of the muffin.

"I read the rest of Arielle's notebook," Hillary said.

"Find a smoking gun?"

"No, but Arielle might have."

"Do tell."

"She began doing research on Moore after recognizing one of the men from the parking garage on the video of his immigration speech."

"I might have a lead on that, by the way," Jackson said.

"Oh? You dream a solution?"

"No. Mouse."

"I beg your pardon."

"Mouse, he's a friend of mine."

"His name is Mouse?"

"Nickname."

She said nothing, her facial expressing conveying her sentiment just perfectly. "Go on."

"If Shelly comes through with a photo of the guy, he can run facial rec on it."

"She already sent it, last night."

"That was quick."

Hillary shrugged. "This Mouse character has access to facial recognition software?"

"Sort of."

"Legal access?"

"No less legal than holding back locker contents from Las Vegas Metro."

She sighed. "There's more."

Jackson took a drink of coffee.

"Arielle Googled Moore, checked public records, and talked to what she termed 'colleagues' about him. She found ties to a man named Richard Holloway."

"Should that name mean something?"

"Not to you, no. But I did see his name yesterday when I was looking at Moore's financial supporters. Holloway has been a major contributor over the years, donating the maximum legally allowed."

"Okay, so what's his tie to Moore? Or's he just like his politics?"

"Arielle did some digging and found a lot of back-scratching between Moore and Holloway. Holloway owns Oasis Las Vegas, and from what she could gather, Moore threw his political weight around to help Holloway get the permits and authorizations needed to buy up several smaller properties and make way for his casino. In return, Holloway was apparently very generous to Moore's re-election campaign and several other initiatives."

"That's not unusual, is it? Wealthy businessmen make big contributions to politicians who in turn push legislation to benefit their businesses? It's the American way."

"It is, and Arielle didn't uncover anything illegal or even shady."

"So what's the tie?" Jackson asked before taking another sip of coffee. "He can't be the only one striking deals with Moore."

"Not until you factor in that Matt Brenner, the man who recruited Arielle, has ties to Holloway too."

"He does?"

Hillary nodded. "He manages a 'concierge' service for guests at Oasis."

"Concierge? That mean what I think it means?"

She nodded again.

"I thought that was only for seedy dives, not glamorous resort properties."

"Well it's not like they have a big sign at the front desk advertising call girls, but if someone made a discreet inquiry, they'd be directed to Matt."

"Any idea who these guys are Arielle was drugging? Is Oasis a pipeline? Are they finding rich whales and blackmailing them or something?"

"I don't know. She didn't either. After her research, she went to Brenner again. Apparently, their ambiguous relationship was only ambiguous as far as description. She asked for details, and he again told her it was best she didn't know. He mentioned the names Moore and Holloway and he warned her again it was best she just dropped it and did what she was paid to do."

"This appears to be pointing to motive."

"Maybe. Anyhow, the last entry in the notebook came after she overheard Brenner on the phone, telling someone that, quote, 'Holloway has the goods, has a paper trail. We might want to get out,' end quote." Hillary looked up. "She wrote that she didn't know if Brenner knew she heard him or not."

Jackson deposited the last of the muffin in his mouth, thought as he chewed, then had a chug of coffee. "You have the notebook?" he asked.

Hillary reached back onto the nightstand and picked it up. She handed it to Jackson, and he flipped to the flow chart Arielle had drawn. It explained why the name Holloway had rung a bell. It was one of several circled and linked to others.

"So she has Moore linked to Holloway, Holloway linked to Brenner, Brenner linked to X, Holloway linked to X with a question mark, and a big question mark linked to X and Moore."

"I assume the last question mark is for the man at the speech," Hillary said.

"Notice a conspicuous absence in all this?"

"My father."

Jackson studied the flow chart for several minutes before checking out all the names, hotels, and dates on the next page. "None of these are real high-class hotels," he said.

"Lack of security footage," she said.

Jackson tossed the notebook onto the bed beside Hillary. "So someone is selecting people, whether they be guys who want hookers or guys who could be seduced by one, and having Arielle and likely others lure them to a hotel room and drug them. They're then carting these guys off to who knows where in a van with government plates—Too bad Arielle didn't get plate number, by the way—then returning the guys to a hotel and selling them on the fact that they just lived *The Hangover*."

"Tell me you haven't watched *The Hangover*."

"Only seen previews. The question is why. What do they want with these guys?"

"And who are 'they'?"

"And how does Moore tie in, besides standing in front of a guy at a speech?"

"And Holloway."

"And your father."

Hillary sighed.

"You know who might be able to tie this all together?" he said.

"Who?"

"Las Vegas's finest."

She sighed again.

"It is kind of why we pay their salary."

"I doubt your tax dollars get funneled to a police department in Nevada."

"You know what I mean." He had more coffee, now cold. "Okay, so what do we do?"

"Research," she said. "We compile a thorough dossier on Holloway, look into Brenner, see if we can get a name for X or identify the man at the speech."

"Research," Jackson muttered. "Super."

Chapter Seventeen

9:59 a.m.

ON SUNDAYS, THE Las Vegas Central Library and Children's Museum opened at ten a.m. Jackson and Hillary were waiting in the parking lot when an employee unlocked the front door one minute before ten. The sky had cleared and more unrelenting sunshine beat down on them as they crossed the asphalt lot.

The building looked nothing like a library. From the conical room out front that was evocative of a NASA escape pod to the silo-esque tower to a pockmarked sandstone wedge at the rear of the building, it resembled a postmodern home more than an academic edifice. Then again, it was nestled in the city's "Cultural Corridor," situated between the Mob Museum and the Burlesque Hall of Fame. Welcome to Vegas.

Before leaving the hotel, Jackson had put in a call to Mouse. He often played video games until dawn, and on the Sundays he did go to church, he still slept until the last possible minute. Mouse didn't pick up so Jackson left a message on his answering machine, asking him to call back when he had a chance. A computer whiz, Mouse didn't own a cell phone, instead sharing a duplex and a landline phone with his sister Pam. Fortunately, she hadn't answered either.

Jackson had watched Senator Moore's immigration speech on YouTube and observed Arielle's mystery man, identifiable from the photo Shelly had e-mailed. He had stood stoically, hands folded in front of his waist, throughout. Jackson had gleaned nothing.

Hillary, meanwhile, had logged onto CD&R's network to begin research on Richard Holloway. Given the restrictions of a tablet or phone for prolonged web searches, and since the library was a federal and state government depository, Jackson and Hillary had opted to continue their research there as soon as it opened.

Inside, the library was sleek and modern with plenty of natural light coming in through windows and skylights. Jackson and Hillary split up, agreeing to meet up in an hour. Jackson spent fifteen minutes at the customer service desk procuring access to a library computer, then went to town.

He Googled Matt Brenner, finding a Twitter profile that was ambiguous and yet rather obvious in identifying him as a "concierge." He found no Facebook page or any other social media sites. A general web search revealed several Matt Brenners in Las Vegas, only one of whom was under forty. He was, apparently, a graduate of UNLV, but that was about all Jackson learned.

He also tried entering "man named X" and similar phrases into the search engine, but that didn't generate much of anything. Hoping Hillary was faring better, Jackson tried a different tack. He combed both internet and library records of Senator Moore, looking for any faces that matched the photo sent by Shelly of the man at the speech. He also pulled up any previous public appearances by Moore, hoping to see the same face, perhaps with some means of identification.

He found next to nothing. He viewed a dozen other speeches by Moore, everything from his victory address after winning the senate seat in 2002 to a park dedication the previous summer. He never spotted Arielle's mystery man. He did identify a former aid named Xavier Stark. He had worked on Moore's senate re-election campaign, but as of 2009, was no longer employed by Moore. He did sort of resemble Antonio the Magnificent's description of the "face" he'd twice spotted in the crowd. That was, if he'd skipped a day shaving and lost some hair.

It was a reach, but it was all Jackson had, so he repeated his searches, this time on Xavier Stark instead of Matt Brenner. He found quite a bit more, all of it regarding Stark's time on Moore's staff, but none of it noticeably helpful. Jackson printed off a few bio sheets with Stark's education, credentials, and physical description in case they became relevant, but he doubted they would lead anywhere.

Jackson had a few minutes before he was supposed to meet up with Hillary, so he wandered outside and called Mouse again. This time his pal answered, sounding very groggy. Hillary had forwarded Shelly's e-mail to Mouse, and Jackson asked him to try to identify the man in the photo. He also asked him to uncover what he could on Matt Brenner and Xavier Stark. Mouse said he hadn't been thrilled about going to church anyway, so why not?

When he reentered the library, Hillary had several books open on a massive desk, a couple more stacked off to the side, and both her laptop and tablet were set up in front of her. She also had Arielle's notebook at her reach, and with a pencil tucked behind her ear, looked very collegial. And, Jackson had to admit, cute as a button.

She informed Jackson that she needed more time, suggesting they meet at noon. He told her he'd pretty much tapped his reservoir and asked if he could help her. She made a crack about the reservoir being dry as the desert to begin with and declined. So he wandered back to his computer terminal and checked e-mail, read a preview of USC's game the following Saturday with Washington, and then hit upon inspiration.

He Googled Warren McKenzie.

It wasn't hard to find a basic bio: school, military service, his career running McKenzie Enterprises, and his philanthropic efforts thereafter. Jackson tried searching his name with words like "scandal," "affair," and "conspiracy," but came up with nothing. Then he tried "Warren McKenzie Las Vegas." It too turned up little. He had this nagging feeling that even if he and Hillary were to figure out the mystery of Arielle Coal, it wouldn't have any tangible tie to Warren. Hillary would be left with a business card in a book and he would be left to figure out how to get out of her employ.

It wasn't even eleven-thirty, so Jackson headed back outside and found a bench in the shade of a palm tree. The air was already stifling. He thought of calling Mouse back, but Mouse would get back to him as soon as he found anything. So on a whim, he dialed another number.

"This is Sam," said a soft voice after three rings.

"Hey, it's Jackson."

"Hey, missed you this morning."

"I'm living in sin," he answered.

"What?"

"Sin City."

"You're in Las Vegas? What for?"

"A case."

"What kind of case?"

He hesitated. Telling Sam about a search for a prostitute wasn't terribly appealing. Neither was lying to her. "It's complicated. I'm with Hillary."

"Grant's fiancée?"

"Yeah. Anyhow, hadn't talked in a while, and I didn't want you to worry."

"I wasn't worried."

Was that just honesty or Sam subtly suggesting that Jackson had better not neglect her? He changed the subject.

"How's Stephanie?" he asked. A few months ago, he had rescued Stephanie Kane from an abusive husband. Jackson's intervention had led to the husband's getting help with his violent temper. During his "rehab," Stephanie was staying with Sam.

"Good," she said. "We're actually on the way to lunch."

"She's with you now?"

"She's in the ladies' room. Then we're headed out."

"How are you holding up? It's been a month and a half now."

"I knew what I was signing up for."

"I kind of conscripted you."

"I could have said no."

"I'm not sure *you* could have."

"And that's why you asked?"

Jackson's silence was a guilty admission.

"Jackson, I don't have any regrets. She's told me several times how much this has meant to her. I've seen her grow so much as a Christian and as a person. And I've grown too."

"Still, it's an adjustment."

"Life's an adjustment."

"I just want you to know I appreciate what you're doing."

"I know you do."

"And I appreciate you."

"I know you do."

As to the earlier remark in question, just honesty.

Jackson smiled. "Look, I don't know how long this deal here is going to drag out. Hillary is setting new records for thoroughness. But when I get back, we'll get together, do something."

"Okay."

"Just the two of us."

"I'd like that."

He nodded, a bad phone habit. "I'll let you go."

"I'll pray for you, Jackson."

"I'll need it."

They said goodbye and he clapped his phone shut. He sat staring at fronds of a palm on the far end of the parking lot. Sam was one of the few good things going in his life right now, a rock in a churning sea. He missed her, and realized he had been foolish for not clinging to that rock more. Best way to get back to it, wrap up the case in Vegas. Best way to do that was to get serious and figure out what, if any, link there was between Arielle's death and Hillary's client or between Arielle and Warren.

To that end, he decided to make a call. Back in the day, he'd worked as an assistant at MTR Investigative Services in San Diego. It had been the launching pad of his career as a private investigator. He'd worked with a girl named Tori Walker, who had herself gone on to a career as a P.I. In Las Vegas, last he'd heard. Maybe in the process of pounding the Vegas pavement, she'd picked up some piece of gossip, a rumor, some little nugget that could point him and Hillary in the right direction. And besides, she hadn't exactly been hard on the eyes. Jackson wouldn't mind seeing her again after four years.

He never got the chance. Before he made it back inside to look up her number, his phone rang. Technically, it played the James Bond theme song. Jackson flipped the phone open and paced back into the shade. "Hey, Mouse."

"Hey, dude. No luck. The guy's a ghost."

"You mean, like a spook ghost?"

"No, like I can't find anything. So, maybe."

Jackson sighed. "Okay."

"But I did find a link between those other guys you gave me, Brenner and Stark."

"That's great. What link?"

"They went to school together."

"At UNLV?"

"Uh, no. Virginia."

"You sure it's the right Matt Brenner?" Jackson asked. The bio he'd found of Xavier Stark said he earned a bachelor's degree at Virginia before getting a master's at Cal-Berkeley. But he hadn't seen anything about Brenner attending UVA.

"Pretty sure, dude," Mouse answered. "Born in Richmond, Virginia, age twenty-nine, current residence in Las Vegas."

"Sounds right," Jackson said. "I thought he went to UNLV."

"He did, after a year at Virginia."

"Aha. He and Stark room together or something?"

"No. But they were both on the rowing team. It's not a huge link, but given the fact they're both players in whatever it is you're into, I thought it was relevant."

"It is, Mouse. Thanks."

"It's what I'm here for, dude."

"You happen to find anything on Stark in the last couple of years? I lost him after he stopped working for Moore."

"Not much. He now lives in Chevy Chase, Maryland, and works for a consulting company in Washington. Newton-Lindley. I looked them up, but they're pretty generic."

"Any ties to Moore?"

"Nothing I saw, but I've only had forty-five minutes."

"You did good work, Mouse. Thanks, man."

"Sure thing. Say, you never told me. What are you doing in Vegas?"

Jackson sighed. "Working."

"Bummer."

"You don't know the half of it. Thanks again, Mouse."

"Yeah."

Jackson clapped his phone shut and headed back inside. It was close enough to noon and now he had info for Hillary. Besides, it was really hot.

She still had her head buried in books and her laptop as he pulled out a chair adjacent to her. "Brenner and Stark knew each other," he said.

She waited a moment before asking, "And how do you know this?" without looking up.

"Mouse."

"Mouse?"

Jackson explained the link Mouse had found between the two men. Only then did Hillary look up. "And how did he find this link?" she asked, closing her book.

"To pull a line from Brenner, 'I think it's best if you don't know.'"

"Is it illegal?"

"Odd that you should ask, Miss Skirt-the-Law."

"I don't skirt the law. I work within its parameters."

"Finding every loophole you can."

"The loopholes exist or haven't been closed for a reason." She sighed and brushed hair out of her face. "I don't want to argue about this."

"You know who's never once said that? The person who won the argument."

She winced. "That's very clever. Help me put these books away."

He did, then followed Hillary out to the Granada. "You find anything?" he asked as he got in.

"A pretty comprehensive profile on Holloway," she answered.

"Where to?" he asked before starting the car.

"Someplace for lunch."

"Got a preference?"

"No."

He felt like a sub and headed for a Jimmy John's he'd scouted from the library. It was on the UNLV campus and not too far from their hotel. Or the twenty-five grand in Hillary's room.

"What'd you find?" he asked as he drove.

"Richard Holloway was born in Jacksonville, Florida, in 1977. He graduated from Bishop Kenny High in 1995 and attended Northwestern University's Kellogg School of Management. He earned a B.A. in three and a half years and began making money almost right away."

"Kid from Jacksonville went to school in Evanston, Illinois?"

"It's one of the best business schools in the country."

"And UF doesn't have at least a passing program?"

Hillary shrugged.

"Go on."

"He opened his first hotel on South Beach just three years later. By the middle of the decade, he had resorts in Florida, the Caribbean, Indonesia, and, as of 2010, here in Las Vegas."

"The Oasis."

"Right. He's never married," Hillary continued, "but did date Leanor for three months back in 2007."

"Who?"

"What's that, Mr. Obscure-Pop-Culture-References doesn't know Leanor?"

Jackson turned right on Maryland Parkway, headed south.

Hillary's taunt having landed, she resumed. "Leanor is a Latina pop star from Miami." She referenced her tablet for the first time. "Holloway's an avid golfer, tennis player, and skier."

"Water or Snow?"

"Both. I didn't look too much into his personal life, but from what I gathered, he's a charismatic and popular guy."

"Of course he is; he's rich."

"It's not just that. He seems to have *it*."

"*It* being eleventy bazillion dollars," Jackson said.

"I didn't find any hint of scandal, no tabloid photos or TMZ cell phone videos at clubs. He keeps a low, clean profile."

They coasted to a stoplight at Charleston Boulevard. A McDonald's on the other side of the intersection suddenly beckoned, but Jackson held out for a sub.

"How did you find all this, anyhow?"

"Why do my methods always amaze you?"

"Because I doubt a real estate mogul's hobbies and love life can be found in library books or a simple Google search."

"I have access to CD&R's database, Pepperdine Law School's online library, and I know people. Green light," she said, and Jackson turned his eyes back to the road. "Besides, I don't think you should be complaining about my sources, considering yours is named after a rodent."

Jackson felt compelled to defend Mouse's honor, but there wasn't that much to defend.

"In addition to owning nearly a dozen resort properties," Hillary continued, "Holloway has a variety of different business ventures, all of which are making good money. Even the ones that weren't have either come around or been transformed into productive endeavors. In addition to running resorts like Oasis, Holloway has part ownership in a Seattle software company, several overseas textile plants, and a couple of chain grocery stores. Those are just diversifications. His big money—other than real estate—comes from his connections to big oil and from his two primary corporations: Sircuit, a major producer of silicone computer chips, processors, and other electrical systems; and RDH Incorporated, a big-time engineering company that makes parts for airplanes, satellites, underwater ROVs—you name it. And of course, he also has a diverse stock portfolio that makes more than you or I could ever dream of."

"I know you didn't find that online."

"Of particular interest were several military contracts his companies earned."

"Which companies?"

"Both Sircuit and RDH. The majority of the contracts were with the Air Force. Guidance systems for both F-22 Raptor fighter jets and HH-60 Pave Hawk helicopters, fuselage components for the F-22s and the F-35 Lightning, and so on," she said, glancing at her tablet only occasionally to fill in details.

"Is that atypical?" Jackson asked.

"No, and everything appears to be on the level."

"So how is this interesting?"

"Because it's another tie in. His companies supplied parts to the Air Force, and Moore and my father were both in the Air Force."

"So are half a million people, Hill."

"There's more. Would you care to take a guess with whom Sircuit and RDH have done business?"

"McKenzie Enterprises?"

Hillary nodded. "They did business with Boeing, Northrop Grumman, Lockheed Martin—the consortium of usual players. But also, in a few instances, with McKenzie Enterprises."

"Okay, that's coincidental, but it doesn't prove anything."

"It does when you factor in that in 2011 Holloway and Dad were both major donors to *Los Rescatados*, a South American charity that rescues children from the streets of half a dozen drug-infested cities and provides them with shelter, schooling, and safety." She lowered the tablet and looked at Jackson. "And since 2008, Holloway has donated over a million dollars to H3."

"To Hummer?"

She sighed in frustration. "H3 is the corporate name for Dad's philanthropic endeavors. Holloway is another player with multiple ties to my father," she said. "Everywhere we look, he turns up."

Chapter Eighteen

12:28 p.m.

JACKSON AND HILLARY took their subs back to the air-conditioned comfort of their hotel. In particular, Hillary's room. The cash was still there.

While they ate—her at the small table in the corner of the room, he pacing back and forth with his sub in one hand and the paper wrapping held beneath it in the other—they recapped what they knew so far. Arielle Coal, who had exchanged phone calls with Hillary's client on the day he allegedly committed the burglary, could have conceivably provided an alibi for Hillary's appeal of his case. Only she had been killed first. This after several months of moonlighting for—presumably—Xavier Stark, luring unsuspecting men to hotel rooms where she drugged them so that they could be carted off to who knew where in a van with government plates. Stark had ties to Senator Carson Moore, as did an unidentified man Arielle had witnessed during the transportation of one of her victims. Stark also had ties to Matt Brenner, Arielle's "friend with benefits." In addition to working for Arielle's agency, Brenner served as a "concierge" at Oasis Las Vegas, owned by Richard Holloway, who himself had ties to Moore. And before she was killed, Arielle had compiled her knowledge in a notebook, which she kept in a bus station locker with twenty-five thousand dollars, presumably part of her payment from Stark.

"Is that it?" Jackson asked as he prepared to take a bite of his Hunter's Club. "Did I leave anything out?"

Hillary watched him pull a fussy piece of roast beef up to his mouth. She shook her head. "Would you sit down? You're dropping lettuce all over the carpet."

"They have vacuums."

She sighed. "Yes, you left out the myriad connections to my father."

"Arielle had his business card, he was stationed at the same base as Moore when both were in the Air Force, he later made contributions to Moore's campaigns, and he did business—both commercial and charitable—with Holloway. Is that it?"

Hillary very delicately took a bite of her sandwich, dabbing her mouth with a napkin afterwards. "Don't forget Roy Donovan's mention of the Silver Dawn project at Blane."

"Right, your dad was instrumental in covering up alien landings or Treadstone mind control or something back in the '80s. Anything else?"

Hillary sighed again. "That's it in a nutshell."

Jackson sat on the corner of Hillary's bed. She eyed him warily.

"So what do you plan on doing next?" Jackson asked.

"We need to gather more intel on Holloway, his connections to Moore, and Dad's connections to both of them. We also need to figure out what Brenner, Stark, the man Arielle tabbed in Moore's speech, and any other players are doing with the men she was drugging."

Jackson shook his head. "Unfortunately, I don't see how any of this ties to your client."

"I don't either, yet."

"Because since the moment we got here, we haven't come any closer to finding an alibi for him, or to anything that would suggest Arielle could provide one. You're not even asking people about it."

Hillary, for just a fraction of a second, blinked.

"Is there something you're not telling me?" Jackson asked.

"No," she said, absent conviction.

"Then, I think it's time we call it quits. The trail is cold, Hill."

She said nothing.

"We're in way over our heads here," Jackson continued. "We should call Baxter and Cruz, tell them all we know, and let them run with it. If they find anything that ties Arielle's death to your client, they can tell us. But I doubt they will because I doubt there's anything to find."

She took a deep breath and stood, walking to the window. "It's not just about Arielle."

"I know, it's your dad. But all you have are business and professional links to a couple of potential players—and for the record, there's no proof Moore or Holloway are involved in any of this—and a business card that could have a hundred explanations."

"That's not all we have," she said softly.

"It's not?"

"No."

He took a bite and chewed thoughtfully. "What am I missing?" he asked after swallowing.

Hillary turned around, looking almost unsure. Lacking confidence. Her facial expression was entirely unfamiliar.

"I haven't been completely forthcoming with you," she said.

"Completely forthcoming? Meaning you lied?"

"Technically, yes."

Jackson sat quietly, waiting to fume until later. He didn't say anything, putting the awkwardness on her.

"There is no client," she said.

"Excuse me?"

"This isn't about a client. I made that part up."

"You made it up?"

"Yes."

He again said nothing, initially angry. Then smugly pleased. She was clearly in the wrong this time, not him. And he had ammunition. And good reason to go home. With any luck, he'd be back on his deck in time to watch the sunset.

"About a month ago," Hillary said, "just before they left for Bangladesh, Mom and Dad were over for dinner and he received a call from a woman named Arielle Coal. When I asked him who she was, he brushed it off."

"What are you, his secretary?"

She sighed. "His cell was on the counter; I saw an incoming call and took it to him. In the process I saw the name. By the time he got the phone, she had already hung up. I didn't think much at the time. But I overheard him call back after dinner, using her name, and that's when I casually asked who she was."

"You haven't ever asked anything casually," Jackson said. "Did he tell you it was none of your business?"

"No, he just said it was someone he knew from the past and that it was nothing."

"And like any daughter, you immediately doubted your father and assumed it was something suspicious."

"No. I let it go and nearly forgot about it. Now will you let me tell this?"

"By all means. Just let me know if you start fabricating again."

She glared at him, but only briefly and without her typical intensity. "A few days later, I was at their place and used his computer to quickly check my e-mails. His account was still open, and I saw a notification of a money transfer. He was out of the room, so instead of asking him about it, I opened it to make sure it wasn't some kind of fraud or something on his account."

"How very diligent of you."

"He'd wired twenty-five thousand dollars to a Las Vegas Western Union."

"Twenty-five thousand?" he asked, his eyes flicking to the stack of cash on the chair.

Hillary nodded.

"In stacks of twenties, by any chance?"

"First of the month, he and Mom left for Bangladesh. She visited a cousin down in Arizona first and flew out of Phoenix. Dad flew from L.A. and met her in Tokyo, but arranged for a last-minute stop-off in Las Vegas."

"Let me guess, as you courteously took his jacket to the drycleaner, you saw the ticket in his breast pocket?"

"He stayed at my place the night before so we could leave early, and I heard him call to change the flights."

"Eavesdrop much?"

Hillary simmered. "I asked him why he was going to Vegas and he again brushed it off, said it was something about business. After he left, I was curious. I researched the name Arielle Coal. When I found out who she was—what she was—I got suspicious."

"So this is all about your fear that your dad's two-timing your mom with a Vegas hooker?"

"No, but thank you for putting it so crudely."

Jackson held out his hands, thus the sub, dropping lettuce onto the comforter. "So then what?"

"I don't know what," Hillary said. "That's why we're here. My plan was to have you find Arielle so that I could confront her and find out what was the nature of her relationship with my father. Obviously that plan didn't work, but since Dad's name keeps popping up, it would suggest my suspicions were on the money."

"Pun intended," Jackson said.

"And there is one other thing."

"What's that?"

"My parents never talk about the time when I was born—about where we lived or what Dad was doing. I knew he was stationed at Blane, but not what he did there, if he and Mom lived on base—or even together—or anything. It's like that period of time has been redacted from their lives." She shrugged. "I always

137

thought it a little strange, but it never seemed relevant. Now, given everything we've turned up, I can't help but wonder why they never talk about 1983 or the first six months of 1984, when Dad was at the base."

Jackson took a deep breath, then a large bite of his sub. He chewed slowly. He had to admit that Warren's ties to Arielle, Las Vegas, Blane Air Force Base, Senator Moore, and Richard Holloway were incredibly coincidental if not indicative of some sort of involvement in whatever was going on. But what that something was and how deeply Warren was involved were questions to which he doubted he and Hillary could find answers.

"Why not just ask him?" he said.

"I told you, he's in Bangladesh."

"So wait till he gets back."

"They aren't coming back until Christmas."

"Okay, but still, what's the urgency?"

"This isn't exactly the kind of thing you ask your father. 'How do you know a call girl and what are your ties to classified military projects?' He probably couldn't and wouldn't tell me."

Jackson wondered how close Hillary and her father truly were if they couldn't discuss something like this. It would be awkward, sure, but if it was his dad . . .

He also felt a little bad for Hillary. This was clearly eating at her, and everything they'd found seemed to implicate Warren further and suggest something sinister. The fact that she had remained so stoic and poised until now spoke volumes about her.

"I am sorry that I lied to you, Jackson."

"Why did you?"

She licked her lips. "Because I wasn't wild about baring my soul to you."

He thought for a moment she was about to break down. He should have known better. Hillary McKenzie didn't break down. Instead, with the smallest of shrugs, she completely re-gathered what little composure she had lost. "This is why I have been so adamant to get to the bottom of things and find the truth. I do not for one second believe my father has ever cheated on my mother, with Arielle or anyone else. But something is clearly going on and I need to know what that is. I need to find the truth. That's why I have pushed you, that's why I have refused to turn everything over to the police and wash my hands of the matter, and that's why I have insisted that we keep working. And that is what I am going to do, with or without you."

"There's no client, no appeal, no phone records ignored by a public defender?"

"No."

"How long did it take you to dream up that little tale?"

"Not long."

He shook his head in disgust.

"I was wrong, and I apologize." She sat back down. "And you're released from your obligation. The debt is paid."

"Just like that?"

"You want it in writing?"

"No, I'm just wondering what I'm supposed to do. Drive back to L.A. and leave you here?"

"I'm a big girl, Jackson. I can handle the rough and tough world of Las Vegas all by myself."

"Without transportation?"

"They have taxis and buses and even car rental agencies."

He exhaled. "Is this a trick?"

"What are you talking about?"

"The jailer unlocking the cell to see if the inmate will try to make a break for it?"

"No tricks. It was a mistake to bring you in the first place, and like I said, I'm sorry about that."

Now she was clearly playing mind games. Telling him he could go if he wanted to. Insulting him so he'd want to stay and prove her wrong. But he was wise to her, and neither tactic would have stood a chance of working if he hadn't felt at least a little sympathy for her and her situation.

He sighed and chased away thoughts of a SoCal sunset from the deck. "Look, Hill, there is one possible avenue we haven't explored."

"What's that?"

"I have a friend who's a P.I. here in Las Vegas. Or, at least, she was last I heard."

"She?"

"Yes, don't be a chauvinist. Women can do any job a man can."

Hillary rolled her eyes.

"I can give her a call. Maybe she knows something about some of this. You have to think Arielle isn't the only person to get curious and ask some questions."

"It sounds like a long shot, but that's what we're down to at this point."

"Use your laptop? I'll look her up."

"Wipe off your hands first."

"Right."

She reached for her sandwich again. "Thank you, Jackson."

"Yeah, sure."

Chapter Nineteen

1:18 p.m.

P&W DETECTIVE AGENCY was located north of downtown and west of I-15, occupying a section of a strip mall between a Chinese take-out and a cell phone provider. It was at least a well-kept strip mall. The parking lot wasn't rife with weeds and the concrete bumpers hadn't crumbled to reveal rebar. A few people were dining at the Chinese place, but for a Sunday afternoon, the mall was pretty quiet.

The W was for Tori Walker, Jackson's acquaintance from his days at MTR in San Diego. Jackson had called the agency from the hotel, expecting to get a voice recording on the weekend before looking up Walker's home number. Instead, a gruff male had answered and told him that Tori Walker was out of town and unavailable. The man had offered his assistance, and since he and Hillary had no better leads, Jackson had accepted. Twenty minutes later, he was opening the all-glass front door of P&W for Hillary.

The office was furnished simply but warmly, with soft carpet, modern wood and glass desks, and sleek computer monitors on the desks rather than stacks of open manila folders. Certificates mounted on one wall advertised the firm's credentials. On another wall, two large LCD monitors were blank while a third displayed a muted cable news feed. Most importantly, the office was air-conditioned.

An electronic chime announced their presence, and a moment later, a man emerged from a back hallway. He was tall and black. His broad shoulders, slight paunch, and muscular arms beneath a maroon Henley hinted at a former athletic career. Former, Jackson concluded, because he placed the guy in his fifties. His head was shaved but for a small goatee that had more salt than pepper, as they said. He had a hard look, but wide, welcoming eyes.

"Danny Pollack," he said, extending a hand like a vice. The voice matched that on the phone. "Mr. Douglas?"

"Jackson. This is my associate, Hillary McKenzie."

"Miss McKenzie, a pleasure."

"Hillary, and likewise."

"We've got a conference room in the back, but we're the only ones here today, so if it's just the same with you, we can sit at my desk," Pollack said, motioning toward one of two desks by the window, identified as his by a small nameplate. The other desk was similarly labeled as belonging to Tori Walker. A third desk on the other side of the room presumably was for a secretary or a non-partner.

"Can I get either of you anything to drink? Coffee, hot or cold tea, water?"

They both declined and took seats that he offered.

"What can I do for you?" Pollack asked, sitting back in his chair, a yellow legal pad on his lap.

Jackson took the lead, explaining that he too was a private investigator and that he had worked with Tori Walker.

"You know Walker?" Pollack said.

"Once upon a time."

"She's a real pistol," he said. "Once she gets a lead, she doesn't let it rest."

"That's the girl I knew," Jackson said.

Pollack regarded him with a sideways glance. Likely deducing if there was anything to that remark, such as romantic interest. Jackson didn't elaborate. "Anyhow, Hillary here's a lawyer, and she hired me to help her track down a woman named Arielle Coal."

"The same Coal who was shot Friday night?"

Jackson nodded. "I had the good fortune of finding her just after she was killed, which earned me a trip downtown to talk to a couple of detectives before Hillary got me out of trouble."

"Which detectives?"

"Messrs. Baxter and Cruz."

Pollack shook his head. "Don't know Cruz, but Baxter is a real hard—" He glanced at Hillary. "One."

She smiled perfunctorily at his decorum.

"Anyhow, we've conducted our own investigation," Jackson said, "and we've identified Richard Holloway as a potential person of interest."

"*The* Richard Holloway?"

Jackson nodded. "Unfortunately, we've kind of hit a roadblock, so I was hoping to chat up an old friend and see if she knew any scuttlebutt about him that might prove helpful. Since she's out of town, I'm hoping you'll engage in a little P.I. to P.I. gossip."

"It's not very professional of us to ask, admittedly," Hillary said in a way that put the idea fully on Jackson, "and it may not lead anywhere. But like he said, we are at a dead end."

Pollack sat forward, setting his blank notepad on the desk. "You got a license?"

Jackson dug for his wallet and pulled out his private investigator's license, which he slid to Pollack.

"How long ago'd you say it was you knew Walker?"

"We worked at a firm in San Diego from July of '06 till June of '08."

"She have her dog then already?"

"Bo? Yeah. He still alive?"

"And kicking," Pollack said, tossing the license back to Jackson. "Has some silver to go with the black now," he said. A black lab, Bo was named for legendary Los Angeles (now Oakland) Raiders running back Bo Jackson. The Raiders wore silver and black.

Pollack reached into a desk drawer to retrieve something, then stood. "Holloway's a good man, at least as far as everybody knows." He walked around the desk toward a filing cabinet against the wall, under the credentials. "He's obviously wealthy, and he lives a good life, but he also puts a lot of money back into this community. Schools, parks, little leagues, all the way up to some pretty major corporate donations and sponsorships." He used a key to open one of the cabinets, pulled out a file, and returned to his desk.

"I'm not going to give you a lot of dirt on the guy because, for one thing, there isn't a lot of dirt to be found. Even if there was, nobody's perfect and I don't like the idea of people taking a smidgen of something and running a guy into the ground."

"Believe me, that's not our intention," Hillary said. "We're just investigating a potential person of interest."

Pollack nodded. He held up a rather thin manila folder. "Six, eight months ago, a client hired us because he thought Holloway was having an affair with his wife. Had no idea who the guy was, but had seen him with her. I didn't want to take the case because I'm tired of celebrity gossip and rumors. But I figured somebody would do it, and they might not be as discreet as I would be. Plus Walker said we owed it to the guy to find the truth. Long story short, we uncovered nothing. No trace of an affair. This," he said, shaking the folder in his hand, "is everything we found on Holloway."

Pollack set the folder back down. "Now, obviously, I can't let you look at this, but I can summarize the key points and let you take your own notes." He spun the legal pad around and set a pen down on top of it. "Fair deal?"

"More than," Jackson said. He looked at Hillary? "You take shorthand?"

With a small sigh, she grabbed the paper and pen.

Pollack opened the folder. He sorted through some handwritten notes, computer printouts, photographs, and a few newspaper clippings. He started by recapping much of what Hillary had found about Holloway's background, schooling, and rise to prominence as a businessman and resort owner.

"It took a little doing to get the Oasis built," Pollack said. "Casinos rise and fall by the day, it seems, but there were several roadblocks to its construction. Holloway was persistent and greased the wheels with a lot of donations to local charities and community support, like I said." He sat back. "Greased the wheels is probably the wrong term. More like proved his goodwill in the community. At any rate, it opened in 2010—on 10/10/10 if I recall. It's as classy as they come, a Five Diamond, and I haven't heard any complaints since it opened."

"What kind of roadblocks?" Hillary asked.

"Mostly buying out properties on Las Vegas Boulevard. The land between Planet Hollywood and the MGM has been void of any major casinos for quite a while, but there were a number of smaller properties on the site, and a couple other bidders who were after it. He also had to get permits and insurance for the Oasis, the aquarium, all the attractions."

"Is there a lot there to insure?" Jackson asked.

"No more than any other resort. Not when you consider roller coasters and bungee jumps and some of the stuff you find on the Strip. But they have a zip-line, a ten-story climbing wall, an infinity pool on the roof. All insurance nightmares, and you wouldn't believe the legal issues and paperwork involved. Not to mention everything required for opening a casino itself."

Hillary looked up. "We have reason to believe that Senator Carson Moore was instrumental in procuring some of the permits and cutting through the red tape. Did you uncover anything along those lines?"

"It's pretty well known that Holloway and Moore worked together to get the casino open. Holloway made generous contributions and Moore twisted what arms he could. They're thick as thieves."

Hillary raised her eyes.

"Just an expression," Pollack said. "I've never met Moore and never heard anything legitimately bad about him."

"Legitimately?" Jackson asked.

"He's a politician. Half the people—or a little less than half if you win re-election as Moore did—are going to hate you. But I haven't heard anything beyond partisan name-calling."

"Fair enough."

Pollack continued. "As for the Oasis, it's a unique place. It's right up there with the Bellagio or the Wynn when it comes to class and sophistication, but it's not just for the upper class. They've got their Strip-view suites that go for five bills a night, but you can also get a decent room for a hundred bucks, and there's plenty to do for everyone." He cracked his first smile. "In fact, the kind of crass nickname detractors gave the place is the Mullet. Business in front, party in the back."

Hillary winced.

"Anyway, Holloway lives at the Oasis, at least when he's in Vegas. He's got a forty thousand-square foot penthouse on the top two floors. Never been, but they say it's a palace."

"Must be a hard life," Jackson said.

"Don't I know it?" Pollack shuffled a few papers. "And speaking of living, Holloway loves to travel. He's gone as often as not. He's been to all the major Asian cities—Hong Kong, Singapore, Tokyo—he hangs out with the sheiks in Dubai and Russian oil tycoons on the Black Sea, and visits the French Riviera once or twice a year. He also craves adventure—an adrenaline rush—either from a neck-and-neck horse race, a high-stakes poker game, or a ballroom full of VIPs. He's skydived, climbed Kilimanjaro, and swam with sharks off Australia. But he's not a radical, risk-taking thrill-seeker. He's a guy who likes adventures and has better means than everybody else."

"I'm getting jealous," Jackson said while Hillary's hand and the pen it held zipped across the pad.

"His first love seems to be sports or any games of chance. He plays golf, tennis, swims, is an avid skier. And the Oasis sports book is fast becoming one of the most distinguished in Las Vegas, mostly because Holloway shows such an interest in the action. Horses to hoops, football to *fútbol*, they've got a line for everything and he's got an eye on it. Rumor has it he's one of several in a partnership trying to bring the NFL or NBA to Las Vegas."

145

Pollack turned a page. "He's also a card shark. It's not unheard of for him to sit in at the Oasis's private poker room or even at one of the regular tables. He'll invite guests up to his private game room for poker or craps tournaments, sometimes with celebrities and A-listers, sometimes just with other guests."

"That seems pretty unusual," Hillary said.

"It is, but it's what makes him who he is. Holloway's as personable as they come, comfortable in a boardroom or chatting up guests in the atrium. He can dress the part of a millionaire or put on a pair of chinos and a cotton shirt and blend in with a thousand tourists."

Pollack turned over his page. "As for his love life, he's thirty-four but never married, never a real serious girlfriend, but never in want of feminine company. But he's not a playboy. He doesn't stay out all night getting hammered, find himself in inappropriate photos, or have a bleary-eyed mugshots taken in some out of the way jail. He doesn't get in trouble, period. The man blends an extravagant lifestyle with personal discretion." He closed the folder. "Like I said, no hint of an affair with our client's wife or of any inappropriate behavior in our research."

Hillary finished jotting a final note.

"That's pretty much it," Pollack said. "There are no obvious ties to Arielle Coal or anyone of her ilk." He shook his head. "Your investigation may prove otherwise, but from what I know, I'd be surprised."

"What about Matt Brenner or Xavier Stark?" Jackson asked. "Did your research come up with anything on either of them?"

"Yes," Pollack said after a moment of thought. He opened the folder again and thumbed through it. "Here we go. Brenner, Matt. He works for Holloway."

"For him?" Hillary asked.

"He's a personal assistant. One of a dozen. We saw him with Holloway several times so we ID'd him, but didn't uncover more than his name and position." Pollack looked up. "Why, who's he?"

"A friend of Arielle's," Hillary said.

"We were also under the impression that he ran a—" Jackson cleared his throat "—concierge service at Oasis."

"You mean call girls?"

"Yes," Hillary said.

"Well, that's news to me. We didn't turn up anything along those lines. Who's Stark?"

"A former aide of Moore's. Arielle was mixed up with some shady people, helping them drug and abduct unsuspecting tourists. We believe Stark is one of the people behind it all."

"Abducting tourists?"

Hillary nodded. "Arielle would slip them a sedative and leave the room, at which time Stark's people would transport the body to an undisclosed location. Other times, they'd dump the tourists back in a hotel room, and she'd stage things to make it look as if the lost time had been spent in a drunken or drug-induced state."

Pollack shook his head. "Afraid I can't tell you anything about him. It's the first time I've heard his name."

Hillary took a deep breath. "Thank you very much for your time."

Pollack nodded and scratched his jaw. "I'm hesitant to mention it, but there's one other person you could talk to."

"Who's that?"

"Holloway's gentleman's gentleman, at least until about two months ago."

"What happened?"

"I don't know. He came up in our investigation and I heard through the grapevine that he'd been let go. Not sure why, not sure if it was amicable, not sure he'd give you the time of day. If it's me, I'd take anything a former employee said with a grain of salt until I knew why he was a former employee. But for the sake of full disclosure, his name's Colin Appleby. Do with that what you will."

After thanking Danny Pollack for his time and the information, Jackson and Hillary headed back out into the heat. The smells from the Chinese take-out place started Jackson's mouth watering even though he had just eaten.

"Honest opinion," Hillary said, looking across the Granada's roof at Jackson. "Do you think it's just coincidence that Holloway's personal assistant and—" she cleared her throat to mimic Jackson a few minutes earlier—"concierge Matt Brenner is also the guy who recruited Arielle to do whatever it is she was doing on the side?"

"Honestly, no," he said with a sigh. "There's too much smoke for no fire."

Chapter Twenty

COLIN APPLEBY, HOLLOWAY'S former personal valet, was a drunken Englishman who hung out in an off-Strip bar, watching soccer on a Sunday afternoon. After tracking him down—ultimately by calling Detective Cruz and giving him the names of Brenner and Stark in exchange for Appleby's address and phone number—Jackson and Hillary met Appleby at his favorite watering hole, west of the Strip just off Harmon Avenue.

While not able to provide them with anything that incriminated Holloway, Moore, Brenner, or Stark, or that tied Warren McKenzie to any of them, Appleby gave the pair some insights into Holloway's personal life. In particular, he described him as a ladies' man whose "little black book" was several volumes thick. Appleby underscored that the women who accompanied Holloway to various parties and dinners were distinguished ladies, not "tramps and trollops." Some were prominent and influential women, some were personal friends, some were even guests he encountered in his hotel. And while it wasn't uncommon for Holloway's dates to spend the night, many were simply social companions in the purest sense of the word.

He also divulged that Holloway made a habit of befriending guests of both sexes. It was not uncommon for him to take a late-morning or afternoon stroll through the pool deck, mingle in his casino, or just chat up guests in passing. Often times these interactions led to invites to private dinners, cocktail receptions, or "penny ante" poker games played for pots of "mere thousands." Appleby admitted most of the invites seemed to be based on a woman's physical attributes, but Holloway was just as likely to entertain a couple or a family as a single female. And aside from an incident in Geneva, Switzerland, a few years back where Holloway had enticed a young woman to leave her boyfriend for him, Appleby said the tycoon was not a homewrecker or poacher.

Aside from commenting on Holloway's social agenda, Appleby provided Jackson and Hillary with little else. He did note that Holloway and Moore,

148

formerly good friends, had gone through a "cooling off" of sorts, their frequent phone calls and visits coming to a halt. He also reported an unusual visitor to Holloway's penthouse office late one night shortly before he was released from Holloway's employ. Unusual in that Holloway didn't often have male guests to his penthouse or conduct business late at night. And earlier that afternoon, Appleby had overheard Holloway reference a "package" on a phone conversation. Appleby described the visitor as a nondescript black man. He hadn't carried any package that Appleby could see, and had only stayed for five or ten minutes.

Appleby talked freely, and drank just as liberally. He wasn't eager to disparage his former employer, but he didn't hold back anything either. Jackson and Hillary left him to watch an Arsenal match on one of the TVs over the bar and exited to sunlight that was even brighter compared to the bar's dark interior.

"What do you think?" Hillary asked as they walked back to the Granada.

"I think I want some ice cream," Jackson said. "And Richard Holloway's little black book."

"Would it kill you not to crack a joke just once?" Hillary asked as she opened her door.

"I don't know, we could try it and see . . ."

He smirked. She didn't. They both got in, and Jackson guided them back to eastbound Harmon Avenue. Hillary had a threatening look on her face, so he offered an olive branch.

"I think it looks like Holloway knows something about whatever Arielle was into. But we don't know what specifically or how it all ties to your father."

"Thank you, Captain Obvious, but I meant what do you think about what we should do next?"

"Well, Miss Parse-My-Words, perhaps you should have said what you meant. As for what we should do now, turn around and be in L.A. by sunset."

"Run away, what a surprise."

"What do you want from me? What other options are there?"

"Why don't you put away your hatred for me for just one minute and pretend I'm some kittenish brunette off the streets who hired you. You'd bend over backwards to find the truth if I was a flirty 'babe' named Monica or Kyla."

"First of all . . . I've never even known anyone named Kyla. Second, I'm getting real sick of your implications that I don't have any moral standards just because I happen to enjoy the opposite sex. And for the record, if you were a 'regular' client—and by regular, I mean paying—I would have dropped you about the time you told me you'd lied to me about everything. The only reason I'm still here is because I am trying to help. And also for the record . . . I like blondes just as much as brunettes."

"See, there you did it again. If you're really trying to help, then help instead of smarting off all the time."

Jackson took several deep breaths, biting his tongue, praying for self-control. He wasn't sure how prayers breathed in anger were received, but it was the best he could do at the moment.

"You're the lawyer," he said. "If this is a trial, what's the evidence against Holloway?"

Hillary took a moment to compose herself. "Circumstantial, at best."

"So what does the D.A. do in that case?"

"Either get more evidence or stage some theatrics."

"Or not prosecute."

She turned her head. "I am not giving up, Jackson. Period."

"Should I be looking for an apartment?"

"Stop being dramatic."

He clicked on his blinker for a left turn on Las Vegas Boulevard just as the light turned red.

"Seriously, how long do you plan to stay here?" he asked.

"Until I get some answers."

"Don't you have to work?"

"I have personal leave coming."

"Great."

She took a deep breath. "Holloway has the answers, right?"

"At the risk of being obvious . . . it would seem so."

"Then we need to find out what he knows."

"Holloway told Brenner he had the goods and a paper trail, but we don't know what the goods are or where the paper trail leads. Appleby said Holloway was ready to make Brenner his second in command, and yet Brenner seemed to be afraid that if the hammer fell, it would fall on him."

"So?"

"So, we have no idea how Holloway's involved. We don't know who Arielle's mystery man is, don't know who Stark is, don't know how—or even if— Moore is involved, and have no clue how your dad is connected to any of this.

Nor do we have any solid evidence that Holloway's 'goods' will give us any of the answers, even if we had access to them, which we don't."

"So we have to find out. It's our only play left."

"How?" Jackson huffed.

"You heard Appleby. Holloway has an eye for women and is fond of inviting guests to private gatherings."

"What are you saying, we check into his hotel and hope he invites us up to tell us his deepest, darkest secrets?"

"No. But we do get close to him so that we can find out what he knows."

"Play him?"

"So to speak."

"And by play, you mean con?" He shook his head. "No. No way. It's too crazy."

"You have a better idea?"

"No."

She shrugged as if that settled it.

Jackson got a green arrow and accelerated. "Lack of good ideas doesn't validate existing ideas," he said as he turned. "In fact, it kind of proves they're bad."

"Fine. I'll do it myself. I'm sick of dragging you along anyhow."

"Dragging me along?"

"From the moment we got here, you've been trying to leave as quickly as possible, only doing the bare minimum to satisfy our agreement. If you're not going to help, then I'd rather go it alone."

"You really think that's a good idea?"

"Getting rid of you is the best idea I've ever had. In fact, drop me off here."

"What?"

"I'll walk back to the hotel. Drop me off."

"Hill, we're in the middle of traffic," he said, slowing for the light at Bellagio's entrance. He'd barely come to a stop before she opened her door.

"Hillary," he called after her, but she kept going. By the time the light turned and he could accelerate, she had crossed two lanes of traffic and was striding along the sidewalk in front of Planet Hollywood. Ignoring two honking cars, he crossed over to the right lane and slowed to match her pace.

"Hill," he called.

She marched with her eyes straight ahead.

"Hillary!"

She ignored him. A driver behind Jackson blasted the horn as he veered into the next lane.

This was absurd. Like a bad movie, him stalking a woman while causing a traffic mess. And for what? For the second time that day, she'd given him his release. So why wasn't he headed for I-15 and SoCal?

Hillary had crossed a narrow drive and was walking in front of a giant facsimile of a hot air balloon, bright blue and yellow with "Paris" emblazoned on its side in red cursive. The entrance to the hotel of the same name was just ahead of the balloon, and Jackson made a sudden sharp right turn, forcing Hillary to stop.

"Will you get in the car?" he asked.

She instead turned and followed the sidewalk along the entrance road. Sculptured hedges lined the walkway on one side; idling cabs the other. Jackson coasted along at five miles per hour, watching Hillary stalk. Petulant was a word to describe bratty kids, but it applied to her now and again too.

Finally, Jackson found a parking place and he zoomed into it. He killed the engine and hopped out, nearly having his door taken off by an incoming shuttle bus. He squeezed against his car until it passed, then stepped onto the sidewalk in front of Hillary. She turned on a dime, crossing the road and heading for a replica of the Arc de Triomphe in the middle of the cul-de-sac.

Huffing, Jackson followed after her. "Hillary, will you wait a second? Hillary!"

She didn't stop and he quickened his pace. He grabbed her arm and spun her around.

"Let go of me!"

"Will you stop for a just a second? Talk about dramatics."

"I am not being dramatic. I am parting ways before I do something I'll regret."

"Like what, slugging me?"

"Perhaps."

"Not being dramatic, huh?"

"Don't tempt me."

"Will you listen to me for just a second, please?"

She said nothing, but didn't leave either.

"You cannot go after a man like Holloway by yourself."

"Why not?"

"For a dozen different reasons."

"Name one."

"I don't know where to start."

"I didn't think so." She turned and he grabbed her elbow again. Her eyes warned him it had better be the last time.

"For starters, you've never run a con in your life, your trial experience notwithstanding."

"And you have?"

"A couple, in fact. Successful ones, too." He took a breath. "For another, he's too powerful. If he is up to something sinister and he catches you, he'll bury you. And third, you can't run a one-man con."

"That's it? You said a dozen."

"Hyperbole. But the point is made."

"And overruled. I'm out of options."

"Hillary, you saw what they did to Arielle. You're gonna get yourself killed."

"What do you care?" She turned and walked away, directly beneath the Arc de Triomphe, toward the entrance to the casino.

"I do care."

She stopped. Then turned. "What?"

"I do care," Jackson said. He walked toward her. "I don't like you. I can't stand you. But I do care if something happens to you."

"Why?"

"Because Grant did. And if he was alive today and he knew that I let you do something this stupid, he'd kill me."

She studied him intensely for several seconds. The fire in her eyes cooled ever so slightly. "Jackson, I already told you, I'm not backing down. I'm getting to the bottom of this, and if running a con on Holloway is the only option I have left, then it's the option I'm taking."

"Look, I've watched enough TV shows. I know how this goes. The girl goes and insists on doing something outlandish so that the guy has to stay and protect her out of guilt. But it's not going to work."

"It seems to be. You're double-parked in an unloading zone, chasing me around the Arch de Triomphe."

"I'm giving you fair warning. That's it."

"Mission accomplished. You can go."

"Hillary, you cannot do this alone."

"Then stay and help me."

He looked away, toward Bellagio across Las Vegas Boulevard. George Clooney and Brad Pitt and Matt Damon popped into his head. That was Hollywood. This was real. That was eleven. This was two. And they at least got along, sort of.

"Please, Jackson," she said as he looked back. Her eyes and face were as vulnerable as he had ever seen. "Help me."

He looked away again, closing his eyes against the desert breeze. Now his phone call to her thirteen months ago popped into his head. He had been utterly desperate, with nowhere to turn but to her. He had hated to call her, dreading her scathing rebuke and terrified that she would say no and leave him with no recourse. Now, the roles were reversed.

Slowly, he turned his head back. Hillary watched him expectantly, hopefully, powerlessly. For once, she wasn't the omnipotent ice queen, enforcing her way with a freezing stare. She was dependent on him.

And so with a labored deep breath, he nodded.

*   *   *

3:50 p.m.

"DO YOU know what you're asking?" Jackson asked. He and Hillary had driven back to their hotel in silence, and now sat in the parked Granada.

"Yeah," she said, "above and beyond our *quid pro quo*."

"No, I mean, to run a game on Holloway, to try to get close to him to get whatever information he has."

"I didn't say it would be easy."

"Easy," Jackson laughed, looking out the window. He looked back and made eye contact with Hillary. "We're talking about—and I'm just thinking out loud here—a Sinbad, a King David, a Robbie Palmer, and a U-2, and that's just to get our foot in the door."

"Please tell me you didn't just make those all up."

"Of course I did. They made them up on *Ocean's Eleven* too, you know. Miss Daisy and Ella Fitzgerald and Leon Spinks aren't the names of real cons."

"And you know this from your subscription to *Confidence Men Monthly*?"

"That's good, *Confidence Men Monthly*." His smile faded. "We don't even know that there's a pot of gold at the end of this rainbow."

154

"Brenner said—"

"That he had the goods, I know."

"And a paper trail."

"Right, but did he mean physical sheets of paper hidden in an uncrackable safe or Word documents saved on an unhackable computer or in the cloud somewhere? Or did he mean that he could construct a paper trail from what's up here?" He tapped his head with his finger. "Even if we successfully pull off the Sinbad, King David, Robbie Palmer, and U-2—which is highly suspect given our inability to eat dinner without almost coming to blows—our chance of success is still minimal unless I turn into Napster and you become Charlize Theron in *The Italian Job*. Which, by the way, I wouldn't mind."

"See, that's the difference between you and me."

"I prefer Charlize Theron and you prefer Napster?"

"No. I see an insurmountable wall in front of me and conclude that I had better find a way to overcome it. You see the wall, make a few wisecracks, and turn around."

"You do realize that by definition it is impossible to overcome something that is insurmountable, right?"

"See?"

"I'm just asking if maybe there might be a different way."

"And I'm telling you, I'm all ears if you have one."

Jackson exhaled.

"But you don't, do you?"

"No."

"Then either we turn around and give up or we find a way to achieve the unachievable."

"I can't believe you. You and Grant always lectured me because you thought I was too lenient with law and order, and here you are begging me to help you break and enter a penthouse suite, then crack a safe or hack a computer network so we can steal something we don't even know exists."

"We're not going to break and enter or steal anything."

He threw up his hands, then dropped them on the steering wheel. "I thought—"

"I said we'd run a con to get close to Holloway."

"But not to give us access to his safe or his computer?"

"No."

"Then how? How are we going to get his 'goods'?"

"We're not. We're going to get him to give them to us."

"And why exactly would he do that?"

"That's what we need to figure out. And that is why I want your help, because despite all the things I say about you, there are actually times when you can be somewhat clever."

"Please, stop, you're embarrassing me with such high praise." He looked out the window again, past the end of the hotel, down the street toward the Strip. He thought of Vegas, a city built on action and chance, high rollers playing with high stakes, of house odds and stacked decks and those who'd actually beaten the system. He thought of Hillary, unflappable, always able to get whatever she set her sights on. Were some people really like that? Could they overcome any obstacle? Did they have some extra strength of will or aptitude? Or was that perception, like so much around him, all an illusion?

"Jackson?"

He sighed.

"What are you thinking?"

"That I should have told Orlando to go blow blunts by himself and had a double cheeseburger."

She was silent.

He sighed one last time, mostly for effect. His way of putting it on the record that he didn't like this plan.

"We do it my way," he said. "I lay it out, I call the shots, and if I say we abort, we abort."

"Why would I ag—"

"Because if you don't agree, I'm going to make it home for the late *SportsCenter*, and I don't care what Grant would say or what trouble you'll get into or how much guilt I have. If we're doing this—if I'm doing this—it's going to be on my terms. That's the deal, no counteroffers, no concessions. You've got ten seconds before I rescind it, start the car, and head home."

"Without your luggage?"

"Nine . . . Eight . . ."

Setting her jaw, Hillary waited until his internal countdown was at one. She wasn't deciding. She, like he had earlier, was making her position clear before conceding.

"Deal," she said.

Jackson dropped his hand from the ignition. "Vegas does it again."

"What's that?"

"Sees the formation of another doomed partnership."

Chapter Twenty-One

THEY WERE QUITE a pair.

He wore baggy jeans, sneakers, and a faded pink T-shirt with "LCA Powder Puff '99" printed on the front and "Coach" stenciled on the back. All the letters had faded from sunlight, wear, and general old age, and were barely distinguishable. The logo on the front of the shirt—depicting a growling girl with eye black streaked on her cheeks and blond hair flowing out from under a San Diego Chargers helmet—had survived the years slightly better. His hair was loose and shaggy, not too long, but still swirling around his temples and ears as it was caught by the San Diego breeze.

She wore a knee-length black skirt, tightly fitted, with ruffles along the uneven bottom. Her blouse was diamond patterned, a mixture of blues and greens outlined in black. It too fit her well, with just enough V in the collar to accentuate a graceful neckline highlighted by a stunning silver locket. Her footwear was a pair of high-heel sandals, subtly adding to her height. Her hair was down, curled away from her face and over her shoulders. Silver hoop earrings, medium in size, complemented the necklace and added a touch more sophistication.

They stood at the beach end of the Oceanside Pier, waiting for the third member of their party. She paced up and down the boardwalk, stopping every few minutes to scan the parking lot, then checking her phone. He couldn't have cared less about the parking lot or the phone, content to watch the waves crash against the pier pylons.

The pier extended over a quarter mile into the Pacific, making it the longest wooden pier on the West Coast and a great spot to fish, catch a sunset, or just people watch. Or grab dinner. Ruby's Diner at the far end of the pier served old-fashioned American food—burgers, dogs, shakes. The smells carried inland to where Jackson waited patiently, albeit hungrily.

Hillary's phone sounded, playing some Mariah Carey song. She quickly thrust the phone to her ear, pacing away from Jackson, then back toward him. He could make out a few phrases: ". . . need to stay?" "How long?" "Are you sure?" She frowned and sighed as she finished the call, stopping in front of him.

"Grant can't make it."

"Grant's ringtone is Mariah Carey?"

She ignored him. "He was involved in a shooting."

"Which end of the gun?" Jackson asked, although Hillary's relatively calm demeanor had already given him the answer.

"His partner shot a suspect who drew on them," she said. "But he's going to be tied up most of the night."

"And he's just calling now?"

"He's been busy all afternoon and finally managed a free minute."

"The life of a cop," Jackson said.

"Compared to a part-time courier?"

He shrugged.

"Anyhow, he said we should go ahead without him," Hillary said.

"Swell. A birthday party without the birthday party."

He grinned at his wordplay. She didn't.

"So is he still coming down for the weekend?" Jackson asked.

"Relax, you're off the hook. You'll only have to drive me to your parents' house."

Jackson tried not to sigh with relief. Hillary had spent the afternoon with her sister, who had dropped her in Oceanside on her way to San Diego to meet an old high school friend. After his shift, Grant was supposed to meet them for dinner, then take Hillary to David and Hannah's house, where the duo would spend the weekend. That part of the plan, at least, was still intact.

"We don't have to go to dinner," Jackson said, "Now that your date has canceled too."

She shot him a glare. Jackson's date had backed out that afternoon, a somewhat puzzling turn of events. Hillary hadn't been wild about a double date to begin with, and even less thrilled about bringing a third wheel along to Grant's birthday dinner. It was the reason Jackson had still insisted on coming.

"I'm sure Mom can heat up leftovers of whatever she made," he added, having no real interest in dining alone with Hillary.

"I don't want to impose," she said. "Besides, Grant thought it might be good for us."

"Good for us?"

"It would give us a sort of second chance. We didn't exactly get off on the right foot."

"No, we didn't."

"What do you say?"

Jackson smiled. "Sure, a fresh start." He stuck out his hand. "Truce."

Her smile, a bit forced, was still beautiful. "Truce."

The armistice lasted all of five minutes, long enough for them to get into his Granada and head half a mile south and several blocks inland. Truth be told, it was hard to say who fired the first shot over the bow. He made an off-handed comment that they could just scrap plans and grab burgers at Ruby's. She replied that they had a reservation, and Béringer's cuisine was worth the cost. She added that she would be paying. He said, innocently enough, that as a lawyer, she should. She made a second reference to his part-time job.

A brief silence ensued. Two would-be combatants, circling, considered whether the battle was worth it, whether they really wanted to engage and risk the cost. They made it to Béringer's with a tenuous peace still presiding. It was broken just as innocuously.

"How'd you find this place, anyhow?" Jackson asked as they got out of the car. The asphalt parking lot was cracked and faded, which pretty much matched the nondescript, yellow-sided building in front of them. It had a flat roof with a green awning over the corner entrance, facing the street.

"Béringer's is one of the finest independently owned French restaurants in Southern California," Hillary answered.

"Too bad they can't afford better real estate. Or a little style," he said, noting the chipped paint on the siding.

"This from the guy wearing a faded pink T-shirt to dinner."

"This is how regular people dress, Hill. And I'm just a regular, average guy."

"You can say that again."

She opened the door for herself and Jackson followed her inside, his eyes needing several seconds to adjust to the darkness. Béringer's didn't have windows, and apparently was plagued by a shortage of light bulbs. At the front desk, a little more than a pulpit in a hallway, the maître d' eyed the two of them with a scowl on his face. He quickly replaced it with a plastic smile as he took their names and checked the reservation book.

"Will there still be four of you this evening?" he asked.

"Just two," Hillary answered.

"I see," he said, making a notation in the book. Then, with a polite wince at Jackson's attire, he led them to a table in the middle of the dining room. He pulled Hillary's chair out for her—Jackson certainly wasn't going to—and provided them with menus. He left them to a romantic evening: soft candlelight, quiet classical music, and a view of an unneeded fireplace on the back wall.

"You have a problem with regular?" Jackson asked.

Hillary glanced over her menu. "When you have the potential to be something more, yes."

Jackson nodded. She returned to reading. He was having trouble with his menu. For one thing, there were no prices. For another, there was no order—salads here, burgers here, entrées here. Everything was scattered all over the place, and he hadn't even heard of half of the dishes. Flamiche. Terrine. Poisson Pané. Huitres. Bigorneaux and Bulots.

He gave up and decided to ask the waiter for a steak and some fries.

"Grant and I are cut from the same cloth," he said.

Hillary peeked at him again. "How's that?"

"I mean, this isn't a reverse *Everafter*. He's not Emily Proctor and I'm not Drew Barrymore."

She scrunched her face. "What on earth are you talking about?"

"We're essentially the same guy. You got a problem with me, you have a problem with him."

A waiter appeared out of nowhere, sensed the tension, and paused for a moment while Jackson and Hillary stared at each other.

"Are *madame* and *monsieur* ready to order?" he asked.

"Uh, we're not married," Jackson said.

"He didn't say we were," Hillary said with a sigh. "Can we have a few more minutes, please?"

"Of course," the waiter said, smiling very politely and backing away.

"You and Grant are not the same."

"We're both just regular guys from a regular family. And no matter how many monogrammed shirts and designer sweaters you buy him, that won't change."

Hillary set down her menu and reached for a glass of water. "My problem with you, Jackson, isn't that you're from an All-American, middle-class family. I don't care if Grant is rich or poor, famous or unknown, a jock or a thespian."

"Okay?"

"It's that you're content to float through life, avoiding serious responsibility, never achieving anything or accomplishing anything or improving yourself in any way. And what's worse, you just make irreverent, smart-aleck comments about anyone who is making something of their life. Like your brother. Like me."

Jackson reached for his water. "Nice speech. But you should check your facts, Counselor."

"Where am I wrong?"

"You think I'm just coasting for the sake of coasting? You think I don't want to make anything of my life? You think I want to be a courier for the rest of time?"

"I don't see any evidence to the contrary."

"Then maybe you haven't been looking close enough."

"Maybe you haven't let me. Any time I try to be serious with you, you get glib and aloof."

"So I have a casual side."

"You don't have a side; you are casual, and incapable of being anything else."

"What's wrong with casual?"

"Nothing, but it can't be a lifestyle."

"Why not?"

"Because sitting around in blue jeans every day, playing video games and squinting out at the ocean won't get you anywhere."

"And defending murderers and rapists and child molesters will?"

"That's not fair."

"Fairness now a sustainable objection?"

The waiter returned, still smiling with all measure of politeness. Hillary snapped off an order, and Jackson caught the words soufflé and something about endives. The rest was a mystery. The waiter turned to him. "Can I get a steak and some fries?" he asked.

"What cut of steak, sir?"

Jackson shrugged. "Something tender."

The waiter winced but his smile didn't fade. "We have an excellent ribeye."

"Sounds great."

"How would you like it prepared?"

"Medium."

"Very good. I'm afraid we don't have French fries, sir."

"At a French restaurant?"

Hillary shook her head.

"I'm sorry, sir," the waiter said. "We offer *aligot*, *tartiflette*, or a baked potato."

"Baked, with butter. And a house salad, ranch dressing."

"Yes, sir."

"Extra croutons."

"Yes, sir."

He collected the menus and left. The staring match resumed.

"You say my lifestyle won't get me anywhere," Jackson said after a while. "Where exactly am I supposed to want to get?"

"You're really content to be forty years old someday, living in an apartment a few blocks from your parents' house with no career, no family, no purpose?"

"I would love to live close to my parents, who are my family, especially if they live a few miles from the ocean. And if I can do that without having a career, that would be even better, because then I have more time to be with my parents and the aforementioned ocean. And as for a purpose, I'm not opposed to the idea if God has one for me. But so far, I haven't seen it."

"Maybe you're not looking hard enough."

"I'm not going to go looking for purpose for the sake of having a purpose. If God has a calling for me, He'll call me."

"And in the meantime you just fritter your life away?"

"I'm not frittering anything. You're the one who spends all day locked away in an office, billing and killing yourself to make partner, getting criminals off on technicalities, and going out of your way to be formal and uptight. I drink iced tea on the beach and kick it with my friends. Who's frittering?"

She opened her mouth, but Jackson beat her to it. "And while we're on the topic, what is your great purpose? And don't give me some fighting for justice and democracy rhetoric. I've read Grisham. I know you're all idealistic in law school, but now you're in the real world. So what are you accomplishing, Hillary? What's your purpose?"

"It's not rhetoric, Jackson."

"Yeah, right. Sure, every once in a while an innocent guy goes to prison, but you all act like it happens half the time."

"'You all'?"

"Defense attorneys."

"Of whom you know so many."

"But what about all the thugs and creeps who are guilty as sin but get off because some rookie forgot to read Miranda in the midst of a free-for-all or because a detective didn't properly bag and tag the murder weapon?"

"Your so-called technicalities exist for a reason, Jackson," she said through gritted teeth. She forced a smile at the waiter as he brought their salads. "Without them, we'd have anarchy. What you can't seem to comprehend is that everyone deserves justice, not just the people you approve."

"So give them justice."

She shook her head. "That's what I'm doing. Even those accused of breaking the law have a right to a fair trial because they have the presumption of innocence until proven guilty. And I don't get to decide their guilt or innocence. All I can do is make sure that their rights are protected so that the legal system can take its course."

Jackson raised his eyebrows as he pushed his salad back and forth on the plate.

"What would you propose otherwise?" Hillary asked. "A Wild West mentality? That didn't exactly breed law and order."

"How about defense attorneys with some scruples?"

"And what is that supposed to mean?" she asked, her eyes flashing.

"It means have a little discretion with your clientele."

"You know nothing about our clients."

"Let me guess, a bunch of choir boys who are misunderstood and wrongly-accused."

"And it doesn't matter anyway. Innocent or guilty, they still have rights that need to be protected. Someone needs to stand up for those rights."

"Well it's a good thing all the drug dealers and pimps and murderers have Saint Hillary to look after them."

Hillary's eyes practically incinerated. Jackson broke off his gaze, looking at his uneaten salad. He waited for her retort, but none came. When he raised his head, it was as if she had pulled a mask down over her face, shutting him out. She started eating her salad, acting as if she was the only one at the table. Jackson picked at his, but the dressing was too light and it tasted like a plate of weeds.

The entrées were served. Jackson's steak was good but a little cold, the potato hard. Hillary's meal was apparently delicious because she consumed it in record time, without compromising her manners. Neither spoke throughout the entire meal. The music, the flicker of the fireplace, and the conversations of other couples seemed to grow deafening.

"Would either of you care for dessert?" the waiter asked as he collected their plates.

"No, thank you," Hillary said before Jackson could ask for a menu. The steak had also been small.

Hillary paid the bill without a word, and they headed out of the restaurant. The sun had set, but the sky was still light blue overhead. It was a beautiful evening.

"Hillary—"

"I think you've said enough for tonight," she said as she started walking.

"The car's this way."

"I'm not going to the car."

"Then what . . ."

"I'll take a cab."

"To San Diego? It will cost a couple hundred bucks."

"Well worth it."

"Hill. Aren't you going to feel a little silly showing up at my parents' place in a cab? Besides, Grant will never let me hear the end of it."

"By all means, let's worry about how Jackson will come out of this ordeal. Now leave me alone."

"Hillary—"

"Jackson, do not say another word. Please tell your parents I won't be coming tonight. I'll spend the night in town and Grant can pick me up tomorrow."

"You're serious?"

"Very."

She turned and strode down the sidewalk. Jackson watched her for a moment, then turned around. If she wanted to play this game, they could play. He quickened his pace, in case she changed her mind. Grant would be ticked, but let him be ticked. He was the one dating a manipulative narcissist.

As he careened out of the parking lot, he cast a quick glance down the sidewalk. He hoped to see Hillary turned around and coming his way. But she was gone.

Partially out of hunger, but mostly because it felt like a way to stick it to her, he drove back to the pier and ordered a milkshake and a burger from Ruby's.

Chapter Twenty-Two

IN A CITY known for extravagance and indulgence, Oasis Las Vegas pushed the envelope. A marvel of engineering design and construction, it formed a giant O that towered almost five hundred feet over the Strip. The sides of the O were approximately eighty feet thick, with open air flowing through its center. Guest rooms and suites on the outside of the O overlooked the Strip, the massive pool deck behind the building, or—in the case of those rooms on the underside of the O's curve—tranquil, garden-encircled pools stocked with colorful fish, manta rays, and sea turtles. There were also rooms on the inside of the O, looking down on a glass-enclosed atrium that was home to "The Lagoon," a forty-thousand-cubic-foot pond surrounded by shops and eateries.

More upscale shops and a variety of restaurants and clubs also filled two arced wings (named the North and South Peninsula) at the base of the O. The wings partially circled a three-story-deep, one-acre park with gardens and cascading water features patterned after the famous Hanging Gardens of Babylon. It was spanned by a forty-foot-wide walkway, made to resemble a rope bridge, that provided quick access to the atrium, shops, and restaurants from the sidewalk along Las Vegas Boulevard.

Behind the O, a fifty-thousand-square-foot casino offered every game of chance known in the city, all in a swank, sophisticated environment. Above the casino and stretching behind it was a pool deck that featured seven pools, a lazy river, and the world's longest waterslide. Additional amenities included various sports courts, an external dance floor, an outdoor gaming section, and an adventure area replete with a rock-climbing wall, a high ropes course, and a zip line. Patrons were also drawn to the H2O Showroom, with its a Grecian-style theater, and Tides, an aquarium boasting over fifty thousand gallons of water home to more than two hundred species of fish and reptiles.

Only open for two years, Oasis was already one of the "it" destinations in Las Vegas and the world. "Whales" and high rollers came to gamble in the opulent, spacious casino. Businesses availed themselves of thirteen different ballrooms and meeting spaces for various conferences and conventions, and hung out in the bars, lounges, and clubs after hours. Couples escaped to a romantic getaway, pampering at the spa, golf at half a dozen area courses with reciprocal deals with the resort, and fashionable shopping at Oasis and neighboring resorts. And families flocked to the fun behind the O, where there were entertainment options for everyone.

No expense had been spared, from the forty-foot LCD screen that graced the marquee out front to high thread count Egyptian cotton sheets in all rooms to a glass exterior that glowed soft blue come nighttime. Lacking no amenities, Oasis received the highest ratings in Las Vegas. *Fortune* and *Forbes* had tabbed Richard Holloway as the next Steve Wynn or Donald Trump. Already there was talk of opening a second Oasis resort in Macau.

None of this was on the mind of Russell "Rusty" Jackson as he guided his rented cobalt blue Dodge Challenger R/T around the two-lane roundabout and under the carport of Oasis Las Vegas, stopping on a dime. All he could think about as he turned down—but not off—the Switchfoot pumping through the Sirius satellite radio was the blond bombshell beside him.

Shannon Hillstrom flashed a bright, toothy smile as she slowly slid butterfly sunglasses down her tanned face. She clipped them over the collar of her fuchsia peasant blouse. The diamond pendant resting against her skin just above the neckline of the blouse and the silver bangles on her wrist, along with perfectly styled blond hair and refined but emphatic makeup, indicated she was anything but a peasant.

Rusty flung open his door and pressed a five-spot into the palm of the blue-vested valet. "Watch it on the corners," he said to the kid, no more than twenty years old. "You go too slow, you won't feel the G's."

"Yes, sir," the kid said with a smile. For good measure, Rusty patted his shoulder as he headed for the trunk. Shannon was already standing at the curb, purse over her shoulder, an attendant closing her door for her. She stared up at the underside of the O, which towered over the carport. A covered colonnade led from the carport, across a turquoise pool, to the main entrance of the resort.

Rusty helped the bellhop load the luggage onto his bellman cart and joined Shannon on the curb. He raised his eyebrows. "Let's go, Peaches."

Peaches strutted down the colonnade, standing every inch of her six-foot-tall frame—plus two inches from the heels on her platform wedge sandals. Her stride was long and confident, the loose curls of her hair bouncing on her back with every step. Exchange the blouse and Capris for an expensive evening gown or some other cutting edge threads, and she could have been working a runway in New York, Milan, or Paris.

Rusty strolled a few paces behind, making small talk with the bellhop. Will the weather hold? Where can I get a good steak around here? Who is headlining this week at H_2O? The conversation was good for the bellhop—it kept him from staring at the lithe figure in front of him as they passed through quiet automatic doors leading to the hotel lobby.

The temperature wasn't quite as high as it had been over the weekend, but the air-conditioned interior of Oasis was still a relief. And the air wasn't the only thing that was cool.

Polished marble, imported from Carrara, Italy, flowed under their feet. Its color was a gray and blue swirl, the latter accentuated by a handful of sleek armchairs and sofas in several shades of blue. They were scattered around the lobby, along with burnished American Cherry end tables. The check-in desk matched the tables, with a wall of marble behind it, over which flowed a sheen of water. Embossed in the marble behind the wall of water in an iridescent sapphire was the word "Oasis." From where they stood, it appeared they had arrived at a Sandals retreat in the Caymans.

Shannon's phone buzzed, and she stepped aside to take the call while Rusty smooth-talked the receptionist, Jola. She was young, with amaretto skin and a perfect smile, and was either attracted by Rusty's charm or just incredibly friendly. She found his reservation—made the night before—for five nights, accepted his cash payment, and put his credit card on file. She also started a tab, billable to the room, for incidentals and hotel services. She provided him with a glossy brochure, highlighted several of the resort's features, and then flipped the brochure over and pointed out the critical locations on a map of the property. She showed him where the casino, the aquarium, the showroom, the North Peninsula and South Peninsula, and several restaurants were located. Lastly, she circled his room, on the thirty-fourth floor.

Jola promised her assistance—as well as that of any of the other resort staff—if it was needed, and with one more flash of her perfect smile, encouraged him to have a wonderful stay at Oasis Las Vegas. With a wink and a return smile, Rusty assured her that he would.

"Ready, Sugar?" Rusty asked, only to find that Shannon had ended the call and was standing right beside him. He smiled at her, and after Jola announced their room number to the bellhop, they followed him toward the atrium.

Covering twenty-five thousand square feet, with a glass ceiling thirty feet above the floor, the atrium felt as massive as it was. In the center, a single column stretched upward and through the ceiling. Around it, a two-story rock feature was home to half a dozen waterfalls, all spilling through the assorted flora to The Lagoon. The water feature curved and flowed around seating areas, a juice bar, and real palm trees, in the process creating several inlets and coves. From their vantage point on the south side of the atrium, the front entrance was to their left and the casino entrance to the right. Across the way was the Healing Waters Spa, a bank of elevators, and Blue, a lounge featuring jazz and blues music. There were more shops and restaurants on their side of the atrium and a place to purchase tickets for various shows. And then there was the Mezzanine Level, also under the atrium, its open walkways looking down on The Lagoon. Ballrooms, a few shops, and the pool deck were all accessible from the Mezzanine Level.

The bellhop let them admire the scene for a moment before turning to the left and leading them to another bank of elevators on the south side of the atrium. They were encased in glass and rode up the inside of the O on a complex system of gyroscopes and balancers that enabled them to always stay level despite the changing contour of the O. The bellhop explained the complexity of their design as they smoothly ascended, then segued to some additional statistics about Oasis—how much it cost to build, average number of visitors per month, biggest slot jackpot ever won. Rusty figured it was a standard speech, and listened nonchalantly, smiling at Shannon's attractive figure. For her part, she pretended not to notice until they were almost to the thirty-fourth floor, at which point she smiled demurely. He clasped the end of her fingers between his middle and index fingers, and gave a light squeeze as they got off.

Room 3415 was on the southeast corner of the floor, high enough up to be over the "hump" of the O and thus not in the shade of higher floors. Sadly, the bellhop said, their suite didn't have a view of the Strip. But it did overlook the pool deck, MGM Grand, and Frenchman Mountain off in the distance. "There's a lot better scenery by the pool than the street anyhow," he said to Rusty as they reached their door. He pushed it open, and the bellhop carried in their luggage. He set it by a small closet, adjacent to a full bathroom. He then walked past a small kitchenette with a sink, refrigerator, microwave, and single-brew coffeepot and across a spacious seating area. In addition to a table and chairs for four, it had a couch and two armchairs that faced a large, flat screen TV. The bellhop pulled back the shear curtains to let in even more afternoon sunlight and encouraged them to check out the view.

He then showed them the attached bedroom, complete with a queen bed, full bathroom, another large TV, and an equally impressive view out the window. Like the living room, the bedroom was plenty spacious. Both were decorated tastefully in soft, elegant blues and greens. Artwork on the walls depicted tranquil Caribbean seas and lush mountain streams.

After showing them where several amenities were, the bellhop directed them to the resort guidebook on the coffee table, and said if they needed anything, not to hesitate to call. Before he left, could he get them anything? Perhaps some ice?

"No, we're good, buddy," Rusty said. He reached for his money clip and peeled off a twenty.

"Thank you, sir."

"Thank you . . . Martin," he said, checking the nametag.

"My pleasure."

Martin backed out of the room, letting the door swing shut behind him. With a familiar thud-click, it settled shut, and the couple was finally alone.

Jackson slapped his hands together. "Pool or craps table?"

"Let's set some gambling guidelines," Hillary said. "I have this horrible picture of you being dragged away, your suit all rumpled, eyes bleary, hair more messed up than usual, pleading for just one more roll of quarters."

"First of all, I won't be playing with quarters."

"Not exactly quelling my fears."

"I'll be in control, Hill. But I've got a role to play."

"And just because you thought of that little slip-of-the-tongue failsafe with our aliases, it doesn't mean you can keep calling me Hill."

"It's a term of endearment."

"Term's up," she said.

"Whatever you say, Cupcake."

She stared at him for several seconds. "You know you're a dork, don't you, naming yourself after a movie character?"

"I don't know, I kind of look like a Rusty, don't you think?" Jackson asked, flopping onto the couch.

"You're obsessed with Brad Pitt is what you are. I think you might fit better as one of those bumbling brothers."

"Turk and Virgil? Yeah, I could see myself as Scotty Caan. More of *Hawaii Five-0* Scotty Caan. And with better hair."

Hillary shook her head. "I'm going to take a quick dip in the pool. It's doubtful I'll run into Holloway yet today, but it will give me a chance to explore and pick a spot for tomorrow."

"Good idea."

"Plus Shannon needs a break after four hours in the car with Rusty."

"Should we decide on sleeping arrangements? You want to go rock, paper, scissors, or maybe a quick game of blackjack?"

She answered by picking up her duffel bag, walking into the bedroom, and closing the door behind her.

Chapter Twenty-Three

5:14 p.m.

MOST VEGAS CASINOS were loud, gaudy, and smoky. They existed for the locals who hadn't been taught fiscal responsibility and the weekenders who didn't mind losing a few hundred bucks as long as they had a good time doing so. Oasis's casino catered to an entirely different crowd. Low-paying slots and dollar blackjack tables were still available, but the majority of the venues had five-, ten-, twenty-, or even fifty-dollar minimums. The tables and machines were spread a little farther apart, half walls and railings creating alcoves with more privacy while still allowing ample foot traffic to flow across the floor.

The carpet in the aisles was royal blue with flecks of color scattered throughout. Lighter shades of blue and soft greens and browns made up the carpet in the lower-traffic areas. A ceiling was recessed several times, and the walls were a sandy taupe, except for two huge aquariums on the west wall, on either side of the main entrance.

And while the video poker and slot machines still hummed and jangled and chirped, they were somewhat muted. Somehow, Oasis had brought sophistication to pulling a lever and hoping the on-screen fruits would match each other. Unobtrusive classical music descended from overhead speakers and swirled among the gaming tables. Even they were high-class, with rich blue velvet surfaces and mahogany wood rimming the edges. The dealers wore dark slacks, pressed white shirts with black ties, and blue Oasis vests. They didn't resemble seedy hucksters like at some joints; rather, these were smiling, congenial, personable men and women who looked as if they couldn't wait to give Richard Holloway's money away.

Jackson, as Rusty, couldn't wait to oblige them. While Hillary had made a quick visit to the pools, he had ordered pay-per-view and absentmindedly watched a few minutes of some yet-to-be-released action movie. He did so to kill time and because it's what his alter ego would do. And because Hillary was picking up the expense tab for their sting.

She had returned just before five, showered quickly, and dressed in a black cocktail dress that looked sensational. Jackson wore a peach shirt under a jacket, no tie. His jeans were designer, purchased at Buckle for almost more than his entire normal wardrobe. Hillary had told him he looked good . . . for Rusty. It was as close as he would get to a compliment.

They had dinner reservations at eight, but first they wanted to give the hotel's security cameras plenty of time to see their faces. If the aliases and backstopping created by Mouse and Wizzy K—a local "artist" recommended by Danny Pollack—were going to fail, they'd rather it be now than halfway through their con. They also hoped Hillary and her black cocktail dress might arouse the attention of Richard Holloway. It was doubtful he sat in the resort's surveillance room scouting for beautiful women, but Colin Appleby had said something about Holloway lingering in his casino, and the sooner she caught his eye, the better.

Jackson strolled confidently toward the cage, a flattened octagon in the center of the casino. He placed a crisp hundred-dollar bill on the counter and asked for five-dollar chips. "Starting small," he said with a grin.

The cashier examined the bill and slid him a small black tray with red-rimmed chips. The off-white centers were stamped with the Oasis logo, a large O with curved palm trees extending from either side over a pool of water in the middle. "Ready to go, Babe?" he said with a wink at Hillary.

She smiled and took his arm. "So far we have Peaches, Sugar, Cupcake, and Babe," she said. "Any others I should know about?"

"Just the typical Hons and Sweeties, and Cupcake wasn't for real."

"Okay."

"Else Dad used to call Mom 'Doll.'"

"I know, I heard it."

"That's right. I forget sometimes you knew them."

Hillary said nothing as she hung loosely to his arm. He walked straight to the craps tables.

"Do you even know how to play craps?" Hillary asked quietly as he waited at a somewhat busy table. The crowds were just starting to fill in.

"It's rolling dice," he said with a shrug. "How hard can it be?"

It proved harder than he thought, as he lost nearly fifty dollars in just over ten minutes. He declared the table "cold" and decided to try his hand at blackjack.

"It'd be great if you didn't deplete my entire savings," she said.

"Relax, Hill. I know my limits."

Five minutes and twenty dollars later, he was down to six red chips. As he had when leaving the craps table, he tipped the dealer a chip. Five remaining.

It hadn't rung, but Jackson plucked his phone from his pocket anyhow. He handed his remaining chips to Hillary. "Here, see if you have any better luck."

"I can't have any worse."

"Yeah?" he said into his phone, then faked a phone call for five minutes. Knowing the eye in the sky would see him and not knowing if Holloway's chief of security had someone on staff who could read lips, he did his best to make his faux conversation seem authentic, staying in character. Just in case. Finished, he clapped his phone shut and sought out Hillary. She wasn't hard to spot, sitting at a pai gow table with a couple of young men.

Jackson slid in between her and another man, placing his hand on her back in the process. "How goes it, Hon?"

"Eight, eight, the lady wins," the dealer announced, removing dominoes from in front of Hillary and sliding chips her way.

Hillary smiled politely and stacked her chips, waiting and betting on the next hand.

The dealer rearranged the dominoes, stacked them, then slid her and two other players stacks of four. The rest he cast to the side. Hillary turned her dominoes over, revealing white and red dots. Jackson watched as she quickly sorted them, turning two sideways, and pushed all four of them forward. When the other players had done so as well, the dealer revealed his dominoes and declared Hillary a winner again.

Jackson frowned. Hillary's two dominoes turned sideways added to nine, and the two perpendicular to them totaled just seven. The dealer's equaled fifteen and ten. Yet he had declared her the winner.

She played a third time, "pushing," which Jackson determined meant winning with one set of dominoes but not the other. She recouped her initial bet, then tipped the dealer and stood to leave. Jackson followed her.

"When did you learn how to play pai gow?" he asked.

"When I was in China," she answered, handing him a stack of chips. His rough estimate was that she had made up what he had lost.

"When were you in China?" he asked.

She stopped walking. "In 2007. What's next?"

He nodded at the roulette wheel.

"You're serious?"

"Yes. What were you doing in China in '07?"

She smirked. "Learning how to play pai gow."

He walked to the roulette wheel and used his chips to buy chips specific to the game and table, enabling the dealer to determine which player—currently it was just Jackson and a middle-aged woman—had placed which bet. He stacked half of his chips on red, then watched as the wheel was spun and the ball landed in a black pocket.

He placed his remaining chips on red for the second spin, and this time won.

"You want in on this?" he asked Hillary.

"No, you just keep going."

"One more," he said, dropping one chip on 34 and one on 15, corresponding to the numbers of their room. He lost, exchanged his chips, tipped the dealer, and moved on.

"Are we going someplace in particular?" she asked.

"Just wandering. I like the casino."

"I couldn't tell. You're going to arouse suspicions."

"That's the idea."

"I meant in a bad way."

"What, I'm playing a character."

"Yes, a slovenly one."

"I'm sampling." He stopped back at a blackjack table and this time won a few hands. He again tipped the dealer on his way out. "Man, the tips get you."

"For two minutes, you could probably tip less than five dollars."

"It's all I have, and Rusty is generous."

"You *are* acting."

"So why China? College trip?"

"No."

"Come on, Hill, dish."

"I went with my boyfriend and his family."

"They took you to China?"

"His dad went to Beijing on business, it was a family thing, and I was invited along."

"Must have been serious between you and this guy?"

She dipped her head to the side. "Semi."

"Did Grant know?"

She looked at him. "There was nothing to know."

"Before you, the furthest Grant took any girl with the family was Olive Garden."

"Are we done?" she asked.

He checked his watch, a new purchase, a genuine-looking knockoff.

"I guess. Maybe we can stroll through a few shops before heading up to change."

"Whatever you say, Rusty."

She took his hand as they exited the casino. He mulled China for a few moments, and then tried to figure out how nine and seven beat fifteen and ten in pai gow.

After browsing through a few of the shops—a sports memorabilia store, a ladies' fashion boutique, a chocolatier named Melt—the duo returned to their room to dress for dinner. Jackson switched shirts, added a tie, and swapped jeans for dress pants. Hillary was busy primping in the master bath, so he strolled to the window and looked down at the pool area.

Night had fallen over the city, but the pools were still lit from within, coloring the water the same soft blue hue as the exterior of the building. Faux tiki torches lined the walkways, and subtle spotlighting accented palm trees and further bathed the deck in soft colors. White stringed lights hung around the dance floor. The sports courts and climbing wall were lit abundantly, and the small "Pool Casino" had just enough neon to stand out.

Jackson spent a moment surveying the various pools and trying to determine where he—were he Richard Holloway—might stroll to look for beautiful women. Then he panned to the south end of the property, where work had already begun on two freestanding structures. Conical in shape and standing ten stories tall, they were just steel skeletons now. Eventually they would house an additional three hundred fifty rooms and suites, most of which had external views. Roughly a third of them would be on the inside of the circle, and instead of a window, would have a large porthole that that looked at massive aquariums. One hundred feet in depth and nearly eighty feet in diameter, the aquariums would contain almost two hundred fifty thousand gallons of water each, playing home to dozens of species of colorful fish, in addition to sea turtles, manta rays, and freshwater sharks. No word on mermaids.

Beyond the construction, the sprawl of MGM Grand ate up most of a city block. A while back, Maggie had tried to talk him in to a weekend in Vegas, bragging up MGM Grand from a previous stay. In a moment of weakness, he'd almost said yes. Thoughts drifting to her, he stared blankly at a distant light that slowly grew until it was multiple lights, a jet descending into McCarran International.

"Are you ready?"

Jackson turned away from the window. Hillary had changed from her black cocktail dress to a red, floor-length halter dress. While it was more than flattering physically, the dress's ruffled neckline drew attention to Hillary's face, as did dangly teardrop earrings and bright red lipstick, to match the dress. Her hair had been curled and styled in a loose side bun, with just a few strands left loose beside her cheek. If she had ever been more beautiful, Jackson couldn't remember it. Then again, he couldn't remember much of anything at the moment.

"Did . . . you say something?" he asked.

"I asked if you were ready."

"Uh, yeah."

"Your collar's popped," she said, and he reached to adjust his jacket. Taking a deep breath, he followed her toward the door.

The O was several hundred feet deep, so from the street it resembled a tube. Suspended in the hollow inside of the tube was a second tube, not quite as deep, and only three stories tall. The sole occupant of the inner tube was Drop, a restaurant offering fine dining with a magnificent view. Supported by a main column that ran from the ground to the top of the O, and by several sweeping vertical beams that blended perfectly with the architecture as they descended from above, the three-story restaurant was another engineering miracle. Two exterior walkways on the twenty-sixth floor connected the guest rooms and suites with the restaurant. From the entrance, it was cantilevered some seventy-five feet in either direction. It was worth the price for the experience alone, never mind the exceptional cuisine.

Jackson and Hillary were led by a maître d' in a tuxedo to the upper level and out onto a balcony that faced the Strip. White linen cloths covered each table. They were set with every imaginable dish and utensil, and lit by flickering long-stem candles. Only one by the railing, however, had a dazzling bouquet of two dozen red and white roses in a field of baby's-breath laid across the plate. Jackson walked a pace behind Hillary as the maître d' guided them to that table and pulled out Hillary's chair.

"For me?" she asked quizzically, looking at the maître d'.

He smiled as he bowed slightly. He gently slid her seat in, then stood back as she cradled the bouquet and sniffed a few of the roses. As she set them down, she spotted a small card tucked into the baby's breath and plucked it out. Her eyes dropped to the handwritten note, then flashed up at Jackson.

With a flourish, the maître d' placed a wine list on the table and announced that their waiter would be with them shortly. He took half a step back and smiled at Hillary. "Would the lady like me to put them in a vase?"

"Yes, thank you."

Still grinning, he accepted the flowers from her and departed.

Hillary again locked her eyes onto Jackson. "That wasn't in the script," she said.

"I thought a gesture like that might catch somebody's attention."

"You could have told me."

"I wanted the surprise factor to be genuine."

"Well, they're very nice. Thank you."

"Don't thank me. You paid for them."

"And there goes the moment, soaring away on the evening breeze."

Drop featured something for everyone, and Jackson and Hillary savored a delicious meal of veal scaloppini and pan-seared salmon. The gentle stirrings of a live string quartet, the scent of the roses, and the exhilaration of the desert air added to the ambiance, and it wasn't hard for the two of them to fall into character. It had seemed silly at the time, but they had planned topics for Rusty and Shannon to talk about during the meal. Security cameras weren't likely to be trained in on their lips all the time, but it would keep them from getting heated over real life topics and help them avoid conversation lulls. It would also help engrain their backstories into their minds. And they had both agreed it was best to stay in character whenever they were out and about.

As the meal was winding down, Hillary broke from the script for a moment. "So what's the agenda for tomorrow?"

"You work on your tan."

"I just lay by the pool all day?"

"You can swim some if you want." Jackson took a bite of a third dinner roll and leaned in slightly. "Appleby said Holloway likes to take a walk late morning or in the afternoon. You need to be in place both times. Besides, with your boyfriend busy all day, what else do you have to do?"

"How about the spa?"

"Your dime."

"So you keep reminding me," she said, reaching for her water. She took a drink. "And what are you going to be doing?"

"I've got business meetings," he said as the waiter returned. He checked on their progress and asked if they would be interested in dessert. They politely declined and he said he'd return with their bill momentarily. "So I have to leave and not be seen," Jackson continued when he was gone.

"Busts your plan to gamble my money away all day."

"Sure does. Guess I'll make a second lap around Red Rock Canyon or see if I can find Area 51 or something." Out of the corner of his eye, he saw the waiter returning. "Then I thought maybe tomorrow night we could take in *Adrift*."

Hillary—in character or out—nodded.

Jackson paid cash for their dinner, left a very handsome tip, and came around to get Hillary's chair for her. Since it was such a pleasant evening and still warm, they decided on a stroll through the Hanging Gardens, after first taking the flowers to their suite. They rode the elevator down one story past the atrium and exited to utter tranquility beneath the Strip.

Over a dozen waterfalls carried the same water that circled the hotel down to a central lagoon, where it was shaded a majestic turquoise. Winding stone walkways led through palm and fern jungles, lavish flowerbeds, and private gazebos and benches perfect for romantic seclusion. Recessed lighting built into the pathway or guardrails provided just enough light to see, without taking away from the natural aura.

Hillary hung loosely on Jackson's arm as they walked. "So I've got a question," she said.

"Shoot."

"You said you gave me the flowers because you wanted to attract attention."

"It's a long shot maybe, but yeah. I doubt Holloway's sitting there watching all his security cameras 24/7, but I'm sure he has a network in place to let him know when his guests do something a little out of the ordinary."

"For most guys, buying flowers for their girlfriend isn't really that out of the ordinary," she said.

"I meant the method of delivery."

"Uh-huh."

"And if it was so ordinary, why'd you smile so big?"

"Because you're not most guys."

"I've never thought so either."

She huffed. "My point is, if it worked and he did take notice, won't it kind of dispel the idea that you're very casual toward me and take me for granted, thus making Holloway less likely to pursue me?"

"Not when I ditch you for the craps table in a few minutes."

Hillary nodded. "I see." She let go of his arm and took a few steps away from him, her heels clicking on the stone. "And you had this all planned from the beginning—the flowers, ditching me?"

"More or less."

"That's what I thought."

He frowned. "Is something wrong?"

"No," she said softly. She reached out and straightened his tie. "You should go play."

"Okay. Are you upset that I didn't really buy you flowers?"

"I'm not upset."

"Because a moment a go you were all prom-date clingy and now I feel like the married guy who blew off dinner with the in-laws to watch the game with his buddies."

"You seriously need to cut back on metaphors."

"Hill, is something the matter?"

"Shannon, remember?" Her shoulders slouched a little. "I thought that maybe you had surprised me with flowers because you were trying to do something sweet. Not because you were getting fresh with me or making a pass at me, but just because you were being nice." She smiled. "And I'm not sure why I would have expected that from you, so it's my own fault for thinking that a very sweet gesture was anything more than the conniving of your master plan."

She turned and started for the atrium and he lagged behind, feeling as if he had been punched in the gut. Was this the Hillary he knew and despised? Was she being vulnerable and showing feelings? Was she hurt that he hadn't bought her flowers out of genuine sweetness? And why did that bother her since, as she'd said, there was no reason for her to expect such a gesture from him?

But none of that was what was bothering him. It was that he *had* had an ulterior motive for buying the flowers. He had surprised her, partially because it would fit well with his character, but also because he wanted to do something nice for her. Not for any romantic reason, but to show her that there was depth beneath the surface. Yet he couldn't bring himself to admit it, to let down the façade, to be real and vulnerable with her for even a moment.

They stood opposite each other as they waited for the elevator. Neither spoke. He loosened his tie and undid the top button of his shirt, then removed his jacket. He rolled his sleeves to the elbow, finishing as the elevator dinged.

"How long are you going to be?" Hillary asked, stepping inside.

"An hour or so, maybe," he said. "Um, you mind?" he asked, holding up the jacket.

She took it wordlessly.

This was too strange, Hillary showing any sort of emotion, any sort of feeling for him. He decided to try and salvage things. "Look, Hillary—"

"It's fine, Jackson. Just forget it."

He opened his mouth, then shut it. "I was just going to say, you look really beautiful tonight."

Her smile lasted only a second. "And you look like a frat boy," she said, then pressed a button and stood back as the doors closed.

He sighed, wondering how stupid he looked in Hillary's eyes right now. He had missed the moment, that fraction in time where he could have actually said the right thing. Instead, as usual, he had tried to be nice and she had verbally smacked him.

He licked his wounds at the craps table. He slowly won a hundred bucks while flirting with a knockout brunette who looked almost as good in a teal evening gown as Hillary had in hers. He kept it light, just banter, and took his winnings back to the baccarat table where he made another fifty. He decided to make a run at blackjack, and over the course of the next half hour, lost all of what he had just won. Then an additional twenty dollars. Then twenty more. It was eleven-thirty and time to quit.

He thought of Hillary, thought of the smug way she always one-upped him, thought of how she had punished him for whatever it was she had punished him for. He decided on his way up to the room he would let another twenty dollars ride on black at the roulette wheel. He lost it with a smile.

Chapter Twenty-Four

Tuesday, September 18
7:39 a.m.

HILLARY HAD BEEN in bed when Jackson returned to the room the night before. Or at least, in the master bedroom with the door closed. He'd spent ten minutes trying to figure out how to get the couch to fold out into a bed, then given up and crashed on it as was. It had taken a while to fall asleep, his mind racing with the events of the day. Had they forgotten something in all their planning? Did they have any chance of catching Holloway's eye? Why was Hillary upset about flowers?

Jackson awoke to the sound of running water. He blinked as he sat up. Hillary was pouring coffee, already dressed in a knee-length floral sundress. Jackson raked his hands through his hair, at the same time noticing that Hillary's was perfect.

"Morning," she said as she walked away from the kitchenette with a mug of coffee.

"What time is it?"

"Twenty till eight. Why'd you sleep on the couch?"

"We had a little spat last night, Muffin."

"I mean, why didn't you pull it out?"

"It doesn't pull," he said, standing up.

Hillary licked her lips, then set her mug back on the counter and crouched down beside the couch. Suddenly it began to whir and the cushions rose before falling onto the floor. As they did, the couch began to unfold. Just that quickly, it retracted and quieted. Hillary stood.

"How—How'd you do that?" Jackson asked.

"Quite easily."

"Exactly how long am I going to be in the doghouse?"

"You're not in the doghouse," she said as she lifted her coffee mug. "Although the smell would suggest otherwise."

182

"And I suppose you smell like potpourri when you wake up."

"I called ahead for a table at Fork. You should get in the shower."

"They serve breakfast?"

"Mm-hmm," she said, taking a sip of coffee.

"I was kind of thinking more along the lines of a few donuts and a stiff cup of coffee. A long, leisurely breakfast doesn't really fit with the cover that I'm busy working and ignoring you most of the day."

"It does if you get a call halfway through breakfast and have to run out suddenly."

"Are you trying to get back at me for something?"

"I'm trying to think of things that might attract attention to us. And me eating breakfast at a five-star restaurant by myself because my boyfriend is too busy for me might just do that."

He scratched his head. "That's not a bad idea."

"We have less than twenty minutes. Get going."

He nodded and gathered some clothes, then stopped to inspect the side of the couch. He spotted a small little switch built into the frame. "Huh."

Fork was the most opulent restaurant at Oasis, and one of the most elegant in all Las Vegas. At the end of the South Peninsula, it looked out at the Strip through two-way glass that provided privacy to those inside. For dinner, gentlemen were required to wear a jacket, but the dress code was relaxed for breakfast. Jackson made the cut—albeit narrowly in the eyes of the hostess—with his button-down shirt and blue jeans from the day before.

Only a handful of people were dining at Fork, given the allure of Tsunami, Oasis's all-you-can-eat breakfast buffet. Jackson and Hillary were seated by the window and served on fine china.

"You're clear on everything for today?" Jackson asked when the waitress was gone.

"Crystal," Hillary said.

"Don't forget your earwig."

"I won't."

"Or the necklace."

"Why again do you need to see everything that's going on?" she asked. "Remember, it's not going to be pointed at me."

"Don't flatter yourself," he said, immediately realizing how absurd he had sounded. "We're doing recon," he added quickly. "An extra set of eyes and ears could be invaluable."

He sipped his orange juice. Pulpy. For $3.95 and barely larger than a shot glass, it ought to at least be smooth.

Hillary mimicked him, only hers was tomato juice. "You know, I also have to wonder if you couldn't have come up with a better plan than this."

"How do you mean?"

"Me lounging around the pool in a bikini is awfully clichéd."

"Clichés work. That's how they become clichés. When was the last time a girl from Saudi Arabia won Miss Universe?"

She shook her head.

"Look, this is your whale hunt, Ahab. You want to call it off, we can."

"I just want to make sure you're really applying yourself."

"Believe it or not, I'm not wild about trotting you out there like a fraternity beauty contestant either. But the cold, hard truth of the matter is, the best way to turn a guy's head is with a pretty girl in skimpy clothes."

She sighed. "I know."

Their breakfast came, fruit and an English muffin for her, scrambled eggs, bacon, and toast for him. The eggs were cold and a little runny, and the bacon was thin and flimsy. It was a good thing he wasn't counting on eating much of it. After a few bites, he faked a phone call, talking a little louder than necessary as he agreed to push up the day's first meeting. He clapped the phone shut a moment later as he saw the waitress approaching.

"Sorry, Babe, but I've got to run."

"Why? What's going on?"

"My 9:30 just became an—" He looked down at his watch. "—five minutes from now."

"I thought we were going to at least enjoy breakfast together," she said, now putting on a show for the waitress.

"It's the business," Jackson said as she stopped at their table.

"Is everything all right?" the waitress asked, frowning as Jackson stood.

"Fine," he said. "I've just got to run. Work."

"Lunch?" Hillary asked hopefully.

"I'll do what I can," he said, slapping a quick kiss on her forehead. "No flirting with any college boys," he called over his shoulder. He didn't pay Hillary another glance as he exited Fork and walked briskly but calmly through the South Peninsula shops and back to the atrium, then to the lobby and out to the carport where he handed the valet the claim check for the Challenger. Five minutes later, he was headed north on Las Vegas Boulevard.

He hung a left at Flamingo Road, then doubled back south on I-15. In ten minutes, he was out of the city and doing seventy-five. The five-point-seven-liter Hemi V8 engine sounded as if it was idling, and he was tempted to push the needle, to see baby reach triple digits. But he didn't want to risk a speeding ticket with a fake ID, so he kept her around the speed limit. After blasting for several miles, he turned around and headed back toward the city.

He picked up a pair of Egg McMuffins and set a course for Town Square, an open-air "mall" just south of the Strip. It contained shops, restaurants, offices, and entertainment venues, all laid out like an intimate European village. He had Hillary's tablet, and thus her subscription to Netflix, and since there was nothing else to do, he thought he'd catch up on some *Leverage*. First he called his grandpa.

"Hey, bud, it's been a while," Leroy Douglas said.

"Yeah, I'm working a case," Jackson said, dropping the last bite of a McMuffin into his mouth and quickly consuming it. "I'm actually in Las Vegas."

"Las Vegas," Leroy said, as if he'd never heard of such a place. "What in the Sam Hill are you doing in Las Vegas?"

"Working. I'm undercover at the Oasis."

"What's the Oasis?"

"Newest mega resort on the Strip. You have heard of the Strip, haven't you, Grandpa?"

"You heard of getting your plow cleaned?"

Jackson smiled.

"Sounds like a big deal. How'd you get roped into this?"

"Hillary."

Leroy was quiet for a moment. "I assume you're talking about the same Hillary I know."

"Yep."

"She must be paying you an awful lot."

"Not a penny."

"Called in your favor then?"

"That she did."

"You two playing nice?"

"Ish."

"Well, you're missing nothing here. Finally rained the last two days, more this afternoon."

"You going to announce seniors' birthdays next?"

"Hardy, har, har. So tell me about this undercover business."

Jackson did, hitting the high points for Leroy. His chuckling turned to outright laughter, mingled with a little bit of concern. That came out in the end. "You be careful, kiddo. People with power and prestige don't like people messing with that power and prestige."

"How do you think I ended up in this situation?"

Another pause. "Has she changed much?"

"Nope. Same delightful girl as always."

"You never did give her much of a chance."

"I gave as given."

"Not sure which metal they assigned to that rule."

"Come on, Grandpa, you didn't like her either."

"I never said that."

"I never said . . . No, I did say that. But you didn't like her."

"We weren't best friends," Leroy said. "But she loved your brother and he loved her. She was family."

"She was family-elect," Jackson said. "And now she's moved on to the next victim."

"Oh?"

"She denies it, but I know better."

"Of course you do."

Jackson grinned. "I'm getting another call. I'll call you later."

"Take care, kiddo."

"I will."

"And take care of Hillary too."

"Yeah," Jackson said, quickly answering his other call. "Hello?"

"Jackson, it's me," Hillary said.

"What's up?"

"I'm headed down to the pool."

"Already?"

"I want to get a good spot."

"Okay. You have—"

"I have the necklace. Pretty dumb, don't you think, wearing a necklace to go tanning?"

"It's a gift from dear old Rusty, and you're not tanning so much as sunning. Is it on?"

"Yes."

Jackson wiped his greasy fingers on his pants before firing up Hillary's tablet. It took him a couple of minutes to access the software Mouse had "adapted" to allow Jackson to see what the small camera embedded in the necklace saw. The necklace with camera had cost them six hundred dollars, but they had been assured by Danny Pollack's "associate" that it was top-of-the-line.

"I can't see anything," Jackson said. "It's hazy."

It appeared as if a sheet was pulled down, and the camera suddenly picked up Hillary in the mirror of her master bathroom. The V-neck of a loose, white cover-up now came just below the graceful but understated silver necklace. The aquamarine birthstone in the center was actually the lens for a miniature camera. Even so, it nearly matched Hillary's eyes. The cover-up was semi-transparent, revealing a purple two-piece swimsuit beneath it. Had Jackson let his eyes linger, he was sure it would have been flattering. Instead, he concentrated on business.

"Try walking around," he said.

She entered the hotel living room and walked over to the window. The camera caught it all, maintaining focus and giving him a sharp image. It was capable of recording four straight hours of video before its microscopic battery needed replacement, and could even be remotely activated or deactivated. Hillary's tablet was fully-charged and Mouse's software was set to record in addition to giving Jackson Hillary's perspective.

"Let's do a quick comms check," Jackson said, activating his earpiece and placing it in his ear. A moment later, Hillary's voice came through loud and clear.

"Okay, we're all set." He thought about pulling a line from *Ocean's Eleven*, telling her she was a natural. But the last thing she ever needed was reassurances from him.

He figured out how to split the screen on the tablet and accessed a game of solitaire as Hillary rode the elevator down to the Mezzanine Level, then proceeded out onto the pool deck. A wide, covered walkway ran between a secluded tropical garden on one side and kiddie pools and the landing pool for the Plunge Waterslide on the other. Both were shielded from view by living palm trees and plants.

The walkway ran into a T intersection, in the center of which was an ornate tiered fountain, reminiscent of some European square. Similar covered walkways ran right and left, leading to two more fountain circles, from which additional paths led to three private, waterfall-fed, adult-only pools, as well as the adventure area and the sports courts at the back of the property. Hillary continued straight ahead, where Oasis's small outdoor casino provided some video poker and slot machines, blackjack and craps tables, and a roulette wheel, all in the shade of canopies. Jackson had never seen people gambling in swimwear before, and he still didn't, seeing as how it was not even ten a.m.

On either side of the casino, secluded areas with cabanas for reading, relaxing, or just avoiding the sun were speckled with palm trees. Straight ahead was Splash, the poolside café and bar with ample shaded seating. More palms, ferns, and flowering bushes cordoned off the cabanas from the casino from the café so that even a pool deck full of people would feel like a private oasis.

But it was not full now. Already there were a few diehard tanners staking out chaise lounges, old folks with books in the shade of a cabana, and lushes at the Splash bar. But the grounds were mostly empty.

Hillary journeyed around the side of Splash, where half a flight of stairs led down to the actual pool area. In addition to a lazy river on the right and a wave pool and surf pool on the left, the area boasted four spacious pools, arranged in a diamond pattern. They were shaped like a club, a diamond, a spade, and a heart. The latter was tucked in another grove of palms and partially encircled by Wade, the swim-up bar. More palm trees dotted the landscape and provided intimacy for the pools while leaving plenty of space for sunlight to beat down on the pools and the concrete deck around them.

Hillary selected a chaise lounge by the spade-shaped pool and oriented it so that she was facing back toward the O. She removed her cover-up and stretched out, giving Jackson a nearly blinding view of the sky.

"Can you sit up a little more?" he asked.

"Excuse me?"

"Unless we're waiting for a solar eclipse, I don't have a view."

"And just what do you want a view of?"

"Hillary, I'm not being a Peeping Tom here. I need to help you keep an eye out for Holloway."

"Fine." She sat up a little, giving Jackson a view of the upper level of the deck.

"That's better. Thank you."

For nearly an hour, Hillary read, at one point turning onto her stomach and giving Jackson a lovely view of the slats of her chaise lounge. She informed him through the earpiece that she was keeping her eyes—hidden behind sunglasses—peeled for signs of Holloway.

After turning back over and back around, she had to rebuff a couple of guys who hit on her and wouldn't take the hint. She threatened to call her boyfriend, and one of them questioned if she had one. Jackson felt a desire to drive over and introduce the guy to his fist. But she eventually got them to leave, which enabled her to strike up a conversation with a brunette two chairs over. That lasted a couple of minutes, and then there was silence.

"You okay?" Jackson asked.

"Why wouldn't I be?"

He just shook his head. The waiting game continued.

At quarter after eleven, Hillary sent a text, which she cleverly kept hidden from Jackson. Her next message, however, popped up on the tablet, interrupting a game of solitaire.

```
ten o clock
```

He typed back:

```
                              Punctuation.
```

She turned her head and upper body slightly and sat up a fraction so Jackson had a view through the necklace. Richard Holloway had emerged onto the pool deck from the same covered walkway Hillary had used. Even from a distance and through a tiny camera, he exuded cool. He strutted, taking his time, smiling at guests—particularly the women—as he made his way in the general direction of Splash. Not untoward Hillary.

Another message appeared on Jackson's screen:

```
fragment
```

He hammered out a reply:

```
                        Quick comback.
```

```
comeback has an e stupid
```

```
                    Says the lady who's
                    never heard of
                    capitalization.
```

Holloway stopped at Splash and spoke with a man in swim trunks and a towel around his neck. Holloway wore a mint green shirt, starched, sleeves up to about the elbow. The top two buttons were open, but he had the physique—and lack of a rug—to pull it off. The pants were white chinos, the belt probably alligator or Chilean otter pelt. Same with the shoes, casual loafers with no socks. Bet they smelled nice.

Go time, Jackson typed.

Hillary's response before she stood was a single period.

Chapter Twenty-Five

HILLARY DIDN'T LOOK at Holloway, didn't act in the least as if she knew he was less than a hundred feet away and this was perhaps her one and only shot. Instead, she wrapped a towel around her waist and sauntered over toward the steps and up to the Splash bar. Her path took her directly in front of Holloway and assured that he would at least see her, along with all the other women currently soaking up the rays. As she walked, Jackson realized the pool deck had filled in.

Hillary ordered a strawberry daiquiri and waited at the bar. The image on the necklace kept shaking, and Jackson realized she was keeping time with the beat of "Call Me Maybe" as it pumped through the bar's speakers. A shadow appeared to her right.

"Neal, this one's on me," the man said. "And I'll have a Johnnie Walker Black, neat."

Hillary turned her head, hair obstructing the camera. "Do you usually buy drinks for strangers?"

"Not always," he said with a grin. Hillary had turned to face him, giving Jackson a perfect view. It wasn't a creepy smile, just casual and charming. For an old dude, anyhow. "But I couldn't help notice the book in your hand," he said, nodding at her copy of Bill O'Reilly's *Killing Lincoln*. Their research had indicated Holloway was an admirer of the Fox News anchor and author. "Are you a fan of Lincoln or O'Reilly?"

"A little of both," she said, neglecting to pick up her room key card—also functioning as a resort-wide charge card—that Neal had slid back to her. "I'm just getting started on this one," she said, opening to where her fingers had her spot marked. Very deftly, she slid the book over the key. "But I've read *The No Spin Zone*, *Culture Warrior*, and my favorite, *Pinheads and Patriots*."

"You're not a fan, you're a connoisseur."

"I don't know about that."

"Here you are, ma'am," Neal said, placing her drink on the bar. A moment later he set down a glass of Scotch. "Mr. H."

"Thank you, Neal."

Hillary lifted the daiquiri with her other hand. "And thank you . . ."

"Richard Holloway," he said. "But you can call me Richie."

"Richie, thank you. I'm Shannon."

"So what brings you to Las Vegas, Shannon?" he asked, cradling his glass but not drinking yet.

Hillary paused before answering, taking a drink of the daiquiri. This was the crucial response, make or break, not just what she said, but how.

"Well, I'm supposed to be here with my boyfriend . . ." She fiddled with the straw for a few seconds and then took another sip. "He's in meetings all day."

"I see. Well, I trust you're finding enough to do?"

"You can't get too much sun," she said. "Which reminds me, I'd better get back there and even my tan."

Jackson winced. Ending the conversation so soon was a risk, but this was her case. He got paid—or rather, didn't get paid—either way.

"Thank you for the drink, Richie."

"My pleasure, Shannon. Enjoy your stay."

Hillary eased away from the bar and strolled back toward her chair. She lay down and Jackson typed out a message. He stopped before sending when a shadow hovered over Hillary.

"You left your key at the bar."

She turned, giving Jackson a view of Holloway as he extended her keycard toward her.

Hillary forced an embarrassed giggle. "I'm always losing things," she said. "Rusty says I'd lose my head if it wasn't screwed on." She reached for the card. "Thank you."

"Not at all."

"That's two favors now," she said. "What can I do to make it up to you?"

Oh, she was good.

"Allow me to sit down?"

"Of course."

Holloway disappeared from view as he presumably took the chair next to Hillary. She inclined hers so that she sat up a little straighter. It gave Jackson a view of a very gorgeous woman in the heart-shaped pool by the swim-up bar, which made it hard to concentrate on Hillary's crucial conversation. Screams from the pools and the background music didn't help any.

"So, Shannon, tell me about yourself."

"What do you want to know?" Her voice went up at the end of each sentence, a little flirty, a little flaky. But just a little. Jackson had sculpted her character as a bit of an airhead, the pretty blond trophy girlfriend of stereotypical fame. Hillary had suggested that Holloway was too sophisticated to fall for a "bimbo" and had said she needed to round out Shannon's character a little if she was going to appeal to him. He couldn't disagree with her argument, as if it would have mattered much had he.

"Where are you from?" Holloway asked.

"Los Angeles," she replied.

"Your first time in Vegas?"

"Um-hmm." She sipped through her straw.

"I hope you've had time to take in some of the sights."

"Not yet. We just got in yesterday."

"How long are you in town?"

"Through the week, but Rusty says that could change. It all depends on work." Her voice was glum. That rotten work.

"What does he do?"

"Well, that's sort of hard to say," Hillary said. "By day he's an insurance broker, but by night he's a documentary filmmaker."

"Oh? What sort of documentaries?"

"Conspiracy theories," she said with ample disgust. "You know, the late-night stuff with a lot of fading images and creepy voiceovers. Shadow government, 9/11 cover-ups, mysterious projects at Area 51." She waved her hand. "I make him sound like one of those kooks with tinfoil on their heads. He actually does his research. He's insistent on not producing anything that isn't verifiable."

"Is he working on a project currently?"

"As a matter of fact, yes. He's got this theory that the Air Force was running some black ops program with the CIA back in the 1980s. His dad was in the Air Force, and Rusty never really bought into the life of a military family. It caused a rift and fueled all this 'expose the government' sort of stuff." She giggled. "I am sorry. That is probably way more than you ever wanted to know." The smile was evident in her voice as she added, "He's an insurance broker."

Holloway was quiet for a moment, sampling the Johnnie Walker Black, Jackson figured.

"How about yourself?" he asked. "What do you do back in Los Angeles?"

"I work part time at my cousin's salon," she said. "I'm trying to get work as a model."

"I like your chances," Holloway said. He kept it not creepy.

"I don't know. It's a who-you-know business."

Another pause. "I might be able to help."

A turn of the head, hair across the necklace. "How so?"

"I know a few people. I can put in a good word."

"Are you in the modeling business?"

"I'm in the business business."

"What exactly does that mean?"

"I own or own parts of several companies," he answered. "I also own a handful of properties around the world."

"Like what?"

"Like . . . this hotel, for example."

"You own this hotel?"

"That's right."

"You're pulling my leg."

"I'm not," Holloway said. "You can look it up online. I also own properties in Atlantic City, South Beach, the Caribbean, Sydney, and Paris, along with oil fields and a variety of technology and manufacturing companies."

"You own all that?"

He nodded.

"How do I know you're really who you say you are?"

Hillary was challenging, but she was doing it with a flirtatious attitude. And, Jackson surmised, a smile that could disarm the Marines.

"Well, I have a business card in my pocket," Holloway said, "but I could have just printed those, I suppose." He too had picked up the playful tone. "I guess you'll just have to trust me."

Hillary took another sip of her daiquiri. "I trust you."

"So what do you and Rusty do for fun?" Holloway asked.

"Oh, we're like all Californians—we go to the beach. Rusty plays tennis. I like to run."

"You a fan of theater?"

"On occasion."

"You should check out *Adrift*. It's a big hit."

"Rusty actually mentioned seeing it tonight. That is if work doesn't take up all day and night."

"Is that why you're here?"

"It was supposed to be a vacation. But his firm is expanding, so he's meeting a few clients in the area. And then he's contacting a couple of potential sources for his documentary. And I'm left to lounge around the pool all day."

"Here," Holloway said. Hillary turned just enough that Jackson could see him reach into his pocket. He withdrew a card, and then a pen. After jotting a moment, he handed it to Hillary. "Take this to the ticket counter in the atrium. Free admission to the show for you and Rusty."

"You don't have to do that."

"I don't have to," he agreed.

"That's three now," Hillary said.

"Trust me, getting to chat with you more than repays the favor."

"You . . . are very charming," Hillary replied.

It was hard to tell who was laying it on thicker, and it was time for Jackson to intervene. He had been waiting for the right moment to tap send on the message he had composed, and he determined this was it.

Hillary's phone buzzed, and she picked it from the small table beside her. "Rusty," she said with no enthusiasm.

"It was nice meeting you," Holloway said, very gallant.

"It's just a text . . ."

"Is something the matter?"

She sighed. "He says he won't be able to make it back for lunch. Meeting 'a source.'"

Holloway kept his charm at bay.

"I guess I ate breakfast alone," she continued. "I can eat lunch alone too. There doesn't happen to be a matinee showing for *Adrift*, does there?"

"I have another thought," Holloway said. "Have lunch with me?"

"With you?"

"That's right. I know a place with a quiet table and a splendid view."

"Is that so?"

"That's so."

Hillary hesitated. "I don't know . . . Rusty—"

"I promise you, just lunch," Holloway said. "No tricks."

She dragged her metaphorical foot.

194

"I tell you what," he said. "You think it over. My private line is on the card I just gave you. I'll have my personal chef, Benoît, serve lunch around one. If you'd like, just give me a buzz and I'll have him set a place for two. If not," he said with a shrug, "then I wish you a lovely stay at Oasis."

"Thank you, Richie."

"It was a pleasure meeting you," he said, standing.

"Likewise."

"Enjoy your book," he said, and slipped off into the crowd.

Jackson fired off another message:

> Don't make the guy
> sweat too long.

im the one sweating
out here

> Well finish your booze
> and hit the showers.

what is that
supposed to mean?

> Nice punctuation, by the
> way. It means, some people
> work better when they get
> a little liquored up.

it was one drink

> Famous last words.

She didn't reply immediately, and for once Jackson thought he'd had the last word.

seems to me i recall
somebody else using
a similar line once

"I hate you" was not an appropriate thing to instant message someone, so Jackson just stewed privately.

is this thing waterproof

> Wouldn't chance it.
> Earwigs either.

then cut transmission

im going to take a brief
dip before i head upstairs
and call richie

           "Richie?"

jealous

           No.

That sounded petulant.

           Of what?

Oh, much better.

ill call you back after
i talk to him

           Who's Ill?

u r a dork

!

           You are an insult to
           the English professors
           at Pepperdine Law School.

that would sting more
coming from a guy with
a diploma

Jackson gave up.

           Enjoy your swim.

i will call you

He sighed as he closed down the software program. He couldn't believe it. His plan had actually worked. Holloway had taken the bait.

But now came the tricky part, reeling in a thousand-pound sport fish.

Chapter Twenty-Six

12:51 p.m.

JACKSON HAD NO idea what sort of fancy, unpronounceable fare Benoît would cook up for Holloway and Hillary, but he doubted it would be any tastier than the spread he'd picked up at Taco Bell. He ate in the parking lot of Town Square, the windows down, an episode of *Leverage* finishing on Hillary's tablet.

Hillary had called Holloway back just after noon, upon returning to their room after a brief swim. He had sounded delighted—according to her—when she had agreed to have lunch with him. He had told her to meet him in the atrium at one o'clock and to come with an appetite. After reporting to Jackson, she had showered and changed, and called him again before preparing to head down.

"Remember, if you need a distraction—"

"I finger my necklace," she said. "I know."

"And if you feel threatened?"

"Jackson, we've been over this. I have all our abort codes and signals memorized."

"Okay. Remember, you don't have to sell him today. Just get him interested."

"I know."

"And don't forget your—"

She disconnected the call.

"Earwig."

He closed Netflix and activated the software that would let him see through the camera again. Hillary was applying lipstick in the mirror. She had changed back into the sundress she'd worn that morning, accentuated now with earrings that complimented the camera necklace. Her hair was down but clipped at the sides, revealing a little more of her face.

"You look good, Hill," Jackson said after placing his earpiece in.

She fixed her eyes on her necklace in the mirror.

"Just trying to give you confidence," he said.

"Thank you." She capped her lipstick. "Now shut up."

Jackson sat back and opened his second chalupa. He ate while Hillary rode the elevator down to the atrium. The restaurants surrounding it were letting out most of the lunch crowd, and an afternoon malaise had settled over the hotel. It didn't last.

Richard Holloway appeared from Hillary's right, changed to a pink dress shirt, no tie, under a white sport jacket. The pants matched. Jackson couldn't decide if he looked ridiculous or very cool.

"Shannon, thank you so much for agreeing to lunch," Holloway said, taking Hillary's hand and kissing it. He immediately let it go. "That is a lovely dress."

"Thank you, Richie. And thank you very much for the invitation."

"Tell him he looks like Don Johnson," Jackson said through the last of a bite of his chalupa.

Hillary, of course, ignored him.

"This way," Holloway said, leading Hillary around a small "bay" of the Lagoon. "I hope you don't mind dining *al fresco*. I had Benoît set a table on the deck."

"That sounds lovely."

He escorted her back toward the center of the atrium, toward the massive rock formation from which the Lagoon's water sprung. They crossed a wooden footbridge, followed a short path through some concealing foliage, and stopped at a door built into the rock and almost invisible to the general public. Holloway placed a thumb on a small biometric scanner and the door recessed into the rock.

"My private elevator," he said, stepping back and gesturing for Hillary to enter. She did, finding herself in an octagonal chamber. "It rides inside the support column that runs through Drop and all the way to the top," Holloway said. The doors closed and the elevator noiselessly began to ascend. The entire ride lasted less than a minute.

"This way," Holloway said as doors parted. Hillary stepped out onto a peach-flecked marble floor and stopped.

"Oh, Richie, this is magnificent."

A wide main hall was flanked on either side by aquariums that reached to the vaulted ceiling some two and a half stories above. Matching staircases curved through the aquariums, which encroached gracefully to funnel the hallway.

Holloway led her straight ahead, beneath a second-story loft, to where the hallway split left and right. Directly ahead, it opened into an elegantly decorated great room.

"I'll give you the full tour later," he said, "but for now, lunch is waiting, and Benoît is very particular about serving his dishes punctually."

Hillary followed him down an equally wide hallway, on either side of which the soft coral-colored walls were adorned with seascapes and nautical artwork. Holloway informed her that the powder room was just down the hall to the right, should she need it, before ushering her through double doors on the left. They opened to a spectacular dining room, the centerpiece of which was a mahogany table that could seat twenty easily. It stretched beneath a crystal chandelier almost as magnificent as the one that had hung between the entry stairways. More nautical-themed artwork decorated the walls of the dining room, painted an understated tan with a wood chair rail that matched the table. It was completely bare.

"I thought all this is a bit much for a two-person luncheon," Holloway said. "This way."

The far wall of the dining room was a bank of windows looking out on the Strip, or rather, the tops of The Cosmopolitan, Aria, Veer Towers, and Mandarin Oriental. In the middle of the windows was a pair of French doors, open to reveal a deck forty-some stories above the ground. Hillary stepped through them and stopped at a small, round table covered by a white tablecloth and set with china equal to that at Fork. A waiter in a white tuxedo stood off to the left, a towel draped over his arm.

"Shannon, please meet Francis, my personal valet," Holloway said as he pulled out Hillary's chair. "Francis, Miss Shannon Hillstrom."

"He's checked our reservation," Jackson said into her ear. "You never gave him your last name."

"A pleasure to meet you, madam," Francis said at the same time. "Would you care for wine?"

"Yes, please," she said, extending her glass to Francis. He had retrieved a bottle from an ice bucket on the table and poured her a glass of white wine.

"Hope you can hold your liquor," Jackson whispered.

Francis also poured a glass for Holloway, then replaced the bottle back in the bucket and disappeared into the dining room.

"Richie, this is too much," Hillary said, looking out at the view, then back at him.

"Not at all. I promised you a quiet table and a splendid view. Aside from the distant sounds of traffic, we have both."

"Thank you very much."

"Think nothing of it." He took a sip of his wine. "So if I may ask, what made you and Rusty choose Oasis?"

"He's fishing already," Jackson said.

"To be honest, Rusty couldn't decide between Wynn or Oasis. In fact, we didn't make reservations until last night. I think the O finally did it for him. That and the casino's high reviews."

"The O?"

"The architecture. I mean, having a theme or a sleek exterior is one thing, but this . . . this is just unheard of before. Where did you ever get the idea?"

"Believe it or not, from blankly staring at a notepad." Holloway folded his hands. "As soon as I knew I wanted to open a Las Vegas resort and casino, I latched onto the name Oasis. It just fit perfectly, given that we're in the middle of a desert and considering the amenities I hoped to provide. But as to how the building should look . . . that took some scheming. I and my team considered everything from the typical three-pronged tower to a Middle Eastern theme that would have been a rip-off of the Sahara, Aladdin, and Luxor. Finally, one day, I was just staring at the word 'Oasis' on a legal pad when my eyes locked onto the O. And it hit me. After that, it was all downhill—aside from several engineering nightmares."

"I can imagine."

Holloway sat back as Francis returned carrying salad plates. "Spinach salad with candied walnuts and goat cheese in honey cider vinaigrette," he announced before departing. They sampled the food, and Hillary quickly complimented Holloway.

"That's delicious."

"Benoît is the best," Holloway said. "He's been with me now for several years, and I've told him he needs to open his own restaurant, fully funded by me. He prefers the anonymity and relaxed life of being a personal chef, however. I can't say as that I blame him some days."

They ate quietly for a few moments.

"Tell me more about your modeling career," Holloway said.

"I'm afraid there isn't a whole lot to tell. I've shot a few spots for local magazines and a mall in San Diego, but that's about it. I'm still waiting for my breakthrough."

"How did you get started?"

Hillary took a bite of her salad before answering. "Some friends and I went to Cabo San Lucas," she answered, tracing the rim of her glass with her finger.

"There was a European ad executive there, shooting a commercial—I don't even remember what for. He needed some stand-ins for a pool shot, and my friends and I were in the right place at the right time . . ."

Holloway was hanging on every word, not touching his salad.

"This ad exec, he sort of . . . noticed me," Hillary said. "I went from an extra to one of the stars of his shoot. He said I had real potential, as a model. That's when I started to think maybe it was true." She reached for her wine. "I know, the young American girl gets duped by the slick European professional, right?"

"Not at all," Holloway replied. "I think this ad executive knew exactly what he was talking about."

"You're not just saying that?"

"I'm not."

She took a drink. "I wish his American counterparts felt the same way."

"Have you thought of modeling overseas?"

"Thought, yes. But it's not very practical for me. I don't have the money, don't know anyone there. And there's Rusty," she said. Perfect, Jackson thought, throwing him in as an afterthought.

"How long have the two of you been together?"

"A little over a year. This trip was actually to celebrate our anniversary. Which," she said as she reached for her glass again, "is why I was a little disappointed when he ditched me at breakfast for work."

"I don't mean to take sides, but I can empathize with the plights of a fellow businessman."

Hillary chuckled in the most polite way possible. "I don't think you and Rusty are exactly on the same level professionally," she said. "He doesn't even own his own home yet, much less this."

Holloway smiled. "I'll tell you something I shouldn't, Shannon." He leaned slightly forward. "I should tell you I got to where I am solely by hard work and determination. Truth is, there was plenty of that. But I also benefited from my share of good fortune along the way. The best inventors, innovators, and artists will usually find a way to shine, but having connections and a little bit of luck turn the road to success into a superhighway."

The small talk continued through the rest of the salads and on into the main course, grilled chicken in a mushroom, garlic, and Merlot sauce, served with fresh vegetables. Hillary again raved about the food while Jackson downed some cinnamon twists. Then Holloway asked about her background, and she told him her parents were immigrants from Sweden. They had come over when they were children, met at the University of Washington, and the rest was history. She made most of it up on the spot. Not bad.

He grew up in Florida, Holloway explained, a child of privilege who wanted out by the time he was eighteen. He briefly tracked his college career, the early days of building his business, and travel to exotic places.

"Does it ever get lonely?" Hillary asked.

"Sometimes," he answered, setting down his glass.

"Yeah, I know the feeling."

They ate in silence for a short while.

Jackson's cell phone interrupted it. He flipped it open and checked the display. Danny Pollack.

He removed his earpiece and answered the call. "Hello?"

"Mr. Douglas, it's Danny Pollack."

"Yeah. What can I do for you?"

"Have you seen the news this morning?"

"No, why? What's up?"

"You were asking about Xavier Stark the other day. Las Vegas Metro found his body in a dumpster this morning."

Jackson sat up straight. "Stark's dead?"

"Shot twice in the back of the head, execution-style."

"By who?"

"No idea. But that's not the reason I'm calling. Stark wasn't alone."

"Brenner?"

"Nope. A former Navy SEAL named Robert Kyle. Killed the same way."

Jackson raked a hand through his hair. "You have anything on Kyle?"

"I didn't, but it was a slow day, so I did some digging. Figured one P.I. could help another."

"I appreciate it."

"I've got a buddy who works as an analyst in Quantico. He told me that Kyle served with distinction in both Iraq and Afghanistan. He was highly decorated, the best of the best, a soldier's soldier. When he was discharged in '09, he got a job at Langley."

"The CIA?"

"That's right."

"Stark worked at a nondescript consulting company in Chevy Chase, just outside Langley. And now the two of them are killed together."

"I've been monitoring local sources," Pollack said, "and Metro has nothing so far. My guess is that's about where they'll stay if this had anything to do with the Company. And by the looks of it, it did."

Jackson looked quickly at the tablet screen. Holloway was listening to Hillary with a smile.

"When you were asking questions the other day, you suggested Stark was mixed up in something underhanded. It's your case and you know it better than I do, but is there any chance you've got the hats switched in this thing?"

Jackson exhaled. "Maybe. You've certainly given me food for thought."

"I haven't given you anything," Pollack said. "In fact, I'm pretty sure I just misdialed."

"Thanks, Pollack."

The P.I. clicked off the phone and Jackson closed his. Was it possible he and Hillary had been reading this all wrong? Just because Kyle was a decorated Navy SEAL it didn't mean he was above reproach. And it definitely didn't mean that the guy he ended up dead in a dumpster with was above reproach. But it certainly suggested that he and Stark had been working together, maybe undercover, and maybe not on the wrong side.

Jackson reinserted his earpiece.

"—by far Paris," Holloway said. "Everything you've ever heard about it is true."

"Hill, make an excuse to go to the powder room."

"Well, I would love to go sometime," she said. "Maybe I can talk Rusty into taking me. Or, I should say, into doing business there."

Holloway smiled. She took a drink.

"Richie, will you excuse me for a minute? I need to visit the powder room."

"Of course," he said, standing as she did. She walked back through the dining room, across the main hall, and down a narrow corridor to the farther of two restrooms, this one marked "Ladies."

"Wow, his house has men's and women's restrooms," Jackson said.

"You didn't call this little powwow to discuss the bathrooms, did you?"

"I just got a call from Danny Pollack. Xavier Stark was found murdered this morning."

"By whom?"

"No idea, but there was another body belonging to a former Navy SEAL named Robert Kyle, a decorated veteran who was now with the CIA."

"Working undercover?"

"That's Pollack's guess and mine. This is a game changer, Hill."

She was slow and measured. "Not necessarily."

"We've got three options. Either Kyle went over to the dark side and he and Stark were up to no good, in which case we've been playing this right all long. But that still begs the question of who popped them and why. Or, Kyle and Stark are the good guys, which means we've had just about everyone tabbed wrong from the beginning. Or, they're the good guys trying to expose the bad guys by pretending to be bad guys, which just muddies the water of who's who. My bet's on one of the latter two, meaning 'Richie' might not be as clean as we'd hoped."

Hillary was quiet for a moment. "So what do we do? Abort?"

"If we proceed as planned, and even if we are able to convince Holloway that I have the means to expose whatever's going on, we don't know any more that it should be exposed. Or, that Holloway wouldn't kill us to keep us from ruining whatever nefarious scheme he has cooked up."

"You don't know that he's up to anything nefarious."

"I don't, but the bodies are starting to stack up. Arielle got too close to the truth and bought it. Now Stark, who might not have been the black hat we thought, is dead along with Kyle. You really want to trust that Richie is on the up and up? I mean, you're the one on the forty-story deck with him."

"I don't see what other options we have."

Jackson sighed. "Just one."

"What?"

"Remember what we said, about getting him to give us the information?"

"Yeah."

"We take it instead."

"What?"

"We find out what information Holloway has, then determine from that who's on what side and which side is the right one."

"How do we do that?" she asked.

"For now, go back to lunch before he thinks something's wrong."

"Do you have a plan?"

"I will. Just listen to the voice in your head."

Chapter Twenty-Seven

HILLARY WAS A pro. She returned to lunch and picked up her conversation with Holloway as if nothing was the matter—as if it wasn't looking more and more like he had blood on his manicured hands. While they talked about travel, art, and Bill O'Reilly books, Jackson pondered some more.

If Xavier Stark was a good guy, then either he had infiltrated whatever group was responsible for using Arielle and other prostitutes to kidnap tourists and cart them off to parts unknown—a group that included Matt Brenner, who worked for Holloway, and the unidentified man from Senator Moore's speech—or Stark was part of the group and they were kidnapping tourists for some altruistic reason. But Jackson couldn't figure out what that would be.

On the other hand, Stark could still be bad. And either way, depending on where loyalties lay, it was hard to pinpoint Holloway's role. Jackson and Hillary had believed that he had been on to something sinister, had thus broken ties with Moore, and gathered evidence to ultimately expose Moore's actions. But was it possible Moore was actually on the right side of things, that Holloway had gone rogue? Or were they both bad?

Or was there just a shortage of dumpsters in Las Vegas in which to dump bodies?

Francis served Holloway and Hillary dessert, a delicious-looking raspberry sorbet. Their small talk continued until he cleared their plates away, leaving the two of them sitting with after dinner coffees. Jackson checked the time on his phone. Lunch had taken almost seventy minutes.

Holloway also glanced at the time, in his case on a gold Rolex. "Would you like to see the rest of the penthouse?" he asked.

Hillary must have nodded, as Jackson heard nothing, but Holloway stood and reached for her hand. He led her inside through another pair of French doors and proceeded to show her an embarrassment of riches. From the massive great room with its dual corner fireplaces and adjacent "parlors" containing additional

205

seating to the billiard room and private poker room to the half tennis court, golf simulator, home theater, and sports memorabilia room, he took her on a tour of the lower level of his penthouse. Then he showed her to his private lounge, where he had a self-serve kitchen, a bar, a dining table and chairs, and a sectional sofa trained on a bank of TVs. He liked to have breakfast there while checking in on world events or take in a late-night ballgame with a little privacy, he explained. Hillary marveled at it all.

Jackson paid loose attention, at the same time plotting a way to still make things work. Their original plan had been for Hillary to merely get Holloway interested in Rusty, a difficult task in its own right, but one she was well on the path toward. Now, he realized, she needed to find out where his safe was, where his computer was, where a potential server might be, all while still enticing him to meet Rusty. And without getting caught.

He perked up when Holloway announced that the stairway in the corner led directly to the master suite.

"Richie, I . . ."

"I promise you, nothing underhanded. I just want to show you the ceiling."

"The ceiling?"

He nodded.

"All right."

She followed him toward the stairs, and he stepped aside to let her go first.

"Find out how many people are there," Jackson said quietly.

Hillary turned over her shoulder as she climbed the stairs. "And you have all this space to yourself?"

"Well, there is my staff. You met Francis, and of course Benoît. And my housekeeper, Rosa. But, still, it does seem rather vacuous at times. So I'm delighted you chose to spend part of an afternoon with me."

They finished the climb into what appeared to be a closet. Or perhaps, the outer chamber of a closet. Holloway directed Hillary through an open door and she stepped into a bedroom fit for a king. The left half was actually the boudoir, separated by a half wall from a spacious, well-lit seating area with a fireplace. Ample windows and a pair of glass doors opened onto another deck.

The bedchamber itself was eye-catching. A four post extra-large bed was draped with silk sheets beneath an elegant, burgundy and gold swirl-patterned duvet and an array of pillows with decorative shams. Elegant, it wasn't exactly manly. Then again, Jackson doubted Holloway's bedroom décor was to impress himself. The floors, cabinets and bookshelves that flanked either side of the bed, headboard, footboard dresser (with a slot from which a flat screen TV could rise up) and the lower half of the wall were all polished honey oak. So too was the ceiling and the floor, except for a gigantic rug beneath the bed and extending out several feet on all sides.

"You must feel the carpet," Holloway said. "Imported from Armenia."

Jackson's view through the necklace camera lowered and tipped down, presumably while Hillary stepped out of her sandals.

"It's magnificent," she said a moment later. "Oh, I would never wear shoes again."

She turned to catch a smile on Holloway's face.

"But I didn't bring you up here to see the floor," he said. He walked beside the bed and pressed a small switch. A soft whirring sound reached Jackson's ears, but he was unable to see what took place. The camera tilted ever so slightly upward, but all Jackson could see were the tops of the walls and bookcases.

"Oh my," Hillary breathed.

"Some of the most exotic species in the world," Richard said. "Moorish idols, yellow tail blue tangs, clown triggers, and several varieties of angelfish," he said, looking upward. Jackson deduced that panels in the wood had recessed to show an aquarium above the bed. "You may not believe it," Holloway said, "but watching them swim around can be an incredibly relaxing way to fall asleep."

"Whereas I listen to Rusty's irregular breathing."

Holloway chuckled.

"Richie, this place is incredible. I'm afraid our rather opulent suite will seem commonplace after this."

"I must admit, at times I almost feel guilty," he said. "But I have worked hard, been very fortunate, and now I'm reaping the fruits."

"You certainly are," Hillary said.

"There's one other thing I must show you," he said. He closed the panels and then led her through the seating area and through yet another set of French doors out into a sunroom. "You would not believe the engineering feat it was to put a couple of skylights into the roof of the building."

"This entire place is an architectural wonder," she said. "Tell me, how do you feed all the fish in these aquariums?"

"It's all automated," he said. "Food, water filtration, water temperature, light—all programmed through a master computer. Have you and Rusty by any chance ventured to Drench?"

Drench was a nightclub located at the bottom level of Oasis, forty feet beneath street level. One entire wall looked out at the underside of the lagoon at the bottom of the Hanging Gardens. Of the multiple clubs and lounges at Oasis, it was the edgiest and most progressive.

"No," Hillary said.

"It takes up approximately one-third of the floor space on the G Level," Holloway said. "The rest is home to a massive computer system that regulates all the water in the Lagoon, the Hanging Gardens, and the rest of the property, as well as maintains a similar food and filtration system for the many aquariums on the premises."

"Just incredible," Hillary said.

"People are amazed by what they see in Las Vegas," Holloway said. "But it's only the proverbial tip of the iceberg. What they don't see—that's what is truly amazing."

They had exited the sunroom and turned to cross an expansive, largely open loft. It looked down on the great room on the right and the entry hall on the left. Farther ahead, an arched passage similar to the one that had connected the sunroom created a portico with a pair of wooden doors.

"I can't even imagine what's through here," Hillary said.

"My office," Holloway said, "but more importantly, the library."

Jackson sat up straight. This was it. "Be sure to get it all on camera," he said to Hillary.

Holloway opened both of the double doors and stepped back. "After you," he said.

Whereas mahogany had dominated the dining room and living room, and honey oak the bedroom, cherry was the theme of Holloway's office. From the floor to the large conference table directly ahead to the trim on windows looking out at the Mandarin Oriental, everything was made of warm, slightly reddish wood. Twelve rolling office chairs were arranged around the table, on which rested two conference phones. A projection system hanging from the ceiling aimed at the right wall. To the left, several plush armchairs surrounded a massive, L-shaped desk—also cherry. A sofa sat against the right wall, which was made entirely of glass, as was the south wall straight ahead. Another deck ringed the office, its views of Monte Carlo, New York-New York, Excalibur, Luxor, Mandalay Bay, MGM Grand, and Tropicana. Not to mention the distant desert and far off mountains.

The left wall of the office had two doors, once of which appeared to be to a private bathroom, and the other presumably leading to the library. The walls were painted turquoise, adorned with blown up photographs of Oasis property from the air, Jack Nicklaus celebrating his signature putt in the 1986 Masters, rolling waves assaulting a rocky coastline, an iconic shot of Michael Jordan's game- and series-winning shot against the Utah Jazz in 1998, and a white lighthouse against a backdrop of choppy water.

Hillary's eyes—and her necklace—swept across it all, then honed in on the desk. It was meticulously clean. No papers, no clutter. Just a pair of flat screen computer monitors in the corner of the L, with a keyboard between them. On the other side of the desk, a closed laptop sat at the ready. Beside the desk, against the east wall, two wooden filing cabinets were joined by a bookcase that had an assortment of collectibles—various business awards, a framed photograph of Holloway shaking hands with George W. Bush, several autographed movie posters and DVD cases, and woodcarvings of various big game animals.

"No safe," Jackson said quietly.

"How do you get any work done?" Hillary asked, approaching the window to admire the view.

"Some days it isn't easy." Holloway's voice grew louder as he presumably stood beside her. "Particularly in the winter when the sun sets in the southwest. I often find myself rotating my chair and staring at the horizon until I lose track of time."

"I bet."

"But come, I must show you the library."

Time was running out, and Jackson needed a diversion, a way to get Hillary some privacy to snoop around. Problem was, he was several miles away and had no idea how to distract Holloway. Unless . . .

As Holloway showed Hillary into a library rimmed on three walls with books—and on the fourth with floor to ceiling windows—an idea began to emerge in Jackson's brain. He wasn't wild about it, seeing as how it struck even him as a little harebrained, but it was all he had. He minimized the view Hillary was giving him and quickly used her tablet to pull up some facts on Google, re-confirming research he and Hillary had conducted previously. The details they'd uncovered were sketchy, and it took him several minutes to fill in a few of the particulars. He hoped it was enough. Meanwhile, Holloway waxed about his book collection, including pointing out several autographed (personally) Bill O'Reilly works.

Taking a deep breath, Jackson pulled out a spare phone—one of several burners purchased for just such an emergency—and dialed Holloway's private line. He heard no ring through his earpiece, which he removed as Holloway stopped mid-pace around a reading table in the center of the library. He removed a phone from his front pants pocket, swiped his finger across the screen, then returned it to his pocket.

Jackson disconnected the call as Holloway apologized to Hillary for the interruption. They exited the library directly onto the deck, and Holloway spieled some gush about the view again. Jackson redialed, then picked up his earpiece.

"Hill, it's me. Get him to answer."

When Holloway looked down at his phone again, she said, "Go ahead and take it. I'll admire the view."

"I apologize," he said. "I'll be brief."

With the camera's image back on one half of the tablet, Jackson watched as Holloway re-entered the library, leaving Hillary alone on the deck. On the other half of the screen, he pecked out a text with one hand.

"This is Richard Holloway."

"Richard. Donny Brisco," Jackson said in a deep, Southern drawl. "Thank you so much for takin' my call."

"Mr. Brisco, I'm afraid this isn't a very good time. Can I possibly arrange to call you back?"

"Well, I'd say yes, but I'm afraid I need to speak with you on a matter of some urgency. About Stricker Oil."

Holloway paused for a moment. "What can I do for you, Mr. Brisco?"

"Are you sitting down?"

"Should I be?"

"Well, I've got something of a proposition for you, Richard."

"Let's hear it."

Jackson pressed send on the message he'd typed to Hillary.

check the office

"My people tell me that you are the primary investor in Stricker Oil, owning fifty-one percent of that company's holdings."

On screen, Hillary turned and found her way to the sliding glass doors that led in from the deck.

"Your people tell you correctly," Holloway answered.

"Well, Richard, they also pulled the records of Stricker Oil, and I see that you boys have quite a successful operation goin' down in Roger Mills County, Oklahoma."

Hillary approached the desk. She knelt down and the camera spotted a black box beneath the corner of the L. An orange light blinked every few seconds, suggesting the machine was in sleep mode.

"Mr. Brisco, I don't mean to be curt, but I don't believe you called just to apprise me of the success Stricker has had down in Roger Mills."

"No, sir, I didn't. Maybe it's time I tell you just who I am."

"I'd appreciate that."

Hillary removed the necklace, and on her hands and knees, moved it around the outside and back of the computer, looking at wires and cables.

Jackson had to remind himself to keep speaking. "Richard, I am the C.E.O., C.F.O., and President of Brisco Oil Limited. Based out of Hondo, Texas, formerly DB Oil, formerly B&R Oil, formerly just a couple of kids what found a bubblin' crude in the backyard," he said with a Texas-sized chuckle. At the same time, he sent Hillary another text.

findthe safe

"You see, Richard," he continued, "we recently acquired the plot of land directly south and west of Stricker Oil's Roger Mills site. Make a fair piece off of it, too."

Hillary stood, quickly clasped the necklace again, and began walking around the office. She scrutinized the bookcase full of knickknacks and the filing cabinets, and peeked behind photo frames. Jackson kept selling. Their research had uncovered Stricker Oil and its Roger Mills County operation, as well as the fact that the plot south and west was up for sale. Everything else was a bluff, one Jackson hoped Mouse could create a significant backstory to substantiate before Holloway did too much digging.

"Here's my proposition to you, Richard, and I said it was urgent and I'll get to that. I want to buy Roger Mills."

"How's that?"

"Now hear my offer before you reject it. I am sure that I cannot offer you what it's worth, and we all know that oil is a rather subjective business. I buy the land and could strike a geyser tomorrow mornin', or it could dry up and I'll be back sellin' used cars in Hondo by the end of the year." He chuckled again as Hillary lifted the photo of Michael Jordan off its hanger. It revealed a safe built into the wall.

Jackson cleared his throat. "In exchange for gettin' such a good deal on Roger Mills, I let you rob me blind on either—or both—of my two hunert'-acre plots in west Texas. I mean whatever price you want to give me to make the deal fair price-wise, and to accommodate you for bein' so accommodatin' to me. Now, of course you can take all the samples you need, bring in your geologists, whatever. I ain't askin' you to sign the contract tonight."

"You did say it was urgent, Mr. Brisco."

Hillary made sure the camera picked up every inch of the safe's visible surface, then carefully replaced the photograph. Jackson desperately needed a second mind to process what he was seeing. The safe had a keypad and, it appeared, a biometric thumbprint scanner on the handle. How were they going to break in?

"Mr. Brisco?"

"I did indeed, Richard, and I'll be brief." He began typing another text to Hillary. "I am leaving tomorrow morning, headed to Sowdy Uh-rabia. I know a sheik over there who's friends with the king and who might be interested in my plots. But afor'n I sell my good ol' American soil to a foreigner, I wanted to give you first crack."

leave the necklace

"Why me?"

"On account of your ownin' Roger Mills."

what?

"And why the swap?" Holloway asked. "Why do you want to unload your plots?"

"Well . . . I'm a thinkin' of movin' my entire business to Oklahoma," Jackson continued. He pressed send.

leave necklace pointed at safe

"You see, I met me a young lady from Lawton, a feisty lil' Boomer Sooner, and I'm fixin' to ask her to be my bride."

where?

"And the plain truth is, she has told me that she won't reside in the state of Texas."

where it wont be ssen

"We take our football rivalries mighty serious 'round these parts."

sene

seen

212

"Now you see, Richard, if we could swap properties, so to speak, it would mean a mighty lot to me and my missus-to-be. And like I said, I'm sellin' my Hondo properties for a song—whatever you think is fair."

Hillary panned around the room, then walked toward the conference table. She set her sandals—which apparently had been in her hand all along—on the table and used one of the chairs to climb up onto the table. The image got shaky and a little blurry as she unclasped the necklace and, if Jackson was right, tried to hang it around the pole descending from the ceiling and supporting the projector.

"Now like I said," Jackson continued, "I don't 'spect you to sign no contract or nothin' right here and now and without lookin' into this matter. But before I offer my business to the A-rabs, I thought I'd at least see if you'd have an interest."

"Well, Mr. Brisco, I appreciate the call, but I can't authorize any sort of dealings without the full approval of the board of Stricker Oil."

"You have an idea on how they might lean?"

"I can't speak for the board, Mr. Brisco, but I will tell you that they are very happy with the current direction of the Roger Mills site."

`done`

He checked the camera. "That sounds like a no, Richard."

`left`

`and down`

"I'm afraid so, Mr. Brisco."

"You won't reconsider?"

`there good`

"I'm afraid not."

`go`

"Well, I understand, and no hard feelins'. I do thank you right kindly for your time, Richard."

"Mr. Brisco."

Jackson closed his phone and scrambled to replace his earpiece. The camera was trained on the Michael Jordan photo that hid the safe, so he had to rely on his hearing to know what was happening.

"I'm down," Hillary said quietly. Then, almost immediately, "Oh, hi, Richie. I'm sorry, I needed to use the ladies' room and I thought I saw one in here. I hope you don't mind."

"Not at all."

"A daiquiri by the pool, wine at lunch, then coffee . . . Everything all right?"

"Just a business proposal," Holloway said. "And not much of one either."

Jackson resisted the urge to feel insulted. He hoped Roger Mills went drier than Death Valley.

"Richie, I can't thank you enough for this afternoon. When I tell Rusty I had lunch with the owner of Oasis, well . . ."

"Speaking of Rusty, do the two of you have plans for tomorrow night?"

"I don't think so," she said. "Why?"

They were moving, Jackson sensed. He hated not being able to see, but it reminded him to remotely deactivate the camera on the necklace, saving battery life for when they would need it.

"I'm having a little get-together," Richie said. "Cocktails, light hors d'oeuvres, perhaps some casual poker. I'd love for the two of you to come."

"Both of us?"

"Absolutely," Holloway said. "I'd like to meet Rusty, and I would certainly like to see you again."

"I'm flattered, Richie, but I can't believe you'd invite a couple of standard guests to your party."

"Don't lay it on too thick," Jackson said. "We want to come."

"There is no such thing as a 'standard' guest," Holloway said. "One of the greatest benefits to owning a property such as Oasis is the people I get to meet. If you have other plans, I'll understand, but if your only hesitancy is feeling undeserving, I assure you, that isn't the case. Please consider it."

"In that case, we'd love to, Richie."

"Super. I'll have Francis see that you get an official invitation. Then just bring it with you and the attendant will let you in."

"You've been too kind," Hillary said. A door opened, and Jackson realized they were at the elevator again. "Thank you again, Richie."

"The pleasure was all mine, Shannon."

There was a pause, then what sounded like a soft kiss. But where? Hand again? Cheek? Lips?

"Your necklace," Holloway said. "You were wearing one earlier."

"Oh, yes. It's in here," Hillary said, presumably patting her purse. "It was starting to chafe. Rusty bought it online, and then I got it wet this morning. A bad combination, I'm afraid."

"It's too bad. It looked lovely on you."

"Thank you. And thanks again, Richie."

"You're most welcome."

Jackson breathed a sigh of relief. He wished he could have seen Holloway's face to know if he bought the story or not. And he wished he could have seen how well the necklace was hidden around the projector support. And he wished he knew how frequently and how thoroughly Rosa cleaned. For that matter, he wished he was back in L.A.

"I'm in the elevator," Hillary announced a moment later.

"Nice cover with the necklace. You think he bought it?"

"If not, he's a spectacular actor."

"Okay, I've got to call Mouse and hope he's not working so he can create a cover story for the deal I just tried to sell Richie on."

"Are you coming back soon? We've got our work cut out for us."

"Tell me about it."

Chapter Twenty-Eight

6:30 p.m.

FOR AN EXTRA fifty bucks, Jackson and Hillary were afforded a table by the water. More accurately, by a giant sheet of glass that looked out at the water. It reflected the myriad colors in the sky, generated by wispy high-level clouds shaded orange, pink, and purple as they caught the last of the day's sunlight. The water itself was smooth as the pane of glass, surrounded by dense, jungle-like foliage to create an intimate feel at the Healing Waters Spa and for the guestrooms with a limited view from the underside of the O.

And for the patrons of Fresh, the upscale seafood restaurant at the base of the North Peninsula. Tables not overlooking the water were situated along one of two slender aquariums teeming with colorful fish and assorted marine life. The lighting was bright and the colors of the walls, floors, and table linens were warm and inviting. A series of murals on the ceiling continued the nautical theme, depicting everything from a pod of humpback whales to the Spanish Armada.

Jackson, playing the boyfriend in need of earning a few points, pulled out Hillary's chair for her. She wore a pink cap-sleeved dress that was the perfect blend of formality and playfulness. Her hair was bunched into a haphazard ponytail with a series of pins holding strands in place here and there. On some women, it would indicate they were about to clean toilets; on others, it hinted of a stroll down a catwalk. Hillary, of course, fell into the latter group.

"Isn't this great, Shan?" Jackson asked as their hostess left them with menus.

"Perhaps not worth fifty dollars though," Hillary answered out of character.

"You gotta go big to make a splash."

"Easy for the guy not paying for anything to say."

"You know a lot of P.I.s that pay for expenses?"

"No, just none that try so hard to get out of them."

They observed a truce while looking at their menus. Jackson had returned to the hotel a little before four, and after getting a full debriefing from Hillary, had begun to lay plans for the next night. First and foremost, he had researched the

Miller 300, the model of safe in Holloway's office. He'd also sent the video Hillary had taken of Holloway's under-desk computer to Mouse, hoping he could identify the specs and any potential interesting aspects.

Hillary, meanwhile, had sketched a thorough diagram of the penthouse, using the video footage and her memory to construct the layout. A basic floor plan wasn't too difficult, but pinning down fast exit routes was a bit trickier. She'd logged in to several public databases, hoping to find blueprints on file, but with no luck. She had also dug up what she could about the deaths of Xavier Stark and Robert Kyle, with little success. Pollack was right, the local cops had nothing.

At six, they'd called a break and decided to make a public appearance. Using the complimentary pass given her by Holloway, they had procured tickets to the 8:00 showing of *Adrift*, the headline show at the H2O Showroom.

By the time they ordered their meals, the sun had set and the pool outside the window was a dark purple trending toward black. Ambient lighting from the city and the O cast enough light to differentiate water from foliage, but not much else.

"I think we should at least discuss walking away," Jackson said.

Hillary glared at him over the centerpiece candle. He'd tried a similar line of conversation upon returning to the room earlier, and it had been a nonstarter.

"No," she said evenly. "We have too much invested."

"It's just money, Hill. You can't take it with you."

"Says the guy who's a month away from broke."

"I'm just say—"

"And it isn't just money. If we walk away now, Holloway will know something's up. Sooner or later he'll find the necklace and run the prints, or he'll run our faces and see past Mouse's smokescreen. We leave this half done, we're more vulnerable than we are now."

"What if we take what we have to the police?"

"We have nothing more than we ever had."

"Except that Stark and Kyle are dead."

"You don't think the police know that?" she asked.

"I think they don't know how they're tied to Holloway, Moore, and Arielle."

"I told Cruz about Stark."

"But not how he's connected."

"We don't know that either," she said more forcefully, yet without raising her voice. "That's what we're trying to find out."

"And need I remind you, we're talking about a felony here?"

"That can be debatable. We're merely looking at something he owns."

Jackson shook his head. "And you accuse me of questionable ethics."

Hillary didn't reply.

He tried his last tack. "What if Holloway suspects something?"

"He doesn't."

"How do you know?"

"Because I'm pretty good at reading people, Jackson. Besides, even if he was suspicious, he's still going to be intrigued by you and your documentaries, so we'll have our opening."

"If you say so."

"I do. It's time to stop second-guessing, because if we're going to pull this off, we need to devote all our energy, effort, and, most importantly, focus to figuring out a plan for tomorrow night."

Jackson took a drink of his ice water, then waited while their waiter set down bowls of she-crab soup in front of each of them. They were steaming, so Jackson crumbled some crackers into his bowl and left it to cool.

"Okay," he said. "We've got the following problems to solve. One, we still aren't sure if it's in the safe or on the computer."

"My money's on the safe. I saw an Ethernet cable on the back of the computer, which means internet, which means it is theoretically hackable. Even if he's got electronic data, I'm guessing it's on an external disk and thus in the safe."

"Okay, fair bet. So how do we crack the safe?"

"I thought that's why I planted the necklace, so we could see the code."

"It was," he said, stirring his soup. He ladled some out and blew on it. "But we have no guarantee he opens the safe." He put the soup in his mouth, then dribbled it back into the bowl.

"You did not just do that."

"Hot."

"We're trying to maintain a cover here, Rusty."

"Well, Rusty doesn't like to sear his taste buds right off his tongue."

"Rusty has some soup on his chin."

Jackson dabbed it with a napkin.

"What if we could get him to open the safe?" Hillary asked.

"How?"

"He mentioned poker tomorrow. We bring enough money to the game that we don't feel comfortable carrying it around all night, and I ask somewhat demurely if he could keep it in the safe for us until later." As she spoke, her voice got a little softer and she tilted her head to the side. She blinked slowly as her eyes widened a fraction and the corners of her mouth tilted upward.

"Um, yeah, that could work," Jackson said.

"Our bigger issue is the thumbprint. We have to procure a legitimate print and figure out some way to lift it."

"We'll research it. It can't be that hard. Finding a valid print somewhere accessible might be the tricky part."

She tried her soup, blowing lightly on her spoon first, then easing it into her mouth. No spitting, dribbling, or red-faced swallowing. Jackson tried his again and found it acceptably cool.

"Two," he continued, "we need access to the safe again. Which means somehow, during the party, one of us needs a reason to sneak back into the office, do so unnoticed, pilfer the safe, sort out what's there, possibly download a file onto a computer, decrypt said file, replace everything, and get out without being noticed."

"And retrieve the necklace."

"Right."

"What else?" she asked as she raised another spoonful of soup from her bowl.

"Three, exit strategy."

"Say 'good night' and 'thank you' at the end of the party?"

"I mean emergency exit strategy. If things go south, we need to get out of the penthouse, the hotel, the city, and perhaps the country."

"Don't be dramatic or anything."

"I'm just trying to be prepared."

They kicked around ideas while finishing their soup. Over main courses of grilled halibut with potatoes and asparagus for her and a grilled shrimp and lobster combo platter for him, they planned out their morning and debated theories about how Stark and Kyle were involved and why they had been killed. But until they knew more, all they had were theories.

They passed on dessert and took the roundabout way to H_2O. From the North Peninsula, a causeway crossed the water that encircled the O. At the end of the causeway, in the corner of the property, was Float, a casual American restaurant with outdoor seating on what looked like a raft hovering on the surface. Turning right, Jackson and Hillary walked along the edge of the lagoon they had overlooked from their table and beside the massive, three-story Tides

Aquarium. The entire pathway was made of bricks lined by a wood railing and lit by actual torches more than a dozen feet off the ground.

They entered through double doors that took them past the entrance to Tsunami, a coffee and donut shop named Dunk, and a smoothie bar, Squirt. Directly ahead of them was H_2O, the five-story showroom, with occupancy for almost five hundred in three different levels of staged seating, all looking down at a huge platform. Like the ancient Roman Coliseum, whose sandy floor could be flooded for staged naval battles, the stage at H_2O could be partially submerged under water to simulate the rising and ebbing tide, a hurricane surge, and even the open ocean. When need be, the water could be drained to reveal a sandy beach. The beach in turn could be lowered, and a tropical jungle raised in its place.

The ceiling was also interactive, with water cannons that simulated a monsoon, realistic lightning and thunder, and artificial light that looked as real as the noonday sun. The backdrop too was realistic, and from their seats in the balcony, Jackson felt as if he was in the South Pacific.

Adrift was an amalgamation of ABC's cult phenomenon *Lost*, the '90s video game franchise *Myst*, and CBS's long-running reality show *Survivor*. Mostly scripted, there was room left for audience participation, particularly when it came time to eliminate cast members. All in all, the show wasn't bad, if a bit long.

At intermission, Jackson floated his arm around Hillary, purely in character. She almost immediately leaned forward, her attention on her phone. He caught her texting again midway through the second act, and casually leaned over to get a look. Purposefully or not, she adjusted her phone so he couldn't see the words. But the look on her face said she wasn't paying bills.

Reminiscent of its inspiration, the ending to *Adrift* left the audience completely confused. It also left them buzzing as they filed out of H_2O and headed for the casino, clubs, or a late-night snack.

"Want to hit the club scene?" Jackson asked.

"I'd rather hit the hay," she said.

"We should at least put in an appearance."

She nodded and took his hand.

They walked through the casino, hand-in-hand, and to the bank of elevators on the north side of the atrium. They entered an elevator with several other people, and Jackson slid his arm around Hillary's waist. He also leaned in close to whisper, "Please don't slap me."

She actually smiled in return.

The elevator made several stops along the way, and Jackson and Hillary were the only two who rode it all the way to the forty-fourth floor of Oasis. In addition to being the launching point for the waterslide, it was also home to Crest, a hip, trendy nightclub. Jackson paid the cover fee, and he and Hillary entered a dark, expansive room that throbbed with almost deafening dance music. Blue, purple, and red lights flashed on a central dance floor, pulsing with the music but doing little to illuminate much of anything. A bar ran around the corner on the right. A few booths were tucked into alcoves on the left. Bistro tables took up space in the immediate center and against the far wall. The rest of the floor was open for dancing, populated with young people grooving and gyrating, flaunting and flirting.

Jackson and Hillary lingered for a few minutes, then exited to the deck. The night air was refreshing after the cloistering interior of Crest, but it wasn't much quieter. More loud music burst from giant speakers in the corners. It was not so loud as to drown out playful shrieks and jovial banter from those "swimming" in and lolling around an infinity pool. This was one establishment at Oasis with no dress code. There were guys in jeans and tees talking with women in cocktail dresses and men in suit jackets flirting with girls in bikini tops.

"So this is what it's like inside an Abercrombie & Fitch," Jackson said to Hillary.

"Are we just going to stand here?"

"You want to go for a dip?"

"Most people do something at a club."

"I have trouble picturing you at this type of environment."

"Oh, why's that?"

"It's too casual. I mean, some of the guys aren't even wearing collared shirts."

Hillary was about to respond, but her phone buzzed and she turned to answer another text. Jackson slipped away to the bar and paid two dollars for bottled water. He returned as she was returning the phone to her purse.

"None for me, thanks," she said.

"I thought you'd want something harder. Besides, it's two bucks a pop."

"So now you're suddenly being frugal?"

He extended the bottle to her, causing her to raise her eyebrows at him.

"We're in love," he said. "We don't have cooties."

Reluctantly she took it and tipped it back. She promptly guzzled it all before handing back the empty container.

"That's great, thanks."

She grinned, then backed away from him and began dancing to the newest Beyoncé hit. Jackson was not a dancer, especially not when it came to the contemporary style of dancing. It looked ridiculous to him, even when cool people did it. Hillary, however, managed to flow in such a way that was perfectly fluid and natural, not the least bit silly.

And of course, she was Hillary, so she looked stunning as she danced. It didn't take long before a couple of guys moved in. She sent them smiles that would entice any man, then made eye contact with Jackson. Her eyes were narrow, taunting. He wasn't sure if she sent him the look as Hillary or as Shannon, but guessed it didn't matter. He took a seat at the end of the bar, ordered another bottle of water, and decided to wait her out.

She danced for thirty minutes, at least once "with" another guy. Jackson pretended to be jealous, including making it known that she was "his girl" when a brunette named Chelsea tried to get friendly. Finally, Hillary sauntered over to him, her face and arms glistening with perspiration.

"Have fun?" he asked.

She answered by reaching for his bottle and promptly chugging the last third of the water. "Why don't you go hit the casino, Rusty?"

"I've got a better idea. Let's head back to the room."

"Okay," she said as if settling on the result of a coin flip. They headed back through the interior of Crest and rode the elevator down a floor, then crossed to the other side of the O and took the south elevators to their floor.

"I take it that was your boy toy you were texting tonight?" Jackson said as they walked to their room.

"It's none of your business."

"In other words, yes."

"I'm sorry, do I need to clear my social agenda with you?"

"Forget I asked."

"That'd be a lot easier if you stopped asking."

"He was my brother, Hill."

"Hillary, and did it ever occur to you that's why I'm not talking to you about it?"

He wanted to retort, but couldn't think of anything. So he shuffled on in silence, hands in his pockets. He did have to stay in character, after all. He thought. He was getting confused anymore as to what was a little bit of tension in

Rusty and Shannon's relationship and what was he and Hillary being at permanent odds.

When they returned to the room, an envelope was waiting for them, having been shoved under the door. Jackson quickly opened it to reveal an invitation specifying the time—9:00 p.m.—and the dress—black tie—for the party the following night, along with a brief schedule of events. Also enclosed was a gift certificate to the spa.

"You must have really turned his head," Jackson said, showing both to Hillary.

"I'm going to shower," was her only response.

"You want dessert? I was thinking of ordering some room service."

She paused, then answered as if on second thought. "A slice of pie actually sounds good. P—"

"Peach, I know."

She nodded and entered her bedroom. Jackson called for two slices of peach pie à la mode, then changed into jeans and a T-shirt. The pie arrived just before Hillary exited her bedroom, smelling like coconut and vanilla, her damp hair loose and wavy. Jackson marveled at how she looked good even in a pair of sweats and a black UCSB T-shirt.

They ate their pie on the couch, the curtains open to reveal the twinkling lights of the Las Vegas night. They discussed their plans for the day ahead one more time, just to make sure they were on the same page and had thought of everything. When they were finished, Hillary took the plates to the sink.

"Want me to unfold the couch for you, or do you think you can figure it out tonight?" she asked.

"I'll manage," he said with a grin. "Hey, you—" he started at the same time as she began speaking.

"Go ahead," she said.

"I was just going to say, you did really good today. That was fast thinking and acting."

"Thank you. And thank you for doing this. It really means a lot to me."

He nodded, shocked that she was exposing true feelings to him.

"Night, Jackson."

"Night," he answered. "Hey," he called and she stopped in the doorway. "Ask you a question, Hill?"

"Not if you call me Hill."

"Ask you a question, Hillary?"

"Mmm, what?"

"When you and 'Richie' said goodbye, where'd he kiss you?"

She didn't answer right away, instead smiling at him. "You really are jealous."

"Rusty is jealous."

"Jackson is too."

"No he's not. He also doesn't know why he's talking in third person."

"Well, *Rusty* can relax. He kissed my hand again."

Jackson didn't respond as she entered her room and closed the door. He changed into something better for sleeping, opened the sofa bed, and then fell asleep wondering why he had cared.

Chapter Twenty-Nine

Wednesday, September 19
8:50 p.m.

"YOU ABOUT READY?" Jackson called as he looked out the window at a descending aircraft. He turned back toward the room. "It's almost ni—"

Hillary stood at the entrance to her bedroom, her hands loosely held behind her back. She should have been standing on a cloud.

Her floor-length evening gown was made of navy blue taffeta with a sweetheart neckline and capped sleeves. It flared marginally from the waist, gathering at the bottom where the hem kissed the carpet. The fabric was draped over the contours of her body as if it had been tailored especially for her, as if she was one with the dress. While alluring, it was neither immodest nor ostentatious. Her hair, in the front, was gently swept aside in a loose braid. The rest was pinned in a bouquet of soft, voluminous curls and wisps that seemed to dance around her face and bare neck. It was adorned by a V-shaped necklace that resembled a tiara, its multiple diamond pendants like snowflakes as they lay against her sternum. Accompanying diamond earrings were reminiscent of miniature chandeliers. Both the necklace and earrings were silver, as was the diamond-encrusted bracelet on her left wrist and the high-heeled dress sandals she dangled in her left hand as she took another few steps into the room.

Hillary's face was angelic and tranquil in its simplicity. Her mascara was just intense enough to catch the eye without overwhelming, and blush subtly called attention to graceful cheeks. Her lipstick was pale pink, delicately accentuating Cupid's bow lips. Her eyes were like lagoons on a sandy beach as she looked at him, a serene smile playing just beneath the surface of her face.

"Wow," he said under his breath. "Hill, you look . . ." None of the words that came to mind—beautiful, gorgeous, stunning—even started to do her justice. She had the magnificence to outshine the most glamorous fashion model and yet the effortless adorability of the girl next door.

Another, "Wow," was all he could utter.

Her mouth parted into a thin smile, her eyes widening in a "thank you" her lips didn't emit.

She glided across the floor and sat down on the couch to fasten her sandals. An intoxicating yet understated fragrance of lilacs or violets or some purple flower wafted over Jackson. He had no idea how to construct a sentence, much less carry out a complicated con and safe-cracking.

"The tux looks good on you," Hillary said softly.

He looked down. It did, but then again, a tux was a tux. It had very little to do with the body underneath it.

"Thanks." He fiddled with his bowtie, which suddenly felt like a choker. "There's just no way to look casual in one of these things."

"That's sort of the point."

"Yeah, I guess."

She stood, smiling wider now. She walked toward him and his throat constricted. He was conscious of every facial movement, every sensation and twitch. Void of saliva, he managed to swallow.

She reached for his tie and straightened it slightly. "Ready?"

He cleared his throat. "Uh, yeah."

She started to back away.

"Hillary."

"Yes?"

He cleared his throat again. "I just wanted to tell you, um . . . if things start going sideways tonight, do what you have to."

Her eyes narrowed.

"If it's time to abort, abort. Don't worry about me making it out or leaving me behind. Get out, get a taxi, get somewhere safe."

She opened her mouth to speak, but he beat her to it.

"And if worst comes to worst, tell them whatever you have to. This was my idea, I forced you into helping. Make something up, whatever you have to to save yourself."

Her eyes honed in on his, then she shook her head slightly. "No. This is my concern."

"You've got a family, Hill. A career. I've got nothing, so if one of us has to bite the bullet . . ."

"No one's biting the bullet, Jackson. We've got this." Her mouth widened in a thin smile. "But it is very sweet of you to say that."

"Maybe we should abort now," Jackson said. "You've complimented me twice in two minutes. You're clearly not feeling well."

"Are you ready?"

"Yeah."

She retreated to her bedroom to grab her purse, and they conducted a quick check to make sure they had everything they would need. At the door, Jackson stopped and snapped his fingers. He walked back to the coffee table and plucked the party invitation off the surface. He tucked it in his jacket pocket. "Seriously, I'm not sure why we're going through all this. The way you look, you could just walk in and ask Holloway for up to half his kingdom and it's probably yours."

"Multiple attempts to compliment my appearance? Now who's not feeling well?"

"Touché," he said as he opened the door.

They walked side by side to the elevators, which they took to the forty-third floor. They walked to the middle of the O, where they used a special code included in the invitation to call the central elevator that would take them to Holloway's penthouse. When it arrived, another younger couple—although not nearly so nattily attired—was already inside.

In character, Jackson nodded at the guy as he entered the elevator. He took Hillary's hand as they stepped to the side. As the elevator began climbing again, he leaned in close to whisper in her ear. "All joking aside, Hillary," he said, remembering the suffix to her name at the last moment, "you look absolutely breathtaking."

She blushed slightly and squeezed his hand.

He had no idea why he felt compelled to declare her beauty. Probably because such splendor couldn't go unacknowledged. He tried to convince himself it was done as a last-minute confidence boost, as if she needed it.

With a soft ding, the doors opened, revealing the marble hallway lined by aquariums Jackson had seen through the camera in Hillary's necklace. In person, it was jaw-dropping. He stared for a moment at walls of water that reached twenty feet to the ceiling. He recovered just in time to hand his invitation to a young man in a tuxedo with long coattails.

"Miss Hillstrom," he said with a slight bow. "And Mr. Jackson. Welcome. Mr. Holloway is receiving guests in the drawing room."

Her arm entwined in his, they walked slowly down the hall and beneath the loft above. The strains of classical violin music reached them first, then the hum of light conversation. They stepped down into the living room, already populated by more than a dozen people. They were young and old, black, white, Hispanic, and Asian. All the gentlemen wore tuxedos, all the women elegant evening gowns. None could hold a candle to Hillary.

Holloway spotted them and a broke away from a young Asian woman. He smiled widely as he approached them. Jackson was wrong about tuxedos. He didn't know what it was, but Holloway's gave him an incredible aura of suave, cool, and charming.

"Shannon," he said, clasping her hand and gently lifting it to his lips. "You look magnificent this evening."

"Thank you, Richie."

"You must be Rusty," he said, turning and extending his hand to Jackson. "It's a pleasure to meet you."

"Likewise, Mr. Holloway."

"Please, call me Richard."

"Likewise, Richard. And I have to thank you for entertaining Shannon yesterday."

"Oh, it was my pleasure."

"And thank you so much for the spa certificate," Hillary said.

"Did you have a chance to visit yet?"

"This morning. It was fantastic."

"Well you're very welcome." He shifted his eyes to Jackson. "Shannon tells me you've been enjoying the casino."

"Not as much as it's been enjoying me, I'm afraid," Jackson answered. "Truth is, I've been too busy with work or wining and dining Shannon here to have much time for serious gambling."

"Speaking of work, I understand you're in the insurance business and something of an entrepreneurial filmmaker on the side."

"Only if entrepreneurial means floundering," Jackson said with a grin.

"Shannon told me a little about your latest project. It sounds fascinating."

"Now I know you're just being polite."

"Not at all. I need to greet some of the other guests, but perhaps we could talk later. I'd love to pick your brain on some things."

"Yeah, sure."

"Excellent. Benoît has prepared some fabulous delicacies," he said with a nod toward the north parlor. "Please help yourself. There's an open bar as well. Until later . . ."

"Oh, Richie, I'm sorry, but could I press upon you for a small favor?" Hillary asked.

"Of course. Name it."

"You mentioned poker the other night, and we brought a fair amount of cash with us. Frankly, I'm a little uncomfortable walking around with it," she said, flexing her clutch purse. "Do you have an office safe or something where you could stash it until later, if it's not too much of an imposition?"

For just a moment, a hint of misgiving played across Holloway's face. It was quickly replaced with a smile. "Of course. Would you like to accompany me?"

"Thank you, Richie."

"Rusty. We'll talk later."

"Absolutely," he said, shaking Holloway's hand again. "I'll grab you a drink, Babe," he said, then watched them exit to the hallway and presumably the stairs. He and Hillary both wore their earpieces, so he listened to her and Holloway make small talk as they climbed the steps. Meanwhile, he probed farther into the room, making a mental list of everyone he saw. Another couple had arrived since them, bringing his count to fifteen, plus Holloway, plus him and Hillary. And the attendant, a bartender, probably several wait staff. It was getting crowded, at least for their purposes. Spatially, the large drawing room still felt empty.

It was not for lack of décor. The peach walls were adorned with priceless artwork. A polished hardwood floor was segmented by wood trim chairs and couches, ornate end and coffee tables, and antique lamps, all arranged around rich, colorful throw rugs. They formed several cozy nooks in a room that still was spacious and flowed naturally.

Two middle-aged ladies sat chatting on a couch to Jackson's left. An older, dark-haired man in army dress blues was holding court with several younger men to his right. From farther into the room, the booming, Southern accent of a heavyset, balding man carried over all the other conversations. From the snatches Jackson heard, he was discussing the decrease in the price of cotton. Then there was the black man in the corner, holding a plate of hors d'oeuvres. In addition to a standard tuxedo, he wore a Chicago White Sox baseball cap, brim flattened, set slightly askew and tilted up on his head. Clinging to his arm was a young woman in a slinky black dress, her blond hair cascading over bare shoulders. She looked familiar to Jackson, but he couldn't place her.

In his ear, he heard Holloway offer to let Hillary accompany him to the office.

"That won't be necessary," she said. "I trust you."

There was a rustling sound, then a soft whistle from Holloway. "That's a lot of money."

Ten thousand, in fact, taken from Arielle's stash. That afternoon, Hillary had contacted Darla Fazekas, who under Nevada law, would be the rightful heir of Arielle's possessions. Darla had confided in Hillary that she was dying of lung cancer and had no interest in Arielle's money. Detective Cruz had then confirmed that Las Vegas Metro had not uncovered any other next of kin, although Hillary hadn't told him why it mattered. She had then, as the legal expert, assured Jackson that the money was as good as theirs.

"Not too much, I hope?" she said to Holloway. "You said 'casual' poker, and I wasn't sure what that meant."

"Different things to everybody. I'll make sure it's safe until you're ready to play."

"Thank you."

"Not at all."

A minute later, as Jackson was waiting on the bartender to mix her Manhattan, Hillary's voice came muted in his ear. "So far, so good."

Chapter Thirty

10:13 p.m.

BENOÎT'S TALENTS HAD not been embellished. The hors d'oeuvres were delicious—prosciutto-wrapped grilled scallops, stuffed mushrooms, paprika- and parsley-dusted deviled eggs, endive spears with sweet potatoes and bacon, crab salad canapés, zucchini and goat cheese tarts, and an assortment of crackers, cheeses, and meats. Then there were desserts: lemon tartlets with meringue caps, chocolate-coconut cheesecake squares, mini raspberry and cream éclairs, key lime whoopie pies, and the old, reliable chocolate-covered strawberries. Jackson was in danger of losing focus on his and Hillary's objective.

Already there were a few glitches. Hillary's necklace had not been disturbed from its position atop the projector in Holloway's office, and, having been activated remotely by Jackson, it had recorded Holloway accessing his safe. When Jackson had slipped out to use the restroom, he had withdrawn Hillary's tablet from his inside jacket pocket and watched the feed on Mouse's app. Holloway had not turned on the lights, so it had taken a quick call to Mouse to enhance the image, enabling Jackson to see the digits Holloway had entered on the keypad: 3-3-9-1-1-3-0-9. The last two digits had been partially obscured because Holloway had chosen that moment to lift with his left hand the stacks of cash Hillary had given him. All Jackson had been able to determine was that the last two keys were higher than the bottom row and possibly a repeat. 2-2, 3-3, maybe 2-3 or 3-2. He'd reported to Hillary, and both had been running numbers in their head, trying to deduce the combination.

Procuring a fingerprint was proving difficult too. Their plan had been to nab a glass or plate or utensil used by Holloway, but so far, he hadn't eaten and hadn't relinquished his Scotch glass. And the crowd had swelled to nearly thirty, making it difficult to do anything undetected.

Then there was the tacky blonde hanging, quite literally, on the guy with the White Sox cap. Jackson was sure he knew her from somewhere, but that somewhere was a mystery. Yet he got the feeling it mattered. So in addition to

231

mulling possible safe combinations and looking for a way to get his hands on Holloway's glass, he was running her face through his brain's facial recognition. So far, no match.

In addition to eating as many crab salad canapés and prosciutto-wrapped scallops as he could, Jackson had made the acquaintance of half the people in attendance, most with Hillary at his side. Not normally one to schmooze at parties, Jackson figured the more he knew about anyone on the premises, the better. He and Hillary also tried to pin down the number of staff members working the party and kept an eye on anyone headed upstairs. So far, the party seemed to be contained to the drawing room, the two side parlors, and the deck.

Having dispatched a few more of Benoît's stuffed mushrooms, Jackson sought out Hillary. She was chatting with a youngish couple in the drawing room, next to a painting of a marina at sunset. He slipped his arms around her waist from behind and planted a kiss on her cheek. "How's it going, Peaches?"

"This would be my boyfriend, Rusty," she announced to the couple. "Rusty, this is Randall and Miranda Betancourt."

"Randy and Randy," the man said with a nervous laugh. He was thin, with an odd-shaped head made more so by square, wire-rimmed glasses that sat atop the high bridge of a very pointed nose. His wife was equally gaunt, pale as death, with eyes like coal. Jackson couldn't tell if she was ill, bored, or preparing to cast a spell on Mordor.

"Nice to meet you," Jackson said, pumping both of their hands. His grip was weak; hers was a wet rag.

"Randall is a software exec from San Jose," Hillary said.

"Ah, a fellow Californian."

"Yes. Shannon says you both are from Los Angeles."

"Born and raised," Jackson said.

"How do you all know Richard?" Miranda asked. Her voice suggested that of Jackson's three choices, she was ill. It was nasally and pitched.

"We actually just met the other day," Shannon said.

"He saw my little angel reclining poolside and the rest is history," Jackson said with a wink and a grin. "How about you two?"

"We met vacationing in Belize, actually," Randall said, thrusting his hands into his pockets. "We had neighboring condos, played a few rounds of golf together, and a friendship formed. We try to make it out here a couple of times a year to see Richard."

Jackson made business-related small talk for a few minutes, then asked if he could ferret "Shannon" away. They found privacy in the south parlor.

"What's up?" Hillary asked.

"Fix my collar or tie or something," Jackson said.

"Why?" she asked, reaching up to do so.

"I've been thinking about the numbers. The nine and one got me thinking about dates, like something that happened in 1991. But Holloway was only thirteen or fourteen then."

"First kiss?"

"If he made out with a number thirty-three maybe."

She gave him the evil eye before lowering her arms. "Thirteen, oh-nine. September 13, 1991, in reverse?"

He shook his head. "I thought so maybe too, but what of the thirty-three?"

"And the last two digits," she sighed.

"And then the thirty-three did it."

"You figured it out?"

"Holloway went to school in Chicago in the mid-'90s, when the Bulls were huge. Scottie Pippen wore number thirty-three, and I'm pretty sure Dennis Rodman wore ninety or ninety-one."

"Which one?"

"Check it out on your phone."

She retrieved it from her purse. A moment later, she announced that Rodman had indeed worn jersey number 91.

"Okay, now check Luc Longley and Ron Harper."

"Who are they?"

"Other starters."

"How do you know that?"

He shrugged. "Common knowledge."

A moment later she confirmed their jersey numbers, 13 and 9.

"Know who's missing?" Jackson asked.

"Michael Jordan."

"Two-three. It fits what I saw."

"And the safe was behind the picture of Jordan," she said.

"Now we just need a print."

"That's good work."

"And Mom said I spent too much time watching sports."

"We should get out of here," Hillary said. "Rejoin the party."

"Hey, that blonde who's only half dressed look familiar to you?"

"With the guy in the baseball cap?"

"Yeah. I've seen her somewhere, but I can't place it."

"Maybe you saw her around the hotel."

"Yeah, maybe."

"Don't worry about it. We've got bigger fish to fry."

"Right."

They exited the parlor and mingled for a while again. Jackson sidled up to a group telling war stories, from the huge fish they'd caught, to modern-day cowboy tall tales, to actual war stories in the case of the man in dress blues. When Holloway joined the group, he introduced Jackson to Colonel Lance Michaels, U.S. Army.

"Retired," Colonel Michaels added with a firm handshake. He had dark hair, graying at the temples, and a mustache that made him resemble Tom Selleck, halfway between his *Magnum P.I.* days and his run on *Blue Bloods*.

The stories continued while the alcohol flowed. Jackson kept an eye on Holloway's glass, which had been refilled since he last saw it. But Holloway nursed his drink slowly, and Jackson was forced to listen—as Rusty—to an impassioned discussion between Michaels and a man named Archie Summers regarding the role the U.S. military should play in the Middle East. Jackson wanted to side with Michaels and say bomb the tar out of anyone who so much as sneezed in the direction of Israel. But Rusty, somewhat disenfranchised with the military, kept his mouth shut.

Eventually Holloway stepped away to greet some early-departing guests, and Jackson used the opportunity to drift away from the conversation as well. He refilled a plate with a few more appetizers and conveniently hung in Holloway's line of sight as he returned to the drawing room. Holloway spotted him and grinned.

"Mr. Jackson, not going to weigh in on Middle East diplomacy."

"We've got enough problems here, frankly."

"Correct me if I'm wrong, but Shannon said you were working on a project about the Air Force and some sort of covert activities?"

Jackson launched into a rehearsed story about his father's time in the Air Force, the traumatic effect it had had on little Rusty, his frustration with so much of the secrecy surrounding the military, and various instances of military oversight. He avoided straying into politically inflammatory waters, instead citing claims of sexual discrimination, lack of quality care for veterans, and the like. He combined a few facts with more rumors and a lot of flat-out imagination. But it sounded good.

By the time he got around to explaining the specific nature of his documentary—a covert, nefarious joint operation between the Air Force and the CIA—they had retired to the south parlor. Originally, Jackson and Hillary's plan had hinged on the hope that Holloway would see Rusty's documentary as a method of disseminating "the goods" he had assembled to the public. They had hoped he would confide in Rusty and divulge details about Silver Dawn, Blane Air Force Base, and, ideally, any connection between the project, the base, or the key players to Arielle or Warren McKenzie. But given the twist of Xavier Stark's death, Jackson now simply tried to deliver a believable backstory that wouldn't cause Holloway to suspect he was being conned. Holloway listened attentively, beyond the extent of a man humoring his guest. He plied Jackson with questions, deftly trying to determine just what Jackson knew about Blane or Silver Dawn. He never actually mentioned their names, and Jackson couched his answers so as not to confirm or deny anything.

Eventually, Hillary floated into the room and hovered over Jackson's shoulder. At a break in the conversation, she asked, "You're not bothering Richie with all your crazy theories, are you?"

"Not at all," Richie said. "It sounds like he's got the making for a very solid project."

"I'm still a ways off," Jackson said.

"I believe I could use a refill, however," Holloway said.

"Allow me," Hillary said, rising. "Scotch?"

"Neat," he said.

"Honey, anything?"

"Just a water."

Hillary took Holloway's glass and headed for the bar. His heart pounding with excitement, Jackson made his closing pitch to Holloway. He listed names of former military members who had gone on the record—and cited several more who had done so under the condition of anonymity—who would testify to some of the alleged incidents his documentary would expose. Originally, he would have spiced it up a little more to get Holloway to dish. Now, he sang a slightly different tune to give credence to his story and keep Holloway's mind from possibly wondering why Hillary had offered to refill his drink.

Before he was finished, Archie Summers and a heretofore unseen woman joined them. She was young and attractive in the snooty, artsy sort of way. Very

Hollywood. Immediately, they dived into the conversation. Dovetailing off Jackson's comments about covert projects and secrecy, Summers launched a tirade about military impropriety, wartime injustices, and a host of other left-wing concerns. His lady friend also got in on the action, her particular gripe seeming to be the flagrant mistreatment of illegal detainees at Gitmo. Jackson was losing control of the conversation, but as Hillary returned and sent him a look of confirmation, he realized that was okay.

Hillary delicately sat in an end chair and pretended to care about the conversation. A few minutes later, as Archie had taken back over from his wife and was railing about the injustices committed in the War on Terror, an elderly man with a not-so-elderly woman in tow appeared in the parlor doorway. "Ah, there you are, Richard," he said in booming, austere voice, tinged with a trace of British influence.

"Lyle, leaving us so soon?"

"I'm afraid so. Eloise has an early flight to Portland tomorrow."

Richard stood, as did Jackson, Hillary, and the left-wingers. "Rusty, I really have enjoyed our conversation," Holloway said. "Shannon mentioned you'd be staying here for a few more days. Perhaps we could get together and chat some more. I'd really like to discuss some of the particulars of your documentary. That is, if you're interested and if you have the time. I don't want to take you away from your beautiful girlfriend any more than necessary."

"I'm sure we can work out something. There's always the spa again."

"Wonderful."

Holloway excused himself to say goodbye to Lyle and Eloise, and Jackson prepared to slip away with Hillary and discuss their plans. But Archie Summers immediately picked up the conversation where they had left off, continuing to harangue on how America had become as bad as the terrorists it pursued. When it became apparent he wasn't stopping anytime soon, Hillary slipped over to Jackson.

"I'm going to get something to eat," she said, then leaned in close. She quickly whispered, "Planter by west entry to north parlor," before brushing her lips against his cheek. She patted his lapel as she retreated, excusing herself from the Summers with a smile.

"Honestly," Janet Summers said, "how can men like Colonel Michaels wear the uniform knowing what they've done to those men at Guantanamo Bay?"

Jackson decided on a quick kill. "I know. If it was up to me, I'd have just shot them all right away."

Archie looked as if he had been slapped in the face. Janet nearly fainted.

"Will you excuse me?" Jackson asked. "Those canapés are just spectacular." He brushed past them and back into the drawing room. The crowd had thinned slightly, with Michaels still telling tales in one corner and several ladies drinking and chatting around one of the two massive fireplaces. Jackson's eyes found the planter Hillary mentioned. It contained a huge fern, and Jackson wondered when he was supposed to dig through it for a Scotch glass without being observed.

Holloway was nowhere to be seen, at the moment, and neither was Hillary. So Jackson wandered out to find the restroom, using the excursion as an excuse to get a better visual of a floor plan he had memorized off blueprints and video from Hillary's necklace. The hallway that led to the north bathrooms (the penthouse had two his and hers powder rooms on the main level alone) also ventured past Holloway's sports memorabilia room to the kitchen. Jackson chanced a quick peek into the kitchen and saw two men at work. One was a waiter Jackson had seen milling about. The other, judging by his white jacket and chef's hat, was Benoît.

From inside the men's room, Jackson spoke into his earpiece. "Hill, what's your ten-twenty?"

"This view really is something," she said a moment later. The feminine voice that replied was unfamiliar to Jackson, but he'd gathered what he needed to.

As he exited the bathroom, he nearly bumped into the familiar-looking blonde. His mind clicked a few times, as if he was getting closer to figuring out her identity. It unnerved him that he couldn't place her, especially since something told him it was relevant.

Depositing his bottle of water in a trash receptacle in the north parlor, Jackson pushed out onto the deck. The air was balmy and invigorating, especially when Jackson saw two beautiful women standing against the railing, backlit by the curved, blue face of the Harmon Hotel across the street. One was Hillary, still as resplendent as she had been a few hours ago. The other was a slightly older woman, maybe in her late-thirties or early-forties. The years had been more than kind. Her youthful face glowed with a placid contentment, and reddish-brown hair fastened in a loose chignon had a luster to match the city lights behind her. She wore an ivory bateau gown to offset well-tanned, flawless skin. The liquid in her champagne flute was perfectly clear and void of bubbles, suggesting the faintest of distensions in her dress was not a result of bad tailoring or the beginnings of mid-life flab, but rather the first signs of a baby bump.

Hillary introduced her to "Rusty" as Tabitha Ellsbury. Her husband Barrett was a spinal surgeon at Summerlin Hospital Medical Center. Jackson emulated Holloway by lifting her extended hand and delicately brushing his lips over the back of it. The gesture appeared to earn him points.

"Would you mind terribly if I borrowed Shannon from you for a moment?" he asked a smiling Tabitha. "This view is far too romantic not to steal a midnight kiss."

"Please. And if you see my husband, pass on a little of your charm."

Grinning widely, Jackson extended his elbow and Hillary latched on. They began strolling ever so slowly northward.

"Smooth," she said, "but I wouldn't call a view of flickering marquees, billboards, and high-rise casinos romantic."

"It's not even eleven-thirty, either," he said.

"Did you find the glass?" Hillary asked.

"No. Still too crowded."

"We'll have to make our play once the poker game starts."

"I've been thinking about that," Jackson said. "I still think it should be me who plays."

"Why's that?" she asked. It had been the one part of the plan they had been unable to settle on during a morning and afternoon of strategizing, or during their late-afternoon trip to Hoover Dam under the auspices of relaxing before "game time."

"It just seems more natural," he said.

"What does that mean, male chauvinism?"

"Think about it, Hill. Which fits better, the guy playing poker while the lady mingles about, maybe wanders around to explore the décor of the penthouse, or the lady playing poker while the guy browses seascapes in the hallway?"

"It is chauvinism."

They had reached the end of the deck, which wrapped partway around the north end of the penthouse. Hillary turned to face him, her back to The Cosmopolitan, Bellagio, Caesar's Palace, and Planet Hollywood. Not sure who was watching, Jackson wrapped his arms loosely around her waist.

"Let's say someone observes one of us sneaking toward Holloway's office," he said. "Which is more believable, me or you, who had been there earlier, who lost a necklace or wanted to see the view again or check out his library?"

"If either of us is caught in his office, I don't know that we can talk our way out of it." She placed her arms loosely around his neck. "And which of us is more likely to hold Holloway's attention at a poker game, you . . ." She leaned in close as she stroked the back of his head with a couple fingers, then gave him the softest, most technically wonderful short kiss ever. "Or me?"

A dozen thoughts raced through his mind, most of them having to do with Hillary's lips. He chased them all away. "Um, you, clearly. But you didn't have to kiss me to prove it."

She smiled sweetly. "We have approaching company at your seven o'clock."

Jackson would have struggled to read a digital clock at the moment, but he got the message.

"So I play?" she asked.

"Can you come up with a good reason why I'm not playing?"

"You have a lousy poker face."

"And why I'm not hanging around to watch you play?"

"I'm sure you'll think of something," she said, drawing him closer. She then gave him a play shove and a leering smile.

He turned as footsteps sounded behind him. It was Randy Betancourt. The male Randy.

"Sorry to interrupt you two lovebirds," he said with an awkward grin, "but Richard is recruiting players for poker. He said the two of you were interested."

"Very," Hillary said, running her hands down Jackson's lapels. "Thank you, Randy," she said, starting past him. She dangled one of her hands behind, blindly finding Jackson's fingers with hers and giving them ever so subtle of a tug.

With a "what are you going to do?" look at Randall, Jackson let her pull him back toward the drawing room. Randall gave them space, and as they neared the doors, Hillary looked back over her shoulder, her eyes dancing with coquettish delight.

"Remind me again, which are worth more, the red or black cards?"

Chapter Thirty-One

RICHARD HOLLOWAY LED most of his remaining guests down the hall, gesturing in turn to a billiard room to the right, his home theater and powder rooms to the left, and to the wall ahead of them where Benoît had moved the remaining hors d'oeuvres. He then ceremoniously drew back the double doors of his poker room and stepped aside to let his guests enter.

Like the rest of the penthouse, it was opulent. Octagonal in shape, four of its walls were paneled with teak wainscoting, their top half painted taupe to match the ceiling. Two more walls with the same design were broken by double doors opening to the hall from which they had just come and, presumably, to the deck. The other two walls, right and left, were floor to ceiling aquariums. Backlit with a dull blueish light, they contained baby sharks.

The floor was Egyptian blue carpet, its softness apparent even through Jackson's wingtips. It matched the velvet on an oval poker table in the center of the room, with seating for ten on leather armchairs. Two unopened decks of cards sat on the table, along with several stacks of brightly colored chips. A middle-aged woman with short, graying blond hair, wearing the official blue vest over white dress shirt of all Oasis casino staff, stood guard at the table. A small self-service bar lined one wall and contained a variety of liquors, mixers, and beers. Several armchairs and sofas were placed along other walls, giving those not playing a vantage point. Even when nearly twenty people had entered the room, it was not crowded.

Holloway pulled Jackson aside as everyone was entering the room. From his pocket, he withdrew an envelope. He discreetly placed it in his hands. "I will not be offended if you count it."

"I never insult a host," Jackson said. "Thank you, Richard."

"Of course," he said, patting Jackson's shoulder.

"But, Shannon's the one who will be playing tonight."

"You're not a poker player?"

Jackson grinned. "No poker face. Craps, blackjack, they're one thing. But I don't have a demeanor suitable to bluffing and calling bluffs."

"It's true," Hillary said, appearing at his shoulder, "He actually tells me if he doesn't like my clothes."

"I have to admit, I didn't take you for a poker player, Shannon."

"I'm afraid I get it honest. Every Saturday night, my dad and my uncles would gather in our basement for their weekly game. Gradually, I learned to play and got hooked. I hope you don't mind losing your money to a woman," she teased.

"In this case, it would be a pleasure."

Holloway broke away from them, and once everyone was gathered, he introduced Patricia, a cashier from Oasis's casino. With the group standing around the table in a circle, he made formal introductions.

He started with Dr. Barrett Ellsbury and his wife Tabitha, then "Randy and Randy" Betancourt. Next came Colonel Lance Michaels, followed by Felipe Ortega. He was a Texas oilman, and Jackson cringed when he heard his occupation. He hoped Holloway didn't drum up a discussion about Brisco Oil Limited during the course of play. Ortega was accompanied by his daughters Sofia and Liana. They were young and attractive, and, if Jackson wasn't mistaken, he had caught Sofia making eyes at him earlier.

Next was Sara Kawahara, the young Asian woman Holloway had been speaking to when Jackson and Hillary had arrived at the party. She wore a high-necked backless dress, black with a blue and green floral print, her dark eyes revealing nothing as they peeked out under straight bangs. "Rusty and Shannon" were the next to be introduced, followed by Logan Guidry, the boisterous Southerner, and his wife Jenny.

Holloway panned the room to the man in the White Sox cap, whom he introduced as Davey Brown, along with his date, Blake. At the mention of her name, bells sounded in Jackson's head. Like a distant object coming into focus, he knew he was about to place her.

The final player was a woman, Vanessa Harris. She was tall and elegant, with creamy black skin and curly hair held behind her head by an ornate clip that probably cost more than Jackson's net worth. Her gown, like Hillary's, was navy blue. A one-shoulder number, it was covered in sequins, and belonged in a Miss America pageant. So did Vanessa Harris. She was attended by her "assistant," Collins Bratton. Short and bald, with a build like a linebacker, he was either a personal valet or a bodyguard. Or both.

Harris's stunning appearance momentarily sidetracked Jackson's brain, but it returned to Blake. Where had he seen her? He tried picturing her with a different hairstyle, a different colored dress, various clothing styles. Where . . .

Holloway announced the rules of the game—no-limit Texas hold 'em. But he reminded everyone it was a gentleman's—and ladies'—game, and asked them to keep that in mind. "Patricia will be happy to change your cash for chips," Holloway said. "Or as always, cash plays."

The room chuckled politely, and at his invitation, the players took their seats. Jackson gave Hillary a good luck peck on the cheek and drifted to the corner. It also happened to be where Sofia Ortega was drifting, and she sent him a cockeyed smile. He returned it, his mind already contemplating how she could become an asset.

Blake. It was coming, coming, coming . . .

Hillary took a seat at one "corner" of the oval table, with Davey Brown on her immediately left. Colonel Michaels, Sara Kawahara, and Logan Guidry were along the left side of the table, in front of Jackson. Holloway and Vanessa Harris rounded out the end opposite Hillary, with Dr. Ellsbury, Felipe Ortega, and Randall Betancourt, who was immediately on Hillary's right, completing the group. Ten seemed like an awful lot for a game of poker until Jackson remembered that in Texas hold 'em, each player was dealt only two cards.

After all the players had exchanged cash for chips, the total potentially in play equaled almost fifty thousand dollars. "So much for a low-stakes poker game," Holloway said with a chuckle. "Just as a precaution, I think we ought to keep this all somewhere secure." He grinned as he put the money in a manila envelope supplied by Patricia. "If anyone doesn't trust me, you're welcome to accompany me to my office safe."

Michaels slowly rose, Jackson thought to take him up on it. "I'll have the 4th Infantry Division at my disposal if you try to cheat me," he said with a crooked grin as he turned toward the bar.

"He's not joking, either," Holloway said, and he slipped from the room with the cash.

"So what part of Texas you from?" Jackson asked, taking a half step closer to Sofia. Her hair was wavy and black, just past her shoulders. Her green halter dress matched her eyes, both of them engraved invitations.

"San Antonio. How 'bout you, cowboy?"

"L.A."

"Ah. Beach bum."

Jackson grinned. Wide. "Among other things."

Liana joined Jackson and Sofia as Holloway returned and the game began. She was older than her sister by a few years, had slightly longer hair, and her dress was a little more modest. Neither of them were exactly Mennonites. The trio made small talk about life in L.A. and San Antonio, their stays in Vegas—the Ortega sisters had been out partying at CatHouse and PURE until four in the morning—and the quality of the alcohol.

"Don't you drink?" Sofia asked, eyeing Jackson's empty hands.

"No, ma'am." In character or out, women from Texas just had to be called ma'am.

"I thought guys from L.A. were loose and hip."

"Who said anything about not being loose and hip," Jackson said with grin that was almost sinful.

Their banter was interrupted by small applause as Colonel Michaels raked in a small pile of chips.

"Showing that iron nerve that won you all those medals in the Gulf War," Holloway said good-naturedly.

"More like beginner's luck," Michaels said, taking a break from puffing on his cigar. Holloway had dealt the first hand, and he now moved a small marker in front of Harris.

Known as the button, it denoted the dealer, and rotated clockwise around the table from hand to hand. The player immediately to the left of the dealer was responsible to open the betting with a bet equal to half the minimum allowable bet, constituting the small blind. In this game, the minimum bet had been set at ten dollars, so the small blind was five dollars, posted by Ellsbury. The next player to the left—Ortega—would post the big blind, double that of the small blind. Once each player was dealt two cards, betting would resume with the player left of the big blind, who could call, raise, or fold. Betting progressed around the table until it was back to the player who had posted the small blind, who would be obligated to add to his or her small blind bet to stay in the game. Betting would continue until any raise above the big blind had been called by all players who wished to continue the hand.

In this case, no one had raised, and Ortega passed on his "option" to raise his original bet, so a mere hundred dollars in chips sat in the middle of the table. After "burning" the top card of the deck, Harris dealt three cards—the "flop"—face-up in the center of the table.

Betting then resumed, starting with the player immediately to the dealer's left. Ellsbury flipped in a red ten-dollar chip, which was matched all around the table to Guidry, who raised an additional ten. All the players called the raise so that two hundred dollars was added to the original hundred.

Harris now dealt "the turn," a fourth face-up card, and another round of betting ensued. Ortega, Brown, and Guidry each added $150 to the pot while all the others folded.

With only three players remaining, Harris dealt the last of the community cards, known as the "river." Players now had two private "hole" cards and five community cards from which to make their best five-card hand. Ortega bet fifty dollars, Brown called, and Guidry raised an additional fifty. Both Ortega and Brown called, putting an additional three hundred into the pot. The total now topped one thousand dollars.

Guidry revealed two kings, which when matched with a king, two jacks, a four, and a five on the board, gave him a full house. It beat Ortega's three of a kind and Brown's two pair, and Guidry guffawed loudly as he stuck a stub of a cigar into his mouth and leaned forward to collect his winnings.

For the next few hands, Jackson balanced his time between trying to observe the players' tells, flirting with the Ortega sisters, and trying to figure out who Blake was. Hillary didn't win much or lose much, while Guidry and Harris both won sizeable pots and Jackson learned a few things about several of the competitors. Guidry played cards like he talked, loud and abrasive. He also grunted at every community card that was turned over, whether good or bad. Michaels acted as if he was playing with Skittles instead of dollars, and Betancourt weighed every raise or call as if he was having a heart attack. Ellsbury seemed to play his cards a little too much. Brown just kept chawing on his coffee stirrer, and Jackson couldn't get a read on his playing style, or that of Ortega or Harris. Holloway was smooth and calm, letting the game come to him, similar to Hillary. It was going to be a long night.

At the start of the sixth hand, Jackson slipped out to "use the restroom." He wandered down the hallway and peeked into various parlors. Two non-poker-playing men were chatting in the entry hallway while looking at the fish from the base of the dual staircases leading to the second floor. Two women, ostensibly their dates, sat by the fireplace in the drawing room, mostly empty wineglasses in their hands. Their backs were to the planter where Hillary had placed Holloway's Scotch glass, but as Jackson moved toward it, he spied two employees cleaning up the food and bar in the north parlor. He decided to wait.

Wandering for a couple more minutes, he determined there was nobody on the deck or in any of the other rooms, except possibly the kitchen. That was good, if he could just chase away the ladies from the drawing room.

Sofia was at the new serving line outside the game room when Jackson returned.

"Hey there," she said.

"Those are particularly tasty," Jackson said, pointing at the lemon tartlets.

"Is that so?"

He nodded.

"Your girlfriend just won a hand," she said. "Pity you missed it."

"It's as good as spent," Jackson said with a wave of his hand.

Sofia added a couple more desserts, then strutted for the game room with a teasing look over her shoulder. Jackson followed a moment later, in time to see the last two rounds of betting on another hand. Brown beat Michaels and celebrated by signaling for Blake to get him another drink. As the cards were collected and passed to Michaels to deal, she obliged.

And for no reason whatsoever, Jackson's brain clicked. He knew where he had seen her. He didn't have time to process potential ramifications as Tabitha Ellsbury approached him and they began to chat. As another hand played out—Michaels won big this time—she informed Jackson that her husband was one of the finest spinal surgeons in the country. She was rich and refined, but pleasant—a complete opposite to Miranda Betancourt. And unlike Sofia or Liana, her interest in Jackson appeared to be purely platonic. Or maybe she was just bored.

After the hand, Holloway called for a fifteen-minute break. Jackson checked in on Hillary, who had nine thousand of her original ten remaining. "I'm biding my time," she explained.

"Is that code for hanging on for dear life?"

"It means I'm biding my time."

"I know who Blake is," he said as they progressed down the hallway toward the main entrance. The men who had been chatting there were gone.

"Who?"

"I saw her face on the Amuse Escorts site when I was looking for Arielle."

"You're sure?"

He nodded. "I doubt she knows anything, but you should maybe chat her up. You know, while you powder your noses or something."

They stopped outside the entrance to the drawing room. The two women still sat on the couch, and Randy and Randy talked in low tones while looking at some of the artwork.

"Did you get the glass yet?" Hillary asked.

"No, those Chatty Cathys and a couple of staffers were lurking about."

"When do you plan to make your move?"

"Soon."

"For what it's worth, Betancourt plays very timidly and won't be around long. Guidry's scraping the bottom of the barrel, and the colonel has been on the verge of bankrupting twice, but he always rebounds. You may not have long while everyone's occupied."

"That's actually okay. Right now, all the action is in the game room. Once a few of the guys bow out, I'm guessing they'll move to the billiard room or find someplace to drink and commiserate. I'll float between the two rooms and thus my absence from one or the other won't be conspicuous."

"Just don't wait too long."

"You afraid you can't hang in there with the sharks?"

"Just the opposite," Hillary said. "I'm afraid I'll clean them all out."

Chapter Thirty-Two

OVER THE COURSE of the next hour, Betancourt, Ortega, and Guidry all busted. Randy and Randy said their goodbyes and headed home, while Guidry persuaded Ortega and Bratton—Vanessa Harris's assistant—to join him in the billiard room. Jenny Guidry and Liana Ortega followed along, and after several players had refilled drinks, the poker resumed.

With Hillary serving as the dealer, Brown and Michaels posted the blinds, five and ten dollars respectively. Since they were playing "no-limit" hold 'em, bets had been escalating such that these trivial blind bets were almost pointless. Yet, protocol was observed.

After Hillary dealt two cards to each player, Kawahara and Holloway both called the ten-dollar bet. Harris raised it to twenty-five. Ellsbury and Hillary matched, and Brown and Michaels contributed twenty and fifteen dollars respectively to bring the pot to $175.

Hillary burned the deck's top card and turned over a king of hearts, an ace of clubs, and a jack of hearts. Brown opened for fifty dollars, Michaels and Kawahara called, and Holloway raised an additional fifty. All six players called. The pot stood at $875.

Next Hillary turned over the king of diamonds. All eyes turned to Brown, whom Jackson had not yet heard speak. After working over his coffee stirrer, he mumbled, "Five hundred."

A few eyebrows raised and Michaels' intake of air was audible as Brown slid the appropriate chips to the center of the table. Michaels took a long puff on his cigar before uttering a firm, "Call," and matching the bet. Kawahara folded, Holloway called, and Harris stared blankly at Brown for lengthening seconds.

"Raise you five hundred," she said, plinking her chips onto those already in the center of the table.

"I'm afraid that's out of my league," Ellsbury said, inching his cards forward.

Hillary wasted no time. "Call," she said flatly, pushing her chips forward.

Brown, Michaels, and Holloway all called as well. Almost six thousand dollars in chips were strewn in the center of the table as Hillary prepared to deal the river card. Holloway took a drink of Scotch. Michaels extracted all he could from his cigar. Brown assaulted the coffee stirrer. Harris matched Hillary's stony expression.

With no added fanfare, Hillary burned the top card one last time, then exposed the ace of diamonds. The board now consisted of two pair—aces and kings—with a jack kicker. It was time for one final round of betting, and Brown again opened.

"A grand."

Jackson wasn't even sure when he had stood, but beside him, Sofia was also on her feet. Tabitha had approached the table, hands draped on her husband's shoulders. Even Blake had turned around to watch.

"I'm afraid it's time to sound the retreat," Michaels said, pushing his cards forward and reaching for his glass of whiskey. He lifted the glass as a toast to the rest of the players as he pushed back from the table.

With Kawahara already out, the play came to Holloway. Like a pro, he didn't peek at his cards. He knew what he had. And after a moment, he too folded. Harris didn't hesitate, raising Brown another thousand. All eyes turned to Hillary. With no expression whatsoever, she announced, "I'm all in."

Several people gasped, none larger than Jackson. Then he bit back a smile. Hillary knew her one objective was to stay in the game. There was no way she would risk everything unless she knew she would win. Not figured. Knew. The smile didn't make it to his lips, but he knew it had to be showing on his face. He steadied himself by focusing on the task that was nearly at hand.

Brown chomped with renewed fervor, then mumbled a "What's the total?"

"Seventy-eight hundred dollars total on the table by Miss Hillstrom," Patricia announced from where she stood behind and to the side of Ellsbury. "By my calculations, Mr. Brown owes $5,675 to call."

The chomping resumed. Four or five times, Brown peered out the side of his eyes at Hillary. Finally, he called, taking nearly a minute to count up and push in his chips.

The attention swung to Harris, who eyed Hillary carefully. Jackson let his eyes follow her stare, and his heart sunk. Hillary, stoic, composed, always in command, had opened her mouth just a fraction, poking the tip of her tongue into the void. Exactly the same as she had on the first hand after the break, when she had mucked her cards after Harris revealed her hand. She had been bluffing then and she was bluffing now, and the faint upturn at the corners of Harris' mouth indicated she knew it.

"I call and raise you everything I have," Harris declared.

More gasps. Holloway chuckled as he shook his head. Michaels' face was not that of a man who had just lost eleven hundred dollars. Rather, it was creased with bemusement.

Hillary didn't blink. Instead, she shifted her gaze to Holloway. "Richie, might I possibly open a line of credit with the casino? I'd like to match the bet."

All heads swiveled his way.

"I'm sure we can work something out," Holloway said. "I'll cover Miss Hillstrom to call."

"You sure about this, Hill?" Jackson said before he could stop himself.

Fortunately, he had based their aliases off their real names for just such a slip, and fortunately, Hillary responded quickly.

"I'm sure, Jack. With Richie's gracious backing, I call."

Brown took his coffee stirrer mashing to a new level before ultimately shoving back from the table in disgust. He joined Blake at the bar and the two women remaining in the game eyed each other icily.

Harris broke first, smiling as she turned over her hole cards, the king of clubs and the king of spades.

"Four kings," she stated smugly.

All eyes in the room turned to Hillary. Given the cards on the board, only one hand could possibly beat Harris's, who sat back with a look of contentment. Next to her, Holloway inched forward. Michaels exhaled a plume of smoke.

To Hillary's credit, she didn't ham it up. Jackson would have been a showman. Instead, she just turned over the ace of hearts and the ace of spades.

"Four aces," she declared.

Holloway started the applause as Patricia quickly totaled the winnings. "Thirty-eight thousand, one hundred fifty dollars," she said as Hillary collected the chips. More applause ensued.

"A fine display," Michaels said.

"Congratulations, Shannon," Holloway said.

She smiled demurely as she began stacking her chips.

"How about we take five?" Holloway asked. Harris stood slowly, gathered her composure, and walked to the bar. Holloway, Michaels, and Ellsbury all stood as well. Only Kawahara and Hillary remained seated.

"Well-played," Kawahara said quietly.

"Thank you."

Jackson walked up, took Hillary's head in his hands, and smooched her on the cheek. "I never doubted you," he said.

Hillary finished arranging her chips and stood. The two of them walked out onto the deck, where Michaels was blowing smoke at the Strip. They sauntered away from him.

"I thought you were bluffing," Jackson said.

"So did she."

"A fake tell?"

Hillary nodded.

"You are good."

Hillary looked around. They were alone. "Aren't you about to go? It's almost two?"

"I still can't get to the planter. Last I checked, their husbands had joined them."

"Think of something."

"I will," he said. "Once you start playing again. Although, what do you say we take the money and run?"

She glared at him.

"I had to ask."

"I'll be sure not to raise anyone too highly, but this may not go a whole lot longer."

"I'm on the move."

The game resumed now with only six players, Hillary, Brown—who was almost bankrupted—Michaels, Kawahara, Holloway, and Ellsbury. Harris stood with a glass of vermouth in her hand and a look that would frighten the sharks in the aquarium beside her. Sofia had gone to check on the billiard in the next room, and Blake and Tabitha Ellsbury had both vacated the game room as well. Jackson lingered for a hand, won by Holloway, then asked Hillary if she wanted a bite of something as he exited to the hallway.

Almost immediately, shrill laughter reached his ears. Fearing the worst, he walked to the drawing room and saw the two women still on the couch. They were reclined back against each other, laughing until they cried, clearly drunk. Their husbands were nowhere to be seen, so Jackson made his move.

He slipped past the women without either of them breaking from their laughter. He saw no one in either parlor, and quickly made his way to the planter where Hillary had left the Scotch glass hours ago. With a look back over his shoulder—the women had controlled themselves but paid him no attention—he used a handkerchief to remove the glass from the planter. He swaddled it and placed it in his pocket, hoping the bulge wasn't obvious.

As he turned around, he heard male voices from the hallway, approaching the drawing room. Figuring he could loop around through the dining room, he headed for the deck and quickly ducked through the French doors. He peeked back into the drawing room as two men in tuxedos returned with bottles of beer, seemingly unaware of his presence. Exhaling, he eased the door shut and turned to the north. A voice stopped him almost immediately.

"What you doin'?"

Jackson whirled his head around to see Sofia leaning coyly against the railing. He quickly suppressed the frown that was trying to form, replacing it with a cockeyed smile.

"Hey," he said.

"Hey," she said back, then slowly sauntered toward him, a martini glass dangling from her right hand. Her walk, her smile, and her eyes suggested this was not just a chance encounter.

"Bored with poker and billiards?" Jackson asked.

"Both getting a little testy," she said. "All that money, all that testosterone, all that ego . . ."

"I suppose."

"So, what are you doing out here all by yourself?"

"Just getting some air."

"Some air," she said, stopping inches in front of him. "I have a theory."

"Oh?"

"I think you're bored just like I am."

He shrugged.

She raised her eyebrows, her green eyes ablaze. "I think maybe we should do something to keep us from being so bored."

"Like what?"

She shrugged, her left hand tracing his lapel. "I'm sure we could think of something."

"Nothing Shannon would mind, I hope."

"I have a theory about her too."

"You're just full of theories, aren't you?" Jackson replied, wondering how to slip away.

251

"Um-hmm," she answered.

"Let's hear it."

"I think the two of you are together because of convenience."

"Convenience," he said with a nod. "As opposed to . . ."

Her eyes locked on. "Passion."

Jackson stared back for a few seconds, then slowly lowered his eyes. "Well, I hate to disappoint you, but there's plenty of passion."

"Prove it."

He smiled. "How?"

"Simple," she said, dropping her glass into a plant behind her. "Just . . ." She reached her hands up around Jackson's neck. ". . . walk . . ." She drew herself to within inches of him. ". . . away."

Sofia kissed him, slow and soft.

He kissed back, but he didn't enjoy it. For one thing, she tasted like gin. And while she was certainly attractive, there was no basis for a real relationship. Rusty would take to a girl like Sofia in the same way she had come on to him. Jackson preferred a little substance to go with the obvious style.

He was about to back away after several seconds, but Sofia beat him to it. "I have one more theory," she breathed. "About you."

"What's that?"

"You're . . ." she said, sliding his jacket off his shoulders and down his arms, ". . . in big trouble." Sofia jerked him around by the collar and pushed him to his knees. Before he could react, he was on the ground, face against the concrete, with Sofia's knee poking into his back. He heard a sickening crack that he at first thought was a rib. He realized there wasn't any pain, and that the crack had actually been a clink, Holloway's Scotch glass breaking in his pocket.

"Who are you?" Sofia hissed, her hair draped across Jackson's neck.

"What are you talking about?"

She dug her knee farther into his back, and wrenched on his arm. He bit off a scream.

"Who are you?" she asked. Her accent had changed, from sultry Hispanic to clipped Middle Eastern.

"Rusty Jackson," he said. "I'm an ins—"

"The truth!" she said. This time he couldn't hold off a growl of pain.

"I'm . . . Miss Hillstrom's bodyguard."

"Lie," she said, and pulled on his arm again. Jackson was prepared for the move, however, and twisted his entire body in the same direction. He nearly dislocated his opposite shoulder, but managed to throw Sofia off him. Ignoring the pain in his arm, shoulder, and back, Jackson pounced, pinning Sofia to the ground and against a potted palm.

"Who are you?" he asked.

She glared at him and tried to wrestle free. He won the battle, grabbing both of her wrists and pinning them to the ground above her head. With his free hand, he reached for her throat. He lifted her chin and squeezed slightly. "Who are you?"

"FBI."

"What are you doing here?"

"I'm investigating—"

Jackson never heard her answer. An explosion sounded at the back of his skull, and he pitched forward, unconscious before he landed half on Sofia and half on the ground beside her.

Chapter Thirty-Three

2:14 a.m.

JACKSON AWOKE TO the view of the side of a toilet. And to long, slender, brown legs in heels. Wincing at the pain, he slowly raised his head. Of course. Liana Ortega. He'd been tag-teamed.

"Who are you?" she asked, without Sofia's emotion, but with the same accent. The Middle Eastern one.

Jackson looked from her to Sofia, who was leaning against the sink, and back to Liana. They were in one of Holloway's powder rooms, if he had to guess. He seriously doubted they had somehow taken him from the penthouse. Just getting him from the deck to the bathroom was an accomplishment.

"I'm not asking again," she said.

He sat up and rubbed his head. "What are you going to do, flirt me to death?"

"No. I will merely turn you over to Richard Holloway. I'm sure he will be more than curious why you had a communications device in your ear," she said, holding up the earpiece.

For the first time, he feared for Hillary's safety. "Like I told your 'sister,' I'm Miss Hillstrom's bodyguard."

"Then why weren't you guarding her?"

"Because I was undercover," he said, looking down at his shirt. His coat was missing, and a small splotch of blood was pooling just above his waste on his left side. Right where he'd had the glass with Holloway's print.

"Why?" Liana asked.

He looked around for his coat, spying it hanging over the sink behind Sofia. "What?"

"Why were you undercover?"

"You ever watch *Human Target*?"

"*Human Target*?"

"Yeah. Mark Valley, Chi McBride, Jackie Earle Haley?"

254

Liana and Sofia both registered blank stares.

"Never mind."

"Why were you undercover?" Liana asked.

"Because I thought it was the best way to keep a low profile," Jackson said. "If nobody knows she's being guarded, they won't think she's worth being guarded."

"And why is she worth being guarded?"

"You see that necklace she's wearing?"

Liana nodded.

"It looks just like a really expensive necklace, but it's actually an old family heirloom. Worth half a million."

Liana smiled. She leaned forward. "Tell me, 'Rusty,' why is a necklace worth half a million dollars around the neck of a Los Angeles attorney, pretending to be a supermodel while playing poker with one of the richest men in America?"

Jackson blanched. Liana grinned. "And why are you, a small-time private investigator, pretending to be the bodyguard of an attorney pretending to be a supermodel?"

"You wouldn't believe me if I told you."

"Try me."

Jackson sighed. He'd long ago learned the lesson, when they call your bluff, all you can do is play your hand. "We're investigating the murder of a call girl that's somehow tied to an assortment of U.S. politicians and businessmen."

"Including Holloway?"

"Yeah. Can I ask who you guys are?"

She studied him for a few seconds before answering. "I'm Agent Attali." She nodded at Sofia. "That's Agent Khoury."

"Agents of what?"

"Mossad."

"Mossad," Jackson said. "The Israeli intelligence agency?"

She nodded.

"What is Mossad doing in Las Vegas?"

Liana—Agent Attali—didn't answer. Instead she looked to Sofia—Agent Khoury—who lifted Jackson's tuxedo jacket and proceeded to go through the pockets. She stopped suddenly and pulled out a bloody finger.

"Uh, careful, the glass cracked middle of round two."

With a glare, she wiped and wrapped her finger with a paper towel. Then, more gingerly, she removed several shards of glass from his pockets, along with a

USB adapter, a penlight, and Hillary's tablet, now with a cracked screen. There was also a bottle of wood glue and a tiny Ziploc of powder graphite. The bottle had cracked and the Ziploc had torn so that the contents had mixed into a light gray, useless glop.

"What were you planning to do?" Attali asked.

"Make a copy of Holloway's fingerprint," Jackson answered.

"For what purpose?"

"Hitchhiking."

Attali turned to Khoury. "Go tell Mr. Holloway that Mr. Jackson and Miss Hillstrom are not who they appear to be."

"If you learned to bluff from your old man, no wonder he's out of the game already."

Khoury froze at the door.

"I'm guessing Mossad didn't obtain Mr. Holloway's permission to infiltrate his party and poker game and thus his penthouse for whatever it is you're doing, probably quasi-legally. Which means you're going to need a pretty good excuse for how two club junkies captured me, and, even more importantly, why you thought to capture me in the first place. I'd also think of something to tell Colonel Michaels, because if he so much as sniffs that you're foreign agents, he'll be in touch with half the Joint Chiefs in about two minutes."

Attali uncrossed her legs. She sighed and crossed them the other way. "What do you propose?"

"You level with me and maybe we can help each other."

"We're not in the business of negotiating with two-bit private eyes."

"Well then, I suggest you knock me out or slit my throat or whatever it is you do, because I've got things to take care of." He pushed to his feet, fighting a bout with nausea and the hammer in his head.

"Sit down," Attali said.

Jackson stopped but remained standing. Attali rose as well.

"We have gathered intelligence to suggest that Richard Holloway may have connections to Hezbollah," she said.

"What kind of connections?"

"Holloway is the primary owner of two corporations, from which we've traced parts sold to several organizations that are known fronts for Hezbollah."

"So you thought you'd have *Abba* play poker with him?"

"Holloway is not our primary target. Besides, because of our relationship with your government, our hands are somewhat tied as far as he is concerned."

"So what is your objective?"

"Finding out who he's working with," Attali replied.

"I thought you identified organizations that were fronts for Hezbollah?"

"We have. However, we don't know who's brokering the deals. Whoever it is, he's likely working with other people like Holloway."

"So let me get this straight. You're going after the middle man?"

"A middle man who can lead us to other suppliers—half a dozen other Holloways."

"Who don't have . . . immunity," Khoury added.

"That still doesn't explain what you're doing here, tonight."

"We think the broker may be one of Holloway's regular business associates, or perhaps a frequent guest at his hotel."

Jackson quickly ran through the players. Betancourt, Ellsbury, Guidry, Harris, Michaels, Brown, Kawahara. None of them jumped out at him as a terrorist, but then again, neither did Holloway. None of their research had disclosed anything to suggest it.

"Who's Felipe?"

"He's an agent under deep cover in an attempt to get close to Holloway," Attali said.

"So why are the two of you here? And why tonight?"

"Because we are," she replied. "And we've answered enough of your questions. Now it's time you answer some of ours."

"I'll save you the time. We think the evidence tying Holloway to the call girl's murder and linking everyone and everything together is in his safe."

"What safe?"

"I see you've done your homework."

Attali stared a hole through him.

"There's a safe in his office," Jackson said. "Behind the picture of MJ."

"Who?"

"Michael Jordan. Played a little basketball in the day. Surely you've heard of him in Israel?"

More glaring.

"We posed as a couple," Jackson said, "checked into the hotel, and worked our way into the poker game to have an opportunity to get into that safe—an opportunity you have just ruined. Not to mention my rental tux." He shook his head. "Why again did Ziva decide to jump me?"

"We were looking for suspicious behavior," Attali said. "You exhibited it."

"How long have I been out?"

"Only a few minutes."

"Then I'm guessing you did your research on me before the seduce-and-abuse routine. You really thought a 'two-bit private eye' was your terrorist broker?"

"We're still considering it," Attali said.

"I guess that makes this the torture scene then."

"Is that a request?"

Jackson took a deep breath. "Look, our absence is going to become noticeable before long. What's it going to take to convince you I'm on the level?"

"A crooked level," Khoury said.

"She got the sense of humor, huh?"

"How about this?" Attali said. "You tell us what you expect to find in the safe. If it's there, you're on the level."

"Modern day *shibboleth*?"

"What?"

Jackson looked from Attali to Khoury and back. He shook his head. "Never mind."

"Do we have a deal?" Attali asked.

"I find evidence in the safe and you don't waterboard me or hand me over to Holloway?"

"That's right."

"Okay. But there's one problem."

"What's that?"

"I don't think we're getting any prints off a bunch of shards of glass, even if my glue hadn't leaked all over my jacket. I'm really going to be on the hook for that," he said with a sigh. "Either of you a safecracker?"

Attali looked down.

"Then it's a good thing I have a Plan B."

*   *   *

2:33 a.m.

THE POKER game was down to four: Hillary, Michaels, Kawahara, and Holloway. They had repositioned themselves so that they sat equally spaced around the table. Hillary and Holloway had mountains of chips. Michaels' stack was much smaller. Kawahara, quite literally, was down to the felt.

Jackson and Khoury sauntered in from off the deck, her letting go of his arm just after he opened the door. They were hoping to play off the suggestion that the two of them had been fooling around, not that any of the players were likely to be thinking about anything other than the fifty thousand dollars in chips on the table in front of them. The others in the room—Harris, Bratton, and "Felipe Ortega"—all sat observing the game. Khoury made no effort that Jackson could detect to contact Ortega.

The hand finished with Kawahara taking a small pot to stave off elimination. Holloway clapped his hands together as Michaels gathered the cards. "Shall we call it a night or keep playing?" he asked.

Hillary quickly shot a glance at Jackson and he very subtly shook his head.

"I'm game," she answered.

"I have nothing to lose," Kawahara answered.

Michaels emitted a puff of smoke before declaring, "The night is young. Unfortunately, I'm not. Take another five to stretch our legs?"

The others agreed and Hillary pushed back from the table. She strode toward Jackson and, as if in on their cover story, she sent Khoury a dirty look.

"I see you're keeping yourself from getting bored," she said to Jackson.

"Sofia and I were just chatting," he said.

"Chat with me for a moment," she said, leading him back out onto the deck. "What's going on?" she asked when they were alone. "I heard you making out and then a bunch of arguing, and then your comm went down."

"First of all, we weren't making out. Second, there's—well, yeah, actually we kind of were, but she started it and I only went along as part of my cover. Anyhow, there's been a slight change of plans. The sisters Ortega are actually undercover Mossad agents."

"Mossad?"

"So they claim. Felipe too. They say they suspect Holloway of selling parts or something to terrorists."

"Are you serious?"

"Yes. They also broke the glass and your tablet and confiscated my earwig."

Hillary looked back toward the door where Khoury lingered. "So what are we going to do? Abort?"

"No. We've got a plan."

"We've?"

"I'm . . ." He trailed off as Harris and Michaels stepped out onto the deck. Jackson guided Hillary away from them. "I'm working with them," he said quietly. "I've got a plan to get into the safe, but I need more time."

"How much more?"

"How much can you give me?"

"I can try to string Michaels or Kawahara along to keep it a three-player game. Otherwise, it will be me and Holloway soon."

"Give me at least half an hour."

"How are you going to break into the safe?"

"Leave that to me. They won't give me back the earwig, I guess because they don't want us in concert."

"But they're letting us talk now?"

"Israelis. Where's everybody else?"

"Brown and Blake left. Dr. Ellsbury's playing pool with Guidry and, until a little while ago, Ortega or whoever he is. Last I heard, Jenny and Tabitha were headed for the theater to watch a movie."

"When they say the city never sleeps . . ."

"Jackson, are you sure about this?"

"Not at all. But we've come this far, and if I don't prove my story, they'll rat me out to Holloway anyhow." He gave her a quick peck on the cheek for show. "You should get back in there. I'm going to see if I can't hustle some guys at pool."

"Be careful."

"I will," he said. He walked her back and, as the players took their seats, made a comment to Khoury about playing some billiard. She followed him over to the next room, where Ellsbury and Guidry had been rejoined by Ortega. Ellsbury, Jackson quickly deduced, had won quite a sum from Guidry, who was red-faced in anger and from massive alcohol consumption. When Ellsbury finished him off again, Guidry stalked off with a curse to refill his glass, and Jackson had an opening.

Ellsbury was a real hustler, and only allowed Jackson three shots in two games. Plopping one more twenty on the table, Jackson challenged him to a third and final game. He lost, shook the doctor's hand, and exited with Khoury in tow.

"You get it?" she asked when they were alone in the hallway.

As they passed the drawing room, he procured a small chalk cube he had slickly pocketed during the game.

The dining room doors opened and Attali quickly strode toward them. "Will this work?" she asked, extending a long-stem candle to Jackson?"

"Perfect. Lighter?"

She handed him a butane lighter, which he stuffed in his pocket. Then he snapped the candle in half and similarly concealed it.

"Let's go," Attali said.

"Not so fast, Golda."

"What are you talking about?"

"Sofia and I would like a little privacy," he said. "Our cover, remember?"

"I can handle it," Khoury said.

"I hear there's a movie playing in the theater," Jackson said. "You should check it out."

"I'll alert you as soon as we find anything," Khoury said. "Or don't."

Attali did not appear to approve of the plan, but she reluctantly went along with it. While she entered the theater, Jackson and Khoury headed for the stairs, her giggling as she held onto his arm. Everyone was accounted for except the staff. The drunk women had vacated the drawing room, and had taken their dates with them. Benoît the chef was likely in bed, and Jackson hadn't seen Francis or any attendants in quite some time. Still they couldn't afford to be too careful.

The loft was dark, the only light coming from the drawing room below. Dropping their pretense, Jackson and Khoury hurried around the corner to Holloway's office. As expected, the door was locked.

"You got picks?" Khoury asked.

Apparently the Mossad agents hadn't frisked him thoroughly. Jackson reached into his pants pocket. "I come pre—"

Khoury took the lock picks from his hand and dropped to a crouch. In a matter of seconds, she had one of the double doors open. They quickly entered the room, closing and locking the door behind them. Ambient light enabled them to see, and Khoury walked to the picture of Michael Jordan. "Here?" she asked.

"Wait," Jackson said as she reached for it.

"What?"

"Thanks to your stop-and-frisk routine earlier, we still need a fingerprint. There might be one on the photo glass. Here," he said, handing her the candle and lighter. "Melt some wax."

"Into what?"

"This," he said, handing her an ashtray off the conference table. He then clambered up onto it.

"What are you doing?"

"Retrieving an investment," he said, unlatching Hillary's necklace and slipping it into his pocket. He climbed back down as Khoury lit the candle. Very carefully, he lifted the photo off the nail that held it in place, revealing the Miller 300 built into the wall. He carefully set the framed photo of Jordan onto the coffee table before walking over to a laser printer on Holloway's desk and removing several sheets of paper. He brought them back to the table and, using his car keys, began sanding the chalk cube, collecting the powder on one of the sheets.

"How much wax do you need?" Khoury asked.

"Enough to make a thumbprint."

"Are you sure about this?"

"Just melt the wax." He leaned over to see how much she had accumulated. "A little bit more."

He gently lifted the paper with the chalk and held it suspended just above the glass surface of the photo frame. Very gently, he blew, sending a fine powder over the glass. He moved around, blowing powder along the edges. When he was done, he stood the frame on end, turning it toward the light. Most of the chalk fell to the table, but in several places, it clung to thumbprints left on the glass. One in particular looked promising.

"Ask you a question?" Agent Khoury said as he laid the frame down again.

"Sure."

"Where'd you learn how to do this stuff?"

"*MacGyver.*"

"What?"

"*MacGyver.* Richard Dean Anderson. Do you not have TVs in Israel?"

"Is that all you Americans think of, television and cinema?"

"You forgot sports."

"Of course."

He checked on her progress again and walked back to Holloway's desk. He rummaged around, hoping to find some duct tape, which he knew was a long shot. There was Scotch tape, but that was next to useless for his intentions.

"I think there's enough," Agent Khoury announced. Jackson closed a drawer and joined her by the conference table. He looked at the ashtray and nodded his agreement.

She blew out the candle. "Now what?"

"Now we wait for it to cool a little," Jackson said. "And in the meantime, you tell me who you really are."

Chapter Thirty-Four

2:56 a.m.

AGENT KHOURY'S GREEN eyes flashed.

"You're not Mossad," Jackson explained with a shake of his head. "You said '*sibboleth.*'"

"What?"

"In the Old Testament, one group of people—and don't ask me to remember the names—tested the legitimacy of this other group by asking them to say '*shibboleth.*' If they mispronounced it, it proved they weren't who they said they were and they were killed. You mispronounced it, ironically, by not knowing the story."

Khoury shook her head. "That's it?"

"You claim to be Israeli. I figure you ought to be familiar with *shibboleth.* Besides, you use contractions."

"What?"

"Foreign agents on TV never use contractions. They're also usually not too good with idioms, but you and What's-her-name have been dropping them all night." He took a step closer to her. "Now my problem is that I don't know who you really are. You're not FBI or CIA, because you would have just flashed a badge and you certainly wouldn't have cooperated with me. And you couldn't claim to be FBI or CIA, because I would expect some sort of ID. So you pick Mossad, figuring it sounds mysterious and a little scary and I won't question you because I'm afraid you'll cane me or something. Which means you're not anything really scary either, because then you wouldn't have to make up something to scare me—you'd just tell me the truth. So who are you? CISEN? CNI? Egyptian freedom fighters?"

Khoury hesitated.

"My second problem," Jackson said, "is I only have about two minutes before that wax is ready, and I need to know if I can trust you or if I'm going to have to incapacitate you. And before it comes to that, I'd really like to know if you're just a girl with some sort of identity complex or a Serbian intelligence officer who could actually incapacitate me. Of course, if that were the case, you wouldn't be using contractions either. At any rate, Agent Sofia Khoury, who are you?"

She replied by throwing the wax at him. He ducked, just in time, and the ashtray clunked against the wall. Khoury ran for the door, but Jackson beat her there, tackling her into the wall.

"Going somewhere?" he asked.

With a snarl, she tried to jam her heel into his instep. Jackson anticipated the move and avoided it, but doing so cost him his leverage. Khoury wrenched herself free and drove an elbow into Jackson's stomach. Doubled over, he was no match for her as she flipped him onto the floor, his body colliding with the legs of several chairs around the meeting table.

His entire body tingled after her Mr. Miyagi flip, and he had banged his elbow on the chairs and his head on the floor, hard enough to smart and cause his left arm to go numb. Leaning toward her being a Serbian intelligence officer, Jackson was content to let Khoury get away. But she apparently had given up on running and wanted to finish the fight. While Jackson winced and tried to shake feeling into his arm, she unstrapped her heels and kicked them aside. Then she pulled several chairs out of the way, giving her a clear run at Jackson.

"You want to talk about this?" he asked.

"Get up."

Either she wanted him to stand so he would be an easier target for some sort of flying scissor kick, or as soon as he started to move and make himself vulnerable, she would break a vital bone. So he stayed where he was.

"Up!" she said. She picked up one of the chairs as if it was a feather and swung it down at Jackson's body. He rolled to the side and against the wall just as the chair thudded on the floor, loud enough to wake everyone in the hotel.

As Jackson stood, Khoury attacked with a sweeping leg kick that would have taken off his head had he not raised an arm to block it. Fortunately, his arm was still numb, and he didn't feel the full force of her leg. For someone who looked more like a young Eva Longoria, Khoury kicked like Jean-Claude Van Damme.

Her kick blocked, she quickly spun around and tried to nail Jackson with her right hand. The blow connected with the side of his head and nearly knocked him loopy. But her combo also provided him an opening to grab her with his left arm, putting her in a headlock. She struggled and kicked, and he pulled tighter, apologizing to his shins. At least she had taken off the heels.

Jackson thought Khoury was about to concede as another flurry of kicks and elbows missed their mark or failed to make him release his grasp. Then, somehow, she got her arms up and around his head. Before he knew it, he was in the air. Jackson flew head over heels, his hands still around Khoury's head. They flipped and crashed onto the floor like a pair of WWE stars. Only they didn't have a padded canvas, nor were they pulling their punches or staging falls.

They both staggered to their feet. Khoury got up first and delivered a kick to the side of Jackson's head that had him seeing stars. But he was able to dodge a follow-up kick, and sliding to the side, swiped at Khoury's ground foot. It was like taking out a punter in mid kick, and she fell hard.

Once again, they both got to their feet. This time Jackson was first, and he charged. He plunged his shoulder into Khoury's stomach and drove her back against the table. She fell backwards and landed with a thud on the mahogany table. Along with her back, her head cracked on the wood, dazing her. Jackson used the opportunity to drag her off the table and onto the floor. He pushed her face down, arms behind her, and applied pressure to her back.

"I . . . can't . . . brea—"

Jackson let up the pressure, just slightly. "Who are you?"

Khoury panted some more. "I . . . can't . . ."

Jackson eased up again, allowing Khoury room to move. She crawled to her knees, breathing in short gasps. Jackson stood, towering over her to send a message. She didn't try anything, and finally, her breath returned.

Seeing that she was okay, Jackson grabbed her by the arm and forced her against the wall. He pinned her, holding both of her arms, his legs against hers. His free hand held her head, tight against the wall.

"Who are you?" he asked. "The truth this time, because I am getting sick of playing *What's My Line?* with you two."

"My name's . . . Adriana Escobar," she said. "I'm a private investigator from Houston."

"You got ID?"

"Not on me."

"Who's your sister?"

"My sister, Teresa."

"She a P.I. too?"

"Yes."

"And Felipe?"

"He's who he says he is. You want to let me go?"

"Not really."

"Truce, I promise."

"Why not? You've been so trustworthy so far." He didn't budge.

Adriana struggled and Jackson pushed harder. "They apparently haven't heard us, by some miracle," Jackson said. "But you try anything, and I guarantee they will."

"I'm terrified."

Jackson resisted the urge to give her head a little tap against the wall. Instead, he released his pressure but continued to hold her tight. "What are you doing here?" he asked.

"Felipe Ortega hired us to investigate Richard Holloway."

"Why?"

"It's confidential."

"Fine. You prefer a quick blow to the head or should I just squeeze your neck until you pass out?"

"Cut the drama, okay? Holloway's in the process of buying land in the Yucatán District of Mexico on which to build a new resort and casino," she explained. Jackson noticed that both accents—Hispanic and Middle Eastern—were gone. "Right now, that land is a high-yield cattle ranch owned by a subsidiary of Felipe Ortega's corporation. Ortega suspects that Holloway has used bribes and threats and a host of other less than ethical tactics to pave the way for his resort. Ortega hired us to vet Holloway and his Mexican operations."

"What are you doing here, tonight?"

"Vetting," she said.

Jackson sighed heavily. According to his and Hillary's research and their talk with Appleby, Holloway had used his connections to Senator Moore to help get Oasis built. Was he running a similar scheme south of the border? Did it have anything to do with Warren, Arielle, or any other part of Jackson and Hillary's investigation?

He sighed again. This wasn't the time to compare case notes. He let go of her and stood back. Adriana took a moment to swipe her hair out of her face and adjust her dress. As she did, he studied her face, looking for signs of truth. He didn't find it so much in her eyes as in her shoulders. They were slightly sagged, resigned. He was far from certain, but for the situation, he would have to trust her.

"Why go MMA with me here?"

"Because you blew my cover, again. I tried to run, then thought the easiest solution might be to take you out and get into the safe myself."

"And now?"

"Now you know the truth. You try to warn Holloway, we're going to fight again."

"I couldn't care less about Mexican cattle."

"Fine."

Jackson let out a heavy breath. "We good?" he asked.

Adriana nodded.

"Are you hurt?"

"Don't flatter yourself."

He rolled his eyes. For the record, his head, back, and elbow were all screaming, but he certainly wasn't telling her that.

"Let's melt some more wax," he said.

It took them ten minutes to burn enough wax and let it cool. Then Jackson placed his thumb in the ashtray, allowing the hot wax to form around it. It had cooled just enough to congeal and so that it didn't sear his flesh.

"Hold the candle over the frame," Jackson said. Adriana did as instructed, and he very carefully lined up his wax-coated thumb with a print made visible by the chalk. Exhaling a deep breath, he pressed his thumb against the powdered residue. He lifted it up and examined his new blue fingerprint.

"Is that really going to work?" she asked.

"We're about to see."

"Don't you still need a code?" she asked, blowing out the candle.

"I have the code," he said. He had even confirmed it was correct earlier, stealing away from the poker game to check the necklace camera's feed of Holloway's two subsequent safe openings. Now, using his left hand, he entered the ten digits into the keypad. Then he circled his fingers around the handle and pushed his thumb against the biometric pad at the base of the handle. It beeped three times, paused, and then beeped a different tone. The beep was followed immediately by a click, and the door unlatched.

Jackson pulled open the door and looked inside. Adriana was right beside him, and it was almost impossible to see. He remembered his penlight and clicked it on as Adriana reached into the safe and pulled out a manila envelope with all the cash from the poker game. Jackson lifted out several additional manila folders and envelopes of various sizes, ignoring the stacks of cash in the back of the safe. There was also a small pistol, various forms of ID, and a satellite phone.

And then, against the left wall, Jackson spotted a pair of small USB flash drives. He quickly scooped them out.

"That's what you want?" Adriana asked.

"We'll see." He took them over to the desk and opened Holloway's laptop. Jackson hoped the PC under the desk was the highly secured, password protected computer and the laptop was more for recreational use. He also hoped there was no alarm that alerted Holloway if someone used it without authorization.

The familiar blue Windows loading screen lit the room. Jackson looked up. Adriana was sorting through various folders on the table.

"Want to summarize what you're finding?" he asked.

"Mostly bank records, titles and deeds, records of business transactions."

The laptop screen went black, then blipped to a picture of the Chicago skyline at dusk. Jackson immediately inserted the two flash drives into ports on the side of the laptop and waited for them to be recognized. When they were, he clicked to open them and began browsing.

The first contained what appeared to be financial records and various business documents—proposals, contracts, annual reports and minutes. Knowing time was of the essence, Jackson switched to the other drive. It contained only one main folder, "GD." He clicked it open and revealed half a dozen other folders: "Audio," "Dossiers," "Events," "Maps," "News," and "Miscellaneous."

Jackson very quickly skimmed a few of them, taking no more than a minute to confirm from the presence of a few names and places that the information was what he wanted. Then he opened an internet browser. The original plan had been for him to copy what he found to Hillary's tablet, but a test had found it unresponsive after his initial tussle with Sofia/Agent Khoury/Adriana. Fortunately, he and Mouse had cooked up a Plan B earlier in the form of a cloud storage site. Jackson quickly accessed it, his fingers stumbling across the keyboard as he entered his password. It took him three tries to type it correctly.

"Find something?" Adriana asked, joining him at the desk.

"Yeah, a jackpot. You?"

"Nothing of interest." She peered at the screen. "What is this?"

"I'm not taking the time to find out," Jackson said, clicking the "Upload" button on his cloud site. He browsed to the flash drive and selected the "GD" folder. Immediately, a small window popped up on the screen and a green progress bar began crawling from left to right. "Time Remaining: About 3 minutes."

"Come on," he said as the time jumped to four minutes. The mouse pointer had become a spinning wheel.

"I'm going to pack up the rest of the files, unless you want to take—"

"What was that?" Jackson asked.

"Sounded like someone unlocking the door," she said.

A moment later, one of the doors started to swing inward. Adriana dived for cover behind the desk and Jackson ducked down just before a figure entered the room.

Chapter Thirty-Five

3:18 a.m.

LIGHT FLOODED THE room and Jackson waited for the inevitable. The Michael Jordan picture was lying on the table, caked with blue chalk. Beside it were an ashtray partially filled with wax, the remains of a candle, half a cube of pool chalk, and the majority of the contents of Holloway's safe. Which was still open. Not to mention chairs had been strewn about during Jackson's fight with Adriana.

A loud curse, followed by some subdued expletives, confirmed the figure was Holloway and that he had seen the mess. Jackson searched Adriana's eyes, hoping his P.I. counterpart had a brilliant idea.

"Help!" she screamed. For good measure, she slapped Jackson on the face and screamed again. "Help! Get off me!"

Jackson grabbed her wrist just before she could slap him again. Playing along, he pinned her underneath the desk. She kicked and flailed and screamed some more, until Richard Holloway appeared beside them both.

"What's going on!" he demanded.

"He's trying . . . to rape me!" Adriana screamed.

"Rape her! I was trying to arrest her," Jackson said, pushing himself up.

"Somebody had better tell me what's going on," Holloway said. "Why is the safe open?" His eyes went to the computer and the files being transferred. He immediately jerked the flash drives out of the ports. "What is going on?"

"She cracked your safe," Jackson said. "She's with Hamas, her and her sister."

"That's a lie!" Adriana stood too. "He attacked me. He dragged me in here and—"

Jackson barked something in what sounded to him like Arabic. Adriana shut up.

"Who are you?" Holloway asked.

"Avery O'Donnell, CIA."

"CIA?"

"That's right, Mr. Holloway. I'm sorry to have misled you, but we were on to Anwar Sharif—a.k.a. Felipe Ortega—and his associates. We thought they might try something tonight during the game. I followed her in here and—"

"He's lying. I am not whatever he claims, and he forced me here against my will."

"I don't believe either of you," Holloway said. "And until I can sort—"

Adriana attacked first, a lightning fast kick that knocked Holloway's recently drawn phone from his hand. Jackson followed it with a quick hook to the jaw that sent Holloway reeling. Adriana pounced, wrapping her arms around his neck.

"No!" Jackson shouted.

She ignored him and squeezed. Holloway blacked out in seconds, and Adriana stood and looked at Jackson. "What, you thought I was going to kill him?"

He shook his head. "We'd better get out of here." He closed the internet window and powered off the computer, hoping enough data had been transmitted to be useful to him and Hillary. He thought about grabbing the flash drives, but they were in Holloway's pocket and he didn't want to take the time to dig. Nor did he want to actually abscond with them. Right now, Holloway had no proof of actual theft, and Jackson didn't want to add any additional crimes to his list.

"Aren't you going to finish the transmission?" Adriana asked.

"Be my guest," he said, turning for the door.

He had only taken a few steps when another figure burst into the room. Jackson crouched instinctively until he recognized Liana/Agent Attali/Teresa.

She saw the carnage and swore. "What's going on?"

"Holloway interrupted us."

"I heard the game was over and came to warn you, but apparently he beat me here."

"Who won?" Jackson asked.

"What?"

"Who won the game?"

"What difference does it make?" Adriana asked.

"Hillary," Teresa said with a frown. "She cleaned out—"

Jackson didn't wait for her to finish. He grabbed the manila envelope containing the poker money and started for the door. "Nice working with you both."

He was out of the office before he could hear their reply. He pulled stacks of cash from the envelope and stuffed them in various pockets of his pants and jacket. It was then for the first time that he realized he'd split one of the jacket's shoulder seams and lost a button during his fight with Adriana. Not that it mattered anymore. Returning a damaged tuxedo was the least of his concerns.

Taking the steps two at a time, he was disgusted with himself for not forcing Adriana and Teresa to give him back his earpiece. He had no way to warn Hillary but to expose himself in the game room. He loosened his tie and was about to open the door when Colonel Michaels pushed it open. He stopped and studied Jackson as he chewed on the stub of a cigar.

"You're a very lucky man," he said, then removed the cigar. "In more ways than one, it appears," he added, appraising Jackson's disheveled appearance.

Jackson forced a lopsided grin to his face as he slipped past Michaels. Hillary sat calmly at the table while Patricia gathered cards and chips. Kawahara stood talking with Harris by the bar. Bratton was nowhere to be seen.

Hillary stood when she saw Jackson.

"Hey, Babe. I hear you won."

She smiled for the sake of the other two women. "Richie's getting my money now."

"Get some air?" he asked.

"I suppose, but he should be right back."

"He'll wait," Jackson said, leading her by the arm. "Come on."

They stepped out onto the deck, the early morning air a touch cool on Jackson's sweaty face.

"What's up?" Hillary asked. They were alone.

"Holloway caught us."

"What?" she asked, her eyes spotting the torn jacket.

"We need to get out of here, now."

They had kept walking and he turned her back into the drawing room. It was vacant and they hurried through it. As they entered the hallway, a female voice screamed from up above.

Jackson looked over his shoulder. Ortega and Bratton had just exited the billiard room. Bratton held a pool cue. Michaels stood next to the stub of a hall leading to the bathrooms.

"Go," Jackson said, pushing Hillary toward the elevator. As soon as she pressed the button, the doors opened. He looked back as they hurried inside. The Escobar sisters had joined Ortega and Bratton, all running toward them while

Michaels and Dr. Ellsbury stood in the background, mouths agape and eyes wide. And from the stairs leading to the loft, a very conscious Richard Holloway and Patricia descended. He held a pistol in his hand.

Jackson mashed the 43 on the side of the elevator with his palm, then repeatedly tapped the "Close" button while pushing Hillary into the corner and out of the way of potential gunfire. None came, and the doors closed on them. The elevator began its descent.

"Take off your sandals," Jackson said.

"What?"

"We're going to need to run. When we exit, throw them left. We're going right."

No sooner had he said the words than the elevator dinged and the doors parted. Jackson ran his hand over the floor buttons, hitting as many of them as he could. Hillary hopped on one foot as she released her other sandal. They stepped into the hallway and she heaved her sandals to the south as Jackson pulled her hand north.

They were in a main hallway that, at this level, could cross the entire structure, bridging the north side of the O to the south. Suites lined either side, but the doors were all closed and the hallway was empty.

"Jackson, where are we going?" Hillary asked.

"Up."

"What?"

"They expect us to go down. We're going up."

"To where?"

"The roof."

"Jackson . . ."

They turned into a side hallway that led to the main elevators. Instead of waiting for them, Jackson opted for the stairs. Holloway would have called security, and they would likely be shutting down the elevators. They would also be coming up from the ground floor, meaning an attempt to escape by going down would lead right to them. That only left one option.

They climbed one flight of stairs and burst out onto the patio by the entrance to Crest. It was open all night, and Jackson led Hillary into the club. At three-thirty in the morning, it was only densely populated, mostly by over-served singles who wouldn't remember anything in the morning. That was perfect.

They hurried around the bar and out onto the deck. Aside from a man and woman making out in the corner of the pool, oblivious to anything around them, the deck was vacant. Hillary's hand in his, Jackson skirted the pool and headed for the wooden platform in the corner.

"Jackson, no," Hillary said.

"It's the only way."

As if to confirm it, the metal fire door exiting from Holloway's private stairway to his helipad opened and two men rushed out. Jackson nearly dragged Hillary up the staircase, keeping low to avoid detection. The darkness of night helped, especially since the few rooftop lights were trained either on the helipad or the pool and deck.

"Jackson, this is nuts," Hillary said as they waited at a landing.

"It's this or a firing squad," he said, pushing her forward when the men on the helipad looked the other way. They reached the top of the stairs and crouched down again. Directly in front of them was a semicircular tube that resembled a plastic bobsled track.

"I'll be right behind you," Jackson said. He took her hand as she stepped into the tube and sat down. As soon as her butt touched the plastic, he gave her shoulders a push to propel her forward. She wasn't quite ready and screamed reflexively.

The sound was quickly swallowed up by the night, but Jackson looked over his shoulder. The men on the helipad had clearly heard it, but had yet to lock on to his location. Before they could, he jumped forward, launching himself after Hillary down the Plunge Waterslide.

Chapter Thirty-Six

FOR THE FIRST few seconds, all Jackson could think about was the immediate sensation of sliding down the Plunge. The water was warm, but unpleasant as it quickly penetrated his clothing. He had hurtled himself into the slide, and thus hadn't gotten into luge form, causing his arms and legs to flail. He tried to compensate by elevating his head, which didn't make any anatomical sense and only made his neck stiff. It was also useless, because almost immediately after its start, the Plunge was covered. The shell was partially translucent, but in the middle of the night, it didn't matter, and he couldn't see to steer himself even if he had the ability to do so.

The slide made three tight loops, two spinning counterclockwise and the one in the middle spinning clockwise. By the time Jackson emerged into a straightaway, he had relaxed a little, realizing he wasn't going to be dashed against the walls of the tube or drown from the rushing water. It allowed his mind to shift to other things.

Like how long it took a person to drop five hundred feet in a waterslide. Like how long it took hotel security to marshal at the base of said slide. Like whether or not the men on the helipad had pinned down the origin of Hillary's scream and put two and two together. He began to formulate a plan for when he and Hillary splashed down. The slide looped and circled over the back portion of the resort—including the H₂O Showroom balcony, offices, the casino security center, and a few eateries—before emptying right behind the O. That meant Jackson and Hillary would have to cross the entire pool deck and the sports courts on foot to reach the parking garage at the back of the property.

Jackson entered a series of larger loops that spun him to the brink of dizziness before reversing and circling the other direction. The loops emulated Jackson's mind as he pondered Holloway's response, his likelihood of contacting the police or meting out justice on his own, what crimes he and Hillary had committed, whether or not the Escobars—or whoever they were—would be in

NATHAN BIRR

trouble with Holloway or side with him, and whether or not it had all been worth it. He had no idea how much data had transferred before Holloway had removed the flash drives from the laptop, nor of what nature the information was.

After another straightaway and more loops, Jackson was thoroughly turned in direction. The slide now ran in a series of short straight sections followed by horseshoe curves. Jackson tried to picture the slide in his mind and concluded they were near the bottom.

His thoughts went to Hillary's poker winnings, which were now in various pockets of his tuxedo. That money was legally theirs. Perhaps it could buy off Holloway. Then again, at least ten grand of it had been Arielle Coal's, and thus was legally either theirs, Darla's, the state of Nevada's, or property of the Las Vegas Metropolitan Police Department pursuant to their investigation.

Jackson made a hard right turn and suddenly sensed he was near the end. Maybe it was an increase in water or an uptick in current, maybe it was the change in sound near the end of the lengthy tube, or maybe it was a faint lightening of his surroundings. A moment later, he made a left and then saw an opening ahead. Before he knew it, he was flying through the air. He saw Hillary directly in front of him, just surfacing, and he tried to orient his body to the side. But being airborne, he had no control. His leg swept over her head, knocking her backwards as he flopped back first into the water.

He sank like a rock, having forgotten to close his mouth in his efforts to avoid Hillary. He struggled for the surface and came up gagging and hacking on chlorinated water.

As soon as he caught his breath, his eyes swept the area. It was vacant. Hillary had resurfaced beside him, wiping water out of her eyes. Her magnificent hair was now plastered to her head, the once elegant braid resembling a tugboat rope due for replacement.

"Are you okay?" Jackson asked.

"Yeah."

He floundered to the edge of the pool and hoisted himself over the lip. Then he reached a hand to pull Hillary out of the water. Her dress clung to her like dense shrink wrap, making it almost impossible to walk. She reached down and clutched the soaked fabric, pulling it to her knees, and followed Jackson through the kiddie pool area.

So far, the coast was clear, but it wouldn't be for long. The eye in the sky had to spot them soon. Jackson decided to avoid the pool deck, because although it would provide them more cover, it was also likely watched by more cameras, considering it was home to the outdoor casino and several restaurants. Instead, he and Hillary crossed to the south end of the deck and raced along an elevated boardwalk that existed to provide access to the dance floor and sports courts without traversing through the pool deck. Most of the way, it was lined by foliage, including palm trees that towered over the walkway and shielded them from view.

They passed the private, adult-only pool area, and crossed the lazy river that wound around the back corner of the pool deck. To their left, a forty-foot by forty-foot wood dance floor was surrounded by palms and tropical flowerbeds, its strings of white lights darkened for the night.

The path joined a similar bypass around the north end of the deck and opened to the sports deck, home to two regulation-size basketball courts, two hard-court tennis surfaces, and two sand volleyball courts, along with a pair of golf simulators, a snack and drink shop named Quench, and a seating area. The entire section was surrounded by more trees and shrubs, effectively trapping Jackson and Hillary.

"Now what?" she asked.

"We blaze a trail," Jackson said, walking purposefully between the basketball and tennis courts. He found a section of bushes that wasn't quite so thick and forced his way through. "Careful," he called to Hillary, mindful of her bare feet. He extended a hand to help her through the bushes. Despite its close proximity to her body, her dress still snagged several times.

The bushes and trees merely hid a six-foot-high brick wall that encircled the property. Jackson needed two tries to hoist himself onto the ledge. He straddled it like a horse, then reached for Hillary. The first time she attempted to climb the wall, she slipped, nearly pulling him down as well. The second time he successfully pulled her onto the ledge with him. Both were breathing heavily, but they knew their getaway depended on speed. Jackson dropped down on the other side of the ledge, then helped Hillary to the ground.

They were in a narrow alley that separated the back of the resort from the parking garage that served it and several of the smaller nearby hotels. To their left, the alley emptied onto a street that led to the resort's official rear entrance and then to Harmon Avenue, the side street off Las Vegas Boulevard. To the right, the alley led to MGM's Garden Arena. Jackson chose to go straight ahead, having much less trouble climbing over a three-foot-high concrete barricade and helping Hillary after him.

He was almost certain cameras would be watching their every move. Thankfully, he had self-parked after returning from Hoover Dam that afternoon, and knew exactly where to find the Challenger. Jogging, Jackson pointed the key fob at the car. It chirped several times, lights flashing. He had the car started before Hillary got in, and was almost out of the garage before she had buckled her seatbelt.

"Are you under control?" Hillary asked as he careened onto Audrie Street.

He glanced at her. Half drowned, shivering from the cold, and most assuredly hopped up on adrenaline, she still had the poise to make sure he did too.

"Yeah. We need to ditch the car. It stands out too much."

She turned around and lifted two bags from the backseat, losing her balance as he careened east onto Harmon Avenue. She raised her eyebrows at him as she settled back. "I have my laptop case and the duffel bag," she said. That afternoon, they had packed a few changes of clothes, their actual phones and IDs and credit cards, and her computer, stashing them all in the car in case they needed to execute an emergency evacuation.

"Your purse?" he asked.

She held it up. "Waterlogged, but I have it."

"They're going to burn through our backstories quickly now," he said. "Adriana and Teresa somehow knew who we were."

"Who?"

"Sofia and Liana."

"I thought you said they were Mossad."

"Yeah, they weren't."

"Who were they?"

He looked at her. "P.I.s. Long story."

He made another turn. Just in case, he had mapped out an escape strategy earlier, and now executed it coldly and calculatedly. He whipped into the parking lot of a fleabag motel and pulled around to the rear.

"They know it's our car," he said, "so there's no point in wiping down prints. Use your phone, not Shannon's, and call for a cab at the corner of Swenson and Naples."

"This isn't Swenson and Naples."

"I know."

While she made the call, he hurriedly removed the license plates from the vehicle. It wouldn't slow down the cops or Holloway's goons for long, because there weren't a lot of cobalt blue Challengers around. But they were his actual plates, transferred from the Granada shortly after they had rented the Challenger. He'd had Connie use her position at the DMV to temporarily alter records so that if Holloway checked, the plates would appear registered to Russell Jackson, not the car rental agency. It had put him in even deeper debt to her, but that was irrelevant now.

When he was finished, he slipped the plates in the duffel bag, which he took from Hillary. She responded by shivering.

"Come on."

They had to walk several blocks, and Jackson kept a constant eye out for surveillance cameras and his ears tuned for police sirens. He had no idea who was coming for them or what resources they would have, but he had to assume the worst.

They arrived at the specified corner, adjacent to the University of Nevada, Las Vegas, and waited in front of a cheap hotel with a vacant billboard above it. Across the street was a saloon. Across the other street was a 7-Eleven. Beside him, Hillary shook like a recovering alcoholic. Kicking himself for not thinking of it sooner, he removed his tuxedo jacket and gave it to her.

"Th-thanks."

"Don't lose it," he said. "It has twenty or thirty grand in the pockets."

"What?"

"I swiped it from the safe. You won it fair and square, I figure."

"Did you g-get anything before he c-caught you?"

"Some," Jackson said, his head on a swivel. A pair of headlights appeared a block away. "I don't know how much."

"I hope this wasn't all for nothing."

"You and me both. I'm pretty sure I violated my parole."

The lights belonged to a cab and it slowed to a halt beside them. The passenger window lowered.

"You call for a cab?" a man with a Middle Eastern accent asked.

"That's right," Jackson said, opening the door. He got in behind Hillary.

"Where . . . to?" the driver asked as he got a good look at them over his shoulder.

"Wild party at Hakkasan," Jackson said with a grin. "North."

"North where?"

"Just north for now," Jackson said, leaning in close to Hillary. "I'm going to get fresh with you and you slap me," he whispered. He stuck his head toward her neck, like a guy looking for an after party.

Hillary turned away in disgust and pushed him to the side.

Jackson leaned back in. "Come on, Kel, we've got a long ride."

"Ugh, get off me," she said, shoving him harder this time.

"Everything all right?" the driver asked, his eyes narrow as they searched the backseat through his mirror.

"Kel," Jackson said, reaching a hand toward her.

She slapped it, hard. "I told you not to take that bet. Don't touch me." She finally looked at the driver. "We're fine."

The driver headed for the interstate, asking again about a direction. Jackson just told him north and assured him they had the money.

As they cruised past the Strip, Jackson surveyed the contents of his pockets. His wallet was waterlogged, but everything in it besides the cash was fake, Rusty's stuff. He collected it in a pile, then discreetly showed Hillary. She got the message and began going through her purse. He had Rusty's cell phone, which he powered off. He then disconnected the battery and the SIM card. Hillary slid Shannon's phone to him, and he did the same with them. His broken bottle of wood glue, the torn bag of graphite powder, and the USB adapter were all throwaways. Hillary's tablet was cracked but possibly still viable, and her necklace camera might also still function. The Challenger keys, penlight, and lock picks were keepers. And, of course, Hillary's poker winnings were also worth saving. The rest—fake IDs, phones, fingerprinting supplies, and a waterlogged USB adapter would all be tossed as soon as possible.

They had left the Strip and downtown behind, and Jackson kept an eye on exit numbers. When they reached Craig Road in North Las Vegas, Jackson directed the driver to head east. A mile later, he pointed out a new brand-name motel on the north side of the street. He paid in cash, tipping the driver well, and waited until he was gone to address Hillary.

"Okay, let's go."

"Go where?"

"Our hotel."

"Is this really necessary?" she asked.

"Look, I want to crash as bad as you do, but the cops will find the Challenger, search cab records, find someone who took a cab from where we ditched it, and find out where we were dropped off. Which is why we can't be there."

"You're assuming Holloway will call the cops."

"You think not?"

"I think he's more likely to have his own people run us down."

"Either way. We're pretty conspicuous, so we shouldn't loiter," he said, glancing down at her feet as they peeked out from under the dress. He'd thought running in wingtips was bad, but she'd been shoeless since the forty-third floor of Oasis. Not to mention, carrying a ton of wet, draping fabric around with her.

"Here," he said, reaching for the strap of the laptop case.

"It's fine," she said.

"I've got it," he said, wincing as he lifted it to his shoulders. The adrenaline had finally worn off and he was feeling the effects of his tussles with a schizophrenic martial artist. "I'd offer to carry you, but that would really look conspicuous."

"I'll be fine," she said and took a few steps to prove it. He shifted the strap for the laptop higher onto his shoulder and caught up with her.

"What happened to your side?" she asked.

"Huh?"

"That looks like blood," she said, her eyes focused on his left side, just above the waist.

"Oh. That would be where the glass for Holloway's fingerprint impaled me when Sofia-Adriana attacked me."

"Is that what happened to your face too?"

"What's wrong with my face?" he asked, immediately frowning at the softball he'd thrown her.

She passed. "You've got a bruise on your jaw and swelling by your eye."

"Yeah, well, you should see the other guy. Who in this case is a Latina-Israeli-Texan who kicks like a mule." He recounted their fight as best he could remember the blow-by-blow.

"You could be concussed," Hillary said.

"I'm fine," Jackson said.

"Why'd she ever attack you in the first place?"

Jackson spent the next ten minutes—while they jaywalked across Craig Road and walked half a mile east—recounting the events of the evening, from Sofia coming on to him on the deck to Liana kayoing him from behind to their interrogation in the bathroom, and from their admission they were Mossad agents to their resolution to work together to his deduction that they weren't Mossad after all, which led to the aforementioned fight with Adriana. He summed up Holloway's arrival in his office to find them at his computer desk and their subsequent attack and escape just as they approached a two-story structure with a bright orange roof. Jackson pointed at a brick landscaping wall that kept a gravel-lined cactus bed at bay. "Have a seat."

"What now?" Hillary asked.

He slid the duffel bag off his shoulder and rummaged in it for a spare T-shirt. He quickly removed his tie and unbuttoned his shirt, then slipped on the T-shirt. His hair had mostly dried, and he tousled it quickly. "Wait here."

In five minutes, he procured a room using just cash. The sleepy clerk at the desk was suspicious at a request for a room at quarter to five in the morning, but Jackson claimed he and his wife had just arrived in town after driving all night and were beat. He paid for two nights—the current night and the next one—without having to produce a credit card. He remained concealed from the waist down, so the clerk never saw the dress pants and wingtips that accompanied his USC T-shirt. And Jackson didn't spy a surveillance camera in the lobby. Feeling good, he returned to Hillary.

"Room 206," he said, picking up the duffel bag and laptop case. They climbed the steps to the exterior hallway and he unlocked a door that matched the roof in color.

The motel wasn't much to look at, but the carpet was clean and the two queen beds might as well have been cushions of clouds. Jackson dropped their luggage, closed and deadbolted and latched the door, and drew the blinds. He promptly collapsed onto the bed.

Hillary set down her purse and leaned against the wall, massaging her foot. "You want to tell me why you picked this lovely place?" she asked.

"Off the beaten track, likely no cameras, no credit card required at check-in, and we're across the street from an IHOP and just down the road from a Wal-Mart and a Budget Car Rental."

"You planned all this?"

"I did."

"When?"

"You take a long time to get ready."

"And look at me now," Hillary said, patting imagined coifs of hair behind her head.

"A joke from Hillary McKenzie. Quick, let me grab a pen and paper and write this down."

Chapter Thirty-Seven

4:56 a.m.

CLIVE CUSSLER'S HERO Dirk Pitt liked to snooze in the shower. Jackson, feeling very much like a Cussler character of late, thought about trying it too. But he didn't have room to stretch out without the water cascading from a rather forceful showerhead into his face. So he settled for leaning his head against the side of the shower and closing his eyes while the water massaged his sore muscles.

Had that really all just happened? Conning their way into a Vegas casino owner and real estate mogul's good graces and private party, winning fifty grand at a poker game, hacking into his safe, being caught, escaping via a forty-five-story waterslide, then MI6-ing their way to a dive motel where they could lay low? Was that all real?

Jackson killed the water and toweled off. He dressed in jeans and the same T-shirt, because when he and Hillary had packed "contingency clothes" the previous afternoon, he hadn't thought of anything to sleep in. He brushed his teeth, looking at a bruised, beleaguered face in the mirror. How long had they been in Vegas now anyhow? How much longer would they be? And had they accomplished anything?

He quietly exited the bathroom, expecting to find Hillary sleeping in one of the motel's two beds. She had showered and changed before him, during which time he'd caught a fifteen-minute catnap. It had been the aroma of a fine meal to a starving man.

But Hillary wasn't sleeping. The lights were on—so was the TV, muted—and she sat cross-legged on the near bed. She wore black running shorts and a pink tank top, her still-damp hair restrained in a hasty ponytail. Her laptop was open on the bed in front of her and she cradled a motel mug of coffee in her left hand.

"Too much adrenaline?" Jackson asked.

"Something like that. And I have to know if we just risked everything for nothing. Besides, it's almost morning anyhow."

And just like that, his prospects for sleep were gone.

"What's the cloud site where you loaded the files?"

He dropped to his knees and spun the laptop toward him. He quickly brought up the site he and Mouse had set up and entered his credentials. Then he turned it back to her. "It had maybe two minutes to copy."

"Just one folder?"

"What's the name?" he asked, leaning over to see.

She angled the screen slightly. "What's 'GD'?"

"Beats me."

She used her touchpad to open the "GD" folder, revealing four subfolders.

"There were five or six," Jackson said.

"Let's see what we have." She scooted over so he could sit beside her and she began browsing the subfolders. The first—"Audio"—contained just two files. Hillary double-clicked the first and waited.

"Go for Reynolds," came a gruff, gravelly voice.

"Ernie, it's me." The second speaker was smooth and refined. Senatorial, even. It sounded just like Moore had on the YouTube videos Jackson had listened to.

"Is there a problem?" the first voice asked.

"No, not a problem. I'm just checking in."

"Why?"

"Making sure everything is still going smoothly."

A pause. Then, *"What makes you ask?"*

"Expenditures, for one. We've gone way over budget. And then there was that . . . incident a few weeks ago."

"My people took care of that. It's contained."

"Containment isn't my concern. The fact that it happened at all is what's alarming."

"Look, Senator, we're walking a very fine line here, probing and testing where we are and the way we are. There are bound to be some irregularities from time to time."

"I understand that. But you have to admit, these are not the results we anticipated."

"Sometimes you have to pick between the end and the means. I can't guarantee you both. You want Golden Dawn to accomplish anything, then you're going to have to give me some latitude to do what I need to do. Besides, we have a competent man looking over things."

Now Moore hesitated. *"I understand that, Ernie. Just promise me you'll do everything you can to keep another . . . situation like this from happening."*

"I'll do what I can."

"And keep me in the loop."

"You're in the loop."

The phone clicked off and the recording stopped.

Jackson and Hillary's eyes met.

"You get a sort of eerie feeling in your gut listening to that?"

She nodded.

"'Incident', 'contained,' 'irregularities.' Why do I suddenly feel like they're covering up alien indwellings or something?"

"Because you're a dork."

"And what's with Golden Dawn? I thought we were looking at Silver Dawn?"

Hillary shrugged and clicked on the next file. Another recording began to play.

"Moore."

"Senator, it's me."

"What's going on, Ernie?"

"We need to talk. About Stark."

"What about him?"

"Not on the phone."

"Okay. I've got appearances all morning, but I can squeeze in lunch. Twelve-thirty, the usual place?"

"Confirmed."

The call ended.

Hillary sat back. "Why these two?" She sipped her coffee.

Jackson eyed her mug enviously.

"And how did he record them?" Her eyes cut to him. "There's more in the pot."

He quickly hopped off the bed. "What are the filenames?" he asked as he poured himself a cup.

"Strings of numbers. 'Two-one-two-four, dash, two-one-two-six, dash, zero-six-two-two-one-two.'"

Jackson took a sip of piping hot coffee. It was weak.

"June 22, 2012."

"What about the first part?"

"Military time? Nine twenty-four to nine twenty-six. Call duration?"

She shrugged.

"What's the second one?"

"'Zero-eight-zero-nine, dash, zero-eight-one-zero, dash, zero-six-two-six-one-two.' A little after eight a.m. on the twenty-sixth of June."

He sat down beside her on the other side of the bed. "What else we got?"

She backtracked and opened a folder named "Maps." It contained half a dozen satellite images of a barren desert, along with close-ups that revealed a complex of buildings and maybe a runway. But they were grainy and zoomed out so far that it was hard to distinguish much detail.

The next folder was entitled "Dossiers," and it had several subfolders: "Alive," "Dead," "Kingman," and "Missing." There were also a handful of other files, each with three-letter filenames.

"C-A-M," Jackson said, pointing at the first one.

"Carson Andrew Moore," Hillary said as she opened the file. It was a thorough dossier on the senator, and at brief glance, didn't reveal anything they didn't already know. Hillary backed out and clicked on a file labeled "EWR."

The file was for General Ernest William Reynolds, U.S. Army. Born in Corpus Christi, Texas, in 1951, Reynolds had attended West Point, served in Vietnam during the late stages of the war, and also spent time in Saudi Arabia and Kuwait during Operations Desert Shield and Desert Storm. He'd received a Purple Heart for injuries suffered in Vietnam, and several other commendations for actions both in the Middle East and during peacetime.

Reynolds lived in Lake Bancroft, Virginia, with his wife Maureen. He was a Republican, an avid hunter, a Redskins season ticket holder, and a smoker. The dossier contained a list of his tours and commands dating back to the 1970s. He was currently stationed in Washington, D.C., where he served as a liaison between the military and Congress.

"Look at this," Hillary said, pointing at the screen. "Reynolds was at Blane."

"Eighty-three to eighty-six. Just over three years." Jackson took another drink of coffee. "Blane's an Air Force Base. Reynolds is an Army man."

"Roy Donovan said something about Army personnel being there."

"Still begs the question of why. And it's that same time as Moore and your dad."

The next file Hillary opened was one named "MJB." It was a profile of Matt Brenner, but it told them little they hadn't already learned. She clicked on the bottom file in the list, labeled "XDS." The file for Xavier Daniel Stark was much smaller. It was heavy on his education at UVA and Berkeley, as well as his time serving on Senator Moore's staff. Aside from that, details were scant.

She closed Stark's profile and selected one of the three remaining files, all with names that meant nothing. The first belonged to an old Hispanic woman named Henrietta Ramirez who had served as a civilian secretary at Blane Air

Force Base in the 1970s and '80s. Jackson had just started skimming the file when Hillary sat up. "Oh my goodness."

"What?"

"It's Aunt Henrietta."

"Aunt?"

"When we were little, we used to get birthday and Christmas cards from an Aunt Henrietta. Dad said it was a sweet old lady he'd worked with, but he never said when or where. The cards stopped when I was in high school, and I just assumed she had died. Dad never spoke of her again. But this must be her."

"Are you sure about that?"

"How many Henrietta's who live in Las Vegas do you think worked with my father?"

"Aunt Henrietta was from Las Vegas?"

"Henderson, but I remember the postmarks were from Las Vegas."

"Shoot, I tore open most birthday cards without even bothering to read the return address, much less the postmark."

"Why is that not a surprise?"

"So why does Holloway have a file on Aunt Henrietta?"

"I don't know," Hillary replied, reading the bio. "It looks like she remained at the base until it closed at the end of 1991, but it doesn't say in what capacity or with whom or why she's of interest."

"Any chance she's why your dad was in Vegas, why he sent the money? Maybe she was sick or in trouble or something."

"No, Arielle had his business card, remember? And they exchanged phone calls."

"Sorry, long night."

"But if she's still alive and still lives in the area, she might be able to shed some light on things."

"Right, because if your dad's old buddy Captain Donovan didn't know anything, I'm sure the lady who answered his phone would be able to tell us all about Silver Dawn or Golden Dawn or Bronze Dawn or *Red Dawn* or whatever."

"It's worth a try."

The two other files were for a man named Isaac Cutler and a woman named Laura Woodson. Cutler, according to the file, worked for the CIA, but in what capacity was unknown. So was his age. A physical description that roughly matched the man Arielle had seen at Moore's speech and also at the "body exchange" suggested he was in his late thirties or early forties, but anything else about him was a mystery.

Laura Woodson also worked for the CIA, and details about her were even scarcer. She was Cutler's superior, but there was nothing to identify what either of them did for the CIA or how they were tied to Moore, Reynolds, or anyone else.

Jackson stood and paced. "We have Stark, who was found dead with a former Navy SEAL and CIA operative named Robert Kyle. Now Holloway has files on two more CIA agents. What the heck are we getting into, Hill?"

She took a drink but didn't answer.

"Is there any chance your dad isn't actually a philanthropist but a CIA hitman or something, like Chuck Woolery or whatever his name was?"

"Chuck Woolery?"

"That guy they made the George Clooney movie about, *Confessions of a* . . . I want to say *Teenage Drama Queen*, but that was Lindsay Lohan."

Hillary stared at him incredulously.

"Help me out here, Hill."

"You mean *Confessions of a Dangerous Mind* about Chuck Barris?"

He snapped his fingers. "That's it."

"No, my dad is not a CIA assassin."

"Okay. But somehow this all ties to Blane, and we've got everybody there—Air Force, Army, a Navy SEAL, the CIA, probably KGB and the SS if we keep digging. And your dad's friend Donovan mentioned the Silver Dawn project from the '80s and now all the players are lumped together again under some reincarnation of the project named Golden Dawn. Or so it would seem."

"Why don't you do some research on Silver Dawn and Golden Dawn? See what you can find out beyond what Donovan told us and learn everything you can about Blane Air Force Base, past and present. I'll see what's in all the subfolders here."

"How am I supposed to conduct this research? Your tablet is cracked and waterlogged."

She sighed. "I'll use my phone. You can have the laptop."

He topped off their coffees and they got to work. Jackson started by researching Blane Air Force Base. As was so often the case when he did online research, he found Wikipedia to be the best blend of straightforward yet comprehensive—if somewhat dubious at times—information. But he learned the basics.

Blane Air Force Base had opened in the 1940s, in the era of nuclear weapons, super bombers, and the Cold War. Blane had been a testing ground for a number of experimental aircraft, and the pilots stationed at Blane made good use of the nearby Nevada Test and Training Range to dump their payloads.

There was also a reference on Wikipedia to top-secret projects at Blane, without any details. There were theories, of course—aliens being the primary one—but no facts to substantiate any of them. What military base in the desert didn't have rumors of aliens, nukes, and CIA experiments?

In the 1980s, several budget cuts had affected the base, resulting in scrapped programs and significant personnel transfers. The January 8, 1988, edition of the *Las Vegas Sun* had painted a pretty bleak picture of the financial situation at Blane, and less than four years later, the base had been decommissioned. According to the page contributors, there had been no activity at the base since.

Jackson spent twenty minutes pecking around, confirming some of the facts about Blane on other websites. He even found the *Sun's* article about the budget cuts in an online repository. It painted the same story about politics and price hikes and military secrecy.

A soft glow was spilling around the edges of the blinds when Jackson took a break to stretch and brew another packet of coffee. While it dripped, he tried a number of Google searches. He keyed combinations of Blane Air Force Base and Senator Moore, Major Moore, Warren McKenzie, General Reynolds, Xavier Stark, Isaac Cutler, Laura Woodson, and Richard Holloway. None turned up anything. He filled his cup and changed his search focus.

Jackson added "Silver Dawn" to his search parameters and, after sorting the semi-credible sites from the completely unreliable sites, read through several pages of theories and pretenses of what had been going on behind the scenes at Blane. Whether or not any of them were factual was another matter.

Aliens stole the show. They had crashed into the desert, or been imported from Roswell, or sprung up from the earth à la *War of the Worlds*. They had been cross-bred with humans, with animals, and with other aliens. Nuclear technology had been applied. Marvel wouldn't have bought half of the ideas people had cooked up and subscribed to on their various blogs and message boards.

But there was more. The idea of superhumans without aliens was also floated. The CIA had genetically engineered a breed of elite fighters, *Captain America* style. Another theory had fallout from nuclear tests turning residents of nearby towns into cannibals and mutants. Brainwashing—by the Air Force, the CIA, the Russians—was yet another common thread.

Not all the theories were quite as absurd. The Air Force had tested smaller versions of the atomic bomb. They had experimented with radar and sonar technology. A weapon that attacked the auditory system had been developed. Green weapons systems had been invented a generation early. As with the crazy theories, they were little more than speculation without any real substantiation. And none of them even hinted at Silver Dawn still operating in the present, especially since the base had been closed for over twenty years.

Nor did Jackson's search of "Golden Dawn" bring up anything even remotely pertinent. As far as the internet knew, it didn't exist.

"How's it coming?" he asked.

Hillary hadn't moved in an hour, her legs still crossed as she peered at her phone. "I'm almost done," she said.

Jackson searched several mapping sites for satellite views of Blane. He got nowhere. Blane was listed on the maps, but whenever he switched to "aerial" or "earth" mode, the picture was scrambled or blurry. It happened sometimes in remote parts of the world, like the middle of the Mojave Desert. It could also happen if the government had purposefully scrambled the image. Either way, he wasn't able to verify if the images from the "Maps" folder were of Blane or not.

It was quarter after six and the light outside the room was getting brighter. Jackson flipped TV channels, keeping the sound muted, looking for early morning news. None of the bottom of the screen scrawls mentioned anything about a burglary at Oasis, and he found nothing online.

Finally, Hillary lowered her phone and looked up.

"What is it?" Jackson asked.

"I don't know," she said. "But something very weird is going on."

Chapter Thirty-Eight

6:21 a.m.

HILLARY SWUNG HER legs off the bed and stood. She set her empty cup on the dresser next to the TV and began as if she was addressing a jury with her opening statement.

"There were four subfolders in the 'Dossiers' folder. The 'Alive' and 'Dead' subfolders each contained twelve bios of people from all over the country, a couple even outside the U.S. Each was the same: age, physical description, education—starting in kindergarten up through college if applicable, with grades and majors—jobs and careers, areas of expertise, marriages, children, and so forth. They included men and women in a variety of fields, with a variety of skills and a variety of educational backgrounds. The only similarity I could find is that they were all in their early thirties, or in a few cases, late twenties."

"The dead ones too?"

"No, some of them had died younger. But there were none who would be over thirty-three in that group." She peeked at her phone. "Of those in the 'Dead' subfolder, one was killed in Iraq in 2008, another died in a head-on collision in Phoenix in 2004, two more were killed in a gang-related shooting in L.A. and an apparent drug deal gone bad in Miami Gardens, and the other eight committed suicide sometime between 2001 and 2011."

"That's a lot of suicides."

"Two of those were murder-suicides."

Jackson squinted.

"That's not all. Of the dozen in the 'Alive' folder, eight had a record. Four assault and batteries, two aggravated assaults, one with repeated domestic violence charges, and one is in Ely State Prison for murder."

"Who are these people?"

Hillary shook her head.

"There's nothing else in common? No similar place of birth, no common school or college, anything?"

"No," she said, "but there's not a place of birth for any of them. Dates of birth are all in a range from 1979 to 1984."

"Strange."

"I randomly searched a few names online, but I didn't find anything there."

"Anything at all?"

"Nothing beyond what was in the file or that amplified it in any way."

Jackson stood too. He paced to the door and back. "Late twenties to early thirties . . ."

"There's more. The 'Kingman' folder listed another seventeen people, all in the same age category, men and women. Thirteen were still alive, but four had died."

"Let me guess, suicides."

"Three of them. One was killed in a knife fight by one of the living persons. It was ruled self-defense. But the killer and three of the thirteen others have violence charges sometime in the last decade."

Jackson shook his head. "Kingman. What's the connection?"

"They all live in the town of Kingman, Nevada," Hillary said.

"Which is where?"

"About an hour's drive north of here, in the middle of the desert."

"Wait, that's—"

"Just across a small mountain range from Blane Air Force Base."

Jackson slowly sat back on the bed. "What in the Sam Hill is going on here?"

"I don't know," she said, also sitting so that she faced him.

"What about the 'Missing' folder?"

"Four names, two men and two women, same demographic. They disappeared in the last decade, one from Kingman, the others from various places across the country. They're cold cases, from what I could tell."

Jackson exhaled. "Did you see Yvonne's name?"

"Arielle's mom? No, why?"

"When I found the folders on the flash drive, I skimmed them quickly. I saw her name there."

"Which folder?"

He held out his hands. "I don't know. It must not have made the jump."

"You're sure it was there?"

"Yeah. It was the only name that stood out. That and a Wyatt Quinn. Sounds like a desperado from an old Western."

"I saw that name," Hillary said. "He was in the 'Kingman' folder too, one of the thirteen living people. He's the sheriff."

"So why's he listed in the group?"

"I don't know. He was the only law enforcement officer in any of the folders."

Jackson stood again. He paced to the window, peeked out at the newly risen sun. "Hill . . . what have we stepped in?"

"I have no idea."

He turned back as she reached for the laptop and lifted it over to her bed. "The fourth folder under 'GD'—'Events'—was empty, so whatever was there must not have had time to copy."

"So that's about the end of what we know?" he said.

"For now. I'm going to research Kingman a little."

"See what you can find on Yvonne too."

"I don't get it," Hillary said. "Everyone else in these folders is the same age. Even Quinn, the sheriff, is only thirty-six. Yvonne had to be older than that."

"Depends how young she had Arielle. And didn't Darla say she had another daughter she gave up for adoption. Back in '84?"

"She'd be the youngest of the bunch, but I'll check it out."

While she did, Jackson sorted the stacks of money on the bed. They were wet and clumped together, and he pulled them apart to let them dry. Wet money was still good money, and just as easy to count in stacks. The total was five hundred short of fifty grand. Ten thousand of that was Hillary's buy-in taken from Arielle's stash, so adding the rest of Arielle's money—which they had packed up as part of their emergency luggage—the total was $64,500. Spread out on a cheap cotton bedspread in a dive motel in the Las Vegas suburbs. While he was on the run with a beautiful woman. All that was missing was Bradley Cooper or Kurt Russell.

"Jackson."

Hillary's voice stopped him cold in mid-recount.

"Yvonne lived in Kingman from 1980 until 1984. Three years before Arielle was born."

He turned around.

"That's the same time Dad was at the base, Moore was at the base, Reynolds was at the base, and Silver Dawn was in operation."

"And it's the same time most of the people on Holloway's list were born."

She nodded. "Kingman is just a little dot on a map, hardly more than a main drag with a few side streets. But it's the nearest town to the base, where some of the families lived and where airmen went to buy what they couldn't get at the BX. It wasn't officially part of the base, but pretty close to it."

"What's a BX?"

"Base exchange."

"I thought it was PX."

"That's the Army."

He shrugged.

"What'd you find out about the base anyhow?" Hillary asked.

He explained his research into Blane and Silver Dawn, starting with the facts and working his way to the fiction.

"Do you ever feel like you have all the puzzle pieces but they don't fit together?" Hillary asked when he was finished.

"All the time."

"Silver Dawn then, Golden Dawn now; Blane and Kingman; all these people dead and alive; the records of violence; the CIA and the Air Force; Moore, Reynolds, Holloway, Dad, Arielle and Yvonne—somehow they're all tied together. But how?" she asked with a frown. "What's the common bond?"

"And how did Holloway compile all this evidence? Those satellite photos of the base weren't just taken off Google or MapQuest. I checked, and the area over the base has been scrambled on all commercial satellite images."

"Reynolds would surely have access to a military satellite," Hillary said.

"But how did Holloway get it? The same with those dossiers."

"That's the other thing. The ones we both looked at seemed more like a compilation of notes. The information varied, wasn't always in the same order, etcetera. The ones I just looked at in the 'Dossiers' folder were minimal but consistent, more professional."

"Prepared by two different people?"

She shrugged. "Same question about the phone calls. Who recorded them, why, and how did Holloway get them?"

"The man Appleby saw delivering a 'package' to Holloway. A P.I. dropping off a flash drive of covertly gathered evidence?"

Another shrug. "I guess how isn't nearly as important as why. We still don't know what it all means, what Holloway intended to do with this info, or what we can do with it."

"You hungry?" Jackson asked.

"I am."

"Take a break, let the info ruminate? There's an IHOP across the street."

"We should keep a low profile."

"Pounding pancakes isn't exactly conspicuous."

She paused for just a moment. "Let me change."

Ten minutes later, she wore blue jeans and a white, cap-sleeved shirt, her hair clipped behind her head. They walked to a new IHOP and were seated in a window booth. Jackson sipped coffee and ice water intermittently while Hillary browsed her menu. Having slept all of a quarter of an hour, he needed the caffeine and the temperature contrast to keep him up. She selected a vegetarian omelet, he a stack of buttermilk pancakes. When the waitress was gone, he leaned forward.

"So what are we going to do?"

"I promised if we didn't find a major link or clue, we'd walk away," she said.

"Did we?"

"I'm leaving that up to you."

He regarded her over a raised glass of water. "That's incredibly fair."

"Were you expecting something else?"

He gulped down some cold water. "We didn't find a link to your father, or to Arielle's death. But we did find solid evidence that the Silver Dawn project is still in existence in some way and apparently renamed Golden Dawn. And while we don't know that anything is going on at the base, something is clearly going on in Kingman, and somehow, forty-some-odd people are being watched and monitored, half of whom are either dead or violent offenders. We're definitely onto something. The question is what, and how deep do we want to dig."

"That's two questions."

"And valid ones. Whatever this is, it's sinister. Incidents and containment and records of a certain age demographic that's assaulting people and hanging themselves. Suddenly Arielle's accounts of drugging people and having them disappear are starting to make sense."

Hillary took a drink of coffee.

"And the other thing we have to ask ourselves," Jackson said, "is how much trouble are we in? It would seem that if Holloway was threatening to expose any of this, he's probably the good guy. But we technically committed a felony last night," he said, looking around and lowering his voice. "I really doubt he just lets that go, even if he doesn't go to the cops."

"What are you saying?"

"What I said earlier. Adriana and Teresa knew who we really were. Which means Holloway might know. If not, he'll certainly find out. We're in over our heads, Hill. We should send him forty grand in poker winnings as an 'I'm sorry' gift, put the other twenty-five in the bus locker, go get the Granada, and call Baxter and Cruz with an anonymous tip from a payphone in Barstow."

Hillary nodded slowly as she reached for her water. "So you're out?"

He sighed. "I didn't say that. I said it's what we should do. But you've still got concerns about your dad, which I understand. And you've got the bulldog McKenzie spirit, so I doubt you'll go back to L.A. even if I do."

"Look, I would turn this over to the cops, I really would. But their jurisdiction ends at the city limits, which means even if they believe us, they'll have to pass it on to the feds. How far do you think the investigation goes with pilfered, partial evidence, and with the military and the CIA trying to keep a lid on it, not to mention a heavily-invested United States senator?"

"So what, Donna Quixote and Sancha go knock over some windmills?"

"It's Sancho, and no. We see what we can find out about General Reynolds and his ties to Moore or Holloway or my father. And we talk to the people in Kingman, see what they have to say. We'll also check into the names on this list in more detail. Maybe there's some other connection that isn't so obvious. It may get us nowhere, but at least we'll have done all we can."

"And you're not worried that we're going to ask the wrong person the wrong question and end up rotting in a rusty barrel of acid behind some barn out in the desert?"

She grimaced. "Where do you come up with these things?"

He shrugged as their breakfasts arrived. He doused his pancakes with an assortment of syrups and cut into the stack with his fork, forming a menu-cover-worthy wedge. "One day," he said as he stabbed the wedge with his fork. "I'll give you one day."

"Thank you."

"But tonight I am going to be back in Vegas, in a nice hotel, with a comfortable bed, which you will pay for."

"Understood."

"That is if we're not in adjoining rooms at the Graybar Motel."

She cut into her omelet. "Thank you, Jackson."

He chewed his bite of pancakes, his stomach immediately begging for more.

"A trip to a small town full of violent people in the middle of nowhere," he said. "What could go wrong?"

Chapter Thirty-Nine

8:04 a.m.

BREAKFAST COMPLETE, JACKSON and Hillary returned to their hotel and split up duties. She tracked down Henrietta Ramirez and used her various contacts to further research General Reynolds. He, meanwhile, reserved a car from the Budget Car Rental just down the street. The Granada was across town, was less than ideal for a drive into the desert, and was sort of conspicuous if anyone was looking for them. To that end, he also checked the local news stations and their websites, none of which were reporting anything about a burglary at Oasis the night before. Shortly after eight, he put in a call to Detective Ashley Larson of the Los Angeles Police Department. He'd saved her and her partner's lives a few months prior, and she had more than repaid him on a trio of cases since. Even so, Jackson was sure he could coax a small favor out of her.

"Detective Larson," she answered in a petite voice that was all business.

"Ashley, it's Jackson."

"Hey, what's up?"

"Wondering if you could do me a very small favor."

"Uh-oh."

"I mean it, very small. Can you check your various sources and back channels and see if the Las Vegas Metro Police Department happens to be looking for me."

"What did you do in Las Vegas?"

"I'd rather not disclose that."

She huffed. "Tell me this is not some frat boy trip gone bad."

"I'm thirty, Ash."

"Is that relevant?"

"Fair point. It's not that. Can you check, please?"

"I'm still at home, so give me a few minutes to log onto my computer. I'll call you back."

He closed his phone. "You find anything?" he asked Hillary.

"Reynolds served on a defense subcommittee with Moore back in 2006 and 2007," she said.

"If we keep digging, we're going to find Kevin Bacon pretty soon."

"He's also been fairly outspoken against gun control and in favor of border security, same as Moore."

"No big surprise."

"No."

Her phone clicked and then a male voice issued a greeting. She tapped the screen to take the call off speaker and stood as she responded. Since the computer was unoccupied while she talked, Jackson did a quick search for Adriana and Teresa Escobar. He found them under the Escobar Detective Agency in the Houston suburb of Stafford. A brief survey of their website suggested they were legit. It did not provide pictures. He hoped they hadn't gotten in trouble with Holloway, but it wasn't his fault they had involved themselves in his and Hillary's affairs.

Ashley called back within five minutes.

"Looks like you're in the clear, Jackson," she said. "No word of any warrants and nothing on the wire about you."

"Good. Thank you, Ashley."

"Whatever you're into, be careful."

"I will. Thanks."

He closed his phone again just as Hillary ended her call. "Looks like Holloway is coming after us vigilante-style," Jackson said. "That was my contact at LAPD. I asked her to check if there was any scuttlebutt surrounding me. All quiet."

"I have a few people putting out some feelers regarding Reynolds, but I didn't learn much other than what I told you earlier. I did get an address for Henrietta, northwest of here off Grand Teton Drive."

"I'll go get the car. You want to pack up here?"

She nodded and he departed. Thirty minutes later, both of them and all their belongings were packed into a silver, two-door Ford Focus. While Jackson had procured the car, Hillary had called ahead and Henrietta Ramirez was expecting them. Hillary had also changed into a pair of denim shorts, whereas Jackson still wore his full-length blue jeans.

Henrietta Ramirez lived in a fourplex that was identical to a dozen more up and down both sides of the street. All were painted in the same brown hue, with a slightly darker roof and slightly lighter shade of dirt and gravel that passed for a yard. They were squeezed close together, with just clumps and stubs of trees beginning to grow in the new subdivision. Jackson parked by the side of the road and he and Hillary got out. The pleasant warmth of morning was quickly turning into an oppressive heat, and Jackson did not relish a trip deep into the desert. Maybe Henrietta could provide some answers that would tie everything up nicely.

She opened the door and Jackson frowned. He had expected a crusty old woman, considering Holloway's bio said she was eighty-seven. But she looked youthful and energetic in her bright blue sweat suit. Her hair was white as snow, but neatly styled. She wore makeup that perhaps disguised a few wrinkles, but her movements were smooth and graceful, lacking the slowness Jackson expected from a woman who'd been born before the Great Depression.

"My, my," she said, regarding Hillary with a wide smile. "I just knew from the photographs your father used to send that you would become a beautiful young woman someday, and you certainly have. Please, please come in."

They entered a very bland living room: off-white walls and ceiling, gray carpet, meager furniture. Very little was hung on the walls, but a small buffet table against the far wall held a cluster of photographs. In a T-shirt and jeans, Jackson was immediately chilled by the temperature, and his hair was parted by the central air. When Henrietta clamped her icy hands on his, he nearly jumped.

"Is this your husband?" she asked Hillary.

"No, this is Jackson."

Henrietta's eyes narrowed, almost to a wink, as she smiled. "Don't let the grass grow under your feet, sonny."

"Uh, we're not dating," Jackson answered.

"We're business associates," Hillary said.

"Oh," Henrietta said as if deeply saddened. Her hands remained a frozen vice on Jackson's. Finally, she unclasped them. "Would you like something to drink? Coffee, tea?"

"No, thank you," Hillary said.

"I would take some coffee," Jackson said.

"Right you are," Henrietta said while Hillary shot Jackson a glare. "Cream or sugar?"

"Black, please."

She disappeared into the kitchen, hollering for them to make themselves comfortable. Hillary sat in an armchair, and Jackson wandered over to the buffet table to examine the photos before taking an adjacent chair. The pictures portrayed people of all ages, presumably Henrietta's children, grandchildren, and great grandchildren. Some were white, some Hispanic, others a mix. Henrietta herself had skin so light that if not for her surname and the demographic info in the dossier, Jackson would never have guessed her ethnicity.

She returned with a cup of steaming coffee. Jackson thanked her and sipped what he counted as his fifth or sixth cup of the day. Sooner or later, he would have to pay the toll, but for now, his bladder was holding.

"Thank you so much for seeing us, Henrietta, especially on short notice," Hillary said.

The old woman smiled. "My pleasure, Hillary. What can I do for you?"

Hillary briefly summed up the reason they were in Las Vegas, leaving out the graphic details of Arielle's death, their con of Richard Holloway, all the reports of violence by and against the people in Holloway's dossiers, and anything else not pertinent to her line of questioning. "We're hoping you can fill in some details for us since you worked with my father at Blane Air Force Base," she concluded.

"How is your father, by the way?"

"He's fine. He and Mom are in Bangladesh right now, doing charity work."

"How lovely. He always had a good heart, your father."

"Thank you."

Henrietta crossed her legs at the ankle and folded her hands in her lap. "I was assigned to your father when he was transferred to the base in January of '83. I took a liking to him right away. He worked hard, demanding nothing more from those under him than he gave himself. And he treated us with respect. It's a hard position, being in command and having to maintain a sense of order and discipline, and your father did so without being harsh or condescending. I always admired that about him."

"Were you aware of a project called Silver Dawn?" Hillary asked.

Henrietta nodded. "I was. It was classified at the time, so I don't know any of the details, but I was aware of its existence."

"Was Dad part of it?"

She nodded again. "As his secretary, I saw the files that came across his desk, knew of appointments, heard phone calls. I'm not certain, but I believe he was transferred to the base specifically for the project."

"And you have no idea what it was about?"

"I'm afraid not. But it was rather extensive. In fact, I even suspected your father was involved . . . more deeply."

Hillary looked at Jackson. Roy Donovan had expressed a similar belief.

"Why do you say that?"

"Like I said, I handled all his appointments and knew when he had visitors. There were typical meetings and appointments, and then there were those with a tighter circle, the Silver Dawn team. But within that group, he met routinely with a much smaller group. Always closed door, not to be disturbed, often after hours. Something was up."

"Do you have any idea what it was?"

"No. Your father didn't say and I didn't ask. It wasn't my place."

Jackson gulped his coffee. It was stronger than an ox. The stuff in the hotel was just hot water by comparison.

Hillary changed gears, asking about Senator Moore—then known as Major Morelli—and General Reynolds. She also brought up the names of Holloway, Stark, Brenner, Cutler, and Woodson. Henrietta knew both Moore and Reynolds, saying Moore was a fine officer and part of the Silver Dawn subset she believed Warren had been part of. Reynolds hadn't arrived until November of 1983 and Henrietta didn't care much for him. She said he was gruff and standoffish, very "regular Army." She didn't divulge anything about him Jackson and Hillary didn't already know or that was helpful, and she'd never heard of the others.

"What about Yvonne Coleman?" Jackson asked over his coffee mug.

The color drained from Henrietta's face.

"You know her?" Hillary asked.

"I do."

"We understand she lived in the nearby town of Kingman while Dad was at Blane."

Henrietta nodded.

"Did she work at the base?"

"No. She was a patient."

"A patient?"

"Of your father's."

"Dad saw patients? Civilians?"

"They were brought to the base," she said. "For several years."

"And Yvonne was one of them?"

"Yes."

"How many?" Jackson asked.

Henrietta shook her head. "I don't know. They were kept secluded from the rest of the base in an old airplane hangar, Hangar 5. Your father trusted me implicitly, and allowed me to schedule his appointments with them. He swore me to confidentiality, assuring me that doctor-patient rights existed in the military as well as civilian sector. All I ever knew were names and appointments."

"And Yvonne was one of them?"

"Yes."

"How long were these civilians on the base?"

"Cumulatively, several years. Individually, I only know when they had appointments with your father, not when they came or went to the base. But based on their appointments, some were there for only a few weeks or months; others over a year."

"Why were civilians brought to the base and why was Dad seeing them?"

"I'm afraid I do not know that," Henrietta answered.

"Was it part of Silver Dawn?"

"I would only be guessing, but I think so."

"Men, women, children?" Jackson asked.

"All women. At least those your father saw."

"Young, old?"

"Very young. Twenties, maybe."

"Were they pregnant?" Jackson asked.

Henrietta nodded. "Many of them. Not all."

"Was Yvonne?" he asked, remembering that she'd had a child before Arielle, in 1984 according to Darla.

"I . . . I think so." Her face had gone from jovial to sad. She wasn't telling them something.

"Henrietta, what is it?" Hillary asked.

"Perhaps I should not say."

"No, please."

She took a deep breath. "I remember Yvonne Coleman because . . . because she met with your father much more frequently than any of the other women. They had several regularly scheduled appointments, a few weeks apart, as he did with all the others. But they also met privately, off the record."

"Off the record," Hillary said.

"Captain McKenzie once informed me that he would be meeting with Yvonne one evening and asked me to make sure no other meetings or appointments were scheduled, but he asked me not to put it in the books or let anyone know. Another time, I caught them meeting together."

"Caught?" Hillary asked.

"I returned to the office after hours and they were just coming out of your father's office. I remember the look on Yvonne's face. She was terrified. Your father asked me not to mention this to anyone and I didn't."

Jackson took a drink of coffee simply because the mug was in his hand. He no longer tasted it.

"Shortly after this, your father stopped seeing her—meeting with her, I mean. I can only presume she was removed from the base. But . . ."

"What is it, Henrietta?"

The old woman wrung her hands so that they turned white to match her hair. "He made several trips off the base in the following months, always very secretive. Like the meeting with Yvonne, I was to schedule these 'appointments' but not let anyone know. They were usually at night."

"Do you remember when this was?" Hillary asked.

"The summer and fall of 1983. I don't know the specific dates, except that the time I 'caught' them meeting together was October 11. I know because it was our anniversary, and I was upset that I had forgotten my purse and had to return to the office and would be late meeting my husband for dinner."

Hillary let a silence hang in the air for a moment. She licked her lips and took a breath as if to reset her composure before speaking. "Henrietta, do you think my father was having an affair with Yvonne Coleman?"

"It is not my place to say."

"But you did suspect it at the time?"

A tear ran down her cheek. "Your father was never anything less than an officer and a gentleman. I told myself these were just the delusions of an old woman and a suspicious mind. I had no proof, no evidence, and I refused to let my thoughts about him be tarnished by conjecture."

Hillary nodded. She looked to Jackson. "Is there anything else you can tell us, Henrietta?"

"No. I am very sorry."

"Don't be. Thank you very much for your time," Hillary said. "It was nice to finally meet you."

Henrietta stood too and embraced Hillary. "I am so sorry," she said again as they separated. "Please, it has been almost thirty years. Do not judge your father based on distant suspicions and coincidences."

"I won't, I assure you."

Jackson returned the mug to her. "Thank you for the coffee, Henrietta."

"Take care of her," she said quietly, her hands even colder as they clamped over his wrist.

"I will," he said, then followed Hillary out the door. The heat was suffocating after the chilly air-conditioned apartment. "You okay?" he asked as they walked to the car.

"I'm fine," she answered cursorily.

"There could be hundreds of explan—"

"Please, Jackson, not right now."

He circled the car and got in. The Focus didn't have the leather seats of the Granada, but it was still roasting. And it was just after nine a.m.

"What's the plan?" he asked when Hillary had buckled in.

"Nothing's changed," she said dourly. "We're going to Kingman."

Chapter Forty

Twenty-one months ago . . .
Saturday, December 25
7:23 a.m.

FOR WHATEVER REASON, the Douglas family had never been one to wake up at the crack of dawn, stagger downstairs in their pajamas, and tear open their Christmas presents like raccoons after garbage. And for that, Jackson was thankful as he alighted from the loft—fully dressed and fully groomed—to the smell of frying bacon and steaming cocoa. Outside, snowflakes were softly falling on the blanket that already covered everything. The fireplace was crackling in the living room, and a professionally decorated tree stood in front of a bay window, a tasteful amount of presents arranged beneath it. The scene was perfect.

"Morning, Son," David said, looking up from an armchair beside the fire. Decked in the reindeer sweater the family had been trying to get him to toss out for a decade, he was reading his Bible and enjoying a cup of coffee. Jackson greeted his father and returned a "Merry Christmas" from Hannah, who was busy in the kitchen.

Getting away for Christmas had generally been considered her idea. Nobody remembered exactly how the discussion had first started back in the spring, or when and how the discussion had evolved into a plan. Douglas Christmases were typically spent at home, or occasionally visiting extended family. But this year, they had opted to trade palms for pines, rain for snow, and the Pacific Ocean for the Rocky Mountains.

The two-bedroom place on the edge of Estes Park, Colorado, had been perfect, and Hannah had booked it over the Fourth of July weekend. With the living area and master suite downstairs, and a second bedroom and living room in the loft, the condo had enough room for four, but was small enough to be cozy and affordable.

Unfortunately, four was on its way to five.

Grant's relationship with Hillary had turned from steady to serious over the summer, and when the family had gathered to celebrate David's birthday, Grant had broached the subject of bringing her along. Her parents were out of the country, her sisters had other arrangements in the works, and she was faced with a Christmas alone, he had argued. David and Hannah had both acquiesced, and to keep his wool light gray, Jackson had made it unanimous.

Sleeping arrangements were the first casualty. David and Hannah got the master suite, leaving just the upstairs bedroom and a pullout sofa in the loft. Grant refused to make Hillary sleep on the pullout, and putting either guy in the bedroom with her was obviously out. So she took one of the double beds, leaving the other unoccupied while Jackson and Grant shared a lumpy doublewide sofa bed.

Food was the next thing to go. Hillary played the would-be daughter-in-law role perfectly, helping Hannah with everything, including meal prep. Goodbye steak and potatoes, hello vegetable courses. Christmas Eve dinner had been split pea soup. Sans ham. Sans any other sustenance. Jackson had sneaked downstairs at midnight and unwrapped Grant's stocking gift of chocolate covered cherries, devouring them all to quiet his stomach. Served his brother right, he figured.

But by far the biggest loss of the week was Jackson's Scrabble dominance. He swore Hillary was making up words until she pulled out her stupid laptop, tapped into the condo's Wi-Fi, and Googled him wrong.

But it was still Christmas, and Jackson had spent his morning shower resolving not to let Hillary ruin it. Other than Thanksgiving, which had an array of football games working in its favor, Christmas was his favorite holiday. This year he had snow, elk bugling in the distance, and reason to wear more than a T-shirt in December. Besides, he'd done a great job on buying presents this year, and couldn't wait to see his parents open their gifts.

"You want some cocoa?" Hannah asked as Jackson leaned over the raised counter and peeked down at her workplace. She was, for the moment, slicing fruit.

"Yeah, sure. I can get it." He walked around the island. "Where are the lovebirds?" he asked as he ladled the creamy brown liquid into his mug.

"Well, Grant went—"

The front door opened, and Grant came in, brushing snow off his hat and shoulders.

"—for a walk."

"Merry Christmas, Jack."

"Merry Christmas, Frosty. What are you doing out there?"

"It's a beautiful morning," Grant answered, stooping to unlace his boots.

That it was, but Jackson enjoyed the view from inside.

"Hillary up yet?" Grant asked, coming over to give Hannah a kiss on the cheek.

"She's in our shower," she answered.

"I'm going to run up and dry off," he announced, and hurried up the stairs.

Jackson took his cocoa into the living room and joined his dad. "What's the word?"

"Immanuel," David replied. "God with us."

"Matthew?"

"And Luke. I'm merging my own Gospels."

"I see."

"I've been studying the prophecies lately," David said, closing the Bible on his finger. "Over three hundred Old Testament prophecies about Christ, every one of them fulfilled. Remarkable."

"You wonder how the Jews missed that."

"'*He has blinded their eyes and hardened their hearts*,'" David said.

"Maybe I should handle the Scripture reading today, Dad. You're not pulling out the most upbeat passages."

David handed him the Bible. "Be my guest."

Douglas family tradition held that just before breakfast, somebody read Luke's account of the birth of Christ. And so when Grant and Hillary joined them in the living room, Jackson read the first twenty verses of chapter two, from the census to Jesus' birth to the arrival of the shepherds. When he was finished, everyone moved to the dining room and Hannah served waffles with custard and fruit, along with bacon and sausage. David offered a blessing and a prayer of thanks, and as soon as he was finished, Jackson reached a fork toward the waffles.

"Before we get started," Grant said with Jackson's fork poised just above the stack of waffles, "I'd like to say a little something."

Jackson's sigh was almost audible.

"What is it, Son?"

"I wanted to say how much I've enjoyed being with you all these last few days, and how thankful I am that Hillary could join us this week."

Jackson cast a glance her way. White sweater and jeans, perfect hair, beaming smile on her face. She was at the same time beautiful, intimidating, and, when her eyes bounced off Jackson's, frightening. White Witch of Narnia-like.

"This last year and a half with her has been the best time of my life. Her smile lights up my world—"

Sensing the heat flowing out of the waffles, Jackson dropped his fork, allowing his exasperation to come out in a light clank against his plate. It went unnoticed.

"—and her presence makes every day a treasure to live."

It was okay about the waffles. Jackson was losing his appetite.

"I feel so blessed to have a family like you guys who have welcomed her and made her feel at ease around us. I couldn't have dreamt of a better scenario than having you all here together."

Great, now he was repeating himself.

"Scenario for what?" David asked.

Jackson's stomach plummeted . . .

"To tell you that Hillary has agreed to marry me!"

. . . and hit the floor.

"Ohhh!" Hannah said, her hands flying to her mouth. Hillary beamed and immediately extended her heretofore hidden hand so Hannah could admire the ring.

"Congratulations, Son," David said, drawing out every syllable and pumping Grant's hand as if he was trying to draw water.

Hannah hugged and kissed her son, then studied the ring and clutched Hillary's arm some more. David came around the table and welcomed her with a hug before continuing on to Grant and pumping his hand again.

Jackson forced a smile to his face, trying hard to make it genuine. But his face started to hurt, so he let the smile fade, picked up his fork, and stabbed at the waffles.

*   *   *

9:38 a.m.

ON THE plus side, nobody else had been very hungry, and Jackson had eaten enough waffles to last him through leftover soup at lunch. On the down side, he had to eat them while listening to a real-time retelling of the proposal the night before. Grant and Hillary had gone off for a moonlit stroll around the property, and he had popped the question to her one minute after midnight. He was lucky he hadn't dropped the ring in a snowbank.

After finishing breakfast and taking care of dishes, the family—it was really true, they were all a family now—moved into the living room. Presents were at a minimum since they had flown to Estes Park, but Jackson was banking on quality over quantity. David's favorite TV show growing up had been *McHale's Navy*, and Jackson had purchased the complete box set on DVD. For Hannah, he had found a plethora of scrapbooking doodads, all the type of stuff she had been admiring when they had been shopping for David's gifts. Grant was getting a couple of CDs, not the greatest gift in the world, but they were ones he'd wanted. For Hillary, he'd picked up an Olive Garden gift card. It was better than a lump of coal.

After opening stocking gifts—containing the usual assortment of candy, knickknacks, perfumes, and lotions—the Douglas family and Hillary moved to the presents under the tree. The happy couple went first, presenting their gift to David and Hannah. It was a simple, flat box, perfectly wrapped of course, that David passed to Hannah to open. She pulled off the bow, gently removed the ribbon, and lifted the lid.

"Ooh."

David leaned over. "What have we got?" He removed a slip of paper. "Carmel?"

"My parents stayed at that bed and breakfast a few years back," Hillary said. "They say it's fabulous."

"Oh, and look at this," Hannah said. "Spa vouchers, the aquarium."

"Golf at Pebble Beach," David added, leaning over her shoulder.

Suddenly Ernest Borgnine and crinkle-cut scissors didn't seem all that great.

"Oh, kids this is too much," Hannah said.

"No it's not," Grant said.

"I quite agree," David said, looking at a brochure for the Pebble Beach Golf Links.

Hillary's grin was just as wide as Grant's. "You both deserve something nice," she said, "and we figured instead of just getting you more stuff, we'd buy you a little romantic getaway."

"This must have cost you a fortune," Hannah continued.

McHale's Navy had been on sale for $39.99.

"We're both doing all right," Grant said.

"But you have a marriage to save for now, and a family."

"Trust us, Mom and Dad, you're worth it. After all you've done for both of us, it was the least we could do."

Well, technically the least that could be done was still to come.

Jackson sighed, letting the euphoria continue for a few minutes, and thinking back on how much he had enjoyed Grant's chocolate covered cherries. He would have eaten Hillary's too, if he'd gotten her any.

To their credit, David and Hannah had the decency to open and appreciate Jackson's gifts for a few minutes before fawning over the vacation package some more. Grant liked his CDs, Hillary smiled her way through the gift card, and Jackson at least got some quality merchandise: A new leather-bound Bible from his parents, along with a digital camera to replace the old 35mm he still used. The newest edition of *Madden* for his Xbox 360 from Grant. And a Blockbuster gift card and several packages of flavored popcorn from Hillary. It was slightly more thoughtful than his gift to her, and yet he couldn't help but feel it had been given with a "you're such a loser that all you do is sit around and watch movies" spirit.

After cleaning up the wrapping paper, ribbons, and bows, they all spent a while playing with or trying out their new gifts. Hillary had a bunch of new clothes and a darling necklace from David and Hannah to model, and Grant had what amounted to a survival kit to examine. Jackson memorized the manual for his camera and tested it on the scenery outside, as well as on a few candid shots of the family when Hillary was away changing.

Hannah heated up leftovers for the hungry for lunch, and soon got a start on Christmas dinner. Preparing for domestication, Grant and Hillary pitched in to help, leaving Jackson and David alone to watch the Lakers on TV. They were getting drubbed by Miami, so they popped in a few episodes of *McHale's Navy*. It wasn't bad, but it was no *Hogan's Heroes*.

Eventually the kitchen trio got everything either prepared, in the oven, or waiting to go in the oven, and Hannah went into the bedroom to call her brother Samuel. Grant cajoled David into going with him to test out his new, state-of-the-art binoculars. Searching the crags for elk and mule deer and bighorns sounded like fun, despite the cold, but Jackson got the feeling they were gearing up for a father-son talk, so he was left to channel surf.

TV Land was airing an *Everybody Loves Raymond* marathon, and TBS had *A Christmas Story* running over and over all day. He flipped back and forth, tuning them both out, wondering how his dream Christmas had slipped away.

"Hey," Hillary said. She was standing over him, holding a steaming cup of hot cocoa and a gingerbread man. "Mind if I sit down?"

There were two other chairs and a loveseat, but she had to sit on the couch he was laying on. Sighing, Jackson retracted his legs and sat up. Hillary sat down a little closer than was necessary, crowding him into the arm of the couch.

"So, a big day, huh?"

"Has been for a few thousand years now," Jackson answered.

Hillary frowned, but only for a moment. "You've been quiet."

"Lot on my mind."

"Me too. I could hardly sleep last night, I was so excited."

Jackson nodded.

"Did Grant tell you what he was planning?"

"Not a word."

"Not even a hint?"

"If he had, I would have talked him out of it."

Hillary's eyes bored into Jackson.

"I'm talking about the way he proposed," Jackson said.

"The way he proposed was perfect."

"Sure, if you like your first engaged kiss to be through dripping snot. How about a walk on the beach, or in an empty field on a warm summer night? Or at least in front of the fireplace?"

"I thought it was perfect."

"Yeah, well . . ."

Hillary snapped the head off the gingerbread man. "You disapprove."

"I never said that."

"You've said it since the day you met me, just not overtly."

"Yeah, well, you're not exactly taken with me, either."

"You never gave me anything to be taken with. From day one, you've acknowledged our relationship with nothing more than smart-aleck asides. Even so, I accepted you, because you're Grant's brother. You're part of the family."

"I guess that was the difference, huh? I do belong to this family. You don't."

"That's what this is all about? Some petty jealousy because I'm taking away your family? Grow up, Jackson. That's called life." Hillary set down her mug and leaned in close. "And for the record, I belong to this family now too. I love your parents, and I am crazy about your brother. So you had better get used to me, because I'm not going anywhere. This is your family now, Jackson. Deal with it."

The front door opened and Grant and David walked in.

"Because if you don't," she added quietly, "I'll make your life miserable."

She patted his knee and smiled, and then hurried over to give her fiancé a kiss.

Jackson furtively drooled into her hot cocoa.

Chapter Forty-One

10:05 a.m.

IT TOOK JACKSON and Hillary twenty minutes to cross back to the east side of the city and join I-15. It took only five more to leave the sprawl of Las Vegas behind them, the white desert sand and tan rock formations appearing otherworldly. The colossal city in the rearview mirror felt like an illusion.

Hillary didn't say a word, staring out her window instead. So Jackson tried to sort things in his own head. They now had it from two sources that Warren McKenzie had been part of Silver Dawn and also likely involved in a component or aspect of the project that others weren't. Nobody knew what Silver Dawn was, but mention of experiments, contained incidents, and pregnant civilians housed in an aircraft hangar gave credence to some of the less civilized rumors Jackson had found online. Maybe genetic experiments and mind-control research weren't so far-fetched after all. Such theories could also explain the outbreak of violence Holloway had documented.

Some things still didn't add up, though. Henrietta had said all of Warren's civilian patients had been women, but Holloway had dossiers for men and women. And what did a top-secret military project back in the 1980s have to do with Arielle and her drugging/kidnapping side jobs thirty years later? Why was the CIA involved? Were Blane Air Force Base and the town of Kingman still relevant today? How did Holloway know what he knew and, more importantly, what was he planning on doing with such knowledge?

Perhaps none of that mattered as much as Henrietta's suspicions that Hillary's father had had an affair with Yvonne Coleman. It was circumstantial evidence at best, the type of thing even a public defender would have thrown out of court. He said as much to Hillary, and she only uttered a soft, "I don't want to talk about it," without even turning her head his way. Not that he could really blame her. Warren had been part of Silver Dawn and had connections to a number of people involved in whatever was going on now. Furthermore, he had some sort of a relationship with Yvonne's second daughter, Arielle. It was circumstantial evidence, true, but there was also that line about where there was smoke . . .

Highway 93 branched off from the interstate, journeying due north. If anything, the terrain grew more barren. With Hillary uncommunicative beside him, Jackson pulled out his phone and called Mouse. He asked him to look into some names for him, and began listing from the dead and alive groups from memory. Mouse grumbled at the number of names, but fortunately for him, Jackson could only remember half of them. And he only was able to list half of that total before the call dropped. He tried to get Mouse back, but as they ventured farther into the desert on the two-lane highway, he had no signal. Awesome.

About thirty miles north of I-15, in a part of the world that made the middle of nowhere look like Manhattan, State Route 323 intersected with Highway 93. Jackson turned east on SR-323, which passed the southern tip of a low, brown mountain range before making a slow curve to run a little east of due north. A dirt road continued straight east toward the next mountain range, this one a hair taller than its counterpart to the west. The two of them created a valley some five to seven miles across, void of any rivers, washes, or arroyos. Aside from sagebrush, it was lifeless.

Since leaving the interstate, they had only encountered a few vehicles, none of them on SR-323. That changed as a brown Dodge Charger passed them headed south. It was emblazoned with the Delamar County Sheriff's Department name and insignia, but easily recognizable as a cop car without them by the radar gun mounted over the driver's mirror and the array of antennas on the back.

"Hope that wasn't Quinn," Jackson said. Hillary was unresponsive, and he speculated she had fallen asleep. Lucky her.

Five miles north of the curve, the heat haze shimmering over the roadway cleared to reveal a small town up ahead. Jackson knew from looking at a somewhat pixelated satellite image that Kingman was tiny, but even so, he was surprised at how few buildings there were. The first was a rundown motel on the right side of the road. It made the one they'd spent the previous night in look like Oasis Las Vegas. A gravel road—identified as "1st Street" by a bent and dinged green sign atop a crooked post—ran due west from the motel, with a couple of shacks and trailers on either side of it, the nearest a quarter of a mile to the west.

The west side of SR-323—which doubled as Main Street—was lined with rundown houses and a bar. On the east side of the road, the sage and sand continued until 2nd Street cut east for a block and a half. A boxy white church with a steeple guarded the corner, looking picturesque against a bright blue sky. It also looked terribly out of place.

The houses on the east side of Main were just as rundown as those on the west, many with boarded windows, all with faded and chipped paint or curled shingles or weeds overgrowing the sidewalk and the foundation. There were a few trees, but they were thin and threadbare, providing little shade. That was okay. According to the thermometer on the Focus's dashboard, it was only 103.

Main and 3rd was clearly the primary intersection in town, seeing as how 3rd Street ran both east and west of Main. Campbell's, a general store from the Old West, sat at the southeast corner, replete with a second story façade, a wooden sidewalk, and a hitching post. There was probably even a jar of licorice in the window.

Jackson crossed 3rd Street and turned into one of six parking spaces in front of the Delamar County Sheriff's Department. Unlike all the other buildings, it had new siding, seamless shingles, clean windows, a freshly paved sidewalk, and an assortment of antennas and a satellite dish on the roof. Another patrol car similar to the one they had seen on the way in was parked at the end of the row of parking spaces, which were otherwise vacant.

Hillary stirred as Jackson put the car in park. "We're here already?" she asked, looking his way.

"Define here," he said as he opened his door. The desert heat hit him like a blast from an oven. He looked at Hillary across the roof of the car and its ripples of heat. She stood tall and wide-eyed, instantly alert and focused. He expected nothing less.

Beyond her, Main Street continued for another block. The last east-west street was 4th, and beyond it more barren wasteland stretched to the horizon. The entire town was less than half a mile long, not half as wide, with ample space between the buildings. Aside from the well-kept sheriff's department, Kingman looked one good dust storm away from disappearing.

"Let me do the talking," Hillary said as they approached the front door.

"Whatever you say."

The door was fiberglass, and as soon as Hillary opened it, Jackson felt the chill from inside. He quickly followed her in, shutting the door and the desert behind him.

The room was large and airy, with a front desk and a half wall separating the entry and a small seating area from the rest of the station. Behind the half wall, four more desks were arranged in twos, facing each other. Each was topped with a desktop computer with a flat screen and a multi-button phone with an LCD display. None were currently manned, nor was the front desk. It too had a new phone and computer. It did not have a bell, so Jackson and Hillary stood and looked around.

The far wall was lined with maps of the country, the southwestern U.S., Nevada, Delamar County, and the town of Kingman—right down to each building in town. There was also a locked gun rack next to an upright safe. The wall to the left had a bank of windows that looked out at 3rd Street. Or rather would have had blinds not been drawn. To the right, immediately behind the front desk, doors led to a unisex bathroom and a hallway that stretched to parts unknown. Only when Jackson wandered to the seating area to look at a Most Wanted poster—circa 2004—and turned back did he spot a pair of computer screens beneath the front desk. They were split to show security feeds of the hallway, a conference room, what looked like a file storage room, and four jail cells.

Jackson walked back to Hillary, mulling the disparity between the fleck-on-a-map town of Kingman and its high-tech sheriff's department. "One car out front, another on the highway. A desk for the sheriff and three deputies, and enough munitions to take down a small country," he said.

"They serve the whole county."

"Which has less occupants than my street."

The door to the bathroom opened and a man stepped out, still zipping his pants. He looked up, failed to startle or show embarrassment, but did frown slightly. "Help you all?"

He was tall and thin, and quite suited to be the sheriff of Nowhere, Nevada, with his long face, strong jaw, protruding chin, and posture to make criminals cower. He had the twang, the gun a little low on his hip, and boots tucked under his dark brown trousers. He didn't wear a cowboy hat, but Jackson saw one on the back desk. He also saw a star pinned to the man's uniform, indicating he was indeed the head lawman.

"We're looking for Sheriff Quinn," Hillary said.

"I'm Wyatt Quinn," he said, offering his hand across the front desk.

The reluctance playing on her face for a second, Hillary shook it.

"What can I do for you all?" Quinn asked.

Hillary had apparently seen her share of Westerns; she knew to shoot straight with the Law. "We're investigating the death of a young woman, and the trail has led us here."

Quinn's cleft of a brow furrowed. "A death, here in Kingman?"

"No. Las Vegas. We think there may be ties to Kingman."

"Are you all detectives?" he asked, looking at Hillary's shorts and Jackson's tee and jeans. More at Hillary's shorts.

"Not exactly," Hillary said. "I'm a lawyer. This is my assistant." She produced a business card from her purse to prove her identity.

"Hillary McKenzie," Quinn said, separating every syllable. "Los Angeles, California."

As if there was another Los Angeles.

"If you all don't mind me asking, how'd a lawyer and her assistant from Los Angeles come to investigate a death in Las Vegas?"

"It's very complicated," Hillary answered. "But we believe her death may be tied to some rather unusual circumstances."

"You're all talking murder?"

Hillary nodded.

"Have you all spoken to the police down in Las Vegas?"

"We met briefly," Jackson said.

"They're investigating," Hillary said. "But we have some alternate theories that we're pursuing."

"And these 'unusual circumstances,' they have something to do with why you all are involved?"

"They do," Hillary said.

"And with Kingman?"

"That's right."

Quinn stroked his jaw, then rested gargantuan hands on the edge of the desk. "Well, I guess that brings me around to my original question: What can I do for you all?"

"We'd like to ask you some questions," Hillary said. "Then, I assume the town has public records that we could peruse?"

Quinn nodded. "Why don't you all come on back to my desk," he said, opening a gate in the half wall. Jackson followed Hillary back to the corner desk, where Quinn offered them seats. He removed the cowboy hat from his desk, tossing it on the adjacent desk. "Can I get either of you all anything to drink? Bottled water, soda? We got coffee, but the weather ain't much for it."

Both declined and Quinn sat down. "What would you all like to know?"

"Have you ever heard of a woman named Arielle Coal?"

Quinn thought for a moment, then shook his head. "Can't say that I have. She the victim?"

Hillary nodded. "What about Yvonne Coleman?"

"Suspect?"

"Her mother. She was a resident of Kingman back in the '80s."

"I've only been here four years," Quinn said. "Hold on a sec." He leaned over and shouted. "Vince!"

Footsteps on the linoleum floor preceded the arrival from the hallway of a man dressed similarly to Quinn, only his star was a deputy's. He was shorter, plumper, and balding. "My deputy, Vince Vickers. Vince, this is Hillary McKenzie and, uh—"

"Jackson Douglas."

"Jackson Douglas. They're from Los Angeles, investigating the murder of a woman named Arielle Coal down in Las Vegas. They've got reason to believe it's somehow tied to Kingman and wanted to ask a few questions. I figure maybe you all'd have some answers for them that I don't."

"I doubt it, Sheriff, but I'll be happy to answer anything I can," he said. He paused to shake hands before pulling over a chair.

"What was that second name you all mentioned?" Quinn asked.

"Yvonne Coleman," Hillary said. "She lived here from 1980 to 1984."

"Before my time, I'm afraid," Vickers said.

Hillary ran down the other names. Quinn and Vickers both knew of Senator Moore, of course, and had heard of Richard Holloway and his business prowess. But Warren McKenzie, Matt Brenner, Xavier Stark, Isaac Cutler, and Laura Woodson were all unknown to them. Only when she asked about General Ernest Reynolds did Quinn's face tighten slightly. "I believe I've heard the name before, in reference to some or other war or military action. But I don't know the man."

Vickers, as had become his custom, shook his head.

"We think the common bond is Blane Air Force Base," Hillary said.

"Blane? It's been closed over twenty years."

"There are rumors of top-secret military projects going on at the base back in the '80s," Hillary said.

Quinn chuckled. "Don't tell me you all believe them?"

"Most of them, no. But Senator Moore, General Reynolds, and Warren McKenzie were all stationed at the base. And they all have connections to the others I mentioned, as does Arielle Coal."

Quinn stroked his jaw again. "Miss McKenzie, it sounds like you all've stumbled into a real mess. Could be something to it, something bound in so much red tape and bureaucracy you all'll never untangle it. More than likely, it's speculation and rumor and coincidence. Either way, I don't know we can tell you all."

"I understand," she said. "But could we at least look at the town's records?"

"Of course. They're in the back. Vince'll show you all where everything is."

"And I do have one more question," Hillary said.

"Fire away."

"It's a bit indelicate, but we did some research on Kingman before we arrived, and we noticed a rather high rate of violent behavior by the residents of town, including a number of suicides."

Quinn's eyes narrowed slightly. "There a question in there?"

"Is there a particular reason why there seems to be such an outbreak in this small of a community?"

Again, the sheriff pulled on his jaw. Having been reclining for most of the interview, he sat up straight. "I'd reckon it has mostly to do with the town being too small for the law of averages to have caught up just yet. And as you all noticed, we're kind of off the beaten path. Some folks don't do too well with the loneliness." He shook his head. "I don't think it's anything more serious than that. There's certainly no underlying cause that we've detected."

Jackson glanced at Vickers, whose face was blank.

"I appreciate your time, Sheriff, Deputy," Hillary said. "And your candor."

"You all's welcome. Like I said, Vince'll show you all to the files."

As if snapping out of a trance, Vickers suddenly stood. "You folks wanna follow me this way?" he said. Jackson and Hillary also rose and followed the deputy to the hallway, past four empty holding cells, and to the file room Jackson had seen on the security feed earlier. A row of filing cabinets lined one wall, a dust-covered computer and monitor (not a flat screen) bowed an old desk against an adjacent wall, and a hodgepodge of boxes, plastic storage containers, and miscellaneous items lined the other. In the middle, what looked like a repurposed kitchen table and chairs provided the only seating in the room.

"Everything's in here," Vickers said, pointing at the filing cabinets. "Labeled, but if you folks have any questions, just ask. The computer requires a password, so I can't authorize that. It's just a glorified storage closet, so please excuse the mess."

Hillary smiled charmingly.

"If you folks need anything, I'm cleaning out cells, so just give a shout. Else the sheriff's at his desk."

"Cleaning out cells," Jackson said. "You all just make a bust?"

"Nothing like that," Vickers answered. "Just weekly cleaning. You folks call if you need anything."

"Thank you, Deputy," Hillary said.

"The A/C doesn't work too well in here for some reason, so I'll leave the door open," he said. He nodded, then disappeared from view.

Jackson and Hillary stared at each other until his footfalls died away.

"There's a camera above the door that feeds to a screen under the front desk," Jackson said.

She acknowledged him with a nod, then procured a list from her purse. She handed it to Jackson before withdrawing a small bottle of hand sanitizer. "Look up those names," she said as she massaged the gel into her hands.

"All of them?"

"I'm going to look for the names from the 'Alive' and 'Dead' folders."

"You think they were Kingman residents too?"

"I think it's worth checking out."

"Okay."

Antiquated, the files were at least neat. There were seventeen names on Jackson's list, thirteen living and four dead. Jackson knocked out the four dead persons first, verifying three suicides and one death caused in self-defense. After checking a couple on the living list, he leaned against a recently closed filing cabinet and waited for Hillary to stop reading and look at him.

"There's nothing here," he said.

"How do you mean?"

"I mean, Holloway's files were twice as complete as anything I'm seeing here. I'm getting nothing but the basics: date of birth, date of death, a few land holdings, a few criminal charges."

"I'm finding the same thing. No official birth certificates. Just a date of birth."

"You know what that means?"

"What?"

"They're the unborn," he said. "Cyborgs from another planet." He raised his eyebrows. "And maybe another time."

"That's very helpful."

"I'll keep looking, but it's a waste of time."

He finished his list in short order, but instead of telling Hillary, pulled a file for Wyatt Quinn. His bio was much thicker, listing both a date of birth—July 1, 1976—and a place of birth—Amarillo, Texas—as well as a host of other details. He'd served two years in the Army out of high school, bought and sold real estate in Dallas, Las Vegas, and Winnemucca, Nevada, and had been a highway patrolman for three years before being elected sheriff in early 2008. According to the file, he owned a house on 3rd Street, just west of the department.

Even with no death record and no criminal record, his file was thicker than anyone on Jackson's list. So he checked a few other random citizens. He found their records matched Quinn's—more details than for those on his list, birth certificates in most cases, and a lack of criminal record. His sample was small and totally haphazard, but conclusive nonetheless.

Hillary closed a filing cabinet with a sigh and announced that she was finished.

"Find anything?" Jackson asked.

"Let's talk elsewhere."

It was getting hot in the file room, but he doubted that was her reason. They retreated down the hall, leaving the room as they had found it. Vickers was not in any of the cells, but was behind his desk, as was Quinn.

"Thank you very much, Sheriff," Hillary said.

"Find what you all needed?"

"Afraid not," she answered.

"Well, like I told you all, it's doubtful we'd be of any help. There's just not much to ol' Kingman."

"I would like to ask a few questions around town," Hillary said. "See if anyone knows anything."

"Folks in Kingman are mighty private," Quinn answered. "They don't take real kindly to strangers."

"Are you telling me I can't speak to them?"

"Far be it from me to tell a lawyer what she can or cannot do. I'm just letting you all know not to expect much. Consider it a fair warning."

Unfazed by his words or the look in his eyes, Hillary smiled. "Thank you again, Sheriff."

"You all's welcome."

"Let's go," she said to Jackson.

Before he turned to follow her, he caught a rather solemn nod from Sheriff Quinn. The silent message was conveyed loud and clear.

Chapter Forty-Two

12:38 p.m.

AS SOON AS Jackson and Hillary exited the office, they were assaulted by the heat. She stood for a moment on the sidewalk, looking up and down Main Street. Jackson wasted no time starting the car. He debated waiting outside it for the air conditioning to kick in, but the lack of a breeze made the air no less oppressive than that in the vehicle.

Hillary joined him a moment later. When her door latched shut, he asked, "Were we just threatened?"

"I don't think he was issuing a threat so much as stating implicit dangers of poking around."

"In a town full of suicidal, violent freaks. Where do we poke first?"

"I found twenty-two of the twenty-four names in the 'Alive' and 'Dead' folders," she said.

"Twenty-two?"

She nodded.

"So why weren't they in the 'Kingman' folder?"

"I'm guessing because they don't live in Kingman anymore. Or didn't when they died."

"But they were born there."

"Not necessarily. I found dates of birth, but no places of birth."

"Well, if they weren't in the Kingman folder but they were in the town's records, isn't it safe to assume they must have been born in Kingman?"

"It's never safe to assume," Hillary said.

"Spare me the lecture. Why is Holloway keeping tabs on a bunch of residents and former residents, half of whom killed themselves or assaulted somebody or both?"

"I don't know." She buckled her seatbelt. "I think we should drive out to the base."

"Why?"

"To see what's there."

"A bunch of abandoned buildings. It's been decommissioned for twenty years."

"There might be something to find."

"What, a folder stuck to the back of a filing cabinet that details Silver Dawn and everyone's involvement?"

Her eyes were heating up. "I don't know what we'll find. But I think we should check it out."

"Fine. But after lunch."

"How can you be hungry the way you ate breakfast?"

"That was hours ago. Besides, you wanted to interrogate the townsfolk. What better place than the local café?"

He put the car in gear and backed onto the street.

"No cell service," Hillary said, looking down at her phone.

"Great. Remember the last time we were in the middle of nowhere with no cell service?"

"Don't remind me."

They drove north a block, past more houses that were fit for the worst neighborhoods of an inner city. Kingman was technically a municipality, but the yards were littered with rubbish like a country junkyard, from rusted out cars and appliances to long-overgrown landscaping arrangements. Most of the homes were closer to condemned than well kept. Those at the corner of Main and 4th Street were a little nicer, and a large apartment building on 4th—while it had all the charm of a 1970s dormitory—was at least maintained. North of 4th, there were only three buildings—a gas station and garage on the east side of the street and a so-so duplex and the Kingman Diner on the west side.

Four vehicles were parked in front of the diner and in a small, cracked lot on the north side. Jackson pulled into a spot directly in front of the entrance. It was elevated several feet, with a ramp going north and steps south. He kept the car and air conditioning running as he asked, "How do you want to play this?"

"How about we look at menus and then order?"

"All right, Snotty Susie, have it your way. But don't complain again about me not helping in this investigation. And time's ticking. You promised me a good night's sleep in a comfortable bed. It's two hours back to Vegas once you factor in finding a hotel and checking in. I want a nice shower and a chance to pick up something to eat, and I want to be in bed by ten. You've got . . . less than seven hours."

Hillary glared at him as she opened her door and got out. He cut the engine and followed suit. She was already halfway up the steps, and with a shake of his head, he followed again. "Guess the honeymoon's over," he mumbled as she let the door close behind her.

The Kingman Diner, like the sheriff's station, was air-conditioned. But it was not nearly as cool, whether because of poor insulation or because the heat of the kitchen came flowing over the Formica countertop that separated it from a row of red, vinyl barstools. There were four booths—two on either side of the door—upholstered similarly. At Johnny Rockets, such décor was vintage. Here, it was just old and sad.

Two waitresses in yellow rayon dresses—also old, not vintage—worked behind the counter. One was in her fifties or sixties, with graying hair and more weight than could be comfortable for a person on her feet all day. The other looked Hillary's age, although not nearly so pretty. She had dark hair with blond roots and a detached expression on her face as she took an order from a guy at the end of the bar. He had the trucker stereotype down pat—jeans, sleeveless shirt, dirty baseball cap covering shaggy hair. Only there was no truck parked outside, and Jackson doubted any commercial freight route had ever led through Kingman.

There were three other patrons. Twins sat on opposite sides of the far booth on the right, dressed similarly but not identically. Like the trucker, they both appeared in their twenties or thirties. It was becoming common. The other person was an old, gray-haired man gumming his sandwich at the opposite end of the bar as the trucker.

Hillary strode to the bar and perched upon a middle barstool, so Jackson did likewise. The older waitress quickly stopped in front of them. Her nametag identified her as Fran.

"What can I get you folks to drink?" she asked as she set down menus.

"Water, please," Hillary said.

"Iced tea, unsweetened, lemon if you got it, and brew another batch," Jackson said.

Fran eyed him from under a raised brow as she retreated to get their drinks. The menu contained the standard fare of burgers, sandwiches, a few entrées, and some greasy appetizers. Unique were something called scorpions. When Fran returned, Jackson had to ask.

"They're deep-fried chili peppers," she said.

"Spicy?"

"They'll make your tongue bleed."

"I'll give 'em a whirl. And a club sandwich on white bread."

"And more tea?" Fran said as she jotted the order on a notepad.

Jackson smiled and winked in return.

"I'll have a house salad," Hillary said.

"Dressing?"

"Do you have maybe a raspberry or balsamic vinaigrette?"

Fran looked at Hillary as if she was speaking Swedish. "Ranch, Caesar, French, Thousand Island."

"Thousand Island," Hillary said.

"Want to tell me what's eating you?" Jackson asked when Fran departed.

"Let's just do what we came for."

"What, bother people while they're eating?"

"You said the local café would be the place to question people."

"And I thought you saw right through that desperate ploy for food."

"Fine, I'll do it." She made eye contact with Fran, who stopped in front of them after tending to the old guy with no teeth. "Do you mind if I ask you a few questions?" Hillary said.

" 'Bout what, honey?"

"We're looking for information about the death of a woman named Arielle Coal. Does that name ring a bell?"

Fran shook her head.

"What about her mom, Yvonne Coleman?"

"I knew an Yvonne Coleman. Not well, but I knew her."

"We understand she lived in Kingman from 1980 to 1984."

"That's about right. I arrived in '81. Course, she wasn't here for about five or six months one summer. Maybe '82 or '83."

"Do you know where she was?"

Fran shook her head. "Came back pregnant is all I know." She excused herself to tend to the old man, who needed a refill. And a bib.

Hillary managed to keep her poise while waiting for Fran to return. "Do you know who the father was?"

Fran shook her head. "I don't even know if the baby was a boy or a girl. Yvonne was always a loner, lived in a trailer outside town. After she came back, it was even worse. I heard one day she'd been evacuated by the county or something, and I remember thinking I'd never even seen her baby. But then again, I hadn't seen her much either. Then she was gone, and I didn't think much of it again."

"Do you know what brought her to Kingman in the first place?" Jackson asked.

"Same as everybody, I imagine."

"The Air Force?"

Fran nodded. "One way or the other."

Hillary changed directions. "What about Senator Moore or General Ernest Reynolds? Do you know either of them?"

"I know of Senator Moore. Voted for him twice."

"Has he ever stopped in the diner?"

"A United States senator in Kingman? Honey, I doubt he's ever heard of the place."

Hillary produced her phone and showed her a picture of Reynolds, but Fran didn't recognize him. Then Hillary swiped the screen to show a photograph of her father.

"Sorry, hon."

Hillary lowered the phone. "They were all stationed at Blane back in the '80s. Surely they must have come into town."

"Along with every other airman on the base," Fran said. "Show me a picture from the 1980s, you got a chance, but even then, I doubt it. Faces were never my thing."

A man and a woman entered the diner and took seats on the other side of Hillary. He was Jackson with another twenty pounds and shorter, darker hair. Save for a few inches in height and added onto her hair, and for a little less appealing pair of shorts—and for the obvious lack of natural beauty—she could have been Hillary. They shared the same despondent look.

Fran turned her attention to them, and Jackson announced to Hillary that he was going to use the bathroom. It was one step up from a pit toilet, and he conducted his business as quickly as possible. Before exiting the privacy of the bathroom, he checked his phone. Still no signal. There was a payphone right outside the door, and after peeking at the bar to see that his meal had not yet arrived, he used it to call Mouse. Collect. He hadn't even been sure if that was still a thing.

"What the heck, dude?" Mouse said when the call was connected.

"Sorry, Mouse, I'll pay you back."

"Lose your phone again?"

"No, we just traveled back to the Stone Age. We're in Kingman, Nevada."

"Where?"

"Exactly. Hey, any luck on those names I gave you?"

"I only got ten names before the call dropped."

"Yeah, sorry."

"I did some checking, but they look pretty random. I hacked some Facebook and Twitter accounts, and the closest thing I can find is that three of them are Green Bay Packers fans and it looks like several of them took trips to Vegas recently."

"How recently?" Jackson asked.

"I don't know. Six months or so, maybe."

"Anything beyond that? Same hotel, airline, anything of that nature?"

"No. And the weird thing is, I didn't find any Vegas pics. I just saw mentions, like 'I'm headed to Vegas, brah' types of posts."

"Hmm. Anything else?"

"No. Hey, are you and that hot chick ever coming back?"

"I sure hope so."

"You didn't elope or something, did you?"

"If I had, would I be calling you collect to ask for info on complete strangers?"

"Good poi—"

A shout interrupted Mouse, and Jackson leaned around the corner. One of the twins was standing at the end of his booth, his face close to Hillary's.

"I gotta go, dude. Later."

Chapter Forty-Three

1:07 p.m.

JACKSON DROPPED THE phone and hurried to Hillary's side. He arrived just as one of the twins grabbed her by the arm, swearing a blue streak that caused everyone in the diner to turn and look. But not move off their chairs to help.

Jackson quickly stepped in front of Hillary, swiping the guy's arm with his own, thus breaking his grip on her. "Step back, pal," he said, then immediately shot a hand out to his twin's chest, keeping him at bay in his booth.

The first twin responded by calling Hillary names Jackson had never even heard, at the same time reaching around Jackson with an outstretched finger. Twice, Jackson told him to knock it off. The third time, he shoved him back into his booth.

The man jumped back up with lightning speed and grabbed Jackson's shirt, pushing him back into Hillary in the process. While the guy gushed more profanity, Jackson shoved down on his arms, creating a tense separation between them. For a second, they stared at each other. The guy's eyes brimmed with hate. For the first time since the altercation began, Jackson calculated his odds in a two-versus-one fistfight.

Before things could escalate further, the bell over the door dinged. Out of the corner of his eye, Jackson saw brown and tan. He flitted a glance to his right and identified Sheriff Quinn, cowboy hat and all.

"What's going on?" he said, tipping his hat back as he hurried toward the group.

"Somebody's off their Tourette's meds," Jackson said, opening the way for another foul tirade from the man.

"Marvin, calm down," Quinn said.

He turned to the side, muttering under his breath.

"What happened?" Quinn asked.

"I was asking them some questions," Hillary said, "and he suddenly jumped up and began yelling at me. He grabbed my arm and that's when Jackson intervened."

327

Quinn nodded for Jackson and Hillary to step away from the booth. They did, and after telling Marvin to sit down and finish his lunch, Quinn joined them by the entrance to the restrooms. "I told you all people in this town wouldn't take lightly to being interrogated."

"I wasn't interrogating him," Hillary said. "I was just asking questions."

"While they were eating lunch."

"I asked if I could talk with them for a minute and the other one said yes."

"Jerry." Quinn exhaled. "Look, I can't stop you all from talking to people. But please, take my advice: finish your all's lunch and hit the road. There's no answers for you all in Kingman."

"What about Howard Hughes over there?" Jackson asked.

"I'll see he doesn't bother you all again."

"Thank you, Sheriff," Hillary said.

Quinn nodded, then returned to Marvin and Jerry's booth. They had calmed down, but he spent several minutes talking to them anyhow. At the counter, everyone had turned back around. Everyone except the old guy gumming his sandwich. He'd never even looked up in the first place.

"Hon, your order's up," Fran said as she caught Jackson's eye. She set two plates on the counter, which he carried over to the far booth. He returned for his tea and Hillary's water. Fran set a pitcher of iced tea down. "Trust me, you'll want it."

"Thanks."

Hillary sat with her back to the rest of the diner and Jackson slid in opposite her. He took a deep breath and a swig of tea. "Guess we finally found someone who likes you less than I do," he said.

"Thank you for stepping in."

"As opposed to letting Marvelous Marvin assault you? What'd you say, anyhow?"

"I asked if they knew Arielle or Yvonne. Jerry said no, and then I asked if they were familiar with Blane Air Force Base. Before the words were out of my mouth, Marvin jumped up and started cursing."

"Did you make out anything other than his thorough grasp of the English language?"

"He said something about having no rights. I couldn't make out much else."

Jackson took the first bite of a scorpion as she spoke. He was about to remark about how they weren't so hot, and then he swallowed. Suddenly the room started spinning. His eyes and nose both ran and he literally couldn't hear

328

Hillary's follow-up statement. He quickly gulped down his remaining glass of tea, splashing it on his chin and cheeks.

"Aahhh!" he gasped.

"Graceful."

He repeated the noise, then poured some more tea and downed it. "Wow. Hill, try one."

"No, thank you."

He tried his club sandwich, but his taste buds had been seared. "Did you say something a minute ago?"

"I tried talking to the other couple, but they weren't responsive. I don't suppose now's the time to talk to either of the other two patrons," she said.

"No," Jackson said, noting that Quinn had taken a seat at the bar. "I wonder if he came here for lunch or was keeping an eye on us." He popped the second half of a scorpion into his mouth. It was again tame until he swallowed, and he had to drain another half glass of tea to bring his senses back into working order.

"Seriously, what is the matter with you?"

"They're growing on me." He bit into another one, chasing it this time with just a standard gulp of tea. "So I talked to Mouse," he said, his voice low. "He looked into about ten of the names for me, the ones I gave him before we entered the wormhole and I lost the call. He said the only connection he could find was that several of them had made trips to Vegas in the last six months."

"That's not that unusual," Hillary said.

"That's what I told him. But there weren't photos of their trips."

"Photos where?"

"Facebook. Who goes to Vegas and doesn't post pictures on Facebook?"

"What are you saying?"

"I don't know. It just struck me as odd."

Speaking for the first time, the old guy at the counter mumbled a holler to Fran that he was leaving. She shouted back that she'd see him tomorrow. A few minutes later, while Jackson was pouring more tea down his throat, Marvin and Jerry stood and departed. He watched them out the window, making sure they didn't touch the Focus. When they had driven away in a pickup truck, he turned back to Hillary.

Carrying half a sandwich with him, Quinn left shortly thereafter. As he did, a young woman entered. She was average looking, with medium-length brown hair. What stood out were her blue jeans—ripped in both knees and one thigh—and a zip-up hooded sweatshirt. Pants were one thing, but who wore a hoodie when the temperature was in the triple digits?

Jackson and Hillary ate quickly, him downing almost the entire pitcher of tea. Hillary said nothing until the other waitress brought them the check.

"Hey, um, how come nobody else has paid?" Jackson asked.

"They all have a tab," the waitress answered quietly.

Hillary reached for the check and took it from under Jackson's hand. "I've got it." She placed a twenty on top of it, more than covering the bill and a generous tip. She lifted her eyes to Jackson. "Let's go."

He exited first, just in case Marvin and Jerry had returned. They hadn't. He turned to Hillary as they reached the car. "This town just gets—"

He stopped as the diner door opened and the "trucker" descended the steps. "You folks are asking questions 'bout Blane?"

"That's right," Hillary said. Jackson took a step forward, in case the man made a move in her direction.

He didn't. Instead, he crossed his arms and leaned against the railing. "If I was you, I'd quit asking and go back to wherever it is you come from."

"Why's that?"

He dropped his arms and started forward. "Just some friendly advice."

Before Jackson could make a move, the man turned and walked past Hillary. He got in a pickup truck at the other end of the lot, and they stood in place and watched as he backed out onto the street. Gunning the engine, he headed into town.

Jackson turned to Hillary and raised his eyebrows. "Warning number two."

She held up her hand, raising three fingers as she circled the car.

"I was only counting Quinn once. Two warners."

"Get in."

"You're driving?"

"I am."

"We'll make good time."

State Route 323 ran on a straight line out of Kingman, still aimed slightly east of north, but never drawing nearer to the mountain range east of town because it fell off to the desert floor. By the time the road made a massive curve to the east, Kingman had disappeared into the haze on the horizon, with nothing but sand, rock, and sage as far as the eye could see, all under a perfectly blue sky. From the air-conditioned interior of the Focus, it was beautiful.

"You notice anything peculiar about the clientele at the diner?" Jackson asked as they drove.

"Any *thing*?"

"The age demographic."

"All young, except for the guy at the end of the counter."

"And Fran. Everybody Holloway had a dossier for was around thirty, and now the majority of the people in the diner match that."

"That's the other thing I found at the station," she said. "The 2010 town census."

"And?"

"Not a single minor."

"What?"

"Mostly white, even balance between the sexes, majority were single, but not one child."

"What sort of weird place is this?"

She shook her head.

"CIA experiments leak into the water table and cause sterility?"

"I'm not sure there is a water table here."

"Good point."

The mountain range that lay to the east of Kingman and that separated it from the base was now directly to their right as they drove due east. Left, no more than a mile, another range—or perhaps the underground continuation of the same one—rose up into a jagged line. Well ahead, another range split to allow the road to pass between. As Jackson studied the sand and scrub beside the highway, he realized the road wasn't alone in cutting through the pass. A very small, totally dry riverbed snaked through the desert. It showed no more signs of life than the rest of the desert, and Jackson wondered when the last time was that it had actually been a river. Circa Noah?

A few miles ahead, a two-lane road intersected SR-323, running south into the valley between two low mountain ranges. There had been no sign publicizing the base, but a weather-beaten, bullet-pierced green sign indicated the road was Blane Road.

Hillary turned south, the whir of tires on concrete changing to a rumble as they drove over aged, cracked asphalt turned light gray by years under the sun. They drove for several miles before buildings began to take shape on the horizon. Heat blistered off the road ahead, making it almost impossible to differentiate sand from scrub from airplane hangars. But Jackson was able to make out dual guard stations less than a mile ahead. Hillary eased off the accelerator and coasted to a stop in front of a sliding chain-link gate that spanned the road between the stations. It was topped with rolling barbed wire, as was the ten-foot-high fence that ran east and west across the desert before disappearing in a blur.

"You much for pole vaulting?" Jackson asked.

Before Hillary could answer, two soldiers in tan and brown fatigues emerged from the left guardhouse, both with automatic weapons slung over their shoulders. Their faces were hard, their mouths set in frowns, their eyes dark and narrow. Jackson wanted to slip under the dashboard.

One of the men moved directly in front of the Focus, holding his weapon against his body with both hands. The other approached Hillary's open window, and his right hand moved an inch toward the pistol strapped at his hip.

"I'm sorry, ma'am, this area is restricted. You'll have to turn around."

"I thought the base was decommissioned," Hillary said.

"That's right."

"Then why can't we get through?"

"Ma'am, I need you to turn the car around now."

"But—"

"Now. Ma'am."

While Hillary capitulated and backed the car into a turn, Jackson scanned the horizon for any clues that would keep this from being a wasted trip. He saw none.

"Well," Hillary said as she turned north and accelerated, "so much for that."

"I told you we wouldn't find anything."

"You expected armed guards?"

"A fence, maybe. Rambo on security, however . . ."

"It doesn't wash," she said. "Something is going on here."

"I guess that shouldn't be a huge surprise," Jackson said. "They have to test *Nightfire* somewhere. It doesn't necessarily mean whatever they're doing is tied to Silver Dawn or Golden Dawn or Senator Moore or your dad."

"No, it doesn't, but I hate coincidence." She stuck her tongue into her cheek.

"You didn't really think that 'why can't we get through' line was going to work, did you?"

"It was worth a try."

"Maybe you should have batted your lashes a little harder."

"Did you glean anything?"

"Yeah, John Cena has two brothers."

"I mean about the base."

"Like what?"

"You claim to have these great observational powers. I thought maybe you observed something."

"You overestimate me."

"You overstate yourself."

Hillary turned back to the west on State Route 323 and Jackson tried to put all the pieces together. Unlike with actual puzzles, the real world didn't have edge and corner pieces to help a person get started. And try as he might, he couldn't figure out what he and Hillary were missing. It wasn't too hard to figure out that something hinky had gone on at Blane and perhaps was still going on. But what exactly, and how all the different parties were involved—most importantly, Warren McKenzie—was a mystery.

"I hate to be a broken record, Hill," Jackson said, "but I don't know how much farther we can push this. The U.S. military isn't exactly known for its transparency, especially if they're doing something off the books."

She didn't answer, instead looking anxiously in the rearview mirror.

"Something up?"

"There's a pickup bearing down on us," she answered.

Jackson sat up and turned around in his seat. It was a beater, faded red, covered in dirt. Probably had a gun rack in the back window. And Hillary was right, it was closing fast.

She clenched the wheel a little tighter and peeked in the mirror again. Jackson watched over his shoulder as the truck veered wildly into the other lane and accelerated. Hillary pushed the Focus to seventy, then seventy-five. They were approaching the big curve that would set them on a southwesterly course toward Kingman, and any more speed would be dangerous. But the truck beside her, although on the verge of falling apart, accelerated even more.

As it passed them, Jackson looked up, expecting to see a couple of rednecks hooting and hollering. Instead, he saw a ski mask covering a head facing forward.

"Stop," he said.

"What?"

"Hit the brakes!"

Before Hillary could respond, the truck swerved back into her lane, cutting her off. She jerked the wheel right, toward the shoulder of the road. She reached for the brake pedal but was too late. They were over the shoulder, continuing straight while the road curved. The car jumped through the air, then landed in sand, the wheels spinning for traction, leaving Hillary to fight to maintain control as they nosedived toward the dry riverbed.

Chapter Forty-Four

1:53 p.m.

HILLARY'S DESPERATE ATTEMPT to steer away from the riverbed only succeeded in turning the car sideways. They had lost enough speed that it didn't flip, but it now teetered on the brink of a precipice that, while not daunting, was steeper than it had appeared from the road. For a moment, the car seemed to hang over the edge. Then, back first, it began to slide down the embankment.

Hillary pumped the brakes to no avail, then floored the accelerator, willing the car to climb. But gravity and the slippery sand won out.

"Let it go," Jackson said as he looked through the back windshield. "Just steer it backwards."

"What?"

"Keep us from crashing."

Hillary whipped her head around, hair flying, as she wrangled the wheel. She had little control as they gained speed and entered the riverbed, but she managed to keep them from hitting a rocky outcropping that jutted into the riverbed. She was not so fortunate when it came to a giant mound of scrub, and suddenly the vehicle stuck and stopped.

"You okay?" Jackson asked as he reached over and turned off the ignition.

"Yeah."

Before the words were out of her mouth, Jackson had unbuckled his seatbelt and thrown open his door. He scrambled up the bank to the edge of the road, just in time to see the blip that was the red pickup disappear in the heat ripples on the horizon.

"Are they gone?" Hillary hollered, struggling to extricate herself from the Focus. Her door only opened a foot before hitting a cactus of some sort. Careful to avoid its spines, she slipped out and plodded up the bank. Jackson met her and extended his hand, pulling her the final measure.

"They're gone," Jackson said.

"That was no accident."

"No. The passenger had a ski mask."

"How could anyone have known where we were?"

"We were followed? Maybe the guards at the base called them? I don't know. You got your phone?"

"In my purse."

"Stay here. If you see anyone coming, shout."

She nodded and he clambered back down the embankment to the car. He thought about searching for the phone in Hillary's purse, decided he didn't want to lose his hand if she caught him, and instead carried the purse back up to her. While she retrieved her phone, he checked his. As feared, there was no signal.

"Nothing," she said a moment later.

"Great," Jackson said, looking down at the car. Even if they were able to free it from the sagebrush, there was no way they were driving it up out of the riverbed. Without built-up highway speed, it would never make it through the sand back to the pavement anyhow. "The only vehicle on the road was the truck," he said, "and before that, the sheriff's car when we were coming in to town, so we could be here a while. We can run the A/C intermittently."

"I say we walk to town," she said.

"It's at least five miles."

"That's not that far."

"It's four thousand degrees and we have no water."

"And what if no one comes? Then we're talking even longer without water, and I don't like the idea of hiking through the desert at night with no means of self-defense. Plus, they could come back."

"They would have by now."

"Maybe. But I say we go for it."

"Okay. But whatever happens, do not get into a semi that will take you into town."

"What?"

"Have you ever watched a movie?"

"This really isn't the time, Jackson."

"Yeah, fair enough." He scanned the desert and sighed. "Probably also not the time to remind you that I drank a gallon of tea at lunch and a pot of coffee this morning."

"Find a cactus and catch up."

Jackson returned to the car a second time and used it for some privacy. He debated bringing Hillary's laptop along, but didn't particularly feel like carrying any additional weight. So he cracked the windows, locked the doors, and started out after Hillary.

He didn't hurry. There was no need to exert himself, and she wasn't exactly splendid company. He set a measured pace, and by the time he caught up to her, Hillary had bound her hair in a ponytail. Her face was flushed and her skin glistened with perspiration. He didn't think about how he looked.

"I used to watch this PBS show called *Square One*, all about math," he said.

"Please tell me you aren't getting delirious already."

"They had this segment at the end called *Mathnet*, a spoof of *Dragnet*, where they solved crimes using math."

"I take it this is relevant somehow?"

"They used to play a game called 'What do we know?'"

"A game."

"They'd state the facts they knew, usually while pacing in opposite directions. We can skip that part."

"Talking will only sap our energy and make our throats dry."

"Fine. I'll talk. You listen."

And so for the next quarter of an hour, he recapped everything, starting with Arielle's death and working his way through the facts as they'd learned them. He included some speculation in with knowledge, feeling like a cow chewing its cud. Hillary plodded along beside him, her face expressionless, her body moving in a steady, resolute rhythm. He had no doubt she would walk back to Vegas if she had to.

"Then we come to Kingman," he said. "Dumpy old town abandoned by the military. Sad enough in its own right, but its citizens are known for violent acts here and abroad and for killing themselves. After a few hours here, though, I can't say I blame them. The entire town seems caught in a 1980s time warp except for the sheriff's department, which is cutting edge. And grossly oversized, although, considering the townsfolk, maybe it's called for."

Hillary continued to match stride for stride for stride.

"Did I miss anything?"

"No," she said quietly.

"Hmm. On *Mathnet*, 'What do we know?' usually led to a break or a deduction of some sort."

"How far do you think we've come?"

He turned and walked backwards for a few steps. "I can't see the curve in the road anymore." He slowly turned back around. "At least a mile or two."

Hillary slowed.

"What?"

"I think I see a car."

Jackson squinted at the shimmering surface of the road. It took a moment, but a vehicle did emerge and take solid shape. Jackson recognized the color. It was a Delamar County Sheriff's Department patrol car, this one an old Crown Victoria instead of a new Dodge Charger. It slowed as it approached, stopping in the middle of the road instead of pulling to the side. The driver's window lowered and an unfamiliar face peered out.

"Trouble?" he asked astutely. He was thin, young, with short-buzzed dark hair under a ranger-style cap. His badge identified him as Deputy McGregor.

"We were run off the road a few miles back," Jackson said.

"Run off the road?"

"Red pickup," Hillary said. "Badly worn. Two men."

"One wore a ski mask."

McGregor studied them for a moment, then nodded at the backseat. "Hop in. You folks look beat."

Jackson got the door for Hillary and slid in after her.

McGregor was already on his radio. "Sheriff, I just picked up two hikers four miles north of town. Said their car was run off the road by an old, red pickup truck. Sounds like the Grange boys."

"Copy that, Tom. You all coming into town?"

McGregor looked over his shoulder. "You think we can get your car back on the road without a wrecker?"

"No," Hillary said.

"Glenn's got a wrecker at the garage. We can either go back to town or we can have him meet us at your car. It's up to you."

"Whatever's quickest," Hillary said.

"Sheriff, we're headed to their car. You wanna call Glenn, have him head out?"

"Copy. I'm on my way."

"Roger." McGregor lowered the radio. "You folks just passing through?"

"More or less," Jackson answered.

McGregor asked no more questions, and when they reached the far end of the turn east, Hillary pointed to where they had gone off the road. He slowed the patrol car and made a U-turn to park on the shoulder, then got out and opened the back doors for them. Jackson led the way some two hundred feet to where the car had stopped in the bottom of the dry riverbed.

"You must have been going at a pretty good clip," McGregor said.

"I sped up to try to outrun them when it became obvious they had malevolent intentions."

McGregor stared briefly at Hillary. Pondering the meaning of malevolent?

He scratched his jaw and looked back at the road. Down to the car. Back at the road. "Glenn's going to have his work cut out getting the wrecker down here."

"Maybe we can get a helo from the base and airlift it," Jackson said.

"The base?"

"Blane," Jackson said.

McGregor shook his head. "The base is closed. Hasn't been operational for twenty years."

"Yeah, so we heard."

A few minutes later, a second patrol car pulled off the road, parking directly in front of McGregor's car. Sheriff Quinn stepped out, his hat low over his eyes. He hesitated for just a moment and then sauntered through the sand.

"Somehow I figured it would be you all," he said.

"You know these folks, Sheriff?"

"Hillary McKenzie and Jackson Douglas. Lawyers from Los Angeles."

Jackson started to object to being tabbed a lawyer, but the protest died on his tongue at a glance from Quinn. "What happened?" the sheriff asked.

Hillary recounted the incident.

"What were you all doing out here?"

"Just seeing the sights," Jackson said.

"Uh-huh."

"We went to check out the base," Hillary said.

"Blane's a restricted military base."

"It's also supposedly decommissioned," she replied.

"Looked more like the border to Mexico," Jackson said.

"You all make a scene?"

"No," Hillary said. "We were sternly told to leave, and we did. That's it."

"And then you all were run off the road by a red pickup?"

"Yes."

"Who are these Grange boys the deputy mentioned?" Jackson asked.

"Couple of brothers that live out this way."

"Troublemakers," McGregor added.

"What kind of trouble?"

"That matter?" Quinn asked.

"If they were the ones responsible, yeah."

"Nothing serious. Some petty vandalism, disorderly conduct, reckless driving."

"Drunkenness," McGregor said

"What he said. Nothing like this."

"But they drive an old, red pickup?"

"They do. And I had Deputy Seaver check it out."

"First names don't happen to be Marvin and Jerry, do they?" Jackson asked.

Quinn shot him another glance.

A grumble from the road ended their conversation, and all four heads turned to see a rusty, rickety tow truck park beside the two patrol cars. The door opened on squeaky hinges and a man in mechanic's coveralls climbed down from the cab. The coveralls were stained and ripped, and his skin was so worn that the tattoos that covered his lower arms were indecipherable. A scraggly red beard hung halfway down his chest, matched in length and style by the hair under a greasy Las Vegas 51s baseball cap. His jaw was lopsided, from either a tumor or a wad of tobacco. The latter, Jackson determined, when he hawked a stream of brown juice that threatened to end the riverbed's dry spell.

"Sheriff," he said in a voice that was too smooth for the body. "Deputy."

"Afternoon, Glenn."

For the first time, Glenn acknowledged Jackson and Hillary. "Let her drive, did ya?" he asked with a grin.

Jackson couldn't help but return it, especially when he saw the brief flare of indignation on Hillary's face.

"Can you get her down here?" McGregor asked.

"Sand's soft, but with the truck, I shouldn't have a problem."

"Tom, you all can head back on patrol," Quinn said. "I'll stay here."

"All right, Sheriff. Folks," he said with a tip of his cap.

"Thank you, Deputy McGregor," Hillary said.

He trudged back up the hill, and Glenn followed. He waited until McGregor backed his car out of the way to begin the slow process of backing down toward the riverbed. Once he was in place, he spent nearly twenty minutes analyzing the terrain and hooking the car to his rig. It took another ten to navigate the sagebrush and rock outcroppings along the riverbank and pull the car back to the shoulder of the road. Having cooled for just a few minutes in the back of McGregor's patrol car, Jackson and Hillary were sweating like hogs again.

Glenn explained that he would tow the vehicle back to town and examine it at the garage, and Quinn gave the duo a lift. Other than a brief radio conversation with Deputy Seaver, who had visited the Grange house and found no one there, the head lawman was silent.

Like most everything else in Kingman, the gas station had seen better days. A cracked concrete lot fronted a one-stall garage attached to a tiny convenience store. The canopy covering the dual pumps in front of the store was painted blue and had long since faded, revealing vacancies where the Chevron name and logo had once been emblazoned.

Quinn waited in the road while Glenn backed the wrecker toward the garage. Quinn then parked at one of the pumps. He got out and opened the doors. "I can't force you all to leave town," he said, "especially not if your all's car's gonna need repairs. But I'd recommend you all keep a low profile."

"Noted," Jackson said.

"If you all need anything, you all know where to find me."

Quinn proceeded to fill his tank, and Jackson and Hillary entered the store. A counter with an old-fashioned cash register ran along the left wall. Behind it were an assortment of small parts and accessories. Two small aisles contained basic snacks, motor oil and other lubricants, and more miscellaneous accessories. A small glass-paneled refrigerator held bottles of water, soda, and beer. Jackson took out two bottles of water. Tossing one to Hillary, he unscrewed the cap on the other and guzzled half of it.

"You're going to have to pay for that."

Jackson turned to see a disheveled man get off a bench beyond the counter. He'd been lying down, a magazine over his head, and Jackson had missed him on his initial scan of the store.

"I will," he said, giving the man a once-over. He was short and stocky, with a mop of curly hair and a beard that would have been long if not compared to Glenn's. Unlike the wrecker driver's, it was jet black. But what caught Jackson's attention was not the man's disheveled appearance or dirty clothes. It was the maniacal look in his dark, deep eyes. They were black as coal, and yet vivid. Drugs, Jackson surmised, and lots of them.

"You work here?" he asked.

"Naw." Nevertheless, the man walked around behind the counter as if he owned the place. "You the out-of-towners?"

"We are."

"The ones asking all sorts of questions?"

"Word travels fast," Jackson said with a look back at Hillary. She was perusing the snacks, likely looking for something healthier than Cheetos or Funyuns. She would be out of luck.

"People don't like being asked questions."

"Yeah, we sort of noticed."

"There's good reason for that," he said, leaning forward. His breath smelled of booze, and Jackson had to brace himself not to take a step back.

"What's that?" he asked.

The man stared at Jackson such that he felt like he was under a spell. Then he leaned back and cackled.

A moment later, Quinn entered the store. "Dime, what are you all doing back there?"

"Nothing, Sheriff."

"Get on out of here. These folks don't want you all lurking around."

"Just watching the store for Glenn."

"Glenn's back. Hit the road."

His head hung low, the man tabbed as Dime shuffled toward the door connecting the store to the garage and pushed through it without a word.

"Sorry about that," Quinn said, rounding the counter. He approached the cash register and proceeded to pay for his gas. "Dime's our resident mental case and town drunk."

"Is he dangerous?" Hillary asked.

"Not so far."

Quinn completed the transaction, tipped his cap, and exited the store.

"Did you take that as a threat?" Jackson asked. "'Not so far.'"

Hillary shrugged.

Jackson watched out the window as Glenn had a word with the sheriff. He entered the store and said, "Good news, bad news."

Hillary approached the counter and stood beside Jackson.

"Good news is, no structural damage. You've got a slightly bent rim that I can easy get back in shape, and your left rear tire's trashed. Besides that, just a few dents and gouges in the fender and some scratches on the sides. Bad news is, I just checked my inventory and I don't have in stock any tires that will fit a Ford Focus. Soonest I can get one delivered," he said, looking back at a clock behind him, "is probably gonna be tomorrow morning."

"What about the spare?" Hillary asked.

"It's got a leaky valve. Where you headed?"

"Ideally, Las Vegas."

"Might get you halfway there, might not."

Hillary's shoulders fell. "Basically you're telling me we have to spend the night in town?"

" 'Fraid so. Kingman Motel's nothing fancy, but it's clean."

Jackson exhaled. "Well, with a slogan like that, it won't be long before they open shop on the Vegas Strip."

Chapter Forty-Five

JACKSON PAID GLENN for two bottles of water and remembered their luggage at the last minute. Glenn procured the duffel bag and Hillary's laptop case from the trunk. With them both over his shoulder, Jackson led Hillary out into the sun and heat.

"It could be worse," he said.

"Than being trapped in this small town? How exactly? Let me carry one of those."

"I was actually hoping you'd know. I got it."

"Stop being heroic," she said, lifting the laptop case off his shoulder.

"Just gallant."

"It's pronounced gal-lant." She hoisted the laptop case around her neck. "Maybe we should chance it on the spare."

"And risk a reprise? I want a nice bed tonight, but not that badly."

"If we made I-15, we'd get a motorist to come along soon, or else be in cell phone range. And even Highway 93 is bound to have some traffic."

"You really want the kind of people that drive across the desert in the middle of the night stopping to assist you?"

She exhaled. "No, you're right."

"Can I get that written down somewhere?"

"Let's go."

"Where exactly?"

"The motel. I need to get out of the heat, shower, and think."

"Maybe if we're lucky they'll have a set of rabbit ears and I can watch some TV."

From one end of town to the other, it was five, maybe six hundred yards. But with the brunt of the afternoon's heat and full sunshine beating down on them, it looked like miles. As they were crossing 4th Street, Hillary nudged Jackson. He looked her way and saw Dime trundling down the opposite side of 4th Street, on a course to intersect them.

"Uh-oh," Jackson said, at the same time plotting a strategy if the man was anything less than civil. "Get ready to run," he mouthed to Hillary.

Neither fast nor slow, Dime kept walking until he was directly in front of them, forcing them to either stop or deliberately walk around him.

"Hello," the man said, his dark eyes aglow.

Hillary returned the greeting. Jackson kept his eyes and body alert.

"Name's Dime. Tenpenny, actually. Darren Tenpenny. But they call me Dime."

Jackson and Hillary both nodded.

"Because a dime's worth ten pennies, you see?"

They both nodded again.

"I saw the sheriff drive away," he said, and Jackson wondered if that gave Dime license to act out or freedom to answer questions. "What do you want to know about Blane Air Force Base?"

"Who said we're asking about the base?" Hillary asked.

"Small town."

She studied him for a second. "Several people we know were stationed at the base." She gave him the rundown of names, but his expression never changed.

"We also heard rumors about a military project called Silver Dawn," Jackson said, watching Dime's face carefully. It gave away nothing.

"Do you know anything about that? Or about Golden Dawn?" Hillary asked.

"I don't know anything about any dawns, but I know all about the base. I know 'cause I've been there."

"You've been on the base?"

"I go every month," Dime said. "They come and get me."

"Who do?"

"The men in white suits." His eyes widened. "They tap into my brain," he said, drumming the side of his head with his finger. "They're coming again soon."

"I see," Jackson said.

"They come for everybody. They'll come for you too!"

"We'll be careful."

"What can you tell us about the base?" Hillary asked. "What are they doing there?"

"That I don't know. But they've seen inside my mind."

"Must be frightening," Jackson muttered.

"They've seen inside my soul." Dime leaned forward. He whispered. "They know who I am."

"And who are you?" Hillary asked.

His voice quieted even more. "I'm one of them."

"One of who?"

"Them," he said in a whisper so quiet it was almost a squeak.

Hillary looked at Jackson. He doubted a "Them who?" would be successful, and she apparently shared that opinion.

"What else can you tell us?" she asked.

"What do you want to know?" he said at normal volume.

"How many people are there?"

"I see three or four."

"Military?"

"No," he said almost with disgust. "The men in white suits."

"Colonel Sanders?" Jackson asked.

Dime just stared at him.

"Do you know any of them?" Hillary asked.

"They don't have names."

"Of course not," Jackson said.

"Jack, be quiet," Hillary said. "What can you tell us about them?"

"They can see inside of me."

"How do they come for you?"

"In a black van." He jerked his thumb over his shoulder. "Right up to the door."

Jackson followed the thumb to a two-story, multi-apartment complex on 4th Street.

"Is that where you live?" Hillary asked.

Dime nodded.

"Alone?"

Another nod.

"Do they ever come for anyone else in your building?"

"They come for everybody," he said. Then, suddenly, his face contorted in pain, he fell to his knees, clamping his hands over his ears. "They're coming!" he shouted.

"Well this isn't awkward or anything," Jackson said, glad to see deserted sidewalks and streets.

"Dime," Hillary said, but he was chanting quietly, his hands still over his ears. She shook his elbow. "Dime."

His eyes popped open, wide and full of fright. Then he stood and took off running back toward the apartment building.

"The guy can move," Jackson said, watching him all the way to the apartment's front door. Dime never once looked back, leaping up the stairs and inside. Jackson turned his eyes to Hillary and they resumed walking.

"What'd you make of that?" she asked a third of the way down the block.

"That this town needs an apothecary."

"You think that's it, he's crazy?"

"Quinn as much as said so. And unless an army of French waiters has taken over the base to practice sautéing brains, I'm inclined to agree with him."

Hillary remained quiet.

"You don't?"

"Oh, he's crazy," Hillary said. "But I think there might be some nuggets of truth embedded in his delusions."

"Like what? You think they're actually drilling into his brain?"

She shrugged.

"And who are the men in white suits? A HAZMAT team? The Navy in their dress whites?"

"How about doctors in lab coats?"

Jackson said nothing, instead mulling the possibilities. He didn't want to admit that Dime's story, crazy as it was, actually fell in line with some of the other things they were discovering. It certainly added to the sinister nature of whatever had been, and perhaps still was, going on at Blane Air Force Base.

As they passed the church at the corner of Main and 2nd Street, Jackson stopped. The white steeple looked so pristine against the pale eastern sky. He half expected a raven to suddenly alight on its apex and begin cawing eerily.

"Come on," Hillary said. "I'm tired."

They arrived at the Kingman Motel with Jackson whistling *The X-Files* theme song and Hillary giving him disdainful looks over her shoulder. The motel was one story, eight rooms that stretched directly north and south so that the southernmost room was farther from the road than was the northernmost. Parking was in a cracked, pitted lot, the lines marking the spaces faded almost to invisibility. It didn't matter; there were no cars.

A covered walkway that led back to an empty swimming pool separated the rooms from the lobby. Over its roof, a rounded trapezoidal sign had once flashed the motel's name and vacancy in neon. Now the tubes were dark. The paint was a faded pink, the doors chipped brown.

"Odds on plumbing?" Jackson asked as they approached the front door.

"One room or two?"

"One, only because I don't like the idea of you being alone."

"How gallant," she said as she opened the door.

The lobby, if it could be called that, was not air-conditioned. An oscillating fan mounted on the desk blew air and a few streamers at a shaggy-haired guy who stared at a magazine until he realized the girl at the counter was better looking than the girl in print. He looked up, words not forming, the fan blowing his hair into his face, then back out of it.

"We'd like a room," Hillary said.

He very slowly licked his lips. Jackson could almost hear his brain coughing and sputtering like an infrequently used car engine. Finally, it caught. "Uh . . . how many nights?"

"Just one."

"You want a suite?"

"You have suites?" Jackson asked.

"King bed, HBO, and complimentary shampoos."

Jackson looked at Hillary. "A bargain like that's hard to pass up."

"Else it's two queens," Shaggy said.

"Two queens," she answered quickly.

Shaggy swallowed as he stood. He knocked over an uncapped bottle of soda. "Um . . ." He bent down to pick it up.

"Imagine if you were all dolled up," Jackson whispered.

"That's, uh, twenty-nine-oh-six with taxes and fees."

Hillary withdrew cash from her purse. She set it on the counter, lest their fingers touch during a handoff, sending the guy into shock.

"Keep the change," she said, and he pushed shut a drawer he had unlocked manually. He turned to a pegboard behind him and retrieved one of eight keys from it.

"Room 3," he said. "There's, uh, an ice machine at the end of the building. You have to kind of bang it a few times to get it to work."

"Thank you," she said.

"Uh, enjoy your stay."

"I doubt that very much," she said as the door closed behind them.

To call the room Spartan would be an understatement. Two beds, a small end table between them, a dresser, a blocky TV, and one padded end chair sat on

347

threadbare carpet. The ivory walls were scarred and smudged, and the one that faced the bathroom had been repainted a different shade of ivory.

Jackson shook his head. "And to think, twenty-four hours ago we were at the Oasis." He dropped their joint duffel on the floor and flopped back onto the bed.

"You touch it, you sleep in it," Hillary said. She placed her laptop case on the nearest bed, then knelt down to adjust the knob on a wall-mounted air conditioner beneath the front window. It rattled and then began humming somewhat steadily. Hillary picked up the duffel, carried it to the other bed, and dug through her end for clean clothes. They were both running low, and clean were getting mixed with dirty. Jackson wondered if Campbell's sold apparel.

While Hillary showered, Jackson flipped through very basic cable, settling on—ironically—*Ocean's Thirteen*. When she was done, he took a long, cold shower. He had only packed one "emergency" pair of jeans, but at least he had clean underwear, socks, and a T-shirt—the last of his clean clothes.

Hillary was seated on the near bed, legs crossed, her laptop balanced on top of them. She wore the jeans she had donned before going to breakfast and a lavender T-shirt.

"You have Wi-Fi?" Jackson asked.

"No. I'm just looking over everything we downloaded from Holloway's flash drive."

"A watched pot never boils."

"What does that have to do with anything?"

"It means you can look at that data all you want, but it's not going to suddenly coalesce into an answer."

She stared at him. "That is not what that saying means."

"Whatever," he said, leaning against the dresser. "What's our plan for the rest of the day?"

"I'm out of socks and down to my last shirt and pants," Hillary said. "I doubt Campbell's carries much in the way of women's fashion, but I'd like to check. I could use a few other things too."

"I think they're only open till five."

She looked at the clock on the desk. "Let's get going."

The heat had not subsided any with sunset still two hours away. As had been the case all day, the sidewalks were empty, the streets were vacant, and yards were void of people or pets. Given the heat, it wasn't surprising, but Jackson would have expected to see some signs of life at some point.

"I called Captain Donovan," Hillary said as they walked.

"Verifying Henrietta's story?"

"She more or less verified his. But we didn't know about Reynolds when we spoke. I wanted to get his take."

"Which was?"

"Reynolds was by the books, no-nonsense, gruff. And Donovan had no idea what he was doing on the base, being an Army general."

"More of the same then."

"Yeah. I also asked him about Yvonne, but the name didn't ring any bells."

Campbell's general store was just that, offering some basic food staples, homecare supplies, personal products, a few rudimentary clothing options, and an assortment of knickknacks. It had a single checkout counter up front, with an actual computer and cash register. A radio mounted above the counter played soft rock with a little static. An old man, at least by Kingman standards, worked the counter and greeted Jackson and Hillary with a friendly smile as they entered. The only other people in the store were a middle-aged woman stocking shelves in the clothing "department" in back and a young woman perusing some ready-made dinners near the front.

Jackson and Hillary both headed for the clothing section, where the woman stocking shelves didn't acknowledge them with so much as a nod. Jackson found packages of underwear and socks and snagged the first T-shirt he spotted. It bore an old Las Vegas slogan above caricatures of several of the more prominent casinos. Folding the socks and underwear inside it, he announced he was going to find some food, as he doubted the Kingman Motel served a continental breakfast.

The young woman avoided him like he had the plague and quickly paid for a few ready-to-eat meals. Jackson overheard the man at the counter call her Sandra, and she identified him as Bobby. His tone was friendly and he made small talk while checking her out. He must have been a commuter.

Jackson found a box of granola bars, another of Pop-Tarts, and some acceptable-looking fruit. He tried to remember if the Kingman Motel had a microwave. Concluding it didn't, he passed on the instant coffee and met Hillary at the checkout counter. She had an armful of purchases that looked decidedly feminine.

"Afternoon," Bobby said as Hillary placed her items on the counter. "You folks new in town?"

"Just visiting," she said.

"Welcome. Name's Bobby." He pushed his glasses onto his nose and began scanning items. "What brings you out this way?"

Hillary cut to the chase. "We're investigating a crime that may involve residents of Kingman or activities at Blane Air Force Base."

Bobby paused for just a second, his hand on a small bottle of shampoo. He took a quick glance toward the back of the store, then swiped the bottle.

"You know about what went on out at the base?" he asked, his voice quieter.

Hillary also lowered her voice. "To an extent."

"About the . . . experiments?"

"We know the military had a top-secret project back in the '80s."

"Military," he said with a huff. He scanned Jackson's socks. "I served two tours in Vietnam. I'm a proud veteran of the United States Army. That wasn't the military running things."

Jackson fought his eyebrows' sudden urge to rise. Not another wackadoo.

"Who was it?" Hillary asked.

Bobby scanned Jackson's T-shirt and looked toward the back of the store again. "I don't know. Everything was shrouded in mystery. The mind control, the genetic research . . ."

"Genetic research?"

He nodded. "Experimentation that didn't work, and this whole town's lived in fear ever since."

"Fear of what?"

Bobby's eyes appeared to glaze over for just a moment. He then flitted them sideways at Hillary. "Them."

Chapter Forty-Six

4:56 p.m.

DESPITE THE HEAT, chills ran down Jackson's spine.

"Them," Hillary said. "Them who?"

Jackson saw movement out the corner of his eye, just before he heard a female voice.

"Bobby, are we out of price tags?"

Jackson turned to see the woman who had been stocking shelves. Medium height and weight, dark hair to her jawline, still no smile or even an acknowledgement the store had customers.

"Uh, I think there are some in the back," Bobby said. "I'll check in just a moment." He quickly scanned the rest of their items. "Thirty-four seventy-seven."

Hillary looked from him to the woman and then to her purse. Forcing a close-lipped smile, she handed him two twenty-dollar bills. He counted out her change, then quickly bagged their items. In the process, he lifted his eyes—out of sight from the woman—to make brief eye contact with Jackson. Although he said nothing, his eyes spoke volumes, uttering fear and a warning his voice couldn't.

Bobby slid the paper bag across the counter to Jackson, smiled, thanked them, and wished them a pleasant stay in Kingman. Then he followed the woman to the back of the store, leaving Jackson and Hillary alone. "What do you say, Mulder?" Jackson asked.

"Mulder was the guy," Hillary said, heading for the door. She lingered in the shade of the porch for a moment before striking out toward the south.

As they crossed 2nd Street, Jackson nodded at the tavern on the other side of Main. "Wanna stop in and see if we can get assaulted?"

She looked at him.

"You want answers. Supposedly talking to drunks works."

"You really think there's anybody there? This whole town is dead."

"Our alternative is sitting and watching the paint peel in the motel all night, and if we don't overturn these rocks now, you'll just want to come back tomorrow."

"Okay. But how do we get them to talk to us?"

"How much cash you got on you?"

"Why?"

"How much?"

With a sigh, she looked into her purse. "A little over fifty."

"Plenty," he said, outlining his plan as they crossed the street.

Bernie's Tavern was a two-story building, the upper half of which appeared to be an apartment. The blinds were all drawn, on both levels. Only a neon "Open" sign in the window and the bar name painted above the entrance indicated it was anything other than a residence. The late afternoon sun bathed the shabby exterior in a golden glow reminiscent of a Western. But as soon as Jackson opened the heavy front door for Hillary, darkness overwhelmed him. Lots of bars were poorly lit, but Bernie's took it to a new level. He and Hillary stood in the entry for nearly a minute as shapes began to form.

The bar ran along the left wall, fading into the murky blackness at the back of the room. Half of the dozen stools were occupied, the patrons men and women, ranging from Jackson and Hillary's age to senior citizens. They weren't watching TVs over the bar, because there was only one and it was off, nor were they chatting, joking, flirting, or pouring out their sad story to the female bartender who was on the constant run. Instead, they cradled shot glasses and beer bottles with looks of despondency and boredom. Their eyes were glazed over, like moles that spent too much time underground.

Jackson leaned over to Hillary. "Beats any advisement the surgeon general could ever issue."

Her eyes swept the room, panning from the bar to a few tables along the right wall and an alcove in the back that appeared to house a pay phone and restrooms. Her eyes settled back at the bar, where one or two patrons had lifted their head to see who had entered. None of them responded in any way.

"Just like walking into Cheers," Jackson said.

"I'm not sure fifty's going to cut it," she said.

"Shoot, here that's probably a week's wages."

Hillary took several steps forward until she caught the eye of the bartender. She was young, no more than thirty—but no less either—with curly brown hair that hung to bare shoulders. Her arms were long and tanned, with several tattoos wrapping around her wrists, forearms, and elbows. Her vest, appropriately, was leather.

"What can I get you?" she barked.

"Next round's on me," Hillary said loudly, holding up all her cash. She slapped it onto the bar. "For everybody."

"You win the lottery or something?"

"And decided to spend our winnings here?" Jackson muttered.

"I was hoping someone might be willing to answer some questions, but there's no strings attached," Hillary said, pushing the money forward.

The bartender pocketed it. "Cops?"

"No."

"Lawyers?"

Hillary didn't bat an eyelash. "Do we look like lawyers?"

The bartender swept her tongue from one side of her mouth to the other. "What questions?"

"We're looking for anyone who knows anything about Arielle Coal, Yvonne Coleman, Warren McKenzie, or activities at Blane Air Force Base."

The room quieted.

At the end of the bar, an old man tipped back a shot glass, draining its clear contents, and clunked it back on the bar. "Sheila, another."

"Coming up, Al," she said without looking his way. "Why are you asking about Blane?" she asked Hillary.

"It's rather complicated."

"So's Blane."

"What can you tell us?"

"Nothing. And nobody else here will either."

"Why not?" Jackson asked.

"Because we don't like strangers poking their noses around. And because there's nothing to do with Blane that's worth talking about."

Sheila went to work pouring Al's drink, then refilling several other patrons' beverages. Hillary looked down the bar, waiting for anyone to make eye contact with her. "Anyone?" she asked. "Just a few questions."

Her answer was a belch and several gulps from various customers.

"Easy come, easy go," Jackson said, shifting the paper bag with their purchases from Campbell's to his other hand. "Shall we repair to our digs?"

"I'll answer your questions."

They both turned to see the speaker. He was an old man, in his sixties or seventies, with a day's growth of gray beard covering a long face. He had approached from the side, where he'd been the loan occupant of a booth. The smell of his clothes or the liquor on his breath were likely reasons why.

"For free," he said, then gestured for them to follow him.

Jackson shrugged at Hillary and followed. The booth faced a window with its blinds drawn, allowing in almost no light. A modest lamp hung over the table, casting light on an open Bible next to a shot glass of brownish liquid. Beside them both was a black baseball cap embroidered with the words "Vietnam Veteran" and a row of military ribbons.

Jackson let Hillary slide into the booth first. He set the bag from Campbell's in the booth behind them and joined her. The man sat opposite them, offering a toothy, disarming smile. It was matched by wide, blue eyes. It was a look that could have been genuine or drug induced, Jackson couldn't tell.

"Names Laplante," he said.

Jackson and Hillary introduced themselves.

"You're not from Kingman, are you?"

"Los Angeles," Hillary said.

"Must be culture shock to you," Laplante said. He wore a plaid shirt, unbuttoned over a ribbed tank top that had at one time presumably been white. It was low enough to reveal a scar on his chest. A bullet hole, it appeared.

"Somewhat," Hillary answered.

"I take it you're the ones who have been asking questions all over town."

"Quite a grapevine here in Kingman," Jackson said.

Laplante smiled.

"We're looking into a murder in Las Vegas last weekend," Hillary said. "The trail has led us to Kingman, and to Blane Air Force Base." She looked over at his cap. "Did you serve?"

"Yes, ma'am, I did."

"Were you ever stationed at Blane?"

"No, ma'am, not as a member of the United States Navy," he said, turning his arm to display a tattoo on the inside of his forearm. "Seventh Fleet, aboard the USS *Blue Ridge*."

"Tonkin Gulf Yacht Club?" she asked, reading the tattoo.

Laplante smiled again. "It's what we called the Seventh Fleet." He sniffed. "I was never on the base, but I know folks who were."

"When was that?"

"Throughout the years. Many of them live in town to this day."

"About how many?" Hillary asked.

"Seventy-seven."

"That many?"

"They weren't all airmen."

"Then what were they?" Jackson asked.

Laplante's smile faded ever so slightly as he turned to look Jackson in the eye. "Test subjects."

Jackson thought the background music might screech to a stop or one of the guys at the bar would fall off his stool in a seizure. Or maybe he'd look down and see blood pouring out of Laplante's scarred-over bullet wound. Nothing so dramatic happened, but he did feel the hair on the back of his neck rising. Again.

"What kind of tests?" Hillary asked.

"All kinds. They had a program, they called it Silver Dawn." Laplante leaned forward. "It was mind control. They were trying to brainwash assassins and super soldiers."

"How do you know this?"

Laplante's mouth formed a smirk. "I have my sources. They were experimenting with breeding too."

"You mean humans?"

He nodded.

Jackson glanced over at the bar, where Sheila was conversing in quiet tones with two of the sullen drinkers. He focused his attention back on Laplante.

"They were making babies," Laplante said, "but not as God intended, with union between a man and a woman. They were using machines."

"Machines?"

"They had a huge laboratory set up in a hangar. They were making genetically altered babies who would come out of the womb programmed to do whatever they wanted them to. Desert Root, they called the project." He leaned farther forward. "It didn't go too well."

"What do you mean?"

"They took science too far. They made babies, but they didn't come out right. They had . . . problems."

"Psychological problems?"

Laplante nodded. "And physical."

Hillary took a deep breath. "You said they made them with machines. But they had to have actual mothers to deliver them, didn't they?"

"Of course. They used anyone they could find. Prostitutes, homeless women, criminals. They didn't care where they got them because they were just incubators."

"Have you ever heard of a woman named Yvonne Coleman?"

He nodded. "She was one of them. One of the surrogate mothers."

Laplante's words barely had time to sink in before the front door was thrown open, temporarily flooding the tavern with light. Jackson glanced over his shoulder to see Sheriff Quinn standing in the doorway, hands on his belt, cowboy hat atop his head. He glanced around for a moment and made his way over to their table.

"Dr. Laplante, I trust you all aren't bothering these folks with more religious mumbo-jumbo," he said.

"Nothing of the sort, Sheriff."

"Doctor?" Hillary asked.

"Doctor of Psychology," Laplante said proudly. "San Jose State, class of 1977."

"Well, Doc, you all mind if I borrow your all's patients for a second?" Quinn asked.

Laplante spread out his hands, and Quinn nodded for Jackson and Hillary to follow him. Reluctantly they did, huddling around an unused coat hanger near the front door.

"What's going on, Sheriff?" Hillary asked.

"I think you all should know that Mr. Laplante is clinically insane."

"Insane?"

Quinn nodded. "He's also a religious nut, and I don't mean that to be derogatory."

"How do you mean it?" Jackson asked.

"Mr. Laplante is a staunch, Bible-thumping, born-again Christian," Quinn said. "Preaches on the street corners, everything."

"What's wrong with that?" Hillary asked.

"Nothing. Except about two years ago he was a devout Mormon."

"People get converted."

Quinn nodded. "That they do. Six months earlier, he converted from Catholicism to Mormonism. And I hear before I arrived in these parts, he was a fervent Muslim, some kind of New Age hippie, and an atheist."

"Gives new meaning to the phrase 'church hopping,'" Jackson said.

"Laplante isn't a true believer. He's just crazy."

"That doesn't mean his other thoughts aren't valid."

"Is he not really a doctor?" Hillary asked.

"Oh, he's got a degree all right, thirty-five years ago. But since then, he's battled clinical depression, anxiety attacks, and severe bouts of hallucinations and delusions—probably all some form of PTSD from his time in 'Nam."

"You know complete medical histories for all the citizens of Kingman?" Hillary asked.

"Nope. Just the ones that could cause a public nuisance. Mr. Laplante's had dinner with the apostles, been Brigham Young—which I'll tell you all was some fine entertainment on the street corner—and for about a month, claimed he was one of the two witnesses from Revelation. The other was Moses, who he thought was beside him the whole time." Quinn looked back and forth between Jackson and Hillary. "He's also claimed that he is the Lord's missionary to the other world."

"Other world?"

Quinn shrugged. "The spirit world, aliens, we don't know and he don't say."

"So in other words, he's completely unreliable," Hillary said.

"I'm sure there's tidbits of truth scattered around in what he tells you all, but I wouldn't take those nuggets to the bank."

Hillary sighed. "Is there anything else?"

"As a matter of fact, I'd appreciate it if you all didn't speak with Mr. Laplante any further. For the last couple of years, since his 'rebirth,' he's been a little less of a hassle . . . Mostly keeps to himself and reads the Bible. I'd rather not get him riled up."

"We weren't riling him," Hillary said. "He was perfectly calm."

"All the same, I'd rather you all stay away from him."

"We were just leaving," Jackson said, pulling on Hillary's elbow.

"One more piece of advice," Quinn said.

"What's that?" Jackson asked when Hillary stayed mute.

"Word's spread around town about you all, and folks are getting a little testy. I wouldn't go asking too many more questions."

"Testy?" Hillary asked.

Quinn nodded. "I talked to Glenn. He said your all's car will be fixed in the morning." He nodded toward the motel. "Go back to your all's motel, lay low, and head on out in the morning."

"Is that an order?" Hillary asked.

Quinn nodded slightly. "If it needs to be."

"Understood," Jackson said. "Thanks, Sheriff."

Quinn tipped his hat as he headed out the door.

Jackson retreated to Laplante's booth and thanked him for his time as he collected their bag from Campbell's.

"He has no legal grounds to bar us from asking questions," Hillary said once they were outside. Quinn was gone.

"I'm not sure he needs legal grounds."

"I smell a cover-up," she said. "And that sounded like another threat."

"Maybe. Or maybe Quinn's right."

"What, you're on his side now?"

"I'm not on his side, Hill." They were walking south, away from Bernie's, toward the motel. "But you've got to know when you're beat."

"Sounds like the words of a quitter."

"Discretion is the bet—"

"Don't give me some old cliché."

"Maybe it'd help if I translated it to Latin first."

"You have enough trouble with English."

As soon as they got back to their motel room, Hillary turned on her laptop and immersed herself in something on screen. Jackson paced, mulling their conversations with Darren "Dime" Tenpenny, Bobby from Campbell's, and now Dr. Laplante. Words and phrases kept coming back to him, each roiling in his stomach.

"They come and get me." . . . *"They tap into my brain"* . . . *"I'm one of them."* . . . *"About the . . . experiments?"* . . . *"That wasn't the military running things."* . . . *"genetic experiments"* . . . *"Them."* . . . *"mind control"* . . . *"breeding"* . . . *"genetically altered babies"* . . . *"Desert Root"* . . . *"It didn't go too well."* . . . *"They had . . . problems."* . . . *"She was one of them. One of the surrogate mothers."*

One guy with a crazy theory about mind-control research and experimentation was one thing. But when three of them told a similar story, it gained credibility. Dime was clearly off his meds and Laplante, while appearing lucid, was allegedly schizophrenic and delusional. But Bobby had seemed to have all his faculties. The more he thought about it, the more Jackson was inclined to believe they were telling the truth, or at least, a facsimile thereof.

He stopped pacing. "Hillary."

"Mmm."

"What if Dime's right about being taken to the base?"

She didn't say anything. Jackson paced the other way. "Arielle said she saw bodies being loaded into a black van."

Again, no response.

Jackson kept walking. Suddenly snatches of conversations and ideas and conclusions were hitting him like a starburst. "Mouse said the common link between the people in Holloway's folders were trips to Vegas that they didn't have pictures of. What if . . . they were born in Kingman?" he said, pacing faster. "No, they weren't born in Kingman, they were actually born on the base, as part of this Desert Root deal, part of Silver Dawn. The base shuts down, these people are released into society, and then . . ." He stopped. "But some of them stay in Kingman . . . the ones that are less stable, maybe? But the ones living elsewhere were instable too." He resumed pacing, thinking, willing himself to tie it all together.

Hillary returned her sole attention to the computer screen.

"What if Silver Dawn and Desert Root were restarted, twenty years after the base was closed?" Jackson asked. "They call it Golden Dawn and study the effects of whatever they were doing to people a quarter century later. Dime and a bunch of the others still live in Kingman, quarantined almost, so they can't wreak havoc on the entire world. That explains the huge police presence and why Quinn doesn't want us digging around and causing trouble. We'll cause volatility.

"Then, on the other hand, you've got the people released into the general public, living normal lives, except half of them are suicidal. The ones that aren't come to Vegas, and maybe, just maybe, are the people Arielle was drugging and passing on to her mysterious guy—who may have been Isaac Cutler—who took them somewhere in a van, like to Blane Air Force Base, where they could study them, jab them with needles, run all sorts of tests, and then dump them back in the care of Arielle or some other moonlighting hooker who would make them think they'd just had a really bad weekend and a movie-worthy hangover."

He finally stopped pacing and looked at Hillary. "I know it sounds absurd, too ridiculous even to mention, but what do you think?"

"Actually, it doesn't," Hillary said, setting aside her laptop and standing.

"What are you looking at, anyhow?"

"Just reviewing, making sure I have my facts straight."

"What specifically?"

It was Hillary's turn to pace, to the door. She turned around, her hands clasped in front of her. "I told you the other day that my parents never talk about the time when I was born, about where we lived or what was going on. I always thought it had to do with Dad being in the military. But there's also a part of me that's known something was off."

"Off how?"

"With Heather and Holly and me."

He waited for her to continue.

"I've seen their baby books. I've seen pictures from the delivery room, even of me holding Holly. There are no pictures of me in the hospital, no mementos in my baby book. And as much as we have in common, I've noticed subtle differences. I've always been more driven, more intense. They're much more laidback and carefree. I'm analytical, whereas they're more artistic. They both have brown eyes, like Mom. I've got Dad's blue eyes."

"Hill, what are you saying?"

"Think about it, Jackson," she said, her voice just above breaking. "Everything we know about Blane and Kingman and Silver Dawn and now Desert Root. About Arielle and what she discovered and was involved in. About the CIA and their association with what's going on. About Dad's close relationship with Yvonne. About her being one of the surrogate mothers. About Dad knowing Arielle, staying in touch with her, helping her out. And the timeline fits."

"The timeline?"

"Yvonne was on the base in the fall of 1983, pregnant by the time she left the base in October. I was born March 29, 1984."

Jackson could hardly speak. "You're . . . You're saying . . ."

"I think Yvonne Coleman is my surrogate mother, Jackson. I think I'm a Desert Root baby."

Chapter Forty-Seven

"NO," JACKSON SAID, shaking his head. "No, that can't be."

"It all makes sense. And remember, Darla said Yvonne gave up her first daughter for adoption. To my parents."

"You don't know that."

"Weren't you just listening?"

"What about your birth certificate? Haven't you seen that?"

"You don't think that could be faked, by these people?"

"And we just heard of Desert Root a few minutes ago, from a guy who thinks he's BYU.

She huffed. "His name wasn't BYU."

"That's beside the point. Dime could be making up nonsense."

"He vocalized it and named it, but Desert Root has been intimated at from the beginning. And his legitimacy, or lack thereof, doesn't change the anomalies with my family."

"Come on, Hillary. If some lame lawyer brought that circumstantial pile of evidence into your courtroom, you'd have him disbarred."

Her look said, "Nice try."

"I mean, you're relying on the testimony of a deadhead and a schizophrenic."

"Five minutes ago you were touting them. Besides, everything we've discovered over the last week points to this conclusion, as you so haphazardly just pointed out. Plus, none of the connections we've found to Dad suggested he was still involved in anything illegal or illicit."

"See?"

"And yet he had all the current ties to Arielle."

"That doesn't prove she's your half-sister."

"I hadn't thought of it yet in those terms, thanks."

"Come on, Hill."

"Hillary!"

"Hillary, calm down."

"Calm down? I've just figured out that I'm a scientifically engineered military test baby, and you want me to calm down?"

"I want you to calm down because you haven't figured that out. It's a theory. You're in shell shock, which is probably a new experience for you, but when you step back and think, you'll realize it's probably not even true. I mean, look at all the examples we have. Desert Root babies had their brains fried. They're genetic freaks."

"Is this supposed to be a pep talk?"

"Yes, because you're not a psychopath, Hillary."

"You've always seemed to think so."

"I never thought that."

Hillary shook her head. Then she put her fingers to her lip.

Before he knew what he was doing, Jackson stepped forward and wrapped his arms around her.

She pulled away. "I need to get out," she said. "Clear my head."

"Okay, let's take a walk."

"Alone," she said, walking over to the duffel bag. She yanked a couple of items out of it and stalked to the bathroom. Jackson sat on the bed, trying to disprove Hillary's assumptions. But the more he thought about them, the more he had to conclude she was right.

She emerged wearing the same pink tank top and black running shorts she'd started the morning in, eons ago. She fastened her hair into a tight ponytail, then sat on the other bed to pull on a pair of new socks and lace up her shoes.

"I still can't believe the U.S. military was messing around with this stuff," Jackson said. "I mean, I know they're not impregnable, but this is pretty sinister. And staging a massive cover-up?"

"Bobby said it wasn't the military. We've seen CIA imprints all over the place, and who knows what private group might have gotten involved."

"Speculation, Your Honor."

"Cut the smart-aleck courtroom references."

"Hillary, even if all this Silver Dawn-Desert Root stuff is true, it's still a stretch to assume you're a product of it."

"No, it's really not. *You* step back and think, Jackson. You'll see I'm not being irrational or jumping to conclusions."

"Hillary . . ."

"Just give me some time to clear my head," she said as she stood.

"Are you sure you should be doing this?"

"I'm going for a run, Jack. I think the AMA is in favor."

"I mean now, in your condition."

"Is it bad for one's health to jog while angry?"

He sighed and tried a different tack. "It's still like a hundred degrees, and it's going to be dark in half an hour."

"No it won't. The sun might set, but I'll have another half hour before it actually gets dark, and I'll be back by then. Besides, I'm wearing a nice bright color and there aren't any cars out here anyhow."

"Just cougars and coyotes."

"They wouldn't dare cross me." She stood and pushed past him toward the door. Jackson followed her and leaned against the faded siding while she stretched. She extended her leg onto the windowsill and bent over it, fingers reaching for her toes. Even at this moment, with his brain overloaded, Jackson couldn't ignore her attractive figure, emphasized by her posture.

"Hill, are you sure you should be going alone?"

She straightened, now facing him. "If you call me Hill one more time I am going to knock your block off."

"Thank you, Lucy Van Pelt."

Hillary did not smile.

"I'm just saying, you're an attractive girl and this town is full of weirdos."

"I'm not running in town, just along the highway. And trust me, no weirdo—no cougar, coyote, or other dangerous mammal—wants a piece of me right now."

He gave up. "Okay."

Hillary finished another stretch, and her lips actually turned up at the corners. "But it's sweet of you to worry."

"I'm going to prove you're wrong," he said, bolstered by having had a female—even Hillary—call him sweet. "Something doesn't add up. We'll get to the bottom of it."

"I appreciate the effort, but we're at the bottom. In every possible way."

Without any other words, Hillary turned and took off across the parking lot, at first walking, soon jogging. Jackson watched until her pink, black, and blond form was just a blip on the horizon, which still shimmered in the early evening heat. Then he headed back inside and got to work.

For half an hour, he paced a hole in the carpet as he mentally reviewed everything: Arielle's death, her connections to Warren McKenzie, her side "job," and her research into what she had gotten involved in. Matt Brenner and Xavier Stark, then Robert Kyle. Senator Moore, Isaac Cutler, Laura Woodson, and all their ties to each other. Richard Holloway, General Reynolds, more connections and ties to Blane Air Force Base. Stories and rumors and stories of rumors about Silver Dawn, mind control, genetic experiments, Desert Root. Kingman with its quirky population. The "Alive" and "Dead" folders and the names of people inside them—people who had been born or lived in Kingman, then moved around the world, many enacting violence on themselves and others. Trips to Las Vegas by several of those same people, with their potential ties to Arielle and Brenner and Stark and Cutler and Woodson again, and similarities to Dime's frenzied tale. Then there were Hillary's personal assessments, memories, and intuition.

His mind contained a mental flow chart with innumerable lines and links, to the point that it all became a jumbled mess. Unfortunately, each time he sorted through the mess, distinct themes seemed to emerge, and they echoed Hillary's conclusion. And yet it was too incredible to be true.

Jackson looked at the clock. 6:33. Hillary had been gone for over half an hour. He walked to the window, and when he didn't spot her, opened the door and stepped outside. The sun was hanging just above the western mountains, its magnificent brightness still baking the desert floor with heat. Jackson turned and scanned the road to the south, but saw nothing.

Half an hour was a long time to jog in this heat, particularly given what Hillary had been through physically and mentally over the previous twenty-four hours. But anger could be a powerful motivator, he knew from personal experience.

He retreated to the coolness of the room and tried to figure out what to do. He wished he could have Mouse hack something or could explore some additional trove of information to find new evidence. But they had turned over every rock, and each clue led them farther down the same path.

Jackson stopped as he realized there was one person who could answer all their questions. But he was in Bangladesh building schools for orphans or running plumbing for field hospitals or some such charitable work. Besides, Hillary had been adamant about not going to her father for answers. Considering what it appeared he had kept from his daughter, Jackson could understand it.

The red numbers on the nightstand clock blipped from 6:44 to 6:45. With the first real pangs of fear gnawing at his gut, Jackson again stepped outside. The western sky was lit a magnificent shade of orange, and the mountains cut a stark, jagged outline against it. To the east, an amber hue was a backdrop for shadowy peaks whose ridges were still traced by a warm, golden glow. On any other night, Jackson would have admired the scenery. But this night, his eyes squinted against the oncoming darkness, pleading for a pink blip to appear on the ribbon of road. It didn't.

A waft of breeze tickled his skin, feeling cool even though it wasn't. He turned and looked north. Kingman was a ghost town, absent of any signs of life. No cars, no people, no glow of lights in buildings. It was as if with the onset of nightfall, darkness consumed the entire town.

Jackson faced south again, his eyes playing tricks with him. First he saw a wavering pink form, then it disappeared into the desert backdrop. The black of Hillary's shorts emerged, only to fade into the lengthening shadows. As he continued to stare, the mirages ceased. Night fell quickly.

Jackson ducked back into the room. The red numbers were vivid heralds.

7:04

Hillary had been gone an hour. No matter how mad she was, that was too long, especially since she had promised to be back by dark.

Jackson exited again, straining his eyes for one last hopeful look down the highway.

All he saw was a strip of concrete bisecting a barren, dusky wilderness.

Chapter Forty-Eight

7:07 p.m.

COUNTLESS SCENARIOS RAN through Jackson's head, none of them pleasant. He blamed himself for letting Hillary go, for ever coming to Kingman, for returning her voicemail in the first place. But none of that would do any good, nor would it make her appear on the horizon.

Returning to the room, he practically tore it apart looking for a pen or pencil and a notepad. When he found one in her laptop case, he scrawled a quick note telling her to wait for him if she returned. Then, with one more futile glance to the south, he jogged a block and a half north to the sheriff's station, sweating profusely by the time he arrived.

Quinn was at his desk, sipping coffee as Jackson burst into the building. He sat up with a frown. "You all look like you all just saw a ghost," he said.

"Hillary's missing."

The frown intensified. "Missing how?"

"She went out for a jog over an hour ago and never came back."

"Maybe she stopped off to get something to eat."

"She went south from the motel, Sheriff. Into the desert."

"Say over an hour ago?"

"Six o'clock, almost on the button."

"Odd time to go running."

"Yeah, well."

Quinn drained the dregs of his coffee and stood. "All right, let me get on the radio." He sidled briskly, if such a thing was possible, to the comm center at the front desk. He yanked an old CB head from its post and raised it to his chin. He squawked it twice, then said, "Mike, what's your all's 10-20?"

The garbled response mentioned something about patrol.

"Roger that. You all see a woman come running out your all's way? Left town about six o'clock?"

The static crackled. "Negative."

"You all wanna make the loop, check it out? Blond girl, tall, pretty, wearing pink—You all can't miss her."

"Copy, Sheriff."

Quinn dropped the radio. "Deputy Klein's stationed about four or five miles south of town. He'll check between 93 and town, including up the old mine road as far as he can. If she's out there, he'll spot her."

"If?"

"Look, Mr. Douglas, there any chance she maybe needed some space?"

"As in ran away?"

"As in maybe she didn't come back to the motel but came back to town and is elsewhere?"

"No, I don't think so. And where would she be? You've thrown us out of every establishment in town."

Quinn leveled his eyes at Jackson.

"Sorry."

"I understand. Look, I'll make some inquiries around town. Klein's making the loop, and Vickers and Clayton are on duty tonight too. I'll put the word out, and if anybody's seen anything, I'll let you all know, pronto."

Jackson nodded.

"You all had dinner?"

"No, why?"

"Why don't you all head over to the diner and get something to eat?"

"I'm not really hungry right now, Sheriff."

"I can appreciate that. But the best thing you all can do right now is take your all's mind off things. Kingman's a small town out in the middle of nowhere. Only so many places she can be."

Jackson sighed with defeat, and he and Quinn both headed for the door. Quinn slapped him on the back before getting into his cruiser. "I'm sure there's an innocent explanation for it."

His head and heart pounding, Jackson started walking north. His stomach was doing flip-flops, all because of something Quinn had said. But what? Jackson replayed the sheriff's last words. *"I'm sure there's an innocent explanation for it."* It wasn't the sentiment, but the way he had said it, casually and matter-of-factly, as if Quinn knew something Jackson didn't.

He walked rapidly to the diner, wondering why that statement had set him off. Or had it been something else Quinn had said? He also prayed, asking for God's protection for Hillary and wisdom for himself. He tried to reassure himself that Quinn was right and there had to be a reasonable explanation for her failure to return, that the irrational ideas in his head were just that. But all evidence was seemingly to the contrary, and the more he thought about it, the more Quinn's statement nagged at him. Like the tinkling of faraway alarm bells.

Jackson barely took notice of half a dozen patrons scattered around the diner, only observing them long enough to determine none of them were Hillary. He took a seat at the counter and stared straight ahead as Fran approached.

"Welcome back, hon. Where's your lady friend?"

"She's . . . missing," Jackson said.

"How's that?"

He looked into Fran's big blue eyes. The face was stern as ever, but the eyes had a touch of compassion.

"She went jogging this evening and never came back."

"Have you been to the sheriff?"

"He's out looking for her now."

"Well why aren't you with him?"

"He said it was best if I came here."

Fran made a tsking sound and checked on an order. The next thing Jackson knew, she had let out a shrill whistle that got the attention of everybody in the place. And half the county. "You all listen up here," Fran said. "This fella's looking for his girlfriend. She went jogging this evening and never came back. Tall, pretty girl, with long blond hair."

Jackson looked over his shoulder hopefully, but none of the patrons so much as stirred.

"Sheriff Quinn's looking for her, so if you see her, let him know."

"Thank you," Jackson said feebly.

"What can I get you?"

"I'm not hungry."

"You need to eat."

"I'll eat when Hillary eats."

Fran turned around and shouted into the kitchen, "Club sandwich, fries." A moment later, she set a glass of iced tea—with lemon—on the counter in front of Jackson. "On the house."

"Thank you," he said. He took a long, refreshing gulp, then chastised himself for enjoying it while Hillary was most likely stranded in the desert or half-eaten by a coyote or . . .

"Your girlfriend missing, huh?"

Jackson turned to see an old-timer taking the seat next to him. Bald head under a wrinkled cap, worn T-shirt, jeans with holes in both knees. His boots were military issue, from the Roosevelt Administration. Jackson didn't bother to correct him on the girlfriend deal. He just nodded.

The man removed his cap and scratched his scalp. "Well, ain't the first time in Kingman, I reckon. We've had a share of folks what disappeared. No outsiders though, I don't recall."

"Henry, I don't think you're helping the boy," another voice chimed in. Jackson glanced over his shoulder. Tall, thirties, dressed better than anyone he'd seen in town yet.

"I'm just saying," Henry replied. " 'Tain't the first time."

Jackson was spared any further word when the door opened and a sheriff's deputy walked in. He was tall and gangly, and he walked like a marionette. He did not seek out Jackson with wonderful news, but instead leaned on the counter.

"Hello, Fran."

"Deputy Clayton." She set a plate in front of a young woman at the end of the counter.

"I'm looking for a missing girl," Clayton said, turning to face the room. "Maybe she stopped in? Six feet tall, blond hair, pink tank top, black running shorts."

Nausea washed over Jackson like a desert sandstorm. It was accompanied by a rock in his gut, an inexorable feeling that something was terribly wrong. It was the same feeling he'd had leaving the sheriff's station, only magnified.

"Last seen this afternoon about six, headed south out of town on foot."

The old guy muttered something about it not being the first time, but the noise in Jackson's head was so loud he could hear nothing else. The room blurred as the tinkling alarm bells turned into full-throated claxons. He pushed his plate forward and slipped past Clayton toward the restroom. He locked himself inside and promptly emptied the contents of his stomach into the toilet.

His throat burning and lungs heaving, he sat back against the wall and tried to come up with an explanation for what he had heard. But there wasn't one. In front of him, Quinn had radioed Deputy Klein and given him a description of Hillary, including the color of her shirt. Deputy Clayton, presumably having been briefed by Quinn, had just specified that she'd been wearing a pink tank top and black running shorts.

But Jackson had never told Quinn anything about her apparel.

Chapter Forty-Nine

7:31 p.m.

STANDING ON WOBBLY knees, Jackson paced in the confines of the small bathroom.

Why would Quinn want Hillary? He had seemed antagonistic to Jackson and Hillary's presence in Kingman and to their questioning, but they had written it off as him not wanting the town's citizens to get riled up. Had his motivations been more sinister? Jackson suddenly remembered General Reynolds' words on the phone conversation Holloway had recorded. "*We have a competent man looking over things.*" Had he meant Quinn, keeping an eye on the Silver Dawn and Desert Root "rejects" at Kingman? Worse yet, was Dime right? Had they had taken Hillary to the base to conduct some sort of experiments on her?

Jackson hunched over and mostly dry heaved into the still open toilet. It felt as if his very innards were going to come out, but no amount of retching could ease the commotion in his brain.

There were other possible reasons Quinn could have taken her—to shut her up and keep her from digging further, which begged the question of why he hadn't also taken Jackson. To learn how much she knew—how dangerous she was. Or, simply because she was an attractive woman with no protection.

Whatever the case, priority number one was finding her. Jackson spat into the sink a few times, wiped his mouth with a paper towel, and returned to the diner. Clayton had gone and the patrons had returned to their business. Jackson asked for his sandwich to go, and while Fran wrapped it, he poured some more tea down his acid-scarred throat. He thanked her and jogged back to the motel, thinking, praying, hoping. He popped in at Bernie's on the off chance Hillary had stopped there to question Laplante again. He knew it was ridiculous, and the same female bartender confirmed Hillary hadn't returned.

He crossed over to the motel, his brain searching for any other explanation other than the one that had already formed. He came up with nothing. He'd left the door unlocked, and as he opened it, a small part of him hoped to find Hillary calmly lounged on one of the beds, watching TV or poring over files on her laptop. But the room was as empty as ever.

The nausea surged through him again, so he went to the bathroom and splashed some water on his face. His eyes were bloodshot, a day and night's worth of growth covering his jaw and chin. He fought off another bout of heaves and exited the bathroom.

At quarter to eight, there was no chance Hillary had just gone for a really long jog. Especially without Klein finding her, although his search could have been a ruse. Without wheels, and since it was dark, Jackson had no hope of going to look for her himself. Which meant the only thing he could do was go to the authorities.

Problem was, the authorities were in on her disappearance. Maybe not all the authorities. Maybe some of the deputies were just honest lawmen, but Jackson had no way of knowing who was with Quinn and who wasn't. And he didn't know what an honest lawman would be able to do with a corrupt sheriff calling the shots. That meant he needed to go up the food chain. But if a three-star Army general, a United States senator, and perhaps the CIA were involved, just whom could Jackson trust? For all he knew, the people running what General Reynolds had referred to as Golden Dawn had moles embedded with the state police or FBI.

An idea began to form in the back of Jackson's head. One he immediately disliked and that made him sick to his stomach all over again. Problem was, he didn't see a lot of other options. He had no idea if and from whence the cavalry might come, or if they'd take his word over Quinn's when they arrived.

He paced as he thought over the idea. He tried to talk himself out of it, he prayed, he pleaded for Hillary to come through the door. He ate a wedge of the club sandwich. The idea took a stronger hold, and his thoughts turned to how he could make it work and avoid getting in a world of trouble. He stopped, realizing the latter condition wasn't likely.

Jackson resumed pacing, now as a method of working up courage. It took a while, and before he did anything drastic, he called Mouse.

Pam answered. "Hello."

"Pam, I need to talk to Mouse."

"Who is this?"

"Jackson."

Pause. "He's busy."

"It's an emergency."

There was no response, and Jackson thought for a moment she had hung up. Then he heard distant, muffled sounds. He knew it was no use, but he shouted, "Pam!"

A minute passed. Then Mouse's sleepy voice sounded. "Yeah?"

"Mouse, I need your help."

"Yeah, what's up?"

There was no way Mouse was sleeping at this time of day, so Jackson assumed his lackadaisical tone was a result of divided attention. A moment later, virtual machine-gun fire proved it.

"I need everything you can get on Wyatt Quinn, the sheriff of Kingman."

" 'Kay."

"Mouse?"

"Yeah."

"I need it now."

"Like, *now* now?"

"Like, Hillary's been kidnapped."

"The hot chick?"

"Mouse, drop your controller and listen. I need you to find anything you can on Quinn, and I need it five minutes ago."

Mouse's voice was suddenly more attentive. "Q-U-I-N-N?"

"Yeah."

"Give me fifteen minutes."

"Make it ten," Jackson said and dropped the phone on its cradle. He stood and paced, counting down the minutes. He plumbed the recesses of his brain for any possible way that Quinn could have known Hillary's apparel without being involved in her disappearance. There was none.

Exactly ten minutes after hanging up the phone, Jackson called Mouse again. This time, he answered.

"Yeah?"

"What you got?"

"Give me a few more minutes."

"Start with what you have."

"I've amassed quite a bit. What are you looking for?"

"Just give it all to me."

Mouse sighed. "Wyatt Jacob Quinn, born July 1, 1976, in Amarillo, Texas, to Garth and Nicole Cutler Quinn."

"What did you say?"

"Nicole Cutler Quinn."

Jackson sat on the bed. That couldn't be a coincidence.

"Did you find anything on Nicole?"

"Wasn't looking."

"Can you? Particularly find out if she has a relative named Isaac Cutler."

"Okay," Mouse said dubiously. The sound of his fingers racing over the keyboard transmitted through the phone. The seconds seemed like hours as Jackson waited for any word from Mouse. Finally, it came.

"Looks like she has a nephew named Isaac Cutler."

"What do you know about him?"

"Seriously?"

"Mouse, come on."

"Okay, okay. Give me a minute." More fingers on keys, more silence otherwise. "I'm not finding much, dude."

"Date of birth, description, anything?"

"I've got a Maryland driver's license that gives him black hair, brown eyes, six feet tall. Date of birth of February 21, 1975."

"That's him."

"Who?"

"Doesn't matter. Thanks, Mouse."

"That's it? What about Quinn?"

"I've got enough. Thanks, man."

"Sure th—"

Jackson hung up the phone. Quinn's knowledge of Hillary's outfit, on its own, was incriminatory. But factor in Quinn's cousin having the same name and description of a suspected CIA agent with believed ties to Arielle and Senator Moore, and it was beyond conclusive. Any faint doubts about what to do faded, replaced only with thoughts of how to go about it.

Chapter Fifty

REGGIE CAMERON DID not answer his phone, which wasn't a huge surprise. As the owner and part-time chef of Cameron's, a happening restaurant on the Santa Monica coastline, he kept pretty busy most nights. Jackson debated leaving him a message, telling him what was going on, in case things went south. But he couldn't bring himself to leave his best friend a voicemail like that. And besides, things were pretty far south already.

He hung up the phone, rubbing his forehead in an effort to remove physical and mental exhaustion. He failed. The carpet already worn to a frazzle, Jackson paced some more, looking for loopholes in his plan. There were too many to count, but he didn't have the luxury of forming a flawless strategy. So before he talked himself out of it, he got to work.

He started by packing up everything but Hillary's laptop. That he left open on the far bed from the door, making sure the screen was turned so it wasn't immediately visible upon entry. Next he unplugged the lamp from the wall and yanked the cord out of the base of the lamp. He tossed it in the corner, and did the same with the cord from the lamp on the other side of the bed. Two lamps, two cords. From the bathroom, he retrieved a hand towel and placed it next to the cords on the floor. He returned to the bathroom and lifted the lid off the toilet tank. He carried the heavy porcelain lid and set it in the corner.

He spent one more moment contemplating his actions. He was at the point of no return, but two images spurred him on. One was Hillary's face as she'd announced her conclusion that she had likely been inseminated as part of Desert Root. The other was the forever etched in his mind panorama of SR-323 at dusk, void of any signs of her return.

Jackson walked over to the phone and called the sheriff's station. Quinn answered.

"Sheriff, it's Jackson. I've been looking at some stuff on Hillary's computer, and I think I might have something. Can you stop by?"

"What exactly did you all find?"

"Easier to show than tell, but she'd apparently found some answers to her questions about the base and this Silver Dawn project."

"I'll be there in five."

"Thank you."

He hung up the phone and took his place by the window. The blinds were drawn, but he was able to peek through the slats and see the road into town. With all but one light off in the room, it was dark enough that he was confident he couldn't be seen, but he crouched low just in case.

While not a theological expert, Jackson was pretty sure the heart that was about to sin couldn't be in the right spirit to also ask for forgiveness. And yet, that's what he found himself doing as he waited for Quinn to arrive. He also watched the clock, counting down the minutes, and counting up from Hillary's disappearance. They were nearing three hours, and Jackson knew she wasn't coming back on her own.

The knock on the door startled him, and he hurried to the peephole. It was Quinn, and Jackson drew back the door, hiding his pile in the corner.

"Come on in, Sheriff," he said.

"There a reason you all's sitting in the dark?" Quinn asked as he entered the room and looked around.

"Headache. Laptop's over there," Jackson said, pointing at where the device was open on the far bed.

Quinn looked at him, then started forward. As he did, Jackson pushed the door shut. He lifted the tank lid from behind the door and raised it over his shoulder. Taking one step forward, he planted his foot and swung at Quinn's head. Unfortunately, Quinn turned at just that moment, saw the attack coming, and was able to duck to the side and avoid a direct hit. The lid clunked off the side of his cowboy hat, knocking it askew and toppling Quinn onto the near bed.

The momentum of the swing brought the lid all the way down to the floor with a second thunk. Jackson knew the blow had not been sufficient to knock Quinn out, and expected the sheriff would have enough wherewithal to reach for his gun. So without even looking over his shoulder, Jackson retightened his grip on the lid and swung again, this time in a roundhouse arc up toward Quinn's head. His aim was off and the lid smacked into Quinn's wrist with a sickening crack, likely breaking bone as it sent his freshly drawn gun flying toward the wall.

Quinn reeled with the blow for just a moment, then stood. Jackson, meanwhile, just kept spinning, using the momentum of his two previous swings to bring the lid around a third time. With a guttural growl, he raised his arc higher and connected with the charging sheriff's temple. He fell like a bag of bricks.

Immediately, Jackson bolted the door. He looked back at the unconscious sheriff, then picked up the cords and towel from the corner. As he did so, he peeked through the blinds at the sheriff's car. He did not see a passenger.

Turning back, he saw Quinn's motionless body quiver and stir. He quickly dropped to the floor and bound Quinn's hands behind his back with one of the lamp cords. Doing so involved moving Quin's broken wrist, and the big sheriff regained consciousness with a growl. Jackson attempted to tie the towel around him as a gag, but Quinn was feisty, and the action was similar to wrestling a bear. Finally, Jackson succeeded, and with Quinn's rage muted to a groan, Jackson bound his ankles with the other cord.

He stood back. Blood streamed down the side of Quinn's head from a gash above his left ear. His eyes flashed with hate. Jackson knew he didn't have much time, so he lifted the sheriff onto the bed. Then he walked around and picked up his gun. It was a Beretta 92FS, the same as Grant's old service weapon, holding ten rounds. Verifying the safety was on, he placed the gun on the dresser and turned to Quinn.

He removed a nightstick and a pair of handcuffs from their holsters, immediately clamping the latter around the sheriff's wrists. This brought a new wave of pain, expressed in a muffled roar. Jackson also went through his pockets and found the keys to the sheriff's Dodge Charger, on a ring with half a dozen others. He placed them beside the gun, which he picked up. He grabbed a pillow off the second bed and placed it over Quinn's knee. He then clicked off the safety of the Beretta and pressed the gun into the pillow with his right hand.

"I'm going to remove the gag from your mouth. Make any noise other than to answer me, and you'll be crippled. Do you understand?"

Quinn's eyes blazed.

Jackson used his left hand to slide the towel from Quinn's mouth.

"You all's a dead man," the sheriff said.

Jackson forced his voice to be even, emotionless, mechanical. "Where is Hillary?"

"How should I know?"

Jackson pushed his gun harder. "I know that you are involved. You knew the color of her shirt, which I never told you, the color of her shorts, which I never told you. And your cousin is Isaac Cutler, who's mixed up in all of this. You know more than you're telling me."

Quinn's face didn't change much, but his eyes narrowed slightly, his mouth tightening a fraction. It confirmed to Jackson that he'd hit the nail on the head and wiped away the final doubts about his course of action.

"I will ask you one more time. Where is Hillary?"

The sheriff's face changed again, to a look of defiance. Jackson pushed the gun harder, wondering if he could actually pull the trigger. His hand began to shake, and he backed away. Quinn sneered.

Jackson turned the big man over, then lightly tapped his broken wrist with the gun. "Where is Hillary?"

Quinn whimpered in response.

He tapped it harder, afraid that he might throw up again.

Quinn only cussed at him.

This time he raised the gun and cracked down on the wrist. Quinn howled in pain, and Jackson buried his head into the bed to silence him. Then he stood beside the bed and rolled him over again.

"We can do this all night, Sheriff. But you're just a peon in this thing. Tell me where she is and you can go back to playing lawman in this freak show of a town. But keep up this tough guy routine, and I'll drag you by the wrist into the bathroom and go Gitmo on you. Got it?"

Quinn said nothing, his eyes watering. The defiance seemed gone.

"Where is Hillary?"

"The . . . mine."

"The mine?"

"South of town, off the old road."

"Why is she at the mine?"

"I don't know. It's where they said to take her."

"They who?"

Quinn shook his head. "I don't know. I get orders, I don't even know who from."

"Cutler?"

Quinn blinked.

"Who's there with her?"

"Nobody."

"Nobody?"

"They left her there."

"Who?"

"The men who took her."

"Cutler's people?"

Quinn looked down.

"Did they hurt her?"

"No."

Jackson studied the sheriff for a moment. Then nodded. "Okay, take me there."

"What?"

"Take me there."

"You're going to have to free my hands."

"You won't need to point. Up."

Quinn struggled to his feet.

"I didn't shoot you because I didn't want to make more noise than I needed to. But if you try anything, I will put a bullet in your dome and make a run for it, *capisci?*"

Quinn nodded.

Carefully, keeping an eye on the sheriff, Jackson packed up Hillary's laptop, then placed both the laptop case and their duffel bag over his shoulder. He picked up the car keys and walked to the window. He saw nothing unusual outside, thankful that the only buildings in sight of his room were Bernie's Tavern and the far off shacks and trailers on 1st Street. He returned to Quinn, and with the gun pointing at his kneecap, untied the lamp cord from around his ankles. He slowly backed away.

"Okay, come to me."

Quinn obeyed.

"Walk nice and normal and get in the passenger seat. No noise."

Quinn nodded, and Jackson motioned for him to exit the room. He followed close on his heels, looking toward the lobby and up and down the length of the motel. With his luck, this would be the time some other occupant would decide they needed ice or it was time for an evening stroll—that is, if any other poor sap was actually staying at the Kingman Motel. But all was calm as he helped Quinn into the passenger seat and quickly circled the car and got behind the wheel.

Jackson backed out onto the street and started south. "Where are your deputies?"

"Vickers is at the desk. Klein and Clayton are on patrol. Seaver and McGregor are off."

"Where on patrol?"

"Clayton's around town. Klein north."

"Where are Seaver and McGregor?"

"I told you all. Off."

"I didn't ask if they were working. I asked where they were."

"I don't know. I assume at home."

Jackson let it pass at that.

"You all's going to fry," Quinn said.

"You're the one who's going down," Jackson said. "You and Cutler and anyone else I can tie to this."

"You all have no idea what you all's talking about."

Jackson ignored him. "Tell me about the mine."

"Tell you all what?"

"Give me the layout, tell me where she is."

Quinn described the mine, stating there were two main shafts that bored into the side of the mountain. From each, tunnels spread out deeper into the earth. He claimed not to know where Hillary was held, as he hadn't been the one to take her there.

Jackson followed the curve of State Road 323 until it bore due west. Then he turned back east on an old, gravel road. Rocks pinged the underside of the Charger as Jackson pushed along as fast as the road and the beam of his headlights would allow. After several miles, the road began to ascend, winding around a dull outcropping of rock and proceeding into a very small swale in the foothills of the mountains.

The car radio crackled. "Sheriff, you there?"

Jackson recognized the voice as that of Deputy Vickers.

"He in on it?"

Quinn shook his head.

"What's your distress signal?"

"We ain't got one."

"You tell him you're investigating a lead," Jackson said, reaching for the radio. "No funny business."

"The cars have GPS. He knows where I am."

"Fine. Tell him to stand down."

"Sheriff?" Vickers called again.

Jackson pressed the talk button. "I'm here, Vickers," Quinn said.

"I tried raising you on your walkie but you didn't answer."

"Dead battery. I'm following a lead on the girl. Douglas is with me."

"You need any assistance?"

"I'll radio you all if I do. In the meantime, stay put."

"Roger that, Sheriff."

Vickers clicked off and Jackson returned the radio to its hook. "Why'd you tell him I was with you?"

"SOP. You all wouldn't want him to get suspicious."

Up ahead, a building took shape. As they neared it, Jackson slowed. It was not so much a building as a pile of rocks with a few rotted boards protruding from the rubble. It was not alone. Several others, all smaller, existed on either side of a narrow drive. With a lot of imagination, one could envision an Old West mining outpost.

"Mine's straight ahead," Quinn said.

Jackson drove through the rubble on a road that grew less and less defined. After a hundred yards, Quinn nodded and Jackson stopped. "Where?" he asked.

"Lower shaft is about a hundred yards ahead," he said. Jackson's headlights illuminated rough and crumbled rock. If there was a path or roadway, it was indistinct. "Upper shaft enters from a few hundred yards to the right."

"Which one?"

"I told you all, I don't know."

"Guess."

"Lower shaft's easier to enter."

Jackson nodded and unbuckled Quinn's seatbelt. "Get out."

Quinn had to twist to open the door with hands cuffed behind his back. By the time he was out, Jackson stood beside him. He made Quinn get down on his knees while he went back to the trunk and sorted through gear. He found a flashlight, clicked it on, and instructed Quinn to stand.

"Now, lead the way."

In the dark and over rough terrain, the going was slow. Twice Jackson detected piles of timbers and rocks that indicated the presence, at one time, of a structure or a sign of some sort. And he could vaguely make out a trail leading up the side of the mountain. Then the terrain leveled and the beam of his flashlight glinted off parallel rails of an old mining track. It disappeared beneath closed wooden doors. They were dilapidated and rotten, with boards missing and corroded. But enough of the timbers remained to restrict entry to the mineshaft, especially since a large board the size of a railroad tie was latched over the top of them. It was bound with a metal chain and a padlock so that even if someone was strong enough to remove the board, they would still be barred from the shaft.

"Where's the key?" Jackson asked.

"Back at the station," Quinn said smugly.

"Okay, back to the car."

"You all're going to march me in to the sheriff's station in handcuffs?"

"Nope. Down."

The climb down was trickier than the climb up, and when they reached the car, Jackson again had Quinn drop to his knees.

"I'm getting sick of your all's ridiculous orders."

"I could shoot you if you'd rather."

With an evil glare, Quinn dropped to the ground. Jackson returned to the trunk and withdrew a Beretta 1301 Tactical shotgun. Then he marched Quinn back up to the entrance to the mine. He again had him drop to his knees.

Jackson approached the door. "Hillary!"

No response.

"Hill, if you can hear me, move away from the door."

He gave her thirty seconds and stepped back, then aimed the shotgun at the lock. He blew it away with the first shot, then used two more to splinter the board that served as a barricade. Throwing the remnants of the board to the side, he pulled back one of the rickety wooden doors. He chucked the shotgun to the side, withdrew the pistol from his jeans, and motioned at Quinn. "You lead."

"In the dark?"

"What are you, scared? I'll shine the light."

The tunnel was low, just over Jackson's head, and only eight to ten feet wide. The old wooden ties of the railroad tracks made tripping a hazard and slowed their progress, as did the faint glow of Jackson's flashlight. They walked for one hundred thirty paces before the air changed and the shaft widened. Jackson called a halt, realizing they had hit a T, with tunnels proceeding right and left. A few feet ahead, the tracks ended in a bumper post.

"Knees," Jackson said, and Quinn listened.

"Hillary!" Jackson shouted, listening until well after his echo had died out. "Hillary!" he shouted again. For another minute, he listened as his voice faded into nothingness.

"Get up."

Jackson marched Quinn down the left shaft, which was just wide enough for a human to pass through. The rock wall was roughly hewn and uneven, supported here and there by aged timbers that had likely lost all structural capacity. Ignoring claustrophobia and air that was growing danker and danker, Jackson counted steps. At fifty paces, a tunnel bored off to the right. It went only about twenty feet before petering out, and they returned to the previous shaft. Twenty-some paces farther, Quinn stopped.

"What?" Jackson asked. He peeked around the sheriff to where his light revealed empty blackness.

"Vertical shaft," Quinn said.

His gun to the sheriff's neck, Jackson stepped beside him and pointed the light all around, up and down. The shaft ended, and the only means of continuing would be down into the inky blackness.

"Hillary!" Jackson shouted as loud as he could. He couldn't tell when the echo he heard was only in his mind, but he concluded she wasn't down the shaft. There were no signs of any pulley or lift mechanism, or any footprints other than theirs in the dirt floor. So Jackson backed up and told Quinn to do likewise. He had the sheriff pass him so that he was leading the way, then directed him back down the shaft.

As they walked, Jackson mulled. Why would they have taken Hillary to the mine? To get her out of the way? To dispose of her? Had they set up a trap that Quinn was leading Jackson toward? Had a mine tunnel been extended from its gold rush days, running all the way through the mountain to the base?

Quinn tripped over the railroad tracks, sprawling so that his shoulder, then face fell into the dirt.

"Get up," Jackson said when he hesitated.

"I think I separated my shoulder," he growled.

Jackson started to reach for the back of his shirt but was stopped by a voice from down the main shaft.

"Take one step and I blow your head off!"

Jackson raised his head and looked up the barrel of a pistol at Deputy Vince Vickers.

Chapter Fifty-One

"DROP YOUR WEAPON!" Vickers instructed.

Jackson obeyed, letting the gun clank on the railroad ties.

"And the flashlight."

He followed suit, and its light extinguished when it hit the ground.

"Lie down on the ground."

He obeyed again.

"Place your palms flat on the ground."

Jackson did so, but turned his head toward the deputy. "He's involved in Hillary's disappearance."

"Shut up!" Vickers shouted. "Sheriff, you all right."

"I'm fine," Quinn said as he pushed to his knees. "Except he broke my wrist!"

Jackson strained his neck to watch as Vickers reached down and removed the cuffs from Quinn's wrists.

"What happened?" the deputy asked.

"He lured me to the motel, then bashed me over the head," Quinn said, standing up and dusting himself off.

"Why'd he do that, Sheriff?"

Quinn strode toward Jackson. "Because he wants to spend the rest of his life in prison." He jerked Jackson up with his good hand and drilled him in the stomach. "You all think you all can get away with assaulting a police officer and taking him hostage?" He backhanded Jackson across the cheek.

"Sheriff."

"Stay out of this, Vince."

"Accuse me of kidnapping your all's girlfriend." He straightened Jackson up and blasted him in the ribs.

"Sheriff, we should take him back to the station. Dale's waiting at the entrance."

"I'll take it from here, Vince. You all go on back."

Vince. Vickers. Quinn always addressed his deputies by their first name. Except on the radio on the way to the mine. Quinn had called him Vickers. A distress signal.

"What are you going to do, Sheriff?"

"Just teach him a lesson about respecting the law. I'll be in soon."

"Don't leave, Deputy," Jackson said.

Quinn's punch to the jaw sent him into the wall of the tunnel, and then to the ground.

"Ask him how he—"

Quinn's boot found its mark just under the ribs, and Jackson sucked in his breath in pain as he fell back on his side.

"How he knew she was wearing pink!" he shouted before Vickers turned down the exit tunnel and Quinn nailed him in the side with another kick.

"What are you talking about?" Vickers asked.

"Nothing, Vince. Get out of here!"

"I never told him what she was wearing, but he radioed Klein and told him she was wearing a pink shirt. Then Deputy Clayton showed up at the diner and announced she was wearing a pink shirt and black shorts." Jackson spat blood. "And I never told him either."

"Sheriff?"

"He's lying!" Quinn said, dragging Jackson to his feet. His stomach hurt so bad he could barely stand up.

Jackson could see that Vickers was at least wavering, and decided to push it. "Ask him about Silver Dawn and the cover-up they're running, and why he's trying to subvert our investigation. Or about his cousin with the CIA."

Jackson knew his last-ditch effort had worked when he saw the look in Vickers's eyes. And Quinn's reaction. He backhanded Jackson across the cheek again, and even though Jackson rolled with the blow, it stung.

"Sheriff, step away from him."

"Stay out of this, Vince."

"Sheriff." Vickers drew his gun.

Quinn let go of Jackson. "What are you all doing, Vince?"

"Step back."

"Are you all out of your all's mind? He assaulted me."

"Yet I'm the one getting the crap kicked out of him," Jackson said.

"Shut up," Vickers said. "Sheriff, we should take him back to the station. Sort things out there."

"You all believe him?"

"I don't know what to believe."

"Deputy Vickers, holster your all's weapon."

"Due respect, Sheriff, but no. If he's lying, we'll be able to verify that easily enough. But if what he says is true, th—"

Quinn lashed out with his good hand, knocking the gun from Vickers' grasp. Jackson summoned what strength he had and lunged at Quinn, colliding shoulder to shoulder and knocking him into the far wall of the tunnel. For his efforts, he received a chop to the chin that nearly knocked him unconscious. He managed to hang on and rolled to his feet.

Vickers' gun was on the ground, and the two lawmen went after it. They tussled in the dirt, kicking Vickers' dropped flashlight down the tunnel. In the semi-darkness, Jackson tried to land a few kicks to Quinn's head and stomach, but missed and was knocked off his feet as the two men wrestled for control of the gun.

Quinn's gun—which Jackson had been using—was still somewhere on the floor of the shaft, and Jackson felt around in the darkness for it. Just as he picked it up, a shot exploded through the tunnel. Vickers fell back, and Quinn jumped to his feet.

Jackson turned and fired, and the bullet tore through Quinn's right shoulder. He reeled backwards in pain, momentarily losing the grip on Vickers' gun. Jackson stepped forward and placed his foot on Quinn's gun hand as he found the pistol again.

"Move and you die," Jackson said.

He pressured with his foot until Quinn released the gun. Jackson then slid the gun backwards with his foot, and backed up himself. He quickly retrieved his flashlight and shined it at Deputy Vickers. His eyes were rolled back in his head, and blood bubbled from a wound in his chest. He'd been shot in the heart, and there was nothing Jackson—or anyone—could do.

"No!" Quinn yelled. "You all killed him!"

His rage was palpable, and Jackson trained the gun on him. "Get up."

Quinn instead knelt by Vickers. "Vince. Vince!"

"Get up, now," Jackson said. When Quinn ignored him, Jackson kicked the sheriff's shoulder. He screamed in pain and fell back, clutching at the wound with his hand.

"Get. Up!" Jackson yelled. "He's dead."

"I will kill you all!" Quinn spat.

Jackson lifted him up by his collar, not an easy task. Then he guided him toward the side of the shaft so that they walked beside the railroad tracks, pushing toward the entrance. Jackson shoved Quinn's gun into the back of his shoulder. "You don't do what I say, I blow it off. Got it?"

Quinn said nothing, and Jackson tapped the back of his head with the gun. "Got it?"

"Got it."

"Walk slowly."

He did, and Jackson kept close on his tail, shining the flashlight in his left hand over Quinn's left shoulder. When another light appeared ahead in the tunnel, Jackson whispered for Quinn to stop. He moved the gun so that it pointed at Quinn's temple. Then he repeated the command, much louder, so that Clayton could hear it too.

"Sheriff?" his voice echoed back.

"This is Jackson Douglas. I have a gun at Sheriff Quinn's head. If you do not drop your weapon, I will shoot him."

Clayton hesitated, and Jackson peeked an eye around Quinn's head, being careful not to give Clayton any opening, even if he was an expert marksman.

"Tell him," Jackson said.

Quinn swore.

"Tell him," Jackson repeated, pushing the gun into Quinn's ear.

"Aagh."

"Sheriff?" Clayton asked.

"I'm not asking again," Jackson said. "Drop your weapon."

"Do it, Dale."

A moment later, the gun clattered on the floor.

"Hands on your head, fingers interlaced, walk slowly toward me," Jackson said.

"What about the flashlight?"

"Extinguish it," Jackson said, relying on his light to track Clayton as he came within thirty feet, then twenty. At ten, Jackson told him to stop. "Very slowly, get to your knees, keeping your hands above your head."

Clayton obeyed. Jackson then pushed Quinn to his knees.

"Where's Vince?" Clayton asked as Jackson came around behind him.

"He shot him," Quinn growled.

"No, he shot Vickers and I shot him," Jackson said. "Ballistics will prove that Deputy Vickers was shot with his own gun. They will also prove that the bullet in Quinn's shoulder came from Quinn's gun, which I'm currently holding." He paused to remove a pair of handcuffs from Clayton's waist. He bound the deputy's hands behind his back, then retrieved a second pair and bound the sheriff's hands in similar fashion. He proceeded to frisk Clayton, removing a secondary firearm, a knife, a nightstick, his radio, and two sets of keys.

"Where's Deputy Klein?" he asked when he had lifted everything from the two men.

"Vince ordered him back to the station after the sheriff used the distress signal."

Jackson picked up the radio and walked over to Quinn. "You're going to tell him to come up here. You'll call him Mike. Tell him you need digging equipment. If he asks if you need anyone besides him, say no, you've got it covered, you just need digging equipment. If he presses for why, tell him he'll have to see it to believe it and that's it. You got that?"

Quinn just stared at him.

"You try anything fishy, or anything I even think is fishy, I'm putting a slug in your deputy. Got it?"

"You all's—"

"Dead, gonna burn, toast, I know. Make the call."

He held the radio to Quinn's mouth, and the sheriff made the call according to plan. Jackson calculated he had ten, maybe fifteen minutes before Deputy Klein arrived.

"What are you going to do?" Clayton asked.

"Deputy, I know this looks bad, but I am not the bad guy in all of this."

"And yet you've shot one lawman and handcuffed two others."

"Technically, I shot one of the two I handcuffed. I don't have time to explain more."

Quinn had a spare set of handcuffs, and Jackson looped them under an exposed section of rail between two railroad ties. He then positioned Quinn and Clayton so that one end of the handcuffs clasped around Quinn's cuffs and one clasped around Clayton's, thus binding them to each other and to the rail. Then he hurried out of the tunnel.

The vehicle Vickers and Clayton had come in was parked directly behind Quinn's cruiser. Its lights were still flashing, their alternating red and blue pulsing across the foothills. The headlights were pointed directly at the mine entrance, clearly illuminating Jackson's path down to where the vehicles were parked. Before hiking down, he surveyed the terrain, surmising where Deputy Klein would park and exit the vehicle, the path he would take to the mine entrance, and anything that might catch his suspicion. He also determined his best ambush location, selecting shelter behind a large outcropping of rock forty or fifty feet from the rear cruiser. It would enable him to see approaching headlights on the gravel road while concealing him from view once Klein arrived.

After taking his position and checking his weapon, Jackson forced himself to breathe deeply. It was all real. He had attacked a county sheriff, assaulted him, threatened torture, and paraded him up to and through the mine like a prisoner of war. He could taste the dried blood on his lip and feel the pain in his head and ribs from Quinn's kicks and punches. The lack of light did nothing to dim the image of Vickers' dying expression, or the memory of shooting Quinn. He was in more trouble than he could imagine, and now he was about to lower the boom on another unsuspecting lawman. He hoped his ambush would sufficiently catch Klein off guard so as to avoid any exchange of gunfire, but what if it didn't? Jackson couldn't bear the thought of shooting a legitimate law enforcement officer, but he also couldn't afford not to take him captive if Klein was complicit. Should the deputy be able to free Quinn and Clayton or contact outside help, Jackson wouldn't have the necessary freedom to rescue Hillary. Besides, he needed Quinn to locate her.

Headlights swept across the distant desert floor, and Jackson realized the time was short. He reminded himself why he was doing this—to save Hillary—and that he had already come this far. Once you broke the antique lamp, you might as well keep playing catch in the living room against Mother's wishes.

The lights disappeared as the car climbed the foothills, then reappeared much closer. Jackson crouched behind the rock, waiting. He saw the lights come to rest on the side of the mountain, just beside the glow from Vickers' car. He heard the engine die, heard a door open and close.

"Sheriff, Deputy Klein, do you copy?"

Klein's voice traveled through the small valley, as did the hiss of static in reply.

"Sheriff, do you copy?" Klein asked again.

Jackson tensed, waiting, straining to hear movement from Klein. He heard the scuffle of boots on gravel, then what sounded like a trunk lid opening. He chanced a peek and saw the thin deputy reaching into the trunk of his car. He came out carrying several shovels and a pickaxe, all hefted over his left shoulder. His right arm was free to reach for his holster, but he had yet to draw.

Jackson waited agonizing seconds as Klein started up the side of the mountain. When the deputy was even with him, Jackson stood and leveled his gun. "Don't move, Deputy."

He froze, mid-stride.

"I have a gun on you. I will shoot. I won't miss."

"Who is it?"

"Jackson Douglas. I don't want to hurt you, but I will do what I have to."

"What's going on? Where's the sheriff?"

"Inside. Very slowly, raise your right hand over your head. . . . Good. Now, lower the shovels with your left." He waited again as Klein obeyed. Jackson then instructed him to turn around, so that he was facing away from Jackson. He had him use the thumb and forefinger of his left hand to remove his gun and drop it on the ground.

"Now, remove your handcuffs and cuff yourself behind your back."

Klein obeyed.

When he was secured, Jackson approached. He frisked him to remove a secondary weapon, a second set of cuffs, a pocketknife, a cell phone, his radio, and his keys. Then he stood back.

"What's this about?"

"Sheriff Quinn told you that Hillary was wearing pink. I never told him that. The only way he could know was if he was involved in her disappearance."

"Why would the sheriff be involved?"

"Because he's working for or with a man named Isaac Cutler, his cousin, who has ties to the CIA. They're conducting top-secret experiments, a rebirth of an '80s-era project called Silver Dawn. And they have Hillary."

"That's absurd."

"Yet true. I took Quinn captive and he told me she was being held here. He used the location as a trap, giving Deputy Vickers a distress signal. Vickers showed up, and when I told my side of the story, he and Quinn got into a fight. Quinn shot him, then I shot Quinn. He and Clayton are handcuffed inside the mine."

"And Vince?"

"Dead."

Klein swore.

"I know you won't believe me, but this is Quinn's doing. I need to find Hillary and he knows where she is. He says you don't, but if you do, it's best you tell me now."

"Or what?"

Jackson didn't answer, in part because he didn't know and in part because he couldn't face the thought.

"Do you know where she is?"

"I have no idea. I can't believe Quinn had anything to do with it."

"He did."

"Because he knew what she was wearing?"

"Ask yourself how he knew."

"All I have is your word you didn't tell him."

"What would my motive be for making this up?"

"How should I know?"

"Just remember, I could have shot you in the back but I didn't." He nodded toward the mine entrance. "Go."

Klein obeyed and Jackson guided him into the mine. He sat him next to Quinn and Clayton and cuffed him to them. Then he stood back, shining his flashlight on Quinn. The bullet wound in his shoulder was through and through, and didn't appear life-threatening. Jackson pointed the gun at him.

"Where is Hillary?"

Quinn swore.

"Is she here in the mines?"

Nothing.

"Deputies, if you know anything about this, now is your one and only chance to tell me."

"What are you talking about?" Clayton asked.

"I don't know anything," Klein said.

Jackson turned back to Quinn. "Sheriff, I am going to ask you one final time. Where is Hillary?"

Quinn spat at him.

Jackson jammed the gun into his kneecap. "So help me, Sheriff, I will put every bullet in this gun into your body before I kill you. Tell me where she is!"

Quinn swore again. He was echoed by Clayton.

"Where is she!"

Quinn spat.

Jackson whipped him with the pistol. "Where is she!"

Quinn broke off his howl of pain to stare defiantly at Jackson.

He split his lip with the barrel of the pistol. "Where!"

Quinn said nothing.

Jackson smashed the gun against his head again. "Where!"

Quinn shouted another curse.

Jackson jammed the gun into his shin and was a half-second from pulling the trigger when Clayton hollered for him to stop. Jackson stared angrily at Quinn until Clayton repeated the command.

"She's not here," Clayton added.

Jackson stood and turned his attention to the deputy. "Where is she?"

"I don't know, but she isn't here."

"How do you know?"

"Because I saw her get into a van headed north."

"What?"

"Shut up, Dale," Quinn said.

Jackson pointed the gun at Clayton. "What do you know?"

"I was the one who grabbed her."

"On whose orders?"

"Shut up, Dale!"

Clayton looked down. "Sheriff Quinn's."

"Where is she now?"

"I don't know."

"You want me to rattle your skull too?"

"We loaded her into the van."

"Dale!"

Jackson swiveled the gun to Quinn. "Shut. Up." Back to Clayton. "What van?"

"Black, unmarked, no windows."

"Dale, so help—"

"Sheriff, the next words you say will be your last," Jackson snarled. "Go on, Deputy."

"I was patrolling south of town when I spotted her jogging, not five minutes after the sheriff radioed and said we were supposed to pick her up if we got the chance. He didn't say why, and I didn't ask. I stopped her and asked her to get into the back of the vehicle. She complied. I radioed the sheriff and he arrived a few minutes later. About fifteen minutes after that, a black van shows up from the north. We loaded her into the back of the van and it returned north. And that's all I know."

"When you came to the diner, you were just putting on a show?"

"Sheriff's orders."

Jackson nodded. "How many men in the van?"

"At least two."

"Describe them."

"I didn't see the driver. The other guy was tall, muscular, wearing fatigues. I only saw him a few seconds."

"You have no idea where they were going?"

"No."

Jackson pushed the gun just under Clayton's jaw. "Did you hurt Hillary?"

"No."

He pulled back and paced for a moment. When he returned, he asked several more questions, probing to see if Clayton knew anything else. It appeared not, that he was just taking orders from Quinn. Jackson circled to look at Klein, and the deputy's expression conveyed shock and confusion. So he returned to Quinn.

"Okay. Where is she?"

"I don't know."

"Playing this game again."

Quinn breathed heavily. "They'd told me to grab her if I got the chance. When Dale saw her, I called them and they said they'd bring a van."

"From the base?"

"I don't know."

"Where else would they take her?"

"I. Don't. Know."

Twenty minutes would be pushing it to come from the base to south of Kingman. But if they were really moving, it was possible. And between scanning the horizon for her and pacing inside the room, Jackson could have easily missed Quinn's cruiser and the van going both ways. It had to be the base. Where else and why else? Still, he would have preferred a confirmation.

Jackson looked back to Quinn. "If there's anything you're not telling me . . ."

Quinn spat and swore at him again.

Jackson resisted the urge to shoot him out of spite. Barely.

"Deputy Klein, I'm sorry for the mistreatment. But I have no other choice."

"What are you going to do?"

"I'm going to get Hillary back."

Chapter Fifty-Two

10:03 p.m.

JACKSON'S BODY ATTEMPTED to vomit as he trekked back down to the trio of parked patrol cars, but he refused to let it, growling and spitting away the urge. He made a quick search of the three vehicles, determining that Quinn's Charger was the best. He shot the GPS devices in the other two and used the butt of Quinn's pistol to bash in his.

Next he sorted through the firearms available to him. Quinn and his deputies all used the same Beretta pistol, so the magazines were interchangeable. He took Quinn's gun and Deputy Klein's as well, along with several extra magazines from the back of one of the cruisers. He also picked up an ARX100 semiautomatic rifle and the 1301 Tactical shotgun, as well as several 30-round magazines, a box of shotgun shells, and a survival knife. And just because, a handful of stun grenades.

He found a set of night-vision goggles, a pair of binoculars, a first-aid and emergency survival kit, and a complex set of lock picks in the trunk and backseat of Vickers' vehicle. He also took the shovel and pickaxe Klein had brought with him, just in case. As he got behind the wheel of Quinn's cruiser, he felt more than ready for battle, until he remembered he would be taking on an untold army at the base.

And it had to be the base. Where else would they have taken her? It still didn't make sense. Why Hillary? Why now? And what were they going to do to her?

Half a mile from the mine, Jackson stopped. He got out and heaved all the extra weapons, sets of keys, and radio equipment—everything he hadn't selected for himself—as far as he could into the desert. If and when someone discovered Quinn and his deputies, Jackson wanted to slow the process of them coming after him as much as possible.

Then he drove back to town. His head was a fog, a jumble of thoughts and ideas, strategies and risks. He kicked himself for not interrogating Quinn further, for not extracting every piece of knowledge from him. At the same time, he was sickened by the short lengths to which he had already gone. Watching Bauer beat intel out of a terrorist was one thing. Pistol-whipping a sheriff and threatening to blast his kneecap was another. What scared Jackson most was his uncertainty as to if he would have really pulled the trigger again had Clayton not caved.

He forced the thoughts from his mind. He couldn't worry about legal ramifications, couldn't debate alternate courses of action, couldn't second-guess his decisions. He forced himself to think tactically, sans emotion. His only focus was on rescuing Hillary.

On high alert, Jackson sped into town, past the Kingman Motel and Bernie's. He felt as if every darkened window harbored eyes watching him intently, but reminded himself there was nothing out of the ordinary about seeing the sheriff's car driving through town.

There was something unusual about seeing another man get out of it, so when he parked at the station, he hurried inside. At twenty after ten, the lights were on in the sheriff's station, but it was empty. Unless Quinn had held back information, he had five deputies. One was dead and two were handcuffed to him in the mine. That left two others, Seaver and McGregor, both of whom were off duty. But Jackson had no idea when that would change.

Locking the front door, he positioned himself behind Quinn's desk and called Mouse. Fortunately, he answered instead of Pam.

"Mouse, I need your help," Jackson said before his friend could finish saying hello.

"What now?"

"I need to find a black van headed northbound on State Route 323 this evening."

"Where's State Route Whatever?"

"Three-two-three in southern Nevada, sixty or seventy miles north of Las Vegas."

"Okay, how am I supposed to find that?"

"I don't know, Mouse. I'm hoping you can hack a satellite."

"With real-time surveillance of the middle of nowhere?"

"I'm desperate. I also need detailed satellite photos of Blane Air Force Base."

"Wher—"

"Same general area. In fact, coordinates are thirty-seven degrees, six minutes, nine seconds north and minus one-fourteen degrees, thirty-eight minutes, and twenty-nine seconds west."

"Say those again?"

Jackson repeated them from memory.

"How detailed?"

"As detailed as you can get. Everything I've found online has been scrambled or pixilated. Else not detailed enough," he added, remembering the photos from Holloway's flash drive.

"What, you want me to hack NASA or the military or something?"

"Can you?"

"No, probably not. Not in one night, anyhow."

"Just get me whatever you can. I need to see that base."

"Why?"

"I think it's where they've taken Hillary. Which is why I need to find that van."

"Who's they?"

Jackson sighed. "You don't want to know."

"Okay, give me some time. Your cell dead?"

"No service out here. Call me at this number. You got it?"

"Yeah."

Jackson hung up the phone and ransacked Quinn's desk and those of his deputies, looking for some power bars or energy drinks, having left the rest of his club sandwich at the motel. He came up empty, but did find a coffee pot. It was better than nothing, so he measured out and brewed a pot of coffee, shaking his head at the absurdity of it. While it brewed, he scoured the office for any detailed maps of the base. But there were none.

With a cup of coffee in hand, he retreated to the records room that he and Hillary had searched earlier. He dug around for several minutes but found no maps of the base there either. He returned to the office and paced and thought while he waited for Mouse to call him back. The black van, the truck that had run them off the road, the decommissioned but guarded military base, repeated allusions to the CIA—it was questionable if even the original Silver Dawn and Desert Root had actually been U.S. military operations, and Jackson was growing more and more dubious about the current occupants of the base.

It didn't matter, he concluded. Whoever they were, they had kidnapped Hillary. Whether it was some shadowy group of former military personnel, a CIA operation, or the U.S. Air Force operating on direct order from the president, they had no right to kidnap a U.S. citizen and hold her against her will. And Jackson had a right—a duty, even—to defend her.

Eleven o'clock came and went, and Jackson thought about recalling Mouse. He decided to give him another quarter of an hour. He paced some more, hoping to alert his brain to anything he might have missed. He checked out the gun rack and the safe, using keys lifted from Quinn. In addition to more tactical rifles and stun grenades, Jackson found teargas and gas masks. The Delamar County Sheriff's Department was ready for World War III. The only question was, were they planning on starting it?

Jackson was about to close the door to the safe when he spotted a crevice along one side. Upon investigation, he concluded it was a false bottom, and he lifted a thin piece of metal flooring and set it beside the safe. In its place was a small cavity with several file folders and envelopes. They were labeled, and one ominously titled "Code Black" caught his attention. He removed it and undid the metal clasp. Inside were several clear sheet protectors with papers inside them. He dropped from a crouch to his knees as he withdrew them.

The first was a list of procedures, emergency steps to take in case of a Code Black. As he skimmed the list, Jackson first deduced it was an evacuation plan. The print appeared to have come from a typewriter, and the paper was yellowed and old. He guessed they were from the 1950s, back when schools conducted bomb drills and folks built shelters to survive a nuclear holocaust.

But as he read on, he realized the directions weren't to be executed in case of an attack. They *were* the attack instructions. Code Black wasn't an evacuation plan. It was an extermination plan.

Morbid fascination growing as fast as the chilling sensation on the back of his neck, Jackson read on. He couldn't believe it. Here was a sheriff's department with step-by-step directions to eliminate every living person in the town of Kingman.

Jackson raked his hand through his hair. Was this real—was he actually seeing what he was seeing? How had something like this taken place under any sort of guise of military involvement? And how could it still be going on, militarily or privately?

He again contemplated calling in some higher authority. But who? The sheriff was crooked. An Army general was corrupt. A U.S. senator was complicit. The CIA, with all its covert and clandestine actions, was, well, the CIA. For all he knew, Silver Dawn then and Golden Dawn now had congressional approval. Maybe even the president had signed off. His country had gone over to the dark side.

Stress and lack of sleep were getting to him. He needed to find Hillary, stash her somewhere safe, and sleep for a week. To do that, he needed help from Mouse. And as he sat down at Quinn's desk, the phone rang. He reached for the extension, then stopped with his hand on the receiver.

The LCD display showed the number of the incoming call, and it wasn't Mouse's number. In fact, the area code was 775, which covered all but far southeastern Nevada. The city code identified the call as coming from Kingman. Jackson removed his hand from the receiver and let the call ring three times before voicemail kicked in.

He rummaged through Quinn's desk for a phonebook. Not finding one, he went to the front desk.

The phone rang again, the front desk phone's display showing the same number.

He didn't like it. A persistent caller was likely to show up, especially in a small town where the sheriff's station was only a block or two away. Jackson opened another drawer and spotted a list of personal numbers. As the call went to voicemail again, Jackson scanned the list, somehow knowing the answer before he found it. The number belonged to the home phone of Deputy Jake Seaver.

Jackson retreated to the safe and quickly replaced the insidious instructions and the false bottom, closing and relocking the safe behind him. He placed the keys in Quinn's desk and retrieved the rifle he'd brought in with him. He took one last slug of coffee and hurried to the front door. He stopped before he got there when he heard the knob turn.

He had locked the door, so it didn't open, but he was sure the deputy would have his keys. Jackson bounded over the gate in the half wall and hit the floor running. He reached the hallway leading to the jail cells and the records room just as the front door swung open.

"Mike! Mike, you here?"

At the end of the hallway, a fire door opened to the outside, but was rigged so that an alarm would go off if it was opened.

"Dale, Vince, Sheriff?"

Jackson quickly debated his options. He could likely get the drop on Seaver, but he was getting sick of taking law enforcement officers captive, and he disliked the options even more if Seaver was armed or managed to get to cover. He could make a break for it, but as of yet, the deputy didn't know he was there. Which left him remaining in hiding, hoping Seaver would leave.

But that also produced a problem. Jackson surmised that Vickers had informed Klein that he had received a distress call before heading out to the mine with Clayton, and that Klein, before going there himself, had alerted one or both of the off-duty deputies, just in case things went haywire. Meaning if Seaver didn't find any answers at the station, he would likely head out to the mine, where he would find and rescue his fellow lawmen. And once rescued, Quinn would immediately notify his cronies that Jackson was coming for Hillary.

As much as he disliked the idea, Jackson had to neutralize Seaver. He tiptoed back to the end of the hall, Quinn's Beretta drawn. By his count, he'd fired three of ten bullets in the current magazine. Just thinking of that made him miss his Glock 19 with its fifteen-round capacity. But now was not the time. He peeked around the corner and saw Seaver reaching for the phone at one of the near desks. It was now or never.

"Don't move, Deputy," Jackson said, spinning around the corner and leveling the gun at Seaver.

Seaver was faced so that he could see Jackson out the corner of his eye, and thus had an ability to assess the situation. Maybe he liked the angles, maybe he saw reticence in Jackson's eyes, or maybe he was just that good. But instead of remaining solitary or raising his hands, Seaver dived for the ground. Immediately, he was behind the desk chair and Jackson's line of fire was restricted. He hesitated, and in that instant, Seaver scampered around behind the desk.

Jackson ducked back behind the corner, gritting his teeth. He hadn't been ready to fire and it had cost him. And now Seaver knew he was tentative.

He peeked around the corner again and saw Seaver eyeing a dash to the gate in the half wall. Jackson aimed and squeezed a round into the gate. Seaver ducked back behind the desk.

"Quinn is responsible for Hillary's disappearance," Jackson said.

Seaver snorted.

"It's the truth. Do you know about Silver Dawn?"

"Everybody knows about it. What's that got to do with anything?"

"They're still operating it. Call it Golden Dawn. They take people out to the base, run tests on them."

"You been talking to Dime?"

"Among others. Now Hillary's gone. Quinn and Clayton are both complicit."

"Where are they?"

"Indisposed."

"What's that supposed to mean?"

"Deputy, I don't have time for all this. I don't know if you're a dedicated civil servant or part of this cover-up, and I don't have time to sort it out. Hillary is missing, and every second she's gone is a second they could be doing something horrible to her. I don't want to shoot you, but I will do what I have to do. Surrender now, and I promise you won't ge—"

A barrage of gunfire interrupted him, and Jackson ducked back behind the corner. As chips of wood exploded, he again kicked himself for not considering that Seaver might have brought his own firearm. He also was mad that he hadn't noticed if he'd had a weapon. The stakes were too critical for him to be messing up.

"You surrender," Seaver called after the shooting stopped. Jackson had counted five or six shots. "Depending on what you've done, maybe this doesn't end with you behind bars for life."

"I do that, and Hillary's dead."

"You really believe all this?"

"I know it sounds crazy, but it's not. Quinn and Clayton as much as admitted it."

"I'll believe that when I talk to them."

"I can't allow that."

"Then you're going to have to shoot your way out of this."

Jackson dropped to the ground while Seaver was talking and peeked his head around the doorframe. He saw no target until it was almost too late, and withdrew his head just in time. Another salvo of bullets exploded into the wood and floor beside his head, and he slid farther down the hall.

He had six bullets in the pistol, and thirty in the ARX100. But he really didn't want to open up a semiautomatic weapon on a sheriff's deputy.

"Give up?" Seaver asked.

"Can't do that, Deputy."

Jackson heard a click, which at first he thought was Seaver emptying an exhausted magazine from his gun. Too late, he realized it was a different sort of click.

Then the hallway exploded.

Chapter Fifty-Three

THE CONCUSSION KNOCKED Jackson back, out of his crouch, sending him sprawling on the floor. He was vaguely aware that he had dropped the pistol, but the explosion had blinded him. His eyelids refused to open against the magnificent whiteness that burned through them. His eardrums felt as if they were going to burst, as if cymbals had gone off inside his skull. He rolled to his side, toward the wall, in a pitiful effort to get away from the din and the blinding light. It was useless.

Against the visual and auditory onslaught, his brain began to function. He wasn't on fire. His flesh hadn't been burned off. Seaver hadn't thrown an actual grenade but a stun grenade—a flashbang. Jackson fully appreciated the moniker as he groped for the pistol or the rifle. His hands found neither.

He knew Seaver would be coming, and he started to crawl. He didn't know where he was going, but he had to get away. He had to survive, even if it was to dash out the fire exit. Hillary's life depended on him, but even so, he couldn't get his body to respond. It was as if he was in sludge, the effects of the grenade reducing the neurons in his brain to half capacity.

A weight fell on his shoulders. At first he thought he'd misjudged the explosion, that perhaps it had been an actual grenade and the ceiling was caving in. But then he felt a hand on the back of his head, pushing it into the floor. The next moment his arms were jerked behind his back, and he felt the cold metal of handcuffs clap against his wrists.

He was lifted to his knees and dragged by the collar out of the hallway and into the office, where he was thrown to the ground. He tried to open his eyes, but they were hesitant to trust that a light as bright as the sun wasn't waiting to sear their retinas.

He rolled onto his stomach, using the dullness of the floor and the shadow of his head to provide his eyes a safe haven. His eyelids fought him, but he forced them open.

The shadow grew. Jackson tipped his neck back as far as he could in his condition and looked up at a squatting Seaver. He saw now how big the man was. Even crouched, his long legs were apparent. They were covered by jeans that hung over scuffed cowboy boots. Seaver wore a white T-shirt, neither tight nor baggy. It failed miserably in concealing a muscular frame. Several tattoos wound around his arms. It was just a hunch, but Jackson sensed this guy was ex-military, and he knew then he was in a world of trouble.

"Where you from?" The voice was calm and collected.

"Uh . . . Los Angeles."

Seaver traced his lower lip with his tongue as he nodded. "Let me tell you how things work here in Kingman. You're sixty miles from the nearest lawyer. Sixty miles from the nearest person who will even listen to your complaint, much less care. You're sixty miles from your nearest possible rescuer. Most folks in Las Vegas don't even know Kingman exists, let alone anybody in L.A."

"That's where you're wrong."

"Oh?"

"I didn't waltz into *The Hills Have Eyes 3* without calling in backup."

"Backup?"

"That's right."

"Another thing we know in Nevada is how to tell if someone's bluffing. And you, my friend, are holding junk." Seaver stood. "What I'm trying to say is, I can make you disappear. Your momma and daddy won't ever know you came to Kingman, much less what happened to you. Your friends, your lawyer, heck, the FBI comes traipsing in here, they'll just see a sleepy little town and an 'aw shucks' sheriff and deputy who don't recall ever seeing you pass by this way."

He continued to speak in an even, detached tone. "The townsfolk might remember you, might not. Either way, they'll never talk. As far as anyone in this town will be concerned, you never even existed."

Jackson didn't like where he was going, and had no doubts Seaver would follow through on the threat he made next.

"So here's the deal, Mr. Douglas. That's right, I know who you are. I'm going to ask you one time where Sheriff Quinn and Deputies Vickers, Clayton, and Klein are. You tell me, and I stand back and let the legal system take its course. How much trouble you're in depends on what you've done." He shook his head slightly. "Don't tell me, and you'll be looking up at the desert floor come sunrise."

Jackson's brain was working again, running at full speed. He thought about telling Seaver the truth. He thought about sending him on a wild goose chase. He thought about telling him they were all at the base. And he thought about pleading with him on Hillary's behalf. But he didn't see any way those scenarios played out favorably. At best, Seaver was the stereotypical, self-inflated, crooked small-town cop. At worst, he was complicit in Hillary's kidnapping and the Silver Dawn cover-up. It only left Jackson one option.

"Can I sit up?"

Seaver lifted him to his knees and stepped back.

"If I tell you where they are," Jackson said with a resigned tone, "and you let the legal system take its course, that means a trial. And in a trial, a lot of stuff is going to get dredged to the surface. A lot of stuff you and your buddies won't want to come to light." He sighed, sizing up Seaver and his small window of opportunity. "Besides," he said, "I don't fancy my chances against four capital murder charges."

His words had the desired effect. Seaver's face slackened in shock for just a second. In that instant, Jackson pushed up off his knees and charged. His hands still behind his back, he used the only weapon he had, his head, driving it straight into Seaver's crotch. It was a desperate plan, one with a low chance for success. But low chance beat no chance, which is what he had if he didn't act.

Seaver responded quickly, reaching for Jackson's midsection to throw him off. But Jackson had momentum on his side, and although it wasn't a fastball to the crotch, his head had caught Seaver in the right—or wrong—place. The deputy staggered backwards, then tripped as Jackson maneuvered his lower body so that it dragged over Seaver's boot. His hope had been that Seaver would fall backwards on the floor, hard enough to knock him unconscious or at least daze him. But Jackson's momentum had carried them so far that his head cracked against the half wall separating the office from the entry area, the thud of bone on drywall and wood almost as loud as the stun grenade.

Jackson immediately stood. Seaver was out cold. Maybe dead. He didn't know and didn't care. He hurriedly looked for handcuff keys, unable to reach those in his pocket. He patted down Seaver, afraid that the deputy would snap to at any moment. He didn't.

Not finding keys on Seaver, Jackson ransacked various desks, a difficult process considering his hands were behind his back. He finally found a set in a drawer in the desk next to Quinn's, and fumbled around to remove his cuffs. All the while he watched Seaver, who remained solitary. Bile rose in Jackson's throat as he feared he was responsible for the death of a second deputy.

Freed from the cuffs, he went over to Seaver and clamped them on his wrists. Then he felt for a pulse. It was there. Relieved but still unsure of the deputy's condition, Jackson relocked the front door.

The clock on the wall showed 11:31. Hillary had been missing for over five hours. She could be dead, cut open, raped, pumped full of drugs, or who knew what else by now. Jackson forced himself to take several deep breaths and think.

His and Seaver's gunfire and the flashbang had likely been heard by someone in town. Whether or not they would take action was questionable, but Jackson couldn't chance it. He especially couldn't risk Deputy McGregor coming down to investigate. He couldn't afford to get involved in another shootout/debate and couldn't risk getting captured a second time. His escape had been lucky, and he didn't want to press it. He also didn't want to have to shoot or injure another deputy.

Jackson stopped. He had to stop thinking of them as deputies. Whatever oath they had sworn to uphold the law had been trumped by their allegiance to Quinn and whoever was calling the Golden Dawn shots. Clayton and Seaver were involved or thoroughly crooked. Klein didn't seem to be. Jackson couldn't take the time to sort it all out. From now on, he had to assume anyone in Kingman who wore a badge was a threat. Hillary's life came first.

He dragged Seaver back into one of the cells and locked the door, making sure this wasn't like the Mayberry jail where the keys were in reach of a prisoner. He retrieved the pistol and the rifle and debated his next course of action. Mouse was long overdue in calling back, but Jackson wasn't sure he wanted to hang around the sheriff's station any longer. He didn't know where he could safely go in town, but settled on the motel. It was as good of a place as any.

He took Quinn's cruiser. Before leaving, he used the knife he'd taken from Quinn's trunk to slash both of the tires in the remaining car. Then he drove back to the motel, entered the room, and locked the door.

The cracked toilet tank lid was on the floor, dried, purplish-black blood smeared along the bottom. The comforter on the near bed was furrowed and wrinkled, and several drops of blood had stained its hideous pattern. The room was poorly lit, with two of the lamps having had their cords pulled out. All eerie reminders of the mess Jackson was in. But he had to keep going.

He called Mouse, noting that it was quarter to midnight.

"Yeah, sorry," Mouse said in answer. He sighed. "I can't find any commercial satellites with live feeds over your coordinates."

"What about non-commercial satellites?"

"Jack, I can hack almost anything, but the military is a different animal. I'm not sure I could even do that, but if I could, it would take all night, at least, and I'd probably be arrested before I got in."

Jackson bit down on his lower lip.

Mouse hesitantly gave him the rest of the news. "I also couldn't find any satellite images of the base. I looked everywhere, man, and I'm getting the same thing you are. Grainy, blurry images. It's the same if you look for Area 51, you can never zoom in far enough to see any detail."

"How close can you get?"

"Not very. I can see a runway and what looks like a bunch of buildings off to one side. That's as far as I can zoom."

Jackson growled under his breath to keep from cursing.

"I'm sorry, dude. I don't know what else to do."

"I know, Mouse, I know." He took several deep breaths. "Okay, what about hacking into radio transmissions."

"Whose?"

"Delamar County Sheriff's Department. Or their phone records. Is something like that even feasible?"

"Maybe, if they're recorded. This isn't the movies, man. Not everything everybody does is actually on camera or overheard by a cosmic listening device."

"I know."

"Look, there is one possibility."

"What?"

"It's remote, but there's a mountain range east of the base, and then there's another range east of that with peaks approaching seven thousand feet. And it looks like there's an old fire road leading up to one of them."

"A fire road?"

"There's some sort of tower up there. It's too grainy to tell, maybe a communications tower, maybe a ranger's station or a fire tower."

"I doubt that. We're talking the middle of nowhere."

"I know, but there are actually some trees out there, a lot of brush. Anyhow, it's something, and there's a road."

"So?"

"So, I've studied the topa—top . . ."

"Topography."

"Right. And that tower is on a peak, Mount Barber, and I think there's a direct line of sight to the base."

"Over the mountain range between them?"

"The peak's twice as high. I did the math, man, twice. If you got a telescope or binoculars or something, you should be able to see the base. At least get the layout and see if there's any activity."

"How far's this mountain range?"

"Twenty, twenty-five miles as the crow flies."

"I'm not a crow, Mouse."

"SR-323 curves just north of town and runs due east to the Utah border. The road leading south is maybe fifteen miles long, but it makes a lot of switchbacks going up the mountain."

Jackson sighed. It would take him at least half an hour, probably closer to forty-five minutes or an hour to get to the peak, just so he could survey the base, and only if Mouse's math calculations were accurate. While he was a computer genius, Jackson wasn't sure on his mathematical skills.

"Run the calculations again," Jackson said.

"I already ran—"

"Run them again. I'll call you in five."

"Whatever."

Jackson slammed the phone down, grabbed his sandwich, and left. He wasn't wild about going back to the sheriff's station and about possibly attracting more attention with his comings and goings. He wanted to leave Kingman behind him and never return. But he also wasn't wild about driving out into the mountains on Mouse's math computations. Even if he had a clear line of sight, he didn't know how much he could see with a pair of binoculars. He hated to make the trip, eating up more valuable time, for nothing. But he also hated to go in blind. He really hated having no good options.

If anyone saw him arrive and enter the sheriff's station, they gave no sign of it. Jackson locked the door behind him again and checked on Seaver. He was conscious and began hollering as soon as he heard the door open. Jackson walked back to the cells and aimed Quinn's pistol at him.

"Shut up."

"You're going to die, boy."

"You might first. Where is Hillary?"

Seaver swore at him, and it took all Jackson's willpower not to put a bullet in him. But he didn't have time. He closed the door to the hallway, muffling the deputy's shouts and retreated to the office. He called Mouse back, studying the magnification power of the binoculars he had absconded. Ten by thirty-five, which if he remembered right, meant ten times zoom and thirty-five millimeter lens. He did the quick math. If the distance was twenty miles, the zoom would make the image appear two miles away. That was still a ways off. Especially at night. Holloway's satellite images, grainy as they were, would likely give him a better overview of the base. But they weren't live. A view from the mountaintop—even a distant view—could reveal current activity at the base.

"I ran them again," Mouse said by way of answering the phone. "It will work."

Jackson logged on to the station's internet and pulled up a satellite map of the area. It took him a moment to overlay altitudes, and then he identified the "fire road" in question. He rummaged for a pencil and did some math while Mouse listened on the phone. If he still had a tenth-grade grasp of geometry, then his view from the top of Mount Barber should indeed give him line of sight over the lower mountain range to the base, with some wiggle room to account for curvature of the earth.

"Okay, Mouse, thanks."

"Anything else I can do?"

"Yeah. If you don't hear from me by eight a.m., call in the national guard."

"How do I do that?"

"I have no idea. And for all I know, they're in on this. Thanks, dude."

Jackson put the phone down. Inertia was fighting against him, both mentally and physically. He forced himself out of the chair and returned to the jail cells.

"You got any stronger binoculars than these?" he asked Seaver.

The deputy suggested where Jackson spend eternity.

He responded by removing Quinn's pistol from the back of his jeans and firing a round two feet to the side of Seaver's head. "Next one goes in your gut. You got any stronger binocs than these?"

"No."

"Sat phone?"

"No. You're going to die."

"So I keep being told." He approached the bars. "What about vests, SWAT gear, anything like that? I didn't see it before."

Seaver repeated his earlier directive.

Jackson compressed his lips and shot the deputy's boot.

He roared in pain, mixing in a few expletives.

"Vests? SWAT gear? Anything like that?"

"You are crazy!"

Jackson steadied the gun. "You want to limp on one leg or hobble on two heels?"

"Back room," Seaver said through gritted teeth.

"With all the records?"

"Tub in the corner. It's marked."

Jackson detoured to the bathroom, returning with a hand towel. He dropped it and the handcuff keys just inside the cell. "Make yourself a tourniquet."

Seaver swore some more, and Jackson ignored him. He quickly located the tub and removed a bulletproof Kevlar vest, emblazoned with DCSD in yellow letters on the front. He also found a hip holster and a silencer for Quinn's pistol, a padded shoulder scabbard for the ARX100 rifle, a knife holster, and a grenade belt to carry several grenades or flashbangs. Loaded for bear, he stopped once more in front of Seaver's cell.

Emptying the partially used magazine from the Beretta 92FS, Jackson replaced it with a fresh one. It was all for show. "If I'm the next person you see, it means Hillary's dead, and that means I'll be the last person you see."

"You're going to get yourself killed."

Jackson turned without a word. He exited the station and got into Quinn's cruiser, hoping and praying that Seaver's words wouldn't prove prophetic.

Chapter Fifty-Four

Friday, September 21
12:14 a.m.

ONCE FREE OF Kingman, Jackson floored the accelerator. Quinn's Dodge Charger hit triple digits on the straightaway of State Route 323. Jackson slowed to seventy-five to take the massive curve east, feeling the G-forces as momentum pushed his body to the left. Once the road straightened again, he mashed the gas pedal and the cruiser shot forward without as much as a gurgle.

He didn't use the sirens or flashing lights because he didn't want to attract any attention, and because there was no one else on the road anyway. He kept one eye on the odometer, knowing from the map he had pulled up on Quinn's computer that he had fourteen miles to go after passing the road to the base. He zipped past it with dread in his gut, knowing time was ticking on Hillary and knowing they could move her at any second. And knowing, if he was completely honest, that it was possible she wasn't at the base to begin with.

A pale crescent moon cast the desert floor in a placid light blue, the mountains in alternating indigo hues and black shadows. He felt a million miles away from anyone and had to choke back emotions over what he had done, what he was yet to do, and the danger Hillary was in. He continued to force his mind to the here and now, resolving to deal with the consequences later.

Fourteen miles east of Blane Road, a gravel turnoff led south. Jackson had to slow his speed considerably, especially when the road began to climb a gradually rising ridge. The ridge turned into a mountain, and Jackson slowed even more as the road grew steeper. Switchbacks enabled it to wind mostly along the top of the ridge, at times dipping into black ravines before cresting the ridge again. There were no guardrails and very little shoulder, and Jackson balanced his own safety with a need for speed. He continued to climb until he crested a small knob and entered a plateau some six or seven thousand feet above sea level and at least half that over the desert floor.

Up ahead a quarter of a mile, one final peak represented the highest summit in the range. It was a scraggly, weathered projection of rock, eerie in the glow of

Jackson's headlights. Beside it, surrounded by a chain-link fence, was a three-legged tower that disappeared into the night sky.

Jackson drove ahead and parked just short of the fence. He got out, using a flashlight to survey the area. The gravel road just ended. There was no turnaround, no defined parking area. But the ground was so hard, barren, and flat that none was needed. Jackson approached the fence, shining his light up at the tower. It was maybe a hundred feet tall, arrayed with satellite dishes and antennas. What was a communications tower doing out here, thirty miles from the nearest town?

As his light slid down, he spotted the answer. Attached to the gate in the chain-link fence was a white sign. "Property of United States Military. Keep Out."

Jackson looked at the double padlock on the gate, then at the barbed wire that ran the length of the fence. As if drawn by magnets, his eyes turned to the west, toward Blane Air Force Base. It started to make sense.

The next mountain range over was much lower than the one he stood atop, and was characterized by three distinct peaks, each a few miles apart. From his vantage point, a line just left of the middle peak looked slightly north of west toward Blane Air Force Base. In the dark, with the naked eye, Jackson could see nothing.

He retrieved the binoculars from the car and activated the night vision. Then, leaning on the roof of the car to steady himself, he peered through them. It took a few minutes to adjust the focus and zoom, line himself up, and zoom farther.

Four airplane hangars came into focus. He adjusted the binoculars to give him a clearer view and realized there were five, all with curved metal roofs, their giant stacker doors facing east, toward him. He squinted through the glasses, identifying shapes in front of the hangars as airplanes. Fighter jets, transports, a small commercial craft, and even an Apache helicopter. He couldn't believe it. Was the base still fully operational? Were planes coming and going? How big was this venture?

Or was this an airplane boneyard? Were these old derelicts that the Air Force hadn't bothered to dispose of? He'd seen photos of such places, storage facilities for retired planes. Sometimes they were used for parts or scrap and sometimes the cheapest option was simply to abandon the aircraft somewhere. From this distance, it was impossible to tell.

Even with the binoculars, Jackson was too far away to see if anyone was moving around. In the middle of the night, he sort of doubted it, save perhaps for a sentry. He saw no vehicular movement, even when he scanned as far north on Blane Road as he could before the middle peak obstructed his vision.

He refocused on the base. The hangars blocked most of his view of any other buildings. He identified the control tower, behind the leftmost and biggest hangar, and one or two buildings beyond and to the south of it. Otherwise, he was restricted to seeing between the hangars, where he made out several other structures but couldn't identify what they were or how many of them there were. The base was small, miniscule in comparison to Nellis Air Force Base, which he and Hillary had skirted the previous morning on their way to Kingman. But it was still plenty big, especially if it was even close to maximum occupancy.

Jackson turned away in disgust. He would still be going in blind. He still had no idea what to expect when he arrived. He still had no idea how many people were on the base, what activities were being conducted, or even if Hillary was there.

Peering through the binoculars one last time in case he had missed something, Jackson concluded he'd learned all he could from his junket to the top of the mountain. He quickly got back into the car, made a Y-turn, and started back down the mountain.

Going downhill, he had to be even more careful, and rode the brakes most of the way to the bottom. Once he hit level terrain, he stepped the pedal to the metal, knowing from his trip in that the road was smooth. He hit seventy on the gravel, having to fight to keep from sliding off the road. When he reached SR-323, he fishtailed onto the pavement and accelerated toward triple digits again. After approximately ten miles, he slowed to fifty miles per hour and cut the headlights. The guard station at the base was roughly five miles south of the highway, and he didn't want to risk having an overly alert guard see him turn onto Blane Road or see headlights on the highway suddenly disappear.

Driving the rest of the way by moonlight, Jackson arrived at the turnoff to the base as the dashboard clock blinked the time. It reminded him to turn down the light switch so that dash lights and dome light wouldn't give off any glow. That left only the brake lights as potential giveaways, and he solved that problem by coasting to a stop approximately one mile north of the guard stations and gate.

He parked to the side of the road and quietly exited the vehicle, making sure he had everything with him. Quinn's pistol—now fitted with a silencer—was strapped to a thigh holster, and he carried the ARX100, loaded with a thirty-round magazine, on his back. He also had the survival knife, a flashlight, a nightstick, and two stun grenades. What he didn't have was a plan. He'd worked his brain to exhaustion on the drive down the mountain, straining to come up with an attack strategy. But he didn't have one because he didn't have enough intel. He was going in blind, and he was going in hot.

Jackson stopped at the side of the road and took several deep breaths, trying to will the words to come. Somehow, they just didn't seem right.

"Lord . . . Forgive me for what I've done and might be about to do. Please, somehow, get Hillary out of this okay."

He looked up at a star-filled sky. None of them twinkled in response.

Lowering the night-vision goggles from the headset strapped around his head, Jackson set off through the desert, aiming for the fence some two hundred or three hundred yards east of the guard station. Everything was green through the goggles, which he used primarily to avoid nocturnal desert-dwellers. Otherwise, the moon would have given him enough light to see, which meant it also gave a guard enough light to see.

He stopped to catch his breath once, then continued. He didn't run because he didn't want to overexert himself, but he couldn't afford to waste time either. He'd lost enough of it already. When he reached the fence, he immediately dropped to the sand and trained his eyes on the guard stations. There was no movement.

He had considered trying to breach the perimeter fence and avoid the main gate altogether. But he didn't know if the fence was electrified and didn't relish the idea of leaving a guard behind him. He wanted to take out resistance as he went along. Besides, he would need the car to transport Hillary.

Jackson waited until his breathing had stilled, then rose to a crouch. He willed himself to the task ahead, knowing it could get bloody. He had taken lives before, all of them gangsters, in an effort to save Detective Larson's life on a case a few months back. He had no idea who he would encounter on the base. They might be members of the United States Armed Forces. They might be CIA agents. They might be mercenaries for hire. He wouldn't have time or opportunity to sort it out. And he couldn't let it matter. Whoever they were, they stood in the way of his rescuing Hillary. He would do everything he could to avoid using lethal force, but if it was required, he couldn't hesitate. If he did, it might not be just his life that was lost, but Hillary's also.

His mind resolved, Jackson took several deep breaths, then stealthily approached the guard stations. They were square buildings, no more than six feet per side, with windows that looked out in all directions. He studied the window that faced him, looking for any signs of movement. He detected none, despite pausing every few dozen paces to look and listen.

A hundred feet away, he stopped when he heard a noise. It was the distant howl of a coyote, eerie but irrelevant. He pushed on until he was crouched at the corner of the east guard station. Again he paused and listened, his own breathing sounding like thunder.

There had been two guards that afternoon, and he strained to remember which of the two buildings they had come from. Not that it mattered now. There could be zero guards or four, housed in one building playing cards or split between both of them. His courage wavering, Jackson forced himself to act.

Instead of using one of the flashbangs, the noise of which might carry to the rest of the base, Jackson picked up a rock the size of a golf ball from the base of the guard station. Leaning to his right, he side-armed it at the window in the door of the west guard station. He missed, and it clattered off the trim instead.

Immediately, Jackson ducked back out of sight, his pistol drawn. The door opened and a guard stepped out, clad in fatigues, a machine gun in his hands. He looked around but didn't come toward Jackson's hiding place on the other side of the guard station. After a moment, the guard retreated back inside.

Jackson waited a minute, picked up another rock, and heaved it at the far guard station. It again ricocheted off the door trim and fell to the pavement. This time the guard burst out of the door, both hands on his weapon. It was not in firing position, and Jackson observed that he didn't come to the east guard station. He deduced this was the sole guard on duty, and determined it was now or never.

While the guard had his head turned to scan the incoming road, Jackson emerged halfway from behind the guard station and leveled his pistol at the man.

"Drop your weapon."

He spun toward the sound, very much not dropping his weapon.

Uttering something between a guttural growl of frustrated resignation and a war whoop, Jackson squeezed the trigger.

His first bullet tore into the man's shoulder. The second sailed wide as the guard reacted to the first and spun. Jackson shot quickly again, hitting the guard in the arm, causing him to release his weapon. He was still standing and began to charge, and Jackson shot two more times, both bullets tearing into flesh but not hitting center mass.

The man continued to charge, himself growling in pain and rage. Jackson stepped out fully from behind the building, planted himself, and took aim. He had one shot before the man was upon him, and he had no choice.

His hands were shaking, and he again missed center mass. His bullet was high, penetrating just below the neck. Blood immediately bubbled to the surface.

The man dropped to his knees, then facedown into the sand, blood gushing from his wounds.

Jackson collapsed onto all fours, vomiting uncontrollably. When he finally stopped, his breath came in gasps. He wanted to lie down and cry. Instead, he pushed himself up with wobbly arms, picked his gun off the sand, and stood. Tipping back the goggles, he checked the man's pulse. It was thready at best, and there was nothing Jackson could do about the blood loss. He found the man's machine gun and tossed it into the desert, then swept his pistol toward the guard stations. It wasn't likely, but it was possible someone was still inside.

He checked both guardhouses and found them empty. They did contain small stocks of ammunition, as well as some energy and protein bars, and bottles of water and energy drinks in a refrigerator. Jackson forced down several protein bars and an energy drink, the food tearing at his freshly agitated esophagus. He feared he might puke again, but gulped down the food and drink anyhow.

While refueling, he searched for anything that would tell him when the next guard came on duty, if there were other sentries or patrols, and most importantly, where Hillary was. All he found was a map of the base that identified the various buildings. Five hangars, the control tower, several barracks, the administration building, a gym and rec center, the mess and base exchange, the infirmary, the armory, a building labeled "SP," and the garage.

Jackson quickly memorized the location of various buildings, then tucked the map into his back pocket. At the last second, he thought to open the gate. It took him a minute to locate the switch, and then the silence was broken by a somewhat rickety chain-link gate sliding open.

The guard was still lying face down in the sand, dead or close to it. Jackson took off jogging down the road back to Quinn's cruiser. As he went, he mentally reconstructed the map. If they were conducting experiments on Hillary, the infirmary was the most likely location to be holding her. Then again, Roy Donovan and Henrietta Ramirez had mentioned Hangar 5 as a housing place for civilians brought to the base. He tabbed it as a second option.

He reached the car in less than ten minutes and quickly accelerated. Still hesitant to use the brake lights, he coasted to a stop just short of the now-open gate. He got out and checked the pulse of the guard, finding him dead. His hands wanted to shake and quiver, but he willed them to be steady. It had taken six shots to fell the man, and that was unacceptable. He needed to be cold and ruthless going forward, because the alternative would be cold and dead.

Chapter Fifty-Five

ONE MILE SOUTH of the guard station, Jackson veered into the desert. He was driving with the night-vision goggles, a tricky task for a newbie, but one that enabled him to make out the terrain. The desert floor was flat and mostly void of scrub for the several hundred yards that separated the road from the westernmost of two parallel, two-mile-long runways. The Charger struggled through the sand but ultimately climbed up onto the near runway unscathed.

The two landing strips marked the easternmost components of the base, and Jackson preferred to come in from a corner rather than from the middle. Plus, if anyone was looking for him or expecting him, they'd be expecting him to come down the main road.

He coasted for another mile and stopped several hundred yards shy of the nearest building, Hangar 5 according to the map. He got out and again used the binoculars to survey the complex. Hangars 4 and 5 extended farther north than the rest of the buildings, such that from his vantage point all he could see was a barracks on the northwest corner of the complex. He did not see any movement as he mentally reviewed the map in his head again, calculating distances, cover angles, and likely entrances.

Blane Road ran south all the way through the complex, intersected by three roads running from the apron on the east side to the base's only other road, one "block" west of Blane Road. One of the three roads marked the south edge of the complex, with only a garage on its south side. The second ran between Hangar 1—by far the biggest of the hangars—and Hangar 2, and also separated the administration building and Officers' Barracks from A Barracks and B Barracks. The mess, base exchange, and infirmary all were clustered around this middle road. The third road marked the north end of the complex, except for Hangars 4 and 5, which were immediately to its north. In all, it was less than a couple thousand feet from the south road to the north road, and only half that from the west road to the runways. As far as military bases went, Blane was tiny.

Jackson was about to proceed when he caught movement out of the corner of his eye. He trained the binoculars on the area and honed in on a single figure walking east along the north road. He was dressed like the guard, in desert fatigues, his head on a swivel as he made steady progress east. He momentarily disappeared behind Hangar 4, then reappeared on the apron, where he promptly turned south, away from Jackson.

He watched the man through the binoculars all the way to the south road, where he turned back to the west. Jackson reached for his cell phone and scrolled through the menus until he found a stopwatch feature, which he quickly activated. Then he waited.

It was a little after three a.m. and he doubted the man was just out for a stroll. He walked like a sentry, purposeful and alert. When he appeared from around B Barracks at the northwest corner of the base ten minutes later, that notion was confirmed. He followed the same path along the north road, between Hangars 3 and 4, and then south on the apron. When he made the turn west again, Jackson checked his phone. The sentry made the loop in just over twenty minutes. He didn't appear to stop and check doors or inspect anything. He just walked the perimeter.

Jackson got back in the car and drove forward. The dual runways extended several hundred yards south of the base complex, according to the map. The apron stretched from the south road—which extended through the apron to provide access from it to the runways—to a similar taxiway even with the northernmost point of Hangar 5. On the apron, maybe seven or eight total aircraft were parked. As Jackson approached, he identified a pair of fighter jets at the north end of the apron, flanked only by an Apache helicopter, which he realized was missing its main rotor blade. Jackson veered onto the runway, driving again by aid of night-vision goggles, and made a tight U-turn so that he was parked in getaway position, facing north, shielded from view of anyone on the base by the Apache's low-riding frame. At night, unless someone was looking for the car, they wouldn't likely spot it.

He got out and checked the time on his phone. The sentry would be turning east on the north road in about five minutes. Clutching the pistol with four remaining rounds, Jackson darted from the cover of the Apache to the northeast corner of Hangar 5. It was maybe two hundred feet in length, with massive stacker garage doors facing the apron. There was also a small, standard-sized door in the corner. There were no windows, in either of the doors or on the north wall.

Jackson crept to the door and gently tested the knob. It was locked. He withdrew the lock picks lifted from Vickers' cruiser and carefully worked the lock. He heard the pins click and grasped the knob with his left hand. He returned the picks to his pocket and raised the pistol, not sure what he would find inside. Hillary strapped to a gurney? Some macabre testing environs? Would he even get the door open before being shot?

He twisted the knob and pushed the door open, waiting by the doorjamb. Nothing happened. The interior was pitch black, and Jackson lowered the goggles before creeping through the open doorway.

Despite the use of the goggles, his vision was still limited due to the lack of ambient light. He was able to make out the far walls of the hangar, as well as the steel trusses in the ceiling. As he swept his head from side to side, he saw that the hangar was completely empty. No airplanes, vehicles, boxes, crates, and no beautiful women being brainwashed. No evidence of any Silver Dawn project a quarter century ago, nor any Golden Dawn now. There were no windows at all in the hangar, and the only other means of egress was a standard door in the south wall, facing Hangar 4.

Jackson checked his phone. The sentry should be about to the apron. He retreated to the door, lay down, and extended his head so that his night-vision goggles peered around the doorframe. He was just in time to see the sentry turn south.

Jackson waited impatiently. It was killing him to hesitate, not knowing what they might be doing to Hillary. Or what if he was wrong and she wasn't here? He was wasting time that could be spent tracking her down. Assuming he had any way of doing so.

When the sentry turned the corner, Jackson exited Hangar 5, locking the door behind him. He hurried to Hangar 4, finding it an exact replica of Hangar 5, right down to being totally vacant inside. Checking his phone, he hurried across the north road and to a door in the corner of Hangar 3. It was slightly larger than the previous two hangars, but just as empty. Leaving the door unlocked, Jackson crouched by the corner of the hangar and peeked his head around, looking west. The sentry had just turned the corner by B Barracks and was headed his way.

Jackson stepped back and stood upright, quietly unsheathing Quinn's nightstick. He held it in his right hand while he gripped the pistol in his left, waiting with his back pressed to the hangar wall. The minutes dragged like hours. The sentry had been walking pretty much down the middle of the road, as near as Jackson could tell, and on previous trips, he had made a wide turn around the hangar so that he walked fifteen to twenty feet away from the massive buildings. Jackson didn't like having to cover open territory, even in the dark and especially since the sentry would be turning his way. Ideally, he would have hid on the other side of the road, but it was too late now.

He heard the sentry's boots scrape the pavement in a steady rhythm. Inspiration—or insanity—hit him, and he pivoted the nightstick so that he could hold it with his mouth. He then used his free right hand to remove a stun grenade from his belt. He waited anxiously, still pressed against the wall of the hangar, until the sentry appeared, striding east. His head turned from side to side, but it was dark enough and Jackson was hidden well enough to avoid detection.

When the sentry's head swiveled to the north one last time before he turned south, Jackson underhanded the stun grenade, pin still in place, in the general direction of Hangar 4. It clanked to the pavement and skittered along the apron, the noise cacophonous compared to the silence it had broken.

The sentry immediately turned toward the sound. At the same time, Jackson rushed forward, sweeping the nightstick from his mouth and raising it over his head. The sentry heard him and turned, reaching for his holstered weapon. He was too late, as Jackson brought the nightstick down toward his temple. His swing connected with a sickening crack, and the sentry slumped to the ground.

There was no doubt he was unconscious, and Jackson quickly dragged him back to the still unlocked Hangar 3. He pulled his body inside and trussed his ankles and wrists with zip ties from the survival kit in Vickers' vehicle. He felt for a pulse and found it steady, although the man was still out cold. Jackson frisked him, removing a utility knife and a keycard, both of which he pocketed. Using the knife, he cut the man's sleeve, ripping it off his arm and using it for a crude gag. If the man was a real soldier, he would still find a way to get free or get to the door and make noise, but it would slow him some.

If he was a real soldier. Jackson hadn't thoroughly examined the guard he had killed, but in tearing off the sentry's sleeve, he had noticed something. Above the left breast pocket, there had been no "tape" identifying the branch of military. Just a name tape above the right breast pocket. Jackson quickly turned the sentry over, spotting no insignia of any kind, no flag on the shoulders. These weren't authentic U.S. military uniforms. They were generic fatigues, bought at a military surplus store or repurposed for unofficial use.

He stood, feeling somewhat vindicated. He wasn't going to battle against the United States Air Force. But as quickly as the feeling had come, it subsided. Regardless of their intent, he would have felt a small measure of solace if Hillary was in the hands of legitimate members of the armed forces. Now, he had no idea whose control she was under.

Jackson closed and locked the door to Hangar 3 behind him and retrieved his un-triggered stun grenade. With the sentry neutralized, he had more freedom of movement. But he also knew that dawn was only a few hours away, and with it light, activity, and almost surely a change of guard. He had to hurry.

Hangar 2 was directly beside Hangar 3, an exact replica of it, with one notable exception. Instead of a keyed lock, the door was electronic, with a keycard swipe mounted beside it. Jackson tested the card he'd picked off the sentry, and with a soft whir, the door unlocked.

An updated, alternate method of entry likely meant the hangar wasn't empty, that it was somehow in use as part of Golden Dawn. Jackson proceeded with caution. As soon as he stepped inside the door, even before his goggles and eyes processed the scene, he sensed that something was different. Then his eyes focused on a Learjet parked in the middle of the hangar. It was sleek and shiny, a far cry from the rusted, partially dismembered jets on the apron. This craft was capable of flight.

It was alone in the hangar, and Jackson circled it to be sure. Hangar 2, like Hangar 3, had a row of offices and separate rooms along its north wall, and since Hangar 2 wasn't abandoned, he checked each of them. They were empty. Aside from some fuel drums along the far wall and a four-wheeler with a small tank on back, the jet was the only object in the hangar.

The airstairs were down, likely a default setting when the plane was in the hangar. He climbed them quickly and looked into the cockpit and down the fuselage of the jet. It was empty. He scurried back down and exited the hangar.

Three were empty, one held a jet. Why Hangar 2 instead of Hangar 1? Was it a size issue? Was Hangar 1 being used for another purpose? Was Hangar 2 just more convenient? He spent a moment debating heading for the infirmary, but decided to check all the hangars before moving on.

Hangar 1 was huge, probably twice the size of Hangars 2 and 3, capable of housing the largest aircraft in the world. In design, however, it was the same, with massive stacker doors that spanned the entire east side and opened to the apron, and a small, standard door in the corner. Like the door to Hangar 2, it had no keyhole but was accessible via a card swipe. As he had in the previous hangars, Jackson entered carefully, the Beretta pistol leading the way.

Once inside, he crouched down, letting his eyes sweep across the hangar. A row of small rooms and offices again lined the north wall, as they had in Hangars

2 and 3. And it appeared that there were offices on the south wall some five hundred feet away. But Jackson's eyes paid them little attention, instead drawn to a huge structure in the middle of the hangar.

Concrete block walls that were close to twenty feet high ran west and south from the northeast corner. They were at least a hundred feet in length, with steel girders running north and south above them. Jackson couldn't see what the girders supported, but he assumed it was a suspended roof or ceiling of some sort, making the structure a building within a building. And despite its size, it was still dwarfed by the massive hangar.

The structure was closer to the hangar's west edge than east, but seemingly centered north-south. The block walls were solid, save for a small break halfway down the east side, containing a pair of steel doors. Jackson's eyes quickly strayed from them to a black panel van parked just feet from the entrance. His heartrate doubled as he realized the ramifications. Dime claimed he had been taken in a black van. Arielle had seen bodies being loaded into a black van. Deputy Clayton said Hillary had been transferred into a black van. And now, a black van was backed up to a mysterious structure inside an airplane hangar on a supposedly decommissioned Air Force base. It gave Jackson chills.

He lifted up the night-vision goggles, allowing his eyes to grow accustomed to meager lighting provided by a series of light fixtures suspended from the hangar's high ceiling. They provided just enough light to see, and while Jackson probably would have been better off with the goggles, he preferred natural lighting and color.

To be thorough, he checked the offices that lined the north wall, then cautiously made his way around the far side of the structure. Its west wall was windowless, just a long row of concrete blocks. Jackson came around to the southeast corner, concluding the only way in was through the doors in the east wall. Before attempting entry, he darted to the hangar's south end and checked out the offices there. All were empty, void of people or furniture, just like the north offices.

Jackson returned to the corner of the structure and stopped to focus and catch his breath. The hangar had four doors, one in each corner, in addition to the stacker doors on the east side. They were closed tight, and Jackson had no idea how to open them if he decided to make a break in the van. But he was getting ahead of himself.

As he approached the doors, he clutched the pistol in his right hand, ready for anything. The van appeared empty, and Jackson circled it to confirm. Peering in the front windows, he saw no signs that anyone was hiding—or hidden—in the back, and the hood was cool to his touch.

Coming around the driver's side of the van, he stopped cold. A small security camera panned slowly back and forth from above the structure's double doors. He ducked back behind the front of the van and out of sight, kicking himself for not noticing it sooner. Surely it had picked up his movement as he had approached the van. He turned his head and spotted a similar red dot in the corner, above the door from which he had entered the hangar.

He bit his lip in frustration, wondering how much else he had missed and how many other times he might have been noticed.

He didn't have long to think about it. In the faint light, he saw a distinction in the shadows by the northeast corner of the concrete structure. Instinctively, he dived to the ground, just before several bullets punctured the side of the van.

Chapter Fifty-Six

4:12 a.m.

THE VAN HAD big tires, and thus was high enough off the ground that Jackson could fit underneath it, even with his array of gear. He quickly scooted under it as more bullets pinged off the epoxy-coated floor. He slid his legs so that he was laying perpendicular to the van, his entire body behind the front tire. Then he reached his gun hand around the side and fired.

His first two bullets sailed wide, forcing the shooter to run for the cover offered by the corner of the building. At the same time, another barrage pinged into the van from the opposite side.

Jackson scooted around on his elbows to see a man coming at him from the south too. He deduced Jackson's location under the van and lowered his assault rifle to fire. Before he got the chance, Jackson took aim and emptied the last two rounds from his magazine. He only needed one, as the first shot tore into the man's chest, dropping him immediately.

Having seen too many movies where a person in a gunfight expelled an empty magazine and thus alerted the enemy that they were temporarily out of ammo, Jackson set down the pistol as he rolled out from under the van. He came up to his knees and withdrew the ARX100 rifle from the scabbard on his back. The man he had just shot was down, not moving. He saw no one else coming from the south. So he crouched behind the front right wheel of the van and listened for the first man.

It took a moment, but his ears detected footsteps. They were quiet, tentative, but growing nearer. Jackson raised the rifle over the hood of the van and fired three quick shots blindly. Immediately, he stood and made for the rear of the van. He'd expected a salvo of return fire, but it didn't come. Instead, he heard the scuff of boots on concrete, and peeked around the rear of the van to see the man again scampering for cover.

Jackson stepped out from behind the van, bringing the rifle to his shoulder. He squeezed four shots and saw the man go down.

Playing video games with Mouse, Jackson often got into trouble by being too bold, too daring. He'd send his character into the open, guns blazing, and get mowed down by an unseen shooter. But he did it because, even in a virtual world, he couldn't stand the waiting, the hiding, the wondering when an enemy would appear. Now, prudence suggested he stay hidden and wait to see if any additional attackers were coming. But since he had been detected and had opened fire with unsilenced rounds, he knew time was short. And the man he'd hit was wounded but not dead, crawling toward the corner and protection.

So Jackson charged, hoping to take the man alive. But his sudden action changed the man's intention. Instead of trying to get away, he turned onto his backside and raised his weapon.

Jackson stopped and fired again, two more shots, one through the shoulder and one into the floor fifty feet behind the man. He dropped backwards, his head hitting the floor with a thud.

Jackson hurried to him, sweeping his weapon away with a kick. He was still breathing, but appeared unconscious. Jackson quickly frisked him, finding— among other things—a SIG Sauer P226 pistol that he jammed into his waistband. Then he zip tied the man's wrists and hurried to the other man, his rifle drawn and ready.

He was already dead, Jackson's bullet having hit a major artery near the heart.

Jackson dealt with this killing much better than the last, adrenaline carrying him straight through phases of shock, grief, and sickness. He retreated to the van, picked up his Beretta, and walked to the double doors in the concrete. They were windowless, without handles or knobs or any means of manually being opened. A swipe pad was built into the concrete on the right, and after knocking the camera off its mount with his rifle, Jackson retrieved the keycard from his pocket and swiped it.

Nothing happened.

He tried again and then again, with the same result.

He searched the dead man and found a keycard, but it was similarly useless. Already knowing the result, he searched the wounded man, found his keycard, and tried it. No good.

Jackson pumped two rounds into the keypad, hoping to short it out and get the doors to open. It too was a useless venture.

He stepped back, breathing heavily, weighing his options. Hillary was behind the doors, he knew it. But his bullets weren't going to gain him access, nor was a stun grenade. He had no means of climbing onto the roof, even if he were able to back the van up to the wall and use it as a launch pad. And the van was too wide for the doors, so he quickly discarded the idea of driving it into them.

He rubbed his hand over his face, pleading with his brain to think. It worked.

He turned and ran for the door on the southeast corner of the hangar. The apron was quiet, the obsolete airplanes creating eerie shadows in the moonlight. Jackson lowered his night-vision goggles and ran along the south wall of the hangar to the southwest corner, where he crouched down. Directly ahead, less than one hundred feet away, was the base's control tower. It was four stories tall, and would serve as an ideal vantage point or command center. But Jackson saw no signs of activity in or near it.

Across the road from the tower was the base garage, in seeming neglect and disrepair. Beyond them both, was the administration building, and to the right, north of the control tower, the armory, base exchange, and the old security police headquarters. None showed any signs of life.

Jackson waited for several minutes, looking for any movement, any indication that the two men who had attacked him were not alone. He had no idea how many men were on the base, who was watching cameras, and why the two men had come to the hangar when they had. But even under the best scenario, the gunfire they had exchanged hadn't been completely muted. Surely his presence wouldn't go undetected for long. He needed to move and move fast.

Sheathing his rifle, Jackson loaded a fresh magazine into the silenced Beretta pistol. He took one more moment to scan for activity and to plan his approach. Operating on the assumption that the control tower was unoccupied, he dashed from cover and sprinted to the near corner of the armory. It was a block concrete building with a south-facing door. His keycard worked on the first swipe, and Jackson ducked inside and quickly closed the door.

It was pitch black inside, and Jackson's goggles only gave him partial sight. But he didn't dare search for and use a light. The same keycard got him past a front counter that faced the side door and a west-facing garage door and into a cage that took up eighty percent of the building. It was lined with metal shelves, most of which were empty. But against the near wall, he found a repository of weapons, everything from pistols and rifles to RPGs, claymore mines, and hand grenades. He identified some traditional "iron pineapple" fragmentation grenades, likely remnants from Blane's official days or even before. For his purposes, Jackson preferred a concussion grenade. He was considering trying to use one of the claymores when he spotted a crate on an adjacent wall. It contained concussion grenades, designed as offensive weapons that relied on the explosive force to cause damage rather than fragments expelled by the explosion. He put five of them in his belt and headed for the exit.

He cracked the door and peeked out, recoiling immediately. Two men were making a fast walk past the control tower toward the hangars. Jackson watched through a slit until they reached the corner of Hangar 1 and continued on along its south edge.

He carefully exited the armory. Seeing no one else, he advanced slowly to the building's southeast corner. Crouched down, he spied two more men entering Hangar 1 from the northwest corner.

Assuming the first duo was headed in via the opposite corner, four men were soon to be inside the hangar. He didn't like the odds. But if they thought he was in Hangar 1, it gave him some freedom of movement.

Changing plans, he crept north, keeping in the shadow of the armory. Pausing at every opportunity along the way, he used the base exchange, SP building, infirmary, and rec center as cover, reaching the southwest corner of Hangar 2 unseen. Breathing hard, he used the keycard to gain entrance to the hangar.

He slipped inside and closed the door. No sooner had it latched than bullets pinged into the hangar wall.

Jackson dived to the ground, begging the night-vision goggles to reveal the shooter. He spotted a figure coming around the back of the plane. He only held a pistol, and his eyes searched the darkness for Jackson. Using his advantage, Jackson crept along the wall. He slowly stood as the man took several steps out from the back of the plane.

Jackson almost pitied him, but he didn't have time. He took two shots, both penetrating the man's shoulder. He fell with a cry, and Jackson heard his pistol clatter on the coated floor.

Watchful for other potential assailants, Jackson hurried over to the man. He kicked his gun aside as he surveyed the wounds. They weren't life threatening, and he noticed the man wasn't wearing fatigues. He was in a polo shirt and dark cargo pants, but with a holster around his waist.

"Who are you?" Jackson asked.

Instead of answering, the man started shouting for help. Jackson dropped to his knees and bashed him with the butt of his pistol. The man blacked out, and Jackson stood and dragged him back to the door. He used one of his remaining zip ties to bind his hands, then rolled him through the door. He closed it behind him and hurried around the plane to the far corner of the hangar.

He inched open the door and looked up and down the apron. He saw nothing. The four men he had seen headed for Hangar 1 were likely still inside, if not searching for him, waiting for him to return. Not finding him, it was possible they would exit the hangar and search the complex for him. Or maybe they'd heard the shots and would come running. Either way, he didn't have time for hide-and-seek, especially since he was likely to lose in a game where he was outnumbered four-to-one. So he decided to make them come out quickly.

Jackson removed one of the grenades from his belt and pulled the pin. He cocked his arm and heaved the grenade across the hangar, aiming for the drums of fuel in the corner. He didn't wait to verify his aim. As soon as the grenade was out of his hand, he burst through the door and took off on a dead run across the apron, headed for the cover of an abandoned fighter jet parked some hundred feet east of the hangar.

He was ten feet short of it when he heard an explosion.

It was a whisper compared to the WHOOMP that followed an instant later. Jackson was lifted off his feet and thrown forward by the concussion. He somersaulted on the pavement and scrambled behind the jet as the corner of the hangar erupted in a giant ball of flame.

Chapter Fifty-Seven

EVEN FROM A distance and partially shielded by the old fighter jet, Jackson felt the scorching heat from the fuel explosion. He crouched with arms over his head and scooted under the jet as bits of debris floated down around him like tiny, fiery parachutists. When he finally dared raise his head, he saw that the south and most of the east wall of the hangar were gone, the doors blown outward and scattered across the apron in a mangled, burning heap. The roof was sagging toward the corner and in danger of collapsing, even as flames raced upward, consuming and melting everything in their wake.

Fearing for the structural integrity of Hangar 1 if the flames spread, Jackson slid out from under the jet and ran south, shielded by a second fighter and a dark gray B-52. With discretion out the window, he switched back to the ARX100 and made a beeline for the southeast entrance to Hangar 1. Two hundred yards north, the roaring fire raged. It enabled him to enter the hangar unbeknownst to two men in fatigues who stood at either end of the van. Jackson mowed them down with several quick bursts from the rifle.

He only paused for a moment to make sure the other two he had seen approaching the building weren't present. Then he removed a second grenade from his belt. He released the lever and pulled the pin, rolling it toward the double doors in the concrete wall. He prayed that if Hillary was inside the structure, she wasn't in close proximity to the doors.

He covered the sixty feet to the hangar door in record time and grabbed onto the doorjamb with his free hand, using it as a fulcrum to pull himself around and out of any potential shrapnel blast range. The bang was only a second later, and as soon as the sound reached his ears, Jackson returned to the hangar, gun drawn.

Both doors had been blown off their hinges. One was completely gone; the other was a mangled mess hanging by the thin metal door closer. The smoke was just clearing, and as it did, Jackson saw a man in fatigues coming toward the opening. He raised the rifle and opened fire, shooting until it clicked. Through it all, the man kept coming, his gun raised. But he never fired, and as Jackson stepped back, out of ammo, the man fell to the floor.

Jackson quickly expelled the empty magazine and replaced it with thirty fresh rounds. Then he advanced. The man was dead, his fifth casualty of the night, at least.

Jackson peered through the doors, down a well-lit hallway with white walls, a drop ceiling, and linoleum flooring. It ended forty feet ahead in a pair of windowless steel doors. On the left side of the hallway, a door opened to a closet, and another led behind what looked like a reception counter. Just beyond it, two more steel doors led to the south. There was nobody in the hallway or behind the desk, and Jackson took a moment to turn over his latest victim.

Blood dribbled out of his mouth and from a bullet through his cheek. Two more had perforated his midsection, and the life was already gone from his eyes. Jackson patted him down, retrieving a keycard that he hoped would gain him access to interior doors.

He stood, scanning the hangar again. He was still alone, the fire in Hangar 2 still snapping and popping loudly. Mindful of the potential consequence of stray bullets, Jackson switched back to the pistol. He stepped through the doorway and into the hall, feeling as if he'd just entered the ER of a hospital.

The door immediately to his left did indeed open to a storage closet, and Jackson quickly shut it. The door leading behind the front counter was ajar, and Jackson entered a very typical reception area. A computer monitor on a desk beneath the counter showed multiple security camera feeds, two of which were snow. The view filled the entire screen, and Jackson saw no way to minimize it. Moving a wireless mouse beside a keyboard did nothing, nor did any of the typical exit or escape keys. Jackson gave up. He searched the desk for anything useful, saw nothing obvious, and decided his time was better spent making a physical search of the building.

A second door led from the reception area to a hall behind the dual steel doors. It was identical to the previous hallway in color and design, but with far more doors on either side. Jackson moved quickly but carefully down the hall, sweeping his gun from room to room. He read signs beside the doors almost in disbelief. Exam 1, 2, and 3. Pharmacy. Lab. OR. He *was* in a hospital. Why, when the base had an infirmary?

The hallway ended with the lab on one side and the OR on the other. All the rooms were empty, and Jackson backtracked. His newly acquired keycard allowed him through the double doors and back to the main hallway. He turned left and used the keycard at the set of doors at the end of the hallway. As they mechanically swung open, he readied his weapon for anything.

All he got were more doors—a set straight ahead some twenty feet and a second pair on the right. They were identical to each other and to those behind him. Above the pair on the right was an unlit red bulb. As the doors automatically closed behind Jackson, he got the feeling he was in an airlock, such as might be found in a nuclear facility or a biochemical lab. Given what he'd encountered so far, nothing would surprise him.

He decided to continue straight first. He again swiped his card, and again crouched in a firing stance. The doors parted to reveal another forty feet of hallway with another set of doors halfway along on the left and a nurse's station dead ahead. A nurse's station, Jackson knew, because a woman stood behind it, decked in aqua scrubs. Short, dark hair was drawn behind her head. Out of place in this clinical scene was the pistol steadied between both hands, aimed at Jackson.

"Drop your weapon," she said.

"Can't do that," he said, advancing first one step, then a second.

"You take another step, I shoot."

"You're a nurse?"

"That's right."

"Where's Hillary?" Jackson said, studying her eyes while never losing sight of her trigger finger. Was she *just* a nurse or was she a nurse with military training? And did it matter, considering she had Jackson in her crosshairs?

"Put it down," she said.

"I don't want to hurt you, but I will."

"I'm not going to tell you again," she said.

Something in her face convinced him she wasn't lying. Nurse or not, military or not, he had no doubt she would indeed shoot. So he squeezed the trigger of his pistol twice. Two bullets thudded into the woman's chest.

At the same time, Jackson felt as if his chest had been smacked with a shovel. He fell back against the doors from the force, instantly looking down to see if the Kevlar vest had indeed absorbed all the impact. His ribs felt as if they had been shattered, but he saw no blood.

He forced himself forward, despite the pain. The woman had fallen behind the counter, and Jackson knew his bullets had hit center mass. But he approached carefully, extending his gun over the counter before peering with his eyes.

The woman was flat on her back, head to the side, eyes closed. The gun lay beside her limp arm, no longer a threat. Blood pooled from a pair of wounds in her chest, staining the aqua scrubs.

Six.

Not counting Vickers.

Or the second victim in the hangar, who while not dead, had been stitched with bullets.

Jackson had killed five gangbangers back in May. Now, in a few hours, he'd more than doubled his kill total. The full weight of that reality slammed against him with more force than the woman's bullet. Scowling away the emotions, he turned toward the double doors in the side of the hallway.

He swallowed the lump in his throat as he swiped the keycard. The doors clicked, then whirred as they opened. He stood back and looked down the barrel of his gun again.

It was another hall, this one dimly lit. Three closed doors on the right, three closed doors on the left. A single steel door straight ahead. Each of the side doors had windows in them, emitting no light. Jackson started with the door on the left, peeking through the window, ready to duck in an instant.

He was looking at a vacant room with a hospital bed, full array of bedside medical equipment, an armchair, even curtains drawn over what could only be an imaginary window.

He crossed the hall and peered in the door on the right. His heart nearly stopped when he saw a body on the bed. It was a man, unresponsive, asleep or sedated. Otherwise, the room was identical to the first.

Jackson's heart didn't stop, instead hammering like a piston inside his chest as he checked the remaining four doors. All led to similar rooms. All were empty, save for the second on the right. It was occupied by another man, also unconscious.

The pounding in Jackson's chest continued, rapid and violent. What had he and Hillary stumbled into? What sort of Orwellian, dystopian place was this? Who was behind it all? And where was Hillary?

None of the other beds had been disturbed. The exam and operating rooms had showed no signs of recent activity. Jackson remembered the unlit red bulb above the door leading to the other half of the building, his mind racing as fast as his heart with possibilities. Red lights meant live—live on-air transmissions, live fire, live electrical power.

He swiped at the door at the end of the hall, and it retracted into the wall. Jackson advanced into a stub of hallway that ended in a door, with another on the right and two more across from it.

Jackson started on the left. The first door opened to a dark room with a window spanning the entire length of the wall on the right. It looked into another room with a table and a pair of chairs. Computer equipment was mounted on a desk on the left, and speakers hung in the corners above the window.

It was an interrogation room, straight out of an episode of *NCIS*.

Jackson returned to the hallway and tried the door at the end of the hall. It opened to a conference room, bare but modern.

Jackson backed out and approached the door on the right. He slid the keycard through the reader mounted beside the door, and it clicked and unlocked. He turned the handle and opened the door inward to his left, stopping immediately.

What he saw made his blood run cold.

Chapter Fifty-Eight

Nineteen months ago . . .
Friday, February 4
3:33 p.m.

"STOP SCRATCHING."

Jackson looked up at his brother. He'd changed from a pair of shorts and a T-shirt into his black LAPD uniform, looking as distinguished as ever.

"I will just as soon as I stop itching," Jackson answered.

"You're just going to make it worse."

"Thanks for the advice, Bildad, but I don't think that's possible." He reached a feeble hand for a plastic bottle. He bent the flexible straw down to his mouth and sucked the lukewarm water. He winced, the sores in his mouth making swallowing painful, albeit necessary. Fluids, fluids, fluids, the doctor had said.

"A refill before you go?" Jackson asked, extending the bottle. "Cold water this time."

Grant sighed. "Are you sure you don't want me to stay?"

"Gangs won't stop banging just because I have chickenpox."

"I can have somebody cover for me."

"You've already switched your shift. Besides, I'm just going to lay here and shiver away my fever. Not much you can do."

Grant refilled the bottle, shaking it as he set it back on the coffee table to prove it was full of ice.

"Thanks."

"Water, phone, remote, Tylenol. Anything else you need?"

"That tribal backscratching stick you bought in Hawaii."

"Hidden away." He pointed at the bottle of Tylenol. "No overdosing. And stop scratching."

Jackson lowered his hand from his head.

"See ya," Grant called as he headed for the door.

"Yeah."

The door closed and he was alone in Grant's apartment. It wasn't a bad place—modern, airy, a decent view if he had the strength to walk to the window and look out at West L.A. But he was so weak he had all he could do to make it to the bathroom or the refrigerator. So he was left to channel surf through a lot of sludge, ultimately settling on ESPN's *Around the Horn* when it came on at four.

For the next hour, he drifted in and out of consciousness, fighting chills, nausea, a distant urge to pee, and itching beyond belief. He tried to avoid scratching, but he couldn't resist, wishing he had something more than fingernails to alleviate the annoyance.

He was half asleep again when a noise jarred him to consciousness. He looked to the TV, where a variety of commentators were discussing the impending Super Bowl. The noise came again, a click, and he turned his head to see the front door swing open. Jackson opened his mouth to make a crack to his brother, but stopped with the words on his tongue when Hillary walked in.

She wore a shirred teal blouse and dark blue jeans. Her hair was glamorous as ever, but several inches shorter, the result of a haircut Jackson had heard about but not yet seen. It was appealing, but no more so than any previous style.

"You have a key?"

She held it up as proof, then returned it to her purse.

"And you just let yourself in?"

"I didn't want you to have to get up."

"I'm sick, not crippled," he said, groaning as he reached for his water.

"Um-hmm. How are you feeling?"

"Peachy." He took a sip and let the bottle fall against his side. "Grant's not here. Working."

"I know that."

Jackson swallowed. "One of the symptoms of chickenpox in adults is apparently malaise, which I seem to be suffering from at the moment."

"How would you know?" Hillary asked with a tight-lipped smile.

"That's great. Do you kick stray puppies in the gutter too?"

Hillary set her purse on an old glider, once Jackson's grandma's, in the corner. Then she sat down in the room's other chair, a lounger at the end of the coffee table, perpendicular to the couch.

Jackson took another drink and returned the bottle to the table. He scratched a particularly itchy pustule on his neck. "Why exactly are you here, Hill?"

She didn't bother to correct him. "Because I thought someone should look in on you."

"Did Grant put you up to this?"

"No. He doesn't know I'm here."

"Ah, brownie points."

"We're going to be family in a few months, Jackson. I thought it was about time we start acting like it."

His eyes drifted to her left hand, particularly her ring finger, to the diamond ring that sparkled as it caught the sunlight. On a cop's salary, Grant had done himself proud with the purchase. Of course, knowing Hillary, she wouldn't have deigned to put anything smaller on her finger.

"You're really here out of the goodness of your heart?"

"Yes. Stop scratching."

"Well, about the only thing I need help with is getting to the bathroom, so that 'We Are Family' vibe is going to get a workout."

"Do you have dinner plans?"

"I know Grant has to work, but still, he's my brother."

She glared at him.

"Leftover pizza in the fridge."

"I think I can do better than that," she said, pushing out of the chair. "I'll see what Grant has on hand."

Jackson attacked the sore on his neck again.

"Stop scratching," she said without looking.

He sighed.

In thirty minutes, Hillary had semi-homemade soup simmering on the stove. Jackson, having made the trip to the bathroom he'd been putting off for the last hour, was back on the couch, shivering under a blanket after his exposure to the apartment's "cool" seventy-two-degree air.

"Have you checked your temperature recently?" Hillary asked from the end of the couch.

"Yeah, absolute Kelvin."

Her thin smile acknowledged the remark without lauding it. Then she turned and disappeared down the hallway. Two minutes later, she returned with a thermometer.

"Really?"

"Open up."

He did.

"How did you manage to avoid chickenpox as a kid?" she asked.

"Mmm, mmm," he answered. Truth was, he'd been pondering that for the last two days. Grant had gotten chickenpox when he was six, but Jackson had remained immune. Until now. Where he had caught it was another mystery. The only kids he'd even seen in the past two weeks were passing Sunday schoolers in the church hallway. Then again, maybe he'd caught it off another adult. None had exhibited symptoms around him, but the virus was communicable several days before it presented.

Hillary tended her soup, then checked Jackson's temperature. It was high but not dangerously so.

"Stop scratching," she said as she placed the thermometer on the table.

"Yes, Florence."

"Cute."

"I've always thought so."

SportsCenter was getting boring, so Jackson flipped channels until he found a rerun of *The Middle*. It was as good as anything.

"Another fifteen minutes or so," Hillary announced.

"How did you make soup in under an hour?"

"I cheated and used store-bought chicken stock."

"Grant has cans of chicken stock on hand?"

She nodded.

"You know you could have just heated up some Campbell's."

"I could have let you eat stale pizza too."

He sighed. "I really can't believe you're here."

She raised her eyebrows.

"I mean, don't you have some art gallery soirée or an indie documentary premiere or some culturally stimulating event to attend? It's Friday, you must have plans."

"Well, I did," she said, tilting her head to the side.

"You mean until Grant had to cancel to switch his shift," Jackson said. "That was the call he had to make that he wouldn't tell me about."

Hillary nodded.

He sighed again. After the diagnosis the day before, Grant had insisted Jackson come stay with him so he could look after him. The night had been particularly grueling, marred by fever and nausea, and Grant had postponed his day shift to tend to Jackson during the worst of his affliction. He hadn't mentioned that doing so meant canceling date night with Hillary.

"So that's it, you're feeling guilty."

"Why would I be feeling guilty?"

"I mean, in reverse. Like . . . I don't know. That malaise again."

"Um-hmm. I'm here because Grant said you were in rough shape and I didn't like the idea of you being alone all night in that condition."

"Well that's really dec—"

"Stop scratching."

"It itches, Hill. It is the natural human response to itching. We scratch."

"Well you're bleeding now."

"It's an old couch and there's a sheet down."

"It's just going to hurt worse."

"Hurt is fine. Hurt I can deal with. It's this conttonpickin' itching I can't stand."

Hillary shook her head and got up to check on the soup. When she returned, she caught Jackson scratching again, this time on his upper chest, hard enough to break the skin.

"Okay, that's enough," she said.

"What?"

She headed down the hallway, leaving Jackson to wonder what was coming. She came back a minute later holding a pair of Grant's skiing mittens.

"You have to be kidding," Jackson said.

"That or I could duct tape your hands to the couch."

"I'd like to see you try."

"Please, a troop of Brownies could subdue you right now."

Physically resisting Hillary seemed absurd, so he allowed her to put the mittens on his hands. When she ducked into the kitchen, he pulled one off and attacked his chest and neck again. He heard her rummaging through kitchen drawers, then saw why as she rounded the counter. She carried a roll of duct tape.

"Not happening, Hill."

"Give me your hand."

"No."

She grabbed his left hand and pinned it to his side, then sat down on his stomach, restraining him and his hand still at his side. She wrested control of his right arm and fitted the glove back on. Then she wrapped his wrist in duct tape, like a corner man taping a boxer before a fight. It briefly gave him the idea to punch her in the head, but he quickly pushed it aside.

Hillary similarly affixed the mitten on his left hand, then stood back. Jackson held up his two paws. "This is pathetic."

"My thoughts exactly."

"I can't even change the channel now."

Hillary bent down and clicked off the TV.

"Hey!"

"That's going to dull your brain. Further," she added as she stood. She entered the kitchen and ladled a bowl of soup. She returned carrying the steaming brew with both hands.

"How am I supposed to eat?"

"I'll feed you. Scoot over."

He slid as far back into the couch as possible, sitting up a little. His neck and chest were driving him mad.

Hillary set the bowl on the coffee table and sat down on the edge of the couch. She turned to face him and tucked several folded paper towels inside the collar of his shirt.

"So this is what it's come to," Jackson said.

"I left out all the 'really gross' vegetables," she said, spooning the first mouthful. "Here."

He opened his mouth to accept the soup. It was hot, which agitated his already sore throat. But it was also tasty. Better than he would have expected from health-nut Hillary.

"Chicken?"

She nodded.

"Let me guess, Grant had a Cornish hen marinating in the fridge?"

"I defrosted a chicken breast in the microwave."

"Very Martha Stewart."

"Just shut up and eat," she said, lifting the spoon to his mouth again.

He did, enjoying the flavor and the sustenance it would hopefully provide. His last meal had been pizza the night before. Then nausea had hit, and he'd thrown up most of what he'd eaten. He'd been on a regimen of soda crackers and buttered toast ever since. By comparison, Hillary's soup was a gourmet meal.

Jackson drained the bowl but passed on a second helping for the time being. Hillary set the empty bowl on the coffee table and lifted the only lightly dribbled-on paper towels from Jackson's shirt. She dabbed at his chin and placed the towels in the bowl. She turned to face him, still seated on the couch.

"Can I ask you something?"

"Yeah."

"Why don't you want me marrying your brother? What is it you really have against me?"

He cleared his throat. "I'd rather not answer that when I can't defend myself," he said, holding up his gloved hands.

She rolled her eyes and stood. "Fine," she said as she picked up the bowl, "just blow off a serious conversation with wisecracks like always." She took the bowl into the kitchen and came back a few minutes later with a bowl of her own. She sat in the chair at the end of the table.

Jackson sat up slightly. "You're too good for me," he said.

"What?"

"That's what it boils down to. You think you're too good for me, and if you're honest, for my parents and even Grant."

"I don't think that. I don't think that at all."

"Maybe not on the surface, but deep down, you believe you're better than us."

She clunked the bowl on the table. "Where did you ever get that idea?"

"From everything you've ever said or done, from day one."

"Like what?"

"Like dressing Grant up in all the clothes you buy, like enlightening us with the movies and books you watch and read, like strutting around as the accomplished CD&R partner-to-be someday, throwing legalese and Latin terms at us, flaunting your knowledge all the time, never once going out without styling your hair and dolling up your face and dressing to the nines. Everything you do is elitist, Hillary, right down to the name Hillary Reagan McKenzie. You play in a different class, you know it, and I think, deep down, you resent us for it. Even Grant. And that is why, while we disagree on so much and you rub me the wrong way and our respective personalities get under each other's skin—that is ultimately why I am opposed to this marriage, because I don't think it's based on a foundation of mutual respect."

Hillary slowly licked her lips, then turned her gaze out the window. When she looked back after a minute, a tear trickled down her cheek, her eyes showing a blankness Jackson had never seen in her before.

"You're right, Jackson, I do feel elite." She swallowed. "I was born into a wonderful family, blessed with riches both material and intangible, provided every opportunity to succeed. And I took advantage of those opportunities. I worked my tail off in college, learned more than I could have imagined, earned my degree, and earned my job at CD&R. I continue to work my tail off, and I'm proud of what I do and how I do it. The reason I dress nice and try to look my best or strive to enrich myself and aspire to sophisticated methods of recreation is because I honestly believe that God would want me to do the most with what I've been given, whether we're talking about a nice physical appearance or the freedom in America to pursue my career. I don't *flaunt* my knowledge, but I don't hide from it either. What I've been given, what I've accomplished, what I've learned, and what I've experienced is all part of who I am, and I'm not going to turn my back on that. And I'm naturally going to share that with the person I love more than any in this world. Is that elite? Yes, but it's not an arrogant superiority. It's a grateful, hard-working striving after excellence."

She swallowed again as she leaned forward. "But if you think for one second that I resent Grant or look down on him—or on your family—because we come from a different social class or have different education levels or have chosen different lifestyles, then you are sadly mistaken. Because I respect everything about Grant, from his upbringing to his godly values to his career choice and passion for what he does, and most of all, for his boundless love for me. And if you can't see that . . . if you haven't seen that after all these months and years . . ."

She lifted the back of her hand to her nose and sniffed. She quietly cleared her throat and locked her eyes onto Jackson one more time. "And I do respect you, Jackson. I think you have *incredible* potential, based on the godly heritage passed down from your parents and grandparents, on your wit and creativity, and based on a resolve and allegiance that I've seen ever so briefly in the past. But you seem content never to capitalize on that potential, never to maximize or make the most of what you've been given. You have no ambition to be elite when it is within your grasp. And that is why, although I respect you, I can't respect so much of the way you live. That's why—despite the personality differences and petty disputes—there is an underlying rift between us. I don't know what to do to fix it, to bridge that gap. And although you'll never believe me, that tears me apart." She flicked her head to the side, as much to keep her composure as to get hair out of her eyes. "Because I love your brother more fiercely than anyone or anything on this earth, and it haunts me to think that my new family might not be as close as the family I've known all my life."

She looked away again.

Jackson swallowed, unable to form cohesive thoughts, let alone words.

Hillary turned back to him, her eyes welling with tears. Then she stood and carried her bowl into the kitchen.

Jackson laid back and closed his eyes. Her words bounced through his brain and he fought to dispel them—to disagree with them. He wasn't sure he could, and the difficulty of attempting to do so—along with the fatigue from his chickenpox—ultimately wore him out. He vacillated between wakefulness and sleep, abstractedly aware of noises from the kitchen. Then he fell fast asleep.

He awoke much later, the room dark. Hillary sat in the chair, her legs and feet pulled up under her. She leaned to the side, her hand and the back of the chair forming a crude pillow. It was too dark to tell, but her lack of movement indicated she was sleeping. In the chair. Keeping watch, so to speak, over him.

Jackson closed his eyes again, unable to avoid wondering if he had seriously misjudged Hillary all along.

Chapter Fifty-Nine

IN THE CENTER of a square room, maybe twenty-five by twenty-five, was a hospital bed. It was backed by an assortment of machines and equipment, and by several screens of medical data. On the near side of the bed, a pole on wheels held an IV drip, an oxygen tank, and a SpO2 monitor, out of which flowed a series of tubes. They were joined by a network of wires and electrodes from the machines on the other side of the bed, and all the tubes and electrodes were in some way affixed to the patient lying on the bed.

Hillary.

She still wore the pink tank top and black running shorts, but her shoes and socks had been removed. Padded leather restraints bound her ankles and wrists to the bed, forcing her to lay perfectly flat. Her head had been inclined slightly, her hair loose around her shoulders. Her eyes were closed, but Jackson saw her torso very gently rise and fall.

She was alive.

A single panel of lamps on a flexible arm shone down on Hillary, leaving a pall over the rest of the room. But they created enough light for Jackson to clearly see the five other people in the room. A man and a woman were seated behind a bar-like counter to the left. They wore casual clothes, not fatigues, not scrubs. A woman in aqua scrubs to match the nurse Jackson had killed moments before stood on the other side of Hillary, next to a man in a white lab coat. A third woman, also in a lab coat, was on the near side of the bed, her back to Jackson as he entered the room. But her head quickly whipped around, a blond ponytail following more slowly.

For a frozen moment, the five people stared at Jackson and he at them. Then he noticed movement to his left. He turned, the gun with him, just in time to see the woman at the counter raise a pistol. He fired first, and she never got the chance. Three bullets spat into her flesh and the counter in front of her. She dropped to the ground almost as quickly as her male companion, who scurried for cover.

The nurse behind Hillary also drew a gun, and was also a touch too slow. Jackson's aim was a little high to assure he didn't shoot Hillary by mistake, and his bullet hit right between her eyes.

The man in the lab coat jumped back, his hands up in the air. Jackson cut his eyes to the man who had dived off the counter. He now stood with his back to the wall, making no effort to reach for a gun.

A blur of movement to Jackson's right drew his attention, and he turned just as the woman in front of the bed swiped at him. He saw it coming but too late, and she made contact with his arm, just above the elbow. He thought it was a knife at first, but the sting was too small. He glanced down and saw that the woman had embedded a syringe into his arm.

He flailed with his hand, striking her in the head with his pistol and knocking her back, into and off one of the machines attached to Hillary.

Immediately, he yanked the syringe from his arm, then transferred his gun to the other hand.

"Up!" he shouted at her. He repeated it when she hesitated.

This time she stood, her hand feeling for her forehead. It came back with blood.

"Take off your coat," Jackson said. "Now."

While she did, he quickly turned the pistol on the other two in the room. "Hands on your heads."

They obeyed, unaware that he had only one bullet left in the gun.

"Tear the sleeve," he said to the woman, and she ripped the sleeve from her coat. He pointed the gun at her stomach. "Now tie it around my arm, tight." He jammed the gun into her stomach, and she met his eyes with a fiery gaze. But she quickly applied the tourniquet, pulling it very tight.

"Step back," he said when she was finished, and she obeyed. "What was that?"

"Benzodiazepine."

"A sedative?"

"That's right."

"How long till it takes effect?"

She shrugged.

"How long!" he barked.

"De-depends on how much entered your system," the man in the lab coat said. "You p-probably didn't get enough of it to f-fully render you unconscious."

442

"Good," Jackson said. "All three of you, hands on your heads. I will not hurt you if you obey, but I will not hesitate to gut you if you try anything." He took a step back. "Now, slowly come around the end of the bed. Follow me," he added when they had complied.

With a quick check to make sure it was still vacant, Jackson backed into the hallway. He motioned for the trio to follow, and they did. He then directed them into the conference room.

"Sit down," he said when he had followed them inside.

All three complied.

"What have you done to her?" Jackson asked.

"Don't answer him," the woman said.

Jackson switched the pistol back to his right hand and aimed at her arm. The bullet tore into the sleeve of a plain blue shirt, sending a splatter of blood onto her arm and face. It was a graze shot, which was fine for his purposes. He dropped the Beretta and tugged the SIG from his waist. He leaned across the table and put it to the woman's forehead.

"What have you done to her?" he asked slowly, his eyes on the man in the lab coat.

"J-just some t-t-te-tests," he answered.

"What kind of tests?"

"We t-took her v-vitals, IATs, response to s-stimuli, be-behavioral response. And w-we probed her m-memory."

"Probed?"

"We just asked her a lot of questions."

"What drugs have you given her?"

"S-sedatives an-and some sodium p-p-p-pen-pentothal."

"You're never going to get out of here," the woman growled.

"I'd be more concerned with whether you survive the next thirty seconds," Jackson said. "I've killed eight people tonight, so one more isn't going to haunt me."

"W-w-we also g-gave her s-some amphetamine and meth-eth-ylth . . . some methylphenidate to enhance her memory," the same man said.

Jackson stepped back but kept the gun on the woman. "How many people on this base?"

"About twenty-five."

"If you leave this room before I leave this base, I will shoot you," Jackson said.

"Wh-when are you l-leaving the base?"

"Now that is the question, isn't it?"

He backed out of the conference room, closed the door, and fired the first round from the SIG into the access panel. Then he dashed back into Hillary's room. He quickly checked his two shooting victims, both of whom were dead, before turning his attention to her.

"Hillary, can you hear me?" he asked. He stepped around the bed and placed a hand on her cheek. "Hill, come on, wake up."

She made no response, so he patted her cheek. She was still unresponsive.

Jackson began removing electrode patches from her arms, sternum, back, waist, and legs. He gently withdrew an oxygen tube from her nose and found that she was breathing on her own. When he slid the IV needle out of her arm, she reflexed slightly but didn't open her eyes.

Next he unfastened the restraints, rubbing her wrist and ankles, trying to get blood flowing, hoping that she wasn't too far gone. He needed a shot of adrenaline, like Tom Cruise had given Keri Russell in *M:i:III*.

He tried holding her face in his hands, calling her name again. She stirred faintly but didn't come around. It had been too long. He would have to carry her. Even if she did suddenly wake up, he doubted she would be able to walk.

Before lifting her off the bed, Jackson peeked around the corner, just in case a feisty needle-stabber had decided to try something stupid. He recoiled for a second when he saw her face at the door, but quickly realized she was unable to open it.

Jackson returned to Hillary's room, clicking the safety on the SIG and returning it to his pants. He then removed the ARX100 from the scabbard on his back, placing it on the counter for a moment.

He pulled Hillary to a sitting position, then came around the bed again. He raised her arm and leaned down, hoisting her onto his back in a fireman's carry. He shrugged her into place, her head over his right shoulder and his left arm looped between her legs. With his right hand, he pulled her left arm back, tight around his neck, so that he could clasp her wrist with his left hand. It kept his right arm and hand free.

Before picking up the rifle, he retrieved the keycard from his pocket, wedging it between fingers of his left hand. Hillary was anything but fat, but she was tall and in good shape, and already the weight was straining Jackson's shoulders. It didn't help that he'd been awake for nearly forty-eight straight hours and had been through a rigorous night. He'd heard stories of soldiers on the battlefield carrying injured comrades—who had to weigh substantially more than Hillary—for miles, and resolved to hike back to Las Vegas with her if he had to.

He exited through the first two doorways, pausing at each to set down the rifle, swipe the card, return the card to two fingers of his left hand, and pick up the rifle. The second time, it dropped from his hand, almost as if he'd had a stroke. He flexed his fingers and shook his arm, not feeling any numbness or deadening, but wondering if he was starting to suffer the effects of the benzodiazepine the woman had injected into him.

With Hillary on his back, bending down to pick up the rifle was a challenge, and he nearly dropped her on her head. Fortunately, her lack of consciousness kept her from complaining.

The nurse had not come back to life, nor was the main hall swarming with reinforcements. If the guy in the lab coat was right and there were twenty-five people on the base, Jackson had killed or captured approximately half of them. So where were the rest? Putting out a fire? Hiding? Still sleeping? Setting an ambush?

Using the same procedure, Jackson made it through the double set of doors, ignoring the pair under the red bulb. It was a mystery that could stay in his imagination. As he approached the blown-open main doors, he raised the rifle, not sure that he could fire it with one hand or what the kick would do if he tried. He spotted the van ahead and decided to use it for his getaway. It was riddled with bullets, but he hoped it still functioned. He didn't know if he could make it all the way back to Quinn's cruiser at the north end of the apron, especially not with Hangar 2 in flames and commandos running around everywhere.

Jackson picked his way across the door debris and out of the chilling hospital. He looked first right, then left. As he did, he spotted movement in the far corner and wished he'd lowered his night-vision goggles. Unable to make out any figures, he kept moving, pushing for the cover of the van. But a shout indicated he had been seen, and an instant later, a burst of bullets smacked into the van.

Then Jackson felt a stab of pain as his leg gave out.

Chapter Sixty

5:01 a.m.

JACKSON WAS FIVE feet from the rear bumper of the van and temporary safety. As he stumbled and ultimately fell, he tried to twist his body in such a way that Hillary fell behind the cover of the van and landed without hitting her head. He mostly succeeded, wrapping his arms around her limp frame and rolling over once so that the rear tire provided them with shelter.

Ignoring the pain in his leg, Jackson looked for the rifle. But he had dropped it during the fall, and it lay just out of reach. So he removed the SIG from his waistband, flipped down his goggles, and prostrated himself to look under the van.

The sight terrified him. He saw two sets of legs to the left, closing fast, almost to the van's rear bumper. To the right, at least two more rushed forward from the hangar's northeast corner, firing rounds that shattered windows. About next, somebody would hit the gas tank and they'd be through.

The closest target was the first priority, and Jackson aimed the SIG to the left, just missing the back tire in an effort to take out the feet of the duo coming at him.

He failed and knew he had only a second before they were on him. He pushed to his knees and reclined back, using his abdominal muscles to support him as he stretched backward. At the same time, he leveled his gun at the rear of the van and started squeezing the trigger. It was a risk, but he was banking on his assailants thinking he was wounded and still on the ground.

This time, his strategy worked. A man in fatigues tried to stop before coming around the corner, but couldn't put the brakes on in time. Jackson's bullets riddled his ribcage and he dropped in a heap.

Jackson dived behind the tire, extending the gun to shoot up past the bumper. The second set of legs was not in view. Jackson swiped for the rifle and sat up. He pushed to his feet, his leg protesting as he crept toward the front of the van. The shooting had stopped, and instead of raising his head to see or fire,

446

Jackson used the butt of the rifle as a club, knocking the rearview mirror loose. He wrenched it the rest of the way free, then crouched behind the tire.

There were three of them and one of him, meaning they could circle the van and come from both sides. Worse yet, if they had raided the armory, they might have grenades like him and could end the fight instantly.

Goggles down, he raised the mirror over the hood, angling it to give him some kind of view. Before he could see anything, it was shot out of his hand, and he crouched again as exploding glass rained down on him. He again lay down, reaching the rifle past the tire and unleashing a volley in the general area he where assumed his attackers were.

Return fire forced him to sit back up, again behind the tire, as bullets pinged into the concrete floor. As he turned, he saw movement behind the van again, in the form of another figure rounding the bumper. It was a woman, and she had a machine gun aimed downward, toward Hillary.

Jackson didn't have time to raise and level the gun in a firing position. But his instincts took over, and he hurled his weapon toward the assailant. She was raising her gun as Jackson's struck, and it jarred her weapon loose. She didn't drop it, but fumbled for the grip as her finger slid off the trigger.

Jackson jumped to his feet. He pushed off on his good leg and lunged toward her. He flew over a still prone Hillary and collided with the woman just as she regained control of the gun. He again knocked it loose, at the same time driving her backwards. He fell on top of her, coiling his fist to strike. But he didn't get the chance.

Before he knew what was happening, the woman raised her legs and flipped him vertically over her. He somersaulted and thunked against the concrete wall. Surprised more than hurt or dazed, he quickly stood. So did the woman, without her gun. Jackson reached for his waistband but the SIG wasn't there.

Then a boot struck him in the side of the head, a lightning fast roundhouse kick that sent him sprawling sideways. His night-vision goggles were knocked askew, only remaining on his head because of the harness. Jackson ripped them off and reached for the van's bumper to pull himself up.

He didn't make it. The woman didn't retreat to grab a weapon but advanced, striking with another kick that snapped Jackson's head to the side. He fell into the bumper, cracking his jaw before crumpling to the pavement. Only sheer determination kept him from blacking out.

The woman advanced again, and Jackson flailed his leg in a weak effort that repelled her for a moment. He quickly crawled under the van, looping around the back tire and hoping to come around to the side and get to the SIG. But she beat him there, stomping one boot down on the gun as Jackson reached for it. The other boot found his chin and lifted him into the air.

He rolled with the kick, feeling warm blood streaming down his chin. She was coming for him again, intent on finishing the fight *mano a mano*. Jackson was overmatched, and he reached for the only thing he had, a grenade. Without pulling the pin, he rolled onto his back so that he could get more arm into a throw. The woman was about to strike again when the grenade bounced off her head.

She stopped cold, staggering backwards. Jackson summoned what little strength he had remaining to get up. Before he could, the woman had already recovered and was coming his way. So he charged forward, wrapping his arms around her midsection as if he was sacking a quarterback. His momentum drove her backward. But instead of falling with her like a defensive lineman who wanted to land on a quarterback with all his girth, Jackson dug his feet in. He released his grip on the woman's midsection, instead grasping for her legs. He got one of two, jerking it up, tipping her farther backward. She fell hard, her back and her head cracking on the pavement.

Almost immediately, gunfire exploded again, the van taking another pounding. The right headlight shattered, sending plastic everywhere. Jackson heard the bullets whizzing past him and into the floor, concrete walls of the hospital, or steel walls of the hangar. He clambered forward, toward Hillary. She appeared to be coming around, either because the drugs were wearing off or because she was in a war zone. Jackson looped his right arm under her left armpit, dragging her back behind the van. At the same time, he reached for the ARX100 with his left hand, grabbing it by the barrel and sliding behind the rear wheel and bumper just as another torrent of bullets scorched the place where he and Hillary had just been.

He unsheathed a stun grenade and launched it like a Kareem skyhook over the van. More bullets riddled the van, zinging into the rear door hinges and sailing wide and into the hospital.

Then the hangar was turned a stunning white, the bang reverberating in Jackson's ears. He spun around the side of the van with the rifle. It took a second to identify a target, a man crouched in the wake of the detonation. Jackson screamed viscerally as he unloaded a dozen rounds, shredding the man where he stood.

He stepped over Hillary and switched the gun to his left hand, looking down the driver's side of the vehicle. He saw a figure running for the corner of the hangar, and chased him there with another half dozen bullets.

And then, there was silence.

The fire in Hangar 2 still crackled, and groans came from the other side of the van. But given the clamor that had just transpired, it was like a tomb. For multiple reasons.

Jackson spat a stream of blood onto the floor. Then another, wiping his chin on his sleeve. He released the magazine from the ARX100 and felt in his belts, pockets, and harnesses for the last one. He rammed it into place and swept both sides of the van again. Content that he was alone, save for Hillary and the unmoving woman he'd fought with, he finally chanced a look down at his leg.

His pant leg was soaked with blood halfway between his knee and foot. Leaning back against the van, he tugged the trouser up, fearful of what he would see.

It wasn't bad. The bullet had gone clear through, just tearing through the edge of his calf muscle. A scrape, by battlefield standards. Never mind the pain.

Jackson checked on the woman again—still immobile, then Hillary. She was groggy, her eyes heavy as she lay on her side, using an arm for a pillow.

"Hill, I need you to wake up," he said, hoping his voice and a command would stimulate her. At the same time, he hurried to the front of the van, wary lest the fourth shooter return. He yanked open the door and was relieved to find keys in the ignition. He had no idea if the van would start, much less run, given all the bullets that had been pumped into and pinged off it. But the engine came to life immediately.

Jackson hastily brushed glass off the seat, slicing his hand in the process. He told the pain to get in the back of the line and knocked a few shards from the passenger seat.

With another look around, he retreated into the structure and behind the reception desk, hoping to spot a button or switch that would open the main doors of the hangar. His eyes fell on a thin, female's sweater hanging on the back of the door. He spent thirty seconds tearing off a sleeve and tying a crude bandage over the wound on his leg. Another thirty seconds of searching for a way to open the hangar doors proved fruitless, and he resorted to Plan B.

Jackson exited the doorway, looked again for attackers, then picked up Hillary. Her eyes fluttered and opened, and her lips parted. No words came out.

"Hang in there, Hill. Hang in there."

He stepped over the fallen woman and dipped Hillary slightly as he opened the van's passenger door. He banged her knees and her feet as he did his best to place her in the seat. She was still only half with it, but managed to keep from falling out of the seat.

He closed the door and quickly gathered his weapons. In addition to the ARX100 with thirty remaining rounds, he had the SIG pistol with four bullets left and the grenade he'd beaned the woman with. It was one of three remaining. Deputy Klein's pistol was still in Quinn's cruiser at the north end of the apron, along with the shotgun. So, for that matter, were all his and Hillary's belongings and sixty-five grand in cash. At the moment, none of those things were a concern.

Jackson pulled the pin on the grenade and heaved it toward the center of the stacker doors. He circled the rear of the van, opening the driver's door again just as the grenade went off. Nearly a hundred feet away, the blast still shook Jackson and rattled the van's remaining window, on Hillary's side. It caused the hangar doors to buckle and tear, but they didn't break apart or open. On to Plan C.

Jackson accelerated slowly, turning to the right. He backed up, turned some more, and advanced until he was facing the blown-out entrance to the hospital. Looking left and right one last time, he put the gearshift into reverse. Straightening the wheel, he stomped on the gas pedal. Tires squealing, they shot backwards.

The doors of the hangar barely registered as the back end of the van tore through their grenade-splintered remains. Jackson fishtailed slightly, then had to apply the brakes so as not to ram into the B-52 parked on the apron. He skidded to a stop, dropped the gear selector into drive, and cranked the wheel hard left.

Hangar 2's roof had totally collapsed, with the doors now smoldering and burning on the apron. The south wall was completely gone, and fire still raged from the center of the hangar. The Learjet must have caught fire. The casualties of war.

Jackson debated circling left and using the runways to get away from the base, but he wasn't wild about a desert crossing. He'd made it in Quinn's cruiser, and the van had high enough clearance that it could very likely make it. But if he hit a divot, punctured a tire, or ran aground on an unseen bump, he and Hillary would be sitting ducks.

He turned west on the south road, between the control tower and the garage. The administration building was straight ahead, and Jackson saw the front door fly open and two men emerge, both carrying weapons. One was a machine gun. The other looked like a grenade launcher.

He turned hard right, cutting across the lawn, aiming for the corner of the armory, planning to clip it like a slalom pole as he turned onto Blane Road.

Bullets riddled the side of the van, plunking as they punctured the steel panels. A hiss was the only warning he had of a grenade coming their way before it crashed into the concrete wall of the armory and exploded, just after Jackson had turned north.

He mashed the accelerator again. The engine was grinding, blue smoke streaming out from under the hood. He heard bullets pelt the rear of the van, hoping none made it through, praying none struck Hillary. At the same time, he kept his eyes roving, looking for any other attackers. He was shocked at the size of the fireball that still consumed Hangar 2, its dark smoke cloud rimmed with ash and thus visible against the night sky.

With a loud pop, the van began to skid. Jackson fought for control, but he was dragging a flat tire that tried to pull him right. He overcompensated and they veered off the left side of road. He cranked the wheel back to the right in a desperate attempt to avoid crashing into A Barracks. He avoided a direct hit, but not the corner of the two-story building. The corner of the van sheered and the engine block collided with the barracks, bringing their getaway to an abrupt halt.

Jackson never saw the actual collision. It happened too fast, and the airbag inflated into his face, blocking his view. Not wearing his seatbelt, he was thrown forward with enough velocity that the airbag snapped his head back. The next thing he knew, the van lifted into the air, its front end thrust into the side of the building. A shockwave and a blast of heat rushed past Jackson at the same time that a deafening whoomp thundered through his ears.

Before it all could process, his head banged against the doorframe, and his world began to dim.

His last thoughts were of Hillary and of the people attacking them. If the van didn't blow up, they would surely be on them in seconds.

Then Jackson blacked out.

Chapter Sixty-One

5:08 a.m.

JACKSON AWOKE WITH surprising lucidity. Their tire had been shot. They had crashed. The van hadn't exploded. Yet. But the shooters were likely closing in.

He fought the airbag for a second. When he got it out of his face, he turned to Hillary. She was draped over hers, blood dripping from her nose and down the side of the airbag. Her eyes were glazed.

"Hill!" Jackson said, reaching for her head. "Hillary—"

He stopped when he saw movement out her cracked window. A Humvee stopped not fifty feet away and several men in fatigues got out.

"Hillary!" he screamed. "We have to go!"

She was still unresponsive, so he pulled her from behind her airbag. His door was jammed, and he had to turn to kick it open. He stuck his head out and pulled it back quickly as a hail of gunfire assaulted the exposed door.

With Hillary half on top of him, he reached for his belt, struggling to extricate one of his last two grenades. He pulled it free as Hillary's window exploded under a torrent of bullets. Shards of glass flew everywhere, and he squinted against the onslaught. He pulled the pin on the grenade as he leaned back. Without looking, he extended his arm and half threw, half rolled the grenade backwards, toward the road. The bullets kept coming, then stopped suddenly.

Seconds later, another concussion shook the ground. Gritting his teeth, Jackson put his arms under Hillary's shoulders and pulled with all his might, using his feet to push off the side of her seat. Banging heads and arms and shoulders and hips and knees on the dash, steering wheel, doorframe, and half-closed door, and fighting two airbags intent on tangling any stray body parts, he dragged her and himself out of the van. They fell to the ground in a heap, and just that quickly, Jackson was on his feet.

He drew the rifle and blindly fired a quick spray of bullets in the general direction of the attackers, even though he saw no one. He then reached for

Hillary. To his surprise, she had already begun to stand, showing the most awareness since he'd rescued her. He looped an arm under hers and carried/drug her toward the side door of the barracks. The door was mostly glass inside an aluminum frame, the kind common on college dorms and businesses. And it was locked.

Jackson leaned Hillary against the wall and withdrew his final stun grenade. He pulled the pin and heaved it toward the rear of the van. Gunfire had continued from the far side of the van, steady machine gun rounds that had all but shredded it. His grenade had quieted the pursuit from behind, but it wouldn't be long.

Using the butt of the ARX100, Jackson smashed the glass in the door, and then swept the barrel of the gun around the edges to get rid of any remaining pieces. Hillary was still barefoot. Not in the mood for a *Die Hard* reenactment, Jackson bent down and lifted her onto his shoulder. He carried her through the opening and into an immediate stairwell. Staggering under her weight, he reached the second floor just as the van exploded.

The ball of fire lit the sky and shattered the window at the end of the second-floor hallway. Jackson turned the corner and pushed down the hallway, Hillary still over his shoulder. When he was sure they were clear of shattered glass and imminent fire danger, he set her down.

They were in a long, unlit hallway. On either side, dorm rooms—some with open doors, some without doors—still housed bunk beds and rudimentary furniture. There were no sheets on the beds, no pillows, no objects on the desks, posters on the walls, or curtains over the windows. The barracks was abandoned.

Going to the second floor had been Jackson's off-the-cuff plan to avoid immediate attack, but it now limited their means of escape. With Jackson supporting her, Hillary managed to walk beside him, albeit slowly, until they reached a two-story common area in the middle of the barracks. The top story was nothing more than a hallway with railings on both sides and a curving staircase that led to a first-floor lounge. Some old furniture was stacked against one wall, but the lounge was otherwise empty. Full panels of glass windows and doors opened onto either side.

"Come on, we have to keep going," Jackson said.

When they reached the north end of the dorm, they found it a duplicate of the south end, with a staircase leading down to an exit. Jackson stopped, doing some quick math in his head. The guard he'd shot, the sentry he'd left in Hangar 3, the first two attackers in Hangar 1, the man he'd taken down in Hangar 2 before he'd blown it sky high, two more inside Hangar 1, the guy coming out the blown-open doors of the hospital, the nurse, five—two of which were dead—who'd been in the room with Hillary, three more as he'd exited with her, and anyone taken out by his last grenade or the van explosion. By his count, that meant seventeen dead or accounted for, of approximately twenty-five. He had twenty-some rounds left in the ARX100, four in the SIG. One grenade. It wasn't a great supply with which to make a stand. But the only other option was to make a break for Quinn's cruiser on the other side of the complex.

He calculated, based on the aggressiveness of recent attacks, that they would come for him and Hillary. And he liked his odds better in an environment he could control than making a run across the base. So he backed Hillary up into one of the rooms on the west side of the building. It might as well have been a college dorm room, with a pair of bunk beds, two desks stacked side by side, and a closet on the near wall.

"Get in the closet," he said.

"What?"

"Wait for me here."

"Jack."

"I'll be right back."

He made eye contact and gave a reassuring nod as he exited the room. He hurried south, to the last two rooms before the common area. The one on the left was empty, but he found a bunk bed in the second and dragged it out into the hallway. It was heavy, and his muscles were fatigued, but he got it positioned so that it blocked the entire hallway. Then he propped the mattress on its side, between the upper and lower bunks. It blocked line of sight, and the bed would have to be moved if anyone was going to get through.

He removed the last grenade from his belt and knelt down. He set the grenade on the floor and lifted the bed, then placed the grenade under the corner post so that the bedpost depressed the lever. It took a little balancing work, but he succeeded in keeping the bed balanced and the grenade deactivated.

He lifted the bed again, pulled out the grenade, and took a deep breath. Then he pulled the pin on the grenade and repeated the procedure, balancing the bed on the grenade.

With the lever depressed, he carefully stood and backed down the hallway. No explosion.

Satisfied that no one was coming at them from the south, he returned to the room and closet where he'd left Hillary. She was slouched in the closet, again catatonic. There was no telling what they had done to her, or how long it would take to reverse the effects. If they were even completely reversible.

To his relief, she stirred when he reached for her hand.

"Can you stand?" he asked.

She nodded, then faltered, then stood.

Jackson stepped back and looked to see if he had missed any obvious injuries. Aside from a small trickle of blood from her nose and an excess of scrapes and scratches, she appeared unscathed. He nodded reassuringly. "We're going to get out of this."

"You're bleeding," she said, her voice soft and croaky.

He took off the grenade belt and unfastened his Kevlar vest.

"Are you okay?" she asked.

"Never better."

"What are you doing?"

"There are more of them," he said. "We're going to make our stand here."

"Can . . . Can I have a gun?"

"Do you know how to shoot?"

"Grant showed me."

He strapped the vest around her midsection. Then he handed her the SIG. "Four bullets left. Safety's on," he said, clicking it to make it so.

"Where should I go?"

"In the closet. Shoot the next person you see unless I tell you it's me."

"Like being back at Gardiners' cabin."

He smiled because her accurate memory was, to him, a good sign. Then he ushered her back into the closet and closed the door. He shoved one of the desks to the north side of the dorm room door and prostrated himself behind it, peeking down the barrel of the ARX100 rifle, past the corner of the desk, and toward the stairway at the end of the hall. He tipped the barrel up slightly and waited, letting his eyes grow accustomed to the shapes in the darkness.

If the twenty-five told him by the man in the lab coat was an accurate count, it left as many as eight potential attackers. More if some of those he had injured and locked up had been set free to fight. The bed and grenade booby-trap might take out one or two, and he'd have the drop on anyone coming up the stairs. But unless they all came at once and he mowed them down like first-level video game baddies, the remaining attackers had him trapped. He and Hillary would have to come out sooner or later. Not to mention the building was potentially on fire.

Jackson forced himself to breathe deeply and slowly, steadying his nerves. Time was imperceptible, and everything paled but Jackson's singular focus on the door to the stairway. His eyes played tricks with him, creating movements and new shadows that weren't there. He blinked them away, willing his brain to function at a high level a little while longer.

Then the walls shook and shrapnel bounced down the hallway, each piece reflecting the orange and yellow hues of a sudden fire. Jackson ignored it all, his focus singularly on the doorway. It flung open a moment later, a pair of legs— then another—charging through.

Jackson sighted in on the first body, a man who swept his gun back and forth down the hall. He was a second from spotting Jackson when he opened fire with the ARX100.

He saw the first few bullets eviscerate the man, and pivoted the gun left. The second attacker had tried to duck back into a bedroom for safety, but Jackson panned with him and took him down.

Immediately, he was on his feet. Through the scope of the weapon, he looked down at the bleeding man, his hands clutched to his stomach, then quickly back toward the booby-trapped bed, now a fire raging in the hallway. Keeping close to the wall, he moved far enough south to see into the room where the second man had gone. He was already dead.

Jackson retreated to the first victim, his breaths coming in short, bubbly gasps. "How many more?"

"Wh-Who . . ."

"How many more are there?"

The eyes closed, and Jackson poked his head with the rifle. "How many?"

"I-I don't know."

"How many were with you?"

"Two . . ." His eyes closed again, but opened voluntarily. "Two from the north, two from the south."

That wasn't enough.

"Two more killed by the grenade."

It was closer.

Jackson picked the machine gun from the ground and lifted a pistol from the man's holster. It slid into his hip holster. The machine gun—an M4 carbine rifle—fit into his shoulder scabbard. He looked back down at the man, his eyes now closed, his breathing hardly discernable.

To his right, the fire was spreading rapidly, eating up the hallway walls. Jackson didn't like the idea of moving Hillary until he knew what they might be facing in the stairwell or outside the barracks, but he couldn't wait much longer. He retreated to the closet, announced himself, and pulled the door open.

"What happened?"

"Come on, we have to move."

"Jackson?"

"Stay behind me and do what I say. If you hear a shot, get to the ground."

She nodded.

"And don't look down."

They started out, her eyes wide each time Jackson checked. They'd been through this once before, on a much smaller scale, stranded in an isolated mountain lodge, cut off from power and help, hunted by professional killers. They'd had Grant then, and numbers to their advantage. And Hillary had kept her poise throughout. Now, hopped up on a variety of drugs, possibly in shock, still emerging from the haze, she kept up gamely.

Jackson paused at the top of the stairwell, at the landing halfway down, and again at the bottom. The first-floor hallway was eerily dark and silent, the only sound the snap and pop and dull moan of the fire above. Jackson quickly swept the first room across the hall and ushered Hillary into it.

"Wait here. Shoot if it's not me."

"Where are you going?"

"Surveying."

He left the room and pushed open the exterior door. That movement didn't draw fire, so he stepped through the doorway, leaving a wood block left by the previous tenant as a prop to keep it from closing and locking.

Jackson crept to the corner unassailed and spent a couple of minutes studying the compound. Hangar 2 was still an inferno, flames and sparks towering into the sky. The smoke was thick and black, reminiscent of the Branch Davidian compound fire Jackson remembered seeing on TV as a child. More flames licked the side of A Barracks, having engulfed the corner. More yet poured out of the roof and several second-story windows.

He spotted a Humvee parked near the far end of the barracks, but otherwise no movement, no signs of life. Had he killed or captured everyone?

He briefly feared for the safety of anyone in Hangar 1, especially the two "patients" he had observed before finding Hillary, as Hangar 2's fire was in danger of jumping the road and taking down Hangar 1. But he couldn't risk Hillary's safety for theirs.

He turned to his left, facing B Barracks, fifty yards away across a field of dead, patchy grass. To the east, the gymnasium would shield him from view of anyone in the vicinity of Hangars 2 and 3. Figuring there was no time like the present, Jackson took off on a dead run for the door to the barracks. He arrived unscathed, looked around, and then broke the glass with his gun. It crinkled down quietly, the noise drowned out by the rampant fires. He stepped through the door and quickly surveyed the building. It was identical to A Barracks.

Jackson tore the mattress off a bunk in an abandoned bedroom and placed it just inside the door, covering most of the glass. He then stepped back outside and jogged back toward A Barracks.

He was just over halfway there when a shot rang out and a bullet bit into the dirt beside him. He stopped instinctively and looked up to see a man approaching from the back corner of the barracks, his machine gun aimed at Jackson's now unprotected chest.

Chapter Sixty-Two

5:30 a.m.

JACKSON'S FIRST THOUGHT was that he shouldn't have stopped, that he should have kept running. But he saw now that he wouldn't have stood a chance. The Hangar 2 fire had grown in intensity, providing just enough light to reveal a sneer on the man's face as he took several steps closer. "Drop the gun," he said, and Jackson let the ARX100 fall from his side.

The man took two more steps. "Where's the girl?"

"In there," Jackson said, nodding backwards.

Suddenly the butt of the machine gun swung up and cracked Jackson in the chin. He bit his tongue as he fell backwards to the ground. When he looked up, it was at the barrel of the gun.

"I will hunt her down and gut her in front of you if you don't tell me," the man snarled.

"Is that what your bosses want?"

"My bosses are dead!"

"Then you're not getting paid."

The man stared at Jackson.

"I have sixty-five grand in my car, over on the runway. Take it and go."

"You expect me to believe that?"

"I'll go with you, and if it's not there—"

Another shot sounded and the man staggered to his side. The barrel of his gun swung away from Jackson, and he lashed out and kicked it from the man's grasp. He ripped the pistol he'd taken off the man in the barracks hallway from the holster, and in a smooth movement, released the safety and emptied the magazine into the man. He collapsed in a bloody heap.

Jackson scrambled to his feet and looked for the second shooter. He spotted her standing in the doorway of A Barracks, a SIG in her hand, glimpses of a pink tank top peeking out beneath a Kevlar vest.

459

Breathing again, Jackson crossed the yard and tentatively approached Hillary. She had lowered the gun to her waist, and he reached out a hand to take it from her. She let it go without a fight and sagged back against the door.

"We need to keep going," he said. "There could be more."

She swallowed hard and nodded.

"Can you run?"

"I don't know. I think so."

"Okay. Wait until I get there. When I signal, come running. No matter what, you don't stop until you get to the door."

She nodded.

"Find whatever reserve you need to and scoot."

She nodded again.

Much more wary, Jackson crossed the yard again, doubting any shooters had come from the north of B Barracks. He took a position just beside the door and signaled for Hillary.

The first few steps weren't graceful, but adrenaline and natural ability took over and she dashed across the lawn. Jackson kept watch through the rifle scope, ready to shoot anything besides Hillary that moved. But nothing did, and twenty seconds later, he followed her inside.

She stood at the end of the mattress, breathing heavily. She was bent over, her hands on her knees, her stomach convulsing under the Kevlar vest.

Jackson put a hand on her back. "You're doing great. We are going to get out of here."

She lifted her head and nodded. For all his complaints about her, he couldn't deny that Hillary was a fighter.

His killed/captured count now stood at twenty-four, adding the four in A Barracks, the two killed by the grenade and van explosion, and the one just gutted in the courtyard. Maybe twenty-three if one had survived the booby-trap in the hallway. There could still be more. But he and Hillary were running out of buildings to hide in. One of them had to make a break for the cruiser.

Carefully, he led her through B Barracks, all the way to the north exit. While she rested in one of the bedrooms, he dragged another bunk into the hallway, figuring it would at least slow down anyone who had followed them. Then he told Hillary his plan.

"I'm going to get the car."

"What car?"

"Quinn's cruiser."

"You have Quinn's cruiser. Where is he?"

"A long story. I'm going to have to circle around the base, so it will take me a little while. Just hang tight. In a few minutes, this will all be over."

She nodded.

"Grant always was a good teacher," he said as he handed the SIG back to her.

Like a pro, she checked the safety.

"I'll be right back," he said, ducking out of the building. The first faint light of dawn was beginning to glow on the eastern horizon, giving distinction to the distant mountains and the billowing black smoke. Just traces of blue, dawn was a welcome sight after an interminable night. But Jackson reminded himself, it wasn't over yet. Not until he and Hillary were off the base, clear of Kingman, and she was safe and sound in a real hospital under qualified supervision.

And he was likely in prison for life.

He peeked around the corner, looking south, toward all the chaos. He saw nothing, and struck out across the intersection of Blane Road and the north road, headed for the corner of Hangar 5 and ultimately the runway. He had just started when he heard a loud, repeating noise. At first he couldn't place it, but he soon realized it was a helicopter.

Jackson was positive there hadn't been any functioning choppers on the apron or in any of the hangars. As he stopped and searched the sky, he saw a white searchlight probing the base and heard the distinctive thup-thup-thup-thup of a helicopter's rotors beating the air. He took a few steps back toward the barracks, but it was too late. The spotlight had found him. The chopper drew closer, and an amplified voice boomed, "Don't move."

Jackson slowly raised his hands, watching as the large aircraft descended toward an open patch of dead grass north of B Barracks and the road. As the chopper swung around, he saw a star emblazoned on its side and the words "United States Army" scrawled beneath it. Even in the darkness, he recognized it as a Sikorsky Black Hawk, a craft popular with multiple governments, including that of the United States.

The chopper touched down, its giant blades whirring incessantly. The wind created by the rotors buffeted him and nearly knocked him off balance, at the same time stirring up dust and sand that stung his eyes.

Two soldiers in full battle gear emerged from the craft, weapons brandished. He immediately spotted flags on their shoulders and insignia on their arms. These were legit G.I.s, and Jackson wanted to drape himself in the flag.

"Sir, drop your weapon!" one of them shouted.

Jackson quickly complied, dropping his rifle and pulling the M4 from the scabbard on his back. He kept his hands up.

"Hillary McKenzie?"

"Inside," Jackson said.

"Who are you?"

"Jackson Douglas. I'm with her."

"Are you all right?"

"I'll live."

The man nodded. "Sergeant John Ravich, United States Army. We're here to rescue you."

Jackson stopped just short of singing "God Bless America."

"She's got a gun," he said to the other man, who had taken a step toward the barracks door. "I told her to shoot anyone that wasn't me."

The man stopped and looked at Ravich, who in turned nodded at Jackson. "Lead us in," he said, then nodded at two other soldiers who had disembarked and kept a vigil on either end of the chopper.

Jackson led them inside. "Hill, it's me. The cavalry's here."

She emerged from the closet, her eyes wide as she spotted the two soldiers.

"I'm going to have to ask you to relinquish your weapon, ma'am," Ravich said.

Hillary nodded and handed Ravich the SIG.

"This way, please," he said.

This time Ravich led the way, back out of the barracks and toward the chopper. "Specialist, take Miss McKenzie to the chopper."

The other soldier nodded. "Aye, Sergeant." He took Hillary by the arm and escorted her to the open door of the helicopter.

Ravich cleared his throat. "I'm sorry, sir," he said, "but we only have room for one passenger."

Jackson frowned.

"We came expecting a firefight," Ravich said, looking around. "It looks like we missed it."

"Uh, yes, sir."

"I've got orders to guard Miss McKenzie with every one of my men," Ravich said. "But as soon as we're airborne, I'll radio for another helo to come and pick you up. Should be less than half an hour."

"I can take my car," Jackson said. "It's parked over on the runway. I'll follow you on land."

Ravich nodded. "That's fine."

Hillary looked back as she climbed aboard, her blond hair swirling around her head.

"Where are you taking her?" Jackson asked.

"My orders are to bring her to North Vista Hospital in Las Vegas for evaluation," Ravich said.

"I'll be there as soon as possible," Jackson said. He extended a hand. "Thank you, Sergeant Ravich."

Ravich quickly clasped his hand. "Just doing my job." He turned and retreated to the chopper. Jackson stepped back and waved at Hillary as the other two soldiers followed Ravich inside and slammed the door shut.

Jackson retreated a few more steps as the engine whined with renewed intensity. He ducked as the Black Hawk lifted off, creating a cloud of dust and debris. It slowly ascended, and Jackson walked out to the place where it had been, craning his neck to watch its flight. The chopper drifted southwest, the pilot eventually turning the nose in that direction. Vegas was maybe fifty miles away. They would be there in a matter of minutes. Jackson would need an hour and a half via roads.

One more time, he swept his eyes over the compound, now bathed in a predawn light. He wasn't exactly sure why they couldn't cram an extra man in the chopper or why Ravich's orders didn't allow for a trained solder to stay behind while Jackson accompanied Hillary to the hospital, but at the moment he didn't really care. She was with the United States Army, on her way to safety.

Jackson took a deep breath and genuinely exhaled for the first time in hours. He cast one more look toward the sky, and frowned. The Black Hawk had banked slightly, turning north of west. And it had stopped ascending.

He watched for another moment as it continued to bank to its right, turning farther north, then east, until the nose of the Black Hawk was facing him.

Reality dawned on Jackson in slow motion, just before the twin guns on the side of the helicopter opened fire.

Chapter Sixty-Three

JACKSON LEAPED FOR the cover of the barracks, sprawling headfirst just before a barrage of high-caliber bullets splintered the corner of the building and gouged into the pavement. He crawled and scrambled to his feet, running again before he was upright.

He was a hundred yards—a football field—from the entrance to either the gym or the burning A Barracks. Either way, the chopper would be on him long before he reached safety.

The chopper. Adorned with U.S. Army markings. And it was firing on him, a U.S. citizen. Had it really come to this? Was the U.S. military actually attacking one of its own, and on American soil? Were they so committed to Silver Dawn-turned-Golden Dawn and the operations at Blane that they would take such drastic measures? Did they see him as a domestic terrorist? Was it because he had launched an attack on an Air Force base? Were they simply following orders from, say, General Reynolds? Was he just following orders from someone even higher?

The questions pounded in his head as he sprinted due south. The Black Hawk's guns had gone silent, but the steady throb of its four blades sounded like war drums announcing impending terror. Jackson reached the southeast corner of the barracks. He knew his one advantage was that he could make sharper, quicker turns than a helicopter, but only if he had a place to hide. Zigging and zagging in an open field would not end well.

Still at full sprint, Jackson angled across the courtyard between the barracks, digging for the northwest corner of A Barracks. It was engulfed in flames, thick black and gray smoke billowing upward in a windless environment. That changed as the Black Hawk approached and the rotors stirred up the smoke. But it also worked to Jackson's advantage, shielding him from view. A few quick bursts from the Black Hawk's guns chased him around the corner, but then he was out of sight.

The smoke also kept the chopper from getting too close. As Jackson ran, he heard it pulling back, circling around to the west side, where it could line him up and open fire. His legs and lungs burning after a hundred-plus-yard dash—and not to mention with the smoke fumes he couldn't help inhaling—he forced himself on.

The thup-thup-thup-thup-thup-thup of the Black Hawk grew louder, so loud and so close that it almost sounded like slow motion. Jackson reached the corner and turned back east, his vision temporarily obscured by the fire that still ate the barracks.

Where to go?

The armory was solid concrete construction, and would provide him with weapons. But he couldn't fight back. Hillary was onboard. And there was no way he could outrun the Black Hawk, even if he somehow made it to Quinn's cruiser. He either had to make them think he was dead or hope they gave up the pursuit.

The guns opened fire again, tearing up the pavement and taking huge divots out of the dead grass beside it. Jackson veered around the remains of the van and hurdled a dead, mutilated body in the street. Then he banked sharply to his left, again using the burning barracks and its smoke for cover. Once again, the fire from the Black Hawk was wild and frivolous, just missing him.

Directly ahead was the mess, and behind it, the infirmary and the rec center. Jackson saw no doors on the west side of the rectangular, one-story mess hall, but knew he didn't have time to scout. He sized up one of the tall windows built into the side wall. He hurtled himself toward it, twisting in mid-air and raising his arms up to the sides of his head.

He slammed against the window, and it shuddered like hockey glass before cracking and giving way. Tiny slivers of glass flew everywhere, tearing at his arms, back, torso, buttocks, and legs. His blue jeans protected his lower body, but his back and arms, clad only in a T-shirt, bore the brunt of the crash.

He landed on a linoleum floor, cracking his elbow on a bench as he sprawled backwards. The firelight shone through the windows to reveal a standard dining hall, with rows of fold-up tables and benches extending from the east and west walls. He was in the center of the room, stunned but cognizant. Against every impulse his body could give him, he staggered to his feet. And not a moment too soon. The dining hall suddenly brightened as the Black Hawk's searchlight found the broken window. A second later, the guns unleashed another torrent.

Jackson was already running, screaming, waiting for a machine gun round to find its target and send him into eternity. Or, more likely, leave him bleeding out on the glass-littered floor.

Straight ahead, he spied the double swinging doors that led to the kitchen. They seemed forever away, his feet on a treadmill as windows exploded, tables were shredded, and the heavy guns kept up their incessant clamor. With a visceral yell, he dived into the door, crashing into a restaurant-style kitchen.

His head throbbed. His lungs begged for air. Each cut and scrape suddenly screamed in pain. But his survival instinct was stronger, and Jackson again stood. The kitchen was stainless steel, with a prep counter in front of him. Ovens, grills, deep fryers, refrigerators, freezers, and more prep and storage space lined the walls. The room was windowless, save for a few transparent glass blocks high in the north wall. It was safe, sort of, but only for a while. Sooner or later, a bullet would pierce a gas line and the entire building would explode.

Then Jackson had an idea. There were two doors leading out of the kitchen, one to the north and one to the east. With bullets still pummeling the dining hall, Jackson quickly searched the kitchen. He found what he wanted in the form of a butane lighter and some dry towels.

Hoping that he knew enough about chemistry and physics and laws of thermodynamics, he cranked the knobs on a double oven, turning it to the max setting. He opened both doors and began throwing towels inside. He left out one, which he ignited with the lighter. He chucked it into the oven and ran, not knowing how long his fuse would take.

Slowing to grab a fire extinguisher from beside the door, he kicked the exit open and stormed through. Back outside, he dashed for the rec center some fifty feet ahead. Its southwest and northwest corners were concaved, making way for a pair of glass doors. He swung the fire extinguisher behind him, then brought it forward into the glass. It shattered into a million pieces and Jackson jumped through the opening, gouging his arm on a shard stuck in the door frame in the process.

He never felt the pain because an instant later, the mess kitchen exploded. The concussion knocked Jackson head over heels. He had the presence of mind to crawl behind a dilapidated sofa before an army of burning debris assailed the west wall of the rec center.

He chanced a look over the sofa and saw a huge ball of fire racing skyward. For a moment, he feared he had taken out the Black Hawk and thus Hillary. But the steady beat of its rotors soon won out over the din of the new inferno.

He listened for several minutes, the chopper circling, searching the wreckage for any signs of him. Had it turned and opened fire on the rec center, he would have been cut to pieces in seconds. But it never happened, and then the thrashing of the rotors began to fade.

When it had completely died, Jackson stood, his entire body on fire from one injury or another. He staggered to the blown-out doorway and looked skyward. He saw no spotlight, heard no beating rotors. He stepped out of the building, the heat from the mess fire blistering his face and arms. He took a few steps to the south, and then spotted the Black Hawk, bearing west.

The sky had lightened enough that it stood out against the glow of dawn, like a dark wraith as it beat a steady course over the mountains.

It had worked. They had given up or assumed him dead.

But his joy was short-lived. Hillary was gone again.

He dropped to one knee, then forced himself to stand. He had not just attacked a military base, blown up a hangar, shot and killed over a dozen people, been beaten and blown up and nearly killed multiple times, just to let her go. Somehow, he would find a way to get her.

He had no idea who the men on the chopper really were. Something about it bugged him, aside from the fact that a United States Army aircraft had opened fire on a U.S. citizen. But he couldn't place it. Maybe it wasn't the chopper. Maybe it was something about Ravich or one of the other men. Maybe it was the entire episode. But his brain had turned to oatmeal, and nothing was processing.

He walked north, angling west toward Blane Road so he could retrieve the ARX100 and the M4 he'd dropped on Ravich's orders. He had a feeling he would still need them.

He paused, remembering that there were still hostiles on the base. At least three inside Hangar 1, which so far, had not succumbed to the flames. Another, possibly, in Hangar 3. The man he'd taken out in Hangar 2 and dragged outside had either been rescued or burned.

There were also two men in the hospital, in the rooms down the secondary hallway. Who knew what condition they were in, now with no one to look after them. That might be good, might be bad. He paused again, considering going back for them. But what could he do? Wheel them outside? Take them with him? He determined that Hillary was his primary and only priority. As soon as he was able, he would send someone back to the base for whoever was left.

As far as Hillary was concerned, it was possible she was actually being taken to the hospital as Ravich said. It depended who he was taking orders from, what they wanted, who they thought Jackson was. At the very least, Jackson saw no further reason to stay at the base.

He reached the intersection of Blane Road and the northernmost east-west road and picked up the guns. He paused again as a distant sound reached his ears. He scanned the sky, fearing the Black Hawk was returning. But this wasn't a pulsing sound. It was a steady drone.

Spinning in circles, he saw a glint of silver in the southern sky, low over the mountains. Then a shape took form. It was an airplane, the roar of its jet engines growing rapidly. Jackson stood transfixed. It was a fighter jet. Landing at Blane?

No. It was coming too fast for a landing, and was still too high as it neared the base. The stress of the night had taken a toll, and Jackson's brain was again slow to process what was happening. Reality crystalized for him when Hangar 1, the remnants of Hangar 2, and Hangar 3 suddenly exploded in gigantic balls of fire.

Chapter Sixty-Four

THE SHOCKWAVE KNOCKED Jackson off his feet.

The jet screamed low over the base and was already fading in the northern sky by the time the deafening roar of its engines concussed the desert floor.

Jackson slowly stood on wobbly legs. He couldn't believe his eyes.

Half of the base—the hangars, the rec center where he'd just taken shelter, half of the gym, and most of the abandoned aircraft on the apron—was gone. In its wake, a crater of flaming debris.

Summoning his last reserves of adrenaline, Jackson took off running, straight across the desert sand toward the runway where the cruiser was parked. Someone was wiping the base off the face of the earth, and he doubted they would stop with one bombing run.

Who?

He couldn't believe the U.S. military was flying sorties on its own soil, no matter what covert, Manhattanesque projects were being conducted. It happened in the movies, but never real life. Or was his viewpoint on the military—based on what he had been taught, based on what he had seen through his father's service—no longer a reality?

Maybe it wasn't the U.S. He hadn't seen the plane well enough to identify it. But the belief that a Russian MiG or a Chinese fighter was responsible was just as far-fetched.

Ultimately, it didn't matter. Someone was bombing the base. The who and why of it could wait until Jackson was safe.

His body was out of gas, but he forced himself to put one leg in front of the other, pounding the sand in a steady rhythm until he reached the concrete of the runway. He had no idea how fast the jet had been flying, other than fast. And he had no idea how long it took a jet at such speed to turn around and make a return run. He had no intention of finding out.

Quinn's Charger was right where he'd left it, a few hundred yards north of Hangar 5. Jackson got behind the wheel and turned the ignition. Casting one final look at the burning destruction, he floored the accelerator. His eyes perceived the carnage, but his mind refused to accept it. This just couldn't be.

Jackson hit 100 on the speedometer, keeping his headlights off so as not to give anyone a potential target. There was enough light from the coming dawn to illuminate the end of the runway. Jackson decelerated and swerved into the desert, praying he would make it across a second time. Twice he nearly bottomed out, but his speed carried him through. The tires gripped solid pavement, and he straightened his course and mashed the accelerator again.

He shot through the open guard station gate, where a few hours earlier, he had taken his first life of the evening. Oh how things had changed.

The jet appeared in the northern sky, approaching incredibly fast. Seconds later, the roar penetrated the Charger's interior as the fighter swooped low overhead. Jackson braced himself, but still jumped when the boom shook the valley. He glanced in the rearview mirror and saw the western half of the base incinerated.

He stomped the pedal even farther, coaxing every ounce of speed from the Charger. If the jet came back for him, he intended to be as far away from the base as possible.

As he reached State Route 323, the sun peeked over the mountains, and with it, despair. Jackson had tortured a sheriff into revealing Hillary's location. He had found her, managing to invade a non-decommissioned decommissioned Air Force Base. He had killed everyone in his path and rescued her, only to have her swooped away by the United States Army. Or a very good facsimile. And now, she was farther gone than ever. All he knew was that they had taken her west.

West. Not south or southwest, but due west. Why weren't they taking her in a straight line? Perhaps because they weren't headed to the North Vista Hospital?

The questions filled his mind. Why had they taken Hillary in the first place? Why hadn't they just shot Jackson right away? Why hadn't they confirmed that he was dead? Why hadn't he been more careful, instead of trusting the helicopter occupants so willingly? And what, as he pictured all the destruction behind him, justified all this? It reminded him of the oil well fires he had seen on TV, when Saddam's troops had practiced scorched earth as they retreated from Kuwait in 1991. Only then, the U.S. military had been the good guys.

And perhaps they still were. Something brought an image of the Black Hawk to the forefront of his mind again. What was it about the chopper that bugged him so?

As he made the turn south toward Kingman, strategy surged to the forefront of his brain. He had no idea what had become of Quinn and his deputies. For that matter, he had no assurance that an F-16 wasn't locking in on Kingman, prepared to wipe the town from the map. Code Black for the twenty-first century.

He thought about stopping to use a phone, but he didn't know who he would call or what he would ask. He determined to keep going, out of the valley, back toward civilization. Maybe Ravich had spoken the truth and the Black Hawk was really going to North Vista Hospital, just taking a less direct route, like an airplane that took off in one direction before banking another. But airplanes did that because of runways; helicopters could take off any direction. Or maybe it was because the jet had been incoming from the south. Maybe that's why the Black Hawk had peeled off so quickly, getting away from the bombing that was coming.

Jackson slowed to fifty as he blew through Kingman. Just after sunrise, the town appeared dead. How apropos.

Out of nowhere, a sheriff's car appeared on his tail. He was almost out of town, passing the motel, and he surmised it had turned onto Main from 2nd Street. He kept driving, increasing his speed, at the same time verifying that the rifles were on the seat beside him.

The radio crackled. "Sheriff, that you?"

Jackson thought about trying to imitate Quinn's voice, but passed. He looked in the rearview mirror as the radio crackled again.

"Sheriff, it's Tom. You there?"

Jackson accelerated and the cruiser behind him did as well. The lights began to flash and the shrill shriek of sirens was next.

He debated trying to outrun the chase car, but it was a modern Dodge Charger like his, meaning he'd have no mechanical advantage. And the last thing he needed was Deputy McGregor having time to call in the state police. So he signaled for the shoulder as he took his foot off the gas. He braked to a stop a little more than a mile south of town. The other cruiser parked a dozen yards behind him.

Deftly, Jackson reached for the ARX100. Clicking off the safety, he rested it on his lap. With his left hand, he unlatched the door without opening it. He tried to still his breathing, watching as a deputy exited the cruiser. His gun was not drawn, but his hand was on his holster as he carefully advanced.

Desperate not to take any more lives, Jackson elevated the rifle slightly, keeping his eye on the mirror. When the deputy entered his blind spot, Jackson shoved the door open with his left hand, at the same time bringing the rifle up with his right. He leaned out of the vehicle and took aim at the deputy, before he could draw his weapon.

"Don't move," Jackson said, feeling for the pavement with his foot.

McGregor froze, his hand just off the handle of his gun.

"Slowly, hands up."

They inched toward his head. "Where are Quinn and the others?" he asked.

"Secure. Take a few steps back."

McGregor obeyed.

Jackson circled around behind him, taking a glance up and down the highway in the process. They were alone. Now behind the deputy, he reached with his left hand for McGregor's gun. Just as he touched it, McGregor spun back, lowering his hand in a chop that knocked the rifle from Jackson's hand. At the same time, the deputy dropped his left hand and swung it toward Jackson. He drilled him in the jaw, knocking him back into the side of the cruiser and all the way to the ground.

Just that quickly, McGregor reached for his holster. But as he had recoiled from the deputy's attack, Jackson had succeeded in prying the gun loose, and it had fallen to the ground in their struggle. McGregor bent to retrieve it, and Jackson scrambled forward, driving into the deputy's shins just before he could pick up the pistol. McGregor tumbled backwards, Jackson entangled with him.

Jackson attempted to get up, to step back and grab one of the guns. But before he got the chance, McGregor swiped him with a leg, knocking him off balance and onto the road. The deputy pounced, turning Jackson over and pushing his face into the concrete. Jackson flailed and struggled and temporarily got free. But again, McGregor was faster, wrapping him in a headlock and pulling him back.

The deputy had him in a sleeper hold, and Jackson felt his windpipe constricting. His right hand was free, but he was unable to pry McGregor's hand free or strike at anything vulnerable. Running out of breath, he remembered the survival knife still at his waist. He struggled to unsheathe it as the corners of his vision started to fade. Finally extricating the knife, he gripped it like a sword and jabbed it behind his back, into McGregor's side.

The deputy winced, a sharp intake of breath, and his grip loosened a fraction. It was all Jackson needed to wiggle to the side, then jam his left elbow under McGregor's ribs. His arms slackened, and Jackson pried himself free.

McGregor rolled to his side, then struggled to rise. By the time he did, Jackson had repossessed the deputy's Beretta. Breathing deeply, he glanced north and south, then steadied his eyes on the deputy. He was bleeding from the side, just above the hip, but the wound didn't appear life-threatening.

"Take out . . . your cuffs, and lock . . . your hands behind your back."

McGregor swore.

"Now, or I shoot."

"You're pronouncing your own death sentence."

"Maybe so."

McGregor defiantly cuffed himself. Jackson then had him kneel in front of his cruiser. He frisked him, removing a cell phone, a second pair of cuffs, and a throwaway weapon in an ankle holster. He removed the radio from the deputy's shoulder and smashed it on the pavement. He did the same with the phone. He emptied all the bullets from the throwaway and heaved it into the desert.

"Where's Quinn?"

"He, Clayton, and Klein are bound at the mine. Seaver is in jail."

"Not anymore."

"Where is he? You let him out? Where is he?"

McGregor said nothing.

Jackson stuck the gun into his neck.

"He's at the doc's house," McGregor said.

"Who?"

"Doc Maynard. Retired MASH doctor. Lives at 4th and Paiute. He said you shot him."

"He was belligerent."

"Where's Vickers."

"Quinn shot him."

McGregor swore to show his disbelief.

Jackson briefly explained what had happened. "Quinn was about to kill me. Deputy Vickers intervened. They fought and Quinn shot Vickers. I then shot Quinn."

"You're a lying sack of—"

"If I'm lying and I'm a cop killer, why are you still breathing?"

McGregor swore under his breath again.

473

"Believe what you want, but it's the truth. I can't have you coming after me, because I need to go save Hillary. But when you get free, you should know that Quinn's been wounded and needs medical attention."

"You're dead when we catch you."

Jackson responded by lifting up the deputy's shirt. "Looks like a flesh wound. I'll put a quick bandage on it."

In not so many words, McGregor told him that wasn't necessary.

"Fine. Then you can bleed all over the backseat. Get up."

Jackson opened the backdoor, then plucked the deputy's badge off his uniform. "I'll crack the windows so you don't suffocate. Sooner or later, someone will come along and help you."

McGregor swore another blue streak, alleviating Jackson's qualms about shoving him into the backseat. He quickly disabled the car's GPS and its radio. He also lowered the rear windows a few inches, then locked and closed the doors. He retrieved his knife and slashed both passenger side tires. He wiped the excess blood on one of the tires, then put the knife back in his holster.

Daylight was literally burning, so he got back into Quinn's cruiser and took off. He reached eighty miles per hour before having to slow on the curve west. As he straightened out again, he saw several dark tendrils of smoke rising above the mountains behind him. Blane Air Force Base was gone. Kingman was behind him once and for all.

And Hillary's location was anyone's guess.

Chapter Sixty-Five

7:11 a.m.

"NORTH VISTA HOSPITAL, this is Rose."

"Rose, this is Deputy Sheriff McGregor from Kingman, Nevada. Badge number 714. Have you admitted a young woman in the last hour? Name is Hillary McKenzie. Blond. Six foot. Likely wearing a pink tank top and black running shorts. May have presented with symptoms of drug-related trauma?"

"Deputy McGregor? Let me check."

Jackson waited as he cruised amidst sparse morning traffic on I-15, just north of Las Vegas. He had slowed to seventy-five, not wanting to arouse unnecessary attention.

"I'm sorry, Deputy, but there's been no one here by that name, or that description. Not this morning."

"Thank you, Rose."

He closed his phone and concentrated on driving. Ravich had lied. No surprise. If Ravich was even his name.

Jackson had spent the past forty minutes waiting for cell service to resume and pondering what might have happened to Hillary. The Black Hawk had left Blane headed west, and presumably had not turned south. If it had, there was no reason it shouldn't have reached the hospital by now, seeing as how the Black Hawk was capable of cruising at speeds over 170 miles per hour. He'd wracked his brain, trying to think of what might be west of Blane Air Force Base, this side of San Francisco. Only one place even roughly matched that vector, and he couldn't bring himself to consider the possibility.

Area 51.

He debated calling Mouse, but doubted his friend could help. He considered waking Reggie, but he had no powers to assist either. He ended up punching in Ashley's number, doubtful that an LAPD detective could do anything. But it was all he had.

Her phone rang four times before she uttered a groggy, "Hello?"

"Ashley, it's Jackson."

She groaned. "What do you wa—It's quarter after seven."

"I'm in trouble."

She groaned again.

"Ashley, listen to me. This is serious."

After a brief pause, she sounded focused. "What's going on?"

As succinctly as possible, Jackson explained the situation. It took five minutes, and he was bearing down on the outskirts of Las Vegas by the time he was done. "I'm sure I'm in huge trouble, probably headed to Leavenworth, and if you need to turn me in, do it. But I've got to get Hillary back somehow."

There was no response.

"Ashley?"

"Jackson, I'm . . . I don't know what to say."

"And I don't know what to ask you to do. Something, please."

"I'll do what I can."

She took down some of the names—Reynolds, Moore, Quinn, Ravich—and promised to push whatever buttons she could. Jackson thanked her and promised he would be careful.

As the North Las Vegas sprawl began to pop up around the interstate, Jackson realized he needed a place to think. He was mentally, physically, and emotionally tapped. He hadn't slept in two full days, hadn't eaten anything but a few energy bars at the Blane guard station, and a glimpse in the mirror showed a face that looked like a *Walking Dead* cast member.

Remembering that the hotel he and Hillary had checked into after escaping from Oasis had been reserved for two nights, he set his course for it and turned into its parking lot just before seven-thirty. Retrieving their luggage from the trunk, Jackson climbed the stairs to Room 206 and let himself into the room without spotting anyone else.

When the door closed behind him, Jackson fell to his knees, his arms on the bed. Everything—failure, fatigue, fear, frustration—came out in a sudden torrent of tears. He squeezed his phone in one hand, balling up a wad of comforter in the other. He allowed it all to pour out of him for a few minutes, then pounded his fists on the bed and emitted a guttural scream. Choking back tears, he forced himself up on shaky legs.

First thing first, he set McGregor's Beretta—Klein's pistol, the rifles, and the shotgun were still in the car—on the dresser. It was joined by the knife, his holsters, and several other accessories, along with his phone, keys, and wallet.

Then Jackson walked to the bathroom, peeling off his clothes and surveying the damage in the mirror.

As much of his body as not was covered in bruises, some red, some purple, some yellowish green. Dried, crusted blood was caked on his chin, above one eye, and on his forehead. Too many cuts and scrapes to count crisscrossed his back and arms. Several of them were sizeable, but none posed any real danger. Then there was the wound in his leg, where a chunk of flesh had been torn away by a grazing bullet. Already, the wound had coagulated. Considering, he'd come through in remarkable shape.

He looked up at his arm, where a makeshift tourniquet hung in tatters. The adrenaline had faded slowly, and now was rushing out of his body. Even so, he didn't feel any ill-effects from the benzodiazepine that had been crudely and briefly administered back in the Hangar 1 hospital.

Going after Hillary was still urgent, but he couldn't go until he knew where to go. And until he figured that out—and figured out how to figure that out—he needed to tend to his own wellbeing. He'd been feeling drowsy on the drive, due to a lack of sleep and extreme physical exertion. And maybe the benzodiazepine had taken some effect after all. He didn't have time to nap, so he brewed a pot of coffee, then stepped into the shower.

The water was like a fresh reminder of every wound, turning pink as it swirled around his feet. Eventually, the warm water became soothing, only adding to Jackson's desire to shut his eyes and end this miserable experience.

He forced Hillary back into his mind. He wanted to scream when he thought of how close they had come to getting away. It was like when his USC Trojans let victory slip away from them, only magnified times a hundred. He used that sick feeling to fuel him, to drive him.

He patted himself dry and dressed, donning clean underwear, socks, and the T-shirt he had purchased at Campbell's. Unfortunately, the only two pair of pants he had available were his dirty, bullet-riddled, blood-soaked jeans or his tuxedo pants. He opted for the latter, and while he dressed, he poured hot coffee down his throat, craving the caffeine and using the pain from the heat to keep his senses sharp.

He poured another cup and paced for a quarter of an hour, trying to think. His stomach began to grumble, and he made the decision to hike across the street to Wal-Mart. It was a risk, showing his face around, because sooner or later, word of what he had done would get out. If he hadn't already done so, Deputy Seaver would put out an APB for Jackson, or somebody would find and rescue Deputy

McGregor and he would send out an alert. Plus whoever had Hillary had tried to neutralize him once. Chances were they would try again.

He hurried, not giving the scarce customers at Wal-Mart chance to observe or judge him for his bruised and scraped flesh or his odd choice of clothes. He ignored any looks he received, grabbing the first pair of jeans in his size off the rack and then snagging two bags of jerky, a six-pack of Mountain Dew, and a loaf of day-old bread from the grocery. He checked out without being indicted and took his purchases back to his hotel room.

He changed into the jeans and sat down on the bed to eat. Nutrition aside, he needed energy quick, and he wolfed down the jerky and bread along with a bottle and a half of soda. As he ate, he sorted through the network morning news programs, wondering if any local stations would break in with an update on what had transpired at Blane. But so far, it was all national coverage of pending elections, celebrity scandal, and dieting tips.

At quarter to nine, Jackson called Sam. She was awake, working at the Santa Monica-UCLA Medical Center. She was also prone to worrying about him, so Jackson tried to shield her from all that had happened. He mentioned that Hillary was missing, and asked if Sam could use her medical contacts to locate Hillary, if she was at any hospital in the Las Vegas area.

Sam asked a few questions, but also accepted Jackson's gentle brush-off. Apparently she grasped the seriousness of the situation. Promising to help and insisting, as had Ashley, that Jackson be careful in whatever he was doing, she said she would call back.

After ending the call, he thought again of calling Reggie. But he couldn't bring himself to do it. What would he say? And what could Reggie do, fly down and help him burn Vegas to the ground? Knowing Reggie, he would if Jackson asked. And that's why he couldn't press send.

Instead, he called Mouse. He again got a groggy female. Pam.

"I need to talk to Mouse."

"He's sleeping."

"Wake him up."

She huffed.

"Pam, do not mess with me today."

"Fine." It came out as two syllables. Fa-ine.

It was almost a minute before Mouse came on, making Ashley and Pam sound chipper by comparison.

"Mouse, I need your help again."

"What?" he asked sleepily.

"Mouse! Focus."

"Yeah, dude."

"I need your help."

"What?"

"Hillary's been taken again."

"To that base or whatever?"

"The base was blown up three hours ago by a fighter jet. Just before that, an Army helicopter took Hill . . ."

"Jack?"

The Army helicopter. It suddenly hit him. Of all the military Black Hawk helicopters he had ever seen—live, on TV, online, or in books—none had borne a white star on the side, and he couldn't remember ever seeing a "United States Army" label as big or as bold as on the chopper that had taken Hillary. Had it been so blatantly labeled in an attempt to prove something that wasn't true? Was it actually proof that it wasn't an authorized military aircraft?

"Jack?"

"Yeah. Look, they took Hillary again, heading west. Maybe headed to another base, or maybe just getting out of the way of the jet. But I have a theory how I can find her, a last-ditch effort."

"What do you need me for?"

Jackson took a deep breath, questioning the plan that was still taking form in his brain. It was crazy, improbable, and full of risk. But it was the only option he could think of.

"Insurance," he said to Mouse. "You're my failsafe."

*   *   *

11:21 a.m.

IT FELT like years since Jackson had been inside Oasis. The marble floors in the halls and plush carpet beneath his feet were quite a contrast from the desert sand, and the air conditioning was a welcome relief from the heat. The absolute luxury and civility worked to ease the pit in Jackson's stomach, but he knew the opulence was just a façade, masking the dark reality that Hillary was gone.

Sam had called back in twenty minutes, unable to turn up any signs of Hillary at any Las Vegas medical center. It had not been a surprise.

Ashley had also called. She had made a dozen phone calls and inquiries, but without proof, no one was willing to act. She had promised to keep trying, but sounded bleak.

Reggie had called five minutes later, quite possibly after talking with Sam. Jackson had felt compelled to take the call, and had broken down while explaining events to his friend. Repeatedly, he'd had to insist that Reggie not join him in Vegas.

"Well what are you going to do, J?" he'd asked.

"I'm going to find Hillary and get her back."

"By yourself?"

"I stormed Blane by myself."

"Jack, you can't take these people alone, man. You don't even know where she is."

"No, but I know where I can apply leverage to find out. And I know where I can apply leverage to the lever."

"You're not making sense, J."

Jackson took a deep breath. "It makes more sense in my head than on my tongue."

"Let me come down there, help you out."

"No. There's no sense two of us throwing our lives away."

"What about the cops? They can't all be crooked just because a hick sheriff is."

"You're forgetting a U.S. Senator, an Army general, the CIA, and a small private army. Plus, it won't be long before they link me to what happened in Kingman, I'm still a person of interest in Arielle's death, and whoever's behind this likely has fabricated ties to Al-Qaeda by now. By the time I can sort this all out legally, she could be dead. If she's not already. I'm going forward. Just promise me you won't do something rash."

"You going to make that promise back to me?"

"Sorry, Hoss."

This time Reggie exhaled. "All right, man. You change your mind, call me. You know I'll be there in a flash."

"I know, Reg. It's why I won't be calling."

His pal inhaled. "Be careful, J. I'll be praying."

Jackson had been unable to say anything in response, and had clapped his phone shut.

That had led to half an hour of internal debate, in which Jackson had convinced himself that his crazy plan was the only viable one. He'd sent everything to Mouse, gone over his role with him multiple times, and then set out for the Strip.

Jackson walked straight to the cages in Oasis's casino and exchanged a hundred dollars into chips. It felt absurd, gambling at a time like this, but he had his reasons.

He took his chips and approached a blackjack table with a five-dollar limit. He tried to place a fifty-dollar bet and was reminded of the table limit. So he moved to a table with a five-dollar minimum and attempted to place a one-dollar bet. When told that wouldn't work, he declared the table cold and moved on. He was halfway through repeating the rigmarole at different tables when a barrel-chested man impeded his path.

"Sir, perhaps you'd like to try your luck at another establishment."

"You kicking me out?"

"It's a recommendation," the man said.

"Maybe I'll hit the pool for a while."

The man raised a hand to his ear, pressing an earpiece tight to block out the clamor of the casino. After a moment, he lowered his hand and made eye contact with Jackson.

"Sir, could you please come with me?"

"Where to?"

"Sir, with me please."

Another man appeared behind Jackson, and he nodded to show he was going peacefully. They led him out of the casino, in the direction of the H$_2$O Showroom. When they reached the hall intersection, they turned right. Almost to the back exit of the resort, they stopped at a recessed doorway. The first man swiped a badge that unlocked the door, then entered the room ahead of Jackson.

It was a storage locker, with steel shelves lining three walls and folding tables and chairs stacked against the other. The man opened a folding chair and set it down. "Please have a seat, sir."

Jackson raised his eyebrows and sat.

The first man nodded at the second, then exited the room. The second man stood guard by the door, hands folded across his waist, his eyes never leaving Jackson but never looking at him either. The waiting began.

In theory, Jackson could have called Richard Holloway or walked up to the front desk and asked to speak with him. But he had surmised this would be the quickest way to get an audience with the man.

Jackson sat patiently at first, but began to fidget as time ticked away. He had no way of passing it, other than to count, which he eventually resorted to after a while. He stopped at thirty minutes.

"Any idea how long we're waiting?"

The man hadn't moved, and he didn't respond, vocally or bodily to Jackson's question.

"Right."

Jackson counted again, this time to fifteen minutes. Was Holloway making him wait as punishment? Was he busy? Was he coordinating with a joint military, FBI, and LVMPD task force to capture him? He considered bull-rushing the man and trying to make a break for it, but he didn't like his odds. Besides, he was here for a reason.

Finally, the door opened and a man stepped in. It was not Richard Holloway but an Oasis employee, judging by the resort logo stamped on his royal blue polo shirt. He was medium height, thick but not heavy, with arms like a stevedore. Light brown hair had been buzzed short, and his eyebrows were almost non-existent. He looked at Jackson with narrow, sloe eyes as he spoke.

"Mr. Douglas, we've been looking for you."

Jackson, for once, kept his mouth shut.

"I'm Jay Davis, Head of Security at Oasis."

"Any chance I could speak to Mr. Holloway?"

"Mr. Holloway is busy at the moment."

"It's incredibly urgent."

"We'll see about that. For right now, you're speaking with me."

Jackson nodded.

"What are you doing here?"

"Uh, I came to talk to Mr. Holloway."

"About what?"

Jackson glanced at the other man in the room, who had yet to move other than to take a step back to make room for Davis.

"It's rather sensitive."

Davis leaned back and looked over his shoulder. "Luther, would you please step outside?"

The man nodded—practically bowed—and obeyed.

"You were saying?"

"Approximately six hours ago, Blane Air Force Base was bombed to oblivion. I escaped by the skin of my teeth, moments after Hillary McKenzie—who Mr. Holloway knew as Shannon Hillstrom—was taken by what I believe to be an imitation U.S. Army helicopter. I need Mr. Holloway's help to find her."

If it was possible, Davis's eyes narrowed. "Assuming that's all true, and it's quite an assumption, why would Mr. Holloway have any interest in helping you? When last you were on the premises, you and Miss McKenzie ran an elaborate and, I must say, effective confidence game, broke into Mr. Holloway's personal safe, and absconded with private property. He is well within his rights to turn you over to the authorities."

"And yet he sent you to talk with me."

Davis licked his lips. "As of this moment, Mr. Holloway is not aware of your presence at Oasis. Whether or not he is ever made aware depends on your answer, which as of yet, you haven't given. Mr. Douglas, why would Mr. Holloway have any interest in helping you?"

Jackson took a deep breath, well aware that he was about to indict himself with testimony that could be admissible in court. Especially with his lawyer in captivity. But he pressed on.

"Because the private property you mentioned was a collection of voice recordings, dossiers, and other incriminating evidence that not only prove the existence of a clandestine regeneration of black-ops genetic experiments conducted at Blane Air Force Base in the 1980s, but also indict Senator Carson Moore, General Ernest Reynolds, and several others in those experiments."

Davis remained stoic as Jackson spoke.

"My hunch," he continued, "is that Mr. Holloway, while at one time involved in some capacity in the project, gathered the evidence as insurance. Assuming an altruistic motive on Mr. Holloway's behalf, and given the recent events that have transpired, I'm hoping that he would provide me with any further potential evidence he might have that would alert me where Hillary has been taken and that would aid in her recovery." He shrugged. "And if I'm wrong about his kindness or the nature of his evidence, then she's as good as dead and so am I."

"You tell quite a tale."

"I wish I were making it up."

Davis nodded. "I'll speak to Mr. Holloway."

"Thank you."

"Don't thank me. I'm merely passing on information. It will be his choice if he wants to see you."

"And if not?"

"The next person through this door will be a member of the Las Vegas Metropolitan Police Department, and you will spend a very long time in prison."

Chapter Sixty-Six

1:24 p.m.

THE NEXT PERSON through the door had actually been Luther, who had stood guard for another lengthy period of time. When Jay Davis re-entered the room, Jackson sighed with relief.

"Mr. Douglas, please come with me."

He stood and followed Davis back through the north wing of the resort, through the casino, and to the private elevator running up through the shaft in the middle of Oasis's atrium. The various gamblers and guests around him felt like a mirage, as if he was in a bubble, isolated from the real world. He and Davis whooshed to the forty-fourth floor of the giant O in no time. The elevator stopped, and with a soft ding, the doors slid open. Davis again asked Jackson to follow him, then led him into Holloway's marbled hallway, up the curving stairs beside the two-story aquarium, and across the loft to the dual wooden doors to Holloway's office. In the bright daylight, the penthouse looked startlingly different than it had thirty-six hours ago. Like everything else, the moment was surreal.

Davis rapped on the right door with his considerable knuckles, then opened it and stepped aside, allowing Jackson to enter the office. He hesitantly took several steps in, turning to face Holloway's desk. Davis entered after him, closed the door, and stood with arms clasped at his waist, directly in front of the doors.

"Mr. Douglas—or is it Mr. Jackson?"

Richard Holloway stood and stepped around his desk. He was dressed in white chinos and a pastel pink shirt, white collar, sleeves rolled to the elbow. His shoes were brown and had cost some sort of reptile its life. The watch on his wrist was gold, and with a glance at it, Holloway indicated he was making a huge sacrifice by meeting with Jackson.

He opened his mouth, but Holloway didn't give him a chance to answer. "Looks a little different, doesn't it, in the daylight, with nothing broken, no safe contents strewn all over? You know," he said, stopping just feet in front of

485

Jackson, his cologne a strong but pleasant aroma, "I have to hand it to you. As upset as I was Wednesday night, you and the Escobar sisters pulled off a pretty brilliant confidence game."

He caught the flicker in Jackson's eye.

"Yeah, I know who they are. I also know that their client, Felipe Ortega, has been bribing officials and falsifying records about the beef raised on his fifty-thousand-acre cattle ranch, several thousand acres of which double as an opium farm. And I told them as much, just before I turned them in to Las Vegas Metro."

Jackson's heart sunk. He had been rather selfish in making his break from the penthouse, copping an "every man for himself" attitude. He had hoped that somehow Adriana and Teresa had also escaped. Although, he had also been less than completely sure they really were who they said they were, and it wasn't like he had forced them to work with him. Either way, Holloway didn't give him much time to think about it.

"Mr. Davis gave me the condensed version of what you told him, but I'd like to hear it from your lips."

So Jackson told him everything. From Hillary's voicemail to the search for Arielle Coal to finding her dead to various connections between her, Warren McKenzie, Senator Moore, and Richard Holloway. Then from further research into the various parties to his and Hillary's belief that Holloway had information that would make sense of everything to their plot to uncover that evidence. From their escape from Oasis to their deduction that they could find answers in Kingman to their discovery of Silver Dawn, Desert Root, and now Golden Dawn to Hillary's belief that she had been a product of the project's genetic experiments. And lastly, from her kidnapping to Jackson's interrogation of Quinn and his deputies to his audacious rescue efforts at Blane to the Black Hawk that had come and taken Hillary away and the jet that had erased the base from the map.

While he spoke, Holloway's face morphed from bemused incredulity to skepticism to surprise, back to incredulity but minus the bemusement, and ultimately to grave comprehension. When Jackson finished, the casino owner nodded at the conference table. "Have a seat."

Jackson obliged.

"So why are you here? What do you want from me?"

"Help. I have no idea where Hillary is, where they've taken her."

"And you think I do?"

"I think when we uploaded the contents of your USB drive to the cloud, we didn't get everything. Maybe you know something more. Or maybe in all your business dealings with Moore and Reynolds and McKenzie, you learned something. Or at the very least, you can tell me who I should go to for answers."

Holloway nodded. His elbow rested on the table as he reclined in his swivel chair, tracing his chin with his finger. "Why haven't you gone to the authorities?"

"Because I don't know who I can trust. The local sheriff was crooked. A U.S. senator is crooked. The CIA operatives involved are crooked, except for the ones who are dead. And the United States Army helicopter that came to our rescue tried to kill me, just before a military jet turned Blane AFB into a crater. The authorities aren't looking so hot."

"And in all of this, you think you can trust me?"

Jackson sat forward. "The way I see it, either you're a good guy who stockpiled information but hasn't yet brought it to the attention of the authorities because the time hasn't been right or you weren't sure it was safe, and who's opposed to what they were doing out there and doesn't want to see harm come to Hillary, in which case I am hoping we can let bygones be bygones and work together . . ." He paused to make eye contact with Holloway. "Or, you're a bad guy, involved up to your armpits, thoroughly complicit, in which case as soon as you've discovered all that I know, you're going to have Mr. Davis over there drive me back to the desert so I can dig my own grave. But if that's the case, I should warn you, that everything I've told you and every shred of evidence we have— from the data we took from your drive to Arielle's notes and observations to our hunches and speculations—is in the hands of my friend right now, and if I don't call him off in—" He glanced at the clock "—the next hour or so, he's going to make it public."

Holloway lowered his hand and sat forward as well. "You're threatening me with a friend who will go to the police? That's the oldest one in the book."

"There's a reason for that," Jackson said. He held up one hand to show he meant no harm, and extracted a piece of paper from his pants pocket. He slid it across the table to Holloway.

"What's this?"

"A web address."

Holloway studied it, then looked up at Jackson. He stood and walked over to his computer.

"Right now, that link is private," Jackson said. "If I don't call off my friend, he blasts it on YouTube, Twitter, Facebook, and anywhere else he can, under the label 'hot Russian chicks.' He's a computer expert, a hacking whiz. If I don't call him in an hour, in two, the whole world will have access to this. And your name is bold, italicized, and highlighted in yellow."

Holloway needed only a minute to look over the site Mouse had created, detailing all Jackson and Hillary's findings and conjecture, outing everyone. It was a last-ditch effort, Jackson's final card in the hole, and also a way to make sure that if he failed, at least the truth was presented.

"You've got a lot of nerve," Holloway said, returning to the table.

"You catch more flies with honey, but it's still good to carry around a flyswatter. Or put another way, use the carrot and the stick."

Holloway sat back down. He smirked. "I've been around gamblers a long time, Mr. Douglas. I'm very good at reading players. I can see it in their eyes when they're desperate. Down to the felt, so to speak. They're on tilt. They start making emotional, impulsive, irrational decisions out of desperation." He leaned forward. "And you, my friend, are displaying all the symptoms. Best advice to players on tilt: walk away."

"I can't do that. Too much skin in the game."

"Then you're going to bust."

Jackson tilted his head. "Maybe. But even that player on tilt, the player who's over his skis, can still win big if he's dealt a royal flush. Please, Mr. Holloway, deal me a fair hand."

He sat back, stroked his chin again. "You really care for this girl, don't you?"

"Honest truth, I can't stand her. But she's family, and you do whatever it takes for family."

"Even if that is waltzing into my casino, confessing to crimes committed, and throwing yourself at my mercy?"

"When a seemingly insane course of action is the only one available, it's not really so insane."

Holloway's face slowly transformed into a smile. "All things considered, I like you, Douglas. You certainly have nerve."

"I get it honest."

"Here's my deal, and I'm not accepting counteroffers: You write down everything you just told me, everything that relates to the activities you and Miss McKenzie conducted in conning me. You leave out nothing, a full confession. You sign it and give it to me. I will, at my discretion, determine whether or not this confession remains in my desk drawer or finds its way onto the desk of a

Metro detective. In return, I will provide you with what information I can. Take it or leave it."

"Where do I sign?"

Holloway opened a drawer from under the table and withdrew a legal notepad. He slapped it on the table in front of Jackson, spun it to face him, and set an engraved pen from his pocket on top of it. For the next twenty minutes, Jackson scribbled furiously, filling eight pages with his recount of his and Hillary's actions. At the bottom, he signed and printed his name and dated it.

Holloway scanned it for a few minutes. "Now, call off your friend."

Jackson looked into the man's intense blue eyes and nodded. He opened his phone and dialed.

"Yeah?" Mouse answered.

"It's me. Hold off."

"You're sure?"

"Yeah."

"Okay, dude."

Jackson clapped the phone shut.

Holloway tore the eight pages out of the legal pad and meticulously folded them, then stuffed them into his shirt's breast pocket, purely for show. "I will hang onto this, and you have my word that if you don't bring me any further hassle, then I will, as you said, 'let bygones be bygones.' But if you besmirch my good name, drag me or Oasis through the mud, or go back on our agreement, then I will turn this in to the authorities without hesitation."

"Understood."

"You were right earlier, that I am a 'good guy.' When I realized the full scope of the Golden Dawn project, realized all that they were doing and undertaking, I withdrew my financial support from it. I began compiling evidence as insurance in case any of the other members sought to implicate me, but as I gathered more evidence, I realized that I couldn't allow the project to continue. I was waiting until I had gathered concrete proof of Golden Dawn and certain persons' collusion before presenting what I'd found to the proper authorities, but as you can no doubt appreciate, it is rather complex."

Jackson nodded to show he was tracking with Holloway.

"Now, an enthusiastic prosecutor could embellish a few illegalities on my part, but nothing my attorneys can't take care of. So rest assured, Mr. Douglas, what I have here—" He patted the papers in his pocket "—does you far more harm than anything you have does me."

"Yes, sir."

Holloway sat back. "Unfortunately, I've had no contact with anyone in the project for quite some time now. The only base of operation I was aware of was Blane Air Force Base, and if that's gone, I'm afraid that I have no idea where they have taken Miss McKenzie."

"Then tell me how I can find somebody who knows. Where do I find Reynolds or Cutler or Woodson or Moore?"

"Why? What are you going to do?"

"Persuade them to tell me where she is."

"I can't advocate that sort of vigilante justice."

"When the legal authorities are compromised, vigilantes are all that's left. I have no idea how high this corruption goes or who has been tainted. And even if I did, by the time I could make my appeal to them and convince them that I was telling the truth, it might be too late. It's been eight hours since they flew off with her. They could be halfway around the world or she could be half dead."

Holloway cleared his throat. "I only met General Reynolds once or twice, and to say I didn't care much for him would be an understatement. He and Moore are quite close, and he's stayed at Oasis a time or two. But I already checked, and he's not registered here currently. I have no idea where to find him," he said with a shake of his head.

"I've never met Cutler or Woodson, or most of the other players, either. The only one I possibly know how to find is Senator Moore. He has a home here in the valley, over in Centennial Hills, where he lives when he's not traveling or in Washington. I'll get you the address," he said, standing, "but only because it's public knowledge and with enough time, you could find it yourself."

"Thank you."

"However, I sincerely doubt Carson knows where Hillary is. He prefers to say out of the 'day-to-day' aspects of the project, keep his hands clean, so to speak."

Holloway retreated to his desk. He quickly consulted his computer, then scratched an address on a small sheet of paper and brought it to Jackson. "Whatever you intend to do, Mr. Douglas, I want to make it perfectly clear, I have no part in it."

"Understood."

"I urge you to be very careful."

"All due respect, I don't have the time to be careful."

Holloway's eyes narrowed.

"Thank you, Mr. Holloway. I do apologize for what Hillary and I did. At the time, we didn't see any other way. I don't suppose that excuses it, and if you have no interest in a handshake, I'll understand. But I need to offer it to you."

He extended his hand, then waited.

Instead of shaking hands, Holloway drew back his fist and, with lightning quick speed, slugged Jackson in the jaw. He recoiled backwards, staggered, tripped over a chair, and caught himself by the elbow on the side of the table. He lost his battle with balance and sagged to a seated position on the floor.

Holloway reached his hand down. "I believe I owed you one, from the other night."

Jackson stood with Holloway's help, rubbing his jaw. "Yes, sir, you did."

"Mr. Davis will escort you out of the casino. I hope you find Hillary."

"Me too."

Chapter Sixty-Seven

3:22 p.m.

AS JACKSON DROVE, he wrestled with the concept of the ends justifying the means. It was a nice principle to adhere to because you could get away with anything under the umbrella of the greater good. But was it right?

Jackson's dad had once told him there was never a good reason to do the wrong thing. But did that include Navy SEALs taking out the leader of a terrorist group like Osama bin Laden? Or non-Nazi Germans trying to assassinate Hitler? Sometimes it wasn't so cut and dried, black and white.

He also asked himself, what would Jesus do? It was a great slogan, but it wasn't always practical. There was no record of Jesus' brother's fiancée being kidnapped by the Sanhedrin, so it was hard to know what Jesus would have done. He had preached to turn the other cheek and love your enemy, but in the Old Testament, God had also commanded the Israelites to slaughter the amoral men, women, and children of the surrounding countries. And Solomon wrote about "a time to kill" in Ecclesiastes. So where did that leave things?

As Jackson neared Centennial Hills, he found his mind drifting to what would Bauer do? As in Jack Bauer. He'd been faced with situations like this. Which was worse, torturing a guy who might be innocent or letting innocent people die by not torturing a guy who was guilty as sin? Confronted with the evidence Jackson had, Bauer would strangle Senator Moore with his necktie until he coughed up Hillary's location. Or his spleen.

But Jack Bauer, despite being the greatest action hero this side of Jason Bourne, was not Jackson's moral compass. His Moral Compass wasn't giving him much direction of late, but that may have been less of a broadcasting issue and more of a tuning problem. It was hard to get direction when you were busy playing G.I. Jackson out in the desert.

And so Jackson wrestled some more, a pit forming in his stomach as he turned off Highway 95 onto West Tropicana Parkway. The pit was partially hunger. He hadn't eaten in hours. But it was mostly fear—for Hillary's safety, of getting caught, and of having to live with himself if he didn't.

492

Jackson had done his homework on Hillary's laptop. He'd scouted Moore's house—it was actually a detached condo, one of two dozen situated around a central lake on La Arena Boulevard. He had surveyed the neighborhood using Google's satellite photos, found a floor plan of the condo on the developer's website, and used them both to plan his assault. Despite his success at the base the night before, raiding a suburban residence in broad daylight was not going to be easy. Especially since Moore would have several bodyguards watching his six. And Jackson refused to kill anyone else he wasn't convinced was dirty and who was not a direct threat to Hillary's wellbeing. As with the deputies in Kingman, he didn't know which of Moore's assistants were just protecting their boss and which of them were conspirators in Moore's nefarious undertakings.

Jackson had called Mouse after leaving the resort, and told him to go public on the internet with Jackson's story if he didn't hear back from him by six p.m. He asked him to scrub Holloway's name from the info as much as possible without altering the facts. It was his final recourse. If things went south and he didn't get a chance to present his evidence, he needed Reynolds and Moore and the other participants to face the music. If the only way to do that was reneging on his word to Holloway and risking his retribution, so be it. Jackson figured if it came to that, Holloway's anger would be the least of his worries.

He nearly called Reggie again, or Leroy, but he couldn't bring himself to the point of telling them what he was about to do. That should have been a warning, but he disregarded it. And he almost called the police, despite all his previous reservations about doing so. But for any good it would do, he feared it would only slow him down. Jackson was on his own, and he decided against what he had generally been taught, that this was one of those extreme situations. The end did justify the means.

He turned onto La Arena Boulevard and flashed Deputy McGregor's badge at the gate. It was a risk, he knew. Along with word of his exploits, his face, Quinn's license plate, and a comprehensive BOLO had to be circulating by now, and every law enforcement officer in the state—not to mention every security camera in Vegas—would be on the lookout for him. But it was a risk he had to take. He told the guard at the gate that he was off duty, there to update Senator Moore on a joint law enforcement task force and to go over some legal matters. The guard didn't know if Moore was at home, but he allowed Jackson through.

The condos were numbered sequentially, regardless of which side of the street they were on. Moore's was near the back of the little community, around a bend in the road, right on the lake. In design, it was the same as all the others—a single story, sprawling, off-white building with stucco walls, orange clay shingles, and a slight Moorish influence over the doors and windows. Like the rest, it had palms in the front yard, more in the back. The lawn was green, which meant heavily irrigated. The garage was detached, separated by a small portico, rimmed with stucco arches. This wasn't a condo. It was a hacienda.

Jackson parked in the driveway, wishing he had a better strategy. He looked for signs of the neighbors. It was a hundred degrees out. They were all in the air conditioning, or at least around back in their pools.

With McGregor's Beretta tucked into the back of his pants, Jackson strolled up the sidewalk to the front gate. He hoped that Moore was so detached from the "day-to-day" operations at Blane and in Kingman that he wouldn't know Deputy McGregor's face. Or at least that the guy answering the door wouldn't.

The guy answering the door was a Latina woman, short and round, clearly identifiable by her dress as the maid. Great way to win the Hispanic vote.

"Yes?" she asked in cracked English.

"Is Senator Moore in?" Jackson asked.

The woman frowned. "Who is asking, please?"

Jackson tried the badge. "Deputy Tom McGregor, Delamar County Sheriff's Department."

The frown didn't go anywhere. "I am sorry, he no is here."

"Perhaps an assistant, a member of his protective detail, someone I could speak with."

"Martina, who is it?" Jackson heard a female voice call out.

The maid turned over her shoulder. "A deputy asking for Senator Moore."

Jackson heard heels clicking on the marble floor, and looked past Martina to see a small, compact woman coming his way. Her stride was quick and confident, sending her straight, raven hair bouncing off her square shoulders. Along with low heels, she wore dark navy pants and a snug-fitting pale blue shirt. She was at most thirty. Not Senator Moore's wife. His mistress? Niece?

She stopped beside Martina. "Can I help you?"

"Deputy Sheriff Tom McGregor," Jackson said, flashing the badge. "I'm looking for Senator Moore."

"Rae. I'm with the Mrs. Moore's security detail. The senator isn't in at the moment. Do you mind if I ask for some identification?"

"Not at all," Jackson said, reaching for his back pocket. He impressed himself with the quick draw, and had a gun on Rae before she could react.

Martina had already gone back to her housework, and the two of them were alone.

"Don't do anything stupid," he said, nodding through the open door. She backed up and he followed her in, feeling for the closing door behind him. He glanced around briefly, then nodded again to a room off the hall, a small den with no other entrance or exit.

"Who are you?" she asked, moving slowly.

"I'll do the talking. Are you armed?"

"No."

"A bodyguard with no weapon?"

"Your lucky day."

They entered the den. "Turn your pockets inside out," Jackson said.

She obeyed.

"Pull up your pant legs."

She did.

"Lift up your shirt."

Rae raised her pale blue shirt high enough to reveal several inches of tanned, hard midriff. And no weapons.

"Sit down," Jackson said, motioning at an armchair. With a glare, Rae obeyed. He sat next to her, just far enough away to be safe.

"What do you want?" she snarled quietly.

"You wouldn't believe me if I told you," he answered. "But here's what you need to know. I have no interest in hurting you, Mrs. Moore, or any of the staff."

"You didn't mention Senator Moore."

"I didn't."

"If you think I'm going to sit here and let you assassinate a United States senator, you're sadly mistaken."

"I'm not going to assassinate anyone."

"Then why the gun?"

"I need to talk to him."

"That's not going to happen."

"Then where do you want the bullet?"

"You talk big."

"And if you watch the news, you know I back it up."

"You're Douglas?"

"That's right."

"What do you want?"

495

"That doesn't matter, because like I said, you won't believe me. What does matter is that you know I'll do whatever it takes to get it. You cooperate, I don't harm you. You try to take this gun from me, try to call for help, I'll do what I have to."

Rae glared some more.

"Who else is in the house? Any other members of your detail?"

"No."

"Staff?"

"Just Martina. It's the butler's day off."

"Where is Martina now?"

"I don't have ESP."

"Nor are you much of a bodyguard, apparently."

Rae's glare intensified.

"Where is she?"

"Changing the linens."

"Where's Mrs. Moore?"

"Shopping."

Jackson shook his head. "Where is she?"

"I told you."

"If that were the case, you'd be with her."

Rae didn't respond.

"I have no beef with Mrs. Moore," Jackson said. "But I will do—"

Out of nowhere, Rae's foot came up and kicked the gun from Jackson's hand. He had no idea how. He wasn't even sitting within kicking distance, and he hadn't let his guard down. But the proof was in the pudding, and his gun had flown across the room.

Worse yet, Rae had leapt out of her chair and was at Jackson's throat. The combined force of her attack and his effort to get away from her tipped the chair backwards with a loud crash.

Rae, who apparently worked out to those MMA videos Jackson always saw advertised, quickly had Jackson on his stomach, face ground into the rug. He tried to roll her off, and succeeded. But in the process, she wrapped her arm around his throat and began to squeeze. Although half the weight of Deputy McGregor, she possessed equal strength when it came to cutting off his air supply.

Even though he was lying on top of her and pulling on her arm, he couldn't get it to budge. He was running out of oxygen, and would pass out long before his weight crushed her. So he used all his strength to roll over again, hoping the sudden jerk would dislodge her grip. It only made it worse.

Jackson's vision was starting to fade, like the slow filter of blood that oozed over the screen when he died in a video game. He reached with his right hand, back behind his own, and came up with hair. Rae stuck a knee or an elbow into the small of his back, and he nearly cried in pain.

Realizing he shouldn't have left the knife in the car, he tried to roll again, like a deer desperately thrashing to get free from an alligator. They crashed into an end table and something heavy fell onto his shoulder and clunked to the floor. He was passing out, and Rae was squeezing harder. Jackson's hand flailed again, found the heavy object. As his last effort, he swung it.

His blow landed with a thud, and the pressure around his neck released slightly. Jackson dropped the weapon and pulled on Rae's arm, and her chokehold slowly loosened. He scrambled free and crawled to the gun. He whipped around, brandishing it as Rae got to her feet.

Her head was cut, just above the eye, and a slow trickle of blood flowed down her cheek. She felt it with her hand, checking the blood and glaring at Jackson.

"On your knees," Jackson tried to say, but his throat wouldn't work. It came out as a scratched growl, something similar to a hissing cat. He swallowed and tried again. "Knees."

Rae understood and obeyed.

Martina appeared in the doorway. "Mees Underwood? Oh!" she gasped when she saw the situation. She also saw the gun, and when Jackson motioned her into the living room, she obeyed.

Wheezing for breath, Jackson directed her to a chair. She was mumbling under her breath, naming saints left and right, and Jackson left her to it and concentrated on Rae. With his left hand, he reached into his back pocket and pulled out a pair of zip ties.

"Hands behind your back," he said, still only able to whisper. "Stay on your knees." Rae obeyed, and Jackson looped one of the ties around her wrists and pulled it tight. It wasn't easy, with only one hand, but he managed. Then he walked around to assess the cut to her head.

"Let me see," he said, but Rae jerked her head away.

He looked past her at the small brass desk clock that had become his billy club. Not exactly the Sean Connery Charlemagne scene from *Indiana Jones and the Last Crusade*, but it had worked.

Keeping an eye on Rae, Jackson asked Martina who else was in the house. Just Meeses Moore. Where was Meeses Moore? In her room. Where was Senator Moore? Golfing. When would he back? Four, maybe five o'clock.

It was already twenty to four, so they didn't have much time. Jackson told Martina and Rae to get up and walk quietly into the kitchen. From there, they took a left, toward the bedrooms. The senator and his wife shared the last room on the right, with a splendid view of the lake through sliding glass doors.

Mrs. Moore had the sculpted look of a politician's wife. High cheeks, a little too much makeup, perfectly coiffed hair dyed blond from gray. She wore a stylish silk blouse and slacks, hose over bare feet, and lay on her side on the bed, knees bent, reading a thick book while casting glances at a nearly muted television.

She looked up as they entered the room, and frowned. Presumably, she then saw the blood on Rae's face and the gun in Jackson's hand. She propped herself up. "Good heavens, what's going on?"

"I'm sorry to intrude, Mrs. Moore, but I need to speak to your husband."

"Rae? Rae, what has he done to you? Martina, are you all right."

"Fine, Meeses Moore."

"Rae, dear—"

"I'm fine, ma'am. Please do what he says."

The senator's wife turned to Jackson. "I demand you tell me what is going on."

"We don't have time. I need you to tie Martina's hands."

"I'll do no such thing."

"Lady, I do not want to hurt you, but I will do whatever I have to."

"Mrs. Moore, please listen to him," Rae said.

She balked for another second, then sat up. Jackson tossed her four zip ties, and instructed her to bind Martina's wrists and ankles, Rae's ankles, and lastly her own ankles. Reluctantly, she obeyed, and he checked the tightness. Satisfactory.

He set down the gun and asked for her hands. Mrs. Moore slapped him.

As much as he detested using force on a fifty-year-old woman, Jackson didn't have time to mess around. Moore could return at any second. He spun her around by the shoulders, grabbed her arms, and bound her wrists.

"You will spend the rest of your life in prison for this!" she said.

"Probably."

As gently as possible, he sat her down on the bed. "How many men are with the senator?"

No one answered. Jackson aimed his gun at Mrs. Moore.

"Two," Rae answered. "And a driver."

"Rae, be quiet."

"One vehicle?"

"Yes."

"Do they park in the garage?"

"Of course."

Jackson nodded. "I'm going to move my car. When I come back, I expect full cooperation. If I get it, you have an unpleasant afternoon and that's it. If not, I will do what I have to, understood?"

Martina's face registered pure fear. Mrs. Moore's, pure indignation. Rae's, pure hate.

Jackson unplugged the phone from the wall and stuffed the cord in his pocket. He quickly checked to make sure there weren't any communication devices in reach—cell phones, tablets, laptops. Convinced that the trio was as secure as possible, he went outside. He drove McGregor's cruiser down the block, around the corner, and hiked back as quickly as possible. He had two ten-round pistols tucked into his waistband and carried a bag with several other accessories.

Mrs. Moore, Rae, and Martina were still in the bedroom, although Rae had scooted toward the door and almost made it. Another five minutes, and she might have been down the hall to a phone.

Jackson pulled a roll of duct tape from his bag. He lifted Rae off the ground—not an easy task—and set her in a desk chair. He taped both legs to one leg of the chair, and taped her left arm to the back of the chair. Then he grabbed Martina by the arm and led her down the hall to the next room. She mixed shrieks with Hail Marys and more supplications to various saints.

"Martina, I am not going to hurt you, okay. But I need you to be calm, and tell me the truth, all right?"

Eyes wide with fear, she nodded.

"When Senator Moore comes home, tell me what happens. What door does he come in? What do his bodyguards do? What about the driver?"

"One of the bodyguards, he come in first. Then Meester Moore."

"Then the other guard?"

Martina shook her head. "He walk around house first. Usually."

"What about the driver?"

"He check vehicle, and sometime take for gas."

"When the other guard comes inside, which door does he use?"

"Through garage. Sometime back door."

"Off the dining room?"

Martina nodded.

"Do these guards have guns?"

"Yes."

"Little guns? Handguns?"

"Yes."

"Where do they carry them?"

"They do not carry. They, how you say, wear?"

Jackson nodded. "On their hip?"

She shook her head.

"Under the arm?" Jackson asked, gesturing as he spoke.

"Yes."

"Very good, Martina." He reached for the duct tape. "I'm going to put this across your mouth," he said. "I'm sorry."

She blinked away tears, and Jackson wanted to turn his guns on himself. He forced an image of Hillary, strapped to the bed in the airplane hangar, into his mind. It stemmed the tide for just a moment.

Scowling resolve onto his face, Jackson returned to the Moores' bedroom. For dramatic effect, he racked the slide of a drawn pistol to chamber a round. "I just asked Martina the same questions I'm going to ask you," he said to Rae. "Your answers don't match, I take it out on Mrs. Moore. *Comprende?*"

Rae nodded.

"You're an animal!" Mrs. Moore spat.

"No, your husband is the animal, and I'm trying to stop him. Rae, walk me through procedure when the senator returns."

He asked her the same questions as he had asked Martina. Aside from using language of her trade—and some other language—Rae's answers matched Martina's.

"Good. Last question. When does your shift end?"

"I get relieved at eight o'clock," Rae answered.

"What about the other guards?"

"Eight and midnight."

"Good." Jackson took out the duct tape and plastered a strip across Rae's mouth. Mrs. Moore uttered more threats as Jackson gagged her, and screamed into the tape as he dragged her into Martina's room. He taped Martina to her desk chair, apologizing in the process. Then he bound Mrs. Moore to the desk itself, making sure there was no way one of their hands could possibly reach the other's tape.

Then he returned to Rae. Her cut had clotted, and he used his thumb to wipe the blood off her cheek. She again jerked her head away.

"I am sorry about this," Jackson said. "But when the truth comes out, I hope you'll understand why I'm doing it."

Rae's brow furrowed, and she stared at him as if he was crazy. Maybe he was.

He dragged her chair down the hallway and into the next bedroom, and reclined her back onto the floor. He closed the blinds, and made a quick sweep of the house. Then he went into the den to wait for Senator Moore to return from the golf course.

Chapter Sixty-Eight

TWO MEMBERS OF the Moores' security detail sat on the floor against the wall, hands and ankles duct taped securely. One was concussed, his head hanging limply on his shoulder; the other was gagged with more duct tape and stared sullenly ahead. Both had avoided being shot. A third bodyguard sat next to them, the gash on her head starting to scab. Her face was in danger of setting in a permanent glare.

Across the table, seated on and taped to a dining room chair, was a young blond driver. He looked as scared as Martina, who was taped to the chair next to him. On her right, nearest to Jackson, was Mrs. Moore. Taped to a chair. Hers was the only mouth not covered with duct tape.

Three bodyguards on the floor, a driver, a maid, and a wife on chairs—all facing the dining room table—formed a makeshift audience, their eyes vacillating between Jackson and the man standing against the wall at the other end of the table: United States Senator Carson Andrew Moore. He too was bound.

Moore looked more like a retired football player than a politician. He was tall and muscular, six-three and maybe two-twenty, two-twenty-five. His skin was well tanned and his mahogany hair was thinning a little, but still plentiful and wavy. He wore a white golf shirt with a red stripe up the left-hand side, stopping at the shoulder. The shirt was soaked with sweat, which also beaded on his forehead and trickled down his neck. The sweat was not residue from the golf course. Jackson had turned off the A/C in the condo.

Moore's defining feature was a set of piercing jade eyes. They were just slits, hidden under an overhanging brow, and they bored into Jackson with an intense loathing. Jackson couldn't blame him. He would have looked at a man who took his wife captive the same way.

Capturing Moore, his bodyguards, and the driver had gone as smoothly as possible. Jackson had waited behind the door, smashed the lead guard with the butt of his pistol, and jabbed the barrel into Moore's kidney. Moore had bound

502

the fallen guard at gunpoint, and then taped his own ankles. Jackson had taped Moore's wrists behind his back. He had then taken the driver in the garage, and the final guard when he came in, both without incident.

The obscenities and curses had all been shouted, and the seven captives had started to resign themselves to their fate. Jackson was nearing the eleven-hour mark since Hillary had been kidnapped the second time. The clock was ticking.

He pulled out the cheap video recorder he had purchased that afternoon on the drive over. It had been another risk, stopping at a public place wired for surveillance, but he'd needed the camera. He turned it on and set it on the counter, making sure it was aimed at Senator Moore. He stepped to the side. "Tell me where Hillary is and confess to everything you've done."

"You're out of your mind."

"I'm going to tell you again, then I'm going to shoot someone."

"You wouldn't dare."

Jackson had seen Jack Bauer shoot a guy's wife once, in the knee. It hadn't worked. The guy hadn't said a word. And for all his bravado, Jackson wasn't Bauer. He knew he couldn't pull the trigger. But he couldn't let Moore know that.

"That's what people keep telling me," Jackson said. "They're finding out the hard way how daring I am. Where's Hillary?"

"Carson, what is he talking about?" Mrs. Moore asked.

"Shut up, Margaret."

"I will not ask again," Jackson said. "Tell me where she is and give me a full confession."

"You honestly think a forced confession will do you any good?" Moore spat, his green eyes glowing demonically. "No one will put any stock in a confession at gunpoint."

"They will when you know what to confess," Jackson said. "I'm not some jihadist in front of a flag in a garage, forcing you to denounce America. There's no script here. So when you come clean, it will be obvious it's the truth."

"It will still be inadmissible in court."

"Who cares about court? I'm betting it will be winner on YouTube. 'Senator Comes Clean on Cover-Up.' Wonder how many hits that will generate."

"You're insane."

"And you're stalling. Confess. Now."

"I don't know what you're talking about."

Jackson walked over to Margaret Moore and placed the gun in her leg, just above the knee.

Senator Moore swore at him.

"Do not make me do this," Jackson said.

Moore scowled and called him a litany of dirty words.

Jackson gritted his teeth. Theoretically, all the guys he had killed or assaulted at the base had been bad guys. Quinn too. Vickers had been shot by Quinn. The other deputies had either been complicit or combative, and Jackson had treated them as well as possible. The assault on Rae and the other bodyguards, the taking people hostage—okay, he was in it pretty deep. Extenuating circumstances might explain some of his actions away. He was hoping for leniency once the truth came out. But if he put a bullet in Margaret Moore, he would cross another line, beyond the reach of clemency. The court's or his own soul's.

"I shot Quinn," Jackson said. "I killed over a dozen men at the base. I drove up to your house in the burbs and took you and your guards captive. Do you really want to take the chance that I'm bluffing," he asked, "that I'll just say 'aw, shucks, you win' and hand over the gun?"

Moore stared at him intently.

"Three seconds," Jackson said, still unsure what to do if Moore called his bluff. "Two . . ." He couldn't shoot her, but if he backed down . . . "One . . ." He pushed the gun deeper into Margaret's leg, and she stifled a yelp.

"Wait!" Moore yelled.

Jackson turned the gun back on him. "Confess!"

"To what?"

"Everything."

"I—I don't know where to start."

"Pick somewhere. Now."

Moore took a deep breath. "I ordered Hillary's abduction."

Margaret gasped.

"Why?" Jackson asked.

"When we learned who she was—what she was—we wanted to study her."

"We who?"

"We don't have a name."

"Do any of you have individual names?"

"Of course."

"Name some. Start at the top."

Moore hesitated and Jackson turned the gun back toward Margaret.

"Myself, General Ernest Reynolds, Laura Woodson, Isaac Cutler."

"Why do you want to study Hillary?" Jackson asked.

"Because she's special."

"Special how?"

"Genetically."

"Quit being evasive. Explain."

Moore sighed, wavered slightly. Jackson only had to start turning the gun toward Margaret this time.

"We have reason to believe that Hillary is a product of Desert Root," Moore said, now sounding defeated.

"What is Desert Root?"

"An offshoot of a military project called Silver Dawn. It was a mind-control research program in the 1980s at Blane Air Force Base. Desert Root took the Silver Dawn research a step farther. The intent was to create test tube babies that would come out of the womb predisposed to certain values and belief constructs."

"How do you know all this?"

"Because I was involved in Silver Dawn and Desert Root."

"When?"

"September, 1978, through June of '85."

"So why the interest now?"

Moore paused.

"Why!"

"Because we're still conducting tests."

"What kind of tests?"

"On the subjects from the old Silver Dawn and Desert Root projects."

"To what end?"

Moore sighed.

"To what end?"

"To see how they've progressed and behaved over the years, to see if we could justify a full re-launch of the project."

"Where are these subjects kept?"

"They're not kept anywhere."

"Then how are you conducting the tests?"

"We have ways."

Jackson took a breath and glanced from Margaret to Rae to the other conscious guard. Their eyes were wide, and maybe, just maybe, their allegiance was wavering.

"I want details," Jackson said. "How are you conducting these 'tests'?"

"We're using . . . government resources to monitor behavior," he said. "Grades, job performance, the occasional introduced stimuli."

"Where?"

"Wherever they live, work, spend their free time."

"Ever in Las Vegas?"

Moore looked down. "Yes."

"How?"

"How what?"

"How do you monitor them in Las Vegas, particularly as it involves now-dead prostitutes?"

Margaret Moore's eyes flashed with astonishment, roving from Jackson, then back to her husband. For the first time, they were absent of fear.

"We used a variety of methods to lure certain promising subjects to Las Vegas. We then hired prostitutes, strippers, and dancers to engage them and ultimately incapacitate them. We transported them to the base, ran a variety of tests, then returned them none the wiser, making it appear as if they had spent a drunken, debauched weekend in Las Vegas. Most of them were too embarrassed by the suggestion to pursue it much further."

"What sort of tests?"

"A wide range of behavioral studies: how they responded to certain mental and physical stimuli, how they reacted in predefined situations and environments, what they believed about a variety of topics."

That was enough for the authorities to investigate. Like Moore had said, this confession would never be admissible in court. But Jackson was sure there was an FBI agent somewhere who would listen to it and spearhead an investigation. That was good enough for him.

"Tell me about Kingman."

"There were some side effects to the Silver Dawn and Desert Root experiments. Violent, often suicidal behavior, hallucinations, an assortment of psychological issues. Those exhibiting these side effects were kept in Kingman. They still are."

"For what purpose?"

Moore sighed. "To protect them, to protect the general public. And so we could easily monitor them."

"Monitor how?"

"We have spies planted in the community, and the sheriff's department works for us."

"Works how?"

"The sheriff is on our payroll."

"He have a name?"

"You know his name!" Moore shouted with a curse. "You shot him last night and left him for dead."

"I've already done my confessing," Jackson said. "His name?"

"Wyatt Quinn."

"Where'd you find him?"

Moore sighed with contempt. "He's Cutler's cousin."

"What about the ones not living in Kingman? Why weren't they quarantined?"

"Because they hadn't yet displayed any symptoms. Sometimes they presented later in life. With the babies . . . we had no idea."

Jackson took a step back and thought for a moment. He figured he had laid enough groundwork to show that Moore was dirty, and that his confession would carry weight.

"Who were the men at the base?" he asked.

"What men?"

"Dressed up like soldiers."

"Mercenaries."

Jackson breathed easier, knowing he hadn't killed members of the United States Armed Forces. But he wasn't sure God made that distinction.

"Where'd you get them?" he asked.

"I didn't. General Reynolds did."

"Where is Hillary now?"

"I don't know."

"You don't know?"

"No."

"Let me refresh your memory," Jackson said. He walked over to Margaret and stuck the gun in her neck. "Where is Hillary?"

"I don't know," Moore said, his voice pleading now. "Killing my wife won't change that."

"You're telling me that you arranged for her to be taken, and then just forgot about her and decided to go play golf?"

"No. I originally ordered McKenzie taken, and she rated higher than any previous subject. She was by far our best case study. When you forced us to evacuate Blane, Reynolds ordered the chopper to secure her. Only he knows where she is now. Maybe Woodson. We agreed it was best if I had plausible deniability."

Ever the politician.

"How do I find Reynolds or Woodson?" Jackson asked.

"Woodson could be anywhere. I never know."

"Cutler?"

"The same."

"Reynolds?"

"Why, you going to torture his wife too?"

"No," Jackson said, lowering the gun and stepping back from Margaret, "I'm going to put a bullet in each star until he gives up Hillary." He locked eyes with Moore. "And if I find out you're lying, that you know where she is, my final act before turning myself into the cops will be to find you and make you a cripple, you got that?"

Moore didn't respond. Jackson took that for a despondent yes.

"Where do I find Reynolds?"

"I don't know."

"Whose head do I put a gun to in order to change that answer?"

"I don't keep tabs on his position. He could be anywhere."

"Not good enough," Jackson said. "I'm trying real hard not to shoot any innocent people today, so maybe I'll just be judge and jury and make Swiss cheese out of your legs. How's that sound?"

Moore sighed. "He has a houseboat, on Lake Mead. It's where he stays when he's in the area, unless he's at the base."

"A houseboat on Lake Mead?"

"That's right. It's owned by a shell corporation. Named the *Leanne*."

Lake Mead was almost due south of Blane, not west as the chopper had flown. Was Moore giving him the runaround, or had the Black Hawk left on a westward bearing to avoid the incoming airstrike or to throw Jackson off? This was his last chance. He couldn't risk not finding Hillary.

"Is there any other place they might have taken her? Any other base, a CIA safe house, a summer home?"

"If there is, I don't know it. Aside from the base, the only location I know of is Woodson's apartment outside Washington. She had a data warehouse there, kept electronic files of everything. I swear, I have no idea where they took her, or where Reynolds is if not at his houseboat."

Jackson nodded. "Where's he dock it?"

"I don't know. I've only been there once, and we took a speedboat out to it."

"One last question. Who killed Arielle Coal?"

Moore looked down. It was his wife who spoke next. "Carson?"

He sighed heavier than all his previous sighs. "Woodson had her killed when she found out what she knew. I don't know who pulled the trigger."

Jackson nodded and turned off the camera. Then he grabbed the duct tape and bound Moore to his chair. He removed the tape from Martina, the driver, the two male bodyguards, and Rae's mouths. Switching his eyes between the three women, he apologized.

"I'm sorry for what I put you through. I'm sorry for my methods, but I had no other choice. Hopefully you see why I did what I did. You see what he's responsible for. He had Hillary kidnapped so he could study the effects of his mind-control project and genetic experiments."

Rae's eyes seemed to believe him. Margaret's were cutting into her husband. Martina was just relieved that the episode was almost over.

"I'm sorry, but I have to leave you tied up. As soon as I can, I'll send help."

He grabbed the camera, his roll of tape, and his guns, and headed for the door.

Chapter Sixty-Nine

5:36 p.m.

LAKE MEAD WAS due east of Las Vegas, but the road there took Jackson south, through Henderson and Boulder City. It also took time. The sun was setting over the valley, reminding him that it had just been rising when he had last seen Hillary. If only he had been more careful, maybe they could have gotten away. Right, from a chopper full of mercenaries. He was lucky he was alive.

While he drove through Vegas sprawl, Jackson called Mouse. He left out the details, but told him Hillary was still in danger. He also advised Mouse on his backup plan. After leaving Senator Moore's house, Jackson had found a Starbucks, parked on a side street, and tapped into their Wi-Fi. He had downloaded Moore's confession from the camera and sent it in an e-mail to Mouse. Now, he verified that his friend had received it.

"Yeah, I've got it."

"Hold onto it. I may need it for my defense."

"Your defense? How bad is this, man?"

"Bad. If I don't call back in a couple of hours, post this thing everywhere. Make sure the whole world sees it."

"You got it."

"Thanks, man."

"Watch your six, dude."

"Yeah."

Across the street from Starbucks, Jackson had also brought up several satellite images of the southwestern shore of Lake Mead. It was confusing in that each seemed to show the harbor in a different location. Some angles showed multiple harbors; some showed none at all. Recent drought conditions had drastically lowered the water level in the lake, and a little research revealed that The Lake Mead Marina had been moved south to combine with the Las Vegas Boat Harbor at Hemenway Harbor. Jackson made it his destination.

The desert was beautiful in the late afternoon, the jagged mountaintops casting long shadows across otherwise brilliantly white sand. It was peaceful and serene. So ironic.

As Jackson neared Boulder City, his phone rang. Or rather, played Point of Grace's "By Heart." He stared at it for several seconds, listening to the harmony. Then he picked it off the seat. "Yeah."

"Jackson, what's going on?" Sam asked. Her voice was heavy with concern.

"Why?"

"I just saw on the news that you're wanted for vandalism, mayhem, assault and battery, and multiple homicides. They say you blew up a military base."

So then, his actions were catching up with him.

"It's a misunderstanding," he said.

"What's going on?"

"Hillary's still missing."

"Have you gone to the police?"

"I can't, for obvious reasons."

"Jackson." She paused, the emotion obvious. "What is going on?"

"Sam . . ."

"Jackson, what is it?"

"I . . . I can't . . ."

"Jackson . . ."

"Look, Sam, I don't have time to explain it now. I really don't. Just promise me . . . promise me you won't believe everything you hear. Don't judge me just yet."

Jackson could hear the sadness in her silence. Or maybe he couldn't.

"Sam? . . . Sam?"

He lowered the phone and saw that the display had gone dark. No amount of button pushing could bring it back to life. The battery had died.

Tossing the phone on the passenger seat, Jackson concentrated on driving. And on the thoughts crawling around inside his head.

He had just tied up a United States senator and his wife and threatened to torture her in front of him if he didn't give Jackson the info he needed. He had lost count of how many people he had shot, threatened to shoot, hit over the head, or otherwise assaulted in the last twenty-four hours. What scared him most is that it was getting easier each time. And now, here he was, on the way to beat the truth out of a U.S. Army general, a Vietnam and Gulf War veteran. He would have cried if he'd had the strength.

Jackson pictured Sam, her heart breaking as she heard the news reports. He thought of Reggie, who had been in the dark since late morning, willing to help but uninvited. He thought of his grandpa, who was completely in the dark. Even Mouse, whose kill number was in the millions online, who had helped him along the way. What would they all think when they learned the totality of the truth?

Jackson took the bypass around Boulder City and, a few miles later, turned off Highway 93 onto Lakeshore Road. At the entrance to the Lake Mead Recreation Area, Jackson used McGregor's badge to bluff his way through the gate. Less than a quarter mile later, he veered right toward the harbor and skidded to a stop in front of what he deemed to be the office. He hurried inside.

A teenage girl was working the counter. Jackson walked up to her and clapped his badge on the glass. "I need a Jet Ski or wave runner or something."

"I'm afraid we're just closing up," she said. "It's going to be dark soon, and personal watercraft aren't allowed on the lake after sunset."

"Let me rephrase," Jackson said. "I need to commandeer a Jet Ski."

The girl looked from the badge to Jackson's face. "Is that real?"

"Is there any way I'd say no to that question?"

She reached for a phone. "I need to call my boss."

Jackson's eyes darted around the room. "Are those the keys?" he asked, nodding at a pegboard on the wall.

Her eyes answered for him, and he hopped over the counter.

"You can't—"

Jackson took her arm, firmly but not violently. "Listen. I am one of the good guys, and I am not going to hurt you. But I need some kind of watercraft and I need it now. A young woman's life is in danger and the man who knows where to find her is on the lake."

The girl swallowed and nodded. "Do you want a personal watercraft or a speedboat?"

"You have two-person Jet Skis?"

She nodded.

"Gassed?"

Another nod.

"I'll go with that."

She lifted a key off the rack and handed it to Jackson. "I'll take you down there."

Jackson followed the girl down a slight hill and onto the dock. In front of him, the dark blue waters of Lake Mead contrasted with the surrounding desert landscape turned orange by a sunset that was lighting up the entire sky. Funny how he noticed the details at a time like this.

The girl gave Jackson a two-minute instructional on a blue and white Jet Ski. He half paid attention and half scanned the lake. In addition to four small islands, he spotted at least a dozen boats zipping across the water. Sailboats, speedboats, cabin cruisers. No houseboats.

"You happen to see a houseboat out there today?"

"I've seen a couple come and go. Pretty standard."

"What about a helicopter?"

"What?"

"Did you see a helicopter land by the dock or maybe drop somebody at a houseboat? Big, green, would have been early this morning."

"I heard one," she said. "Probably seven a.m. I didn't see where it went, but it sounded low."

"Here?"

"I live at a trailer park just north of here."

Jackson nodded. "Anything else?"

She stepped back. "You're all set."

"Thank you," he said, revving the engine. It was his first time on a Jet Ski, and it took several minutes to get the hang of it. When he finally did, he opened the throttle and skimmed across the surface of the lake.

Since he hadn't spotted a houseboat from land, Jackson decided to swing around the southern end of three islands stacked in a row a couple miles offshore. As he zoomed across the water, he considered all the ways this could fail. Moore could have lied to him to get him to leave the house. Or he could have been telling the truth as far as he knew it. That still didn't mean Reynolds was on his houseboat. It certainly didn't mean Hillary was there, no matter what the girl from the marina had heard. Her ears might have mistaken a charter chopper on its way to the Grand Canyon for a low-flying Black Hawk. Even if Hillary had been brought to the houseboat, it didn't mean she was there now. Or that if she was, Jackson would be able to rescue her. He'd been living by the skin of his teeth all night and day. Sooner or later, the odds would catch up to him.

Not to mention the law in hot pursuit. News had already reached Los Angeles. It was only a matter of time before the dragnet closed in. If he didn't find Hillary on Lake Mead, he wasn't sure he'd have time or opportunity to continue the chase.

Jackson's mind also raced with invasion scenarios. He was familiar with houseboats since Leroy lived on one anchored in Marina del Rey. But not knowing the make or model of the boat, not knowing who was on it or how they might be armed, he was going in blind. Again.

He rounded the southernmost island and turned into the shadows, which he figured worked in his favor. Wide open at fifty miles per hour, Jackson scanned the horizon for a houseboat. Just off the northernmost island, he saw a speck that he first mistook for a small rock outcropping. As he approached it, he realized it was a houseboat drifting a quarter mile east of the island.

Jackson eased back on the throttle, made a circle, and coasted to a stop. He harkened back to his childhood, playing red light, green light. There were two ways to play: make a mad rush for the signal caller, or try to sneak up on them foot by foot. Both had their merits, and both had a chance of getting a person spotted. And in this case, killed.

There was a third option. Jackson could buzz the boat and scope out the scene, posing as just another pleasure-seeker out on the lake. But if anyone on the boat saw him the first time, he'd be in trouble the second time.

Darkness was coming fast. Jackson watched the sunset play out against the cliffs on the east side of the lake. When the vivid yellow light dimmed, then disappeared, he circled the southernmost island in the string. There was no sign yet of a police presence at or approaching the dock. He finished the circle, and eyed the houseboat again. It hadn't gone anywhere.

Jackson decided to make his move. He opened the throttle and took off, aiming a little bit left of the houseboat, as if to shoot between it and the island. He hoped that if anyone spotted him, they would remain unsuspicious as long as possible.

Jackson drew within a mile, then closed to a thousand yards. Muted light emanated from several windows, suggesting at least someone was onboard.

Five hundred yards, then five hundred feet. No movement aboard the boat, which he realized was a much larger model—and much newer—than his grandpa's. There were two full levels, plus a covered deck on top. It had a small deck forward, a larger one aft, and walkways along either side.

Merging the direct approach and the buzz-the-boat approach, Jackson continued through the opening between the boat and the island, confirming it was indeed the *Leanne*. His blood tried to run cold.

Coming around the north side of the houseboat, Jackson saw a small speedboat tethered to the front deck. He kicked himself for not questioning the girl at the dock about seeing a man matching Reynolds' description. Or a tall blond woman.

A hundred yards past the boat, Jackson started to make a wide turn to the left, as if to circle the northernmost island. But then he cranked hard right on the handlebars, nearly throwing himself off the Jet Ski. He made a one-eighty turn and took dead aim at the houseboat.

Entrance strategy had always been a missing part of the plan, but Jackson settled on the most direct method. He gunned the engine, planning to jump the Jet Ski onto the back deck of the *Leanne*. Then he would jump off, gun blazing, and shoot anything not blond and beautiful.

The report of a gunshot blew that plan to smithereens. Jackson wasn't hit, but he wasn't about to press his luck. Pushing the throttle for all it was worth, Jackson stood and threw himself into the water as another shot echoed through the night. Jackson stayed underwater, stroking toward the rear of the houseboat. Even beneath the surface, he heard the collision.

Jackson surfaced and saw the Jet Ski explode into a ball of flames as it banged into the side of the houseboat. He quickly submerged to avoid debris, and pushed hard toward a ladder on the stern. He peeked his head up again, ducked under, and made one more push. He grabbed onto the ladder and surfaced again, reaching for one of the Beretta pistols with his right hand.

A bullet pinged off the ladder just above his head, and he flinched. Holding onto the ladder with his left hand, Jackson swung his body to the right, around the corner of the deck. He peeked over the deck and raised his gun hand. His target stood in the doorway, and when he saw Jackson, he pivoted and unleashed a volley to the starboard corner.

Counting on that move, Jackson had dropped back down. At the same time, he used his left hand to pull his upper body as far left as possible. He brought his gun hand up again and fired three shots before the shooter could reorient his aim. All three hit center mass. The man staggered, and Jackson steadied himself before shooting once more. The man dropped his gun and fell backwards through the open doorway.

Jackson quickly clambered onto the deck and peeked carefully through the doorway before advancing. He was in a hallway, with two bedrooms and a bathroom on each side. All were empty, although one of the beds appeared to have been disturbed. Jackson moved past them and emerged into the kitchen. To his left, a curved stairway led to the second level. It was dark, and Jackson's glance up the stairs over the barrel of the gun revealed nothing.

He crept into the kitchen, lit by a single recessed light over the sink. An island counter doubled as a bistro dining table, surrounded by slat-backed barstools. The kitchen was separated from a living area with a sofa, two chairs, and a fireplace by a half wall between two support columns. They were set several feet in from the outside walls, leaving dual passages to the living room. Beyond it, sliding glass doors opened to the forward deck. He carefully peeked around the columns, then advanced into the living room. It was empty, unlit, with no signs that anyone had been there recently.

The curving staircase creaked. Jackson spun around and ducked just before bullets sailed over his head. Crouching behind the half wall, he listened until a barrage of fire terminated with a click. The shooter had exhausted his magazine.

Jackson popped up and took aim, seeing a man duck behind the kitchen island. He was in no mood for another duck-and-fire gun battle, so he rushed forward, around the left column. He skidded into the kitchen just as the man rammed another magazine into his machine gun and raised it.

Before he could fire, Jackson expended his final six bullets into the man's chest. He dropped in a pool of blood.

Something whoomped and Jackson momentarily recoiled. The *Leanne* could blow at any moment, but he couldn't abandon ship until he confirmed neither Reynolds nor Hillary was onboard.

Jackson drew the second Beretta—Klein's or McGregor's, he'd lost track—from the waistband of his jeans and approached the stairs. He climbed slowly, every creak giving away his presence. He had no idea what he would find on the second level, or if his eyes would even be able to process the scene before his head was blown off.

The staircase curved so that it exited perpendicular to the length of the boat. Jackson paused with his eyes at floor level, thankful that the room was dark, drawing only faint ambient light from up the stairs and from the fire that flickered translucently beyond windows covered by blinds. His eyes took a moment to acclimate, spotting what looked like a boardroom to the left and sliding glass doors right. They did not spot people.

He carefully raised his entire head above floor level, then climbed the rest of the way. The doors to the right opened to a deck that encompassed a hot tub. He turned left, facing a long table, surrounded by an array of chairs, cabinets, a wet bar, and an entertainment console. Coffee mugs, empty plates and glasses, multiple folders and pieces of paper, a laptop computer, and basic medical equipment—a blood pressure cuff, a heartrate monitor, and another object he couldn't identify—sat at the far end of the table. But the room was empty.

At the far end of the room, a set of double wooden doors were both closed, presumably leading to the master bedroom. Jackson crept toward them, twice glancing back over his shoulder to make sure no one was coming at him from the hot tub deck. When he reached the doors, he paused and listened. He could hear the fire, see its light growing brighter out the starboard window. He put his hand on the door handle and it felt hot. The fire was growing fast, and he realized he didn't have time to be cautious.

He jerked on the handle and prepared to fire. Instead, all he got was a billow of smoke and the searing heat from a fire that was going to engulf the houseboat in minutes.

He turned and ran forward. He threw open the sliding glass doors and stepped onto the deck that circled the hot tub. Both port and starboard walkways ran aft, and he peeked down each of them. Flames licked the walls on both sides, obscuring any possible path to the top deck from the boat's stern. So he circled the hot tub, debating between climbing a circular staircase to the top and retreating below.

The choice was taken away from him when he peered over the railing and saw blond hair down below on the open forward deck of the boat. It was unkempt and lay over an army green long-sleeved shirt, but there was no doubt it was Hillary's. She leaned on the front railing like a seasick passenger while a thin, wiry man worked to untie the speedboat tethered to the houseboat. A woman with dark hair drawn into a ponytail stood beside Hillary. When Jackson saw the pistol in her hand, he acted.

He aimed his Beretta at the woman's back and fired. Somehow, at the last moment, she turned to look back at him. Instead of pulverizing her spine, Jackson's two bullets tore into her right shoulder. She staggered, her gun limp at her side. Jackson re-aimed and fired again, as she dived for cover. Both bullets missed, and he readjusted and shot a fifth time, hitting the woman in the small of the back as she dived toward the starboard walkway and out of his line of fire.

Jackson redirected his attention to the man, who had climbed out of the boat and wrapped his arms around Hillary, using her as a human shield. He hadn't drawn a gun, but he gave Jackson no line of fire. And his arm was positioned tightly around Hillary's neck. Her arms flailed, but to no avail. Jackson still had no shot, so he did the only thing he could.

He jumped, stepping up onto the railing and launching himself forward, toward the man and Hillary. He'd estimated the distance incorrectly, and instead of landing on the deck beside the man where he could free Hillary from his clutches, he sailed long and his foot snagged the railing. It grabbed him, slowing his momentum, and he pitched forward and tumbled headfirst into the boat.

He cracked his head, banged his shoulder, and nearly split his kneecap on the gunwale of the boat. Those pains were quickly forgotten when the man jumped upon him, pummeling his head and face with lightning quick and well-trained fists.

It felt like minutes passed as Jackson attempted to dodge blows that pounded his head into the deck. At the same time, he tried to wrestle free, tried to plant a knee in the man's groin, and tried to reach his dropped gun. He failed in all three pursuits, but before the guy beat his brains in, Hillary came to the rescue. She jumped into the boat, wrapped her arms around the man's head, and pulled back.

She didn't have the strength to break his neck or do any serious damage, but she did give Jackson an opening. He drilled the man in the chin, and as he shook Hillary off, Jackson slid out from under him.

The guy was quick, and before Jackson could regain his feet, he popped him in the jaw with a hook that sent him sprawling. Jackson landed against the front console of the boat, and used it as a springboard to charge the man. He put all fighting tactics aside, and as Hillary jumped back onto the bench and out of his way, he hurled himself at the man. They both fell and a head cracked against the deck of the boat. It wasn't Jackson's.

The guy was momentarily dazed, and Jackson went for the knockout blow. Metaphorically. He stood and jumped, WWE style, landing knee first. Right in the crotch. The guy's eyeballs nearly hit Jackson in the face, and while he dealt with his reduced manhood, Jackson remodeled his face.

When he was sure no further resistance was coming, he stooped down to pick up his gun. Combined with the blows he had taken and with the adrenaline draining from his body, bending over nearly caused him to black out.

A gunshot roused him from his mini-stupor, and he jerked his head around.

Just in time to see Hillary pitch over the side of the boat into the dark waters of Lake Mead.

Chapter Seventy

JACKSON'S HEAD WHIRLED back to the houseboat. Leaning against the wall, her right hand on her bleeding stomach and her left clutching a gun, was the woman Jackson had just shot. She could barely stand, and the gun in her hand was aimed down at the floor. She tried to raise it to fire again, but Jackson didn't give her a chance.

He emptied his magazine into her midsection, dropped the gun, and dived overboard.

Lake Mead was known for its clean, clear, warm water. That changed after dark. Jackson felt like he was swimming through ink, looking for some sign of Hillary. He hadn't seen where the bullet hit. For all he knew, it had gone through her head or her heart and she was dead when she hit the water.

He was frantic, searching left, right, up, down. He saw no sign of her. His lungs on fire, he surfaced, hoping that maybe she had too, and was clinging to the side of the houseboat.

She wasn't.

Gulping in air, Jackson submerged again, widening his circle, fighting off panic that was far colder and darker than the lake waters. He tried to widen his search circle, but without markers or buoys, it was haphazard at best. Jackson flailed, pleading with his lungs for more time. Hillary had been under twice as long, and hadn't surfaced. He had to find her.

Jackson knew his time was up. He kicked for the surface, searching desperately through the darkness for some sign of Hillary. Unless she had sunk straight to the bottom, he couldn't understand . . .

He spotted something floating in the water to his right. Drifting aimlessly away from the houseboat, and down deeper into the murkiness. A body, maybe.

Jackson's lungs were on fire. He popped through the water, like a dolphin at Sea World, sucking in as much air as possible before gravity carried him back beneath the surface. He kicked toward the shape, knowing that if it wasn't Hillary, it wouldn't matter if he did find her.

He saw a leg, then a blip of pink. Two strokes and he had her. Michael Phelps couldn't have reached the surface more quickly.

Holding Hillary on top of him, Jackson backstroked and thrashed toward the speedboat. She was unconscious, not breathing, maybe not even alive.

An explosion rocked the night, the concussion spinning Jackson sideways and submerging him and Hillary under the water. He came up spitting and coughing as fiery debris rained down all around them. He pulled her under again, giving the wreckage several seconds to fall. When he surfaced, half of the houseboat was gone, and the rest was a sinking inferno.

Jackson kicked urgently for the speedboat, untethered from the *Leanne* and drifting several feet away from it as the houseboat was consumed. He heaved Hillary's body over the side, amazed at how much a six-foot-tall woman in an army button-down shirt weighed when wet. He crawled into the boat after her, and rolled her onto her back, away from the unconscious man. He put his head to her chest. She was deadly still. He looked for a bullet wound, but the water had washed away all the blood. He grabbed her green shirt by the collar and ripped it down the front, tearing loose the buttons.

There it was, under her right shoulder, just inside the strap of her pink tank top. He didn't see the bullet, but the wound was beginning to bleed again. He wasn't a surgeon and didn't dare probe for it with his bare hands. So he started CPR, tipping her head back slightly, pinching her nose, and exhaling slowly into her mouth. Then he began giving her chest compressions, counting as he did.

Another smaller explosion shook the speedboat, and Jackson instinctively hunched down over Hillary, like a *M*A*S*H* doctor during a shelling. He continued with the CPR, while out of the side of his eye, he saw the houseboat imitating the *Titanic*, ready to sink backwards into the lake.

"Come on, Hillary," Jackson said, returning to the chest compressions. "Come on!"

She was unresponsive.

Jackson heard a helicopter in the distance, and maybe a police siren too. Even if it was a water ambulance, it would never arrive in time. They were going on five minutes since she had been shot and fallen into the water.

"Hillary, breathe!" he screamed as he finished a round of compressions. He again pinched her nose and exhaled into her mouth twice. The effort had him short of breath, and Hillary remained lifeless.

"No!" he yelled, and started the compressions again. "No! Not again! Breathe, Hillary! Breathe!"

The sirens were there and growing closer. The helicopter was almost directly overhead, its spotlight circling around them. The speedboat was rocking from the waves caused by the sinking houseboat. Jackson was aware of it all, but almost subconsciously. He was on the verge of tears as he screamed again and again for Hillary to breathe.

A gurgle.

He stopped.

A cough.

Then an outright sputter.

"Hillary!" Jackson slid behind her and lifted her head as she coughed and spat water. She rolled over onto her knees, her whole body shaking as her lungs fought to expel the water in them.

Finally, it was out, and with wheezing gasps, Hillary drew in fresh air. Jackson turned her back over and knelt beside her. "Hillary. Hillary, are you with me?"

Her eyes blinked several times and locked onto his. "Jackson?"

"Yeah. I'm here. Just keep breathing."

She did, sucking in several lungfuls of air.

"Is it . . . Is it over?"

"Yeah, it's over."

*   *   *

Three and a half years ago . . .
Friday, May 15
7:54 p.m.

GRANT RETURNED carrying nachos, two hot dogs, and two sodas. He excused himself past a family of four and sidestepped his way toward Jackson.

"Hurry up, dude. I think the Pads might actually score a run."

"Sorry, long lines." Grant looked up at the scoreboard in consternation before sitting down. "*Five* to nothing?"

Jackson grinned. "Manny being Manny."

Grant sighed.

"A soaring, towering, magnificent two-run shot to left-center," Jackson said, imitating the legendary Dodgers broadcaster, Vin Scully. "Ramirez does it again, and the Dodgers are dominating the last-place Padres."

"Here's your hot dog, Vinny," Grant said.

"Brought to you by the fine people at Hebrew National," Jackson continued, "proudly supporting another stellar season of Dodger baseball."

Grant handed him the soda next. "Another? When was the last time you guys won a World Series?"

"Ten years to the day before the Padres were swept by the Yankees in only their second ever appearance in the Fall Classic. It was the sixth world championship for the Dodgers, paced by the phenomenal, fantastic pitching of Orel Hershiser and—"

"Can the Scully, will you?"

Jackson turned his attention to the field, where the Los Angeles pitcher induced a ground ball to the second baseman.

"Ooh, four-six-three double play, and the inning is over," Jackson mimicked. "The Padres come up empty yet again."

Grant elbowed him in the ribs.

"Hey, it's my birthday. I can talk like Scully all day if I want to."

"Yesterday was your birthday, and I paid for the tickets, so shut up."

"Always a gracious giver," Jackson said. He concentrated on his hot dog and the early evening view. Unlike the old Jack Murphy Stadium (it would forever be known as Jack Murphy to Jackson) the Padres' new ballpark provided great views of downtown San Diego. The sun had set, but still warmed the western half of a cloudless sky. Lights in the office buildings of downtown shone yellow and orange, contrasting with the amber glow on the eastern horizon. The air was warm but accompanied by a gentle breeze. It was a perfect night for baseball. And needling loser Padre fans.

"I can't believe you still have that hat," Jackson said, nodding at the brown and orange San Diego cap Grant wore. "Or the complete lack of fashion sense to wear it."

"This from a guy who wears jeans and T-shirts every day."

"Brett Favre wears jeans and a T-shirt."

"Brett Favre is a washed up, retired old man," Grant said.

"For today at least."

Grant took a slurp of his soda. "Speaking of, any prospects on a steady line of work?"

"What's un-steady about driving an airport shuttle?"

"If you're a retired guy named Max, nothing."

"Yeah, well, I'm toying with another idea. Pass the nachos."

"Let's hear it."

"You'll just laugh."

"So?"

Jackson shrugged. "I'm thinking of becoming a private eye."

Grant laughed.

"See, I told you."

"Are you trying to imitate your little brother?"

"Not while you're wearing that hat."

"Seriously, Jack. A private investigator?"

Jackson dipped into the nacho cheese. "What's so bad about that?"

"Nothing if you're a washed up Marine mooching off of a millionaire."

"Okay, first, you're using 'washed up' way too much. Second, I assume you're talking about Magnum, who was not a Marine and wasn't washed up. He just—"

"Realized at thirty-three that he hadn't been twenty-three," Grant finished. "Yeah, I've seen 'em all just like you."

"It's not a ridiculous reason," Jackson said.

"Is it yours?"

He shrugged and went for more cheese. "All I hear is how I'm not maximizing my life, hopping from college to job to whatever. Well . . ."

"You think a private investigator is the answer? Not psychic detective or something?"

"Too special of a niche, not that I couldn't pull it off."

"Come on, Jack. Level."

"I told you, I'm just toying. With motivation too."

The crack of the bat drew them back to the game. The Dodgers were in business with a double to left that put runners at second and third with no outs. The San Diego manager started a slow walk to the mound, and Jackson began humming "Hit the Road Jack."

"My sentiments exactly," Grant said with a glare at his brother.

Jackson turned toward him while the replacement pitcher made his warm-up tosses. "So what's your secret?"

"What do you mean?"

"I mean you've been acting weird all day. A strange sort of smirky expression. Starting sentences and pausing as if you're changing your mind about what to say. You aren't complaining about Padre strategy—or lack thereof—and you haven't said word one about that ultra-hot chick four rows in front of us.

523

She's wearing Padres swag and is still smoking. She might even look good in your hat."

Grant shrugged. "I hadn't noticed."

"You didn't notice," Jackson said. "Every guy in the upper deck has noticed. Every red-blooded, sing—" He turned his head. "You've got a girl."

Grant's face didn't change.

"That's it, isn't it?" Jackson asked. He watched the Los Angeles shortstop pop up to third. "You've got a girl. You might as well tell me."

Grant took a long drink of soda. "Yeah."

"Is she cute?"

He smiled. "Yeah."

"Like, really cute, or Grant girlfriend cute?"

"Like, Miss Four Rows Down would be jealous."

"Dang, baby brother. How'd you pull that off?"

Grant shrugged, now unable to contain that ear-to-ear grin that had been just behind the surface all night.

"Blond, brunette? What's she do? What's her name? Come on, bro, give me the scoop."

"Her name's Hillary," Grant said. "She's a defense lawyer in L.A."

"A lawyer? Really?"

He nodded.

"Does she know you're a cop?"

"Yeah."

A base hit scored a run and sent the drunks two rows behind Jackson and Grant into a profanity-laden fit. Five runs was bad. Six runs, apparently, was just unacceptable.

"Meatballs," Jackson muttered under his breath. "You don't get classless fans like this at Dodger Stadium."

"Um-hmm."

"So tell me about her. How long you been dating?"

"Just a few weeks. But she's good for me, Jack. She's intense, sound in her convictions, not afraid to speak her mind. She's brilliant, confident, witty. I—"

"Please stop before you tell me you think she might be the one. Not until after at least a month."

"I wasn't going to say that," Grant said. "I just think there's potential."

"Well that's good, Grant. I mean it."

"Thanks."

"This could be fun, you finally having a serious relationship."

"Me finally having one?"

Jackson ignored him. "I could get used to the idea of having a kid sister. She is a kid, right. Not some cougar partner at her firm."

"Four months older than me, to the day."

"I guess that will work." Jackson stuffed the last bite of hot dog into his mouth.

"I'm thinking of bringing her down on Memorial Day to meet the family."

"Good deal." Jackson swallowed. "Especially if she's as hot as you say she is."

Chapter Seventy-One

THE LAS VEGAS Metropolitan Police Department had taken Jackson into custody shortly before seven p.m. That was two minutes after first responders had pulled Hillary from Jackson's arms in the speedboat and approximately five minutes after the *Leanne* had disappeared beneath the murky waters of Lake Mead.

They had brought him back to shore via boat, just in time to see an ambulance—perhaps containing Hillary, perhaps containing the man he had rendered unconscious in the speedboat—race away from the marina. They had handcuffed and ankle-cuffed Jackson and brought him downtown for processing, where they had fingerprinted and photographed him before leading him to an interrogation room. He had waited for almost an hour without food or drink and without basic medical attention.

He needed it. A look in the two-way mirror showed him a bruised, bloodied, smudged face he didn't even recognize. His head was pounding, from the stress and from the repeated blows from the man he had concluded was Isaac Cutler. It had yet to be confirmed, but the description fit. The physical exertion aboard the houseboat and in the waters of Lake Mead—not to mention over the past twenty-four hours—had worn him past the point of exhaustion. He had also suffered countless minor to moderate injuries throughout the course of events. A routine checkup wouldn't have been out of order.

He had also not been given any information on Hillary. She had nearly drowned, which in itself was grounds for grave concern. She had also been shot, and for all Jackson knew, the bullet had pierced an important artery. She could have lost untold amounts of blood, swept away by the waters of Lake Mead. And this all on top of a day of physical, mental, and emotional abuse and repeated drug inoculations.

Finally, the door to his interrogation room opened. A man and a woman walked in. She was dressed in slacks, a wide-open V-necked blouse over a black camisole. Her hair was clipped up behind her head but strands hung loose in front of each ear. She wore too much mascara and a scowl that was matched by the man, Detective Marshall Baxter. Apparently this would be a game of bad cop-bad cop.

Baxter actually smiled as he sat down. "You're going to prison for a very long time."

"I'd like to see my lawyer. Where is she?"

"This is Assistant District Attorney Ronnie Miranda. She's going to talk deal."

Jackson turned his eyes to the woman, passing on a joke about an attorney being named Miranda or asking if she had adopted the name from a soap opera character.

She tucked one of the loose strands behind her ear and leaned on the table, hard enough that her fingers turned white.

"Mr. Douglas, I'm going to make you this offer once and only once and you have one minute to take it or leave it. Confess to the murders of Arielle Coal, Xavier Stark, and Robert Kyle, and I will do everything in my power to see that you are tried in the state of Nevada and I will take the death penalty off the table."

"I'd like to speak to my attorney first."

"Fifty-five seconds."

He smiled. "Somehow I get the feeling that this limited-time offer isn't being made for my benefit as much as yours. So I have to wonder, why the urgency on your behalf?"

"Forty-five seconds."

"Afraid the feds are going to swoop in and take me away?"

"I'm not joking, Mr. Douglas." She made a show of looking at her watch, even though she hadn't consulted it when she'd started her countdown. "Thirty-five seconds."

He sat back. "If I'm going to confess to three murders I didn't commit and, in the process, commit myself to a life in prison, I ought to at least get five minutes to think it over."

"Twenty-five seconds."

"Not until I talk to my lawyer."

"Twenty."

"Where is she?"

"Fifteen."

"Miss Miranda, I'm sorry to drag you out here on a Friday night for nothing, but I'm not confessing to anything."

"Five seconds. Last chance."

He pursed his lips and waited. Her final five seconds lasted at least fifteen. Then she stood. "Fine." She looked at Baxter with pity and exited the room.

He paced back and forth a few times, then pulled out a chair and sat down.

"You're in deep trouble."

"Oh, really?"

"You really want to wisecrack right now?"

"Detective, I have been shot at hundreds of times, beaten up, blown up, bombed, all to save the life of a woman who was injected with drugs and treated like a guinea pig by factions in her own government, shot, nearly drowned, and whose location and medical condition I have yet to be told. So when you and Ms. Miranda stage a little dramatic episode for me and then try to tell me how much trouble I'm in, yes, I very much would like to wisecrack."

Baxter sat back. He stared at Jackson for what seemed like minutes. Then he leaned all the way forward, resting his arms on the table. "Just between you and me, why? I get that you were trying to save the girl, but why Coal? What did she have to do with any of this?"

"Just between you and me?" Jackson asked.

"Yeah."

"Because, what, we're girlfriends up late with a pint of ice cream?"

Baxter sat back with the beginnings of anger on his face.

"And the cameras and microphones and the A.D.A. behind the glass will plug their ears and hum while we talk?" Jackson asked.

Baxter now glared.

"I'm not saying another word until I get to speak to Hillary."

Baxter tried for fifteen more minutes before giving up. He left the room, and Jackson bowed his head and prayed. He wasn't real big on creating a major mess and then asking God to spare him consequences, but he prayed that he wouldn't get railroaded. He had no idea how high the Silver Dawn/Golden Dawn conspiracy went or what the key figures involved would do to protect themselves. Moore's confession, if Mouse had followed the plan, had been broadcast on the internet. And Jackson was pretty sure the woman he'd shot on the *Leanne* had been Laura Woodson. Cutler—if the man was Cutler—had been taken into some sort of custody. But Reynolds was in the wind, and who knew what other parties were at play. Jackson was on shaky ground legally as it was, much more so he if was set up.

He also prayed for Hillary, for her health and recovery and mental state. Even if she hadn't suffered any long-term effects from being under water so long, and even if the bullet wound hadn't hit anything major, and even if all the drugs could be flushed from her system, she was still left to deal with the very real possibility that she was a product of Desert Root. Everything she had known about her family had changed. The thought that she was coming to grips with all this alone tormented Jackson.

At some point in time—its passage was hard to determine—Jackson heard raised voices in the hall outside the interrogation room. A last-ditch plea by the local authorities to maintain jurisdiction, he figured. They lost.

Jackson was transferred to the FBI's John Lawrence Bailey Memorial Building, where Special Agents Hodge and Asbury went to work on him. Hodge was short, black, and loud. Asbury was tall and white and smelled of garlic. Hodge took the first go-round, berating Jackson with rapid-fire questions, looking to trip him up. Jackson kept his composure and didn't push back, but asked to speak with his lawyer. Hodge told him only guilty people needed a lawyer, and Jackson filed that remark away for later.

With Hodge ready to blow a gasket, Asbury took over and put his partner to shame. Jackson was looking at life in prison, and Asbury said that he didn't think Jackson was prison material. But he would personally see to it that Jackson lived a long and healthy life so that his sentence was maximized. Or better yet, since Jackson's acts could be construed as domestic terrorism, maybe they'd ship him to Gitmo and let a few months in the yard with the Al-Qaeda boys work on him. The interrogation room grew darker and clammier by the minute, and Jackson was having visions of scenes from the early part of *The Count of Monte Cristo*. Only he doubted there would be a friendly but crazy old abbé in his adjoining cell.

Thinking of Hillary—he pictured her tall, regal, and beautiful as opposed to hopped up on drugs and bullet-riddled—Jackson continued to keep his mouth shut, refusing to answer questions and risk incriminating himself until he could speak with counsel. Then Hodge joined Asbury and they tag-teamed Jackson, battering him with threats until he realized they were mostly bluster. So he broke his silence.

"What exactly do you want from me?" he asked. "If you've got such incriminatory evidence that you can throw me in with a bunch of terrorists, then do it already. But I haven't slept in about a week, I haven't eaten since breakfast yesterday—assuming today is tomorrow by now—and until I get to speak with a lawyer—my lawyer!—I am not answering anything. So either do what you will to me or let me sleep."

He glared at each of them, then lay his head on the desk.

One of them, he guessed Hodge, slammed his palm on it.

Jackson sat up, waiting until the ringing in his ears stopped, and then lay his head right back down.

"You want to play games with us," Asbury said, "fine. We'll play games. Maybe you'd like us to take you back to Las Vegas Metro and have them throw you in the drunk tank for a few hours."

Without raising his head, almost as if bored, he answered. "Right, because you're alleging I just killed twenty-five people, some of them in cold blood, and am possibly a terrorist, so having to share a cell with a couple of drunks, dealers, and pimps is really going to scare me. What's next, going to my room without dinner?"

He had no idea why he was being so lippy. Maybe it was the lack of sleep. Or food. Or the fact that they were denying him constitutional rights and refusing to tell him how Hillary was doing. Or maybe it was because, despite all he had done and the guilt he felt, he knew he wasn't the savage they wanted to portray.

Nearly foaming at the mouth, the two agents left. An inordinate amount of time later, a third man entered the room. He wore a suit coat and tie and wire-rim glasses, and set a Styrofoam cup of water in front of Jackson. It wasn't a cheeseburger and a shake, but it was something. He introduced himself as Special Agent Richter, apologized for the conduct of his colleagues, and got down to business. Clearly playing the good cop, he appealed to Jackson's common sense, obvious physical strain, and even his sense of civic and patriotic duty. Just answer a few questions, and it will all be better, okay?

Jackson took a long drink of water, before it was taken away, and told Special Agent Richter that he was not answering any questions until he spoke with his lawyer.

"I'm afraid we can't do that right now."

"Why not?"

Richter didn't answer.

"Is she dead?"

"Mr. Douglas, I can arrange for you to speak with another lawyer from her firm, or you can select one from the phonebook."

"I want Hillary."

"That's not possible right now."

Jackson breathed slowly, lest he say something he'd regret. He tried to take hope from the repeated phrase "right now." After nearly a minute, he leaned forward.

"I am not saying anything until I speak to Hillary, and I don't care if you march the Director of the FBI in here. Is that clear?"

Richter cleared his throat and adjusted his glasses. "Perfectly." He turned around and spoke into the two-way mirror behind him. "Have Mr. Douglas transferred to Holding One."

Five minutes later he was in a white square room with a bench and a stainless steel toilet. No windows, not even bars on his cell door. It was a standard steel door with a small window in the middle, out of which Jackson could see nothing but a hallway and the cell across from him.

Baxter was right, he was in deep trouble.

Chapter Seventy-Two

Saturday, September 22
6:03 a.m.

"MR. DOUGLAS, I'M General Thomas W. Bradford, Vice Chief of Staff of the United States Air Force."

Jackson looked into the flinty eyes of a man with a voice like muted thunder. He was not physically intimidating, with a round head, wrinkles in his forehead and beneath his neck, and crisp silver hair. His uniform, on the other hand, was daunting. The dark blue three-button coat was immaculate, the four stars on his epaulets shining like their namesakes. A rainbow of ribbons decorated the left breast, and a blue tie to match the coat hung perfectly straight. Jackson had no doubt the trousers were flawlessly creased and the shoes buffed to a shine. Bradford sat ramrod straight, his peaked service cap placed on the table to his left. A manila folder with a pen on top lay on the table in front of him. To its right were two steaming cups of store-bought coffee. He eased one of them toward Jackson.

"Thank you, sir," he said, his throat froggy. He cleared it.

"I'm here on behalf of the Secretary of the Air Force, in conjunction with the Department of Defense and the Department of Justice, for starters. This situation is no longer under the jurisdiction of the Las Vegas Metro Police or the FBI."

Jackson reached his un-cuffed hands for the coffee. He was barely cognizant, and now the titles and agencies were flying fast. He guessed he'd had four or five hours in isolation, during which he had drifted in and out of fitful sleep. His mind had not stopped, worrying about Hillary, worrying about his own fate, worrying about what Leroy and Reggie and Sam would think. But most of all, he couldn't stop reliving the events of the last so-many hours. He'd been running on pure adrenaline, and as it finally washed from his system, not only was he more thoroughly drained than all but once in his life, but also struggling to believe it had been real. He hoped the coffee was strong.

"In a few moments, I'm going to bring in an officer from the JAG Corps who will be able to advise you on some legal matters. I'm also working on upgrading your accommodations for the time being. I realize this is a stressful time, but I'd encourage you to be patient. It's going to take a little while to sort things out."

Jackson sat forward, forcing his brain to be attentive. This actually sounded positive. Not just the words, but the general's tone. Was there a light at the end of the tunnel? Or was the breeze that carried hope just the wind produced by an oncoming train?

"I also want to inform you that Miss McKenzie is out of surgery and recovering at Desert Springs Hospital."

Jackson's body involuntarily slumped with relief.

"I spoke to Dr. Sears just a few moments ago," Bradford continued. "He said you pulled her from the water just in time. There should be no long-term damage from being submerged in the water and the bullet didn't strike any major organs or arteries. She was under the influence of several narcotics when she was admitted, and as soon as she's recovered from the surgery, they'll work on flushing them from her system."

"Thank you, General."

He nodded. "Just sit tight, Mr. Douglas."

Bradford stood and exited the room—by all appearances the same one in which Jackson had been questioned by Hodge, Asbury, and Richter—leaving Jackson alone with his coffee and his thoughts. He gulped the coffee while trying to make sense of everything. Was the Air Force on his side? It almost sounded that way. Or was this another good cop routine?

He didn't have long to think. The door opened and a petite woman entered. She was dressed in blue to match General Bradford, only with a tie tab in place of the tie and a knee-length skirt instead of trousers. A garrison cap was tucked under her arm. She carried a small attaché case, which she set on the table as she smiled briefly at Jackson. She was young and pretty, her short auburn hair tied in a low chignon. Sitting down, she placed her cap in the same place Bradford had and opened her briefcase.

"I'm Lieutenant Alison Paige," she said. "I work for the JAG Corps, and I have been asked by Secretary Wittingham to offer my services on behalf of the United States Air Force."

"Offer your services?"

She smiled again. Under any other circumstances, it would have been alluring. Now, it was at least comforting. "That's correct. Secretary Wittingham wants to make sure you receive proper representation."

"I thought JAG only represented members of the armed forces."

"Typically, that's correct. However, this is a rather unique scenario, and since you haven't yet spoken to an attorney, I was asked to meet with you."

Jackson took another swig of coffee. He was going to need full brainpower.

"Now, you are certainly under no obligation to retain my services, but if you so choose, you can have full assurance that anything you say will be held in the strictest of confidence, as would be the case if you spoke to any civilian attorney. Furthermore, I will be representing you only, so there will be conflict of interest where the Air Force is concerned."

"Forgive me, Lieutenant, but this all strikes me as a little odd."

"Me as well, Mr. Douglas, but I am following orders."

He nodded and had more coffee.

"Before you make a decision, I should point out a few things. Right now, you are facing the following potential charges."

She had extracted a tablet from her briefcase and consulted it with quick downward flits of her eyes. Mostly, she spoke from memory. Considering she had likely been awakened in the middle of the night and briefed in transit, Jackson was impressed.

"First, the Las Vegas Metropolitan Police Department considers you their primary suspect in the murders of Arielle Coal, Xavier Stark, and Robert Kyle."

Jackson nodded, confident he could at least beat that rap.

"Second, Sheriff Wyatt Quinn of the Delamar County Sheriff's Department is charging you with murder, attempted murder, assault and battery, false imprisonment, grand theft auto, and a litany of smaller crimes."

Jackson wanted to ask how ol' Wyatt was doing, but left the question on his tongue.

"Third—and here is where it gets murky—are the deaths of some twenty-four persons reported to be on or at Blane Air Force Base on Thursday evening. Their deaths are under investigation by the Delamar County Sheriff's Department; the state of Nevada; the FBI; and the Departments of Homeland Security, Defense, and Justice; as well as the United States Air Force. You are, to put it mildly, a person of interest."

Jackson rubbed the considerable stubble on his jaw, realizing that the fighter jet that had bombed the base had wiped away most evidence that could incriminate him, as well as any witnesses who might testify about the events that had transpired. He wasn't sure if that was good or bad.

"Fourth, according to the testimony of Senator Carson Moore, you detained him, his wife, and five members of their staff at gunpoint, threatening bodily harm to at least two of them."

She looked up. He nodded.

"Fifth, we have the deaths of three persons aboard a now-sunken houseboat on Lake Mead, as well as a fourth victim who is in intensive care as we speak. Las Vegas Metro, the state of Nevada, and a host of other agencies are interested in this episode as well."

Lieutenant Paige set down her tablet. "And lastly, we have a variety of other, smaller charges and claims that amount to nuisances in light of the issues I mentioned." She traced her forehead with her finger, in the process lifting a stray strand of hair out of the way. She looked at Jackson with bright green eyes. "Now, you are certainly welcome to seek your own counsel, but it is my understanding that you have been asking for an attorney, and specifically Miss McKenzie. Since she is unavailable at the moment, as I said a bit earlier, I have been asked by Secretary Wittingham to offer my services. I have the necessary paperwork here if you'd like to look it over."

"All due respect, Lieutenant, I greatly appreciate the offer and your taking the time to come down here. But the fact is, I did what I did and I didn't do what I didn't do. Nothing's going to change that, and I'm ready and willing to face the music for my actions."

For the first time, her pleasant face clouded. "It was my understanding you refused to cooperate with the FBI until you spoke to your attorney."

"That's because I had yet to confirm that my attorney was still alive. And were she here now, I'm sure she'd berate me for it, but I don't need an attorney to negotiate technicalities. Like I said, I did what I did."

"May I be frank, Mr. Douglas?"

He lifted his cup. "Please," he said before taking a drink.

"I commend you for your valor, but I don't think you fully appreciate the situation. Right now, no less than eight agencies are seeking to find the truth behind what happened here in Las Vegas, on Lake Mead, in Kingman, and at Blane Air Force Base. Your honesty and integrity aside, this could get very sticky. My advice would be that you retain me as your legal counsel until Miss McKenzie or another lawyer of your choice is available or until you see fit. You'll be under no obligation to employ my services any longer than you wish. But allow me to make sure that you get a fair deal and do not get coerced or pressured into anything."

Jackson mulled.

"Some of these men and women are very eager to nail somebody to the wall, and I'm not entirely sure they care who. Like I said, you're under no obligation, but I'd strongly advise you avail yourself of my counsel."

He nodded. "May I be candid in return?"

"Of course."

"I don't have the money to retain you, even until Hillary can sit up in her hospital bed and make a few cranky phone calls." He thought of the money that had been in the trunk of Quinn's car, that now was who knew where, and that was likely going to be impounded as evidence. Without it, he really couldn't afford Lieutenant Paige or the most rookie street lawyer from a Grisham novel.

Paige's lips parted in a thin smile. "I guess I wasn't clear. My services will be *pro bono*—no charge to you whatsoever."

Jackson leaned back in his folding chair. "Why?"

"You'd have to ask Secretary Wittingham."

This was too good to be true, but Jackson didn't see the harm. If the Secretary of the Air Force was involved in the Silver Dawn/Golden Dawn conspiracy, then it truly went all the way to the top and there was nothing Jackson could do to save himself. If this was some sort of legal trap, he was sure Hillary could get him out of it. And while he was prepared to accept responsibility for his actions, he'd rather not accept any more than necessary.

"Okay," he said, "on one condition."

"Name it."

"I'm starved. I haven't eaten since breakfast yesterday. Any chance you can find someone in this building who will get me something to eat?"

"I think I can manage that," she said. She retrieved several forms from her briefcase and placed them in front of Jackson, along with a pen. "Read those over, and I'll answer any questions you may have. In the meantime, I'll see if I can rustle up some breakfast."

Jackson skimmed the legalese, knowing that if he were properly rested and not facing life in prison, he still wouldn't understand half of it. He signed and initialed where necessary and slid the forms to Paige's side of the desk just as she returned, carrying a small tray. It held a pair of microwaved breakfast sandwiches, a side of hash browns, a glass of orange juice, and a refill of coffee.

"It's nothing special," she said, "but it's what was on hand."

"Thank you," Jackson said, tossing manners to the wind and gorging himself.

Lieutenant Paige looked over the forms, returned them to her briefcase, and drew out a small digital recorder. She set it on the desk and clicked a button. "All right, Mr. Douglas, tell me everything."

Chapter Seventy-Three

2:44 p.m.

JACKSON HAD BEEN transferred again, this time to a nondescript building somewhere on Nellis Air Force Base. (He was pretty sure it wasn't in the middle of an airplane hangar.) There he had been allowed to shower and shave, and he took advantage of both opportunities. He'd been provided a change of clothes, albeit to blue Air Force physical training gear. Someone had requisitioned a lunch of a cold cut sub sandwich and potato chips, and he had downed it voraciously. And he'd been updated on Hillary's condition—she was resting comfortably— although not allowed to speak with her.

Now he sat in a huge conference room, in the middle of the wide side of a long mahogany table. Lieutenant Alison Paige sat to his left, smelling pleasantly like cinnamon. Over a dozen others were wrapped around the far side and both ends of the table. They were men and women, white, black, Latino, and Asian. They wore everything from military uniforms to business dress. Some had laptops or tablets in front of them, some notepads or a folder. A few looked bored and a couple appeared angry. None were smiling.

Two cameras were aimed at Jackson, both from the far side of the table, each at a slight angle. A thin microphone as might be found on a podium was positioned directly in front of him. Several carafes of water were spaced around the table, and each person had a glass in front of them. Jackson's was filled with ice water, which he sipped to wet a suddenly dry mouth. And lest he think the relaxed environment was an invitation to try to escape, two armed airmen stood on either side of the door, with two more posted in the hall.

The man directly across the table from Jackson cleared his throat. He was nondescript as far as build and appearance, but his eyes were mere slits, the heart of a no-nonsense face. He looked through them, over the top of bifocals perched at the end of his nose, as he addressed Jackson.

"Mr. Douglas, I'm Deputy Secretary of Defense James Duval. I understand that you have retained Lieutenant Paige as your legal counsel for the purpose of these proceedings?"

Jackson too cleared his throat, leaning slightly toward the microphone. "Yes, uh . . . I'm sorry, how do I address you?"

"'Mr. Deputy Secretary' is a bit wordy, so 'sir' will be fine."

"Yes, sir."

"And Lieutenant Paige has briefed you?"

"Yes, sir."

"Then you understand that anything you say here is admissible in a court of law and could be used against you?"

"I do."

As they spoke, a woman several seats to his right, around the corner of the table, typed on a very small laptop, the tapping of keys almost inaudible.

Duval cleared his throat again. "Then let me introduce you to everyone here, starting on my right with Associate Attorney General of the United States, Adrienne Porter; Secretary of the Air Force, Theodore Wittingham; Chief of Staff of the Air Force, General Dalton Hollis; Vice Chief of Staff of the Air Force, General Thomas W. Bradford; and Special Agent Nghia Nguyen of the Air Force Office of Special Investigations."

To his right, Wittingham coughed.

"Of course, my apologies. Airman First Class Kimberly Armstrong will be acting as secretary for these proceedings." Duval turned his head. "On my left, Assistant Director Neil Simpson Dykes of the Federal Bureau of Investigation; Associate Deputy Director Mitch Cooper of the Central Intelligence Agency; Chief of Staff of the Army, General Felix G. Masterson; Attorney General for the State of Nevada Madeline Graves; Sheriff Sergio Cortez of the Las Vegas Metropolitan Police Department; and Clark County District Attorney Paloma Aguilar."

Jackson looked around the room, trying to breathe. Two of the Joint Chiefs, multiple secretaries and undersecretaries and assistant directors and deputy associates—his head was spinning. Lieutenant Paige had only given him the outline of what would happen, so he was learning as they went.

"Mr. Douglas," Duval continued, "the purpose of this meeting is to determine the precise course of events that led up to your arrival at Blane Air Force Base on the morning of Friday, September 21, 2012, and the actions taken thereupon and in the subsequent hours leading up to your arrest by LVMPD." He turned to Paige. "Lieutenant Paige, you have outlined for Mr. Douglas the potential charges he faces?"

"I have, sir."

Duval's eyes swiveled back to Jackson. "Then I will assume, Mr. Douglas, that you fully appreciate the gravity of this situation. Rest assured, we will find the truth. It will go much easier for you if you do not withhold from us initially."

"Yes, sir."

Duval relaxed slightly. He took off his glasses. "Please tell us your side of the story."

Paige beat him to it. "Mr. Deputy Secretary, please let the record reflect that I have advised Mr. Douglas not to answer any questions or make any statements at this time. And let it reflect that he has waived that advice because he would like to set the record straight."

Duval glanced at Armstrong, the acting secretary. "So noted."

Jackson sat up straighter. This was it. If he owned his actions, there was no walking back his testimony in court later. But he had no intentions of walking back, and the evidence of his actions in Kingman and at Moore's house was undeniable, even if any evidence at Blane had been bombed to smithereens. And as far as his fears of going to the authorities were concerned, the authority didn't get much higher than this room. If the Department of Defense, Department of Justice, CIA, FBI, and Joint Chiefs were all compromised, his plight was pretty much hopeless anyhow.

So he told them everything, starting with Hillary's voicemail and finishing with his being led to the conference room ten minutes prior. It took him the better part of an hour, recounting every detail he could remember and citing motivations and thought processes along the way. He did his best to minimize any possible suspicion of Richard Holloway, and took responsibility for all decisions he and Hillary had made. Otherwise, he was thoroughly truthful.

He finished and gulped from a sweating glass of water. Throughout his speech, Armstrong had typed along with him, and several on the panel had taken their own notes. None had interrupted or asked any questions, and Lieutenant Paige had sat silently beside him, jotting occasionally on a legal pad.

Duval looked left and right. "Questions?"

Paloma Aguilar, a heavyset, frowning Latina woman led off, asking several accusatory questions about the death of Arielle Coal. Jackson answered each one, repeating much of what he had said earlier. Aguilar's questions served as a gateway for Mitch Cooper, the appropriately furtive associate deputy director of the CIA, to inquire about Stark and Kyle. Jackson said he'd never met either of them, and had just come to suspect Stark when he'd been informed of the dual murder by private investigator Danny Pollack. Cooper scribbled a few notes and sat back.

"How did you know that Miss McKenzie was being held on the *Leanne* on Lake Mead?" Madeline Graves asked after a short pause. The attorney general for the state of Nevada was a thin black woman with dark brown eyes and straight, slick hair. She wore a burgundy pantsuit that matched wide, circular glasses attached to a chain. Thus far, they had been off her nose and back a dozen times.

"Um, I didn't, ma'am."

"But you went there to find her."

"I went there hoping to find General Reynolds and possibly Hillary."

"What made you think either of them might be there?"

He'd already explained it all during his statement, but he sensed Graves was fishing. He had no choice but to swim toward her shiny lure.

"Senator Moore informed me that Reynolds often stayed on that boat."

"Why did he volunteer this information?"

"Objection," Paige said. "Mr. Douglas has already provided the answers to these questions."

"This isn't a courtroom, Lieutenant," Duval said. His heavy eyes shifted to Jackson.

"I coerced the information out of him," he said.

"At gunpoint?"

"Yes, ma'am."

"So just to confirm, you placed a gun to the head of a United States senator?"

"If you want to be totally accurate, I placed the gun to the kneecap and neck of his wife."

"And you find this behavior acceptable?"

"Quite the contrary, ma'am. It is one of the most reprehensible things I've ever done."

She shook her head, removing her glasses. "Then why did you do it?"

"Because it was the only possible way I thought I could find Hillary."

"Why didn't you contact the police?" Sheriff Cortez asked.

"At that point, I had evidence that multiple members of the Delamar County Sheriff's Department, a U.S. senator, a three-star general in the United States Army, and members of the CIA were complicit in Hillary's kidnapping. I had been shot at by Army soldiers in a Black Hawk helicopter and nearly bombed by an American fighter jet. With all due respect, I think my trust issues were somewhat warranted."

"I can assure you, those were not United States Army soldiers," General Masterson said. He was an old crusty with drooping jowls and a mouth full of mush. But he had the ribbons to demand respect, and while the skin around them was sagged and creased, his eyes were strong and vivid. "Sergeant John Ravich was dishonorably discharged in August of 2009 after striking a superior officer." He glanced down to consult his notes. "Last we knew, he was working with a private military contractor named GrayLine." He looked up. "I would bet my pension the other men in the chopper were similarly disgruntled former military or wannabes. But they were not acting on behalf of the United States Army."

"Thank you, General, that's a relief to know."

"I'm afraid the same cannot be said for the F-22 that bombed Blane Air Force Base," General Hollis said. He was black, half the age of General Masterson, but just as decorated. "We're still tracking the chain of command, but the jet was scrambled from right here at Nellis, we believe at the behest of General Reynolds."

"Isn't Reynolds Army?" Neil Simpson Dykes, the FBI assistant director, asked.

"Yes, he is, which is why tracing the chain of command is a little confusing. You all have my assurance that any members of the United States Air Force who were willing conspirators will be dealt with most severely."

"Can we get back to Mr. Douglas's blatant disregard for the law?" Graves asked. "I'd like to know what evidence he had to prove that members of the Delamar County Sheriff's Department were complicit in the kidnapping."

Jackson took a drink of water. "As I stated previously, Sheriff Quinn made several comments about the apparel Hillary was wearing to go jogging. She had changed just prior to departing from our motel at the southern end of Kingman. Unless he had seen her jogging and withheld that information, there was no way for him to know what she was wearing."

"And based on that, you attacked a sworn officer of the law and took him as your prisoner?"

"Yes, ma'am, along with his ties to Isaac Cutler, a man believed to be part of the conspiracy, along with some circumstantial evidence and a hunch, I did. And if I hadn't, Hillary may not be alive at this moment."

The questioning continued, with several members on the panel on a witch hunt, several earnestly seeking the truth, and a few seemingly disinterested. They covered almost everything in detail a second time, by which point their meeting had lasted nearly two hours. Jackson knew because Duval announced it as he called a ten-minute recess.

"You're doing great," Paige said as she and Jackson stood in the corner of the room by themselves. He had needed to stretch his legs but had been asked not to leave the conference room.

"Says the lady who didn't want me to say anything."

"As your legal counsel, I have to advise you as I deem best. But given your insistence on telling your side of the story, you've done very well. You've answered every question with honesty and aplomb, which isn't easy when you're being attacked."

"How much longer do you think this lasts?"

She licked her lips. "I think Deputy Secretary Duval is looking for something to make a decision. What that is, I don't know."

"It's his decision?"

"I should say, he's looking on behalf of his boss, Secretary Chambers. Ultimately, he and the attorney general will likely make the decision."

Jackson nodded.

"The fact that Deputy Secretary Duval is chairing this committee is a good sign," she said.

"How's that?"

"Because the Department of Justice would be the body to bring federal charges against you," Paige answered. "The Department of Defense is more interested in getting answers about what was going on at Blane and with the Golden Dawn project as it pertains to national defense."

She offered a thin smile, her eyes sparkling with confidence.

Jackson determined he'd send her a gift when this was all over, maybe a handcrafted vanity license plate, courtesy of the federal pen.

The inquisition reconvened, and Duval took over the questioning. "Mr. Douglas, I commend you on a very methodical recounting of events. However, there is one area in which you were somewhat vague, and I'd like to clarify a few points."

"Yes, sir."

"Forgive me if I'm treading over familiar ground, but what caused you to suspect Richard Holloway's involvement in Golden Dawn and Blane Air Force Base?"

Jackson took a deep breath. He had promised not to drag Holloway's name through the mud, and he'd done his best to keep him out of it. But now, staring at so much brass, he figured he'd better come clean.

"As I mentioned, Miss Coal overheard a man named Matt Brenner mention that Holloway had the goods in the form of a paper trail and that it was time for Brenner and an associate to 'get out.' We assumed, based on the rest of her notes, that the goods in question were in relation to Senator Moore and the mysterious man we later pegged as Isaac Cutler. Brenner worked for Holloway, and we also noticed several business and political connections between Holloway and Moore. We suspected that whatever it was Holloway held that Brenner was afraid of might be something to incriminate Moore and shine a light on what was truly going on. It was then that we decided to make an effort to learn what Holloway knew."

"And this led to your break-in of his safe?" Duval asked.

"Ultimately, yes, sir. We had hoped to get him to reveal the information to us. But when we learned of the death of Xavier Stark, a man we suspected to be in cahoots with Moore but who was found murdered with a former Navy SEAL and CIA operative—"

"Kyle," Duval interjected.

"Correct. At that point, we began to question Holloway's involvement and, frankly, which side—if either—was the quote unquote 'good guys.' Unsure as to whether Holloway was part of something sinister or not, we opted for a more direct method of obtaining his information."

"By stealing from him," Graves said.

"I'm not sure on the legal term," Jackson said. "We didn't ever plan to, nor did we actually, deprive him of anything."

"Whose idea was this, Mr. Douglas?" Duval asked.

"Mine, sir."

"What role did Miss McKenzie play in your decision?"

"Hillary hired me as a private investigator. I made it very clear that we would do things my way. I take full responsibility for all decisions and actions."

Adrienne Porter, the U.S. associate attorney general, leaned forward. She was in her late fifties or early sixties, with short blondish-brown hair coiffed stylishly. She wore an assortment of jewelry, gold bracelets jangling as she rested her arms on the table. "Are you telling us that the decision to con Mr. Holloway and the decision to break into his safe were yours and yours alone?"

"Yes, ma'am. Hillary was my client. As such, all final decisions were mine."

"Just to be clear, the decision to investigate Richard Holloway was yours?"

Jackson hesitated for a moment. He concluded that it wouldn't be a lie to say yes, because he had—albeit at Hillary's insistence—made the choice to stay in Las Vegas and continue their investigation. So he nodded.

"Please answer orally," Porter said.

"Yes, ma'am, it was my decision."

"And the decision to run a confidence game on Mr. Holloway was yours?"

"Yes."

"And the decision to break into his safe was yours?"

"Yes."

"And the decision to pursue your investigations in Kingman was yours?"

"Yes," he said, using the same internal reasoning as before.

"Mr. Douglas, you're certain that the two of you, working together, didn't make any of these decisions jointly?"

Jackson actually grinned. "I'm pretty sure Hillary and I have never made a joint decision."

Armstrong hit the last key on her laptop and the room went silent.

"Anything further?" Duval asked after a few moments.

No one spoke.

"Mr. Douglas, do you have anything to add?"

"Yes, sir, thank you. I just want to underscore that I am well aware that I crossed lines, and I am willing to pay whatever price I must. But every single decision I made, I made with the belief that it was the best—if not only—way to rescue Hillary from people who, by all accounts, were acting in a sinister and often illegal manner. As far as the things we did in our investigation, again, they were my responsibility, and any punishment should fall on me."

He licked dry lips in conclusion.

"Thank you, Mr. Douglas. That concludes this hearing. You will now be confined to your quarters, pending our decision."

"I'll come talk to you as soon as I know anything," Paige whispered with a light touch on his arm. Then a pair of airmen took him away.

Chapter Seventy-Four

LIEUTENANT PAIGE WORE the same Air Force blue uniform as the day before, only minus the jacket. She stood in the entrance to Jackson's holding cell, her briefcase clutched in front of her. As was the case the day before, her auburn hair was bound in a loose chignon.

"May I come in?"

"Yeah," Jackson said, sitting up a little straighter on his bed. Cot, more accurately. "I'd offer you a seat," he said, nodding at the second cot in the room, across from him, "but given the nature of the seat, I'm not sure it'd be gentlemanly."

She smiled sweetly. "I can only stay a minute. I wanted to give you an update."

Jackson nodded, feigning calmness for some reason. As much as he was willing to accept due punishment, he was far from eager for it. Having a night to himself to think hadn't helped matters. His attempts to sleep had been marred by memories that stirred up incredible guilt. The urgency to save Hillary and the intensity of the moment had masked it initially, but the taking of nearly twenty lives had caught up with him.

And he'd counted, too. He couldn't be sure in some cases who had died because of bullet wounds or grenade explosions and who had died in a bombing thereafter, but his best guess was that, between the base and the houseboat, he had killed or been directly responsible for the death of approximately twenty people. Twenty! Not to mention those he felt responsible for, like Vickers, or those he had merely seriously injured. And what about Moore and his wife, whom he had put through horrible trauma?

The pain had been too raw for tears as the full weight of his actions had taken hold of him. Everything he had done over the last few days had been done in an effort to rescue Hillary, but that didn't make it right. Could end and means always be reconciled so easily, with one justifying the other? Was there sometimes no right way to do the thing that had to be done?

He'd also been tormented by thoughts of his parents. What would they think, were they still alive, of their son? What would Leroy think now of his grandson, or Reggie of his best friend? And what about Sam?

It had been too much to bear, and Jackson had finally succumbed to an hour or two of restless sleep before he'd been awakened with news that he had a visitor. Now, here she was, smelling like cinnamon again as she sat down beside him. And he tried to pretend that his heart wasn't thumping in his chest, hoping that her update would be positive, even though he felt more and more that he didn't deserve a positive outcome.

"I spoke to Secretary Wittingham this morning," Paige said. "He and the others are meeting again at ten a.m. My understanding is that they first wanted to speak with Miss McKenzie."

He nodded.

"I called the hospital this morning. She's doing very well. The doctor doesn't believe there will be any lasting effects."

"Is there any way I can talk to her?"

Paige's smile was sympathetic. "I'm afraid not, at least not until the committee has wrapped up its investigation."

He nodded again.

"I really don't know much more than that," she said. "As soon as I do, I'll let you know."

"Thank you."

She stood to leave. Just before she reached the door, he called out, "Lieutenant."

"Yes?" she asked, turning around.

"Can I ask you a personal question?"

She squinted one eye at him, then nodded.

"How old are you?"

Paige smiled curiously. "Thirty-one."

"And how long have you been with JAG Corps?"

"Five years."

He nodded. "What are my chances?"

Paige took a few steps toward him. "To be perfectly honest, I have no idea. I think the tenor of the investigation has been positive, from your perspective. But with this many agencies and departments in the room, this many personalities and agendas—not to mention, egos—it'd be nothing more than a guess."

Jackson nodded once more. "Well, thank you, whatever happens."

"You're welcome. I'll see about getting you something to eat."

She left and after an airman brought him breakfast, Jackson was alone again. He ate a little, but his appetite was absent and the food was bland. He finally gave up and tried to pray. He knew that the blood of Christ covered all his sins, that he didn't have to pay any penance. And yet, a few murmured pleas seemed a wholly inadequate response to the carnage he had caused. It wasn't just what he'd done. It was how. Almost as if it was second nature, instinctive. Taking prisoners, killing, torturing. What did it say about him that he so easily turned into an instrument of death and destruction?

Regardless of what the committee decreed, even if he agreed to some plea deal and a reduced sentence, he knew his life would never be the same again.

*   *   *

11:56 a.m.

THE SAME conference room seemed much emptier this time. Jackson sat in the same chair. Lieutenant Paige sat in the same place beside him. And Secretary of the Air Force Theodore Wittingham sat across the table. No military personnel, no heads of assorted bureaus and agencies, no airman taking notes. And, Jackson noted, no guards stationed at the door. Just Wittiningham, Paige, and Jackson.

The secretary was a middle-aged man who bore a slight resemblance to an older Scott Bakula. The previous afternoon, Jackson had been unable to determine if he was aloof, contemplative, bored, or angry. As he looked across the table at him now, clad in a perfectly tailored suit, striped tie, American flag pin on the lapel, Jackson still couldn't tell.

"Mr. Douglas, I want you to know that I am here on behalf of both the Department of Justice and the Department of Defense," Wittingham started. His voice was calm and measured. "Given that most of the events in question either took place at Blane Air Force Base or originated there in some fashion, and since it was an Air Force fighter jet dropping Air Force ordnance that obliterated the base, the Air Force is clearly in this up to our epaulets. I should also inform you that everything I am about to tell you on behalf of the DOD and the DOJ has been consented to by the appropriate persons at the CIA, FBI, DHS, the state of

Nevada, Las Vegas Metro PD, and AFOSI." He grinned for the first time Jackson could remember. "I know that's a large bowl of alphabet soup, but I mention it so that you know that what I'm going to tell you is binding. There are no loopholes because some agency or director didn't sign off on it."

Jackson nodded.

"Members of our panel, including myself, spoke at length with Richard Holloway last night. He confirmed everything you said yesterday and turned over to us all evidence he had compiled against Senator Moore, General Reynolds, and the entire Golden Dawn team. Suffice to say, it is damning."

Jackson nodded again.

"He also gave us this, and asked that it be returned to you." Wittingham reached into his folder and withdrew a sheaf of yellow papers, folded. He slid them across the table to Jackson, who quickly confirmed his suspicion by opening them. It was his confession to Richard Holloway.

"He said he had no further use for it," Wittingham stated.

Jackson stared at the papers, dumbstruck.

"Several of us also spoke to Miss McKenzie this morning. Her story matches yours, with one notable difference."

Jackson frowned. "What's that?"

Wittingham grinned again. "There appears to be some discrepancy as to who was in charge of your operation and who made decisions. You claim that they were all your responsibility. Miss McKenzie made a similar claim."

"I'm sure she would, but I hones—"

Wittingham held up his hand. "Small potatoes, Mr. Douglas. We also interviewed Sheriff Quinn and his four deputies, as well as Senator Moore, his wife, and his staff, and we watched the video you shot and shared on the internet. Based on the confession of Moore, the testimony of his wife and staff, the testimony primarily of Deputy Mike Klein of the Delamar County Sheriff's Department, and the testimony and evidence provided by Richard Holloway, it is the decision of the DOJ and DOD that you will not be indicted with any federal charges at this time."

Jackson couldn't believe it, and looked at Paige for some cue.

"At this time?" she asked, her eyes on Secretary Wittingham.

"That caveat is in place given the hasty conclusion of the committee. The DOJ and DOD will be extensively questioning Senator Moore, Sheriff Quinn, residents of Kingman, Nevada, and all persons believed to have been part of the Golden Dawn project, as well as poring over Mr. Holloway's evidence, evidence believed to have been gathered and submitted to the CIA by Xavier Stark prior to his death, several servers seized from the home of Laura Woodson by the FBI, and any forensic evidence that can be gleaned from the remains of Blane Air Force Base." He made eye contact with Jackson. "We expect that this will corroborate your and Miss McKenzie's stories. But, should the evidence point in a different direction, I can't guarantee we won't come knocking on your door in the future."

Jackson wasn't too worried about corroboration, although he was curious what sort of things might be on Woodson's server. He'd seen all the movies about the CIA cooking up conspiracies and taking illicit covert action, and now, he'd seen it in real life. The people involved had likely been rogue agents, but it was still a little disconcerting.

"You said federal charges," Paige stated, ever the advocate.

"Correct. The State of Nevada, and in particular, Delamar County and Clark County, have agreed to abide by the DOJ and DOD's joint decision and not bring any charges against you either."

Jackson's eyes widened, and he wondered if he might faint.

"Now, there are a number of provisions," Wittingham said.

"I'm listening."

"You will be placed on temporary probation. Your license as a private investigator will be indefinitely suspended."

Jackson nodded.

"You will be expected to cooperate fully with our investigation, including potentially serving as a witness at trial, at your own expense."

"Done."

"The money you found in the locker will need to be turned over to Las Vegas Metro PD pursuant to their investigation into the murder of Arielle Coal. And since that appears tied to the Golden Dawn investigation, it will likely ultimately be property of the DOJ until such time as it is no longer needed as evidence. Even then, it's murky as to its rightful owner."

"Understood."

"To that end, Las Vegas Metro isn't real pleased with you and Miss McKenzie's withholding evidence. As part of the deal we reached, they have agreed not to pursue any charges against you, but I wouldn't recommend so much as jaywalking in this city anytime soon."

"Not a problem."

"As I mentioned, neither the DOJ, the state of Nevada, nor any of its municipalities will be filing criminal charges against you. However, should any parties involved seek to file a civil suit, they will be entirely within their legal right to do so. Given the evidence we've uncovered so far, it is unlikely a court would rule in favor of Senator Moore, especially since his wife and staff have turned on him, or with Sheriff Quinn or Isaac Cutler or anyone else. But be advised, that is a possibility."

Jackson nodded.

"And finally, many of the events that have transpired, things you have seen, and facts you have been told are highly classified and likely to remain so. Conditional to your release, you will sign a confidentiality agreement that you will not disclose any classified information. If you do, you'll be taken into custody before your words reach your own ears. Is that clear?"

"Absolutely."

"You'll be provided with a sanitized, redacted version of events that you can tell your family and friends and for any legal requirements you may have down the road. And frankly, given the nature of all that went on as part of Golden Dawn, a sanitized version is for the best. Other than that, I will need some signatures and it will take a little while to process everything, but you will be free to go." He sat back. "Do you have any questions for me?"

"What about Hillary? Is she facing any sort of discipline?"

"No. She's subject to the same exposure to a potential civil suit, but I don't believe Mr. Holloway has any interest in pursuing one."

"Mr. Secretary, I . . . I don't know how to thank you. I'm still shocked, frankly. If you don't mind my asking, why am I not in a heap of trouble?"

Wittingham nodded. "As we speak, the DOJ is preparing to indict Senator Carson Moore; Sheriff Wyatt Quinn; Deputies Clayton, Seaver, and McGregor; possibly several residents of Kingman; various members of Moore's staff; Matt Brenner; and a host of other people on charges ranging from kidnapping to fraud to treason. The CIA is working with the DOJ to root out and deal with any remaining conspirators. And all three branches of the armed forces are combing their ranks to find any potential personnel, past or present, tied to Golden Dawn."

Jackson waited for the answer to his question, sensing Wittingham was building to it.

"For several years now, a number of law enforcement agencies and the U.S. military have also been tracking a private militia group named RASER. They've been on the fringe of the law for a while, and while no one has been able to concretely tie them to anything prosecutable, it has been widely suspected that they were a dangerous element that was growing in size and influence. Preliminary research would suggest that the majority of people you encountered at Blane were members of RASER, hired as a private army to guard the base."

"Ravich too?"

"Likely." He reached for a glass of water before continuing. "There were also a number of rogue CIA operatives working at the base, part of a group Langley was monitoring but was short of having enough evidence to indict or expose. Robert Kyle and Xavier Stark were working to that end when they were killed, Stark as a deep-cover double agent embedded within Golden Dawn. Anyhow, all this has come to a head now, largely because you and Miss McKenzie pursued things as you did. Your actions, while highly dubious and ill-advised, were instrumental in taking down RASER and the rogue CIA operatives, as well as exposing Golden Dawn. Because of that—and because of the cooperation and consent of Mrs. Moore, members of her and Senator Moore's detail, and Ms. Santiago—the decision was made to grant you immunity out of recognition and appreciation for the part you played and, to be quite frank, because there are bigger fish to fry."

"I see." Jackson too took a drink of water. "You mentioned exposing Golden Dawn. Is that why the base was bombed, because it had been exposed?"

"Sort of. It appears that was the work of General Reynolds, using loyal and unwitting members of the U.S. Air Force and acting on behalf of the Golden Dawn team. He was destroying evidence, we believe."

"And all their research, records, not to mention two—the words are sticking in my mouth—test subjects."

Wittingham nodded. "We found a cache of info at Laura Woodson's home, as I mentioned. The working theory is that any research and records they had were duplicated on her servers."

"So Golden Dawn . . . Is it over?"

"Yes. And I was asked by almost everyone on the committee to underscore that the Golden Dawn project was not a legitimate Air Force, Army, CIA, or DOD project. Senator Moore, General Reynolds, Laura Woodson, and those running it were doing so entirely of their own volition and with their own backing. Admittedly, they likely siphoned taxpayer dollars for some of their funding, used legitimate people and resources to their own end, and covered their tracks incredibly well. But they were operating solely on their own, as a rogue faction."

"What about, if you don't mind my asking, the original Silver Dawn program and the Desert Root phase of it? Were they sanctioned military ops?"

"I don't mind you asking, but I'm afraid that is classified."

Jackson nodded. "You haven't mentioned General Reynolds. What's happening to him?"

"He is being dealt with."

"Does that mean—"

"It means he is being dealt with."

Jackson nodded yet again.

"Is there anything else?"

"One more question. What ties does Warren McKenzie have to all of this? Is he involved?"

"Not in any way that we could discover. He was stationed at Blane Air Force Base in the 1980s, and thus knew and may have developed relationships with Senator Moore and General Reynolds. But any current relationship appears to be purely personal, as do his ties to Miss Coal."

Jackson shook his head.

"Something bother you?"

"I'm just not a big fan of coincidence."

"Me either, Mr. Douglas. But we could find no link."

Jackson placed his palms on the table, exhaling. "Mr. Secretary, I can't thank you all enough. I wish I could undo everything that happened. I wish Hillary and I had never come to Las Vegas."

Wittingham cleared his throat. "A lot of very bad things happened over the last few days, and I won't sugarcoat it—you caused some of them. But some very good things happened as well. Men who committed some heinous acts have been brought to justice. You caused much of that as well. Don't forget that."

Jackson looked down. "Do you know what they did to Hillary?"

"I don't have the full toxicology report, but my understanding is they administered sedatives, some truth serum, and several nootropics. According to Dr. Sears and Miss McKenzie herself, there's no reason to believe she was physically or sexually abused. It appears they just—and I use that word reticently—questioned her intensely."

Jackson nodded and raised his head. "Thank you, sir. I really do appreciate it."

"You're welcome, Mr. Douglas. Like I said, it will take some time to process everything before you can be released. I'll leave the necessary forms with Lieutenant Paige and she can answer any legal questions you have."

Jackson nodded for what felt like the hundredth time.

Secretary Wittingham stood, and Jackson and Paige did as well. Wittingham extended his hand across the table, and Jackson shook it.

"Mr. Douglas, I understand your position these last few days, but I encourage you, in the future, please go to the proper authorities. I assure you, the majority of them are honest, loyal, and hardworking men and women who are truly seeking justice."

"Yes, sir."

Wittingham nodded and exited the conference room, leaving Jackson and Lieutenant Paige. They sat back down.

"The forms will only take a few minutes," she said. "I just need some signatures."

"Yeah, sure. Actually, could I just have a couple of minutes first?"

"Of course," she gathered her things into her briefcase and stood. She placed one hand on his shoulder. "Just let me know when you're ready."

He nodded as she left the room. Then, all alone, he dropped his head onto the table and cried.

Chapter Seventy-Five

INHALING A HUGE breath, Jackson smiled into the bright sunshine bathing the parking lot of the Desert Springs Hospital. The sky was clear blue, the mountains in the distance a hazy brown, and the palm trees to his right a lush shade of green. The air was hot and dry, but not terribly unpleasant, a change from the past few weeks. Jackson inhaled again, letting the air fill him. Forty-eight hours ago, he hadn't been sure he'd ever breathe fresh air again.

After composing himself in the conference room, Jackson had spent fifteen minutes with Lieutenant Paige, going over various releases and confidentiality forms. She had also provided him a very detailed list of non-classified facts and events, scrubbed thoroughly to indemnify certain persons and agencies. Paige had emphasized that anything not specifically detailed should remain confidential, and he'd promised her it would. Hillary would be provided a similar list, minus some of the details she wasn't aware of. If they had any questions about it or ran into any legal issues, Paige had said to contact JAG Corps, promising that as long as she was an officer with the corps, she would be happy to help.

It had taken another hour to officially process his release and return his belongings—minus Arielle's twenty-five thousand dollars and plus all his and Hillary's belongings left at Oasis, which Holloway had magnanimously returned. Jackson had been shown off the base and provided cab fare to wherever he wanted to go. He'd collected the Granada from the park and ride south of town, then checked into a hotel. After showering and changing, he had felt refreshed. But the aches and pains of all his physical turmoil had remained, and the water could never wash away the mental, emotional, and psychological scars he'd suffered.

Jackson stood beside the Granada, basking in the sun and warmth and fresh air for several more moments. Life had taught him that he had to take joy in the little things, because the big things were often monsters waiting to cause nightmares. So for those few seconds, warm sun and a gentle desert breeze on his face were enough.

The tacos in his hand were turning to slop, so Jackson pulled himself from the reverie and strolled into the hospital. As soon as he stepped through the whooshing glass doors, the desert was forgotten as a blast of artic air washed over him. This experience, too, was incredible, another little thing to savor.

Hillary was on the third floor, and Jackson took the elevator. He had called from the hotel, spoken to the front desk, and learned that she was stable, awake, and able to have a visitor. He had also called Leroy, Reggie, and Mouse from the hotel or in transit. He owed them all a detailed explanation—a DOD- and DOJ-redacted one—and probably a few apologies. Dinner on his deck, maybe, once he returned home.

He also had taken the time to return the six messages Connie had left on his phone. Her lawn was past due for another mowing. Had he moved in with one of those girlfriends of his? Was he out of the country on some undercover mission? He had promised her he would be home soon and would explain everything then, and would definitely mow her lawn as soon as he got back. It might take two cuttings she had said, with the mower deck at different levels. He would use a scissors, if necessary, he said. She let him off the phone. He'd also asked her to undo the changes she had made at the DMV, and she had promised to do so first thing in the morning.

He had not called Sam. For whatever reason, he just couldn't bring himself to tell her what had happened, despite several pleading voicemails she had left him over the weekend. He wasn't sure he could ever redact enough from what had transpired to look her in the eye again.

Hillary was in bed, her eyes closed, hair tangled, without makeup, still hooked to oxygen and an IV, dressed in a typical hospital gown. Yet, she was beautiful. The TV was off, and the room was quiet except for the noise made by the machines beside her bed.

Jackson set her duffel bag in the corner and sat down in a chair by the window, looking out at the mountains. It was a beautiful view, but he missed the ocean. Desert mountains now had connotations that might never go away. Jackson decided that when he got home, mowed his and Connie's lawns, and explained everything to everyone who needed an explanation, he would go sit at the beach and stare at the ocean until his head cleared. If it ever did.

With Hillary sleeping peacefully, Jackson quietly unwrapped his tacos. His last legitimate meal had been at the Kingman Diner on Thursday afternoon, and even that had been harried. Since then, it had been what he could get when he could get it, and that had usually been nothing. Or Air Force-requisitioned food.

So he enjoyed his tacos, which were still warm, but in that been-out-in-the-heat-and-melted-together sort of way. Tacos nonetheless.

"Did you bring me any?"

Jackson looked up with a taco halfway to his mouth as Hillary stirred. Tomatoes, lettuce, and cheese promptly fell onto his shirt.

"Hey," he said. "You're awake."

Hillary inched her way higher onto the bed. "Are you here on work release?"

"That's funny."

Her smile faded. "I didn't think I'd ever see you again. When the chopper started . . ."

Jackson stood. "Hey, it's okay."

"I thought you were dead."

"And that didn't make you happy?"

"Jackson."

"I'm fine. I pulled a fast one, ducked out of the mess hall and hid behind a rec center couch."

She shook her head. "They knocked me out right after opening fire. I just assumed . . ."

"Yeah, well, I made it," he said, taking her hand.

She squeezed it for a moment, then lifted it to his face. "You look terrible," she said.

Jackson knew what she meant. Bags underlined hollow eyes. His skin was a lifeless gray color, except where bruises shaded it yellow and purple. He was unshaven, his hair styled only by the breeze.

Hillary dropped her hand. "Do I look half as bad as you?"

"Not hardly."

She smiled.

"How are you feeling?" Jackson asked.

"Exhausted. Like I was hit by the proverbial truck."

"What have the doctors told you?"

"That I need rest. But I'm sick of resting." She yawned.

"Well, you're clearly showing them with all these displays of energy."

"Shut up."

"Seriously, Hill, you okay?"

She leveled her eyes at him.

"Hillary," he corrected.

"The doctor said my scar should be minimal." She sat up a little higher. "I didn't suffer any brain damage from being in the water so long, and none of the drugs caused any permanent damage."

"That's good."

"I am, however, still dealing with the ramifications of not being real," she said. "Of being a research project, of my parents lying to me my whole life."

Jackson looked down.

"I guess that will take time," she said.

"I guess." He cleared his throat. "Have you called your sisters?"

"This afternoon."

"I'm surprised they aren't here."

"They wanted to come, but I told them it wasn't necessary. I knew you were getting out. I told them I was in good hands."

He raised his eyebrow.

"Besides," she said, letting her voice trail off for a moment, "they didn't even know I was in Las Vegas."

"You didn't tell them what you were doing?"

"Tell them I was investigating Dad's relationship with a prostitute while suspecting he'd been covering up something in my past? No, I didn't get around to mentioning that." She sighed. "We have a big conversation coming up, and I'd rather not do it here or over the phone."

He nodded.

She beckoned at the bag. "So are any of those for me or not?"

"Have you been cleared for solid food?"

"I've been eating so-called solid food all day," she said. "They say if I can have a bowel movement, I can get off the IV and go home in the morning."

"Well, these will give you a bowel movement," Jackson said, sliding a rolling table over her bed. He set the bag of tacos on top of it. "I hope it's okay, they have red meat in them."

"I eat red meat."

"Prove it."

With a mischievous twinkle in her brilliant blue eyes, Hillary reached into the bag and pulled out a soft-shell taco.

"I hear you had an interview with half the government too," Jackson said once she had taken and savored a few bites. He was back in his chair.

"They were here for a good hour. I couldn't stay awake."

A nurse came in, checked Hillary's vitals, frowned at the taco and at Jackson, and then left. Hillary kept eating.

"How much did they tell you?" Jackson asked.

"Just the basics. I still have no idea how you found me, or how I ended up on a boat in the middle of the lake." She frowned. "Lake Mead?"

He nodded.

"How did I get there?"

"I don't know. I assume the chopper."

"A helicopter can't land on a houseboat."

Jackson shrugged. "You don't remember anything after they knocked you out?"

"I don't remember much of anything from the night. I remember being in a strange room, machines all around me, doctors hovering over me, lots of questions. It was blurry though . . . I don't know where I was."

"Do you remember me rescuing you?"

"I remember getting shot, and thinking I was going to drown. Then I remember your scruffy mug leaning over me."

He smiled. "I mean at the base."

She frowned. "I remember hiding in a barracks and . . ." Her face clouded. "Did I kill someone?"

"No."

"But I shot him?"

"You saved my life."

Her eyes closed as she sighed. When they opened, they found his. "The next thing I remember is the Army showing up and taking me away and . . ."

"Trying to kill me."

Hillary shook her head. "Why did they do that?"

"I'm guessing because Reynolds told them to. And it wasn't the real Army."

"They didn't say anything about General Reynolds earlier."

"To me either. I'm guessing it's over our pay grade."

"Do you think this is really over then?"

"Yeah. The head may still be alive, but it's got no snake body to be attached to."

"How colorful." She took the last bite of her taco and coyly peeked into the bag for another. Great, her first bowel movement would be a gut-buster.

"Did they say anything about your father?" Jackson asked as she unwrapped it.

Hillary looked up. "No. Should they have?"

"If it's any consolation, Secretary Wittingham told me he thought your dad's involvement was just coincidence, that he knew Moore and Arielle personally, but wasn't involved in Golden Dawn."

"Do you believe that?"

"I don't know. It tracks, I guess."

She took a bite and chewed slowly. "Thanks, but it isn't much consolation. Even if he wasn't part of anything criminal, he still . . ."

Jackson politely stared out the window, letting her have a moment.

When he looked back a minute later, Hillary's head had fallen against the pillow, her hand about to pull the taco off the table and onto her blue scrubs. He lifted it from her grasp, a move that caused her to stir.

"You must be tired if you can fall asleep mid-taco."

"Sorry," she said, yawning again. "Like I said, exhausted."

"More like narcoleptic. I'll let you sleep."

"No, I want to talk to you."

"You must still be under the influence."

She gave him a glare. "I want to know . . . I want to know what happened— where I went, how you found me. Both times."

Jackson shook his head. "No you don't."

"What does that mean?"

He looked down, then away.

"Jackson?"

"I did what I had to do to find you. And you're safe. You're going to be all right. That's all that matters."

"What aren't you telling me?"

"You get some rest," he said, standing. "I'll be back in the morning. We have a five-hour ride home. We can talk then."

She nodded, and he left her room, dreading telling her at what price her rescue had come.

Chapter Seventy-Six

Monday, September 24
9:37 a.m.

THE SKY OVER Las Vegas was overcast as Jackson drove from the hotel to the hospital. The temperature was in the low seventies and the breeze actually felt cool. The cloud cover intimated at rain, but also at eventual clearing that would usher in the heat. But the weather wasn't really on Jackson's mind. Foremost in his thoughts was the medical opinion of Dr. Sears, who would determine if Hillary—and thus Jackson—could go home or not.

The night had done wonders for her. She was dressed in denim shorts and a charcoal gray T-shirt, casual yet somehow chic. Her hair had been washed and brushed and restrained in a loose ponytail. And she was standing, awake, her eyes vivid and her body possessing energy and enthusiasm he hadn't seen in a while. She was the old Hillary.

He was the new Jackson. For the second night in a row, he had been tormented with guilt, by thoughts and images of what he had done. This on the heels of three nights with hardly any sleep, one escaping from Holloway's penthouse, one storming a decommissioned military base, and one being questioned by everyone from local cops to the Department of Justice. Even one last all-you-can-eat Vegas breakfast buffet—for $4.99—couldn't invigorate him. Nor could fresh air or hospital air conditioning. It was the problem with the little things—their effectiveness was usually short lasting.

"I take it you're good to go," Jackson said as he rapped on her door. She turned from the bedside table, where she was putting on jewelry, and smiled. Before he knew what happened, she had crossed the room and wrapped him in a tight embrace—as tight as her bandaged collarbone would allow, anyhow. She squeezed for several seconds, her perfume and shampoo floating into his nostrils, and if he wasn't mistaken, warm tears dripping down her cheek onto his neck.

She backed away, smiling sheepishly and wiping her eyes.

"I'm going to call the doctor," Jackson said. "I'm not sure you're ready to be released."

Hillary smiled. "My father called me this morning," she said.

"Oh?"

"Stop playing coy, Jackson. I know that you called him."

"I told him not to say anything."

"He doesn't take orders from you."

"He told me the same thing."

She returned to the table, fastening her left earring and slipping a bracelet over her wrist. How many women accessorized to drive home from the hospital?

"Does his call account for the good mood, or are you just excited about five hours in a Granada?"

Hillary's face actually fell. "I forgot about that."

"We have money," Jackson said. "Although, not as much as before. But you can buy a plane ticket or rent a car."

"Um-mm," she said. "We have things to talk about."

"Like what?"

"Like how you got a hold of my father, and how you tracked me down, and how much trouble we're in. But I'd rather put Nevada behind us first."

"You read my mind. Clark Griswold had a better time in Vegas than we did."

Hillary's discharge paperwork took a few minutes, and then they headed for the car with Jackson carrying Hillary's bag for her. Because she was still Hillary, she complained about the leather seats as he opened her door for her. Because he was Jackson, he reminded her that he had parked facing west, so that the passenger side of the car was in the shade. She pointed out that it was cloudy and direction didn't matter, and he countered by asking why she had complained about the seats if it was cloudy. Some things never changed.

Fifty minutes later, they were in California. The clouds had actually intensified, threatening a storm. They also kept the Granada relatively cool, so that the front and rear windows didn't have to be all the way down. As a result, Jackson and Hillary were able to converse.

"So how did you get a hold of my father?" Hillary asked.

"I made some phone calls, asked for a few favors."

"From who?"

"Among others, a Starbucks barista in Santa Monica and the Secretary of the Air Force."

Hillary shook her head. "Why?"

"Because I figured he owed you an explanation."

"He said you were kind of curt on the phone."

"I've been through a lot."

"I want to talk about that too."

"You just think you do," Jackson said.

Hillary shook her head again. "How did Mouse and Secretary Wittingham get you to my father?"

"Wittingham used his assortment of contacts to pinpoint your parents' location fifty miles north of Dhaka, which let me tell you, was not an Embassy Suites. Mouse found an online translator so I could talk to the brothel clerk—"

"You mean hostel?"

"Are they different?"

"A little bit."

"Whatever. He told me, or rather the translator told me, that your parents were on an early morning tour of a new school, and Wittingham used another contact to get a call through to the headmaster, whose English was passing, and who put me in touch with your father." He took a deep breath. "So what'd he have to say, if I may pry?"

"Just what we feared, that I was a Desert Root baby," Hillary said, looking down. "He was hesitant at first, but when he learned everything that had happened . . ." She swallowed. "He said Yvonne was brought in as a surrogate mother, about the same time as he became involved in Desert Root. His job was to monitor the surrogates, to make sure the babies were healthy, to study the development of the baby compared to a . . . a normal baby."

Jackson nodded.

"He said the extra meetings with Yvonne were about faking a false negative."

"A false negative?" he asked.

"That's right, to get her out of the program. My father had a conversion of sorts, a spiritual awakening, about what they were doing—about Desert Root. He convinced Yvonne to go along with his plan, and their 'extra' appointments were to discuss how he would fake this false negative and get her discharged from the base; how he would continue to provide for her prenatal care; and ultimately, since Yvonne didn't want a baby, how he and Mom would adopt me, off the record."

Jackson had nothing to say.

"They weren't having an affair," Hillary continued, "and although he was a part of Desert Root, my father tried to right the wrongs they were doing at Blane. They transferred him before he could convince any other women to do what Yvonne did."

"Why her? Why you?"

"He said he had to approach the women carefully to avoid getting caught. And they had to agree to go along with everything. They were paid meager amounts to be surrogates, but that was still better than some of them were making. It wasn't an easy sale to get them to opt out. And they had to agree to either keep the baby or put it up for adoption. Abortion wasn't an option for him."

"Did he mention Arielle? Moore? Holloway?"

"He kept in touch with Yvonne, loosely. He found out she had a daughter and sort of monitored her from a distance. He was in Vegas once and looked her up. He said he gave her the card, in case she was ever in any trouble. She had called last month because she feared her life was in jeopardy. She wanted to meet with him. He wired her twenty-five thousand dollars so she could get away and start over, but she didn't do it. When they met a few weeks ago on his way to Bangladesh, she told him a few of the details of what she suspected, and he urged her to get out. He promised to look into things, and contacted a colleague of his at the DOD. But, apparently they didn't act fast enough."

"Or his colleague was stymied by someone higher up the food chain who didn't want an investigation."

"Yeah." Hillary shrugged. "As for connections to Moore and Holloway, they were just coincidence. He said."

"You don't believe him?"

"With Dad, I've always known there were secrets, things he couldn't—or wouldn't—tell us. I think there might be some in this case too."

Jackson nodded. "But you're okay?"

"I will be," she said. "It takes some getting used to, this idea of being adopted. And being a product of a military mind-control project."

They drove silently for a few miles.

"Your turn," Hillary said. "I want to know what happened. How did you find me, how did you track me from Kingman to Blane and Lake Mead?"

Jackson told his story yet again, hitting the high points. When he was finished, Hillary made him pull over. She got out of the car and bent down, hands on her knees, losing her hospital breakfast. Jackson got out and joined her on her side of the car.

"I had no idea," she said.

He brushed loose hair off her cheek. "I did what I had to."

"All because . . ." She turned away, the breeze playing with her hair, dragging strands back across her face. She let them blow.

Raindrops started to fall. Big, splotchy droplets that kicked up dust as they pelted the ground. Hillary slowly turned back to Jackson. "How many?" she asked.

"How many what?"

"How many people did you have to kill to save me?"

He shrugged and pried at a rock with his shoe. A semi swept past them at seventy-five miles per hour, the gush of wind nearly knocking them over. "What with the grenades and the bombs, I sort of lost count."

"How many?"

"Twenty, give or take."

"Oh my goodness," Hillary said, and she sagged against the door of the car.

The rain began to pelt, but she was oblivious. Jackson put a hand on her shoulder. "They were mercenaries, hired by Reynolds and Moore and Woodson. They were bad guys."

"They were still people."

"I know. But it was the only way."

She turned and buried her head in his shoulder, and he held her for several minutes while the rain became a steady shower. Eventually, he became aware of Hillary's body shaking, heaving in sobs. He'd never seen this reaction from her—weakness.

"How did this happen?" she asked, wiping her eyes. "How did we get here?"

"It started with an apple in a garden."

"Don't get cute with me right now."

"Sorry. But it's the only answer I can come up with. This world is depraved, Hillary. And sometimes you have to do bad things in a depraved world. Like bombing terrorists or shooting teenage gangbangers. Or slaughtering mercenaries to rescue the damsel in distress."

She raised her head and stared at him, raindrops mixing with tears on her face. She let them both slide down her cheeks.

Jackson stepped closer and cupped her face in his hands. "It's over, Hillary. You're safe. Your parents and your sisters love you more than anything in this world. That's all that matters. The rest is . . . I don't know. But it's not your fault, and it's behind you now."

Hillary swallowed. "Do you really believe that?"

Jackson lied. "I do."

She slowly nodded. Then, with lips tightly pursed, she turned away and got back into the car. His back drenched, Jackson waited for a caravan of cars to pass. Then he got in and they merged back onto the interstate.

They didn't talk for a while. Hillary stared out her window, and Jackson focused on I-15. They stopped for lunch in Barstow again, taking their food to go. Eating seemed to help.

"Are you going to need a lawyer?" Hillary asked.

"Let's not start that cycle again."

It drew a thin smile, then a graceful slurp of her diet soda. "Seriously, Jackson, how much trouble are you in?"

"Surprisingly little," he said. "We've still got our poker winnings—minus some expenses that still need to be taken care of—late fees, towing, repairs, miscellaneous expenses, and I totaled a Jet Ski."

Hillary blanched.

"Don't worry, I took care of it all last night. Connie and Mouse are canceling our aliases as we speak, Hertz and Budget are going to bill me, and Lieutenant Paige said something about Reynold's shell company having to pay for the Jet Ski. We're good."

She sat back, far from relieved.

Jackson continued. "My P.I. license has been revoked, and I may be spending the rest of my life in a civil courtroom. But I won't be in jail, and Holloway won't be dogging me like Terry Benedict."

Hillary frowned at him, and he explained, taking fifteen minutes to walk through his conversations with Secretary Wittingham, particularly Holloway's compassion and cooperation and Margaret Moore's confirmation of Jackson's side of things. As he laid out the full terms of the deal, Hillary's despondency returned.

"I am so sorry," she said.

"It's okay."

"No it's not okay."

"But you are," he said, turning her way. "That's all that matters."

Another thin smile.

"You know, I don't get it," he said after a while. "How come you're not . . ."

"Not what?"

"Not messed up? You don't talk to yourself or see ghosts or randomly assault people or anything."

"Well, I am intense, driven, thorough, hard-working, strong in my convictions. Those are all attributes the Desert Root program was trying to generate."

"Where'd you hear that?"

"Dad."

Jackson nodded. "So you're one of the ones that . . . came out right?"

"Eloquently put, but yeah."

"Or, you're intense, driven, thorough, hard-working, and strong in your convictions. God makes people that way too."

"Yeah." She looked out the window. "But unfortunately, the paternity test doesn't lie."

*   *   *

3:41 p.m.

HILLARY SLEPT the last hour and a half of the trip, and they arrived at her condominium as another ring of rain was sweeping across southern California. Jackson carried her duffel bag inside, dropping it in the hallway.

"So, 'thanks' seems a little trite," Hillary said, tilting her head to one side.

"I could use a reference for my résumé. And if any of those civil suits ever do come my way . . ."

"It's on the house."

"You sure you still have a room at the house after all this?"

"I called my boss this morning and explained everything. He said to take my time, there'd be a mountain of paperwork waiting for me when I got back."

He nodded. "You, uh, need a ride to get your car or anything?"

"Heather's coming to stay with me tonight and tomorrow. We'll figure something out in the morning."

"Okay."

"I mean it, Jackson. Thank you for everything."

"Everything?"

"You really shouldn't play modest," she said, smiling archly. "It doesn't become you."

He smirked back.

"For everything," she repeated. "Like honoring your commitment when you really didn't want to, propositioning Arielle, staying on the case when I know you thought I was losing it—"

"Was is that obvious?"

She nodded. "Being a gentleman while we were undercover, risking your life and saving mine. And for this." She pulled a small slip of paper from her pocket. Jackson recognized it as a sheet from a bedside pad at the hotel, the one on which he had written the Psalm he had looked up the previous afternoon. He had hidden the paper in her duffel bag before bringing it to her room, thinking maybe she would need some scriptural comfort.

"I found it this morning while packing," she said, handing it to him. He read the verses again.

> *For you created my inmost being;*
>> *you knit me together in my mother's womb.*
> *I praise you because I am fearfully and wonderfully made;*
>> *your works are wonderful,*
>> *I know that full well.*
> *My frame was not hidden from you*
>> *when I was made in the secret place,*
>> *when I was woven together in the depths of the earth.*
> *Your eyes saw my unformed body;*
>> *all the days ordained for me were written in your book*
>> *before one of them came to be.*

"Huh?" Jackson asked, realizing she had said something.

"When did you write this?"

"Uh, I didn't. David did."

She glared playfully.

"Yesterday, right before coming to the hospital. I was thinking . . ."

"About me being an artificial human being," Hillary said.

Jackson shook his head. "There's no such thing, Hillary. I just wanted to make sure you knew that."

"I do," she said. "And that's very sweet."

"I have my moments."

"So I've seen."

"Well, I should get going. I have lawns to mow."

"It's raining."

"Yeah, it is."

Hillary traced the edge of a floor tile with the toe of her shoe. "Would you mind staying until Heather gets here? I really don't want to be alone right now."

He nodded. "Sure."

They settled in the living room, at opposite ends of the couch. Across the way, he saw the picture of Dark and Handsome.

"What's his name?" he asked, nodding at the photo.

Hillary kept her defenses down. "Brian."

"I hope it works out for you."

"It's just casual," she said. "We're taking it slow."

"Have you called him?"

"He didn't know I was in Vegas either. I wasn't ready to share everything with him just yet. He's in Seattle for work until the end of the month, anyhow."

"You should call him, Hill."

She rolled her head his way. "Now you're encouraging me?"

He shrugged and looked down. "I'm sorry about what I said the other day, about you not suffering as much as I did and implying you didn't care for Grant. Blame it on pain talking." He raised his eyes to meet hers. "And stupidity."

"Well, I think I finally understand why Grant always defended you to me. I see what he saw."

They sat in silence for a while. Then Hillary shivered and got up to get a sweatshirt. On her way back, she asked if Jackson wanted something to drink. The rain and the adjustment from the heat of the desert had made him a little cold, so he accepted a coffee. She brewed a single cup and brought it to him, and they sat mostly in silence again.

"We should have tried this before," Jackson said.

"What?"

"Mutual silent treatment."

She smiled as he drained his coffee and carried the cup to the kitchen. He had just placed it in the dishwasher when the doorbell rang. Since he was closer, he opened the door.

Heather McKenzie stood on the front stoop, protected from the rain by the roof's overhang. She wore cuffed skinny jeans, a teal sweater, and a flowing scarf. Breathtakingly beautiful, Heather was plain ordinary compared to Hillary.

As soon as Jackson opened the door, Heather attacked him in a hug that caused him to stagger backwards. "Thank you, Jackson," she said, mashing her cheek against his and rocking from side to side. "Thank you so much."

"You're welcome," he said as they separated. She turned and spied Hillary, who had stepped out of the living room. Heather rushed to her and engulfed her older sister in a tearful embrace. As they laughed, wiped tears, and hugged again, Jackson realized how much they resembled each other for not being blood relatives.

"I'll let the two of you catch up," he said, starting for the door.

"Wait," Hillary called. She came over and gave him another hug. "I'd kiss you on the cheek, but it seems so trite."

"Besides, I'd get frostbite."

She smiled, then slowly licked her lips. "If you need anything, Jackson, I'm here."

He nodded. "Me too. Just no more *quid pro quos.*"

"Agreed."

He turned to Heather, offering a small wave, and made eye contact with Hillary one more time. They said nothing, their eyes expressing something words couldn't.

Then he opened the door and walked out into the rain.

Acknowledgements

I'VE BEEN TO Las Vegas twice. I don't gamble, drink, or party. And yet I love America's Playground. The majestic, themed architecture and energetic atmosphere cut a sharp contrast to the barren desert and unchecked sky. Somehow, it creates magic. To be sure, Vegas fully earns its reputation as Sin City. It's a den of iniquity, and I don't love that part of it. But for a long time, I've known I had to set a novel here and allow the city to play a character all its own, both good and bad.

Oasis Las Vegas exists only in the deep recesses of my imagination. I hope those whose real-life properties were fictitiously imploded to make way for my creation won't hold it against me. The rest of the city, to the best of my ability, was depicted accurately. Well, mostly. I wouldn't go looking for Alex at Seven-7 either.

For the sake of my story, I painted some members of the military and law enforcement community in a less than flattering light. I hold the men and women in uniform in the highest regard, and want to stress that any negative depictions of individuals exist only to drive the plot. In no way are they meant to reflect my views of the institutions as a whole or of the vast majority of those who serve.

I owe a great deal of thanks to several people for their tireless work proofing manuscripts and redrafts, helping me dress and style my characters, and answering questions like, "Does this plot make any sense at all?" (Blame them if it doesn't!) Beyond the nuts and bolts of writing and editing, they also reinvigorated me time and time again.

Sierra, you unfortunately are at the mercy of my incessant thoughts and questions. Thank you for answering them patiently and pushing me to keep going. Mom and Dad, thanks for reading and reading and for offering your feedback and critique. (Also, thanks for amending that '03 vacation to include Vegas. It was the dawn of my inspiration.) Mark and Tiff, thanks for editing and proofing, for validating the good ideas and politely questioning the not so good ones.

A special thanks to my readers for coming along for the ride. Your words of appreciation and encouragement mean the world to me. I hope it's been worth your while too.

Despite all the research, exhaustive editing, and multiple revisions, I am sure mistakes still exist. I take full responsibility for them. I'll try to do better next time.

About the Author

NATHAN BIRR IS the author of *Overnight Delivery*, *Black Male*, and *Three's a Crowd*. After reading his first Hardy Boys novel, he was hooked on tales of adventure and mystery, and has been writing the stories he wants to read ever since. When not plotting, drafting, and editing, Nathan enjoys spending time with his family, traveling, and watching college football. He lives in Sheboygan, Wisconsin, with his wife, Sierra.

If you enjoyed *All an Illusion*, Nathan would love to hear from you. To interact with him or to find out more about his other writing projects, visit www.nathanbirr.com or follow him on Twitter @atruebluehusker.

Deleted Scenes

IF YOU HATE coming to the end of a novel, if you want all the details and backstory, if you crave just a little more character interaction, then check out the *All an Illusion* Deleted Scenes. All part of the original story, these seven additional "chapters" will give you a fuller adventure by providing further background and context as well as additional humor and banter. And they're yours FREE in EPUB, MOBI, or PDF format. Simply go to www.nathanbirr.com/more and follow the instructions to download the Deleted Scenes!